TEN MODERN MASTERS

Borges

Chekhov

Conrad

Faulkner

Joyce

Lawrence

Malamud

Mann

O'Connor

Welty

Ten Modern Masters

AN ANTHOLOGY OF THE SHORT STORY

Third Edition

Edited by

ROBERT GORHAM DAVIS

Columbia University

HARCOURT BRACE JOVANOVICH, INC.

NEW YORK / CHICAGO / SAN FRANCISCO / ATLANTA

ISBN: 0-15-590281-4

Library of Congress Catalog Card Number: 70-183244

Printed in the United States of America

Contents

Introduction

Though descended from the folk tale, one of the oldest of literary forms, the modern short story is one of the youngest, younger even than the British novel, which dates back to the mid-eighteenth century, to the time of *Pamela* by Richardson and *Tom Jones* by Fielding.

In this sense "modern" means something more than "contemporary" or "recent." It refers to a type of brief fiction combining in a quite distinctive way the representative realism of the modern novel with emotional and artistic effects that only the short story can achieve.

The most famous definition of these effects peculiar to the short story occurred in Edgar Allan Poe's reviews in the 1840's of Hawthorne's fiction. Poe felt that anyone who was interested in pure beauty should write poetry. But if one wanted to unite thought and feeling, to reveal truth and at the same time create intensities of suspense, passion and terror, then the short tale, as he called it, was superior to both the poem and the novel. As the novel "cannot be read at one sitting, it deprives itself, of course, of the immense force derivable from *totality*."

Poe prided himself on his intellectuality. His formulas made the writing of a short story sound a little too deliberate and scientific. In his review of Hawthorne, his description of the artistic possibilities of the short story suggested the conscious artistry of Borges rather than the more intuitive, exploratory approach of Chekhov or Frank O'Connor.

Poe supposed that the author "conceived with deliberate care a certain unique or single *effect* to be wrought out." Having done this, he then "invents such incidents—he then combines such events as may best aid him in establishing this preconceived effect. If his very initial sentence tend not to the outbringing of this effect, then he has failed in his first step. In the whole composition there should be no word written, of which the tendency, direct or indirect, is not to the one pre-established design. And by such means, with such care and skill, a picture is at length painted which leaves in the mind of him who contemplates it with a kindred art, a sense of the fullest satisfaction." Poe criticized Hawthorne's stories for being too allegorical. Allegory, Poe said, is fatally injurious "to the most vitally important point in fiction—that of earnestness or verisimilitude."

In his usual dogmatic manner, Poe laid down rules that have governed the best short story writing ever since. Naturally his stating these principles did not by itself bring the modern short story into being. Literature does not develop that way. It is simply that Poe defined with clarity possibilities in the short story form which writers in Europe were also beginning to discover and to work toward in their fiction. One of them was the Russian, Nikolai Gogol, Poe's exact contemporary. His tale "The Overcoat" is sometimes said to be the ancestor of the modern realistic short story.

Despite his awareness of these new possibilities for the short story, the examples Poe himself knew best were the romantic tales written in Germany by Ludwig Tieck and by E. T. A. Hoffman, of the famous "Tales of Hoffman." These were imitated and adapted in America by Washington Irving, Nathaniel Hawthorne and Poe himself. In Poe's time, the most imaginative of the short story writers still had as their models the wonder-tales of folk tradition, tales of supernatural and legendary events. Everyday plausibility, matter-of-factness in little things, was not important to them. They did not try to give the reader the illusion that their imaginative world was the same world in which he had social existence.

This "verisimilitude," this sense of immediate relationship with the reader's own kind of experience, or the experience of the kind of people he knows, developed principally in Russia and France. In Russia the men who contributed most were Nikolai Gogol, Ivan Turgeniev and Anton Chekhov; in France they were Alphonse Daudet, Gustave Flaubert and Guy de Maupassant. Though there were some forerunners, like Gogol, and though there was important work in the 1860's and 1870's, it was not until the 1880's that the modern short story—usually a story of from five to fifteen pages—firmly established itself. This was when Maupassant and Chekhov, the most prolific and influential originators, began producing their best work. They became famous through the popular daily and weekly newspapers which offered a vast new audience for the writers of such stories. These papers helped to give the modern short story its character.

In 1888, Henry James took account of this new form in *Partial Portraits,* a collection of important critical essays on Daudet, Maupassant, Turgeniev, and on "The Art of Fiction." As Poe had done before him, James defined the distinguishing characteristics of the modern short story. But he was a less dogmatic critic than Poe, and he had more than thirty years of new material to work on. Unlike Poe he did not reject beauty as one of the proper effects of prose fiction. Of Turgeniev's stories he said, "I was struck afresh with their combination of beauty and reality," and of Daudet's, "Benevolent nature has placed him at that exquisite point where poetry ends and reality begins."

"Reality" is one of James's key terms. He meant by it very much what Poe had meant by "verisimilitude." James says that "the air of reality" is the supreme virtue in fiction, the merit on which all other merits depend. The purpose of the writer is "to represent life," to give "a personal, a direct impression of life." The greater the intensity of the impression, the greater the value of his fiction.

The reader of this anthology will discover from the introductions, the appendices and the stories themselves, that nearly every writer in this volume defines his purpose in almost precisely these terms. Chekhov put it most directly: "The aim of fiction is absolute and honest truth."

At first this insistence on truth by fiction writers seems a little puzzling. If they are interested primarily in truth, why do they write fiction? Fiction is supposed to be the opposite of fact. It is something "made up," imagined, invented. The short story in the past has been, above all, the form used for the unreal and untrue, for accounts of magic, witches and fairies, strange quests, impossible tasks, miraculous transformations. Now it claims to be equal to science and philosophy in conveying truth. Or even superior to them. How can this be?

Much depends, of course, on our definition of truth or reality. Maupassant had his own, which most people would not be willing to accept. "How childish," he wrote, "to believe in reality, since we each carry our own in our thought and in our organs. Our eyes, our ears, our sense of smell, of taste, differing from one person to another, create as many truths as there are men upon earth. And our minds, taking instruction from these organs so diversely impressed, understand, analyze, judge, as if each of us belonged to a different race."

Maupassant is obviously exaggerating human separateness. And yet this separateness is something which we all feel acutely at times. A sense of isolation is one of the causes of anxiety in this age of alienation. Philosophers propose ideas, inconsistent with each other, which they hold to be true for all men. But these are ideas abstracted from experience, with meaning for most people only as they directly transform immediate experience. Experience itself, however, is always individual, occurring here and now to a particular body and mind, different from all the other bodies and minds in the world.

Everyone has to view the world—or reality—from his own limited perspective, with such faculties as his birth and upbringing have given him. He can never view life from inside anyone else, except in imagination. He can never be angry with other people's anger. He can never remember with their memories, feel their toothaches or their thrills of ecstasy. He can never even know whether the color red looks to them as it looks to him. And yet experience—which is life itself—is made up much more of sensations, feelings, observations, emotions and memories than of ideas.

What imaginative literature does is to break through the barriers of personal identity, of personal separateness. In this it is like religion, though it does not have a church, or a ritual, or dogmas. It lets us know what goes on inside other minds, what it is like to be another person. It brings the two worlds of the inner and outer, of the private and the public, into creative harmony. It literally "communicates", that is, makes common, or available to others, what otherwise would have been shut up within a single self. It extends immeasurably our sense of direct experience of life.

When someone has gone through an intense or unusual experience, we ask him eagerly, "What was it like?" We identify ourselves imaginatively with the person who has acted or suffered, we try to imagine how we would have felt or acted in the same circumstances. This takes as much imagination as thinking up something purely fanciful. And since no experience ever repeats itself exactly, and since we are looking to the future as well as to the past, our question really is, "What is it like to be that *kind* of person going through that *kind* of experience?"

This is the question these stories answer. What is it like to own a failing grocery store? What is it like to be on a burning ship in the middle of the ocean? What is it like to take part in a lynching? What was it like to be an officer in the Imperial German Army?

Poe's more literary term *verisimilitude* means likeness to truth, the appearance or illusion of reality. Since experience cannot be communicated directly, the writer chooses words, images, symbols, dramatic actions, that give its qualities, suggesting what it is like, enabling us to imagine it. A writer in command of his medium can often define the quality of an experience with a single adjective or metaphor.

Like is a connecting word. It relates one thing to another because they have qualities in common. A short story makes what began as a unique experience meaningful and communicable by relating it to other experiences, by "placing" it in the broad context of life, by showing what kind of experience it is. In doing this the author can shift facts about or substitute others for them as long as they are true to the kind of experience he is struggling to comprehend. Since events always occur in a particular time and place to particular people, the modern short story, unlike the fairy tale, usually tries to create the illusion of particularity. It may not matter whether the events occurred on Wednesday in Cleveland or on Friday in Minneapolis, but specification adds to the illusion of reality. Notice how this is done, in a matter-of-fact, unadorned way, at the beginning of Conrad's "Amy Foster": "Kennedy is a country doctor and lives in Colebrook, on the shores of Eastbay." And usually the time and place do make a difference. See how important the historical moment is in Thomas Mann's "Disorder and Early Sorrow," and the sense of place in Frank O'Connor's "Uprooted."

The characters in modern short stories, as Henry James said of those in Turgenev's, must be at once individuals of the most concrete sort and yet types, "so strangely, fascinatingly particular, and yet so recognizably general." That the stories in this volume deal with typical characters and typical situations is shown by the very titles, such as "The Infant Prodigy," "The Intruder," "The Dead," "The New Villa." A child performer faces his audience. Two brothers fall in love with the same woman. Thoughts of the dead come between a man and the wife he loves. City people, building a house in the country, find themselves baffled and defeated by peasant obduracy.

These are general situations. They have happened before, they will happen again. And yet nothing could be more concrete and individual than the means by which they are made real. We remember a hair-ribbon on a little boy, a tenement dance where the bodies of the dancers must not touch, a horse walking round a statue, a cucumber covered with crumbs of rye bread.

Stories both generalize and particularize, and it is in the relation of particulars to generals that meaning lies. Faulkner's "Dry September" is a kind of case study of a typical lynching, and of the psychological motivations that lie behind it. The implications we must discern for ourselves. Poe said that to get the full benefit of the writer's art, the reader must read with "kindred art." He must keep in mind all the elements of a story, and see the different ways in which they are interrelated. Though the theme or subject of a story can be stated in a few sentences, this is not the full meaning of the story. If it were, there would be no point in reading the story—or writing it. In a good story every detail should have meaning, should add to the implication.

Modern short story writers do not tell *about* events. They present experience in its most immediately sensuous, concrete and graphic form. Obviously, this makes the story more vivid, but that is not their only purpose. They are not trying primarily to entertain or excite or convince, but to show what life is like. Atmosphere, moods, feelings, sensuous details are essential ingredients of our sense of life at any given moment. If a story is to be completely faithful to life, it must render these essentials insofar as they can be rendered in words. This holds even for a writer like Hemingway, who seems at times to write so objectively, so much from the outside. His statement quoted in the appendix of this book (p. 577), tells us what great pains he took to describe external events and details in such a way as to create in the reader precisely the inner feeling that he had resolved to evoke.

At once objective and subjective, general and particular, social and personal, the short story views life with a double vision. It gives us the illusion of immediate experience, and yet at the same time permits us to see this experience in perspective, to understand its meaning in a way that is seldom possible while we are in the midst of life.

The classic distinction between fiction and history appears in Aristotle's *Poetics*. It was written in the fourth century B.C., but still holds good. In fact, most modern textbooks on short stories can add little to Aristotle's rules for plot construction. Aristotle said that poetry— by which he meant imaginative literature generally—"is a more philosophic and higher thing than history: for poetry tends to express the universal; history, the particular." The business of the poet, he said, is not to state what *did* happen, but to describe what *may* happen;

that is, how a person of a certain type will behave and feel in a certain situation "according to the laws of probability."

What Aristotle says is consistent with ordinary experience. History does not repeat itself. The mere fact that a thing has happened once does not mean that it will happen again. No science of history has yet been developed that enables us to predict the future any more certainly than the science of psychology enables us to predict certainly the behavior of our friends. How many historians anticipated the pact in 1939 between Hitler and Stalin? Who could have predicted the outburst of the "Cultural Revolution" in the late sixties in Mao's China or the dramatic changes of American student attitudes and values during the same period?

And yet in living our lives, in planning for the future, we have to try to predict. In making the decisions that constantly face us, we ask what is *likely* to happen, what consequences, moral and otherwise, are *likely* to follow from our decisions, how people are *likely* to feel about it, how the values we cherish or the larger ends we seek are *likely* to be affected. These are the probabilities of which Aristotle spoke. Given this beginning, what is likely to follow? Given this complication, how is it all likely to end? Another way of putting it is to say that authors choose to write about consequential actions, actions which make a difference. The nature of that difference is what they communicate to the reader.

Fiction, in its likeness to life, deals with probabilities rather than certainties. Expectation, suspense, surprise, and revelation provide the dramatic interest in a plot. What happens must not be fully predictable, at least not in the way it happens. In "The Secret Sharer," for instance, the captain does not himself know what he is going to do about the fugitive. Full predictability would not only be boring, but untrue to life. The accidental, the immeasurable, the unaccounted-for, play their essential parts in life as in fiction. If they seem more common in fiction, it is because fiction prepares us imaginatively for what we do not expect or are likely to overlook. This is part of its great value.

On the other hand, even a fairy tale or fantasy must have its inner logic. How is the princess in "Rumpelstiltskin" to get out of her contract with the dwarf or meet its terms? Once the initial conditions in a story have been established, what follows must seem appropriate and even, in a sense, inevitable. The final incident in "The Tree" by Dylan Thomas is quite unexpected, yet looking back we see that all the apparently random events in the story have prepared us for it, and that it, in turn, reveals their latent meaning.

A major short story writer, then, must be able to discern the patterns that give experience its shape and meaning. He must be able to represent them in such vivid detail, through such highly individualized characters and actions and circumstances, that he seems to be describing events that actually occurred. For this he needs mastery of his medium—of words, images and symbols. He must be able to imitate the speech and thought of a wide variety of characters. He must have a sharply observant eye, a sense of drama, and know how to use effects of suspense and sudden revelation. And he must be serious—or "earnest," as Poe called it—even though he expresses his seriousness in comic or satiric fashion. He must feel deeply the joys and anguish, the tragedy and beauty, the grandeur and misery of life.

A writer who combines these qualities in a marked degree is rare, and interests us as a personality. We value the writer for what he puts into the writing, but we are conscious that he stands behind the writing and that it would not exist except for him. "The deepest quality of a work of art," Henry James said, "will always be the quality of the mind of the producer." "Art," Emile Zola said, "is a corner of nature seen through a temperament."

When we study the qualities that distinguish a writer's work as a whole, we are studying his literary personality. This may be quite different from the personality he presents to his family and friends, and is often superior to it. Our appreciation of Shakespeare's plays has probably not suffered because of the little we know of his private life. But nearly all of Shakespeare's plays have the stamp of his genius, his literary personality, on them. This is what the name Shakespeare means to us.

Writers have an importance as writers which transcends any single work. We speak of the genius of D. H. Lawrence or William Faulkner quite apart from the individual stories in which it shows itself, though we can know it only through them. The distinctive character, art, and gifts of a major writer are evident in nearly everything he writes. The style is the man, and we can learn to identify it in passages chosen almost at random, and in parodies, or imitations by his followers. We could hardly mistake a story by Lawrence for one by Nabokov if we had read many stories by either. Moreover, we often identify situations in life with the names of authors whose works we know well. We say, "That would make a perfect Maupassant plot," or "That dialogue was straight out of Hemingway," or "That is a very Proustian approach."

The purpose of this anthology is to enable the student to know authors as well as stories. If his acquaintance is to be a first-hand, original one, it is not enough that he be told *about* the author, though some biographical facts are useful. He must have an opportunity to read several stories and discover for himself the qualities they have in common which reveal the author's literary personality, his particular sensibilities and view of life. Each of nine major modern short story writers is here represented by three stories. The tenth, Conrad, is represented by two, simply because his best stories are so very long. Printing three would make his share of the book disproportionate.

The number three is not chosen arbitrarily. Generalizations from a single example are obviously unsound, though people frequently make them. Generalizations from two examples have more validity, though the resemblances noted may be coincidental. With three examples, if they are well chosen, we have a real basis for comparison, for an inductive approach. Three is the traditional number of comparison, and has always been so recognized in popular art and legend, where it can also have profound religious and psychological significance. Portia had to choose among three suitors; Paris, among three goddesses. The hero of a fairy tale is frequently the third son. The three bears and the three little pigs are among our earliest literary acquaintances.

If more than three stories by each author were printed, however, a sufficient number of authors could not be included, and the possibilities of another kind of comparison would be too restricted. Definition requires that we should be able to say what a thing is not, as well as what it is. To see what qualities an author possesses, we need to be able to examine a representative range of his work. To see what qualities he lacks, and to distinguish him from other writers, negatively as well as positively, we need to examine his work side by side with the representative work of a number of his contemporaries. It is the purpose of this anthology to make such a direct examination possible.

Quality, of course, is the prime consideration. Are these the very best stories by the very best writers? No absolute standards exist which permit a final answer. Anthology choices and the standards implied by them always provoke lively disagreement, as do the annual National Book Award choices. In practice what the editor does is to select what are certainly very good stories by unquestionably important writers, stories he likes to read and teach. His personal taste and judgment give the volume its homogeneity, but he also takes into account the prevailing judgments of literary historians and critics. What writers and stories should a student know well if he is to follow current literary discussion intelligently? In a collection like the present one, the stories should be both representative and widely varied. They should offer such parallels in theme and subject matter, such contrasts in form and style, that one can learn a great deal about the art of the short story simply by comparing them.

To increase the range of comparison, Appendix A has been added. It reprints a number of significant stories by writers of distinction who were not, for various reasons, included in the basic list. These stories further exemplify what has been said in the introduction, introduce important themes, and suggest very specific parallels and contrasts with other stories in the book.

Many stories in this volume treat childhood experiences or look at life through youthful eyes. In this, too, the collection seeks to be representative. Reviewers of the annual collections of prize stories and of the work of the more sensitive and imaginative younger short story writers frequently comment on the dominance of a youthful or even childlike point of view. The reason is not hard to find. As this introduction has explained, the fiction writer seeks to unify, to communicate. He enables us to share the experiences of persons quite unlike ourselves. He joins image and idea, the personal and the social, the unconscious and the conscious, the present and the past. One past that is especially important to us is our own past as children, when the imaginative world and the world of immediate physical experience had a richness of connotation and a wonder which for most grown-ups it has since lost. This is particularly true in an age of science and rationality when religion, rites, and symbols play so much less a part in our public life than they did in other times. Adults no longer have a shared imaginative life based on an accepted scheme of values. The values of a child may be sounder than his elders' in many ways. How tawdry adult goals can become is shown in Lawrence's "The Rocking-Horse Winner." By seeing with the double vision, which is both that of a child and an adult, the short story writer is able to recapture kinds of feelings that give us a new or revived sense of what life can be if we dive below the merely rational surface of things.

The reader of *Ten Modern Masters* will observe that although many of the stories deal with action—sometimes very violent action—their authors are never interested in action purely for its own sake. There is always a complex relationship between outer event and inner awareness, and this relationship is usually so developed and dramatized that the reader becomes himself involved as a moral and sentient being. In proportion to the demands for attention and understanding that the stories may make, they provide increased self-understanding, an increased knowledge of the richness and intensity of fully lived life.

In Appendix B are selections showing how the authors in this anthology feel about their work and about the art of writing. These statements were chosen to represent the particular attitudes of the individual writers. But they will be found to have a general coherence or agreement also. If one reads them thoughtfully along with the stories, one discovers that the term *modern short story* is not just a loosely descriptive term, but that it suggests a very definite kind of intention and revelation, and that its authors are strikingly similar not only in their attitude toward their art but in their appreciation of life itself.

Jorge Luis Borges

1899–

THE GARDEN OF FORKING PATHS ·
PIERRE MENARD, AUTHOR OF DON QUIXOTE · THE
INTRUDER

Borges is descended from distinguished military leaders who fought Indians and fellow countrymen in the turbulent Argentina of the nineteenth century. He spent his earliest boyhood in a drab suburb of Buenos Aires where the knife duels of petty gangsters took obsessive and lasting hold on his imagination. A frail, lonely, nearsighted boy, Jorge Luis stayed mostly indoors, reading and inventing stories with his younger sister. His paternal grandmother was English, and her language was spoken in the family almost as frequently as Spanish. At nine Jorge translated "The Happy Prince" by Oscar Wilde into Spanish and sent it to one of the leading newspapers where the editor, not realizing it was the work of a boy, published it on its merits.

Borges' father was an anarchist lawyer who admired the idealist philosopher Bishop Berkeley and taught courses in philosophy, using as his text William James's *Principles of Psychology*, with its famous chapters on "The Stream of Consciousness" and "The Self." His library contained many books on Eastern mysticism. Such early influences encouraged in his son the solipsism, the introspectiveness, and the preoccupation with occultism, erudition, and the powers of the mind that characterize much of Borges' writing. They link him with Edgar Allan Poe and the French tradition—mentioned in "Pierre Menard"—that stems from Poe and runs from Baudelaire to Paul Valéry.

Seeking a cure for his own impending blindness, Borges' father took the family to Europe just before the First World War broke out. Borges' education was in French-speaking Swiss institutions. Under the influence of Carlyle's *Sartor Resartus* he taught himself German. He began publishing poems in Spain, where he associated with an avant-garde group called the "ultraists."

Coming back to his greatly changed native city after seven years was a strange experience which he celebrates in a volume of poems called *Fervor de Buenos Aires* (1923). Argentina, Borges tells us, left off being Spanish in 1816, when it won independence. It slaughtered most of its Indians, imported few black slaves. Archeologically and ethnically it had little in common with other South American countries. The flood of immigrants from Europe who had poured into Argentina while Borges was away created a new kind of society. Fascinated, Borges studied it, particularly in some of its less exalted aspects, such as the cult of the tango and the activities of semicriminal political bosses.

Through the twenties and thirties, Borges threw himself into a variety of literary activities—editing "little" magazines, translating Woolf and Faulkner, writing science fiction and detective stories in collaboration with Adolfo Bioy Casares. His *Universal History of Infamy* tells invented stories about actual criminals. His *Book of Fantastic Beasts* does something comparable for the animal world. To help support himself Borges took an ill-paying but undemanding job as cataloguer in a public library, an occupation often reflected in his writing.

In 1938 Borges had a traumatic illness that made him fear for the powers of his mind, but it was after this illness that he produced the stories by which he is now best known. The first was "Pierre Menard, Author of Don Quixote," written in a kind of self-testing, immediately after he began to recover. When the dictator Perón came to power in Argentina, Borges, who courageously opposed him, was removed from his library post and offered a job as inspector of poultry at fairs. Instead he gave public lectures on American and British literature, and later taught at the University of Buenos Aires. After Perón's fall Borges was appointed (at the request of the writers of Argentina) Director of the National Library. By now he was beset by the affliction that ran in his family. "I inherited," he says, "800,000 books and darkness."

His nearly total blindness did not prevent him from continuing to teach at the university, specializing in Anglo-Saxon and Old Norse, or from lecturing extensively abroad, particularly in the United States where he has received many honors.

Like Poe, Borges admires concentrated, ingenious short stories that achieve their effects very quickly and engage the intellect as well as the emotions. "The Garden of Forking Paths" begins like a spy thriller by Graham Greene or Ian Fleming, and ends with a plot device typical of that tradition. But meanwhile the teller has received from a mysteriously recovered ancestral past a dizzying glimpse into the arbitrary relationship of the real and the possible, of time and contingency.

"Pierre Menard, Author of Don Quixote"—what Borges calls an "essay-story"—is even more subtle in its treatment of time and identity. While projecting ideas about literature that carry further the ideas of T. S. Eliot's "Tradition and the Individual Talent," Borges has great fun with his fictional bibliography of Menard's works and with the vanities of literary patronesses. The bibliography runs, we notice, from the year of Borges' birth to the time of the production of this story, and embodies many of Borges' own interests and those of eccentric poets whom he had known in Spain or Buenos Aires. The complicated game of identities played out in the second part of the original *Don Quixote* suggests that Cervantes himself would have been delighted by Borges' *tour de force*, which deserves very careful reading.

Borges describes the genesis and development of "The Intruder" on page 561 of Appendix B: The Writers on their Art. We might suppose that no new pattern of triangular love tragedy could possibly be conceived, especially one involving members of a family. But Borges has given it to us, putting aside his usual erudition and play of mind and using the straightforward simplicity of a neighborhood legend. Behind his apparent objectivity, he studies the way in which love, loyalty, and pity can be modified or denied by the strong customs of a place or time.

THE GARDEN OF FORKING PATHS

To Victoria Ocampo

In his *A History of the World War* (page 212), Captain Liddell Hart reports that a planned offensive by thirteen British divisions, supported by fourteen hundred artillery pieces, against the German line at Serre-Montauban, scheduled for July 24, 1916, had to be postponed until the morning of the 29th. He comments that torrential rain caused this delay—which lacked any special significance. The following deposition, dictated by, read over, and then signed by Dr. Yu Tsun, former teacher of English at the Tsingtao *Hochschule,* casts unsuspected light upon this event. The first two pages are missing.

* * *

. . . and I hung up the phone. Immediately I recollected the voice that had spoken in German. It was that of Captain Richard Madden. Madden, in Viktor Runeberg's office, meant the end of all our work and—though this seemed a secondary matter, *or should have seemed so to me*—of our lives also. His being there meant that Runeberg had been arrested or murdered.* Before the sun set on this same day, I ran the same risk. Madden was implacable. Rather, to be more accurate, he was obliged to be implacable. An Irishman in the service of England, a man suspected of equivocal feelings if not of actual treachery, how could he fail to welcome and seize upon this extraordinary piece of luck: the discovery, capture and perhaps the deaths of two agents of Imperial Germany?

* A malicious and outlandish statement. In point of fact, Captain Richard Madden had been attacked by the Prussian spy Hans Rabener, alias Viktor Runeberg, who drew an automatic pistol when Madden appeared with orders for the spy's arrest. Madden, in self defense, had inflicted wounds of which the spy later died.—*Note by the manuscript editor.*

THE GARDEN OF FORKING PATHS. From *Ficciones* by Jorge Luis Borges. Edited by Anthony Kerrigan. Copyright © 1962 by Grove Press, Inc. Translated from the Spanish © 1956 by Emecé Editores, S.A., Buenos Aires. Reprinted by permission of Grove Press, Inc.

I went up to my bedroom. Absurd though the gesture was, I closed and locked the door. I threw myself down on my narrow iron bed, and waited on my back. The never changing rooftops filled the window, and the hazy six o'clock sun hung in the sky. It seemed incredible that this day, a day without warnings or omens, might be that of my implacable death. In despite of my dead father, in despite of having been a child in one of the symmetrical gardens of Hai Feng, was I to die now?

Then I reflected that all things happen, happen to one, precisely *now*. Century follows century, and things happen only in the present. There are countless men in the air, on land and at sea, and all that really happens happens to me. . . . The almost unbearable memory of Madden's long horseface put an end to these wandering thoughts.

In the midst of my hatred and terror (now that it no longer matters to me to speak of terror, now that I have outwitted Richard Madden, now that my neck hankers for the hangman's noose), I knew that the fast-moving and doubtless happy soldier did not suspect that I possessed the Secret—the name of the exact site of the new British artillery park on the Ancre. A bird streaked across the misty sky and, absently, I turned it into an airplane and then that airplane into many in the skies of France, shattering the artillery park under a rain of bombs. If only my mouth, before it should be silenced by a bullet, could shout this name in such a way that it could be heard in Germany. . . . My voice, my human voice, was weak. How could it reach the ear of the Chief? The ear of that sick and hateful man who knew nothing of Runeberg or of me except that we were in Staffordshire. A man who, sitting in his arid Berlin office, leafed infinitely through newspapers, looking in vain for news from us. I said aloud, "I must flee."

I sat up on the bed, in senseless and perfect silence, as if Madden was already peering at me. Something—perhaps merely a desire to prove my total penury to myself—made me empty out my pockets. I found just what I knew I was going to find. The American watch, the nickel-plated chain and the square coin, the key ring with the useless but compromising keys to Runeberg's office, the notebook, a letter which I decided to destroy at once (and which I did not destroy), a five shilling piece, two single shillings and some pennies, a red and blue pencil, a handkerchief—and a revolver with a single bullet. Absurdly I held it and weighed it in my hand, to give myself courage. Vaguely I thought that a pistol shot can be heard for a great distance.

In ten minutes I had developed my plan. The telephone directory gave me the name of the one person capable of passing on the information. He lived in a suburb of Fenton, less than half an hour away by train.

I am a timorous man. I can say it now, now that I have brought my incredibly risky plan to an end. It was not easy to bring about, and I know that its execution was terrible. I did not do it for Germany—no! Such a barbarous country is of no importance to me, particularly since it had degraded me by making me become a spy. Furthermore, I knew an Englishman—a modest man—who, for me, is as great as Goethe. I did not speak with him for more than an hour, but during that time, he *was* Goethe.

I carried out my plan because I felt the Chief had some fear of those of my race, of those uncountable forebears whose culmination lies in me. I wished to prove to him that a yellow man could save his armies. Besides, I had to escape the Captain. His hands and voice could, at any moment, knock and beckon at my door.

Silently, I dressed, took leave of myself in the mirror, went down the stairs, sneaked a look at the quiet street, and went out. The station was not far from my house, but I thought it more prudent to take a cab. I told myself that I thus ran less chance of being recognized. The truth is that, in the deserted street, I felt infinitely visible and vulnerable. I recall that I told the driver to stop short of the main entrance. I got out with a painful and deliberate slowness.

I was going to the village of Ashgrove, but took a ticket for a station further on. The train would leave in a few minutes, at eight-fifty. I hurried, for the next would not go until half past nine. There was almost no one on the platform. I walked through the carriages. I remember some farmers, a woman dressed in mourning, a youth deep in Tacitus' *Annals* and a wounded, happy soldier.

At last the train pulled out. A man I recognized ran furiously, but vainly, the length of the platform. It was Captain Richard Madden. Shattered, trembling, I huddled in the distant corner of the seat, as far as possible from the fearful window.

From utter terror I passed into a state of almost abject happiness. I told myself that the duel had already started and that I had won the first encounter by besting my adversary in his first attack—even if it was only for forty minutes—by an accident of fate. I argued that so small a victory prefigured a total victory. I argued that it was not so trivial, that were it not for the precious accident of the train schedule, I would be in prison or dead. I argued, with no less sophism, that my timorous happiness was proof that I was man enough to bring this adventure to a successful conclusion. From my weakness I drew strength that never left me.

I foresee that man will resign himself each day to new abominations, that soon only soldiers and bandits will be left. To them I offer this advice: *Whosoever would undertake some atrocious enterprise should act as if it were already accomplished, should impose upon himself a future as irrevocable as the past.*

Thus I proceeded, while with the eyes of a man already dead, I contemplated the fluctuations of the day which would probably be my last, and watched the diffuse coming of night.

The train crept along gently, amid ash trees. It slowed down and stopped, almost in the middle of a field. No one called the name of a station. "Ashgrove?" I asked some children on the platform. "Ashgrove," they replied. I got out.

A lamp lit the platform, but the children's faces remained in a shadow. One of them asked me: "Are you going to Dr. Stephen Albert's house?" Without waiting for my answer, another said: "The house is a good distance away but you won't get lost if you take the road to the left and bear to the left at every crossroad." I threw them a coin (my last), went down some stone steps and started along a deserted road. At a slight incline, the road ran downhill. It was a plain dirt way, and overhead the branches of trees intermingled, while a round moon hung low in the sky as if to keep me company.

For a moment I thought that Richard Madden might in some way have divined my desperate intent. At once I realized that this would be impossible. The advice about turning always to the left reminded me that such was the common formula for finding the central courtyard of certain labyrinths. I know something about labyrinths. Not for nothing am I the great-grandson of Ts'ui Pên. He was Governor of Yunnan and gave up temporal power to write a novel with more characters than there are in the *Hung Lou Mêng,* and to create a maze in which all men would lose themselves. He spent thirteen years on these oddly assorted tasks before he was assassinated by a stranger. His novel had no sense to it and nobody ever found his labyrinth.

Under the trees of England I meditated on this lost and perhaps mythical labyrinth. I imagined it untouched and perfect on the secret summit of some mountain; I imagined it drowned under rice paddies or beneath the sea; I imagined it infinite, made not only of eight-sided pavilions and of twisting paths but also of rivers, provinces and kingdoms. . . . I thought of a maze of mazes, of a sinuous, ever-growing maze which would take in both past and future and would somehow involve the stars.

Lost in these imaginary illusions I forgot my destiny—that of the hunted. For an undetermined period of time I felt myself cut off from the world, an abstract spectator. The hazy and murmuring countryside, the moon, the decline of the evening, stirred within me. Going down the gently sloping road I could not feel fatigue. The evening was at once intimate and infinite.

The road kept descending and branching off, through meadows misty in the twilight. A high-pitched and almost syllabic music kept coming and going, moving with the breeze, blurred by the leaves and by distance.

I thought that a man might be an enemy of other men, of the differing moments of other men, but never an enemy of a country: not of fireflies, words, gardens, streams, or the West wind.

Meditating thus I arrived at a high, rusty iron gate. Through the railings I could see an avenue bordered with poplar trees and also a kind of summer house or pavilion. Two things dawned on me at once, the first trivial and the second almost incredible: the music came from the pavilion and that music was Chinese. That was why I had accepted it fully, without paying it any attention. I do not remember whether there was a bell, a push-button, or whether I attracted attention by clapping my hands. The stuttering sparks of the music kept on.

But from the end of the avenue, from the main house, a lantern approached; a lantern which alternately, from moment to moment, was crisscrossed or put out by the trunks of the trees; a paper lantern shaped like a drum and colored like the moon. A tall man carried it. I could not see his face for the light blinded me.

He opened the gate and spoke slowly in my language.

"I see that the worthy Hsi P'eng has troubled himself to see to relieving my solitude. No doubt you want to see the garden?"

Recognizing the name of one of our consuls, I replied, somewhat taken aback.

"The garden?"

"The garden of forking paths."

Something stirred in my memory and I said, with incomprehensible assurance:

"The garden of my ancestor, Ts'ui Pên."

"Your ancestor? Your illustrious ancestor? Come in."

The damp path zigzagged like those of my childhood. When we reached the house, we went into a library filled with books from both East and West. I recognized some large volumes bound in yellow silk—manuscripts of the Lost Encyclopedia which was edited by the Third Emperor of the Luminous Dynasty. They had never been printed. A phonograph record was spinning near a bronze phoenix. I remember also a rose-glazed jar and yet another, older by many centuries, of that blue color which our potters copied from the Persians. . . .

Stephen Albert was watching me with a smile on his face. He was, as I have said, remarkably tall. His face was deeply lined and he had gray eyes and a gray beard. There was about him something of the priest, and something of the sailor. Later, he told me he had been a missionary in Tientsin before he "had aspired to become a Sinologist."

We sat down, I upon a large, low divan, he with his back to the window and to a large circular clock. I calculated that my pursuer, Richard Madden, could not arrive in less than an hour. My irrevocable decision could wait.

"A strange destiny," said Stephen Albert, "that of Ts'ui Pên— Governor of his native province, learned in astronomy, in astrology and tireless in the interpretation of the canonical books, a chess player, a famous poet and a calligrapher. Yet he abandoned all to make a book and a labyrinth. He gave up all the pleasures of oppression, justice, of a well-stocked bed, of banquets, and even of erudition, and shut himself up in the Pavilion of the Limpid Sun for thirteen years. At his death, his heirs found only a mess of manuscripts. The family, as you doubtless know, wished to consign them to the fire, but the executor of the estate—a Taoist or a Buddhist monk—insisted on their publication."

"Those of the blood of Ts'ui Pên," I replied, "still curse the memory of that monk. Such a publication was madness. The book is a shapeless mass of contradictory rough drafts. I examined it once upon a time: the hero dies in the third chapter, while in the fourth he is alive. As for that other enterprise of Ts'ui Pên . . . his Labyrinth. . . ."

"Here is the Labyrinth," Albert said, pointing to a tall, lacquered writing cabinet.

"An ivory labyrinth?" I exclaimed. "A tiny labyrinth indeed . . . !"

"A symbolic labyrinth," he corrected me. "An invisible labyrinth of time. I, a barbarous Englishman, have been given the key to this transparent mystery. After more than a hundred years most of the details are irrecoverable, lost beyond all recall, but it isn't hard to imagine what must have happened. At one time, T'sui Pên must have said; 'I am going into seclusion to write a book,' and at another, 'I am retiring to construct a maze.' Everyone assumed these were separate activities. No one realized that the book and the labyrinth were one and the same. The Pavilion of the Limpid Sun was set in the middle of an intricate garden. This may have suggested the idea of a physical maze.

"Ts'ui Pên died. In all the vast lands which once belonged to your family, no one could find the labyrinth. The novel's confusion suggested that *it* was the labyrinth. Two circumstances showed me the direct solution to the problem. First, the curious legend that Ts'ui Pên had proposed to create an infinite maze, second, a fragment of a letter which I discovered."

Albert rose. For a few moments he turned his back to me. He opened the top drawer in the high black and gilded writing cabinet. He returned holding in his hand a piece of paper which had once been crimson but which had faded with the passage of time: it was rose colored, tenuous, quadrangular. Ts'ui Pên's calligraphy was justly famous. Eagerly, but without understanding, I read the words which a man of my own blood had written with a small brush: "I leave to various future times, but not to all, my garden of forking paths."

I handed back the sheet of paper in silence. Albert went on:

"Before I discovered this letter, I kept asking myself how a book could be infinite. I could not imagine any other than a cyclic volume, circular. A volume whose last page would be the same as the first and so have the possibility of continuing indefinitely. I recalled, too, the night in the middle of *The Thousand and One Nights* when Queen Scheherezade, through a magical mistake on the part of her copyist, started to tell the story of *The Thousand and One Nights,* with the risk of again arriving at the night upon which she will relate it, and thus on to infinity. I also imagined a Platonic hereditary work, passed on from father to son, to which each individual would add a new chapter or correct, with pious care, the work of his elders.

"These conjectures gave me amusement, but none seemed to have the remotest application to the contradictory chapters of Ts'ui Pên. At this point, I was sent from Oxford the manuscript you have just seen.

"Naturally, my attention was caught by the sentence, 'I leave to various future times, but not to all, my garden of forking paths.' I had no sooner read this, than I understood. *The Garden of Forking Paths* was the chaotic novel itself. The phrase 'to various future times, but not to all' suggested the image of bifurcating in time, not in space. Rereading the whole work confirmed this theory. In all fiction, when a man is faced with alternatives he chooses one at the expense of the others. In the almost unfathomable Ts'ui Pên, he chooses— simultaneously—all of them. He thus *creates* various futures, various times which start others that will in their turn branch out and bifurcate in other times. This is the cause of the contradictions in the novel.

"Fang, let us say, has a secret. A stranger knocks at his door. Fang makes up his mind to kill him. Naturally there are various possible outcomes. Fang can kill the intruder, the intruder can kill Fang, both can be saved, both can die and so on and so on. In Ts'ui Pên's work, all the possible solutions occur, each one being the point of departure for other bifurcations. Sometimes the pathways of this labyrinth converge. For example, you come to this house; but in other possible pasts you are my enemy; in others my friend.

"If you will put up with my atrocious pronunciation, I would like to read you a few pages of your ancestor's work."

His countenance, in the bright circle of lamplight, was certainly that of an ancient, but it shone with something unyielding, even immortal.

With slow precision, he read two versions of the same epic chapter. In the first, an army marches into battle over a desolate mountain pass. The bleak and somber aspect of the rocky landscape made the soldiers feel that life itself was of little value, and so they won the battle easily. In the second, the same army passes through a palace where a banquet is in progress. The splendor of the feast remained a memory throughout the glorious battle, and so victory followed.

With proper veneration I listened to these old tales, although perhaps with less admiration for them in themselves than for the fact that they had been thought out by one of my own blood, and that a man of a distant empire had given them back to me, in the last stage of a desperate adventure, on a Western island. I remember the final words, repeated at the end of each version like a secret command: "Thus the heroes fought, with tranquil heart and bloody sword. They were resigned to killing and to dying."

At that moment I felt within me and around me something invisible and intangible pullulating. It was not the pullulation of two divergent, parallel, and finally converging armies, but an agitation more inaccessible, more intimate, prefigured by them in some way. Stephen Albert continued:

"I do not think that your illustrious ancestor toyed idly with variations. I do not find it believable that he would waste thirteen years laboring over a never ending experiment in rhetoric. In your country the novel is an inferior genre; in Ts'ui Pên's period, it was a despised one. Ts'ui Pên was a fine novelist but he was also a man of letters who, doubtless, considered himself more than a mere novelist. The testimony of his contemporaries attests to this, and certainly the known facts of his life confirm his leanings toward the metaphysical and the mystical. Philosophical conjectures take up the greater part of his novel. I know that of all problems, none disquieted him more, and none concerned him more than the profound one of time. Now then, this is the *only* problem that does not figure in the pages of *The Garden*. He does not even use the word which means *time*. How can these voluntary omissions be explained?"

I proposed various solutions, all of them inadequate. We discussed them. Finally Stephen Albert said: "In a guessing game to which the answer is chess, which word is the only one prohibited?" I thought for a moment and then replied:

"The word is *chess*."

"Precisely," said Albert. "*The Garden of Forking Paths* is an enormous guessing game, or parable, in which the subject is time. The rules of the game forbid the use of the word itself. To eliminate a word completely, to refer to it by means of inept phrases and obvious paraphrases, is perhaps the best way of drawing attention to it. This, then, is the tortuous method of approach preferred by the oblique Ts'ui Pên in every meandering of his interminable novel. I have gone over hundreds of manuscripts, I have corrected errors introduced by careless copyists, I have worked out the plan from this chaos, I have restored, or believe I have restored, the original. I have translated the whole work. I can state categorically that not once has the word *time* been used in the whole book.

"The explanation is obvious. *The Garden of Forking Paths* is a picture, incomplete yet not false, of the universe such as Ts'ui Pên conceived it to be. Differing from Newton and Schopenhauer, your ancestor did not think of time as absolute and uniform. He believed in an infinite series of times, in a dizzily growing, ever spreading network of diverging, converging and parallel times. This web of time— the strands of which approach one another, bifurcate, intersect or ignore each other through the centuries—embraces *every* possibility. We do not exist in most of them. In some you exist and not I, while in others I do, and you do not, and in yet others both of us exist. In this one, in which chance has favored me, you have come to my gate. In another, you, crossing the garden, have found me dead. In yet another, I say these very same words, but am an error, a phantom."

"In all of them," I enunciated, with a tremor in my voice. "I deeply appreciate and am grateful to you for the restoration of Ts'ui Pên's garden."

"Not in *all*," he murmured with a smile. "Time is forever dividing itself toward innumerable futures and in one of them I am your enemy."

Once again I sensed the pullulation of which I have already spoken. It seemed to me that the dew-damp garden surrounding the house was infinitely saturated with invisible people. All were Albert and myself, secretive, busy and multiform in other dimensions of time. I lifted my eyes and the short nightmare disappeared. In the black and yellow garden there was only a single man, but this man was as strong as a statue and this man was walking up the path and he was Captain Richard Madden.

"The future exists now," I replied. "But I am your friend. Can I take another look at the letter?"

Albert rose from his seat. He stood up tall as he opened the top drawer of the high writing cabinet. For a moment his back was again turned to me. I had the revolver ready. I fired with the utmost care: Albert fell without a murmur, at once. I swear that his death was instantaneous, as if he had been struck by lightning.

What remains is unreal and unimportant. Madden broke in and arrested me. I have been condemned to hang. Abominably, I have yet triumphed! The secret name of the city to be attacked got through to Berlin. Yesterday it was bombed. I read the news in the same English newspapers which were trying to solve the riddle of the murder of the learned Sinologist Stephen Albert by the unknown Yu Tsun. The Chief, however, had already solved this mystery. He knew that my problem was to shout, with my feeble voice, above the tumult of war, the name of the city called Albert, and that I had no other course open to me than to kill someone of that name. He does not know, for no one can, of my infinite penitence and sickness of the heart.

PIERRE MENARD, AUTHOR OF DON QUIXOTE

To Silvina Ocampo

The *visible* works left by this novelist are easily and briefly enumerated. It is therefore impossible to forgive the omissions and additions perpetrated by Madame Henri Bachelier in a fallacious catalogue that a certain newspaper, whose Protestant tendencies are no secret, was inconsiderate enough to inflict on its wretched readers— even though they are few and Calvinist, if not Masonic and circumcised. Menard's true friends regarded this catalogue with alarm, and even with a certain sadness. It is as if yesterday we were gathered together before the final marble and the fateful cypresses, and already

PIERRE MENARD, AUTHOR OF DON QUIXOTE. From *Ficciones* by Jorge Luis Borges. Edited by Anthony Kerrigan. Copyright © 1962 by Grove Press, Inc. Translated from the Spanish © 1956 by Emecé Editores, S.A., Buenos Aires. Reprinted by permission of Grove Press, Inc.

Error is trying to tarnish his Memory. . . . Decidedly, a brief rectification is inevitable.

I am certain that it would be very easy to challenge my meager authority. I hope, nevertheless, that I will not be prevented from mentioning two important testimonials. The Baroness de Bacourt (at whose unforgettable *vendredis* I had the honor of becoming acquainted with the late lamented poet) has seen fit to approve these lines. The Countess de Bagnoregio, one of the most refined minds in the Principality of Monaco (and now of Pittsburgh, Pennsylvania, since her recent marriage to the international philanthropist Simon Kautsch who, alas, has been so slandered by the victims of his disinterested handiwork) has sacrificed to "truth and death" (those are her words) that majestic reserve which distinguishes her, and in an open letter published in the magazine *Luxe* also grants me her consent. These authorizations, I believe, are not insufficient.

I have said that Menard's *visible* lifework is easily enumerated. Having carefully examined his private archives, I have been able to verify that it consists of the following:

a) A symbolist sonnet which appeared twice (with variations) in the magazine *La Conque* (the March and October issues of 1899).

b) A monograph on the possibility of constructing a poetic vocabulary of concepts that would not be synonyms or periphrases of those which make up ordinary language, "but ideal objects created by means of common agreement and destined essentially to fill poetic needs" (Nîmes, 1901).

c) A monograph on "certain connections or affinities" among the ideas of Descartes, Leibnitz and John Wilkins (Nîmes, 1903).

d) A monograph on the *Characteristica Universalis* of Leibnitz (Nîmes, 1904).

e) A technical article on the possibility of enriching the game of chess by means of eliminating one of the rooks' pawns. Menard proposes, recommends, disputes, and ends by rejecting this innovation.

f) A monograph on the *Ars Magna Generalis* of Ramón Lull (Nîmes, 1906).

g) A translation with prologue and notes of the *Libro de la invención y arte del juego del axedrez* by Ruy López de Segura (Paris, 1907).

h) The rough draft of a monograph on the symbolic logic of George Boole.

i) An examination of the metric laws essential to French prose, illustrated with examples from Saint-Simon (*Revue des langues romanes*, Montpellier, October, 1909).

j) An answer to Luc Durtain (who had denied the existence of such laws) illustrated with examples from Luc Durtain (*Revue des langues romanes*, Montpellier, December, 1909).

k) A manuscript translation of the *Aguja de navegar cultos* of Quevedo, entitled *La boussole des précieux*.

l) A preface to the catalogue of the exposition of lithographs by Carolus Hourcade (Nîmes, 1914).

m) His work, *Les problèmes d'un problème* (Paris, 1917), which takes up in chronological order the various solutions of the famous problem of Achilles and the tortoise. Two editions of this book have appeared so far; the second has as an epigraph Leibnitz' advice "Ne craignez point, monsieur, la tortue," and contains revisions of the chapters dedicated to Russell and Descartes.

n) An obstinate analysis of the "syntactic habits" of Toulet (*N.R.F.*, March, 1921). I remember that Menard used to declare that censuring and praising were sentimental operations which had nothing to do with criticism.

o) A transposition into Alexandrines of *Le Cimetière marin* of Paul Valéry (*N.R.F.*, January, 1928).

p) An invective against Paul Valéry in the *Journal for the Suppression of Reality* of Jacques Reboul. (This invective, it should be stated parenthetically, is the exact reverse of his true opinion of Valéry. The latter understood it as such, and the old friendship between the two was never endangered.)

q) A "definition" of the Countess of Bagnoregio in the "victorious volume"—the phrase is that of another collaborator, Gabriele d'Annunzio—which this lady publishes yearly to rectify the inevitable falsifications of journalism and to present "to the world and to Italy" an authentic effigy of her person, which is so exposed (by reason of her beauty and her activities) to erroneous or hasty interpretations.

r) A cycle of admirable sonnets for the Baroness de Bacourt (1934).

s) A manuscript list of verses which owe their effectiveness to punctuation.*

* Madame Henri Bachelier also lists a literal translation of a literal translation done by Quevedo of the *Introduction à la vie dévote* of Saint Francis of

Up to this point (with no other omission than that of some vague, circumstantial sonnets for the hospitable, or greedy, album of Madame Henri Bachelier) we have the *visible* part of Menard's works in chronological order. Now I will pass over to that other part, which is subterranean, interminably heroic, and unequalled, and which is also—oh, the possibilities inherent in the man!—inconclusive. This work, possibly the most significant of our time, consists of the ninth and thirty-eighth chapters of Part One of *Don Quixote* and a fragment of the twenty-second chapter. I realize that such an affirmation seems absurd; but the justification of this "absurdity" is the primary object of this note.*

Two texts of unequal value inspired the undertaking. One was that philological fragment of Novalis—No. 2005 of the Dresden edition—which outlines the theme of *total* identification with a specific author. The other was one of those parasitic books which places Christ on a boulevard, Hamlet on the Cannebière and Don Quixote on Wall Street. Like any man of good taste, Menard detested these useless carnivals, only suitable—he used to say—for evoking plebeian delight in anachronism, or (what is worse) charming us with the primary idea that all epochs are the same, or that they are different. He considered more interesting, even though it had been carried out in a contradictory and superficial way, Daudet's famous plan: to unite in *one* figure, Tartarin, the Ingenious Gentleman and his squire. . . . Any insinuation that Menard dedicated his life to the writing of a contemporary *Don Quixote* is a calumny of his illustrious memory.

He did not want to compose another *Don Quixote*—which would be easy—but *the Don Quixote*. It is unnecessary to add that his aim was never to produce a mechanical transcription of the original; he did not propose to copy it. His admirable ambition was to produce pages which would coincide—word for word and line for line—with those of Miguel de Cervantes.

"My intent is merely astonishing," he wrote me from Bayonne on

Sales. In Pierre Menard's library there are no traces of such a work. She must have misunderstood a remark of his which he had intended as a joke.
* I also had another, secondary intent—that of sketching a portrait of Pierre Menard. But how would I dare to compete with the golden pages the Baroness de Bacourt tells me she is preparing, or with the delicate and precise pencil of Carolus Hourcade?

December 30th, 1934. "The ultimate goal of a theological or metaphysical demonstration—the external world, God, chance, universal forms—are no less anterior or common than this novel which I am now developing. The only difference is that philosophers publish in pleasant volumes the intermediary stages of their work and that I have decided to lose them." And, in fact, not one page of a rough draft remains to bear witness to this work of years.

The initial method he conceived was relatively simple: to know Spanish well, to re-embrace the Catholic faith, to fight against Moors and Turks, to forget European history between 1602 and 1918, and to *be* Miguel de Cervantes. Pierre Menard studied this procedure (I know that he arrived at a rather faithful handling of seventeenth-century Spanish) but rejected it as too easy. Rather because it was impossible, the reader will say! I agree, but the undertaking was impossible from the start, and of all the possible means of carrying it out, this one was the least interesting. To be, in the twentieth century, a popular novelist of the seventeenth seemed to him a diminution. To be, in some way, Cervantes and to arrive at *Don Quixote* seemed to him less arduous—and consequently less interesting—than to continue being Pierre Menard and to arrive at *Don Quixote* through the experiences of Pierre Menard. (This conviction, let it be said in passing, forced him to exclude the autobiographical prologue of the second part of *Don Quixote*. To include this prologue would have meant creating another personage—Cervantes—but it would also have meant presenting *Don Quixote* as the work of this personage and not of Menard. He naturally denied himself such an easy solution.) "My undertaking is not essentially difficult," I read in another part of the same letter. "I would only have to be immortal in order to carry it out." Shall I confess that I often imagine that he finished it and that I am reading *Don Quixote*—the entire work—as if Menard had conceived it? Several nights ago, while leafing through Chapter XXVI—which he had never attempted—I recognized our friend's style and, as it were, his voice in this exceptional phrase: *the nymphs of the rivers, mournful and humid Echo.* This effective combination of two adjectives, one moral and the other physical, reminded me of a line from Shakespeare which we discussed one afternoon:

Where a malignant and turbaned Turk . . .

Why precisely *Don Quixote,* our reader will ask. Such a preference would not have been inexplicable in a Spaniard; but it undoubtedly was in a symbolist from Nîmes, essentially devoted to Poe, who engendered Baudelaire, who engendered Mallarmé, who engendered Valéry, who engendered Edmond Teste. The letter quoted above clarifies this point. *"Don Quixote,"* Menard explains, "interests me profoundly, but it does not seem to me to have been— how shall I say it—inevitable. I cannot imagine the universe without the interjection of Edgar Allan Poe

> Ah, bear in mind this garden was enchanted!

or without the *Bateau ivre* or the *Ancient Mariner,* but I know that I am capable of imagining it without *Don Quixote.* (I speak, naturally, of my personal capacity, not of the historical repercussions of these works.) *Don Quixote* is an accidental book, *Don Quixote* is unnecessary. I can premeditate writing, I can write it, without incurring a tautology. When I was twelve or thirteen years old I read it, perhaps in its entirety. Since then I have reread several chapters attentively, but not the ones I am going to undertake. I have likewise studied the *entremeses,* the comedies, the *Galatea,* the exemplary novels, and the undoubtedly laborious efforts of *Pérsiles y Sigismunda* and the *Viaje al Parnaso.* . . . My general memory of *Don Quixote,* simplified by forgetfulness and indifference, is much the same as the imprecise, anterior image of a book not yet written. Once this image (which no one can deny me in good faith) has been postulated, my problems are undeniably considerably more difficult than those which Cervantes faced. My affable precursor did not refuse the collaboration of fate; he went along composing his immortal works a little *à la diable,* swept along by inertias of language and invention. I have contracted the mysterious duty of reconstructing literally his spontaneous work. My solitary game is governed by two polar laws. The first permits me to attempt variants of a formal and psychological nature; the second obliges me to sacrifice them to the 'original' text and irrefutably to rationalize this annihilation. . . . To these artificial obstacles one must add another congenital one. To compose *Don Quixote* at the beginning of the seventeenth century was a reasonable, necessary and perhaps inevitable undertaking; at the beginning of the twentieth century it is almost impossible. It is not in vain that three hundred years have passed, charged with the most complex happenings—among them, to mention only one, that same *Don Quixote*."

In spite of these three obstacles, the fragmentary *Don Quixote* of Menard is more subtle than that of Cervantes. The latter indulges in a rather coarse opposition between tales of knighthood and the meager, provincial reality of his country; Menard chooses as "reality" the land of Carmen during the century of Lepanto and Lope. What Hispanophile would not have advised Maurice Barrès or Dr. Rodriguez Larreta to make such a choice! Menard, as if it were the most natural thing in the world, eludes them. In his work there are neither bands of gypsies, conquistadors, mystics, Philip the Seconds, nor autos-da-fé. He disregards or proscribes local color. This disdain indicates a new approach to the historical novel. This disdain condemns *Salammbô* without appeal.

It is no less astonishing to consider isolated chapters. Let us examine, for instance, Chapter XXXVIII of Part One "which treats of the curious discourse that Don Quixote delivered on the subject of arms and letters." As is known, Don Quixote (like Quevedo in a later, analogous passage of *La hora de todos*) passes judgment against letters and in favor of arms. Cervantes was an old soldier, which explains such a judgment. But that the *Don Quixote* of Pierre Menard —a contemporary of *La trahison des clercs* and Bertrand Russell— should relapse into these nebulous sophistries! Madame Bachelier has seen in them an admirable and typical subordination of the author to the psychology of the hero; others (by no means perspicaciously) a *transcription* of *Don Quixote;* the Baroness de Bacourt, the influence of Nietzsche. To this third interpretation (which seems to me irrefutable) I do not know if I would dare to add a fourth, which coincides very well with the divine modesty of Pierre Menard: his resigned or ironic habit of propounding ideas which were the strict reverse of those he preferred. (One will remember his diatribe against Paul Valéry in the ephemeral journal of the superrealist Jacques Reboul.) The text of Cervantes and that of Menard are verbally identical, but the second is almost infinitely richer. (More ambiguous, his detractors will say; but ambiguity is a richness.) It is a revelation to compare the *Don Quixote* of Menard with that of Cervantes. The latter, for instance, wrote (*Don Quixote,* Part One, Chapter Nine):

. . . *la verdad, cuya madre es la historia, émula del tiempo, depósito de las acciones, testigo de lo pasado, ejemplo y aviso de lo presente, advertencia de lo por venir.*

[. . . truth, whose mother is history, who is the rival of time, depository of deeds, witness of the past, example and lesson to the present, and warning to the future.]

Written in the seventeenth century, written by the "ingenious layman" Cervantes, this enumeration is a mere rhetorical eulogy of history. Menard, on the other hand, writes:

. . . *la verdad, cuya madre es la historia, émula del tiempo, depósito de las acciones, testigo de lo pasado, ejemplo y aviso de lo presente, advertencia de lo por venir.*

[. . . truth, whose mother is history, who is the rival of time, depository of deeds, witness of the past, example and lesson to the present, and warning to the future.]

History, *mother* of truth; the idea is astounding. Menard, a contemporary of William James, does not define history as an investigation of reality, but as its origin. Historical truth, for him, is not what took place; it is what we think took place. The final clauses—*example and lesson to the present, and warning to the future*—are shamelessly pragmatic.

Equally vivid is the contrast in styles. The archaic style of Menard —in the last analysis, a foreigner—suffers from a certain affectation. Not so that of his precursor, who handles easily the ordinary Spanish of his time.

There is no intellectual exercise which is not ultimately useless. A philosophical doctrine is in the beginning a seemingly true description of the universe; as the years pass it becomes a mere chapter— if not a paragraph or a noun—in the history of philosophy. In literature, this ultimate decay is even more notorious. *"Don Quixote,"* Menard once told me, "was above all an agreeable book; now it is an occasion for patriotic toasts, grammatical arrogance and obscene deluxe editions. Glory is an incomprehension, and perhaps the worst."

These nihilist arguments contain nothing new; what is unusual is the decision Pierre Menard derived from them. He resolved to outstrip that vanity which awaits all the woes of mankind; he undertook a task that was complex in the extreme and futile from the out-set. He dedicated his conscience and nightly studies to the repetition of a pre-existing book in a foreign tongue. The number of rough drafts kept on increasing; he tenaciously made corrections and tore up thousands of manuscript pages.* He did not permit them to be examined, and he took great care that they would not survive him. It is in vain that I have tried to reconstruct them.

I have thought that it is legitimate to consider the "final" *Don Quixote* as a kind of palimpsest, in which should appear traces—tenuous but not undecipherable—of the "previous" handwriting of our friend. Unfortunately, only a second Pierre Menard, inverting the work of the former, could exhume and resuscitate these Troys. . . .

"To think, analyze and invent," he also wrote me, "are not anomalous acts, but the normal respiration of the intelligence. To glorify the occasional fulfillment of this function, to treasure ancient thoughts of others, to remember with incredulous amazement what the *doctor universalis* thought, is to confess our languor or barbarism. Every man should be capable of all ideas, and I believe that in the future he will be."

Menard (perhaps without wishing to) has enriched, by means of a new technique, the hesitant and rudimentary art of reading: the technique is one of deliberate anachronism and erroneous attributions. This technique, with its infinite applications, urges us to run through the *Odyssey* as if it were written after the *Aeneid*, and to read *Le jardin du Centaure* by Madame Henri Bachelier as if it were by Madame Henri Bachelier. This technique would fill the dullest books with adventure. Would not the attributing of *The Imitation of Christ* to Louis Ferdinand Céline or James Joyce be a sufficient renovation of its tenuous spiritual counsels?

Nîmes
1939

---

* I remember his square-ruled notebooks, the black streaks where he had crossed out words, his peculiar typographical symbols and his insect-like handwriting. In the late afternoon he liked to go for walks on the outskirts of Nîmes; he would take a notebook with him and make a gay bonfire.

THE INTRUDER

> *. . . passing the love of women.*
> 2 Samuel 1:26

People say (but this is unlikely) that the story was first told by Eduardo, the younger of the Nelsons, at the wake of his elder brother Cristián, who died in his sleep sometime back in the nineties out in the district of Morón. The fact is that someone got it from someone else during the course of that drawn-out and now dim night, between one sip of maté and the next, and told it to Santiago Dabove, from whom I heard it. Years later, in Turdera, where the story had taken place, I heard it again. The second and more elaborate version closely followed the one Santiago told, with the usual minor variations and discrepancies. I set down the story now because I see in it, if I'm not mistaken, a brief and tragic mirror of the character of those hard-bitten men living on the edge of Buenos Aires before the turn of the century. I hope to do this in a straightforward way, but I see in advance that I shall give in to the writer's temptation of emphasizing or adding certain details.

In Turdera, where they lived, they were called the Nilsens. The priest there told me that his predecessor remembered having seen in the house of these people—somewhat in amazement—a worn Bible with a dark binding and black-letter type; on the back flyleaf he caught a glimpse of names and dates written in by hand. It was the only book in the house—the roaming chronicle of the Nilsens, lost as one day all things will be lost. The rambling old house, which no longer stands, was of unplastered brick; through the arched entranceway you could make out a patio paved with red tiles and beyond it a second one of hard-packed earth. Few people, at any rate, ever set foot inside; the Nilsens kept to themselves. In their

THE INTRUDER. From the book *The Aleph And Other Stories: 1939–1969* by Jorge Luis Borges. Eng. trans. copyright © 1968, 1969, 1970 by Emecé Editores, S.A. and Norman Thomas di Giovanni; copyright © 1970 by Jorge Luis Borges, Adolfo Bioy-Caseres and Norman Thomas di Giovanni. Published by E. P. Dutton & Co., Inc. and reprinted with their permission.

almost bare rooms they slept on cots. Their extravagances were horses, silver-trimmed riding gear, the short-bladed dagger, and getting dressed up on Saturday nights, when they blew their money freely and got themselves into boozy brawls. They were both tall, I know, and wore their red hair long. Denmark or Ireland, which they probably never heard of, ran in the blood of these two Argentine brothers. The neighborhood feared the Redheads; it is likely that one of them, at least, had killed his man. Once, shoulder to shoulder, they tangled with the police. It is said that the younger brother was in a fight with Juan Iberra in which he didn't do too badly, and that, according to those in the know, is saying something. They were drovers, teamsters, horse thieves, and, once in a while, professional gamblers. They had a reputation for stinginess, except when drink and cardplaying turned them into spenders. Of their relatives or where they themselves came from, nothing is known. They owned a cart and a yoke of oxen.

Their physical makeup differed from that of the rest of the toughs who gave the Costa Brava its unsavory reputation. This, and a lot that we don't know, helps us understand the close ties between them. To fall out with one of them was to reckon with two enemies.

The Nilsens liked carousing with women, but up until then their amorous escapades had always been carried out in darkened passageways or in whorehouses. There was no end of talk, then, when Cristián brought Juliana Burgos to live with him. Admittedly, in this way he gained a servant, but it is also true that he took to squandering on her the most hideous junk jewelry and showing her off at parties. At those dingy parties held in tenements, where suggestive dance steps were strictly forbidden and where, at that time, partners still danced with a good six inches of light showing between them. Juliana was a dark girl and her eyes had a slight slant to them; all anyone had to do was look at her and she'd break into a smile. For a poor neighborhood, where drudgery and neglect wear women out, she was not bad-looking.

In the beginning, Eduardo went places with them. Later, at one point, he set out on a journey north to Arrecifes on some business or other, returning home with a girl he had picked up along the way. But after a few days he threw her out. He turned more sullen; he took to drinking alone at the corner saloon and kept completely to himself. He had fallen in love with Cristián's woman. The whole neighborhood, which may have realized it before he did, maliciously and cheerfully looked forward to the enmity about to break out between the two brothers.

Late one night, on coming home from the corner, Eduardo saw Cristián's horse, a big bay, tied to the hitching post. Inside in the patio, dressed in his Sunday best, his older brother was waiting for him. The woman shuttled in and out serving maté. Cristián said to Eduardo, "I'm on my way over to Farias' place, where they're throwing a party. Juliana stays here with you; if you want her, use her."

His tone was half commanding, half friendly. Eduardo stood there a while staring at him, not knowing what to do. Cristián got up, said goodbye—to his brother, not to Juliana, who was no more than an object—mounted his horse, and rode off at a jog, casually.

From that night on they shared her. Nobody will ever know the details of this strange partnership which outraged even the Costa Brava's sense of decency. The arrangement went well for several weeks, but it could not last. Between them the brothers never mentioned her name, not even to call her, but they kept looking for, and finding, reasons to be at odds. They argued over the sale of some hides, but what they were really arguing about was something else. Cristián took to raising his voice, while Eduardo kept silent. Without knowing it, they were watching each other. In tough neighborhoods a man never admits to anyone—not even to himself—that a woman matters beyond lust and possession, but the two brothers were in love. This, in some way, made them feel ashamed.

One afternoon, in the square in Lomas, Eduardo ran into Juan Iberra, who congratulated him on this beauty he'd got hold of. It was then, I believe, that Eduardo let him have it. Nobody—not to *his* face—was going to poke fun at Cristián.

The woman attended both men's wants with an animal submission, but she was unable to keep hidden a certain preference, probably for the younger man, who had not refused sharing her but who had not proposed it either.

One day, they ordered Juliana to bring two chairs out into the first patio and then not show her face for a while because they had things to talk over. Expecting a long session between them, she lay down for a nap, but before very long they woke her up. She was to fill a sack with all her belongings, including her glass-bead rosary and the tiny crucifix her mother had left her. Without any explanation, they lifted her onto the oxcart and set out on a long, tiresome, and silent journey. It had rained; the roads were heavy with mud and it was nearly daybreak before they reached Morón. There they sold her to the woman who ran the whorehouse. The terms had already been agreed to; Cristián pocketed the money and later on split it with his brother.

Back in Turdera, the Nilsens, up till then trapped in the web (which was also a routine) of this monstrous love affair, tried to take up their old life of men among men. They went back to card-playing, to cockfights, to their Saturday night binges. At times, perhaps, they felt they were saved, but they often indulged—each on his own—in unaccountable or only too accountable absences. A little before the year was out, the younger brother said he had business in the city. Immediately, Cristián went off to Morón; at the hitching post of the whorehouse he recognized Eduardo's piebald. Cristián walked in; there was his brother, sure enough, waiting his turn. It is said that Cristián told him, "If we go on this way, we'll wear out the horses. We'd be better off keeping her close at hand."

He spoke with the owner of the place, drew a handful of coins out of his money belt, and they took the girl away. Juliana rode with Cristián. Eduardo dug his spurs into his horse, not wanting to see them together.

They went back to what has already been told. Their solution had ended in failure, for the two had fallen into cheating. Cain was on the loose here, but the affection between the Nilsens was great—who knows what hard times and what dangers they may have faced together!—and they preferred taking their feelings out on others. On strangers, on the dogs, on Juliana, who had set this wedge between them.

The month of March was coming to a close and there was no sign of the heat's letting up. One Sunday (on Sundays people go to bed early), Eduardo, on his way home from the corner saloon, saw that Cristián was yoking the oxen. Cristián said to him, "Come on. We have to leave some hides off at Pardo's place. I've already loaded them; let's make the best of the night air."

Pardo's warehouse lay, I believe, farther south; they took the old cattle trail, then turned down a side road. As night fell, the countryside seemed wider and wider.

They skirted a growth of tall reeds; Cristián threw down the cigar he had just lit and said evenly, "Let's get busy, brother. In a while the buzzards will take over. This afternoon I killed her. Let her stay here with all her trinkets, she won't cause us any more harm."

They threw their arms around each other, on the verge of tears. One more link bound them now—the woman they had cruelly sacrificed and their common need to forget her.

Anton Chekhov

1860–1904

A TRIFLE FROM REAL LIFE · THE STUDENT · THE
NEW VILLA

Anton Chekhov's father, born in serfdom, was a petty shop-keeper in the southern Russian seaport of Taganrog. Passionately devoted to church music, the father often roused his large family at three in the morning to go to sing matins in the church choir which he directed. Because Anton had a good head for figures, his father made him work evenings in the shop when he should have been studying, and beat him frequently. Nevertheless, Anton somehow developed into a high-spirited boy, given to mimicry and practical jokes.

When Anton was seventeen, his bankrupt father had to flee to Moscow to escape creditors. The rest of the family joined him there, except for Anton. Fortunately for his development, he was allowed to stay behind for three years and finish his courses at the Taganrog Gymnasium. Always enthusiastic about such the-ater as he had been able to attend or take part in as an amateur, Chekhov began writing plays.

In Moscow, Chekhov found that his two older brothers were helping to support the desperately impoverished family by selling skits and illustrations to the comic weeklies. Anton contributed too. Though he was working hard for a medical degree, he soon became the chief money-earner in the family. In 1883, his most difficult year at medical school, he sold over a hundred jokes and short stories. Much of this was conventional humor of a low order, written hastily for small sums. But as Chekhov continued writing, his social satire became more original, and he showed more sympathy for his characters. Above all, he learned to write with forcefulness and economy what was then called the "little story."

Chekhov's work rapidly attracted the attention of serious literary men, including influential editors. When he made his first visit to St. Petersburg at the age of twenty-five, he was amazed at the extent of his reputation. By 1888, the year in which he was awarded the Pushkin Prize, three collections of his stories had appeared in book form.

His fellow writers found it hard to define Chekhov's tendencies. This was a period of severe censorship under a reactionary government, when there was great eagerness to know where a writer stood politically. Chekhov wrote a few stories that seemed to advocate the principles of humility and renunciation being preached by the great Russian writer, Leo Tolstoy. He omitted these, however, from his collected works. He also wrote a few clinical studies of pathological cases which seemed to ally him with the French naturalist school of Emile Zola. But mostly his stories were quite unique blends of humorous, sharply observant truthfulness about human nature, and sympathetic, even lyrical, re-creations of his characters' moods.

In 1889 Chekhov, tubercular himself, became deeply depressed by the death from tuberculosis of an older brother. He decided suddenly to set off alone to investigate one of the remotest of the Siberian prison camps, on Sakhalin Island, and to write a book about it. He spent a whole year on this courageous adventure and was deeply affected by what he saw. He published the book, though without hope that it would lead to real reform. After his return, he devoted himself to a variety of philanthropies in the towns where he lived, doctoring the peasants free, building schools and clinics, supporting libraries.

In 1900 Chekhov was included in the first group of writers ever to be elected to the Russian Academy of Sciences. Two years later the leftist novelist Maxim Gorky was also elected, but his election was canceled by direct order of the Tsar. Chekhov immediately resigned in protest. He had also spoken out against the unjust treatment of Dreyfus in France. He retained a hardheaded skepticism, however, in most practical and political matters. He admired Tolstoy as a man and writer, but could not go along with Tolstoy's attempt to re-create in Russia the mode of life of primitive Christianity. Chekhov had no illusions about the peasants, and thought nothing would be gained by the attempts of intellectuals to live like them.

In the latter part of his career, suffering from severe tubercular attacks, Chekhov wrote far less fiction, though some of his best stories date from this period. But he collaborated actively with the Moscow Art Theatre, founded in 1898. In its first year it had a distinguished success with his drama *The Sea Gull,* which had failed with another company. The great director Stanislavsky found Chekhov's plays perfectly suited to his ideal of making all the elements of a theatrical production into one artistic whole. This in turn encouraged Chekhov to write such masterpieces as *The Three Sisters* and *The Cherry Orchard.* In their humor, lyricism, sudden shifts of mood, mingling of the trivial and profound, the plays are like the short stories. Three years before his death, Chekhov married one of the principal actresses in the Art Theatre.

"A Trifle from Real Life," the story of the callous, imperceptive betrayal of a child by an adult, establishes a pattern that was to become familiar in the work of Joyce, O'Connor, Katherine Mansfield, and more recent writers. Though Chekhov makes this theme explicit, he is not surpassed by any of his successors in his imaginative grasp of a child's mode of thought or in his ironical judgment of adult insensitivity. "The Student," brief though it is, resembles the plays in its identification of a temporary mood and an immediate physical scene with a sense of past and future, and of values that transcend individual lives and give them their meaning. "The New Villa," primarily a commentary on human irrationality and malevolence, is also a soberly realistic report to the Tolstoyans and other political theorists by one who was sympathetic to the peasants and had worked hard to improve their lot.

A TRIFLE FROM REAL LIFE

Nikolai Ilitch Belayeff was a young gentleman of St. Petersburg, aged thirty-two, rosy, well fed, and a patron of the race-tracks. Once, toward evening, he went to pay a call on Olga Ivanovna with whom, to use his own expression, he was dragging through a long and tedious love-affair. And the truth was that the first thrilling, inspiring pages of this romance had long since been read, and that the story was now dragging wearily on, presenting nothing that was either interesting or novel.

Not finding Olga at home, my hero threw himself upon a couch and prepared to await her return.

"Good evening, Nikolai Ilitch!" he heard a child's voice say. "Mamma will soon be home. She has gone to the dressmaker's with Sonia."

On the divan in the same room lay Aliosha, Olga's son, a small boy of eight, immaculately and picturesquely dressed in a little velvet suit and long black stockings. He had been lying on a satin pillow, mimicking the antics of an acrobat he had seen at the circus. First he stretched up one pretty leg, then another; then, when they were tired, he brought his arms into play, and at last jumped up galvanically, throwing himself on all fours in an effort to stand on his head. He went through all these motions with the most serious face in the world, puffing like a martyr, as if he himself regretted that God had given him such a restless little body.

"Ah, good evening, my boy!" said Belayeff. "Is that you? I did not know you were here. Is mamma well?"

Aliosha seized the toe of his left shoe in his right hand, assumed the most unnatural position in the world, rolled over, jumped up, and peeped out at Belayeff from under the heavy fringes of the lampshade.

"Not very," he said shrugging his shoulders. "Mamma is never really well. She is a woman, you see, and women always have something the matter with them."

From lack of anything better to do, Belayeff began scrutinizing Aliosha's face. During all his acquaintance with Olga he had never bestowed any consideration upon the boy or noticed his existence at all. He had seen the child about, but what he was doing there Belayeff, somehow, had never cared to think.

Now, in the dusk of evening, Aliosha's pale face and fixed, dark eyes unexpectedly reminded Belayeff of Olga as she had appeared in the first pages of their romance. He wanted to pet the boy.

"Come here, little monkey," he said, "and let me look at you!"

The boy jumped down from the sofa and ran to Belayeff.

"Well," the latter began, laying his hand on the boy's thin shoulder. "And how are you? Is everything all right with you?"

"No, not very. It used to be much better."

"In what way?"

"That's easy to answer. Sonia and I used to learn only music and reading before, but now we have French verses, too. You have cut your beard!"

"Yes."

"So I noticed. It is shorter than it was. Please let me touch it— does that hurt?"

"No, not a bit."

"Why does it hurt if you pull one hair at a time, and not a bit if you pull lots? Ha! Ha! I'll tell you something. You ought to wear whiskers. You could shave here on the sides, here, and here you could let the hair grow—"

The boy nestled close to Belayeff and began to play with his watch-chain.

"Mamma is going to give me a watch when I go to school, and I am going to ask her to give me a chain just like yours— Oh, what a lovely locket! Papa has a locket just like that; only yours has little stripes on it, and papa's has letters. He has a portrait of mamma in his locket. Papa wears another watch-chain now made of ribbon."

"How do you know? Do you ever see your papa?"

"I—n-no—I—"

Aliosha blushed deeply at being caught telling a fib and began to scratch the locket furiously with his nail. Belayeff looked searchingly into his face and repeated:

"Do you ever see your papa?"

"N-no!"

"Come, tell me honestly! I can see by your face that you are not telling the truth. It's no use quibbling now that the cat is out of the bag. Tell me, do you see him? Now then, as between friends!"

Aliosha reflected.

"You won't tell mamma?" he asked.

"What an idea!"

"Honour bright?"

"Honour bright!"

"Promise!"

"Oh, you insufferable child! What do you take me for?"

Aliosha glanced around, opened his eyes wide, and said:

"For heaven's sake don't tell mamma! Don't tell a soul, because it's a secret. I don't know what would happen to Sonia and Pelagia and me if mamma should find out. Now, listen. Sonia and I see papa every Thursday and every Friday. When Pelagia takes us out walking before dinner we go to Anfel's confectionery and there we find papa already waiting for us. He is always sitting in the little private room with the marble table and the ash-tray that's made like a goose without a back."

"What do you do in there?"

"We don't do anything. First we say how do you do, and then papa orders coffee and pasties for us. Sonia likes pasties with meat, you know, but I can't abide them with meat. I like mine with cabbage or eggs. We eat so much that we have a hard time eating our dinner afterward so that mamma won't guess anything."

"What do you talk about?"

"With papa? Oh, about everything. He kisses us and hugs us and tells us the funniest jokes. Do you know what? He says that when we grow bigger he is going to take us to live with him. Sonia doesn't want to go, but I wouldn't mind. Of course it would be lonely without mamma, but I could write letters to her. Isn't it funny, we might go and see her then on Sundays, mightn't we? Papa says, too, he is going to buy me a pony. He is such a nice man! I don't know why mamma doesn't ask him to live with her and why she won't let us see him. He loves mamma very much. He always asks how she is and what she has been doing. When she was ill he took hold of his head just like this—and ran about the room. He always asks us whether we are obedient and respectful to her. Tell me, is it true that we are unfortunate?"

"H'm—why do you ask?"

"Because papa says we are. He says we are unfortunate children, and that he is unfortunate, and that mamma is unfortunate. He tells us to pray to God for her and for ourselves."

Aliosha fixed his eyes on the figure of a stuffed bird, and became lost in thought.

"Well, I declare—" muttered Belayeff. "So, that's what you do, you hold meetings at a confectioner's? And your mamma doesn't know it?"

"N-no. How could she? Pelagia wouldn't tell her for the world. Day before yesterday papa gave us pears. They were as sweet as sugar. I ate two!"

"H'm. But—listen to me, does papa ever say anything about me?"

"About you? What shall I say?" Aliosha looked searchingly into Belayeff's face and shrugged his shoulders. "Nothing special," he answered.

"Well, what does he say, for instance?"

"You won't be angry if I tell you?"

"What an idea! Does he abuse me?"

"No, he doesn't abuse you, but, you know, he is angry with you. He says that it is your fault that mamma is unhappy, and that you have ruined mamma. He is such a funny man! I tell him that you are kind and that you never scold mamma, but he only shakes his head."

"So he says I have ruined her?"

"Yes—don't be angry, Nikolai Ilitch!"

Belayeff rose and began pacing up and down the room.

"How strange this is—and how ridiculous!" he muttered shrugging his shoulders and smiling sarcastically. "It is all *his* fault and yet he says *I* have ruined her! What an innocent baby this is! And so he told you I had ruined your mother?"

"Yes, but—you promised not to be angry!"

"I'm not angry and—and it is none of your business anyway. Yes, this is—this is really ridiculous! Here I have been caught like a mouse in a trap, and now it seems it is all my fault!"

The door-bell rang. The boy tore himself from Belayeff's arms and ran out of the room. A moment later a lady entered with a little girl. It was Aliosha's mother, Olga Ivanovna. Aliosha skipped into the room behind her, singing loudly and clapping his hands. Belayeff nodded and continued to walk up and down.

"Of course!" he muttered. "Whom should he blame but me? He has right on his side! He is the injured husband."

"What is that you are saying?" asked Olga Ivanovna.

"What am I saying? Just listen to what your young hopeful here has been preaching. It appears that I am a wicked scoundrel and that I have ruined you and your children. You are all unhappy, and I alone am frightfully happy. Frightfully, frightfully happy!"

"I don't understand you, Nikolai. What is the matter?"

"Just listen to what this young gentleman here has to say!" cried Belayeff pointing to Aliosha.

Aliosha flushed and then grew suddenly pale and his face became distorted with fear.

"Nikolai Ilitch!" he whispered loudly. "Hush!"

Olga Ivanovna looked at Aliosha in surprise, and then at Belayeff, and then back again at Aliosha.

"Ask him!" Belayeff continued. "That idiot of yours, Pelagia, takes them to a confectioner's and arranges meetings there between them and their papa. But that isn't the point. The point is that papa is the victim, and that I am an abandoned scoundrel who has wrecked the lives of both of you!"

"Nikolai Ilitch!" groaned Aliosha. "You gave me your word of honour!"

"Leave me alone!" Belayeff motioned to him impatiently. "This is more important than words of honour. This hypocrisy, these lies are intolerable!"

"I don't understand!" cried Olga Ivanovna, the tears glistening in her eyes. "Listen, Aliosha," she asked, turning to her son. "Do you really see your father?"

But Aliosha did not hear her, his eyes were fixed with horror on Belayeff.

"It cannot be possible!" his mother exclaimed. "I must go and ask Pelagia."

Olga Ivanovna left the room.

"But Nikolai Ilitch, you gave me your word of honour!" cried Aliosha trembling all over.

Belayeff made an impatient gesture and went on pacing the floor. He was absorbed in thoughts of the wrong that had been done him, and, as before, was unconscious of the boy's presence: a serious, grown-up person like him could not be bothered with little boys. But Aliosha crept into a corner and told Sonia with horror how he had been deceived. He trembled and hiccoughed and cried. This was the first time in his life that he had come roughly face to face with deceit; he had never imagined till now that there were things in this world besides pasties and watches and sweet pears, things for which no name could be found in the vocabulary of childhood.

THE STUDENT

At first the weather was fine and still. The thrushes were calling, and in the swamps close by something alive droned pitifully with a sound like blowing into an empty bottle. A snipe flew by, and the shot aimed at it rang out with a gay, resounding note in the spring air. But when it began to get dark in the forest a cold, penetrating wind blew inappropriately from the east, and everything sank into silence. Needles of ice stretched across the pools, and it felt cheerless, remote, and lonely in the forest. There was a whiff of winter.

Ivan Velikopolsky, the son of a sacristan, and a student of the clerical academy, returning home from shooting, walked all the time by the path in the water-side meadow. His fingers were numb and his face was burning with the wind. It seemed to him that the cold that had suddenly come on had destroyed the order and harmony of things, that nature itself felt ill at ease, and that was why the evening darkness was falling more rapidly than usual. All around it was deserted and peculiarly gloomy. The only light was one gleaming in the widows' gardens near the river; the village, over three miles away, and everything in the distance all round was plunged in the cold evening mist. The student remembered that, as he went out from the house, his mother was sitting barefoot on the floor in the entry, cleaning the samovar, while his father lay on the stove coughing; as it was Good Friday nothing had been cooked, and the student was terribly hungry. And now, shrinking from the cold, he thought that just such a wind had blown in the days of Rurik and in the time of Ivan the Terrible and Peter, and in their time there had been just the same desperate poverty and hunger, the same thatched roofs with holes in them, ignorance, misery, the same desolation around, the same darkness, the same feeling of oppression—all these had existed,

THE STUDENT. From *The Witch and Other Stories* by Anton Chekhov. Translated by Constance Garnett. Reprinted by permission of The Macmillan Company and Chatto & Windus, Ltd.

did exist, and would exist, and the lapse of a thousand years would make life no better. And he did not want to go home.

The gardens were called the widows' because they were kept by two widows, mother and daughter. A camp fire was burning brightly with a crackling sound, throwing out light far around on the ploughed earth. The widow Vasilisa, a tall, fat old woman in a man's coat, was standing by and looking thoughtfully into the fire; her daughter Lukerya, a little pock-marked woman with a stupid-looking face, was sitting on the ground, washing a caldron and spoons. Apparently they had just had supper. There was a sound of men's voices; it was the labourers watering their horses at the river.

"Here you have winter back again," said the student, going up to the camp fire. "Good evening."

Vasilisa started, but at once recognized him and smiled cordially.

"I did not know you; God bless you," she said. "You'll be rich."

They talked. Vasilisa, a woman of experience, who had been in service with the gentry, first as a wet-nurse, afterwards as a children's nurse, expressed herself with refinement, and a soft, sedate smile never left her face; her daughter Lukerya, a village peasant woman, who had been crushed by her husband, simply screwed up her eyes at the student and said nothing, and she had a strange expression like that of a deaf mute.

"At just such a fire the Apostle Peter warmed himself," said the student, stretching out his hands to the fire, "so it must have been cold then, too. Ah, what a terrible night it must have been, granny! An utterly dismal long night!"

He looked round at the darkness, shook his head abruptly and asked:

"No doubt you have been at the reading of the Twelve Gospels?"

"Yes, I have," answered Vasilisa.

"If you remember at the Last Supper Peter said to Jesus, 'I am ready to go with Thee into darkness and unto death.' And our Lord answered him thus: 'I say unto thee, Peter, before the cock croweth thou wilt have denied Me thrice.' After the supper Jesus went through the agony of death in the garden and prayed, and poor Peter was weary in spirit and faint, his eyelids were heavy and he could not struggle against sleep. He fell asleep. Then you heard how Judas the same night kissed Jesus and betrayed Him to His tormentors. They took Him bound to the high priest and beat Him, while Peter, exhausted, worn out with misery and alarm, hardly awake, you know, feeling that something awful was just going to happen on earth, followed behind. . . . He loved Jesus passionately, intensely, and now he saw from far off how He was beaten. . . .'

Lukerya left the spoons and fixed an immovable stare upon the student.

"They came to the high priest's," he went on; "they began to question Jesus, and meantime the labourers made a fire in the yard as it was cold, and warmed themselves. Peter, too, stood with them near the fire and warmed himself as I am doing. A woman, seeing him, said: 'He was with Jesus, too'—that is as much as to say that he, too, should be taken to be questioned. And all the labourers that were standing near the fire must have looked sourly and suspiciously at him, because he was confused and said: 'I don't know Him.' A little while after again someone recognized him as one of Jesus' disciples and said: 'Thou, too, art one of them,' but again he denied it. And for the third time someone turned to him: 'Why, did I not see thee with Him in the garden to-day?' For the third time he denied it. And immediately after that time the cock crowed, and Peter, looking from afar off at Jesus, remembered the words He had said to him in the evening. . . . He remembered, he came to himself, went out of the yard and wept bitterly—bitterly. In the Gospel it is written: 'He went out and wept bitterly.' I imagine it: the still, still, dark, dark garden, and in the stillness, faintly audible, smothered sobbing. . . ."

The student sighed and sang into thought. Still smiling, Vasilisa suddenly gave a gulp, big tears flowed freely down her cheeks, and she screened her face from the fire with her sleeve as though ashamed of her tears, and Lukerya, staring immovably at the student, flushed crimson, and her expression became strained and heavy like that of someone enduring intense pain.

The labourers came back from the river, and one of them riding a horse was quite near, and the light from the fire quivered upon him. The student said good-night to the widows and went on. And again the darkness was about him and his fingers began to be numb. A cruel wind was blowing, winter really had come back and it did not feel as though Easter would be the day after to-morrow.

Now the student was thinking about Vasilisa: since she had shed tears all that had happened to Peter the night before the Crucifixion must have some relation to her. . . .

He looked round. The solitary light was still gleaming in the darkness and no figures could be seen near it now. The student thought again that if Vasilisa had shed tears, and her daughter had been troubled, it was evident that what he had just been telling them about, which had happened nineteen centuries ago, had a relation to the present—to both women, to the desolate village, to himself, to all people. The old woman had wept, not because he could tell the story touchingly, but because Peter was near to her, because her whole being was interested in what was passing in Peter's soul.

And joy suddenly stirred in his soul, and he even stopped for a minute to take breath. "The past," he thought, "is linked with the present by an unbroken chain of events flowing one out of another." And it seemed to him that he had just seen both ends of that chain; that when he touched one end the other quivered.

When he crossed the river by the ferry boat and afterwards, mounting the hill, looked at his village and towards the west where the cold purple sunset lay a narrow streak of light, he thought that truth and beauty which had guided human life there in the garden and in the yard of the high priest had continued without interruption to this day, and had evidently always been the chief thing in human life and in all earthly life, indeed; and the feeling of youth, health, vigour—he was only twenty-two—and the inexpressible sweet expectation of happiness, of unknown mysterious happiness, took possession of him little by little, and life seemed to him enchanting, marvellous, and full of lofty meaning.

THE NEW VILLA

Two miles from the village of Obrutchanovo a huge bridge was being built. From the village, which stood up high on the steep river-bank, its trellis-like skeleton could be seen, and in foggy weather and on still winter days, when its delicate iron girders and all the

THE NEW VILLA. From *The Witch and Other Stories* by Anton Chekhov. Translated by Constance Garnett. Reprinted by permission of The Macmillan Company and Chatto & Windus, Ltd.

scaffolding around was covered with hoar frost, it presented a picturesque and even fantastic spectacle. Kutcherov, the engineer who was building the bridge, a stout, broad-shouldered, bearded man in a soft crumpled cap drove through the village in his racing droshky or his open carriage. Now and then on holidays navvies working on the bridge would come to the village; they begged for alms, laughed at the women, and sometimes carried off something. But that was rare; as a rule the days passed quietly and peacefully as though no bridge-building were going on, and only in the evening, when camp fires gleamed near the bridge, the wind faintly wafted the songs of the navvies. And by day there was sometimes the mournful clang of metal, don-don-don.

It happened that the engineer's wife came to see him. She was pleased with the river-banks and the gorgeous view over the green valley with trees, churches, flocks, and she began begging her husband to buy a small piece of ground and to build them a cottage on it. Her husband agreed. They bought sixty acres of land, and on the high bank in a field, where in earlier days the cows of Obrutchanovo used to wander, they built a pretty house of two storeys with a terrace and a verandah, with a tower and a flagstaff on which a flag fluttered on Sundays—they built it in about three months, and then all the winter they were planting big trees, and when spring came and everything began to be green there were already avenues to the new house, a gardener and two labourers in white aprons were digging near it, there was a little fountain, and a globe of looking-glass flashed so brilliantly that it was painful to look at. The house had already been named the New Villa.

On a bright, warm morning at the end of May two horses were brought to Obrutchanovo to the village blacksmith, Rodion Petrov. They came from the New Villa. The horses were sleek, graceful beasts, as white as snow, and strikingly alike.

"Perfect swans!" said Rodion, gazing at them with reverent admiration.

His wife Stepanida, his children and grandchildren came out into the street to look at them. By degrees a crowd collected. The Lytchkovs, father and son, both men with swollen faces and entirely beardless, came up bareheaded. Kozov, a tall, thin old man with a long, narrow beard, came up leaning on a stick with a crook handle: he kept winking with his crafty eyes and smiling ironically as though he knew something.

"It's only that they are white; what is there in them?" he said. "Put mine on oats, and they will be just as sleek. They ought to be in a plough and with a whip, too. . . ."

The coachman simply looked at him with disdain, but did not utter a word. And afterwards, while they were blowing up the fire at the forge, the coachman talked while he smoked cigarettes. The peasants learned from him various details: his employers were wealthy people; his mistress, Elena Ivanovna, had till her marriage lived in Moscow in a poor way as a governess; she was kind-hearted, compassionate, and fond of helping the poor. On the new estate, he told them, they were not going to plough or to sow, but simply to live for their pleasure, live only to breathe the fresh air. When he had finished and led the horses back a crowd of boys followed him, the dogs barked, and Kozov, looking after him, winked sarcastically.

"Landowners, too-oo!" he said. "They have built a house and set up horses, but I bet they are nobodies—landowners, too-oo."

Kozov for some reason took a dislike from the first to the new house, to the white horses, and to the handsome, well-fed coachman. Kozov was a solitary man, a widower; he had a dreary life (he was prevented from working by a disease which he sometimes called a rupture and sometimes worms); he was maintained by his son, who worked at a confectioner's in Harkov and sent him money; and from early morning till evening he sauntered at leisure about the river or about the village; if he saw, for instance, a peasant carting a log, or fishing, he would say: "That log's dry wood—it is rotten," or, "They won't bite in weather like this." In times of drought he would declare that there would not be a drop of rain till the frost came; and when the rains came he would say that everything would rot in the fields, that everything was ruined. And as he said these things he would wink as though he knew something.

At the New Villa they burned Bengal lights and sent up fireworks in the evenings, and a sailing-boat with red lanterns floated by Obrutchanovo. One morning the engineer's wife, Elena Ivanovna, and her little daughter drove to the village in a carriage with yellow wheels and a pair of dark bay ponies; both mother and daughter were wearing broadbrimmed straw hats, bent down over their ears.

This was exactly at the time when they were carting manure, and the blacksmith Rodion, a tall, gaunt old man, bareheaded and bare-footed, was standing near his dirty and repulsive-looking cart and, flustered, looked at the ponies, and it was evident by his face that he had never seen such little horses before.

"The Kutcherov lady has come!" was whispered around. "Look, the Kutcherov lady has come!"

Elena Ivanovna looked at the huts as though she were selecting one, and then stopped at the very poorest, at the windows of which there were so many children's heads—flaxen, red, and dark. Stepanida, Rodion's wife, a stout woman, came running out of the hut; her ker-chief slipped off her grey head; she looked at the carriage facing the sun, and her face smiled and wrinkled up as though she were blind.

"This is for your children," said Elena Ivanovna, and she gave her three roubles.

Stepanida suddenly burst into tears and bowed down to the ground. Rodion, too, flopped to the ground, displaying his brownish bald head, and as he did so he almost caught his wife in the ribs with the fork. Elena Ivanovna was overcome with confusion and drove back.

II

The Lytchkovs, father and son, caught in their meadows two cart-horses, a pony, and a broad-faced Aalhaus bull-calf, and with the help of red-headed Volodka, son of the blacksmith Rodion, drove them to the village. They called the village elder, collected witnesses, and went to look at the damage.

"All right, let 'em!" said Kozov, winking, "le-et 'em! Let them get out of it if they can, the engineers! Do you think there is no such thing as law? All right! Send for the police inspector, draw up a statement! . . ."

"Draw up a statement," repeated Volodka.

"I don't want to let this pass!" shouted the younger Lytchkov. He shouted louder and louder, and his beardless face seemed to be more and more swollen. "They've set up a nice fashion! Leave them free, and they will ruin all the meadows! You've no sort of right to ill-treat people! We are not serfs now!"

"We are not serfs now," repeated Volodka.

"We got on all right without a bridge," said the elder Lytchkov gloomily, "we did not ask for it. What do we want a bridge for? We don't want it!"

"Brothers, good Christians, we cannot leave it like this!"

"All right, let 'em!" said Kozov, winking. "Let them get out of it if they can! Landowners, indeed!"

They went back to the village, and as they walked the younger Lytchkov beat himself on the breast with his fist and shouted all the way, and Volodka shouted, too, repeating his words. And meanwhile quite a crowd had gathered in the village round the thoroughbred bull-calf and the horses. The bull-calf was embarrassed and looked up from under his brows, but suddenly lowered his muzzle to the ground and took to his heels, kicking up his hind legs; Kozov was frightened and waved his stick at him, and they all burst out laughing. Then they locked up the beasts and waited.

In the evening the engineer sent five roubles for the damage, and the two horses, the pony and the bull-calf, without being fed or given water, returned home, their heads hanging with a guilty air as though they were convicted criminals.

On getting the five roubles the Lytchkovs, father and son, the village elder and Volodka, punted over the river in a boat and went to a hamlet on the other side where there was a tavern, and there had a long carousal. Their singing and the shouting of the younger Lytchkov could be heard from the village. Their women were uneasy and did not sleep all night. Rodion did not sleep either.

"It's a bad business," he said, sighing and turning from side to side. "The gentleman will be angry, and then there will be trouble. . . . They have insulted the gentleman. . . . Oh, they've insulted him. It's a bad business. . . ."

It happened that the peasants, Rodion amongst them, went into their forest to divide the clearings for mowing, and as they were returning home they were met by the engineer. He was wearing a red cotton shirt and high boots; a setter dog with its long tongue hanging out, followed behind him.

"Good-day, brothers," he said.

The peasants stopped and took off their hats.

"I have long wanted to have a talk with you, friends," he went on. "This is what it is. Ever since the early spring your cattle have been in my copse and garden every day. Everything is trampled down; the pigs have rooted up the meadow, are ruining everything in the kitchen garden, and all the undergrowth in the copse is destroyed. There is no getting on with your herdsmen; one asks them civilly, and they are rude. Damage is done on my estate every day and I do nothing—I don't fine you or make a complaint; meanwhile you impounded my horses and my bull-calf and exacted five roubles. Was that right? Is that neighbourly?" he went on, and his face was so soft and persuasive, and his expression was not forbidding. "Is that the way decent people behave? A week ago one of your people cut down two oak saplings in my copse. You have dug up the road to Eresnevo, and now I have to go two miles round. Why do you injure me at every step? What harm have I done you? For God's sake, tell me! My wife and I do our utmost to live with you in peace and harmony; we help the peasants as we can. My wife is a kind, warm-hearted woman; she never refuses you help. That is her dream —to be of use to you and your children. You reward us with evil for our good. You are unjust, my friends. Think of that. I ask you earnestly to think it over. We treat you humanely; repay us in the same coin."

He turned and went away. The peasants stood a little longer, put on their caps and walked away. Rodion, who always understood everything that was said to him in some peculiar way of his own, heaved a sigh and said:

"We must pay. 'Repay in coin, my friends' . . . he said."

They walked to the village in silence. On reaching home Rodion said his prayer, took off his boots, and sat down on the bench beside his wife. Stepanida and he always sat side by side when they were at home, and always walked side by side in the street; they ate and they drank and they slept always together, and the older they grew the more they loved one another. It was hot and crowded in their hut, and there were children everywhere—on the floors, in the windows, on the stove. . . . In spite of her advanced years Stepanida was still bearing children, and now, looking at the crowd of children, it was hard to distinguish which were Rodion's and which were Volodka's. Volodka's wife, Lukerya, a plain young woman with prominent eyes and a nose like the beak of a bird, was kneading dough in a tub; Volodka was sitting on the stove with his legs hanging.

"On the road near Nikita's buckwheat . . . the engineer with his dog . . ." Rodion began, after a rest, scratching his ribs and his elbow. " 'You must pay,' says he . . . 'coin,' says he. . . . Coin or no coin, we shall have to collect ten kopecks from every hut. We've offended the gentleman very much. I am sorry for him. . . ."

"We've lived without a bridge," said Volodka, not looking at anyone, "and we don't want one."

"What next; the bridge is a government business."

"We don't want it."

"Your opinion is not asked. What is it to you?"

" 'Your opinion is not asked,' " Volodka mimicked him. "We don't want to drive anywhere; what do we want with a bridge? If we have to, we can cross by the boat."

Someone from the yard outside knocked at the window so violently that it seemed to shake the whole hut.

"Is Volodka at home?" he heard the voice of the younger Lytch-kov. "Volodka, come out, come along."

Volodka jumped down off the stove and began looking for his cap.

"Don't go, Volodka," said Rodion diffidently. "Don't go with them, son. You are foolish, like a little child; they will teach you no good; don't go!"

"Don't go, son," said Stepanida, and she blinked as though about to shed tears. "I bet they are calling you to the tavern."

" 'To the tavern,' " Volodka mimicked.

"You'll come back drunk again, you currish Herod," said Lukerya, looking at him angrily. "Go along, go along, and may you burn up with vodka, you tailless Satan!"

"You hold your tongue," shouted Volodka.

"They've married me to a fool, they've ruined me, a luckless orphan, you red-headed drunkard . . ." wailed Lukerya, wiping her face with a hand covered with dough. "I wish I had never set eyes on you."

Volodka gave her a blow on the ear and went off.

III

Elena Ivanovna and her little daughter visited the village on foot. They were out for a walk. It was a Sunday, and the peasant women and girls were walking up and down the street in their brightly-coloured dresses. Rodion and Stepanida, sitting side by side at their door, bowed and smiled to Elena Ivanovna and her little daughter as to acquaintances. From the windows more than a dozen children stared at them; their faces expressed amazement and curiosity, and they could be heard whispering:

"The Kutcherov lady has come! The Kutcherov lady!"

"Good-morning," said Elena Ivanovna, and she stopped; she paused, and then asked: "Well, how are you getting on?"

"We get along all right, thank God," answered Rodion, speaking rapidly. "To be sure we get along."

"The life we lead!" smiled Stepanida. "You can see our poverty yourself, dear lady! The family is fourteen souls in all, and only two bread-winners. We are supposed to be blacksmiths, but when they bring us a horse to shoe we have no coal, nothing to buy it with. We are worried to death, lady," she went on, and laughed. "Oh, oh, we are worried to death."

Elena Ivanovna sat down at the entrance and, putting her arm round her little girl, pondered something, and judging from the little girl's expression melancholy thoughts were straying through her mind, too; as she brooded she played with the sumptuous lace on the parasol she had taken out of her mother's hands.

"Poverty," said Rodion, "is a great deal of anxiety—you see no end to it. Here, God sends no rain . . . our life is not easy, there is no denying it."

"You have a hard time in this life," said Elena Ivanovna, "but in the other world you will be happy."

Rodion did not understand her, and simply coughed into his clenched hand by way of reply. Stepanida said:

"Dear lady, the rich men will be all right in the next world, too. The rich put up candles, pay for services; the rich give to beggars, but what can the poor man do? He has no time to make the sign of the cross. He is the beggar of beggars himself; how can he think of his soul? And many sins come from poverty; from trouble we snarl at one another like dogs, we haven't a good word to say to one another, and all sorts of things happen, dear lady—God forbid! It seems we have no luck in this world nor the next. All the luck has fallen to the rich."

She spoke gaily; she was evidently used to talking of her hard life. And Rodion smiled, too; he was pleased that his old woman was so clever, so ready of speech.

"It is only on the surface that the rich seem to be happy," said Elena Ivanovna. "Every man has his sorrow. Here my husband and

I do not live poorly, we have means, but are we happy? I am young, but I have had four children; my children are always being ill. I am ill, too, and constantly being doctored."

"And what is your illness?" asked Rodion.

"A woman's complaint. I get no sleep; a continual headache gives me no peace. Here I am sitting and talking, but my head is bad, I am weak all over, and I should prefer the hardest labour to such a condition. My soul, too, is troubled; I am in continual fear for my children, my husband. Every family has its own trouble of some sort; we have ours. I am not of noble birth. My grandfather was a simple peasant, my father was a tradesman in Moscow; he was a plain, uneducated man, too, while my husband's parents were wealthy and distinguished. They did not want him to marry me, but he disobeyed them, quarrelled with them, and they have not forgiven us to this day. That worries my husband; it troubles him and keeps him in constant agitation; he loves his mother, loves her dearly. So I am uneasy, too, my soul is in pain."

Peasants, men and women, were by now standing round Rodion's hut and listening. Kozov came up, too, and stood twitching his long, narrow beard. The Lytchkovs, father and son, drew near.

"And say what you like, one cannot be happy and satisfied if one does not feel in one's proper place." Elena Ivanovna went on. "Each of you has his strip of land, each of you works and knows what he is working for; my husband builds bridges—in short, everyone has his place, while I, I simply walk about. I have not my bit to work. I don't work, and feel as though I were an outsider. I am saying all this that you may not judge from outward appearances; if a man is expensively dressed and has means it does not prove that he is satisfied with his life."

She got up to go away and took her daughter by the hand.

"I like your place here very much," she said, and smiled, and from that faint, diffident smile one could tell how unwell she really was, how young and how pretty; she had a pale, thinnish face with dark eyebrows and fair hair. And the little girl was just such another as her mother: thin, fair, and slender. There was a fragrance of scent about them.

"I like the river and the forest and the village," Elena Ivanovna went on; "I could live here all my life, and I feel as though here I should get strong and find my place. I want to help you—I want to dreadfully—to be of use, to be a real friend to you. I know your need, and what I don't know I feel, my heart guesses. I am sick, feeble, and for me perhaps it is not possible to change my life as I would. But I have children. I will try to bring them up that they may be of use to you, may love you. I shall impress upon them continually that their life does not belong to them, but to you. Only I beg you earnestly, I beseech you, trust us, live in friendship with us. My husband is a kind, good man. Don't worry him, don't irritate him. He is sensitive to every trifle, and yesterday, for instance, your cattle were in our vegetable garden, and one of your people broke down the fence to the bee-hives, and such an attitude to us drives my husband to despair. I beg you," she went on in an imploring voice, and she clasped her hands on her bosom—"I beg you to treat us as good neighbours; let us live in peace! There is a saying, you know, that even a bad peace is better than a good quarrel, and, 'Don't buy property, but buy neighbours.' I repeat my husband is a kind man and good; if all goes well we promise to do everything in our power for you; we will mend the roads, we will build a school for your children. I promise you."

"Of course we thank you humbly, lady," said Lytchkov the father, looking at the ground; "you are educated people; it is for you to know best. Only, you see, Voronov, a rich peasant at Eresnevo, promised to build a school; he, too, said, 'I will do this for you,' 'I will do that for you,' and he only put up the framework and refused to go on. And then they made the peasants put the roof on and finish it; it cost them a thousand roubles. Voronov did not care; he only stroked his beard, but the peasants felt it a bit hard."

"That was a crow, but now there's a rook, too," said Kozov, and he winked.

There was the sound of laughter.

"We don't want a school," said Volodka sullenly. "Our children go to Petrovskoe, and they can go on going there; we don't want it."

Elena Ivanovna seemed suddenly intimidated; her face looked paler and thinner, she shrank into herself as though she had been touched with something coarse, and walked away without uttering another word. And she walked more and more quickly, without looking round.

"Lady," said Rodion, walking after her, "lady, wait a bit; hear what I would say to you."

He followed her without his cap, and spoke softly as though begging.

"Lady, wait and hear what I will say to you."

They had walked out of the village, and Elena Ivanovna stopped beside a cart in the shade of an old mountain ash.

"Don't be offended, lady," said Rodion. "What does it mean? Have patience. Have patience for a couple of years. You will live here, you will have patience, and it will all come round. Our folks are good and peaceable; there's no harm in them; it's God's truth I'm telling you. Don't mind Kozov and the Lytchkovs, and don't mind Volodka. He's a fool; he listens to the first that speaks. The others are quiet folks; they are silent. Some would be glad, you know, to say a word from the heart and to stand up for themselves, but cannot. They have a heart and a conscience, but no tongue. Don't be offended· . . . have patience. . . . What does it matter?"

Elena Ivanovna looked at the broad, tranquil river, pondering, and tears flowed down her cheeks. And Rodion was troubled by those tears; he almost cried himself.

"Never mind . . ." he muttered. "Have patience for a couple of years. You can have the school, you can have the roads, only not all at once. If you went, let us say, to sow corn on that mound you would first have to weed it out, to pick out all the stones, and then to plough, and work and work . . . and with the people, you see, it is the same . . . you must work and work until you overcome them."

The crowd had moved away from Rodion's hut, and was coming along the street towards the mountain ash. They began singing songs and playing the concertina, and they kept coming closer and closer. . . .

"Mamma, let us go away from here," said the little girl, huddling up to her mother, pale and shaking all over; "let us go away, mamma!"

"Where?"

"To Moscow. . . . Let us go, mamma."

The child began crying.

Rodion was utterly overcome; his face broke into profuse perspiration; he took out of his pocket a little crooked cucumber, like a half-moon, covered with crumbs of rye bread, and began thrusting it into the little girl's hands.

"Come, come," he muttered, scowling severely; "take the little cucumber, eat it up. . . . You mustn't cry, Mamma will whip you. . . . She'll tell your father of you when you get home. Come, come. . . ."

They walked on, and he still followed behind them, wanting to say something friendly and persuasive to them. And seeing that they were both absorbed in their own thoughts and their own griefs, and not noticing him, he stopped and, shading his eyes from the sun, looked after them for a long time till they disappeared into their copse.

I V

The engineer seemed to grow irritable and petty, and in every trivial incident saw an act of robbery or outrage. His gate was kept bolted even by day, and at night two watchmen walked up and down the garden beating a board; and they gave up employing anyone from Obrutchanovo as a labourer. As ill-luck would have it someone (either a peasant or one of the workmen) took the new wheels off the cart and replaced them by old ones, then soon afterwards two bridles and a pair of pincers were carried off, and murmurs arose even in the village. People began to say that a search should be made at the Lytchkovs' and at Volodka's, and then the bridles and the pincers were found under the hedge in the engineer's garden; someone had thrown them down there.

It happened that the peasants were coming in a crowd out of the forest, and again they met the engineer on the road. He stopped, and without wishing them good-day he began, looking angrily first at one, then at another:

"I have begged you not to gather mushrooms in the park and near the yard, but to leave them for my wife and children, but your girls come before daybreak and there is not a mushroom left. . . . Whether one asks you or not it makes no difference. Entreaties, and friendliness, and persuasion I see are all useless."

He fixed his indignant eyes on Rodion and went on:

"My wife and I behaved to you as human beings, as to our equals, and you? But what's the use of talking! It will end by our looking down upon you. There is nothing left!"

And making an effort to restrain his anger, not to say too much, he turned and went on.

On getting home Rodion said his prayer, took off his boots, and sat down beside his wife.

"Yes . . ." he began with a sigh. "We were walking along just now, and Mr. Kutcherov met us. . . . Yes. . . . He saw the girls at daybreak. . . . 'Why don't they bring mushrooms,' he said . . . 'to my wife and children?' he said. . . . And then he looked at me and he said: 'I and my wife will look after you,' he said. I wanted to fall down at his feet, but I hadn't the courage. . . . God give him health. . . . God bless him! . . ."

Stepanida crossed herself and sighed.

"They are kind, simple-hearted people," Rodion went on. " 'We shall look after you.' . . . He promised me that before everyone. In our old age . . . it wouldn't be a bad thing. . . . I should always pray for them. . . . Holy Mother, bless them. . . ."

The Feast of the Exaltation of the Cross, the fourteenth of September, was the festival of the village church. The Lytchkovs, father and son, went across the river early in the morning and returned to dinner drunk; they spent a long time going about the village, alternately singing and swearing; then they had a fight and went to the New Villa to complain. First Lytchkov the father went into the yard with a long ashen stick in his hands. He stopped irresolutely and took off his hat. Just at that moment the engineer and his family were sitting on the verandah, drinking tea.

"What do you want?" shouted the engineer.

"Your honour . . ." Lytchkov began, and burst into tears. "Show the Divine mercy, protect me . . . my son makes my life a misery . . . your honour. . . ."

Lytchkov the son walked up, too; he, too, was bareheaded and had a stick in his hand; he stopped and fixed his drunken senseless eyes on the verandah.

"It is not my business to settle your affairs," said the engineer. "Go to the rural captain or the police officer."

"I have been everywhere. . . . I have lodged a petition . . ." said Lytchkov the father, and he sobbed. "Where can I go now? He can kill me now, it seems. He can do anything. Is that the way to treat a father? A father?"

He raised his stick and hit his son on the head; the son raised his stick and struck his father just on his bald patch such a blow that the stick bounced back. The father did not even flinch, but hit his son again and again on the head. And so they stood and kept hitting one another on the head, and it looked not so much like a fight as some sort of a game. And peasants, men and women, stood in a crowd at the gate and looked into the garden, and the faces of all were grave. They were the peasants who had come to greet them for the holiday, but seeing the Lytchkovs, they were ashamed and did not go in.

The next morning Elena Ivanovna went with the children to Moscow. And there was a rumour that the engineer was selling his house. . . .

v

The peasants had long ago grown used to the sight of the bridge, and it was difficult to imagine the river at that place without a bridge. The heap of rubble left from the building of it had long been overgrown with grass, the navvies were forgotten, and instead of the strains of the "Dubinushka" that they used to sing, the peasants heard almost every hour the sounds of a passing train.

The New Villa has long ago been sold; now it belongs to a government clerk who comes here from the town for the holidays with his family, drinks tea on the terrace, and then goes back to the town again. He wears a cockade on his cap; he talks and clears his throat as though he were a very important official, though he is only of the rank of a collegiate secretary, and when the peasants bow he makes no response.

In Obrutchanovo everyone has grown older; Kozov is dead. In Rodion's hut there are even more children. Volodka has grown a long red beard. They are still as poor as ever.

In the early spring the Obrutchanovo peasants were sawing wood near the station. And after work they were going home; they walked without haste one after the other. Broad saws curved over their shoulders; the sun was reflected in them. The nightingales were singing in the bushes on the bank, larks were trilling in the heavens. It was quiet at the New Villa; there was not a soul there, and only golden pigeons—golden because the sunlight was streaming upon them—were flying over the house. All of them—Rodion, the two Lytchkovs, and Volodka—thought of the white horses, the little ponies, the fireworks, the boat with the lanterns; they remembered how the engineer's wife, so beautiful and so grandly dressed, had come into the village and talked to them in such a friendly way. And it seemed as though all that had never been; it was like a dream or a fairy-tale.

They trudged along, tired out, and mused as they went. . . . In their village, they mused, the people were good, quiet, sensible, fearing God, and Elena Ivanovna, too, was quiet, kind, and gentle; it made one sad to look at her, but why had they not got on together? Why had they parted like enemies? How was it that some mist had shrouded from their eyes what mattered most, and had let them see nothing but damage done by cattle, bridles, pincers, and all those trivial things which now, as they remembered them, seemed so non-sensical? How was it that with the new owner they lived in peace, and yet had been on bad terms with the engineer?

And not knowing what answer to make to these questions they were all silent except Volodka, who muttered something.

"What is it?" Rodion asked.

"We lived without a bridge . . ." said Volodka gloomily. "We lived without a bridge, and did not ask for one . . . and we don't want it. . . ."

No one answered him and they walked on in silence with drooping heads.

Joseph Conrad

1857–1924

AMY FOSTER · THE SECRET SHARER

Joseph Conrad's parents were aristocratic, highly cultivated Poles, who had suffered for their resistance to Tsarism and to the Russian domination of Poland. When Joseph was less than ten he read aloud to his sick father in exile the proofs of Victor Hugo's *Toilers of the Sea,* which his father had translated into Polish. The novels of James Fenimore Cooper and Frederick Marryat excited his imagination, and at eleven he had already determined to visit the Congo region which provided him, years later, with the material of his short novel, *Heart of Darkness* (1920). Before he was twenty-one, Conrad had been twice to the West Indies, had smuggled guns to Carlist conspirators in Spain, had made love to the beautiful woman who financed the conspiracy, and had been wounded in a duel.

Conrad's romanticism was balanced by a deep moral and political conservatism, which grew stronger as he grew older. After his parents' early deaths from the hardships of exile, Conrad was brought up by an uncle who was unsympathetic to their revolutionary ardor. Most of his relatives, however, felt that the young Conrad had deserted Poland and the nationalist struggle when he remained at sea for many years and then settled in England. Conrad's inner conflicts over this question and his sense of guilt appear, often disguised, throughout his stories.

Conrad roamed the world as a ship's officer for twenty years before he became a writer of fiction. He had, in a rather desultory way, begun his novel *Almayer's Folly* when he sailed as second mate on a Congo river steamer. The Congo experience was decisive so far as the rest of his life, both literary and personal, was concerned. First he nearly drowned, and then he became very ill with tropical fever, an illness which was followed by an incapacitating period of mental depression. Though he returned to the sea for a brief period, he was never completely well again, either in body or spirit. In 1896 he settled down in the countryside in England with his wife, an Englishwoman, and devoted himself entirely to writing.

Of Conrad's major novels, only one, *The Nigger of the Narcissus* (1897), takes place entirely at sea. This is the story of extraordinary tensions created on a voyage by the presence aboard ship of a remarkable dying Negro. But nearly all Conrad's fiction describes places he visited, people he had known, and experiences that had happened to him, or that he had heard about from others. *Almayer's Folly* (1895) and *An Outcast of the Islands* (1896) describe intrigues and betrayals at a trading post on a river in Borneo. *Nostromo* (1904) is the history of a South American revolution and of buried treasure. *The Secret Agent* (1907) and *Under Western Eyes* (1911) deal with international revolutionaries and the government spies working against them. *Victory* (1915) is a tale of love, villainy, and spiritual isolation on a tropical island. *Lord Jim* (1900), the most popular of Conrad's novels, portrays a man with a romantic idea of his own possibilities who, having once failed himself grievously, regains his self-respect only at the moment of his death.

Conrad wrote English with difficulty, quarrying the words, he said, like precious stones from a dark mine, with "unremitting, never-discouraged care for the shape and ring of sentences." In achieving the somber majesty and musical brilliance of his style, he was as great a perfectionist as Henry James, whom he profoundly admired. In a way, James had set himself a less difficult task, for Conrad tried to re-create exotic scenes and adventures in their full color and at the same time do justice to the abiding complexities of the human soul. His material was romantic, but his moral sense was thoroughly realistic. Like Hemingway, he spoke of the "absolute loyalty toward his feelings and sensations" which an author must maintain, "even in the most exalted moments of creation." He liked to write of life at sea and on islands, and up remote rivers, because isolation and danger made universal human problems stand out with a particular force and clarity.

Because Conrad's best stories are all very long, only two are included here. Both "Amy Foster" and "The Secret Sharer" describe situations of extreme alienation. Strangers are totally dependent on such good will as they may happen to encounter. In one case, the stranger is tragically betrayed by a woman who had seemed capable of giving him love if not understanding. In the other case, the risky and perhaps unwarranted help given the stranger seems mysteriously to protect his protector.

In "Amy Foster," as in some of his best novels, Conrad uses the indirect method of narration. Two narrators and their generalizing comments come between us and the events themselves, yet the events have unforgettable vividness. This method enables Conrad to express what the principal characters themselves could never have expressed, the emotions aroused when two kinds of primitivism come into conflict. It takes special power of imagination to see how the world presents itself to the innocent and ignorant. Little as Conrad resembled his character Yanko in other respects, we remember that he, a central European, always felt himself a stranger in England.

"The Secret Sharer" describes in the first person the kind of dramatic adventure Conrad could have experienced as ship's officer, yet the incidents have some of the quality of allegory. What is primary is what is going on within the self. An inner duality is suggested by the employment of the "double," the other self, a phenomenon that fascinated a number of nineteenth-century writers—Hoffmann and Dostoevsky in Europe, for instance, and Hawthorne and Poe in America.

AMY FOSTER

Kennedy is a country doctor, and lives in Colebrook, on the shores of Eastbay. The high ground rising abruptly behind the red roofs of the little town crowds the quaint High Street against the wall which defends it from the sea. Beyond the sea-wall there curves for miles in a vast and regular sweep the barren beach of shingle, with the village of Brenzett standing out darkly across the water, a spire in a clump of trees; and still further out the perpendicular column of a lighthouse, looking in the distance no better than a lead-pencil, marks

AMY FOSTER by Joseph Conrad. Reprinted by permission of J. M. Dent & Sons Ltd., London.

the vanishing point of the land. The country at the back of Brenzett is low and flat; but the bay is fairly well sheltered from the seas, and occasionally a big ship, windbound or through stress of weather, makes use of the anchoring ground a mile and a half due north from you as you stand at the back door of the "Ship Inn" in Brenzett. A dilapidated windmill near by, lifting its shattered arms from a mound no loftier than a rubbish-heap, and a Martello tower squatting at the water's edge half a mile to the south of the Coastguard cottages, are familiar to the skippers of small craft. These are the official sea-marks for the patch of trustworthy bottom represented on the Admiralty charts by an irregular oval of dots enclosing several figures six, with a tiny anchor engraved among them, and the legend "mud and shells" over all.

The brow of the upland overtops the square tower of the Cole-brook Church. The slope is green and looped by a white road. Ascending along this road, you open a valley broad and shallow, a wide green trough of pastures and hedges merging inland into a vista of purple tints and flowing lines closing the view.

In this valley down to Brenzett and Colebrook and up to Darnford, the market town fourteen miles away, lies the practice of my friend Kennedy. He had begun life as surgeon in the Navy, and afterwards had been the companion of a famous traveller, in the days when there were continents with unexplored interiors. His papers on the fauna and flora made him known to scientific societies. And now he had come to a country practice—from choice. The penetrating power of his mind, acting like a corrosive fluid, had destroyed his ambition, I fancy. His intelligence is of a scientific order, of an investigating habit, and of that unappeasable curiosity which believes that there is a particle of a general truth in every mystery.

A good many years ago now, on my return from abroad, he invited me to stay with him. I came readily enough, and as he could not neglect his patients to keep me company, he took me on his rounds—thirty miles or so of an afternoon, sometimes. I waited for him on the roads; the horse reached after the leafy twigs, and, sitting high in the dogcart, I could hear Kennedy's laugh through the half-open door of some cottage. He had a big, hearty laugh that would have fitted a man twice his size, a brisk manner, a bronzed face, and a pair of gray, profoundly attentive eyes. He had the talent of making people talk to him freely, and an inexhaustible patience in listening to their tales.

One day, as we trotted out of a large village into a shady bit of road, I saw on our left hand a low, black cottage, with diamond panes in the windows, a creeper on the end wall, a roof of shingle, and some roses climbing on the rickety trellis-work of the tiny porch. Kennedy pulled up to a walk. A woman, in full sunlight, was throwing a dripping blanket over a line stretched between two old apple-trees. And as the bobtailed, long-necked chestnut, trying to get his head, jerked the left hand, covered by a thick dogskin glove, the doctor raised his voice over the hedge: "How's your child, Amy?"

I had the time to see her dull face, red, not with a mantling blush, but as if her flat cheeks had been vigorously slapped, and to take in the squat figure, the scanty, dusty brown hair drawn into a tight knot at the back of the head. She looked quite young. With a distinct catch in her breath, her voice sounded low and timid.

"He's well, thank you."

We trotted again. "A young patient of yours," I said; and the doctor, flicking the chestnut absently, muttered, "Her husband used to be."

"She seems a dull creature," I remarked, listlessly.

"Precisely," said Kennedy. "She is very passive. It's enough to look at the red hands hanging at the end of those short arms, at those slow, prominent brown eyes, to know the inertness of her mind—an inertness that one would think made it everlastingly safe from all the surprises of imagination. And yet which of us is safe? At any rate, such as you see her, she had enough imagination to fall in love. She's the daughter of one Isaac Foster, who from a small farmer has sunk into a shepherd; the beginning of his misfortunes dating from his runaway marriage with the cook of his widowed father—a well-to-do apoplectic grazier, who passionately struck his name off his will, and had been heard to utter threats against his life. But this old affair, scandalous enough to serve as a motive for a Greek tragedy, arose from the similarity of their characters. There are other tragedies, less scandalous and of a subtler poignancy, arising from irreconcilable differences and from that fear of the Incomprehensible that hangs over all our heads—over all our heads. . . ."

The tired chestnut dropped into a walk; and the rim of the sun, all red in a speckless sky, touched familiarly the smooth top of a ploughed rise near the road as I had seen it times innumerable touch the distant horizon of the sea. The uniform brownness of the harrowed field glowed with a rose tinge, as though the powdered clods had sweated out in minute pearls of blood the toil of uncounted ploughmen. From the edge of a copse a waggon with two horses was rolling gently along the ridge. Raised above our heads upon the sky-line, it loomed up against the red sun, triumphantly big, enormous, like a chariot of giants drawn by two slow-stepping steeds of legendary proportions. And the clumsy figure of the man plodding at the head of the leading horse projected itself on the background of the Infinite with a heroic uncouthness. The end of his carter's whip quivered high up in the blue. Kennedy discoursed.

"She's the eldest of a large family. At the age of fifteen they put her out to service at the New Barns Farm. I attended Mrs. Smith, the tenant's wife, and saw that girl there for the first time. Mrs. Smith, a genteel person with a sharp nose, made her put on a black dress every afternoon. I don't know what induced me to notice her at all. There are faces that call your attention by a curious want of definiteness in their whole aspect, as, walking in a mist, you peer attentively at a vague shape which, after all, may be nothing more curious or strange than a signpost. The only peculiarity I perceived in her was a slight hesitation in her utterance, a sort of preliminary stammer which passes away with the first word. When sharply spoken to, she was apt to lose her head at once; but her heart was of the kindest. She had never been heard to express a dislike for a single human being, and she was tender to every living creature. She was devoted to Mrs. Smith, to Mr. Smith, to their dogs, cats, canaries; and as to Mrs. Smith's gray parrot, its peculiarities exercised upon her a positive fascination. Nevertheless, when that outlandish bird, attacked by the cat, shrieked for help in human accents, she ran out into the yard stopping her ears, and did not prevent the crime. For Mrs. Smith this was another evidence of her stupidity; on the other hand, her want of charm, in view of Smith's well-known frivolousness, was a great recommendation. Her short-sighted eyes would swim with pity for a poor mouse in a trap, and she had been seen once by some boys on her knees in the wet grass helping a toad in difficulties. If it's true, as some German fellow has said, that without phosphorus there is no thought, it is still more true that there is no kindness of heart without a certain amount of imagination. She had some.

She had even more than is necessary to understand suffering and to be moved by pity. She fell in love under circumstances that leave no room for doubt in the matter; for you need imagination to form a notion of beauty at all, and still more to discover your ideal in an unfamiliar shape.

"How this aptitude came to her, what it did feed upon, is an inscrutable mystery. She was born in the village, and had never been further away from it than Colebrook or perhaps Darnford. She lived for four years with the Smiths. New Barns is an isolated farmhouse a mile away from the road, and she was content to look day after day at the same fields, hollows, rises; at the trees and the hedgerows; at the faces of the four men about the farm, always the same—day after day, month after month, year after year. She never showed a desire for conversation, and, as it seemed to me, she did not know how to smile. Sometimes of a fine Sunday afternoon she would put on her best dress, a pair of stout boots, a large gray hat trimmed with a black feather (I've seen her in that finery), seize an absurdly slender parasol, climb over two stiles, tramp over three fields and along two hundred yards of road—never further. There stood Foster's cottage. She would help her mother to give their tea to the younger children, wash up the crockery, kiss the little ones, and go back to the farm. That was all. All the rest, all the change, all the relaxation. She never seemed to wish for anything more. And then she fell in love. She fell in love silently, obstinately—perhaps helplessly. It came slowly, but when it came it worked like a powerful spell; it was love as the Ancients understood it: an irresistible and fateful impulse—a possession! Yes, it was in her to become haunted and possessed by a face, by a presence, fatally, as though she had been a pagan worshipper of form under a joyous sky—and to be awakened at last from that mysterious forgetfulness of self, from that enchantment, from that transport, by a fear resembling the unaccountable terror of a brute. . . ."

With the sun hanging low on its western limit, the expanse of the grass-lands framed in the counterscarps of the rising ground took on a gorgeous and sombre aspect. A sense of penetrating sadness, like that inspired by a grave strain of music, disengaged itself from the silence of the fields. The men we met walked past, slow, unsmiling, with downcast eyes, as if the melancholy of an overburdened earth had weighted their feet, bowed their shoulders, borne down their glances.

"Yes," said the doctor to my remark, "one would think the earth is under a curse, since of all her children these that cling to her the closest are uncouth in body and as leaden of gait as if their very hearts were loaded with chains. But here on this same road you might have seen amongst these heavy men a being lithe, supple and long-limbed, straight like a pine, with something striving upwards in his appearance as though the heart within him had been buoyant. Perhaps it was only the force of the contrast, but when he was passing one of these villagers here, the soles of his feet did not seem to me to touch the dust of the road. He vaulted over the stiles, paced these slopes with a long elastic stride that made him noticeable at a great distance, and had lustrous black eyes. He was so different from the mankind around that, with his freedom of movement, his soft—a little startled —glance, his olive complexion and graceful bearing, his humanity suggested to me the nature of a woodland creature. He came from there."

The doctor pointed with his whip, and from the summit of the descent seen over the rolling tops of the trees in a park by the side of the road, appeared the level sea far below us, like the floor of an immense edifice inlaid with bands of dark ripple, with still trails of glitter, ending in a belt of glassy water at the foot of the sky. The light blur of smoke, from an invisible steamer, faded on the great clearness of the horizon like the mist of a breath on a mirror; and, inshore, the white sails of a coaster, with the appearance of disentangling themselves slowly from under the branches, floated clear of the foliage of the trees.

"Shipwrecked in the bay?" I said.

"Yes; he was a castaway. A poor emigrant from Central Europe bound to America and washed ashore here in a storm. And for him, who knew nothing of the earth, England was an undiscovered country. It was some time before he learned its name; and for all I know he might have expected to find wild beasts or wild men here, when, crawling in the dark over the sea-wall, he rolled down the other side into a dyke, where it was another miracle he didn't get drowned. But he struggled instinctively like an animal under a net, and this blind struggle threw him out into a field. He must have been, indeed, of a tougher fibre than he looked to withstand without expiring such buffetings, the violence of his exertions, and so much fear. Later on, in his broken English that resembled curiously the speech of a young child, he told me himself that he put his trust in God, believing he was no longer in this world. And truly—he would add—how was he to know? He fought his way against the rain and the gale on all fours, and crawled at last among some sheep huddled close under the lee of a hedge. They ran off in all directions, bleating in the darkness, and he welcomed the first familiar sound he heard on these shores. It must have been two in the morning then. And this is all we know of the manner of his landing, though he did not arrive unattended by any means. Only his grisly company did not begin to come ashore till much later in the day."

The doctor gathered the reins, clicked his tongue; we trotted down the hill. Then turning, almost directly, a sharp corner into High Street, we rattled over the stones and were home.

Late in the evening Kennedy, breaking a spell of moodiness that had come over him, returned to the story. Smoking his pipe, he paced the long room from end to end. A reading-lamp concentrated all its light upon the papers on his desk; and, sitting by the open window, I saw, after the windless, scorching day, the frigid splendour of a hazy sea lying motionless under the moon. Not a whisper, not a splash, not a stir of the shingle, not a footstep, not a sigh came up from the earth below—never a sign of life but the scent of climbing jasmine: and Kennedy's voice, speaking behind me, passed through the wide casement, to vanish outside in a chill and sumptuous stillness.

". . . The relations of shipwrecks in the olden time tell us of much suffering. Often the castaways were only saved from drowning to die miserably from starvation on a barren coast; others suffered violent death or else slavery, passing through years of precarious existence with people to whom their strangeness was an object of suspicion, dislike or fear. We read about these things, and they are very pitiful. It is indeed hard upon a man to find himself a lost stranger, helpless, incomprehensible, and of a mysterious origin, in some obscure corner of the earth. Yet amongst all the adventurers shipwrecked in all the wild parts of the world, there is not one, it seems to me, that ever had to suffer a fate so simply tragic as the man I am speaking of, the most innocent of adventurers cast out by the sea in the bight of this bay, almost within sight from this very window.

"He did not know the name of his ship. Indeed, in the course of time we discovered he did not even know that ships had names— 'like Christian people'; and when, one day, from the top of Talfourd Hill, he beheld the sea lying open to his view, his eyes roamed afar, lost in an air of wild surprise, as though he had never seen such a sight before. And probably he had not. As far as I could make out, he had been hustled together with many others on board an emigrant ship at the mouth of the Elbe, too bewildered to take note of his surroundings, too weary to see anything, too anxious to care. They were driven below into the 'tween-deck and battened down from the very start. It was a low timber dwelling—he would say—with wooden beams overhead, like the houses in his country, but you went into it down a ladder. It was very large, very cold, damp and sombre, with places in the manner of wooden boxes where people had to sleep one above another, and it kept on rocking all ways at once all the time. He crept into one of these boxes and lay down there in the clothes in which he had left his home many days before, keeping his bundle and his stick by his side. People groaned, children cried, water dripped, the lights went out, the walls of the place creaked, and everything was being shaken so that in one's little box one dared not lift one's head. He had lost touch with his only companion (a young man from the same valley, he said), and all the time a great noise of wind went on outside and heavy blows fell—boom! boom! An awful sickness overcame him, even to the point of making him neglect his prayers. Besides, one could not tell whether it was morning or evening. It seemed always to be night in that place.

"Before that he had been travelling a long, long time on the iron track. He looked out of the window, which had a wonderfully clear glass in it, and the trees, the houses, the fields, and the long roads seemed to fly round and round about him till his head swam. He gave me to understand that he had on his passage beheld uncounted multitudes of people—whole nations—all dressed in such clothes as the rich wear. Once he was made to get out of the carriage, and slept through a night on a bench in a house of bricks with his bundle under his head; and once for many hours he had to sit on a floor of flat stones, dozing, with his knees up and with his bundle between his feet. There was a roof over him, which seemed made of glass, and was so high that the tallest mountain-pine he had ever seen would have had room to grow under it. Steam-machines rolled in at one end and out at the other. People swarmed more than you can see on a feast-day round the miraculous Holy Image in the yard of the Carmelite Convent down in the plains where, before he left his home, he drove his mother in a wooden cart—a pious old woman who wanted to offer prayers and make a vow for his safety. He could not give me an idea of how large and lofty and full of noise and smoke and gloom, and clang of iron, the place was, but someone had told him it was called Berlin. Then they rang a bell, and another steam-machine came in, and again he was taken on and on through a land that wearied his eyes by its flatness without a single bit of a hill to be seen anywhere. One more night he spent shut up in a building like a good stable with a litter of straw on the floor, guarding his bundle amongst a lot of men, of whom not one could understand a single word he said. In the morning they were all led down to the stony shores of an extremely broad muddy river, flowing not between hills but between houses that seemed immense. There was a steam-machine that went on the water, and they all stood upon it packed tight, only now there were with them many women and children who made much noise. A cold rain fell, the wind blew in his face; he was wet through, and his teeth chattered. He and the young man from the same valley took each other by the hand.

"They thought they were being taken to America straight away, but suddenly the steam-machine bumped against the side of a thing like a great house on the water. The walls were smooth and black, and there uprose, growing from the roof as it were, bare trees in the shape of crosses, extremely high. That's how it appeared to him then, for he had never seen a ship before. This was the ship that was going to swim all the way to America. Voices shouted, everything swayed; there was a ladder dipping up and down. He went up on his hands and knees in mortal fear of falling into the water below, which made a great splashing. He got separated from his companion, and when he descended into the bottom of that ship his heart seemed to melt suddenly within him.

"It was then also, as he told me, that he lost contact for good and all with one of those three men who the summer before had been going about through all the little towns in the foothills of his country. They would arrive on market-days driving in a peasant's cart, and would set up an office in an inn or some other Jew's house. There were three of them, of whom one with a long beard looked venerable; and they had red cloth collars round their necks and gold lace on their sleeves like Government officials. They sat proudly behind a long table; and in the next room, so that the common people shouldn't hear, they kept a cunning telegraph machine, through which they could talk to the Emperor of America. The fathers hung about the door, but the young men of the mountains would crowd up to the table asking many questions, for there was work to be got all the year round at three dollars a day in America, and no military service to do.

"But the American Kaiser would not take everybody. Oh, no! He himself had a great difficulty in getting accepted, and the venerable man in uniform had to go out of the room several times to work the telegraph on his behalf. The American Kaiser engaged him at last at three dollars, he being young and strong. However, many able young men backed out, afraid of the great distance; besides, those only who had some money could be taken. There were some who sold their huts and their land because it cost a lot of money to get to America; but then, once there, you had three dollars a day, and if you were clever you could find places where true gold could be picked up on the ground. His father's house was getting over full. Two of his brothers were married and had children. He promised to send money home from America by post twice a year. His father sold an old cow, a pair of piebald mountain ponies of his own raising, and a cleared plot of fair pasture land on the sunny slope of a pine-clad pass to a Jew inn-keeper, in order to pay the people of the ship that took men to America to get rich in a short time.

"He must have been a real adventurer at heart, for how many of the greatest enterprises in the conquest of the earth had for their beginning just such a bargaining away of the paternal cow for the mirage of true gold far away! I have been telling you more or less in my own words what I learned fragmentarily in the course of two or three years, during which I seldom missed an opportunity of a friendly chat with him. He told me this story of his adventure with many flashes of white teeth and lively glances of black eyes, at first in a sort of anxious baby-talk, then, as he acquired the language, with great fluency, but always with that singing, soft, and at the same time vibrating intonation that instilled a strangely penetrating power into the sound of the most familiar English words, as if they had been the words of an unearthly language. And he always would come to an end, with many emphatic shakes of his head, upon that awful sensation of his heart melting within him directly he set foot on board that ship. Afterwards there seemed to come for him a period of blank ignorance, at any rate as to facts. No doubt he must have been abominably seasick and abominably unhappy—this soft and passionate adventurer, taken thus out of his knowledge, and feeling bitterly as he lay in his emigrant bunk his utter loneliness; for his was a highly sensitive nature. The next thing we know of him for certain is that he had been hiding in Hammond's pig-pound by the side of the road to Norton, six miles, as the crow flies, from the sea. Of these experiences he was unwilling to speak: they seemed to have seared into his soul a sombre sort of wonder and indignation. Through the rumours of the country-side, which lasted for a good many days after his arrival, we know that the fishermen of West Colebrook had been disturbed and startled by heavy knocks against the walls of weatherboard cottages, and by a voice crying piercingly strange words in the night. Several of them turned out even, but, no doubt, he had fled in sudden alarm at their rough angry tones hailing each other in the darkness. A sort of frenzy must have helped him up the steep Norton hill. It was he, no doubt, who early the following morning had been seen lying (in a swoon, I should say) on the roadside grass by the Brenzett carrier, who actually got down to have a nearer look, but drew back, intimidated by the perfect immobility, and by something queer in the aspect of that tramp, sleeping so still under the showers. As the day advanced, some children came dashing into school at Norton in such a fright that the schoolmistress went out and spoke indignantly to a 'horrid-looking man' on the road. He edged away, hanging his head, for a few steps, and then suddenly ran off with extraordinary fleetness. The driver of Mr. Bradley's milk-cart made no secret of it that he had lashed with his whip at a hairy sort of gipsy fellow who, jumping up at a turn of the road by the Vents, made a snatch at the pony's bridle. And he caught him a good one, too, right over the face, he said, that made him drop down in the mud a jolly sight quicker than he had jumped up; but it was a good half a mile before he could stop the pony. Maybe that in his desperate endeavours to get help, and in his need to get in touch with someone, the poor devil had tried to stop the cart. Also three boys confessed afterwards to throwing stones at a funny tramp, knocking about all wet and muddy, and, it seemed, very drunk, in the narrow deep lane by the limekilns. All this was the talk of three villages for days; but we have Mrs. Finn's (the wife of Smith's waggoner) unimpeachable testimony that she saw him get over the low wall of Hammond's pig-pound and lurch straight at her, babbling aloud in a voice that was enough to make one die of fright. Having the baby with her in a perambulator, Mrs. Finn called out to him to go away, and as he persisted in coming nearer, she hit him courageously with her umbrella over the head, and, without once looking back, ran like the wind with the perambulator as far as the first house in the village. She stopped then, out of breath, and spoke to old Lewis, hammering there at a heap of stones; and the old chap, taking off his immense black wire goggles, got up on his shaky legs to look where she pointed. Together they followed with their eyes the figure of the man running over a field; they saw him fall down, pick himself up, and run on again, staggering and waving his long arms above his head, in the direction of the New Barns Farm. From that moment on he is plainly in the toils of his obscure and touching destiny. There is no doubt after this of what happened to him. All is certain now: Mrs. Smith's intense terror; Amy Foster's stolid conviction held against the other's nervous attack, that the man 'meant no harm': Smith's exasperation (on his return from Darnford Market) at finding the dog barking himself into a fit, the back-door locked, his wife in hysterics; and all for an unfortunate dirty tramp, supposed to be even then lurking in his stackyard. Was he? He would teach him to frighten women.

"Smith is notoriously hot-tempered, but the sight of some nondescript and miry creature sitting cross-legged against a lot of loose straw, and swinging itself to and fro like a bear in a cage, made him pause. Then this tramp stood up silently before him, one mass of mud and filth from head to foot. Smith, alone amongst his stacks with this apparition, in the stormy twilight ringing with the infuriated barking of the dog, felt the dread of an inexplicable strangeness. But when that being, parting with his black hands the long matted locks that hung before his face, as you part the two halfs of a curtain, looked out at him with glistening, wild, black-and-white eyes, the weirdness of this silent encounter fairly staggered him. He has admitted since (for the story has been a legitimate subject of conversation about here for years) that he made more than one step backwards. Then a sudden burst of rapid, senseless speech persuaded him at once that he had to do with an escaped lunatic. In fact, that impression never wore off completely. Smith has not in his heart given up his secret conviction of the man's essential insanity to this very day.

"As the creature approached him, jabbering in a most discomposing manner, Smith (unaware that he was being addressed as 'gracious lord,' and adjured in God's name to afford food and shelter) kept on speaking firmly but gently to it, and retreating all the time into the other yard. At last, watching his chance, by a sudden charge he bundled him headlong into the wood-lodge, and instantly shot the bolt. Thereupon he wiped his brow, though the day was cold. He had done his duty to the community by shutting up a wandering and probably dangerous maniac. Smith isn't a hard man at all, but he had room in his brain only for that one idea of lunacy. He was not imaginative enough to ask himself whether the man might not be perishing with cold and hunger. Meantime, at first, the maniac made a great deal of noise in the lodge. Mrs. Smith was screaming upstairs, where she had locked herself in her bedroom; but Amy Foster sobbed piteously at the kitchen-door, wringing her hands and muttering, 'Don't! don't!' I daresay Smith had a rough time of it that evening with one noise and another, and this insane, disturbing voice crying obstinately through the door only added to his irritation. He couldn't possibly have connected this troublesome lunatic with the sinking of a ship in Eastbay, of which there had been a rumour in the Darnford market place. And I daresay the man inside had been very near to insanity on that night. Before his excitement collapsed and he became unconscious he was throwing himself violently about in the dark, rolling on some dirty sacks, and biting his fists with rage, cold, hunger, amazement, and despair.

"He was a mountaineer of the eastern range of the Carpathians, and the vessel sunk the night before in Eastbay was the Hamburg emigrant-ship *Herzogin Sophia-Dorothea,* of appalling memory.

"A few months later we could read in the papers the accounts of the bogus 'Emigration Agencies' among the Sclavonian peasantry in the more remote provinces of Austria. The object of these scoundrels was to get hold of the poor ignorant people's homesteads, and they were in league with the local usurers. They exported their victims through Hamburg mostly. As to the ship, I had watched her out of this very window, reaching close-hauled under short canvas into the bay on a dark, threatening afternoon. She came to an anchor, correctly by the chart, off the Brenzett Coastguard station. I remember before the night fell looking out again at the outlines of her spars and rigging that stood out dark and pointed on a background of ragged, slaty clouds like another and a slighter spire to the left of the Brenzett church-tower. In the evening the wind rose. At midnight I could hear in my bed the terrific gusts and the sounds of a driving deluge.

"About that time the Coastguardmen thought they saw the lights of a steamer over the anchoring-ground. In a moment they vanished; but it is clear that another vessel of some sort had tried for shelter in the bay on that awful, blind night, had rammed the German ship amidships (a breach—as one of the divers told me afterwards—'that you could sail a Thames barge through'), and then had gone out either scathless or damaged, who shall say; but had gone out, unknown, unseen, and fatal, to perish mysteriously at sea. Of her nothing ever came to light, and yet the hue and cry that was raised all over the world would have found her out if she had been in existence anywhere on the face of the waters.

"A completeness without a clue, and a stealthy silence as of a neatly executed crime, characterize this murderous disaster, which, as you may remember, had its gruesome celebrity. The wind would have prevented the loudest outcries from reaching the shore; there had been evidently no time for signals of distress. It was death without any sort of fuss. The Hamburg ship, filling all at once, capsized as she sank, and at daylight there was not even the end of a spar to be seen above water. She was missed, of course, and at first the Coastguardmen surmised that she had either dragged her anchor or parted her cable some time during the night, and had been blown out to sea. Then, after the tide turned, the wreck must have shifted a little and released some of the bodies, because a child—a little fair-haired child in a red frock—came ashore abreast of the Martello tower. By the afternoon you could see along three miles of beach dark figures with bare legs dashing in and out of the tumbling foam, and rough-looking men, women with hard faces, children, mostly fair-haired, were being carried, stiff and dripping, on stretchers, on wattles, on ladders, in a long procession past the door of the "Ship Inn," to be laid out in a row under the north wall of the Brenzett Church.

"Officially, the body of the little girl in the red frock is the first thing that came ashore from that ship. But I have patients amongst the seafaring population of West Colebrook, and, unofficially, I am informed that very early that morning two brothers, who went down to look after their cobble hauled up on the beach, found a good way from Brenzett, an ordinary ship's hencoop, lying high and dry on the shore, with eleven drowned ducks inside. Their families ate the birds, and the hencoop was split into firewood with a hatchet. It is possible that a man (supposing he happened to be on deck at the time of the accident) might have floated ashore on that hencoop. He might. I admit it is improbable, but there was the man—and for days, nay, for weeks—it didn't enter our heads that we had amongst us the only living soul that had escaped from that disaster. The man himself, even when he learned to speak intelligibly, could tell us very little. He remembered he had felt better (after the ship had anchored, I suppose), and that the darkness, the wind, and the rain took his breath away. This looks as if he had been on deck some time during that night. But we mustn't forget he had been taken out of his knowledge, that he had been sea-sick and battened down below for four days, that he had no general notion of a ship or of the sea, and therefore could have no definite idea of what was happening to him. The rain, the wind, the darkness he knew; he understood the bleating of the sheep, and he remembered the pain of his wretchedness and misery, his heartbroken astonishment that it was neither seen nor understood, his dismay at finding all the men angry and all the women fierce. He had approached them as a beggar, it is true, he said; but in his country, even if they gave nothing, they spoke gently to beggars. The children in his country were not taught to throw stones at those who asked for compassion. Smith's strategy overcame him completely. The wood-lodge presented the horrible aspect of a dungeon. What would be done to him next?. . . No wonder that Amy Foster appeared to his eyes with the aureole of an angel of light. The girl had not been able to sleep for thinking of the poor man, and in the morning, before the Smiths were up, she slipped out across the back yard. Holding the door of the wood-lodge ajar, she looked in and extended to him half a loaf of white bread—'such bread as the rich eat in my country,' he used to say.

"At this he got up slowly from amongst all sorts of rubbish, stiff, hungry, trembling, miserable, and doubtful. 'Can you eat this?' she asked in her soft and timid voice. He must have taken her for a 'gracious lady.' He devoured ferociously, and tears were falling on the crust. Suddenly he dropped the bread, seized her wrist, and imprinted a kiss on her hand. She was not frightened. Through his forlorn condition she had observed that he was good-looking. She shut the door and walked back slowly to the kitchen. Much later on, she told Mrs. Smith, who shuddered at the bare idea of being touched by that creature.

"Through this act of impulsive pity he was brought back again within the pale of human relations with his new surroundings. He never forgot it—never.

"That very same morning old Mr. Swaffer (Smith's nearest neighbor) came over to give his advice, and ended by carrying him off. He stood, unsteady on his legs, meek, and caked over in half-dried mud, while the two men talked around him in an incomprehensible tongue. Mrs. Smith had refused to come downstairs till the madman was off the premises; Amy Foster, far from within the dark kitchen, watched through the open back-door; and he obeyed the signs that were made to him to the best of his ability. But Smith was full of mistrust. 'Mind, sir! It may be all his cunning,' he cried repeatedly in a tone of warning. When Mr. Swaffer started the mare, the deplorable being sitting humbly by his side, through weakness, nearly fell out over the back of the high two-wheeled cart. Swaffer took him straight home. And it is then that I come upon the scene.

"I was called in by the simple process of the old man beckoning to me with his forefinger over the gate of his house as I happened to be driving past. I got down, of course.

"'I've got something here,' he mumbled, leading the way to an outhouse at a little distance from his other farm buildings.

"It was there that I saw him first, in a long, low room taken upon the space of that sort of coach-house. It was bare and whitewashed, with a small square aperture glazed with one cracked, dusty pane at its further end. He was lying on his back upon a straw pallet; they had given him a couple of horse-blankets, and he seemed to have spent the remainder of his strength in the exertion of cleaning himself. He was almost speechless; his quick breathing under the blankets pulled up to his chin, his glittering, restless black eyes reminded me of a wild bird caught in a snare. While I was examining him, old Swaffer stood silently by the door, passing the tips of his fingers along his shaven upper lip. I gave some directions, promised to send a bottle of medicine, and naturally made some inquiries.

" 'Smith caught him in the stackyard at New Barns,' said the old chap in his deliberate, unmoved manner, and as if the other had been indeed a sort of wild animal. 'That's how I came by him. Quite a curiosity, isn't he? Now tell me, doctor—you've been all over the world—don't you think that's a bit of a Hindoo we've got hold of here?'

"I was greatly surprised. His long black hair scattered over the straw bolster contrasted with the olive pallor of his face. It occurred to me he might be a Basque. It didn't necessarily follow that he should understand Spanish; but I tried him with the few words I know, and also with some French. The whispered sounds I caught by bending my ear to his lips puzzled me utterly. That afternoon the young ladies from the rectory (one of them read Goethe with a dictionary, and the other had struggled with Dante for years), coming to see Miss Swaffer, tried their German and Italian on him from the doorway. They retreated, just the least bit scared by the flood of passionate speech which, turning on his pallet, he let out at them. They admitted that the sound was pleasant, soft, musical—but, in conjunction with his looks perhaps, it was startling—so excitable, so utterly unlike anything one had ever heard. The village boys climbed up the bank to have a peep through the little square aperture. Everybody was wondering what Mr. Swaffer would do with him.

"He simply kept him.

"Swaffer would be called eccentric were he not so much respected. They will tell you that Mr. Swaffer sits up as late as ten o'clock at night to read books, and they will tell you also that he can write a cheque for two hundred pounds without thinking twice about it. He himself would tell you that the Swaffers had owned land between this and Darnford for these three hundred years. He must be eighty-five to-day, but he does not look a bit older than when I first came here. He is a great breeder of sheep, and deals extensively in cattle. He attends market days for miles around in every sort of weather, and drives sitting bowed low over the reins, his lank gray hair curling over the collar of his warm coat, and with a green plaid rug round his legs. The calmness of advanced age gives a solemnity to his manner. He is clean-shaved; his lips are thin and sensitive; something rigid and monachal in the set of his features lends a certain elevation to the character of his face. He has been known to drive miles in the rain to see a new kind of rose in somebody's garden, or a monstrous cabbage grown by a cottager. He loves to hear tell of or to be shown something that he calls 'outlandish.' Perhaps it was just that outlandishness of the man which influenced old Swaffer. Perhaps it was only an inexplicable caprice. All I know is that at the end of three weeks I caught sight of Smith's lunatic digging in Swaffer's kitchen garden. They had found out he could use a spade. He dug barefooted.

"His black hair flowed over his shoulders. I suppose it was Swaffer who had given him the striped old cotton shirt; but he wore still the national brown cloth trousers (in which he had been washed ashore) fitting to the leg almost like tights; was belted with a broad leathern belt studded with little brass discs; and had never yet ventured into the village. The land he looked upon seemed to him kept neatly, like the grounds round a landowner's house; the size of the cart-horses struck him with astonishment; the roads resembled garden walks, and the aspect of the people, especially on Sundays, spoke of opulence. He wondered what made them so hardhearted and their children so bold. He got his food at the back door, carried it in both hands, carefully, to his outhouse, and, sitting alone on his pallet, would make the sign of the cross before he began. Beside the same pallet, kneeling in the early darkness of the short days, he recited aloud the Lord's Prayer before he slept. Whenever he saw old Swaffer he would bow with veneration from his waist, and stand erect while the old man, with his fingers over his upper lip, surveyed him silently. He bowed also to Miss Swaffer, who kept house frugally for her father—a broadshouldered, big-boned woman of forty-five, with the pocket of her dress full of keys, and a gray, steady eye. She was Church—as people said (while her father was one of the trustees of the Baptist Chapel)—and wore a little steel cross at her waist. She dressed severely in black, in memory of one of the innumerable Bradleys of the neighbourhood, to whom she had been engaged some twenty-five years ago—a young farmer who broke his neck out hunting on the eve of the wedding-day. She had the unmoved countenance of the deaf, spoke very seldom, and her lips, thin like her father's, astonished one sometimes by a mysteriously ironic curl.

"These were the people to whom he owed allegiance, and an overwhelming loneliness seemed to fall from the leaden sky of that winter without sunshine. All the faces were sad. He could talk to no one, and had no hope of ever understanding anybody. It was as if these had been the faces of people from the other world—dead people—he used to tell me years afterwards. Upon my word, I wonder he did not go mad. He didn't know where he was. Somewhere very far from his mountains—somewhere over the water. Was this America, he wondered?

"If it hadn't been for the steel cross at Miss Swaffer's belt he would not, he confessed, have known whether he was in a Christian country at all. He used to cast stealthy glances at it, and feel comforted. There was nothing here the same as in his country! The earth and the water were different; there were no images of the Redeemer by the roadside. The very grass was different, and the trees. All the trees but the three old Norway pines on the bit of lawn before Swaffer's house, and these reminded him of his country. He had been detected once, after dusk, with his forehead against the trunk of them, sobbing, and talking to himself. They had been like brothers to him at that time, he affirmed. Everything else was strange. Conceive you the kind of an existence overshadowed, oppressed, by the everyday material appearances, as if by the visions of a nightmare. At night, when he could not sleep, he kept on thinking of the girl who gave him the first piece of bread he had eaten in this foreign land. She had been neither fierce nor angry, nor frightened. Her face he remembered as the only comprehensible face amongst all these faces that were as closed, as mysterious, and as mute as the faces of the dead who are possessed of a knowledge beyond the comprehension of the living. I wonder whether the memory of her compassion prevented him from cutting his throat. But there! I suppose I am an old sentimentalist, and forget the instinctive love of life which it takes all the strength of an uncommon despair to overcome.

"He did the work which was given him with an intelligence which surprised old Swaffer. By-and-by it was discovered that he could help at the ploughing, could milk the cows, feed the bullocks in the cattleyard, and was of some use with the sheep. He began to pick up words, too, very fast; and suddenly, one fine morning in spring, he rescued from an untimely death a grandchild of old Swaffer.

"Swaffer's younger daughter is married to Willcox, a solicitor and the Town Clerk of Colebrook. Regularly twice a year they come to stay with the old man for a few days. Their only child, a little girl not three years old at the time, ran out of the house alone in her little white pinafore, and, toddling across the grass of a terraced garden, pitched herself over a low wall head first into the horsepond in the yard below.

"Our man was out with the waggoner and the plough in the field nearest to the house, and as he was leading the team round to begin a fresh furrow, he saw, through the gap of a gate, what for anybody else would have been a mere flutter of something white. But he had straight-glancing, quick, far-reaching eyes, that only seemed to flinch and lose their amazing power before the immensity of the sea. He was barefooted, and looking as outlandish as the heart of Swaffer could desire. Leaving the horses on the turn, to the inexpressible disgust of the waggoner he bounded off, going over the ploughed ground in long leaps, and suddenly appeared before the mother, thrust the child into her arms, and strode away.

"The pond was not very deep; but still, if he had not had such good eyes, the child would have perished—miserably suffocated in the foot or so of sticky mud at the bottom. Old Swaffer walked out slowly into the field, waited till the plough came over to his side, had a good look at him, and without saying a word went back to the house. But from that time they laid out his meals on the kitchen table; and at first, Miss Swaffer, all in black and with an inscrutable face, would come and stand in the doorway of the living-room to see him make a big sign of the cross before he fell to. I believe that from that day, too, Swaffer began to pay him regular wages.

"I can't follow step by step his development. He cut his hair short, was seen in the village and along the road going to and fro to his work like any other man. Children ceased to shout after him. He became aware of social differences, but remained for a long time surprised at the bare poverty of the churches among so much wealth. He couldn't understand either why they were kept shut up on weekdays. There was nothing to steal in them. Was it to keep people from praying too often? The rectory took much notice of him about that time, and I believe the young ladies attempted to prepare the ground for his conversion. They could not, however, break him of his habit of crossing himself, but he went so far as to take off the string with a couple of brass medals the size of a sixpence, a tiny metal cross, and a square sort of scapulary which he wore round his neck. He hung them on the wall by the side of his bed, and he was still to be heard every evening reciting the Lord's Prayer, in incomprehensible words and in a slow, fervent tone, as he had heard his old father do at the head of all the kneeling family, big and little, on every evening of his life. And though he wore corduroys at work, and a shop-made pepper-and-salt suit on Sundays, strangers would turn round to look after him on the road. His foreignness had a peculiar and indelible stamp. At last people became used to see him. But they never became used to him. His rapid, skimming walk; his swarthy complexion; his hat cocked on the left ear; his habit, on warm evenings, of wearing his coat over one shoulder, like a hussar's dolman; his manner of leaping over the stiles, not as a feat of agility, but in the ordinary course of progression—all these peculiarities were, as one may say, so many causes of scorn and offence to the inhabitants of the village. *They* wouldn't in their dinner hour lie flat on their backs on the grass to stare at the sky. Neither did they go about the fields screaming dismal tunes. Many times I have heard his high-pitched voice from behind the ridge of some sloping sheep-walk, a voice light and soaring, like a lark's, but with a melancholy human note, over our fields that hear only the song of birds. And I would be startled myself. Ah! He was different; innocent of heart, and full of good will, which nobody wanted, this castaway, that, like a man transplanted into another planet, was separated by an immense space from his past and by an immense ignorance from his future. His quick, fervent utterance positively shocked everybody. 'An excitable devil,' they called him. One evening, in the tap-room of the Coach and Horses, (having drunk some whisky), he upset them all by singing a love-song of his country. They hooted him down, and he was pained; but Preble, the lame wheelwright, and Vincent, the fat blacksmith, and the other notables, too, wanted to drink their evening beer in peace. On another occasion he tried to show them how to dance. The dust rose in clouds from the sanded floor; he leaped straight up amongst the deal tables, struck his heels together, squatted on one heel in front of old Preble, shooting out the other leg, uttered wild and exulting cries, jumped up to whirl on one foot, snapping his fingers above his head—and a strange carter who was having a drink in there began to swear, and cleared out with his half-pint in his hand into the bar. But when suddenly he sprang upon a table and continued to dance among the glasses, the landlord interfered. He didn't want any 'acrobat tricks in the tap-room.' They laid their hands on him. Having had a glass or two, Mr. Swaffer's foreigner tried to expostulate: was ejected forcibly: got a black eye.

"I believe he felt the hostility of his human surroundings. But he was tough—tough in spirit, too, as well as in body. Only the memory of the sea frightened him, with that vague terror that is left by a bad dream. His home was far away; and he did not want now to go to America. I had often explained to him that there is no place on earth where true gold can be found lying ready and to be got for the trouble of the picking up. How, then, he asked, could he ever return home with empty hands when there had been sold a cow, two ponies, and a bit of land to pay for his going? His eyes would fill with tears, and, averting them from the immense shimmer of the sea, he would throw himself face down on the grass. But sometimes, cocking his hat with a little conquering air, he would defy my wisdom. He had found his bit of true gold. That was Amy Foster's heart; which was 'a golden heart, and soft to people's misery,' he would say in the accents of overwhelming conviction.

"He was called Yanko. He had explained that this meant Little John; but as he would also repeat very often that he was a mountaineer (some word sounding in the dialect of his country like Goorall) he got it for his surname. And this is the only trace of him that the succeeding ages may find in the marriage register of the parish. There it stands—Yanko Goorall—in the rector's handwriting. The crooked cross made by the castaway, a cross whose tracing no doubt seemed to him the most solemn part of the whole ceremony, is all that remains now to perpetuate the memory of his name.

"His courtship had lasted some time—ever since he got his precarious footing in the community. It began by his buying for Amy Foster a green satin ribbon in Darnford. This was what you did in his country. You bought a ribbon at a Jew's stall on a fair-day. I don't suppose the girl knew what to do with it, but he seemed to think that his honourable intentions could not be mistaken.

"It was only when he declared his purpose to get married that I fully understood how, for a hundred futile and inappreciable reasons, how—shall I say odious?—he was to all the countryside. Every old woman in the village was up in arms. Smith, coming upon him near the farm, promised to break his head for him if he found him about again. But he twisted his little black moustache with such a bellicose air and rolled such big, black fierce eyes at Smith that this promise came to nothing. Smith, however, told the girl that she must be mad to take up with a man who was surely wrong in his head. All the same, when she heard him in the gloaming whistle from beyond the orchard a couple of bars of a weird and mournful tune, she would drop whatever she had in her hand—she would leave Mrs. Smith in the middle of a sentence—and she would run out to his call. Mrs. Smith called her a shameless hussy. She answered nothing. She said nothing at all to anybody, and went on her way as if she had been deaf. She and I alone in all the land, I fancy, could see his very real beauty. He was very good-looking, and most graceful in his bearing, with that something wild as of a woodland creature in his aspect. Her mother moaned over her dismally. whenever the girl came to see her on her day out. The father was surly, but pretended not to know; and Mrs. Finn once told her plainly that 'this man, my dear, will do you some harm some day yet.' And so it went on. They could be seen on the roads, she tramping stolidly in her finery—gray dress, black feather, stout boots, prominent white cotton gloves that caught your eye a hundred yards away; and he, his coat slung picturesquely over one shoulder, pacing by her side, gallant of bearing and casting tender glances upon the girl with the golden heart. I wonder whether he saw how plain she was. Perhaps among types so different from what he had ever seen, he had not the power to judge; or perhaps he was seduced by the divine quality of her pity.

"Yanko was in great trouble meantime. In his country you get an old man for an ambassador in marriage affairs. He did not know how to proceed. However, one day in the midst of sheep in a field (he was now Swaffer's under-shepherd with Foster) he took off his hat to the father and declared himself humbly. 'I daresay she's fool enough to marry you,' was all Foster said. 'And then,' he used to relate, 'he puts his hat on his head, looks black at me as if he wanted to cut my throat, whistles the dog, and off he goes, leaving me to do the work.' The Fosters, of course, didn't like to lose the wages the girl earned: Amy used to give all her money to her mother. But there was in Foster a very genuine aversion to that match. He contended that the fellow was very good with sheep, but was not fit for any girl to marry. For one thing, he used to go along the hedges muttering to himself like a dam' fool; and then, these foreigners behave very queerly to women sometimes. And perhaps he would want to carry her off somewhere—or run off himself. It was not safe. He preached it to his daughter that the fellow might ill-use her in some way. She made no answer. It was, they said in the village, as if the man had done something to her. People discussed the matter. It was quite an excitement, and the two went on 'walking out' together in the face of opposition. Then something unexpected happened.

"I don't know whether old Swaffer ever understood how much he was regarded in the light of a father by his foreign retainer. Anyway the relation was curiously feudal. So when Yanko asked formally for an interview—'and the Miss, too' (he called the severe, deaf Miss Swaffer simply *Miss*)—it was to obtain their permission to marry. Swaffer heard him unmoved, dismissed him by a nod, and then shouted the intelligence into Miss Swaffer's best ear. She showed no surprise, and only remarked grimly, in a veiled blank voice, 'He certainly won't get any other girl to marry him.'

"It is Miss Swaffer who has all the credit of the munificence: but in a very few days it came out that Mr. Swaffer had presented Yanko with a cottage (the cottage you've seen this morning) and something like an acre of ground—had made it over to him in absolute property. Willcox expedited the deed, and I remember him telling me he had a great pleasure in making it ready. It recited: 'In consideration of saving the life of my beloved grandchild, Bertha Willcox.'

"Of course, after that no power on earth could prevent them from getting married.

"Her infatuation endured. People saw her going out to meet him in the evening. She stared with unblinking, fascinated eyes up the road where he was expected to appear, walking freely, with a swing from the hip, and humming one of the love-tunes of his country. When the boy was born, he got elevated at the 'Coach and Horses,' essayed again a song and a dance, and was again ejected. People expressed their commiseration for a woman married to that Jack-in-the-box. He didn't care. There was a man now (he told me boastfully) to whom he could sing and talk in the language of his country, and show how to dance by-and-by.

"But I don't know. To me he appeared to have grown less springy of step, heavier in body, less keen of eye. Imagination, no doubt; but it seems to me now as if the net of fate had been drawn closer round him already.

"One day I met him on the footpath over the Talfourd Hill. He told me that 'women were funny.' I had heard already of domestic differences. People were saying that Amy Foster was beginning to find out what sort of man she had married. He looked upon the sea with indifferent, unseeing eyes. His wife had snatched the child out of his arms one day as he sat on the doorstep crooning to it a song such as the mothers sing to babies in his mountains. She seemed to think he was doing it some harm. Women are funny. And she had objected to him praying aloud in the evening. Why? He expected the boy to repeat the prayer aloud after him by-and-by, as he used to do after his old father when he was a child—in his own country. And I discovered he longed for their boy to grow up so that he could have a man to talk with in that language that to our ears sounded so disturbing, so passionate, and so bizarre. Why his wife should dislike the idea he couldn't tell. But that would pass, he said. And tilting his head knowingly, he tapped his breastbone to indicate that she had a good heart: not hard, not fierce, open to compassion, charitable to the poor!

"I walked away thoughtfully; I wondered whether his difference, his strangeness, were not penetrating with repulsion that dull nature they had begun by irresistibly attracting. I wondered. . . ."

The Doctor came to the window and looked out at the frigid splendour of the sea, immense in the haze, as if enclosing all the earth with all the hearts lost among the passions of love and fear.

"Physiologically, now," he said, turning away abruptly, "it was possible. It was possible."

He remained silent. Then went on—

"At all events, the next time I saw him he was ill—lung trouble. He was tough, but I daresay he was not acclimatized as well as I had supposed. It was a bad winter; and, of course, these mountaineers do get fits of home sickness; and a state of depression would make him vulnerable. He was lying half dressed on a couch downstairs.

"A table covered with a dark oilcloth took up all the middle of the little room. There was a wicker cradle on the floor, a kettle spouting steam on the hob, and some child's linen lay drying on the fender. The room was warm, but the door opens right into the garden, as you noticed perhaps.

"He was very feverish, and kept on muttering to himself. She sat on a chair and looked at him fixedly across the table with her brown, blurred eyes. 'Why don't you have him upstairs?' I asked. With a start and a confused stammer she said, 'Oh! ah! I couldn't sit with him upstairs, sir.'

"I gave her certain directions; and going outside, I said again that he ought to be in bed upstairs. She wrung her hands. 'I couldn't. I couldn't. He keeps on saying something—I don't know what.' With the memory of all the talk against the man that had been dinned into her ears, I looked at her narrowly. I looked into her short-sighted eyes, at her dumb eyes that once in her life had seen an enticing shape, but seemed, staring at me, to see nothing at all now. But I saw she was uneasy.

" 'What's the matter with him?' she asked in a sort of vacant trepidation. 'He doesn't look very ill. I never did see anybody look like this before. . . .'

" 'Do you think,' I asked indignantly, 'he is shamming?'

" 'I can't help it, sir,' she said, stolidly. And suddenly she clapped her hands and looked right and left. 'And there's the baby. I am so frightened. He wanted me just now to give him the baby. I can't understand what he says to it.'

" 'Can't you ask a neighbour to come in to-night?' I asked.

" 'Please, sir, nobody seems to care to come,' she muttered, dully resigned all at once.

"I impressed upon her the necessity of the greatest care, and then had to go. There was a good deal of sickness that winter. 'Oh, I hope he won't talk!' she exclaimed softly just as I was going away.

"I don't know how it is I did not see—but I didn't. And yet, turning in my trap, I saw her lingering before the door, very still, and as if meditating a flight up the miry road.

"Towards the night his fever increased.

"He tossed, moaned, and now and then muttered a complaint. And she sat with the table between her and the couch, watching every movement and every sound, with the terror, the unreasonable terror, of that man she could not understand creeping over her. She had drawn the wicker cradle close to her feet. There was nothing in her now but the maternal instinct and that unaccountable fear.

"Suddenly coming to himself, parched, he demanded a drink of water. She did not move. She had not understood, though he may have thought he was speaking in English. He waited, looking at her, burning with fever, amazed at her silence and immobility, and then he shouted impatiently, 'Water! Give me water!'

"She jumped to her feet, snatched up the child, and stood still. He spoke to her, and his passionate remonstrances only increased her fear of that strange man. I believe he spoke to her for a long time, entreating, wondering, pleading, ordering, I suppose. She says she bore it as long as she could. And then a gust of rage came over him.

"He sat up and called out terribly one word—some word. Then he got up as though he hadn't been ill at all, she says. And as in fevered dismay, indignation, and wonder he tried to get to her round the table, she simply opened the door and ran out with the child in her arms. She heard him call twice after her down the road in a terrible voice—and fled. . . . Ah! but you should have seen the stirring behind the dull, blurred glance of those eyes the spectre of the fear which had hunted her on that night three miles and a half to the door of Foster's cottage! I did the next day.

"And it was I who found him lying face down and his body in a puddle, just outside the little wicker gate.

"I had been called out that night to an urgent case in the village, and on my way home at daybreak passed by the cottage. The door stood open. My man helped me to carry him in. We laid him on the couch. The lamp smoked, the fire was out, the chill of the stormy night oozed from the cheerless yellow paper on the wall. 'Amy!' I called aloud, and my voice seemed to lose itself in the emptiness of this tiny house as if I had cried in a desert. He opened his eyes. 'Gone!' he said, distinctly. 'I had only asked for water—only for a little water. . . .'

"He was muddy. I covered him up and stood waiting in silence, catching a painfully gasped word now and then. They were no longer in his own language. The fever had left him, taking with it the heat of life. And with his panting breast and lustrous eyes he reminded me again of a wild creature under the net; of a bird caught in a snare. She had left him. She had left him—sick—helpless—thirsty. The spear of the hunter had entered his very soul. 'Why?' he cried, in the penetrating and indignant voice of a man calling to a responsible Maker. A gust of wind and a swish of rain answered.

"And as I turned away to shut the door he pronounced the word 'Merciful!' and expired.

"Eventually I certified heart-failure as the immediate cause of death. His heart must have indeed failed him, or else he might have stood this night of storm and exposure, too. I closed his eyes and drove away. Not very far from the cottage I met Foster walking sturdily between the dripping hedges with his collie at his heels.

" 'Do you know where your daughter is?' I asked.

" 'Don't I!' he cried. 'I am going to talk to him a bit. Frightening a poor woman like this.'

" 'He won't frighten her any more,' I said. 'He is dead.'

"He struck with his stick at the mud.

" 'And there's the child.'

"Then, after thinking deeply for a while—

" 'I don't know that it isn't for the best.'

"That's what he said. And she says nothing at all now. Not a word of him. Never. Is his image as utterly gone from her mind as his lithe and striding figure, his carolling voice are gone from our fields? He is no longer before her eyes to excite her imagination into a passion of love or fear; and his memory seems to have vanished from her dull brain as a shadow passes away upon a white screen. She lives in the cottage and works for Miss Swaffer. She is Amy Foster for everybody, and the child is 'Amy Foster's boy.' She calls him Johnny —which means Little John.

"It is impossible to say whether this name recalls anything to her. Does she ever think of the past? I have seen her hanging over the boy's cot in a very passion of maternal tenderness. The little fellow was lying on his back, a little frightened at me, but very still, with his big black eyes, with his fluttered air of a bird in a snare. And looking at him I seemed to see again the other one—the father, cast out mysteriously by the sea to perish in the supreme disaster of loneliness and despair."

THE SECRET SHARER

On my right hand there were lines of fishing stakes resembling a mysterious system of half-submerged bamboo fences, incomprehensible in its division of the domain of tropical fishes, and crazy of aspect as if abandoned forever by some nomad tribe of fishermen now

THE SECRET SHARER by Joseph Conrad. Reprinted by permission of J. M. Dent & Sons Ltd., London.

gone to the other end of the ocean; for there was no sign of human habitation as far as the eye could reach. To the left a group of barren islets, suggesting ruins of stone walls, towers, and blockhouses, had its foundations set in a blue sea that itself looked solid, so still and stable did it lie below my feet; even the track of light from the westering sun shone smoothly, without that animated glitter which tells of an imperceptible ripple. And when I turned my head to take a parting glance at the tug which had just left us anchored outside the bar, I saw the straight line of the flat shore joined to the stable sea, edge to edge, with a perfect and unmarked closeness, in one leveled floor half brown, half blue under the enormous dome of the sky. Corresponding in their significance to the islets of the sea, two small clumps of trees, one on each side of the only fault in the impeccable joint, marked the mouth of the river Meinam we had just left on the first preparatory stage of our homeward journey; and, far back on the inland level, a larger and loftier mass, the grove surrounding the great Paknam pagoda, was the only thing on which the eye could rest from the vain task of exploring the monotonous sweep of the horizon. Here and there gleams as of a few scattered pieces of silver marked the windings of the great river; and on the nearest of them, just within the bar, the tug steaming right into the land became lost to my sight, hull and funnel and masts, as though the impassive earth had swallowed her up without an effort, without a tremor. My eye followed the light cloud of her smoke, now here, now there, above the plain, according to the devious curves of the stream, but always fainter and farther away, till I lost it at last behind the miter-shaped hill of the great pagoda. And then I was left alone with my ship, anchored at the head of the Gulf of Siam.

She floated at the starting point of a long journey, very still in an immense stillness, the shadows of her spars flung far to the eastward by the setting sun. At that moment I was alone on her decks. There was not a sound in her—and around us nothing moved, nothing lived, not a canoe on the water, not a bird in the air, not a cloud in the sky. In this breathless pause at the threshold of a long passage we seemed to be measuring out fitness for a long and arduous enterprise, the appointed task of both our existences to be carried out, far from all human eyes, with only sky and sea for spectators and for judges.

There must have been some glare in the air to interfere with one's sight, because it was only just before the sun left us that my roaming eyes made out beyond the highest ridge of the principal islet of the group something which did away with the solemnity of perfect solitude. The tide of darkness flowed on swiftly; and with tropical suddenness a swarm of stars came out above the shadowy earth, while I lingered yet, my hand resting lightly on my ship's rail as if on the shoulder of a trusted friend. But, with all that multitude of celestial bodies staring down at one, the comfort of quiet communion with her was gone for good. And there were also disturbing sounds by this time—voices, footsteps forward; the steward flitted along the main deck, a busily ministering spirit; a hand bell tinkled urgently under the poop deck. . . .

I found my two officers waiting for me near the supper table, in the lighted cuddy. We sat down at once, and as I helped the chief mate, I said:

"Are you aware that there is a ship anchored inside the islands? I saw her mastheads above the ridge as the sun went down."

He raised sharply his simple face, overcharged by a terrible growth of whisker, and emitted his usual ejaculations: "Bless my soul, sir! You don't say so!"

My second mate was a round-cheeked, silent young man, grave beyond his years, I thought; but as our eyes happened to meet I detected a slight quiver on his lips. I looked down at once. It was not my part to encourage sneering on board my ship. It must be said, too, that I knew very little of my officers. In consequence of certain events of no particular significance, except to myself, I had been appointed to the command only a fortnight before. Neither did I know much of the hands forward. All these people had been together for eighteen months or so, and my position was that of the only stranger on board. I mention this because it has some bearing on what is to follow. But what I felt most was my being a stranger to the ship; and if all the truth must be told, I was somewhat of a stranger to myself. The youngest man on board (barring the second mate), and untried as yet by a position of the fullest responsibility, I was willing to take the adequacy of the others for granted. They had simply to be equal to their tasks; but I wondered how far I should turn out faithful to that ideal conception of one's own personality every man sets up for himself secretly.

Meantime the chief mate, with an almost visible effect of collaboration on the part of his round eyes and frightful whiskers, was trying to evolve a theory of the anchored ship. His dominant trait was to take all things into earnest consideration. He was of a painstaking turn of mind. As he used to say, he "liked to account to himself" for practically everything that came in his way, down to a miserable scorpion he had found in his cabin a week before. The why and the wherefore of that scorpion—how it got on board and came to select his room rather than the pantry (which was a dark place and more what a scorpion would be partial to), and how on earth it managed to drown itself in the inkwell of his writing desk—had exercised him infinitely. The ship within the islands was much more easily accounted for; and just as we were about to rise from the table he made his pronouncement. She was, he doubted not, a ship from home lately arrived. Probably she drew too much water to cross the bar except at the top of spring tides. Therefore she went into that natural harbor to wait for a few days in preference to remaining in an open roadstead.

"That's so," confirmed the second mate, suddenly, in his slightly hoarse voice. "She draws over twenty feet. She's the Liverpool ship *Sephora* with a cargo of coal. Hundred and twenty-three days from Cardiff."

We looked at him in surprise.

"The tugboat skipper told me when he came on board for your letters, sir," explained the young man. "He expects to take her up the river the day after tomorrow."

After thus overwhelming us with the extent of his information he slipped out of the cabin. The mate observed regretfully that he "could not account for that young fellow's whims." What prevented him telling us all about it at once, he wanted to know.

I detained him as he was making a move. For the last two days the crew had had plenty of hard work, and the night before they had very little sleep. I felt painfully that I—a stranger—was doing something unusual when I directed him to let all hands turn in without setting an anchor watch. I proposed to keep on deck myself till one o'clock or thereabouts. I would get the second mate to relieve me at that hour.

"He will turn out the cook and the steward at four," I concluded, "and then give you a call. Of course at the slightest sign of any sort of wind we'll have the hands up and make a start at once."

He concealed his astonishment. "Very well, sir." Outside the cuddy he put his head in the second mate's door to inform him of my unheard-of caprice to take a five hours' anchor watch on myself. I heard the other raise his voice incredulously: "What? The captain himself?"

Then a few more murmurs, a door closed, then another. A few moments later I went on deck.

My strangeness, which had made me sleepless, had prompted that unconventional arrangement, as if I had expected in those solitary hours of the night to get on terms with the ship of which I knew nothing, manned by men of whom I knew very little more. Fast alongside a wharf, littered like any ship in port with a tangle of unrelated things, invaded by unrelated shore people, I had hardly seen her yet properly. Now, as she lay cleared for sea, the stretch of her main deck seemed to me very fine under the stars. Very fine, very roomy for her size, and very inviting. I descended the poop and paced the waist, my mind picturing to myself the coming passage through the Malay Archipelago, down the Indian Ocean, and up the Atlantic. All its phases were familiar enough to me, every characteristic, all the alternatives which were likely to face me on the high seas—everything! . . . except the novel responsibility of command. But I took heart from the reasonable thought that the ship was like other ships, the men like other men, and that the sea was not likely to keep any special surprises expressly for my discomfiture.

Arrived at that comforting conclusion, I bethought myself of a cigar and went below to get it. All was still down there. Everybody at the after end of the ship was sleeping profoundly. I came out again on the quarter-deck, agreeably at ease in my sleeping suit on that warm breathless night, barefooted, a glowing cigar in my teeth, and, going forward, I was met by the profound silence of the fore end of the ship. Only as I passed the door of the forecastle I heard a deep, quiet, trustful sigh of some sleeper inside. And suddenly I rejoiced in the great security of the sea as compared with the unrest of the land, in my choice of that untempted life presenting no disquieting problems, invested with an elementary moral beauty by the absolute straightforwardness of its appeal and by the singleness of its purpose.

The riding light in the fore-rigging burned with a clear, untroubled, as if symbolic, flame, confident and bright in the mysterious shades of the night. Passing on my way aft along the other side of the ship, I observed that the rope side ladder, put over, no doubt, for the master of the tug when he came to fetch away our letters, had not been hauled in as it should have been. I became annoyed at this, for exactitude in small matters is the very soul of discipline. Then I reflected that I had myself peremptorily dismissed my officers from duty, and by my own act had prevented the anchor watch being formally set and things properly attended to. I asked myself whether it was wise ever to interfere with the established routine of duties even from the kindest of motives. My action might have made me appear eccentric. Goodness only knew how that absurdly whiskered mate would "account" for my conduct, and what the whole ship thought of that informality of their new captain. I was vexed with myself.

Not from compunction certainly, but, as it were mechanically, I proceeded to get the ladder in myself. Now a side ladder of that sort is a light affair and comes in easily, yet my vigorous tug, which should have brought it flying on board, merely recoiled upon my body in a totally unexpected jerk. What the devil! . . . I was so astounded by the immovableness of that ladder that I remained stock-still, trying to account for it to myself like that imbecile mate of mine. In the end, of course, I put my head over the rail.

The side of the ship made an opaque belt of shadow on the darkling glassy shimmer of the sea. But I saw at once something elongated and pale floating very close to the ladder. Before I could form a guess a faint flash of phosphorescent light, which seemed to issue suddenly from the naked body of a man, flickered in the sleeping water with the elusive, silent play of summer lightning in a night sky. With a gasp I saw revealed to my stare a pair of feet, the long legs, a broad livid back immersed right up to the neck in a greenish cadaverous glow. One hand, awash, clutched the bottom rung of the ladder. He was complete but for the head. A headless corpse! The cigar dropped out of my gaping mouth with a tiny plop and a short hiss quite audible in the absolute stillness of all things under heaven. At that I suppose he raised up his face, a dimly pale oval in the shadow of the ship's side. But even then I could only barely make out down there the shape of his blackhaired head. However, it was enough for the horrid, frostbound sensation which had gripped me about the chest to pass off. The moment of vain exclamations was past, too. I only climbed on the spare spar and leaned over the rail as far as I could, to bring my eyes nearer to that mystery floating alongside.

As he hung by the ladder, like a resting swimmer, the sea lightning played about his limbs at every stir; and he appeared in it ghastly, silvery, fishlike. He remained as mute as a fish, too. He made no motion to get out of the water, either. It was inconceivable that he should not attempt to come on board, and strangely troubling to suspect that perhaps he did not want to. And my first words were prompted by just that troubled incertitude.

"What's the matter?" I asked in my ordinary tone; speaking down to the face upturned exactly under mine.

"Cramp," it answered, no louder. Then slightly anxious, "I say, no need to call anyone."

"I was not going to," I said.

"Are you alone on deck?"

"Yes."

I had somehow the impression that he was on the point of letting go the ladder to swim away beyond my ken—mysterious as he came. But, for the moment, this being appearing as if he had risen from the bottom of the sea (it was certainly the nearest land to the ship) wanted only to know the time. I told him. And he, down there, tentatively:

"I suppose your captain's turned in?"

"I am sure he isn't," I said.

He seemed to struggle with himself, for I heard something like the low, bitter murmur of doubt. "What's the good?" His next words came out with a hesitating effort.

"Look here, my man. Could you call him out quietly?"

I thought the time had come to declare myself.

"*I* am the captain."

I heard a "By Jove!" whispered at the level of the water. The phosphorescence flashed in the swirl of the water all about his limbs, his other hand seized the ladder.

"My name's Leggatt."

The voice was calm and resolute. A good voice. The self-possession of that man had somehow induced a corresponding state in myself. It was very quietly that I remarked:

"You must be a good swimmer."

"Yes. I've been in the water practically since nine o'clock. The question for me now is whether I am to let go this ladder and go on swimming till I sink from exhaustion, or—to come on board here."

I felt this was no mere formula of desperate speech, but a real alternative in the view of a strong soul. I should have gathered from this that he was young; indeed, it is only the young who are ever confronted by such clear issues. But at the time it was pure intuition on my part. A mysterious communication was established already between us two—in the face of that silent, darkened tropical sea. I was young, too; young enough to make no comment. The man in the water began suddenly to climb up the ladder, and I hastened away from the rail to fetch some clothes.

Before entering the cabin I stood still, listening in the lobby at the foot of the stairs. A faint snore came through the closed door of the chief mate's room. The second mate's door was on the hook, but the darkness in there was absolutely soundless. He, too, was young and could sleep like a stone. Remained the steward, but he was not likely to wake up before he was called. I got a sleeping suit out of my room and, coming back on deck, saw the naked man from the sea sitting on the main hatch, glimmering white in the darkness, his elbows on his knees and his head in his hands. In a moment he had concealed his damp body in a sleeping suit of the same gray-stripe pattern as the one I was wearing and followed me like my double on the poop. Together we moved right aft, barefooted, silent.

"What is it?" I asked in a deadened voice, taking the lighted lamp out of the binnacle, and raising it to his face.

"An ugly business."

He had rather regular features; a good mouth; light eyes under somewhat heavy, dark eyebrows; a smooth, square forehead; no growth on his cheeks; a small, brown mustache, and a well-shaped, round chin. His expression was concentrated, meditative, under the inspecting light of the lamp I held up to his face; such as a man thinking hard in solitude might wear. My sleeping suit was just right for his size. A well-knit young fellow of twenty-five at most. He caught his lower lip with the edge of white, even teeth.

"Yes," I said, replacing the lamp in the binnacle. The warm, heavy tropical night closed upon his head again.

"There's a ship over there," he murmured.

"Yes, I know. The *Sephora*. Did you know of us?"

"Hadn't the slightest idea. I am the mate of her—" He paused and corrected himself. "I should say I *was*."

"Aha! Something wrong?"

"Yes. Very wrong indeed. I've killed a man."

"What do you mean? Just now?"

"No, on the passage. Weeks ago. Thirty-nine south. When I say a man—"

"Fit of temper," I suggested, confidently.

The shadowy, dark head, like mine, seemed to nod imperceptibly above the ghostly gray of my sleeping suit. It was, in the night, as though I had been faced by my own reflection in the depths of a somber and immense mirror.

"A pretty thing to have to own up to for a *Conway* boy," murmured my double, distinctly.

"You're a *Conway* boy?"

"I am," he said, as if startled. Then, slowly . . . "Perhaps you too—"

It was so; but being a couple of years older I had left before he joined. After a quick interchange of dates a silence fell; and I thought suddenly of my absurd mate with his terrific whiskers and the "Bless my soul—you don't say so" type of intellect. My double gave me an inkling of his thoughts by saying:

"My father's a parson in Norfolk. Do you see me before a judge and jury on that charge? For myself I can't see the necessity. There are fellows that an angel from heaven— And I am not that. He was one of those creatures that are just simmering all the time with a silly sort of wickedness. Miserable devils that have no business to live at all. He wouldn't do his duty and wouldn't let anybody else do theirs. But what's the good of talking! You know well enough the sort of ill-conditioned snarling cur—"

He appealed to me as if our experiences had been as identical as our clothes. And I knew well enough the pestiferous danger of such a character where there are no means of legal repression. And I knew well enough also that my double there was no homicidal ruffian. I did not think of asking him for details, and he told me the story roughly in brusque, disconnected sentences. I needed no more. I saw it all going on as though I were myself inside that other sleeping suit.

"It happened while we were setting a reefed foresail, at dusk. Reefed foresail! You understand the sort of weather. The only sail we had left to keep the ship running; so you may guess what it had been like for days. Anxious sort of job, that. He gave me some of his cursed insolence at the sheet. I tell you I was overdone with this terrific weather that seemed to have no end to it. Terrific, I tell you—and a deep ship. I believe the fellow himself was half crazed with funk. It was no time for gentlemanly reproof, so I turned round and felled him like an ox. He up and at me. We closed just as an awful sea made for the ship. All hands saw it coming and took to the rigging, but I had him by the throat, and went on shaking him like a rat, the men above us yelling,

'Look out! look out!' Then a crash as if the sky had fallen on my head. They say that for over ten minutes hardly anything was to be seen of the ship—just the three masts and a bit of the forecastle head and of the poop all awash driving along in a smother of foam. It was a miracle that they found us, jammed together behind the forebits. It's clear that I meant business, because I was holding him by the throat still when they picked us up. He was black in the face. It was too much for them. It seems they rushed us aft together, gripped as we were, screaming 'Murder!' like a lot of lunatics, and broke into the cuddy. And the ship running for her life, touch and go all the time, any minute her last in a sea fit to turn your hair gray only a-looking at it. I understand that the skipper, too, started raving like the rest of them. The man had been deprived of sleep for more than a week, and to have this sprung on him at the height of a furious gale nearly drove him out of his mind. I wonder they didn't fling me overboard after getting the carcass of their precious shipmate out of my fingers. They had rather a job to separate us, I've been told. A sufficiently fierce story to make an old judge and a respectable jury sit up a bit. The first thing I heard when I came to myself was the maddening howling of that endless gale, and on that the voice of the old man. He was hanging on to my bunk, staring into my face out of his sou'wester.

" 'Mr. Leggatt, you have killed a man. You can act no longer as chief mate of this ship.' "

His care to subdue his voice made it sound monotonous. He rested a hand on the end of the skylight to steady himself with, and all that time did not stir a limb, so far as I could see. "Nice little tale for a quiet tea party," he concluded in the same tone.

One of my hands, too, rested on the end of the skylight; neither did I stir a limb, so far as I knew. We stood less than a foot from each other. It occurred to me that if old "Bless my soul—you don't say so" were to put his head up the companion and catch sight of us, he would think he was seeing double, or imagine himself come upon a scene of weird witchcraft; the strange captain having a quiet confabulation by the wheel with his own gray ghost. I became very much concerned to prevent anything of the sort. I heard the other's soothing undertone.

"My father's a parson in Norfolk," it said. Evidently he had forgotten he had told me this important fact before. Truly a nice little tale.

"You had better slip down into my stateroom now," I said, moving off stealthily. My double followed my movements; our bare feet made no sound; I let him in, closed the door with care, and, after giving a call to the second mate, returned on deck for my relief.

"Not much sign of any wind yet," I remarked when he approached.

"No, sir. Not much," he assented, sleepily, in his hoarse voice, with just enough deference, no more, and barely suppressing a yawn.

"Well, that's all you have to look out for. You have got your orders."

"Yes, sir."

I paced a turn or two on the poop and saw him take up his position face forward with his elbow in the ratlines of the mizzen-rigging before I went below. The mate's faint snoring was still going on peacefully. The cuddy lamp was burning over the table on which stood a vase with flowers, a polite attention from the ship's provision merchant— the last flowers we should see for the next three months at the very least. Two bunches of bananas hung from the beam symmetrically, one on each side of the rudder casing. Everything was as before in the ship—except that two of her captain's sleeping suits were simultaneously in use, one motionless in the cuddy, the other keeping very still in the captain's stateroom.

It must be explained here that my cabin had the form of the capital letter L, the door being within the angle and opening into the short part of the letter. A couch was to the left, the bed-place to the right; my writing desk and the chronometers' table faced the door. But anyone opening it, unless he stepped right inside, had no view of what I call the long (or vertical) part of the letter. It contained some lockers surmounted by a book case; and a few clothes, a thick jacket or two, caps, oilskin coat, and such like, hung on hooks. There was at the bottom of that part a door opening into my bathroom, which could be entered also directly from the saloon. But that way was never used.

The mysterious arrival had discovered the advantage of this particular shape. Entering my room, lighted strongly by a big bulkhead lamp swung on gimbals above my writing desk, I did not see him anywhere till he stepped out quietly from behind the coats hung in the recessed part.

"I heard somebody moving about, and went in there at once," he whispered.

I, too, spoke under my breath.

"Nobody is likely to come in here without knocking and getting permission."

He nodded. His face was thin and the sunburn faded, as though he had been ill. And no wonder. He had been, I heard presently, kept under arrest in his cabin for nearly seven weeks. But there was nothing sickly in his eyes or in his expression. He was not a bit like me, really; yet, as we stood leaning over my bed-place, whispering side by side, with our dark heads together and our backs to the door, anybody bold enough to open it stealthily would have been treated to the uncanny sight of a double captain busy talking in whispers with his other self.

"But all this doesn't tell me how you came to hang on to our side ladder," I inquired, in the hardly audible murmurs we used, after he had told me something more of the proceedings on board the *Sephora* once the bad weather was over.

"When we sighted Java Head I had had time to think all those matters out several times over. I had six weeks of doing nothing else, and with only an hour or so every evening for a tramp on the quarter deck."

He whispered, his arms folded on the side of my bed-place, staring through the open port. And I could imagine perfectly the manner of this thinking out—a stubborn if not a steadfast operation; something of which I should have been perfectly incapable.

"I reckoned it would be dark before we closed with the land," he continued, so low that I had to strain my hearing, near as we were to each other, shoulder touching shoulder almost. "So I asked to speak to the old man. He always seemed very sick when he came to see me—as if he could not look me in the face. You know, that foresail saved the ship. She was too deep to have run long under bare poles. And it was I that managed to set it for him. Anyway, he came. When I had him in my cabin—he stood by the door looking at me as if I had the halter around my neck already—I asked him right away to leave my cabin door unlocked at night while the ship was going through Sunda Straits. There would be the Java coast within two or three miles, off Angier Point. I wanted nothing more. I've had a prize for swimming my second year in the *Conway*."

"I can believe it," I breathed out.

"God only knows why they locked me in every night. To see some of their faces you'd have thought they were afraid I'd go about at night strangling people. Am I a murdering brute? Do I look it? By Jove! if I had been he wouldn't have trusted himself like that into my room. You'll say I might have chucked him aside and bolted out, there and then—it was dark already. Well, no. And for the same reason I wouldn't think of trying to smash the door. There would have been a rush to stop me at the noise, and I did not mean to get into a confounded scrimmage. Somebody else might have got killed —for I would not have broken out only to get chucked back, and I did not want any more of that work. He refused, looking more sick than ever. He was afraid of the men, and also of that old second mate of his who had been sailing with him for years—a gray-headed old humbug; and his steward, too, had been with him devil knows how long—seventeen years or more—a dogmatic sort of loafer who hated me like poison, just because I was the chief mate. No chief mate ever made more than one voyage in the *Sephora,* you know. Those two old chaps ran the ship. Devil only knows what the skipper wasn't afraid of (all his nerve went to pieces altogether in that hellish spell of bad weather we had)—of what the law would do to him—of his wife, perhaps. Oh, yes! she's on board. Though I don't think she would have meddled. She would have been only too glad to have me out of the ship in any way. The 'brand of Cain' business, don't you see. That's all right. I was ready enough to go off wandering on the face of the earth—and that was price enough to pay for an Abel of that sort. Anyhow, he wouldn't listen to me. 'This thing must take its course. I represent the law here.' He was shaking like a leaf. 'So you won't?' 'No!' 'Then I hope you will be able to sleep on that,' I said, and turned my back on him. 'I wonder that *you* can,' cries he, and locks the door.

"Well, after that, I couldn't. Not very well. That was three weeks ago. We have had a slow passage through the Java Sea; drifted about Carimata for ten days. When we anchored here they thought, I suppose, it was all right. The nearest land (and that's five miles) is the ship's destination; the consul would soon set about catching me; and there would have been no object in bolting to these islets there. I don't suppose there's a drop of water on them. I don't know how it was, but tonight that steward, after bringing me my supper, went out to let me eat it, and left the door unlocked. And I ate it—all there was, too. After I had finished I strolled out on the quarter-deck. I don't know that I meant to do anything. A breath of fresh air was all

I wanted, I believe. Then a sudden temptation came over me. I kicked off my slippers and was in the water before I had made up my mind fairly. Somebody heard the splash and they raised an awful hullabaloo. 'He's gone! Lower the boats! He's committed suicide! No, he's swimming.' Certainly I was swimming. It's not so easy for a swimmer like me to commit suicide by drowning. I landed on the nearest islet before the boat left the ship's side. I heard them pulling about in the dark, hailing, and so on, but after a bit they gave up. Everything quieted down and the anchorage became as still as death. I sat down on a stone and began to think. I felt certain they would start searching for me at daylight. There was no place to hide on those stony things—and if there had been, what would have been the good? But now I was clear of that ship, I was not going back. So after a while I took off all my clothes, tied them up in a bundle with a stone inside, and dropped them in the deep water on the outer side of that islet. That was suicide enough for me. Let them think what they liked, but I didn't mean to drown myself. I meant to swim till I sank—but that's not the same thing. I struck out for another of these little islands, and it was from that one that I first saw your riding light. Something to swim for. I went on easily, and on the way I came upon a flat rock a foot or two above water. In the daytime, I dare say, you might make it out with a glass from your poop. I scrambled up on it and rested myself for a bit. Then I made another start. That last spell must have been over a mile."

His whisper was getting fainter and fainter, and all the time he stared straight out through the porthole, in which there was not even a star to be seen. I had not interrupted him. There was something that made comment impossible in his narrative, or perhaps in himself; a sort of feeling, a quality, which I can't find a name for. And when he ceased, all I found was a futile whisper: "So you swam for our light?"

"Yes—straight for it. It was something to swim for. I couldn't see any stars low down because the coast was in the way, and I couldn't see the land, either. The water was like glass. One might have been swimming in a confounded thousand-feet deep cistern with no place for scrambling out anywhere; but what I didn't like was the notion of swimming round and round like a crazed bullock before I gave out; and as I didn't mean to go back . . . No. Do you see me being hauled back, stark naked, off one of these little islands by the scruff of the neck and fighting like a wild beast? Somebody would have got killed for certain, and I did not want any of that. So I went on. Then your ladder—"

"Why didn't you hail the ship?" I asked, a little louder.

He touched my shoulder lightly. Lazy footsteps came right over our heads and stopped. The second mate had crossed from the other side of the poop and might have been hanging over the rail, for all we knew.

"He couldn't hear us talking—could he?" My double breathed into my very ear, anxiously.

His anxiety was an answer, a sufficient answer, to the question I had put to him. An answer containing all the difficulty of that situation. I closed the porthole quietly, to make sure. A louder word might have been overheard.

"Who's that?" he whispered then.

"My second mate. But I don't know much more of the fellow than you do."

And I told him a little about myself. I had been appointed to take charge while I least expected anything of the sort, not quite a fortnight ago. I didn't know either the ship or the people. Hadn't had the time in port to look about me or size anybody up. And as to the crew, all they knew was that I was appointed to take the ship home. For the rest, I was almost as much of a stranger on board as himself, I said. And at the moment I felt it most acutely. I felt that it would take very little to make me a suspect person in the eyes of the ship's company.

He had turned about meantime; and we, the two strangers in the ship, faced each other in identical attitudes.

"Your ladder—" he murmured, after a silence. "Who'd have thought of finding a ladder hanging over at night in a ship anchored out here! I felt just then a very unpleasant faintness. After the life I've been leading for nine weeks, anybody would have got out of condition. I wasn't capable of swimming round as far as your rudder chains. And, lo and behold! there was a ladder to get hold of. After I gripped it I said to myself, 'What's the good?' When I saw a man's head looking over I thought I would swim away presently and leave him shouting—in whatever language it was. I didn't mind being looked at. I—I liked it. And then you speaking to me so quietly—as if you had expected me—made me hold on a little longer. It had been a confounded lonely time—I don't mean while swimming. I was glad to talk a little to somebody that didn't belong to the *Sephora*. As to asking for the captain, that was a mere impulse. It could have been no use, with all the ship knowing about me and the other people pretty certain to be round here in the morning. I don't know—I wanted to be seen, to talk with somebody, before I went on. I don't know what I would have said. . . . 'Fine night, isn't it?' or something of the sort."

"Do you think they will be round here presently?" I asked with some incredulity.

"Quite likely," he said, faintly.

He looked extremely haggard all of a sudden. His head rolled on his shoulders.

"H'm. We shall see then. Meantime get into that bed," I whispered. "Want help? There."

It was a rather high bed-place with a set of drawers underneath. This amazing swimmer really needed the lift I gave him by seizing his leg. He tumbled in, rolled over on his back, and flung one arm across his eyes. And then, with his face nearly hidden, he must have looked exactly as I used to look in that bed. I gazed upon my other self for a while before drawing across carefully the two green serge curtains which ran on a brass rod. I thought for a moment of pinning them together for greater safety, but I sat down on the couch, and once there I felt unwilling to rise and hunt for a pin. I would do it in a moment. I was extremely tired, in a peculiarly intimate way, by the strain of stealthiness, by the effort of whispering and the general secrecy of this excitement. It was three o'clock by now and I had been on my feet since nine, but I was not sleepy; I could not have gone to sleep. I sat there, fagged out, looking at the curtains, trying to clear my mind of the confused sensation of being in two places at once, and greatly bothered by an exasperating knocking in my head. It was a relief to discover suddenly that it was not in my head at all, but on the outside of the door. Before I could collect myself the words "Come in" were out of my mouth, and the steward entered with a tray, bringing in my morning coffee. I had slept, after all, and I was so frightened that I shouted, "This way! I am here, steward," as though he had been miles away. He put down the tray on the table next the couch and only then said, very quietly, "I can see you are here, sir." I felt him give me a keen look, but I dared not meet his eyes just then. He must have wondered why I had drawn the curtains of my bed before going to sleep on the couch. He went out, hooking the door open as usual.

I heard the crew washing decks above me. I knew I would have been told at once if there had been any wind. Calm, I thought, and I was doubly vexed. Indeed, I felt dual more than ever. The steward reappeared suddenly in the doorway. I jumped up from the couch so quickly that he gave a start.

"What do you want here?"

"Close your port, sir—they are washing decks."

"It is closed," I said, reddening.

"Very well, sir." But he did not move from the doorway and re- turned my stare in an extraordinary, equivocal manner for a time. Then his eyes wavered, all his expression changed, and in a voice unusually gentle, almost coaxingly:

"May I come in to take the empty cup away, sir?"

"Of course!" I turned my back on him while he popped in and out. Then I unhooked and closed the door and even pushed the bolt. This sort of thing could not go on very long. The cabin was as hot as an oven, too. I took a peep at my double, and discovered that he had not moved, his arm was still over his eyes; but his chest heaved; his hair was wet; his chin glistened with perspiration. I reached over him and opened the port.

"I must show myself on deck," I reflected.

Of course, theoretically, I could do what I liked, with no one to say nay to me within the whole circle of the horizon; but to lock my cabin door and take the key away I did not dare. Directly I put my head out of the companion I saw the group of my two officers, the second mate barefooted, the chief mate in long india-rubber boots, near the break of the poop, and the steward halfway down the poop ladder talking to them eagerly. He happened to catch sight of me and dived, the second ran down on the main desk shouting some order or other, and the chief mate came to meet me, touching his cap.

There was a sort of curiosity in his eye that I did not like. I don't know whether the steward had told them that I was "queer" only, or downright drunk, but I know the man meant to have a good look at me. I watched him coming with a smile which, as he got into point- blank range, took effect and froze his very whiskers. I did not give him time to open his lips.

"Square the yards by lifts and braces before the hands go to breakfast."

It was the first particular order I had given on board that ship; and I stayed on deck to see it executed, too. I had felt the need of asserting myself without loss of time. That sneering young cub got taken down a peg or two on that occasion, and I also seized the opportunity of having a good look at the face of every foremast man as they filed past me to go to the after braces. At breakfast time, eating nothing myself, I presided with such frigid dignity that the two mates were only too glad to escape from the cabin as soon as decency permitted; and all the time the dual working of my mind distracted me almost to the point of insanity. I was constantly watching myself, my secret self, as dependent on my actions as my own personality, sleeping in that bed, behind that door which faced me as I sat at the head of the table. It was very much like being mad, only it was worse because one was aware of it.

I had to shake him for a solid minute, but when at last he opened his eyes it was in the full possession of his senses, with an inquiring look.

"All's well so far," I whispered. "Now you must vanish into the bathroom."

He did so, as noiseless as a ghost, and I then rang for the steward, and facing him boldly, directed him to tidy up my stateroom while I was having my bath—"and be quick about it." As my tone admitted of no excuses, he said, "Yes, sir," and ran off to fetch his dustpan and brushes. I took a bath and did most of my dressing, splashing, and whistling softly for the steward's edification, while the secret sharer of my life stood drawn up bolt upright in that little space, his face looking very sunken in daylight, his eyelids lowered under the stern, dark line of his eyebrows drawn together by a slight frown.

When I left him there to go back to my room the steward was finishing dusting. I sent for the mate and engaged him in some insignificant conversation. It was, as it were, trifling with the terrific character of his whiskers; but my object was to give him an opportunity for a good look at my cabin. And then I could at last shut, with a clear conscience, the door of my stateroom and get my double back into the recessed part. There was nothing else for it. He had to sit still on a small folding stool, half smothered by the heavy coats hanging there. We listened to the steward going into the bathroom out of the saloon, filling the water bottles there, scrubbing the bath, setting things to rights, whisk, bang, clatter—out again into the saloon—turn the key—click. Such was my scheme for keeping my second self invisible. Nothing better could be contrived under the circumstances. And there we sat; I at my writing desk ready to appear busy with some papers, he behind me, out of sight of the door. It would not have been prudent to talk in daytime; and I could not have stood the excitement of that queer sense of whispering to myself. Now and then, glancing over my shoulder, I saw him far back there, sitting rigidly on the low stool, his bare feet close together, his arms folded, his head hanging on his breast—and perfectly still. Anybody would have taken him for me.

I was fascinated by it myself. Every moment I had to glance over my shoulder. I was looking at him when a voice outside the door said: "Beg pardon, sir."

"Well!" . . . I kept my eyes on him, and so, when the voice outside the door announced, "There's a ship's boat coming our way, sir," I saw him give a start—the first movement he had made for hours. But he did not raise his bowed head.

"All right. Get the ladder over."

I hesitated. Should I whisper something to him? But what? His immobility seemed to have been never disturbed. What could I tell him he did not know already? . . . Finally I went on deck.

II

The skipper of the *Sephora* had a thin red whisker all round his face, and the sort of complexion that goes with hair of that color; also the particular, rather smeary shade of blue in the eyes. He was not exactly a showy figure; his shoulders were high, his stature but middling—one leg slightly more bandy than the other. He shook hands, looking vaguely around. A spiritless tenacity was his main characteristic, I judged. I behaved with a politeness which seemed to disconcert him. Perhaps he was shy. He mumbled to me as if he were ashamed of what he was saying; gave his name (it was something like Archbold—but at this distance of years I hardly am sure), his ship's name, and a few other particulars of that sort, in the manner of a criminal making a reluctant and doleful confession. He had had terrible weather on the passage out—terrible—terrible—wife aboard, too.

By this time we were seated in the cabin and the steward brought in a tray with a bottle and glasses. "Thanks! No." Never took liquor. Would have some water, though. He drank two tumblerfuls. Terrible thirsty work. Ever since daylight had been exploring the islands round his ship.

"What was that for—fun?" I asked, with an appearance of polite interest.

"No!" He sighed. "Painful duty."

As he persisted in his mumbling and I wanted my double to hear every word, I hit upon the notion of informing him that I regretted to say I was hard of hearing.

"Such a young man, too!" he nodded, keeping his smeary blue, unintelligent eyes fastened upon me. What was the cause of it—some disease? he inquired, without the least sympathy and as if he thought that, if so, I'd got no more than I deserved.

"Yes; disease," I admitted in a cheerful tone which seemed to shock him. But my point was gained, because he had to raise his voice to give me his tale. It is not worth while to record that version. It was just over two months since all this had happened, and he had thought so much about it that he seemed completely muddled as to its bearings, but still immensely impressed.

"What would you think of such a thing happening on board your own ship? I've had the *Sephora* for these fifteen years. I am a well-known shipmaster."

He was densely distressed—and perhaps I should have sympathized with him if I had been able to detach my mental vision from the unsuspected sharer of my cabin as though he were my second self. There he was on the other side of the bulkhead, four or five feet from us, no more, as we sat in the saloon. I looked politely at Captain Archbold (if that was his name), but it was the other I saw, in a gray sleeping suit, seated on a low stool, his bare feet close together, his arms folded, and every word said between us falling into the ears of his dark head bowed on his chest.

"I have been at sea now, man and boy, for seven-and-thirty years, and I've never heard of such a thing happening in an English ship. And that it should be my ship. Wife on board, too."

I was hardly listening to him.

"Don't you think," I said, "that the heavy sea which, you told me, came aboard just then might have killed the man? I have seen the sheer weight of a sea kill a man very neatly, by simply breaking his neck."

"Good God!" he uttered, impressively, fixing his smeary blue eyes on me. "The sea! No man killed by the sea ever looked like that." He seemed positively scandalized at my suggestion. And as I gazed at him, certainly not prepared for anything original on his part, he advanced his head close to mine and thrust his tongue out at me so suddenly that I couldn't help starting back.

After scoring over my calmness in this graphic way he nodded wisely. If I had seen the sight, he assured me, I would never forget it as long as I lived. The weather was too bad to give the corpse a proper sea burial. So next day at dawn they took it up on the poop, covering its face with a bit of bunting; he read a short prayer, and then, just as it was, in its oilskins and long boots, they launched it amongst those mountainous seas that seemed ready every moment to swallow up the ship herself and the terrified lives on board of her.

"That reefed foresail saved you," I threw in.

"Under God—it did," he exclaimed fervently. "It was by a special mercy, I firmly believe, that it stood some of those hurricane squalls."

"It was the setting of that sail which—" I began.

"God's own hand in it," he interrupted me. "Nothing less could have done it. I don't mind telling you that I hardly dared give the order. It seemed impossible that we could touch anything without losing it, and then our last hope would have been gone."

The terror of that gale was on him yet. I let him go on for a bit, then said, casually—as if returning to a minor subject:

"You were very anxious to give up your mate to the shore people, I believe?"

He was. To the law. His obscure tenacity on that point had in it something incomprehensible and a little awful; something, as it were, mystical, quite apart from his anxiety that he should not be suspected of "countenancing any doings of that sort." Seven-and-thirty virtuous years at sea, of which over twenty of immaculate command, and the last fifteen in the *Sephora,* seemed to have laid him under some pitiless obligation.

"And you know," he went on, groping shamefacedly amongst his feelings, "I did not engage that young fellow. His people had some interest with my owners. I was in a way forced to take him on. He looked very smart, very gentlemanly, and all that. But do you know

—I never liked him, somehow. I am a plain man. You see, he wasn't exactly the sort for the chief mate of a ship like the *Sephora*."

I had become so connected in thoughts and impressions with the secret sharer of my cabin that I felt as if I, personally, were being given to understand that I, too, was not the sort that would have done for the chief mate of a ship like the *Sephora*. I had no doubt of it in my mind.

"Not at all the style of man. You understand," he insisted superfluously, looking hard at me.

I smiled urbanely. He seemed at a loss for a while.

"I suppose I must report a suicide."

"Beg pardon?"

"Sui-cide! That's what I'll have to write to my owners directly I get in."

"Unless you manage to recover him before tomorrow," I assented, dispassionately. . . . "I mean, alive."

He mumbled something which I really did not catch, and I turned my ear to him in a puzzled manner. He fairly bawled:

"The land—I say, the mainland is at least seven miles off my anchorage."

"About that."

My lack of excitement, of curiosity, of surprise, of any sort of pronounced interest, began to arouse his distrust. But except for the felicitous pretense of deafness I had not tried to pretend anything. I had felt utterly incapable of playing the part of ignorance properly, and therefore was afraid to try. It is also certain that he had brought some ready-made suspicions with him, and that he viewed my politeness as a strange and unnatural phenomenon. And yet how else could I have received him? Not heartily! That was impossible for psychological reasons, which I need not state here. My only object was to keep off his inquiries. Surlily? Yes, but surliness might have provoked a point-blank question. From its novelty to him and from its nature, punctilious courtesy was the manner best calculated to restrain the man. But there was the danger of his breaking through my defense bluntly. I could not, I think, have met him by a direct lie, also for psychological (not moral) reasons. If he had only known how afraid I was of his putting my feeling of identity with the other to the test! But, strangely enough—(I thought of it only afterward)—I believe that he was not a little disconcerted by the reverse side of that weird situa-

tion, by something in me that reminded him of the man he was seeking—suggested a mysterious similitude to the young fellow he had
distrusted and disliked from the first.

However that might have been, the silence was not very prolonged.
He took another oblique step.

"I reckon I had no more than a two-mile pull to your ship. Not a
bit more."

"And quite enough, too, in this awful heat," I said.

Another pause full of mistrust followed. Necessity, they say, is
mother of invention, but fear, too, is not barren of ingenious sugges-
tions. And I was afraid he would ask me point-blank for news of
my other self.

"Nice little saloon, isn't it?" I remarked, as if noticing for the first
time the way his eyes roamed from one closed door to the other. "And
very well fitted out, too. Here, for instance," I continued, reaching
over the back of my seat negligently and flinging the door open, "is
my bathroom."

He made an eager movement, but hardly gave it a glance. I got
up, shut the door of the bathroom, and invited him to have a look
round, as if I were very proud of my accommodation. He had to rise
and be shown round, but he went through the business without any
raptures whatever.

"And now we'll have a look at my stateroom," I declared, in a voice
as loud as I dared to make it, crossing the cabin to the starboard side
with purposely heavy steps.

He followed me in and gazed around. My intelligent double had
vanished. I played my part.

"Very convenient—isn't it?"

"Very nice. Very com . . ." He didn't finish, and went out
brusquely as if to escape from some unrighteous wiles of mine. But
it was not to be. I had been too frightened not to feel vengeful; I felt
I had him on the run, and I meant to keep him on the run. My polite
insistence must have had something menacing in it, because he gave
in suddenly. And I did not let him off a single item; mate's room,
pantry, storerooms, the very sail locker which was also under the
poop—he had to look into them all. When at last I showed him out
on the quarter-deck he drew a long, spiritless sigh, and mumbled dismally that he must really be going back to his ship now. I desired my
mate, who had joined us, to see to the captain's boat.

The man of whiskers gave a blast on the whistle which he used to wear hanging round his neck, and yelled, *"Sephora* away!" My double down there in my cabin must have heard, and certainly could not feel more relieved than I. Four fellows came running out from somewhere forward and went over the side, while my own men, appearing on deck too, lined the rail. I escorted my visitor to the gangway ceremoniously, and nearly overdid it. He was a tenacious beast. On the very ladder he lingered, and in that unique, guiltily consciousness manner of sticking to the point:

"I say . . . you . . . you don't think that—"

I covered his voice loudly:

"Certainly not. . . . I am delighted. Good-by."

I had an idea of what he meant to say, and just saved myself by the privilege of defective hearing. He was too shaken generally to insist, but my mate, close witness of that parting, looked mystified and his face took on a thoughtful cast. As I did not want to appear as if I wished to avoid all communication with my officers, he had the opportunity to address me.

"Seems a very nice man. His boat's crew told our chaps a very extraordinary story, if what I am told by the steward is true. I suppose you had it from the captain, sir?"

"Yes. I had a story from the captain."

"A very horrible affair—isn't it, sir?"

"It is."

"Beats all these tales we hear about murders in Yankee ships."

"I don't think it beats them. I don't think it resembles them in the least."

"Bless my soul—you don't say so! But of course I've no acquaintance whatever with American ships, not I, so I couldn't go against your knowledge. It's horrible enough for me. . . . But the queerest part is that those fellows seemed to have some idea the man was hidden aboard here. They had really. Did you ever hear of such a thing?"

"Preposterous—isn't it?"

We were walking to and fro athwart the quarter-deck. No one of the crew forward could be seen (the day was Sunday), and the mate pursued:

"There was some little dispute about it. Our chaps took offense. 'As if we would harbor a thing like that,' they said. 'Wouldn't you like to look for him in our coal hole?' Quite a tiff. But they made it up in the end. I suppose he did drown himself. Don't you, sir?"

"I don't suppose anything."

"You have no doubt in the matter, sir?"

"None whatever."

I left him suddenly. I felt I was producing a bad impression, but with my double down there it was most trying to be on deck. And it was almost as trying to be below. Altogether a nerve-trying situation. But on the whole I felt less torn in two when I was with him. There was no one in the whole ship whom I dared take into my confidence. Since the hands had got to know his story, it would have been impossible to pass him off for anyone else, and an accidental discovery was to be dreaded now more than ever. . . .

The steward being engaged in laying the table for dinner, we could talk only with our eyes when I first went down. Later in the afternoon we had a cautious try at whispering. The Sunday quietness of the ship was against us; the stillness of air and water around her was against us; the elements, the men were against us—everything was against us in our secret partnership; time itself—for this could not go on forever. The very trust in Providence was, I suppose, denied to his guilt. Shall I confess that this thought cast me down very much? And as to the chapter of accidents which counts for so much in the book of success, I could only hope that it was closed. For what favorable accident could be expected?

"Did you hear everything?" were my first words as soon as we took up our position side by side, leaning over my bed-place.

He had. And the proof of it was his earnest whisper, "The man told you he hardly dared to give the order."

I understood the reference to be to that saving foresail.

"Yes. He was afraid of it being lost in the setting."

"I assure you he never gave the order. He may think he did, but he never gave it. He stood there with me on the break of the poop after the maintopsail blew away, and whimpered about our last hope—positively whimpered about it and nothing else—and the night coming on! To hear one's skipper go on like that in such weather was enough to drive any fellow out of his mind. It worked me up into a sort of desperation. I just took it into my own hands and went away from him, boiling, and—. But what's the use telling you? *You* know! . . . Do you think that if I had not been pretty fierce with them I should have got the men to do anything? Not it! The bosun perhaps? Perhaps! It wasn't a heavy sea—it was a sea gone mad! I suppose the end of the world will be something like that; and a man may have the heart to see it coming once and be done with it—but to have to face it day after day—I don't blame anybody. I was precious little better than the rest. Only—I was an officer of that old coal-wagon, anyhow—"

"I quite understand," I conveyed that sincere assurance into his ear. He was out of breath with whispering; I could hear him pant slightly. It was all very simple. The same strung-up force which had given twenty-four men a chance, at least, for their lives, had, in a sort of recoil, crushed an unworthy mutinous existence.

But I had no leisure to weigh the merits of the matter—footsteps in the saloon, a heavy knock. "There's enough wind to get under way with, sir." Here was the call of a new claim upon my thoughts and even upon my feelings.

"Turn the hands up," I cried through the door. "I'll be on deck directly."

I was going out to make the acquaintance of my ship. Before I left the cabin our eyes met—the eyes of the only two strangers on board. I pointed to the recessed part where the little campstool awaited him and laid my finger on my lips. He made a gesture—somewhat vague —a little mysterious, accompanied by a faint smile, as if of regret.

This is not the place to enlarge upon the sensations of a man who feels for the first time a ship move under his feet to his own independent word. In my case they were not unalloyed. I was not wholly alone with my command; for there was that stranger in my cabin. Or rather, I was not completely and wholly with her. Part of me was absent. That mental feeling of being in two places at once affected me physically as if the mood of secrecy had penetrated my very soul. Before an hour had elapsed since the ship had begun to move, having occasion to ask the mate (he stood by my side) to take a compass bearing of the Pagoda, I caught myself reaching up to his ear in whispers. I say I caught myself, but enough had escaped to startle the man. I can't describe it otherwise than by saying that he shied. A grave, preoccupied manner, as though he were in possession of some perplexing intelligence, did not leave him henceforth. A little later I moved away from the rail to look at the compass with such a stealthy gait that the helmsman noticed it—and I could not help noticing the unusual roundness of his eyes. These are trifling instances, though it's to no commander's advantage to be suspected of ludicrous eccentricities. But I was also more seriously affected. There are to a seaman certain words, gestures, that should in given conditions come as naturally, as instinctively as the winking of a menaced eye. A certain order should spring on to his lips without thinking; a certain sign should get itself made, so to speak, without reflection. But all unconscious alertness had abandoned me. I had to make an effort of will to recall myself back (from the cabin) to the conditions of the moment. I felt that I was appearing an irresolute commander to those people who were watching me more or less critically.

And, besides, there were the scares. On the second day out, for instance, coming off the deck in the afternoon (I had straw slippers on my bare feet) I stopped at the open pantry door and spoke to the steward. He was doing something there with his back to me. At the sound of my voice he nearly jumped out of his skin, as the saying is, and incidentally broke a cup.

"What on earth's the matter with you?" I asked astonished.

He was extremely confused. "Beg pardon, sir. I made sure you were in your cabin."

"You see I wasn't."

"No, sir. I could have sworn I had heard you moving in there not a moment ago. It's most extraordinary . . . very sorry, sir."

I passed on with an inward shudder. I was so identified with my secret double that I did not even mention the fact in those scanty, fearful whispers we exchanged. I suppose he had made some slight noise of some kind or other. It would have been miraculous if he hadn't at one time or another. And yet, haggard as he appeared, he looked always perfectly self-controlled, more than calm—almost invulnerable. On my suggestion he remained almost entirely in the bathroom, which, upon the whole, was the safest place. There could be really no shadow of an excuse for anyone ever wanting to go in there, once the steward had done with it. It was a very tiny place. Sometimes he reclined on the floor, his legs bent, his head sustained on one elbow. At others I would find him on the campstool, sitting in his gray sleeping suit and with his cropped dark hair like a patient, unmoved convict. At night I would smuggle him into my bed-place, and we would whisper together, with the regular footfalls of the officer of the watch passing and repassing over our heads. It was an infinitely miserable time. It was lucky that some tins of fine preserves were stowed in a locker in my stateroom; hard bread I could always get hold of; and so he lived on stewed chicken, paté de foie gras, asparagus, cooked oysters, sardines—on all sorts of abominable sham delicacies out of tins. My early morning coffee he always drank; and it was all I dared do for him in that respect.

Every day there was the horrible maneuvering to go through so that my room and then the bathroom should be done in the usual way. I came to hate the sight of the steward, to abhor the voice of that harmless man. I felt that it was he who would bring on the disaster of discovery. It hung like a sword over our heads.

The fourth day out, I think (we were then working down the east side of the Gulf of Siam, tack for tack, in light winds and smooth water)—the fourth day, I say, of this miserable juggling with the unavoidable, as we sat at our evening meal, that man, whose slightest movement I dreaded, after putting down the dishes ran upon deck busily. This could not be dangerous. Presently he came down again; and then it appeared that he had remembered a coat of mine which I had thrown over a rail to dry after having been wetted in a shower which had passed over the ship in the afternoon. Sitting stolidly at the head of the table I became terrified at the sight of the garment on his arm. Of course he made for my door. There was no time to lose.

"Steward," I thundered. My nerves were so shaken that I could not govern my voice and conceal my agitation. This was the sort of thing that made my terrifically whiskered mate tap his forehead with his forefinger. I had detected him using that gesture while talking on deck with a confidential air to the carpenter. It was too far to hear a word, but I had no doubt that this pantomime could only refer to the strange new captain.

"Yes, sir," the pale-faced steward turned resignedly to me. It was this maddening course of being shouted at, checked without rhyme or reason, arbitrarily chased out of my cabin, suddenly called into it, sent flying out of his pantry on incomprehensible errands, that accounted for the growing wretchedness of his expression.

"Where are you going with that coat?"

"To your room, sir."

"Is there another shower coming?"

"I'm sure I don't know, sir. Shall I go up again and see, sir?"

"No! Never mind."

My object was attained, as of course my other self in there would have heard everything that passed. During this interlude my two officers never raised their eyes off their respective plates; but the lip of that confounded cub, the second mate, quivered visibly.

I expected the steward to hook my coat on and come out at once. He was very slow about it; but I dominated by nervousness sufficiently not to shout after him. Suddenly I became aware (it could be heard plainly enough) that the fellow for some reason or other was opening the door of the bathroom. It was the end. The place was literally not big enough to swing a cat in. My voice died in my throat and I went stony all over. I expected to hear a yell of surprise and terror, and made a movement, but had not the strength to get on my legs. Everything remained still. Had my second self taken the poor wretch by the throat? I don't know what I would have done next moment if I had not seen the steward come out of my room, close the door, and then stand quietly by the sideboard.

Saved, I thought. But, no! Lost! Gone! He was gone!

I laid my knife and fork down and leaned back in my chair. My head swam. After a while, when sufficiently recovered to speak in a steady voice, I instructed my mate to put the ship round at eight o'clock himself.

"I won't come on deck," I went on. "I think I'll turn in, and unless the wind shifts I don't want to be disturbed before midnight. I feel a bit seedy."

"You did look middling bad a little while ago," the chief mate remarked without showing any great concern.

They both went out, and I stared at the steward clearing the table. There was nothing to be read on that wretched man's face. But why did he avoid my eyes I asked myself. Then I thought I should like to hear the sound of his voice.

"Steward!"

"Sir!" Startled as usual.

"Where did you hang up that coat?"

"In the bathroom, sir." The usual anxious tone. "It's not quite dry yet, sir."

For some time longer I sat in the cuddy. Had my double vanished as he had come? But of his coming there was an explanation, whereas his disappearance would be inexplicable. . . . I went slowly into my dark room, shut the door, lighted the lamp, and for a time dared not turn round. When at last I did I saw him standing bolt upright in the narrow recessed part. It would not be true to say I had a shock, but an irresistible doubt of his bodily existence flitted through my mind. Can it be, I asked myself, that he is not visible to other eyes than mine? It was like being haunted. Motionless, with a grave face, he raised his hands slightly at me in a gesture which meant clearly, "Heavens! what a narrow escape!" Narrow indeed. I think I had come creeping quietly as near insanity as any man who has not actually gone over the border. That gesture restrained me, so to speak.

The mate with the terrific whiskers was now putting the ship on the other tack. In the moment of profound silence which follows upon the hands going to their stations I heard on the poop his raised voice: "Hard alee!" and the distant shout of the order repeated on the maindeck. The sails, in that light breeze, made but a faint fluttering noise. It ceased. The ship was coming round slowly; I held my breath in the renewed stillness of expectation; one wouldn't have thought that there was a single living soul on her decks. A sudden brisk shout, "Mainsail haul!" broke the spell, and in the noisy cries and rush overhead of the men running away with the main brace we two, down in my cabin, came together in our usual position by the bed-place.

He did not wait for my question. "I heard him fumbling here and just managed to squat myself down in the bath," he whispered to me. "The fellow only opened the door and put his arm in to hang the coat up. All the same—"

"I never thought of that," I whispered back, even more appalled than before at the closeness of the shave, and marveling at that something unyielding in his character which was carrying him through so finely. There was no agitation in his whisper. Whoever was being driven distracted, it was not he. He was sane. And the proof of his sanity was continued when he took up the whispering again.

"It would never do for me to come to life again."

It was something that a ghost might have said. But what he was alluding to was his old captain's reluctant admission of the theory of suicide. It would obviously serve his turn—if I had understood at all the view which seemed to govern the unalterable purpose of his action.

"You must maroon me as soon as ever you can get amongst these islands off the Cambodje shore," he went on.

"Maroon you! We are not living in a boy's adventure tale," I protested. His scornful whispering took me up.

"We aren't indeed! There's nothing of a boy's tale in this. But there's nothing else for it. I want no more. You don't suppose I am afraid of what can be done to me? Prison or gallows or whatever they may please. But you don't see me coming back to explain such things to an old fellow in a wig and twelve respectable tradesmen, do you? What can they know whether I am guilty or not—or of *what* I am guilty, either? That's my affair. What does the Bible say? 'Driven off the face of the earth.' Very well. I am off the face of the earth now. As I came at night so I shall go."

"Impossible!" I murmured. "You can't."

"Can't? . . . Not naked like a soul on the Day of Judgment. I shall freeze on to this sleeping suit. The Last Day is not yet—and . . . you have understood thoroughly. Didn't you?"

I felt suddenly ashamed of myself. I may say truly that I under-stood—and my hesitation in letting that man swim away from my ship's side had been a mere sham sentiment, a sort of cowardice.

"It can't be done now till next night," I breathed out. "The ship is on the offshore tack and the wind may fail us."

"As long as I know that you understand," he whispered. "But of course you do. It's a great satisfaction to have got somebody to under-stand. You seem to have been there on purpose." And in the same whisper, as if we two whenever we talked had to say things to each other which were not fit for the world to hear, he added, "It's very wonderful."

We remained side by side talking in our secret way—but sometimes silent or just exchanging a whispered word or two at long intervals.

And as usual he stared through the port. A breath of wind came now and again into our faces. The ship might have been moored in dock, so gently and on an even keel she slipped through the water, that did not murmur even at our passage, shadowy and silent like a phantom sea.

At midnight I went on deck, and to my mate's great surprise put the ship round on the other tack. His terrible whiskers flitted round me in silent criticism. I certainly should not have done it if it had been only a question of getting out of that sleepy gulf as quickly as possible. I believe he told the second mate, who relieved him, that it was a great want of judgment. The other only yawned. That intoler-able cub shuffled about so sleepily and lolled against the rails in such a slack, improper fashion that I came down on him sharply.

"Aren't you properly awake yet?"

"Yes, sir! I am awake."

"Well, then, be good enough to hold yourself as if you were. And keep a lookout. If there's any current we'll be closing with some islands before daylight."

The east side of the gulf is fringed with islands, some solitary, others in groups. On the blue background of the high coast they seem to float on silvery patches of calm water, arid and gray, or dark green and rounded like clumps of evergreen bushes, with the larger ones, a mile or two long, showing the outlines of ridges, ribs of gray rock under the dark mantle of matted leafage. Unknown to trade, to travel, almost to geography, the manner of life they harbor is an unsolved secret. There must be villages—settlements of fishermen at least—on the largest of them, and some communication with the world is probably kept up by native craft. But all that forenoon, as we headed for them, fanned along by the faintest of breezes, I saw no sign of man or canoe in the field of the telescope I kept on pointing at the scattered group.

At noon I gave no orders for a change of course, and the mate's whiskers became much concerned and seemed to be offering themselves unduly to my notice. At last I said:

"I am going to stand right in. Quite in—as far as I can take her."

The stare of extreme surprise imparted an air of ferocity also to his eyes, and he looked truly terrific for a moment.

"We're not doing well in the middle of the gulf," I continued, casually. "I am going to look for the land breezes tonight."

"Bless my soul! Do you mean, sir, in the dark amongst the lot of all them islands and reefs and shoals?"

"Well—if there are any regular land breezes at all on this coast one must get close inshore to find them, mustn't one?"

"Bless my soul!" he exclaimed again under his breath. All that afternoon he wore a dreamy, contemplative appearance which in him was a mark of perplexity. After dinner I went into my stateroom as if I meant to take some rest. There we two bent our dark heads over a half-unrolled chart lying on my bed.

"There," I said. "It's got to be Koh-ring. I've been looking at it ever since sunrise. It has got two hills and a low point. It must be inhabited. And on the coast opposite there is what looks like the mouth of a biggish river—with some town, no doubt, not far up. It's the best chance for you that I can see."

"Anything. Koh-ring let it be."

He looked thoughtfully at the chart as if surveying chances and distances from a lofty height—and following with his eyes his own figure wandering on the blank land of Cochin-China, and then passing off that piece of paper clean out of sight into uncharted regions. And it was as if the ship had two captains to plan her course for her. I had been so worried and restless running up and down that I had not had the patience to dress that day. I had remained in my sleeping suit, with straw slippers and a soft floppy hat. The closeness of the heat in the gulf had been most oppressive, and the crew were used to see me wandering in that airy attire.

"She will clear the south point as she heads now," I whispered into his ear. "Goodness only knows when, though, but certainly after dark. I'll edge her in to half a mile, as far as I may be able to judge in the dark—"

"Be careful," he murmured, warningly—and I realized suddenly that all my future, the only future for which I was fit, would perhaps go irretrievably to pieces in any mishap to my first command.

I could not stop a moment longer in the room. I motioned him to get out of sight and made my way on the poop. That unplayful cub had the watch. I walked up and down for a while thinking things out, then beckoned him over.

"Send a couple of hands to open the two quarter-deck ports," I said, mildly.

He actually had the impudence, or else so forgot himself in his wonder at such an incomprehensible order, as to repeat:

"Open the quarter-deck ports! What for, sir?"

"The only reason you need concern yourself about is because I tell you to do so. Have them open wide and fastened properly."

He reddened and went off, but I believe made some jeering remark to the carpenter as to the sensible practice of ventilating a ship's quarter-deck. I know he popped into the mate's cabin to impart the fact to him because the whiskers came on deck, as it were by chance, and stole glances at me from below—for signs of lunacy or drunkenness, I suppose.

A little before supper, feeling more restless than ever, I rejoined, for a moment, my second self. And to find him sitting so quietly was surprising, like something against nature, inhuman.

I developed my plan in a hurried whisper.

"I shall stand in as close as I dare and then put her round. I shall presently find means to smuggle you out of here into the sail locker, which communicates with the lobby. But there is an opening, a sort of square for hauling the sails out which gives straight on the quarter-deck and which is never closed in fine weather, so as to give air to the sails. When the ship's way is deadened in stays and all the hands are aft at the main braces you shall have a clear road to slip out and get overboard through the open quarter-deck port. I've had them both fastened up. Use a rope's end to lower yourself into the water so as to avoid a splash—you know. It could be heard and cause some beastly complication."

He kept silent for a while, then whispered, "I understand."

"I won't be there to see you go," I began with an effort. "The rest . . . I only hope I have understood, too."

"You have. From first to last," and for the first time there seemed to be a faltering, something strained in his whisper. He caught hold of my arm, but the ringing of the supper bell made me start. He didn't, though; he only released his grip.

After supper I didn't come below again till well past eight o'clock. The faint, steady breeze was loaded with dew; and the wet, darkened sails held all there was of propelling power in it. The night, clear and starry, sparkled darkly, and the opaque, lightless patches shifting slowly against the low stars were the drifting islets. On the port bow there was a big one more distant and shadowily imposing by the great space of sky it eclipsed.

On opening the door I had a back view of my very own self looking at a chart. He had come out of the recess and was standing near the table.

"Quite dark enough," I whispered.

He stepped back and leaned against my bed with a level, quiet glance. I sat on the couch. We had nothing to say to each other. Over our heads the officer of the watch moved here and there. Then I heard him move quickly. I knew what that meant. He was making for the companion; and presently his voice was outside my door.

"We are drawing in pretty fast, sir. Land looks rather close."

"Very well," I answered. "I am coming on deck directly."

I waited till he was gone out of the cuddy, then rose. My double moved too. The time had come to exchange our last whispers, for neither of us was ever to hear each other's natural voice.

"Look here!" I opened a drawer and took out three sovereigns. "Take this, anyhow. I've got six and I'd give you the lot, only I must keep a little money to buy some fruit and vegetables for the crew from native boats as we go through Sunda straits."

He shook his head.

"Take it," I urged him, whispering desperately. "No one can tell what—"

He smiled and slapped meaningly the only pocket of the sleeping jacket. It was not safe, certainly. But I produced a large old silk handkerchief of mine, and tying the three pieces of gold in a corner, pressed it on him. He was touched, I suppose, because he took it at last and tied it quickly round his waist under the jacket, on his bare skin.

Our eyes met; several seconds elapsed, till, our glances still mingled, I extended my hand and turned the lamp out. Then I passed through the cuddy, leaving the door of my room wide open. . . . "Steward!"

He was still lingering in the pantry in the greatness of his zeal, giving a rub-up to a plated cruet stand the last thing before going to bed. Being careful not to wake up the mate, whose room was opposite, I spoke in an undertone.

He looked round anxiously. "Sir!"

"Can you get me a little hot water from the galley?"

"I am afraid, sir, the galley fire's been out for some time now."

"Go and see."

He fled up the stairs.

"Now," I whispered, loudly, into the saloon—too loudly, perhaps, but I was afraid I couldn't make a sound. He was by my side in an instant—the double captain slipped past the stairs—through the tiny dark passage—a sliding door. We were in the sail locker, scrambling on our knees over the sails. A sudden thought struck me. I saw myself wandering barefooted, bareheaded, the sun beating on my dark poll. I snatched off my floppy hat and tried hurriedly in the dark to ram it on my other self. He dodged and fended off silently. I wonder what he thought had come to me before he understood and suddenly desisted. Our hands met gropingly, lingered united in a steady, motionless clasp for a second. . . . No word was breathed by either of us when they separated.

I was standing quietly by the pantry door when the steward returned.

"Sorry, sir. Kettle barely warm. Shall I light the spirit lamp?"

"Never mind."

I came out on deck slowly. It was now a matter of conscience to shave the land as close as possible—for now he must go overboard whenever the ship was put in stays. Must! There could be no going back for him. After a moment I walked over to leeward and my heart flew into my mouth at the nearness of the land on the bow. Under any other circumstances I would not have held on a minute longer. The second mate had followed me anxiously.

I looked on till I felt I could command my voice.

"She will weather," I said then in a quiet tone.

"Are you going to try that, sir?" he stammered out incredulously.

I took no notice of him and raised my tone just enough to be heard by the helmsman.

"Keep her good full."

"Good full, sir."

The wind fanned my cheek, the sails slept, the world was silent. The strain of watching the dark loom of the land grow bigger and denser was too much for me. I had shut my eyes—because the ship must go closer. She must! The stillness was intolerable. Were we standing still?

When I opened my eyes the second view started my heart with a thump. The black southern hill of Koh-ring seemed to hang right over the ship like a towering fragment of the everlasting night. On that enormous mass of blackness there was not a gleam to be seen, not a sound to be heard. It was gliding irresistibly toward us and yet seemed already within reach of the hand. I saw the vague figures of the watch grouped in the waist, gazing in awed silence.

"Are you going on, sir?" inquired an unsteady voice at my elbow. I ignored it. I had to go on.

"Keep her full. Don't check her way. That won't do now," I said warningly.

"I can't see the sails very well," the helmsman answered me, in strange, quavering tones.

Was she close enough? Already she was, I won't say in the shadow of the land, but in the very blackness of it, already swallowed up as it were, gone too close to be recalled, gone from me altogether.

"Give the mate a call," I said to the young man who stood at my elbow as still as death. "And turn all hands up."

My tone had a borrowed loudness reverberated from the height of the land. Several voices cried out together: "We are all on deck, sir."

Then stillness again, with the great shadow gliding closer, towering higher, without a light, without a sound. Such a hush had fallen on the ship that she might have been a bark of the dead floating in slowly under the very gate of Erebus.

"My God! Where are we?"

It was the mate moaning at my elbow. He was thunderstruck, and as it were deprived of the moral support of his whiskers. He clapped his hands and absolutely cried out, "Lost!"

"Be quiet," I said sternly.

He lowered his tone, but I saw the shadowy gesture of his despair. "What are we doing here?"

"Looking for the land wind."

He made as if to tear his hair, and addressed me recklessly.

"She will never get out. You have done it, sir. I knew it'd end in something like this. She will never weather, and you are too close now to stay. She'll drift ashore before she's round. O my God!"

I caught his arm as he was raising it to batter his poor devoted head, and shook it violently.

"She's ashore already," he wailed, trying to tear himself away.

"Is she? . . . Keep good full there!"

"Good full, sir," cried the helmsman in a frightened, thin, childlike voice.

I hadn't let go the mate's arm and went on shaking it. "Ready about, do you hear? You go forward"—shake—"and stop there"—shake—"and hold your noise"—shake—"and see these head sheets properly overhauled"—shake, shake—shake.

And all the time I dared not look toward the land lest my heart should fail me. I released my grip at last and he ran forward as if fleeing for dear life.

I wondered what my double there in the sail locker thought of this commotion. He was able to hear everything—and perhaps he was able to understand why, on my conscience, it had to be thus close—no less. My first order, "Hard alee!" re-echoed ominously under the towering shadow of Koh-ring as if I had shouted in a mountain gorge. And then I watched the land intently. In that smooth water and light wind it was impossible to feel the ship coming-to. No! I could not feel her. And my second self was making now ready to slip out and lower himself overboard. Perhaps he was gone already . . . ?

The great black mass brooding over our very mastheads began to pivot away from the ship's side silently. And now I forgot the secret stranger ready to depart, and remembered only that I was a total stranger to the ship. I did not know her. Would she do it? How was she to be handled?

I swung the mainyard and waited helplessly. She was perhaps stopped, and her very fate hung in the balance, with the black mass of Koh-ring like the gate of the everlasting night towering over her taffrail. What would she do now? Had she way on her yet? I stepped to the side swiftly, and on the shadowy water I could see nothing except a faint phosphorescent flash revealing the glassy smoothness of the sleeping surface. It was impossible to tell—and I had not learned yet the feel of my ship. Was she moving? What I needed was something easily seen, a piece of paper, which I could throw overboard and watch. I had nothing on me. To run down for it I didn't dare. There was no time. All at once my strained, yearning stare distinguished a white object floating within a yard of the ship's side. White on the black water. A phosphorescent flash passed under it. What was that thing? . . . I recognized my own floppy hat. It must have fallen off his head . . . and he didn't bother. Now I had what I wanted—the saving mark for my eyes. But I hardly thought of my other self, now gone from the ship, to be hidden forever from all friendly faces, to be a fugitive and a vagabond on the earth, with no brand of the curse on his sane forehead to stay a slaying hand . . . too proud to explain.

And I watched the hat—the expression of my sudden pity for his mere flesh. It had been meant to save his homeless head from the dangers of the sun. And now—behold—it was saving the ship, by serving me for a mark to help out the ignorance of my strangeness. Ha! It was drifting forward, warning me just in time that the ship had gathered sternway.

"Shift the helm," I said in a low voice to the seaman standing still like a statue.

The man's eyes glistened wildly in the binnacle light as he jumped round to the other side and spun round the wheel.

I walked to the break of the poop. On the overshadowed deck all hands stood by the forebraces waiting for my order. The stars ahead seemed to be gliding from right to left. And all was so still in the world that I heard the quiet remark "She's round," passed in a tone of intense relief between two seamen.

"Let go and haul."

The foreyards ran round with a great noise, amidst cheery cries. And now the frightful whiskers made themselves heard giving various orders. Already the ship was drawing ahead. And I was alone with her. Nothing! no one in the world should stand now between us, throwing a shadow on the way of silent knowledge and mute affection, the perfect communion of a seaman with his first command.

Walking to the taffrail, I was in time to make out, on the very edge of a darkness thrown by a towering black mass like the very gateway of Erebus—yes, I was in time to catch an evanescent glimpse of my white hat left behind to mark the spot where the secret sharer of my cabin and of my thoughts, as though he were my second self, had lowered himself into the water to take his punishment: a free man, a proud swimmer striking out for a new destiny.

William Faulkner

1897–1962

DRY SEPTEMBER · SHINGLES FOR THE LORD · THE
OLD PEOPLE

As a boy in Oxford, Mississippi, where his father was treasurer of the university, William Faulkner became acquainted with the legendary Southern past through family reminiscences. One great-grandfather, for example, had been a Mexican War veteran, a guerrilla leader in the Civil War, a railroad builder, and author of the best-selling novel *The White Rose of Memphis*. Perhaps because he associated the American army with the Union army of the Civil War, young William Faulkner preferred to join the British Air Force during the First World War.

While training in England, before active service (in which he may have been wounded—the details of Faulkner's military service are still unclear), Faulkner took courses at Oxford University that were open to servicemen. His formal education, however, was scanty and sporadic. For a decade or so after the war, until his books began selling well, he supported himself in his home town, as Thoreau had in Concord, by odd jobs of farming and carpentry. Two of his best early novels were written in the slack hours while he was night engineer in a power plant. On a prolonged visit to New Orleans in 1924 he became a friend of Sherwood Anderson, who helped place his work with publishers. For the next quarter of a century, except for occasional writing assignments in Hollywood, Faulkner stayed in Oxford, Mississippi, refusing all contact with the literary and academic world. After 1950, however, when he received the Nobel Prize, Faulkner made trips to Europe and Japan as a semiofficial representative of American culture. He declared himself publicly on such questions as that of racial segregation, and his informal talks to students at West Point, the University of Virginia, and elsewhere were very fully recorded.

The postwar disillusionment of the twenties intensified Faulkner's preoccupation with the defeat or self-destruction of Southern chivalry in the Civil War. From a doomed and disintegrating present, his novels look back to a romantic, though often terrible past. Faulkner's literary tastes are romantic also—he liked Keats, Shelley, Swinburne, Housman, the later Elizabethans—and in his fiction violent extremes of action and emotion are expressed with lyrical and rhetorical exuberance. His formal experiments, his use of flashbacks, interior monologues, and incredibly long and involved sentences, make his work sometimes bewildering and difficult to read. But much of it is well worth the effort.

As the novelist Balzac did for early nineteenth-century France, Faulkner created in his work a sociologically true picture of the region he knew well. His imaginary Yoknapatawpha County is peopled with a wide range of profoundly representative characters—gentlemen and scoundrels, planters and traders, Negroes, Indians, and poor whites. The same characters turn up in different novels, now in a major role, now in a minor one, and from book to book we piece together the eventful family histories of the Sartoris, Snopes, McCaslin, Bundren, and other clans. Each work illuminates some of the others, though they cannot be arranged in any ordered sequence.

Like D. H. Lawrence, Faulkner has a strong feeling for man's relation to nature, to animals, and to the past, especially when the human imagination has made that past more or less legendary or mythical. Unlike Lawrence, Faulkner limits himself to a single area where he himself has roots. But what his work ultimately dramatizes, he says, is "the human heart in conflict with itself." In his Nobel Prize acceptance speech, he referred in very much the same terms as Conrad's to the "old universal truths lacking which any story is ephemeral and doomed—love and honor and pity and pride and compassion and sacrifice."

Faulkner has been the subject of more critical discussion than any other modern American novelist except Henry James. Because his works are all related, it can be seen that even imperfect ones like *Sanctuary* (1931), *The Wild Palms* (1939), and *Requiem for a Nun* (1951), contribute significantly to the whole. Among the best novels are *The Sound and the Fury* (1929), *As I Lay Dying* (1930), *Light in August* (1932), *Absalom, Absalom!* (1936), *The Hamlet* (1940), and *Intruder in the Dust* (1948). The critical response to *A Fable* (1954), an elaborate allegorical treatment of Christianity and war, was largely unfavorable. *The Town* (1957) and *The Mansion* (1959) continued from *The Hamlet* to form a major trilogy describing the South after the Civil War, with the emergent Snopes family as principal characters. His final work was *The Reivers, a Reminiscence* (1962).

Faulkner often gives more unity of form and feeling to his short stories than to his novels. "Dry September" is one of the most famous of all tales of a lynching. Despite the emotional charge of the material and Faulkner's deep identification with the South, he describes the event from several perspectives with perfect truth and humanity. Comic tales of swapping, outwitting, and malingering were very popular in the local-color tradition from which Faulkner's work in part derives. Faulkner is a master of such story-telling, but "Shingles for the Lord" develops into something of deeper significance as the characters of the clergyman and father define themselves in the climactic scene at the end. Imagined through his family's eyes, the father is a disturbing and complicated figure. In "The Old People," the sense of the past, of race, and of soil is so much alive that it seems perfectly appropriate to make the hunting experience a kind of initiation rite, as among primitive peoples, and to suggest the supernaturalism of myth.

DRY SEPTEMBER

Through the bloody September twilight, aftermath of sixty-two rainless days, it had gone like fire in a dry grass—the rumor, the story, whatever it was. Something about Miss Minnie Cooper and a Negro. Attacked, insulted, frightened: none of them, gathered in the barbershop on that Saturday evening where the ceiling fan stirred, without freshening it, the vitiated air, sending back upon them, in recurrent surges of stale pomade and lotion, their own stale breath and odors, knew exactly what had happened.

"Except it wasn't Will Mayes," a barber said. He was a man of middle age; a thin, sand-colored man with a mild face, who was shaving a client. "I know Will Mayes. He's a good nigger. And I know Miss Minnie Cooper, too."

"What do you know about her?" a second barber said.

"Who is she?" the client said. "A girl?'"

"No," the barber said. "She's about forty, I reckon. She ain't married. That's why I don't believe—"

"Believe hell!" a hulking youth in a sweat-stained silk shirt said. "Won't you take a white woman's word before a nigger's?"

"I don't believe Will Mayes did it," the barber said. "I know Will Mayes."

"Maybe you know who did it, then. Maybe you already got him out of town, you damn nigger-lover."

"I don't believe anybody did anything. I don't believe anything happened. I leave it to you fellows if them ladies that gets old without getting married don't have notions that a man can't—"

"Then you're a hell of a white man," the client said. He moved under the cloth. The youth had sprung to his feet.

"You don't?" he said. "Do you accuse a white woman of telling a lie?"

The barber held the razor poised above the half-risen client. He did not look around.

"It's this durn weather," another said. "It's enough to make any man do anything. Even to her."

Nobody laughed. The barber said in his mild, stubborn tone: "I ain't accusing nobody of nothing. I just know and you fellows know how a woman that never——"

"You damn nigger-lover!" the youth said.

"Shut up, Butch," another said. "We'll get the facts in plenty of time to act."

"Who is? Who's getting them?" the youth said. "Facts, hell! I—"

"You're a fine white man," the client said. "Ain't you?" In his frothy beard he looked like a desert-rat in the moving pictures. "You tell them, Jack," he said to the youth. "If they ain't any white men in this town, you can count on me, even if I ain't only a drummer and a stranger."

"That's right, boys," the barber said. "Find out the truth first. I know Will Mayes."

"Well, by God!" the youth shouted. "To think that a white man in this town—"

"Shut up, Butch," the second speaker said. "We got plenty of time."

The client sat up. He looked at the speaker. "Do you claim that anything excuses a nigger attacking a white woman? Do you mean to tell me that you're a white man and you'll stand for it? You better go back North where vou come from. The South don't want your kind here."

"North what?" the second said. "I was born and raised in this town."

"Well, by God!" the youth said. He looked about with a strained, baffled gaze, as if he was trying to remember what it was he wanted to say or to do. He drew his sleeve across his sweating face. "Damn if I'm going to let a white woman—"

"You tell them, Jack," the drummer said. "By God, if they—"

The screen-door crashed open. A man stood in the floor, his feet apart and his heavy-set body poised easily. His white shirt was open at the throat; he wore a felt hat. His hot, bold glance swept the group. His name was Plunkett. He had commanded troops at the front in France and had been decorated for valor.

"Well," he said, "are you going to sit there and let a black son rape a white woman on the streets of Jefferson?"

Butch sprang up again. The silk of his shirt clung flat to his heavy shoulders. At each armpit was a dark half-moon. "That's what I been telling them! That's what I—"

"Did it really happen?" a third said. "This ain't the first man-scare she ever had, like Hawkshaw says. Wasn't there something about a man on the kitchen roof, watching her undress, about a year ago?"

"What?" the client said. "What's that?" The barber had been slowly forcing him back into the chair; he arrested himself reclining, his head lifted, the barber still pressing him down.

Plunkett whirled on the third speaker. "Happen? What the hell difference does it make? Are you going to let the black sons get away with it until one really does it?"

"That's what I'm telling them!" Butch shouted. He cursed, long and steady, pointless.

"Here, here," a fourth said. "Not so loud. Don't talk so loud."

"Sure," Plunkett said; "no talking necessary at all. I've done my talking. Who's with me?" He poised on the balls of his feet, roving his gaze.

The barber held the client's face down, the razor poised. "Find out the facts first, boys. I know Willy Mayes. It wasn't him. Let's get the sheriff and do this thing right."

Plunkett whirled upon him his furious, rigid face. The barber did not look away. They looked like men of different races. The other barbers had ceased also above their prone clients. "You mean to tell me," Plunkett said, "that you'd take a nigger's word before a white woman's? Why, you damn nigger-loving—"

The third rose and grasped Plunkett's arm; he too had been a soldier. "Now, now! Let's figure this thing out. Who knows anything about what really happened?"

"Figure out hell!" Plunkett jerked his arm free. "All that're with me get up from there. The ones that ain't—" He roved his gaze, dragging his sleeve across his face.

Three men rose. The client in the chair sat up. "Here," he said, jerking at the cloth around his neck; "get this rag off me. I'm with him. I don't live here, but, by God, if our mothers and wives and sisters—" He smeared the cloth over his face and flung it to the floor. Plunkett stood in the floor and cursed the others. Another rose and moved toward him. The remainder sat uncomfortably, not looking at one another, then one by one they rose and joined him.

The barber picked the cloth from the floor. He began to fold it neatly. "Boys, don't do that. Will Mayes never done it. I know."

"Come on," Plunkett said. He whirled. From his hip pocket protruded the butt of a heavy automatic pistol. They went out. The screen-door crashed behind them reverberant in the dead air.

The barber wiped the razor carefully and swiftly, and put it away, and ran to the rear, and took his hat from the wall. "I'll be back soon as I can," he said to the other barbers. "I can't let—" He went out, running. The two other barbers followed him to the door and caught it on the rebound, leaning out and looking up the street after him. The air was flat and dead. It had a metallic taste at the base of the tongue.

"What can he do?" the first said. The second one was saying "Jees Christ, Jees Christ" under his breath. "I'd just as lief be Will Mayes as Hawk, if he gets Plunkett riled."

"Jees Christ, Jees Christ," the second whispered.

"You reckon he really done it to her?" the first said.

11

She was thirty-eight or thirty-nine. She lived in a small frame house with her invalid mother and a thin, sallow, unflagging aunt, where each morning, between ten and eleven, she would appear on the porch in a lace-trimmed boudoir cap, to sit swinging in the porch swing until noon. After dinner she lay down for a while, until the afternoon began to cool. Then, in one of the three or four new voile dresses which she had each summer, she would go down-town to spend the afternoon in the stores with the other ladies, where they would handle the goods and haggle over prices in cold, immediate voices, without any intention of buying.

She was of comfortable people—not the best in Jefferson, but good people enough—and she was still on the slender side of ordinary-looking, with a bright, faintly haggard manner and dress. When she was young she had had a slender, nervous body and a sort of hard vivacity which had enabled her to ride for the time upon the crest of the town's social life as exemplified by the high-school party and church-social period of her contemporaries while still children enough to be un-class-conscious.

She was the last to realize that she was losing ground; that those among whom she had been a little brighter and louder flame than any other were beginning to learn the pleasure of snobbery—male—and retaliation—female. That was when her face began to wear that bright, haggard look. She still carried it to parties on shadowy porticos and summer lawns, like a mask or a flag, with that bafflement and furious repudiation of truth in her eyes. One evening at a party she heard a boy and two girls, all schoolmates, talking. She never accepted another invitation.

She watched the girls with whom she had grown up as they married and got houses and children, but no man ever called on her steadily until the children of the other girls had been calling her "aunty" for several years, the while their mothers told them in bright voices about how popular Minnie had been as a girl. Then the town began to see her driving on Sunday afternoons with the cashier in the bank. He was a widower of about forty—a high-colored man, smelling always faintly of the barbershop or of whiskey. He owned the first automobile in town, a red runabout; Minnie had the first motoring bonnet and veil the town ever saw. Then the town began to say: "Poor Minnie!" "But she is old enough to take care of herself," others said. That was when she first asked her schoolmates that the children call her "cousin" instead of "aunty."

It was twelve years now since she had been relegated into adultery by public opinion, and eight years since the cashier had gone to a Memphis bank, returning for one day each Christmas, which he spent at an annual bachelors' party in a hunting-club on the river. From behind their curtains the neighbors would see him pass, and during the across-the-street Christmas-day visiting they would tell her about him, about how well he looked, and how they heard that he was prospering in the city, watching with bright, secret eyes her haggard, bright face. Usually by that hour there would be the scent of whiskey on her breath. It was supplied her by a youth, a clerk at the soda-fountain: "Sure; I buy it for the old gal. I reckon she's entitled to a little fun."

Her mother kept to her room altogether now; the gaunt aunt ran the house. Against that background Minnie's bright dresses, her idle and empty days, had a quality of furious unreality. She went out in the evenings only with women now, neighbors, to the moving pictures. Each afternoon she dressed in one of the new dresses and went down-town alone, where her young cousins were already strolling in the late afternoons with their delicate, silken heads and thin, awkward arms and conscious hips, clinging to one another or shrieking and giggling with paired boys in the soda-fountain when she passed and went on along the serried stores, in the doors of which sitting and lounging men did not even follow her with their eyes any more.

III

The barber went swiftly up the street where the sparse lights, insect-swirled, glared in rigid and violent suspension in the lifeless air. The day had died in a pall of dust; above the darkened square, shrouded by the spent dust, the sky was clear as the inside of a brass bell. Below the east was a rumor of the twice-waxed moon.

When he overtook them Plunkett and three others were getting into a car parked in an alley. Plunkett stooped his thick head, peering out beneath the top. "Changed your mind, did you?" he said. "Damn good thing; by God, tomorrow when this town hears about how you talked tonight—"

"Now, now," the other ex-soldier said. "Hawkshaw's all right. Come on, Hawk; jump in!"

"Will Mayes never done it, boys," the barber said. "If anybody done it. Why, you all know well as I do there ain't any town where they got better niggers than us. And you know how a lady will kind of think things about men when there ain't any reason to, and Miss Minnie anyway—"

"Sure, sure," the soldier said. "We're just going to talk to him a little; that's all."

"Talk hell!" Butch said. "When we're done with the—"

"Shut up, for God's sake!" the soldier said. "Do you want everybody in town—"

"Tell them, by God!" Plunkett said. "Tell every one of the sons that'll let a white woman—"

"Let's go; let's go: here's the other car." The second car slid squealing out of a cloud of dust at the alley-mouth. Plunkett started his car and backed out and took the lead. Dust lay like fog in the street. The street lights hung nimbused as in water. They drove on out of town.

A rutted lane turned at right angles. Dust hung above it too, and above all the land. The dark bulk of the ice-plant, where the Negro Mayes was night-watchman, rose against the sky. "Better stop here, hadn't we?" the soldier said. Plunkett did not reply. He hurled the car up and slammed to a stop, the headlights glaring on the blank wall.

"Listen here, boys," the barber said; "if he's here, don't that prove he never done it? Don't it? If it was him, he would run. Don't you see he would?" The second car came up and stopped. Plunkett got down; Butch sprang down beside him. "Listen, boys," the barber said.

"Cut the lights off!" Plunkett said. The breathless darkness rushed down. There was no sound in it save their lungs as they sought air in the parched dust in which for two months they had lived; then the diminishing crunch of Plunkett's and Butch's feet, and a moment later, Plunkett's voice:

"Will! . . . Will!"

Below the east the wan hemorrhage of the moon increased. It heaved above the ridge, silvering the air, the dust, so that they seemed to breathe, live, in a bowl of molten lead. There was no sound of night-bird nor insect, no sound save their breathing and a faint ticking of contracting metal about the cars. Where their bodies touched one another they seemed to sweat dryly, for no more moisture came. "Christ!" a voice said; "let's get out of here."

But they didn't move until vague noises began to grow out of the darkness ahead; then they got out and waited tensely in the breathless dark. There was another sound: a blow, a hissing expulsion of breath and Plunkett cursing in undertone. They stood a moment longer, then they ran forward. They ran in a stumbling clump, as though they were fleeing something. "Kill him, kill the son!" a voice whispered. Plunkett flung them back.

"Not here," he said. "Get him into the car." They hauled the Negro up. "Kill him, kill the black son!" the voice murmured. They dragged the Negro to the car. The barber had waited beside the car. He could feel himself sweating and he knew he was going to be sick at the stomach.

"What is it, captains?" the Negro said. "I ain't done nothing. 'Fore God, Mr. John." Someone produced handcuffs. They worked busily about him as though he were a post, quiet, intent, getting in one another's way. He submitted to the handcuffs, looking swiftly and constantly from dim face to face. "Who's here, captains?" he said, leaning to peer into the faces until they could feel his breath and smell his sweaty reek. He spoke a name or two. "What you-all say I done, Mr. John?"

Plunkett jerked the car-door open. "Get in!" he said.

The Negro did not move. "What you-all going to do with me, Mr. John? I ain't done nothing. White folks, captains, I ain't done nothing: I swear 'fore God." He called another name.

"Get in!" Plunkett said. He struck the Negro. The others expelled their breath in a dry hissing and struck him with random blows, and he whirled and cursed them, and swept his manacled hands across their faces and slashed the barber upon the mouth, and the barber struck him also. "Get him in there," Plunkett said. They pushed at him. He ceased struggling and got in, and sat quietly as the others took their places. He sat between the barber and the soldier, drawing his limbs in so as not to touch them, his eyes going swiftly and constantly from face to face. Butch clung to the running-board. The car moved on. The barber nursed his mouth in his handkerchief.

"What's the matter, Hawk?" the soldier said.

"Nothing," the barber said. They regained the high road and turned away from town. The second car dropped back out of the dust. They went on, gaining speed; the final fringe of houses dropped behind.

"Goddam, he stinks!" the soldier said.

"We'll fix that," the man in front beside Plunkett said. On the running-board Butch cursed into the hot rush of air. The barber leaned suddenly forward and touched Plunkett's shoulder.

"Let me out, John."

"Jump out, nigger-lover," Plunkett said without turning his head. He drove swiftly. Behind them the sourceless lights of the second car glared in the dust. Presently Plunkett turned into a narrow road. It too was rutted in disuse. It led back to an old brick-kiln—a series of reddish mounds and weed-and-vine-choked vats without bottom. It had been used for pasture once, until one day the owner missed one of his mules. Although he prodded carefully in the vats with a long pole, he could not even find the bottom of them.

"John," the barber said.

"Jump out, then," Plunkett said, hurling the car along the ruts. Beside the barber the Negro spoke:

"Mr. Henry."

The barber sat forward. The narrow tunnel of the road rushed up and past. Their motion was like an extinct furnace blast: cooler, but utterly dead. The car bounded from rut to rut.

"Mr. Henry," the Negro said.

The barber began to tug furiously at the door. "Look out, there!" the soldier said, but he had already kicked the door open and swung onto the running-board. The soldier leaned across the Negro and grasped at him, but he had already jumped. The car went on without checking speed.

The impetus hurled him crashing, through dust-sheathed weeds, into the ditch. Dust puffed about him, and in a thin, vicious crackling of sapless stems he lay choking and retching until the second car passed and died away. Then he rose and limped on until he reached the high road and turned toward town, brushing at his clothes with his hands. The moon was higher, riding high and clear of the dust at last, and after a while the town began to glare beneath the dust. He went on, limping. Presently he heard the cars and the glow of them grew in the dust behind him and he left the road and crouched again in the weeds until they passed. Plunkett's car came last now. There were four people in it and Butch was not on the running-board.

They went on; the dust swallowed them; the glare and the sound died away. The dust of them hung for a while, but soon the eternal dust absorbed it again. The barber climbed back onto the road and limped on toward town.

IV

As she dressed after supper, on that Saturday evening, her own flesh felt like fever. Her hands trembled among the hooks and eyes, and her eyes had a feverish look, and her hair swirled crisp and crackling under the comb. While she was still dressing, the friends called for her and sat while she donned her sheerest underthings and stockings and a new voile dress. "Do you feel strong enough to go out?" they said, their eyes bright too, with a dark glitter. "When you have had time to get over the shock, you must tell us what happened. What he said and did; everything."

In the leafed darkness, as they walked toward the square, she began to breathe deeply, something like a swimmer preparing to dive, until she ceased trembling, the four of them walking slowly because of the terrible heat and out of solicitude for her. But as they neared the square she began to tremble again, walking with her head up, her hands clinched at her sides, their voices about her murmurous, also with that feverish, glittering quality of their eyes.

They entered the square, she in the center of the group, fragile in her fresh dress. She was trembling worse. She walked slower and slower, as children eat ice-cream, her head up and her eyes bright in the haggard banner of her face, passing the hotel and the coatless drummers in chairs along the curb looking around at her: "That's the one: see? The one in pink in the middle." "Is that her? What did they do with the nigger? Did they—?" "Sure. He's all right." "All right, is he?" "Sure. He went on a little trip." Then the drug-store, where even the young men lounging in the doorway tipped their hats and followed with their eyes the motion of her hips and legs when she passed.

They went on, passing the lifted hats of the gentlemen, the suddenly ceased voices, protective, deferent. "Do you see?" the friends said. Their voices sounded like long hovering sighs of hissing exultation. "There's not a Negro on the square. Not one."

They reached the picture-show. It was like a miniature fairyland with its lighted lobby and colored lithographs of life caught in its terrible and beautiful mutations. Her lips began to tingle. In the dark, when the picture began, it would be all right; she could hold back the laughing so it would not waste away so fast and so soon. So she hurried on before the turning faces, the undertones of low astonishment, and they took their accustomed places where she could see the aisle against the silver glare and the young men and girls coming in two and two against it.

The lights flicked away; the screen glowed silver, and soon life began to unfold, beautiful and passionate and sad, while still the young men and girls entered, scented and sibilant in the half-dark, their paired backs in silhouette delicate and sleek, their slim, quick bodies awkward, divinely young, while beyond them the silver dream accumulated, inevitably on and on. She began to laugh. In trying to suppress it, it made more noise than ever; heads began to turn. Still laughing, her friends raised her and led her out, and she stood at the curb, laughing on a high, sustained note, until the taxi came up and they helped her in.

They removed the pink voile and the sheer underthings, and the stockings, and put her to bed, and cracked ice for her temples, and sent for the doctor. He was hard to locate, so they ministered to her with hushed ejaculations, renewing the ice and fanning her. While the ice was fresh and cold she stopped laughing and lay still for a time, moaning only a little. But soon the laughing welled again and her voice rose screaming.

"Shhhhhhhhhhh! Shhhhhhhhhhh!" they said, freshening the ice-pack, smoothing her hair, examining it for gray; "poor girl!" Then to one another: "Do you suppose anything really happened?" their eyes darkly aglitter, secret and passionate. "Shhhhhhhhhhh! Poor girl! Poor Minnie!"

v

It was midnight when Plunkett drove up to his neat new house. It was trim and fresh as a bird-cage and almost as small, with its clean green-and-white paint. He locked the car and mounted the porch and entered. His wife rose from a chair beside the reading-lamp. Plunkett stopped in the floor and stared at her until she looked down.

"Look at that clock!" he said, lifting his arm, pointing. She stood before him, her face lowered, a magazine in her hands. Her face was pale, strained, and weary-looking. "Haven't I told you about sitting up like this, waiting to see when I come in?"

"John!" she said. She laid the magazine down. Poised on the balls of his feet, he glared at her with his hot eyes, his sweating face.

"Didn't I tell you?" He went toward her. She looked up then. He caught her shoulder. She stood passive, looking at him.

"Don't, John. I couldn't sleep. . . . The heat; something. Please, John. You're hurting me."

"Didn't I tell you?" He released her and half struck, half flung her across the chair, and she lay there and watched him quietly as he left the room.

He went on through the house, ripping off his shirt, and on the dark, screened porch at the rear he stood and mopped his head and shoulders with the shirt and flung it away. He took the pistol from his hip and laid it on the table beside the bed, and sat on the bed and removed his shoes, and rose and slipped his trousers off. He was sweating again already, and he stooped and hunted furiously for the shirt. At last he found it and wiped his body again, and, with his body pressed against the dusty screen, he stood panting. There was no movement, no sound, not even an insect. The dark world seemed to lie stricken beneath the cold moon and the lidless stars.

SHINGLES FOR THE LORD

Pap got up a good hour before daylight and caught the mule and rid down to Killegrew's to borrow the froe and maul. He ought to been back with it in forty minutes. But the sun had rose and I had done milked and fed and was eating my breakfast when he got back, with the mule not only in a lather but right on the edge of the thumps too.

"Fox hunting," he said. "Fox hunting. A seventy-year-old man, with both feet and one knee, too, already in the grave, squatting all night on a hill and calling himself listening to a fox race that he couldn't even hear unless they had come right up onto the same log he was setting on and bayed into his ear trumpet. Give me my breakfast," he told maw. "Whitfield is standing there right this minute, straddle of that board tree with his watch in his hand."

And he was. We rid on past the church, and there was not only Solon Quick's school-bus truck but Reverend Whitfield's old mare too. We tied the mule to a sapling and hung our dinner bucket on a limb, and with pap toting Killegrew's froe and maul and the wedges and me toting our ax, we went on to the board tree where Solon and Homer Bookwright, with their froes and mauls and axes and wedges, was setting on two upended cuts, and Whitfield was standing jest like pap said, in his boiled shirt and his black hat and pants and necktie, holding his watch in his hand. It was gold and in the morning sunlight it looked big as a full-growed squash.

"You're late," he said.

So pap told again about how Old Man Killegrew had been off fox hunting all night, and nobody at home to lend him the froe but Mrs. Killegrew and the cook. And naturally, the cook wasn't going to lend none of Killegrew's tools out, and Mrs. Killegrew was worser deaf than even Killegrew. If you was to run in and tell her the house was afire, she would jest keep on rocking and say she thought so, too, unless she began to holler back to the cook to turn the dogs loose before you could even open your mouth.

"You could have gone yesterday and borrowed the froe," Whitfield said. "You have known for a month now that you had promised this one day out of a whole summer toward putting a roof on the house of God."

"We ain't but two hours late," pap said. "I reckon the Lord will forgive it. He ain't interested in time, nohow. He's interested in salvation."

Whitfield never even waited for pap to finish. It looked to me like he even got taller, thundering down at pap like a cloudburst. "He ain't interested in neither! Why should He be, when He owns them both? And why He should turn around for the poor, mizzling souls of men that can't even borrow tools in time to replace the shingles on His church, I don't know either. Maybe it's just because He made them. Maybe He just said to Himself: 'I made them; I don't know why. But since I did, I Godfrey, I'll roll My sleeves up and drag them into glory whether they will or no!' "

But that wasn't here nor there either now, and I reckon he knowed it, jest like he knowed there wasn't going to be nothing atall here as long as he stayed. So he put the watch back into his pocket and motioned Solon and Homer up, and we all taken off our hats except him while he stood there with his face raised into the sun and his eyes shut and his eyebrows looking like a big iron-gray caterpillar lying along the edge of a cliff. "Lord," he said, "make them good straight shingles to lay smooth, and let them split out easy; they're for You," and opened his eyes and looked at us again, mostly at pap, and went and untied his mare and clumb up slow and stiff, like old men do, and rid away.

Pap put down the froe and maul and laid the three wedges in a neat row on the ground and taken up the ax.

"Well, men," he said, "let's get started. We're already late."

"Me and Homer ain't," Solon said. "We was here." This time him and Homer didn't set on the cuts. They squatted on their heels. Then I seen that Homer was whittling on a stick. I hadn't noticed it before.

"I make it two hours and a little over," Solon said. "More or less."

Pap was still about half stooped over, holding the ax. "It's nigher one," he said. "But call it two for the sake of the argument. What about it?"

"What argument?" Homer said.

"All right," pap said. "Two hours then. What about it?"

"Which is three man-hour units a hour, multiplied by two hours," Solon said. "Or a total of six work units." When the WPA first come to Yoknapatawpha County and started to giving out jobs and grub and mattresses, Solon went in to Jefferson to get on it. He would drive his school-bus truck the twenty-two miles in to town every morning and come back that night. He done that for almost a week before he found out he would not only have to sign his farm off into somebody else's name, he couldn't even own and run the school bus that he had built himself. So he come back that night and never went back no more, and since then hadn't nobody better mention WPA to him unless they aimed to fight, too, though every now and then he would turn up with something all figured down into work units like he done now. "Six units short."

"Four of which you and Homer could have already worked out while you was setting here waiting on me," pap said.

"Except that we didn't," Solon said. "We promised Whitfield two units of twelve three-unit hours toward getting some new shingles on the church roof. We been here ever since sunup, waiting for the third unit to show up, so we could start. You don't seem to kept up with these modren ideas about work that's been flooding and uplifting the country in the last few years."

"What modren ideas?" pap said. "I didn't know there was but one idea about work—until it is done, it ain't done, and when it is done, it is."

Homer made another long, steady whittle on the stick. His knife was sharp as a razor.

Solon taken out his snuffbox and filled the top and tilted the snuff into his lip and offered the box to Homer, and Homer shaken his head, and Solon put the top back on the box and put the box back into his pocket.

"So," pap said, "jest because I had to wait two hours for a old seventy-year man to get back from fox hunting that never had no more business setting out in the woods all night than he would 'a' had setting all night in a highway juke joint, we all three have got to come back here tomorrow to finish them two hours that you and Homer—"

"I ain't," Solon said. "I don't know about Homer. I promised Whitfield one day. I was here at sunup to start it. When the sun goes down, I will consider I have done finished it."

"I see," pap said. "I see. It's me that's got to come back. By myself. I got to break into a full morning to make up them two hours that you and Homer spent resting. I got to spend two hours of the next day making up for the two hours of the day before that you and Homer never even worked."

"It's going to more than jest break into a morning," Solon said. "It's going to wreck it. There's six units left over. Six one-man-hour units. Maybe you can work twice as fast as me and Homer put together and finish them in four hours, but I don't believe you can work three times as fast and finish in two."

Pap was standing up now. He was breathing hard. We could hear him. "So," he said. "So." He swung the ax and druv the blade into one of the cuts and snatched it up onto its flat end, ready to split. "So I'm to be penalized a half day of my own time, from my own work that's waiting for me at home right this minute, to do six hours more work than the work you fellers lacked two hours of even doing atall, purely and simply because I am jest a average hard-working farmer trying to do the best he can, instead of a durn froe-owning millionaire named Quick or Bookwright."

They went to work then, splitting the cuts into bolts and riving the bolts into shingles for Tull and Snopes and the others that had promised for tomorrow to start nailing onto the church roof when they finished pulling the old shingles off. They set flat on the ground in a kind of circle, with their legs spraddled out on either side of the propped-up bolt, Solon and Homer working light and easy and steady as two clocks ticking, but pap making every lick of hisn like he was killing a moccasin. If he had jest swung the maul half as fast as he swung it hard, he would have rove as many shingles as Solon and Homer together, swinging the maul up over his head and holding it there for what looked like a whole minute sometimes and then swinging it down onto the blade of the froe, and not only a shingle flying off every lick but the froe going on into the ground clean up to the helve eye, and pap setting there wrenching at it slow and steady and hard, like he jest wished it would try to hang on a root or a rock and stay there.

"Here, here," Solon said. "If you don't watch out you won't have nothing to do neither during the six extra units tomorrow morning but rest."

Pap never even looked up. "Get out of the way," he said. And Solon done it. If he hadn't moved the water bucket, pap would have split it, too, right on top of the bolt, and this time the whole shingle went whirling past Solon's shin jest like a scythe blade.

"What you ought to do is to hire somebody to work out them extra overtime units," Solon said.

"With what?" pap said. "I ain't had no WPA experience in dickering over labor. Get out of the way."

But Solon had already moved this time. Pap would have had to change his whole position or else made this one curve. So this one missed Solon, too, and pap set there wrenching the froe, slow and hard and steady, back out of the ground.

"Maybe there's something else besides cash you might be able to trade with," Solon said. "You might use that dog."

That was when pap actually stopped. I didn't know it myself then either, but I found it out a good long time before Solon did. Pap set there with the maul up over his head and the blade of the froe set against the block for the next lick, looking up at Solon. "The dog?" he said.

It was a kind of mixed hound, with a little bird dog and some collie and maybe a considerable of almost anything else, but it would ease through the woods without no more noise than a hant and pick up a squirrel's trail on the ground and bark jest once, unless it knowed you was where you could see it, and then tiptoe that trail out jest like a man and never make another sound until it treed, and only then when it knowed you hadn't kept in sight of it. It belonged to pap and Vernon Tull together. Will Varner give it to Tull as a puppy, and pap raised it for a half interest; me and him trained it and it slept in my bed with me until it got so big maw finally run it out of the house, and for the last six months Solon had been trying to buy it. Him and Tull had agreed on two dollars for Tull's half of it, but Solon and pap was still six dollars apart on ourn, because pap said it was worth ten dollars of anybody's money and if Tull wasn't going to collect his full half of that, he was going to collect it for him.

"So that's it," pap said. "Them things wasn't work units atall. They was dog units."

"Jest a suggestion," Solon said. "Jest a friendly offer to keep them runaway shingles from breaking up your private business for six hours tomorrow morning. You sell me your half of that trick overgrown fyce and I'll finish these shingles for you."

"Naturally including them six extra units of one dollars," pap said.

"No, no," Solon said. "I'll pay you the same two dollars for your half of that dog that me and Tull agreed on for his half of it. You meet me here tomorrow morning with the dog and you can go on back home or wherever them urgent private affairs are located, and forget about that church roof."

For about ten seconds more, pap set there with the maul up over his head, looking at Solon. Then for about three seconds he wasn't looking at Solon or at nothing else. Then he was looking at Solon again. It was jest exactly like after about two and nine-tenths seconds he found out he wasn't looking at Solon, so he looked back at him as quick as he could. "Hah," he said. Then he began to laugh. It was laughing all right, because his mouth was open and that's what it sounded like. But it never went no further back than his teeth and it never come nowhere near reaching as high up as his eyes. And he never said "Look out" this time neither. He jest shifted fast on his hips and swung the maul down, the froe done already druv through the bolt and into the ground while the shingle was still whirling off to slap Solon across the shin.

Then they went back at it again. Up to this time I could tell pap's licks from Solon's and Homer's, even with my back turned, not because they was louder or steadier, because Solon and Homer worked steady, too, and the froe never made no especial noise jest going into the ground, but because they was so infrequent; you would hear five or six of Solon's and Homer's little polite chipping licks before you would hear pap's froe go "chug!" and know that another shingle had went whirling off somewhere. But from now on pap's sounded jest as light and quick and polite as Solon's or Homer's either, and, if anything, even a little faster, with the shingles piling up steadier than I could stack them, almost; until now there was going to be more than a plenty of them for Tull and the others to shingle with tomorrow, right on up to noon, when we heard Armstid's farm bell, and Solon laid his froe and maul down and looked at his watch too. And I wasn't so far away neither, but by the time I caught up with pap he had untied the mule from the sapling and was already on it. And maybe Solon and Homer thought they had pap, and maybe for a minute I did, too, but I jest wish they could have seen his face then. He reached our dinner bucket down from the limb and handed it to me.

"Go on and eat," he said. "Don't wait for me. Him and his work units. If he wants to know where I went, tell him I forgot something and went home to get it. Tell him I had to go back home to get two spoons for us to eat our dinner with. No, don't tell him that. If he hears I went somewhere to get something I needed to use, even if it's jest a tool to eat with, he will refuse to believe I jest went home, for the reason that I don't own anything there that even I would borrow." He hauled the mule around and heeled him in the flank. Then he pulled up again. "And when I come back, no matter what I say, don't pay no attention to it. No matter what happens, don't you say nothing. Don't open your mouth a-tall, you hear?"

Then he went on, and I went back to where Solon and Homer was setting on the running board of Solon's school-bus truck, eating, and sho enough Solon said jest exactly what pap said he was going to.

"I admire his optimism, but he's mistaken. If it's something he needs that he can't use his natural hands and feet for, he's going somewhere else than jest his own house."

We had jest went back to the shingles when pap rid up and got down and tied the mule back to the sapling and come and taken up the ax and snicked the blade into the next cut.

"Well, men," he said, "I been thinking about it. I still don't think it's right, but I still ain't thought of anything to do about it. But somebody's got to make up for them two hours nobody worked this morning, and since you fellers are two to one against me, it looks like it's going to be me that makes them up. But I got work waiting at home for me tomorrow. I got corn that's crying out loud for me right now. Or maybe that's jest a lie too. Maybe the whole thing is, I don't mind admitting here in private that I been outfigured, but I be dog if I'm going to set here by myself tomorrow morning admitting it in public. Anyway, I ain't. So I'm going to trade with you, Solon. You can have the dog."

Solon looked at pap. "I don't know as I want to trade now," he said.

"I see," pap said. The ax was still stuck in the cut. He began to pump it up and down to back it out.

"Wait," Solon said. "Put that durn ax down." But pap held the ax raised for the lick, looking at Solon and waiting. "You're swapping me half a dog for a half a day's work," Solon said.

"Your half of the dog for that half a day's work you still owe on these shingles."

"And the two dollars," pap said. "That you and Tull agreed on. I sell you half the dog for two dollars, and you come back here tomorrow and finish the shingles. You give me the two dollars now, and I'll meet you here in the morning with the dog, and you can show me the receipt from Tull for his half then."

"Me and Tull have already agreed," Solon said.

"All right," pap said. "Then you can pay Tull his two dollars and bring his receipt with you without no trouble."

"Tull will be at the church tomorrow morning, pulling off them old shingles," Solon said.

"All right," pap said. "Then it won't be no trouble at all for you to get a receipt from him. You can stop at the church when you pass. Tull ain't named Grier. He won't need to be off somewhere borrowing a crowbar."

So Solon taken out his purse and paid pap the two dollars and they went back to work. And now it looked like they really was trying to finish that afternoon, not jest Solon, but even Homer, that didn't seem to be concerned in it nohow, and pap, that had already swapped a half a dog to get rid of whatever work Solon claimed would be left over. I quit trying to stay up with them; I jest stacked shingles.

Then Solon laid his froe and maul down. "Well, men," he said, "I don't know what you fellers think, but I consider this a day."

"All right," pap said. "You are the one to decide when to quit, since whatever elbow units you consider are going to be shy tomorrow will be yourn."

"That's a fact," Solon said. "And since I am giving a day and a half to the church instead of jest a day, like I started out doing, I reckon I better get on home and tend to a little of my own work." He picked up his froe and maul and ax, and went to his truck and stood waiting for Homer to come and get in.

"I'll be here in the morning with the dog," pap said.

"Sholy," Solon said. It sounded like he had forgot about the dog, or that it wasn't no longer any importance. But he stood there again and looked hard and quiet at pap for about a second. "And a bill of sale from Tull for his half of it. As you say, it won't be no trouble a-tall to get that from him." Him and Homer got into the truck and he started the engine. You couldn't say jest what it was. It was almost like Solon was hurrying himself, so pap wouldn't have to make any excuse or pretense toward doing or not doing anything. "I have always understood the fact that lightning don't have to hit twice is one of the reasons why they named it lightning. So getting lightning-struck is a mistake that might happen to any man. The mistake I seem to made is, I never realized in time that what I was looking at was a cloud. I'll see you in the morning."

"With the dog," pap said.

"Certainly," Solon said, again like it had slipped his mind completely. "With the dog."

Then him and Homer drove off. Then pap got up.

"What?" I said. "What? You swapped him your half of Tull's dog for that half a day's work tomorrow. Now what?"

"Yes," pap said. "Only before that I had already swapped Tull a half a day's work pulling off them old shingles tomorrow, for Tull's half of that dog. Only we ain't going to wait until tomorrow. We're going to pull them shingles off tonight, and without no more racket about it than is necessary. I don't aim to have nothing on my mind tomorrow but watching Mr. Solon Work-Unit Quick trying to get a bill of sale for two dollars or ten dollars either on the other half of that dog. And we'll do it tonight. I don't want him jest to find out at sunup tomorrow that he is too late. I want him to find out then that even when he laid down to sleep he was already too late."

So we went back home and I fed and milked while pap went down to Killegrew's to carry the froe and maul back and to borrow a crowbar. But of all places in the world and doing what under the sun with it, Old Man Killegrew had went and lost his crowbar out of a boat into forty feet of water. And pap said how he come within a inch of going to Solon's and borrowing his crowbar out of pure poetic justice, only Solon might have smelled the rat jest from the idea of the crowbar. So pap went to Armstid's and borrowed hisn and come back and we et supper and cleaned and filled the lantern while maw still tried to find out what we was up to that couldn't wait till morning.

We left her still talking, even as far as the front gate, and come on back to the church, walking this time, with the rope and crowbar and a hammer for me, and the lantern still dark. Whitfield and Snopes was unloading a ladder from Snopes' wagon when we passed the church on the way home before dark, so all we had to do was to set the ladder up against the church. Then pap clumb up onto the roof with the lantern and pulled off shingles until he could hang the lantern inside behind the decking, where it could shine out through the cracks in the planks, but you couldn't see it unless you was passing in the road, and by that time anybody would 'a' already heard us. Then I clumb up with the rope, and pap reached it through the decking and around a rafter and back and tied the ends around our waists, and we started. And we went at it. We had them old shingles jest raining down, me using the claw hammer and pap using the crowbar, working the bar under a whole patch of shingles at one time and then laying back on the bar like in one more lick or if the crowbar ever happened for one second to get a solid holt, he would tilt up that whole roof at one time like a hinged box lid.

That's exactly what he finally done. He laid back on the bar and this time it got a holt. It wasn't jest a patch of shingles, it was a whole section of decking, so that when he lunged back he snatched that whole section of roof from around the lantern like you would shuck a corn nubbin. The lantern was hanging on a nail. He never even moved the nail, he just pulled the board off of it, so that it looked like for a whole minute I watched the lantern, and the crowbar, too, setting there in the empty air in a little mess of floating shingles, with the empty nail still sticking through the bail of the lantern, before the whole thing started down into the church. It hit the floor and bounced once. Then it hit the floor again, and this time the whole church jest blowed up into a pit of yellow jumping fire, with me and pap hanging over the edge of it on two ropes.

I don't know what become of the rope nor how we got out of it. I don't remember climbing down. Jest pap yelling behind me and pushing me about halfway down the ladder and then throwing me the rest of the way by a handful of my overhalls, and then we was both on the ground, running for the water barrel. It set under the gutter spout at the side, and Armstid was there then; he had happened to go out to his lot about a hour back and seen the lantern on the church roof, and it stayed on his mind until finally he come up to see what was going on, and got there jest in time to stand yelling back and forth with pap across the water barrel. And I believe we still would have put it out. Pap turned and squatted against the barrel and got a holt of it over his shoulder and stood up with that barrel that was almost full and run around the corner and up the steps of the church and hooked his toe on the top step and come down with the barrel busting on top of him and knocking him cold out as a wedge.

So we had to drag him back first, and maw was there then, and Mrs. Armstid about the same time, and me and Armstid run with the two fire buckets to the spring, and when we got back there was a plenty there, Whitfield, too, with more buckets, and we done what we could, but the spring was two hundred yards away and ten buckets emptied it and it taken five minutes to fill again, and so finally we all jest stood around where pap had come to again with a big cut on his head and watched it go. It was a old church, long dried out, and full of old colored-picture charts that Whitfield had accumulated for more than fifty years, that the lantern had lit right in the middle of when it finally exploded. There was a special nail where he would keep a old long nightshirt he would wear to baptize in. I would use to watch it all the time during church and Sunday school, and me and the other boys would go past the church sometimes jest to peep in at it, because to a boy of ten it wasn't jest a cloth garment or even a iron armor; it was the old strong Archangel Michael his self, that had fit and strove and conquered sin for so long that it finally had the same contempt for the human beings that returned always to sin as hogs and dogs done that the old strong archangel his self must have had.

For a long time it never burned, even after everything else inside had. We could watch it, hanging there among the fire, not like it had knowed in its time too much water to burn easy, but like it had strove and fit with the devil and all the hosts of hell too long to burn in jest a fire that Res Grier started, trying to beat Solon Quick out of half a dog. But at last it went, too, not in a hurry still, but jest all at once, kind of roaring right on up and out against the stars and the far dark spaces. And then there wasn't nothing but jest pap, drenched and groggy-looking, on the ground, with the rest of us around him, and Whitfield like always in his boiled shirt and his black hat and pants, standing there with his hat on, too, like he had strove too long to save what hadn't ought to been created in the first place, from the damnation it didn't even want to escape, to bother to need to take his hat off in any presence. He looked around at us from under it; we was all there now, all that belonged to that church and used it to be born and marry and die from—us and the Armstids and Tulls, and Bookwright and Quick and Snopes.

"I was wrong," Whitfield said. "I told you we would meet here tomorrow to roof a church. We'll meet here in the morning to raise one."

"Of course we got to have a church," pap said. "We're going to have one. And we're going to have it soon. But there's some of us done already give a day or so this week, at the cost of our own work. Which is right and just, and we're going to give more, and glad to. But I don't believe that the Lord—"

Whitfield let him finish. He never moved. He jest stood there until pap finally run down of his own accord and hushed and set there on the ground mostly not looking at maw, before Whitfield opened his mouth.

"Not you," Whitfield said. "Arsonist."

"Arsonist?" pap said.

"Yes," Whitfield said. "If there is any pursuit in which you can engage without carrying flood and fire and destruction and death behind you, do it. But not one hand shall you lay to this new house until you have proved to us that you are to be trusted again with the powers and capacities of a man." He looked about at us again. "Tull and Snopes and Armstid have already promised for tomorrow. I understand that Quick had another half day he intended—"

"I can give another day," Solon said.

"I can give the rest of the week," Homer said.

"I ain't rushed neither," Snopes said.

"That will be enough to start with, then," Whitfield said. "It's late now. Let us all go home."

He went first. He didn't look back once, at the church or at us. He went to the old mare and clumb up slow and stiff and powerful, and was gone, and we went too, scattering. But I looked back at it. It was jest a shell now, with a red and fading core, and I had hated it at times and feared it at others, and I should have been glad. But there was something that even that fire hadn't even touched. Maybe that's all it was—jest indestructibility, endurability—that old man that could plan to build it back while its walls was still fire-fierce and then calmly turn his back and go away because he knowed that the men that never had nothing to give toward the new one but their work would be there at sunup tomorrow, and the day after that, and the day after that, too, as long as it was needed, to give that work to build it back again. So it hadn't gone a-tall; it didn't no more care for that little fire and flood than Whitfield's old baptizing gown had done. Then we was home. Maw had left so fast the lamp was still lit, and we could see pap now, still leaving a puddle where he stood, with a cut across the back of his head where the barrel had busted and the blood-streaked water soaking him to the waist.

"Get them wet clothes off," maw said.

"I don't know as I will or not," pap said. "I been publicly notified that I ain't fitten to associate with white folks, so I publicly notify them same white folks and Methodists, too, not to try to associate with me, or the devil can have the hindmost."

But maw hadn't even listened. When she come back with a pan of water and a towel and the liniment bottle, pap was already in his nightshirt.

"I don't want none of that neither," he said. "If my head wasn't worth busting, it ain't worth patching." But she never paid no mind to that neither. She washed his head off and dried it and put the bandage on and went out again, and pap went and got into bed.

"Hand me my snuff; then you get out of here and stay out too," he said.

But before I could do that maw come back. She had a glass of hot toddy, and she went to the bed and stood there with it, and pap turned his head and looked at it.

"What's that?" he said.

But maw never answered, and then he set up in bed and drawed a long, shuddering breath—we could hear it—and after a minute he put out his hand for the toddy and set there holding it and drawing his breath, and then he taken a sip of it.

"I Godfrey, if him and all of them put together think they can keep me from working on my own church like ary other man, he better be a good man to try it." He taken another sip of the toddy. Then he taken a long one. "Arsonist," he said. "Work units. Dog units. And now arsonist. I Godfrey, what a day!"

THE OLD PEOPLE

At first there was nothing. There was the faint, cold, steady rain, the gray and constant light of the late November dawn, with the voices of the hounds converging somewhere in it and toward them. Then Sam Fathers, standing just behind the boy as he had been standing when the boy shot his first running rabbit with his first gun and almost with the first load it ever carried, touched his shoulder and he began to shake, not with any cold. Then the buck was there. He did not come into sight; he was just there, looking not like a ghost but as if all of light were condensed in him and he were the source of it, not only moving in it but disseminating it, already running, seen first as you always see the deer, in that split second after he has already seen

THE OLD PEOPLE. From *Go Down Moses and Other Stories* by William Faulkner. Copyright 1940 by William Faulkner. Reprinted by permission of Random House, Inc.

you, already slanting away in that first soaring bound, the antlers even in that dim light looking like a small rocking-chair balanced on his head.

"Now," Sam Fathers said, "shoot quick, and slow."

The boy did not remember that shot at all. He would live to be eighty, as his father and his father's twin brother and their father in his turn had lived to be, but he would never hear that shot nor remember even the shock of the gun-butt. He didn't even remember what he did with the gun afterward. He was running. Then he was standing over the buck where it lay on the wet earth still in the attitude of speed and not looking at all dead, standing over it shaking and jerking, with Sam Fathers beside him again, extending the knife. "Don't walk up to him in front," Sam said. "If he ain't dead, he will cut you all to pieces with his feet. Walk up to him from behind and take him by the horn first, so you can hold his head down until you can jump away. Then slip your other hand down and hook your fingers in his nostrils."

The boy did that—drew the head back and the throat taut and drew Sam Fathers' knife across the throat and Sam stooped and dipped his hands in the hot smoking blood and wiped them back and forth across the boy's face. Then Sam's horn rang in the wet gray woods and again and again; there was a boiling wave of dogs about them, with Tennie's Jim and Boon Hogganbeck whipping them back after each had had a taste of the blood, then the men, the true hunters— Walter Ewell whose rifle never missed, and Major de Spain and old General Compson and the boy's cousin, McCaslin Edmonds, grandson of his father's sister, sixteen years his senior and, since both he and McCaslin were only children and the boy's father had been nearing seventy when he was born, more his brother than his cousin and more his father than either—sitting their horses and looking down at them: at the old man of seventy who had been a Negro for two generations now but whose face and bearing were still those of the Chickasaw chief who had been his father; and the white boy of twelve with the prints of the bloody hands on his face, who had nothing to do now but stand straight and not let the trembling show.

"Did he do all right, Sam?" his cousin McCaslin said.

"He done all right," Sam Fathers said.

They were the white boy, marked forever, and the old dark man sired on both sides by savage kings, who had marked him, whose bloody hands had merely formally consecrated him to that which, under the man's tutelage, he had already accepted, humbly and joyfully, with abnegation and with pride too; the hands, the touch, the first worthy blood which he had been found at last worthy to draw, joining him and the man forever, so that the man would continue to live past the boy's seventy years and then eighty years, long after the man himself had entered the earth as chiefs and kings entered it;—the child, not yet a man, whose grandfather had lived in the same country and in almost the same manner as the boy himself would grow up to live, leaving his descendants in the land in his turn as his grandfather had done, and the old man past seventy whose grandfathers had owned the land long before the white men ever saw it and who had vanished from it now with all their kind, what of blood they left behind them running now in another race and for a while even in bondage and now drawing toward the end of its alien and irrevocable course, barren, since Sam Fathers had no children.

His father was Ikkemotubbe himself, who had named himself Doom. Sam told the boy about that—how Ikkemotubbe, old Issetibbeha's sister's son, had run away to New Orleans in his youth and returned seven years later with a French companion calling himself the Chevalier Soeur-Blonde de Vitry, who must have been the Ikkemotubbe of his family too and who was already addressing Ikkemotubbe as *Du Homme;*—returned, came home again, with his foreign Aramis and the quadroon slave woman who was to be Sam's mother, and a gold-laced hat and coat and a wicker wine-hamper containing a litter of month-old puppies and a gold snuff-box filled with a white powder resembling fine sugar. And how he was met at the River landing by three or four companions of his bachelor youth, and while the light of a smoking torch gleamed on the glittering braid of the hat and coat Doom squatted in the mud of the land and took one of the puppies from the hamper and put a pinch of the white powder on its tongue and the puppy died before the one who was holding it could cast it away. And how they returned to the Plantation where Issetibbeha, dead now, had been succeeded by his son, Doom's fat cousin Moketubbe, and the next day Moketubbe's eight-year-old son died suddenly and that afternoon, in the presence of Moketubbe and most of the others (the People, Sam Fathers called them) Doom produced another puppy from the wine-hamper and put a pinch of the white powder on its tongue and Moketubbe abdicated and Doom became in fact The Man which his French friend already called him. And how on the day after that, during the ceremony of accession, Doom pronounced a marriage between the pregnant quadroon and one of the slave men which he had just inherited (that was how Sam Fathers got his name, which in Chickasaw had been Had-Two-Fathers) and two years later sold the man and woman and the child who was his own son to his white neighbor, Carothers McCaslin.

That was seventy years ago. The Sam Fathers whom the boy knew was already sixty—a man not tall, squat rather, almost sedentary, flabby-looking though he actually was not, with hair like a horse's mane which even at seventy showed no trace of white and a face which showed no age until he smiled, whose only visible trace of Negro blood was a slight dullness of the hair and the fingernails, and something else which you did notice about the eyes, which you noticed because it was not always there, only in repose and not always then —something not in their shape nor pigment but in their expression, and the boy's cousin McCaslin told him what that was: not the heritage of Ham, not the mark of servitude but of bondage; the knowledge that for a while that part of his blood had been the blood of slaves. "Like an old lion or a bear in a cage," McCaslin said. "He was born in the cage and has been in it all his life; he knows nothing else. Then he smells something. It might be anything, any breeze blowing past anything and then into his nostrils. But there for a second was the hot sand or the cane-brake that he never even saw himself, might not even know if he did see it and probably does know he couldn't hold his own with it if he got back to it. But that's not what he smells then. It was the cage he smelled. He hadn't smelled the cage until that minute. Then the hot sand or the brake blew into his nostrils and blew away, and all he could smell was the cage. That's what makes his eyes look like that."

"Then let him go!" the boy cried. "Let him go!"

His cousin laughed shortly. Then he stopped laughing, making the sound, that is. It had never been laughing. "His cage aint McCaslins," he said. "He was a wild man. When he was born, all his blood on both sides, except the little white part, knew things that had been tamed out of our blood so long ago that we have not only forgotten them, we have to live together in herds to protect ourselves from our own sources. He was the direct son not only of a warrior but of a chief. Then he grew up and began to learn things, and all of a sudden one day he found out that he had been betrayed, the blood of the warriors and chiefs had been betrayed. Not by his father," he added quickly. "He probably never held it against old Doom for selling him and his mother into slavery, because he probably believed the damage was already done before then and it was the same warriors' and chiefs' blood in him and Doom both that was betrayed through the black blood which his mother gave him. Not betrayed by the black blood and not wilfully betrayed by his mother, but betrayed by her all the same, who had bequeathed him not only the blood of slaves but even a little of the very blood which had enslaved it; himself his own battleground, the scene of his own vanquishment and the mausoleum of his defeat. His cage aint us," McCaslin said. "Did you ever know anybody yet, even your father and Uncle Buddy, that ever told him to do or not do anything that he ever paid any attention to?"

That was true. The boy first remembered him as sitting in the door of the plantation blacksmith-shop, where he sharpened plow-points and mended tools and even did rough carpenter-work when he was not in the woods. And sometimes, even when the woods had not drawn him, even with the shop cluttered with work which the farm waited on, Sam would sit there, doing nothing at all for half a day or a whole one, and no man, neither the boy's father and twin uncle in their day nor his cousin McCaslin after he became practical though not yet titular master, ever to say to him, "I want this finished by sundown" or "why wasn't this done yesterday?" And once each year, in the late fall, in November, the boy would watch the wagon, the hooped canvas top erected now, being loaded—the food, hams and sausage from the smokehouse, coffee and flour and molasses from the commissary, a whole beef killed just last night for the dogs until there would be meat in camp, the crate containing the dogs themselves, then the bedding, the guns, the horns and lanterns and axes, and his cousin McCaslin and Sam Fathers in their hunting clothes would mount to the seat and with Tennie's Jim sitting on the dog-crate they would drive away to Jefferson, to join Major de Spain and General Compson and Boon Hogganbeck and Walter Ewell and go on into the big bottom of the Tallahatchie where the deer and bear were, to be gone two weeks. But before the wagon was even loaded the boy would find that he could watch no longer. He would go away, running almost, to stand behind the corner where he could not see the wagon and nobody could see him, not crying, holding himself rigid except for the trembling, whispering to himself: "Soon now. Soon now. Just three more years" (or two more or one more) "and I will be ten. Then Cass said I can go."

White man's work, when Sam did work. Because he did nothing else: farmed no allotted acres of his own, as the other ex-slaves of old Carothers McCaslin did, performed no field-work for daily wages as the younger and newer Negroes did—and the boy never knew just how that had been settled between Sam and old Carothers, or perhaps with old Carothers' twin sons after him. For, although Sam lived among the Negroes, in a cabin among the other cabins in the quarters, and consorted with Negroes (what of consorting with any-one Sam did after the boy got big enough to walk alone from the house to the blacksmith-shop and then to carry a gun) and dressed like them and talked like them and even went with them to the Negro church now and then, he was still the son of that Chickasaw chief and the Negroes knew it. And, it seemed to the boy, not only Negroes. Boon Hogganbeck's grandmother had been a Chickasaw woman too, and although the blood had run white since and Boon was a white man, it was not chief's blood. To the boy at least, the difference was apparent immediately you saw Boon and Sam to-gether, and even Boon seemed to know it was there—even Boon, to whom in his tradition it had never occurred that anyone might be better born than himself. A man might be smarter, he admitted that, or richer (luckier, he called it) but not better born. Boon was a mastiff, absolutely faithful, dividing his fidelity equally between Major de Spain and the boy's cousin McCaslin, absolutely dependent for his very bread and dividing that impartially too between Major de Spain and McCaslin, hardy, generous, courageous enough, a slave to all the appetites and almost unratiocinative. In the boy's eyes at least it was Sam Fathers, the Negro, who bore himself not only to-ward his cousin McCaslin and Major de Spain but toward all white men, with gravity and dignity and without servility or recourse to that impenetrable wall of ready and easy mirth which Negroes sus-tain between themselves and white men, bearing himself toward his cousin McCaslin not only as one man to another but as an older man to a younger.

He taught the boy the woods, to hunt, when to shoot and when not to shoot, when to kill and when not to kill, and better, what to do with it afterward. Then he would talk to the boy, the two of them sitting beneath the close fierce stars on a summer hilltop while they waited for the hounds to bring the fox back within hearing, or beside a fire in the November or December woods while the dogs worked out a coon's trail along the creek, or fireless in the pitch dark and heavy dew of April mornings while they squatted beneath a turkey-roost. The boy would never question him; Sam did not react to questions. The boy would just wait and then listen and Sam would begin, talking about the old days and the People whom he had not had time ever to know and so could not remember (he did not remember ever having seen his father's face), and in place of whom the other race into which his blood had run supplied him with no substitute.

And as he talked about those old times and those dead and vanished men of another race from either that the boy knew, gradually to the boy those old times would cease to be old times and would become a part of the boy's present, not only as if they had happened yesterday but as if they were still happening, the men who walked through them actually walking in breath and air and casting an actual shadow on the earth they had not quitted. And more: as if some of them had not happened yet but would occur tomorrow, until at last it would seem to the boy that he himself had not come into existence yet, that none of his race nor the other subject race which his people had brought with them into the land had come here yet; that although it had been his grandfather's and then his father's and uncle's and was now his cousin's and someday would be his own land which he and Sam hunted over, their hold upon it actually was as trivial and without reality as the now faded and archaic script in the chancery book in Jefferson which allocated it to them and that it was he, the boy, who was the guest here and Sam Fathers' voice the mouthpiece of the host.

Until three years ago there had been two of them, the other a full-blood Chickasaw, in a sense even more incredibly lost than Sam Fathers. He called himself Jobaker, as if it were one word. Nobody knew his history at all. He was a hermit, living in a foul little shack at the forks of the creek five miles from the plantation and about that far from any other habitation. He was a market hunter and fisherman and he consorted with nobody, black or white; no Negro would even cross his path and no man dared approach his hut except Sam. And perhaps once a month the boy would find them in Sam's shop—two old men squatting on their heels on the dirt floor, talking in a mixture of Negroid English and flat hill dialect and now and then a phrase of that old tongue which as time went on and the boy squatted there too listening, he began to learn. Then Jobaker died. That is, nobody had seen him in some time. Then one morning Sam was missing, nobody, not even the boy, knew when nor where, until that night when some Negroes hunting in the creek bottom saw the sudden burst of flame and approached. It was Jobaker's hut, but before they got anywhere near it, someone shot at them from the shadows beyond it. It was Sam who fired, but nobody ever found Jobaker's grave.

The next morning, sitting at breakfast with his cousin, the boy saw Sam pass the dining-room window and he remembered then that never in his life before had he seen Sam nearer the house than the blacksmith-shop. He stopped eating even; he sat there and he and his cousin both heard the voices from beyond the pantry door, then the door opened and Sam entered, carrying his hat in his hand but without knocking as anyone else on the place except a house servant would have done, entered just far enough for the door to close behind him and stood looking at neither of them—the Indian face above the nigger clothes, looking at something over their heads or at something not even in the room.

"I want to go," he said. "I want to go to the Big Bottom to live."

"To live?" the boy's cousin said.

"At Major de Spain's and your camp, where you go to hunt," Sam said. "I could take care of it for you all while you aint there. I will build me a little house in the woods, if you rather I didn't stay in the big one."

"What about Isaac here?" his cousin said. "How will you get away from him? Are you going to take him with you?" But still Sam looked at neither of them, standing just inside the room with that face which showed nothing, which showed that he was an old man only when it smiled.

"I want to go," he said. "Let me go."

"Yes," the cousin said quietly. "Of course. I'll fix it with Major de Spain. You want to go soon?"

"I'm going now," Sam said. He went out. And that was all. The boy was nine then; it seemed perfectly natural that nobody, not even his cousin McCaslin, should argue with Sam. Also, since he was nine now, he could understand that Sam could leave him and their days and nights in the woods together without any wrench. He believed that he and Sam both knew that this was not only temporary but that the exigencies of his maturing, of that for which Sam had been training him all his life some day to dedicate himself, required it. They had settled that one night last summer while they listened to the hounds bringing a fox back up the creek valley; now the boy discerned in that very talk under the high, fierce August stars a presage, a warning, of this moment today. "I done taught you all there is of this settled country," Sam said. "You can hunt it good as I can now. You are ready for the Big Bottom now, for bear and deer. Hunter's meat," he said. "Next year you will be ten. You will write your age in two numbers and you will be ready to become a man. Your pa" (Sam always referred to the boy's cousin as his father, establishing even before the boy's orphanhood did that relation between them not of the ward to his guardian and kinsman and chief and head of his blood, but of the child to the man who sired his flesh and his thinking too) "promised you can go with us then." So the boy could understand Sam's going. But he couldn't understand why now, in March, six months before the moon for hunting.

"If Jobaker's dead like they say," he said, "and Sam hasn't got anybody but us at all kin to him, why does he want to go to the Big Bottom now, when it will be six months before we get there?"

"Maybe that's what he wants," McCaslin said. "Maybe he wants to get away from you a little while."

But that was all right. McCaslin and other grown people often said things like that and he paid no attention to them, just as he paid no attention to Sam saying he wanted to go to the Big Bottom to live. After all, he would have to live there for six months, because there would be no use in going at all if he was going to turn right around and come back. And, as Sam himself had told him, he already knew all about hunting in this settled country that Sam or anybody else could teach him. So it would be all right. Summer, then the bright days after the first frost, then the cold and himself on the wagon with McCaslin this time and the moment would come and he would draw the blood, the big blood which would make him a man, a hunter, and Sam would come back home with them and he too would have outgrown the child's pursuit of rabbits and 'possums. Then he too would make one before the winter fire, talking of the old hunts and the hunts to come as hunters talked.

So Sam departed. He owned so little that he could carry it. He walked. He would neither let McCaslin send him in the wagon, nor take a mule to ride. No one saw him go even. He was just gone one morning, the cabin which had never had very much in it, vacant and empty, the shop in which there never had been very much done, standing idle. Then November came at last, and now the boy made one—himself and his cousin McCaslin and Tennie's Jim, and Major de Spain and General Compson and Walter Ewell and Boon and old Uncle Ash to do the cooking, waiting for them in Jefferson with the other wagon, and the surrey in which he and McCaslin and General Compson and Major de Spain would ride.

Sam was waiting at the camp to meet them. If he was glad to see them, he did not show it. And if, when they broke camp two weeks later to return home, he was sorry to see them go, he did not show that either. Because he did not come back with them. It was only the boy who returned, returning solitary and alone to the settled familiar land, to follow for eleven months the childish business of rabbits and such while he waited to go back, having brought with him, even from his brief first sojourn, an unforgettable sense of the big woods—not a quality dangerous or particularly inimical, but profound, sentient, gigantic and brooding, amid which he had been permitted to go to and fro at will, unscathed, why he knew not, but dwarfed and, until he had drawn honorably blood worthy of being drawn, alien.

Then November, and they would come back. Each morning Sam would take the boy out to the stand allotted him. It would be one of the poorer stands of course, since he was only ten and eleven and twelve and he had never even seen a deer running yet. But they would stand there, Sam a little behind him and without a gun himself, as he had been standing when the boy shot the running rabbit when he was eight years old. They would stand there in the November dawns, and after a while they would hear the dogs. Sometimes the chase would sweep up and past quite close, belling and invisible; once they heard the two heavy reports of Boon Hogganbeck's old gun with which he had never killed anything larger than a squirrel and that sitting, and twice they heard the flat unreverberant clap of Walter Ewell's rifle, following which you did not even wait to hear his horn.

"I'll never get a shot," the boy said. "I'll never kill one."

"Yes, you will," Sam said. "You wait. You'll be a hunter. You'll be a man."

But Sam wouldn't come out. They would leave him there. He would come as far as the road where the surrey waited, to take the riding horses back, and that was all. The men would ride the horses and Uncle Ash and Tennie's Jim and the boy would follow in the wagon with Sam, with the camp equipment and the trophies, the meat, the heads, the antlers, the good ones, the wagon winding on among the tremendous gums and cypresses and oaks where no axe save that of the hunter had ever sounded, between the impenetrable walls of cane and brier—the two changing yet constant walls just beyond which the wilderness whose mark he had brought away forever on his spirit even from that first two weeks seemed to lean, stooping a little, watching them and listening, not quite inimical because they were too small, even those such as Walter and Major de Spain and old General Compson who had killed many deer and bear, their sojourn too brief and too harmless to excite to that, but just brooding, secret, tremendous, almost inattentive.

Then they would emerge, they would be out of it, the line as sharp as the demarcation of a doored wall. Suddenly skeleton cotton- and corn-fields would flow away on either hand, gaunt and motionless beneath the gray rain; there would be a house, barns, fences, where the hand of man had clawed for an instant, holding, the wall of the wilderness behind them now, tremendous and still and seemingly impenetrable in the gray and fading light, the very tiny orifice through which they had emerged apparently swallowed up. The surrey would be waiting, his cousin McCaslin and Major de Spain and General Compson and Walter and Boon dismounted beside it. Then Sam would get down from the wagon and mount one of the horses and, with the others on a rope behind him, he would turn back. The boy would watch him for a while against that tall and secret wall, growing smaller and smaller against it, never looking back. Then he would enter it, returning to what the boy believed, and thought that his cousin McCaslin believed, was his loneliness and solitude.

II

So the instant came. He pulled trigger and Sam Fathers marked his face with the hot blood which he had spilled and he ceased to be a child and became a hunter and a man. It was the last day. They broke camp that afternoon and went out, his cousin and Major de Spain and General Compson and Boon on the horses. Walter Ewell and the Negroes in the wagon with him and Sam and his hide and antlers. There could have been (and were) other trophies in the wagon. But for him they did not exist, just as for all practical purposes he and Sam Fathers were still alone together as they had been that morning. The wagon wound and jolted between the slow and shifting yet constant walls from beyond and above which the wilderness watched them pass, less than inimical now and never to be inimical again since the buck still and forever leaped, the shaking gun-barrels coming constantly and forever steady at last, crashing, and still out of his instant of immortality the buck sprang, forever immortal;—the wagon jolting and bouncing on, the moment of the buck, the shot, Sam Fathers and himself and the blood with which Sam had marked him forever one with the wilderness which had accepted him since Sam said that he had done all right, when suddenly Sam reined back and stopped the wagon and they all heard the unmistakable and unforgettable sound of a deer breaking cover.

Then Boon shouted from beyond the bend of the trail and while they sat motionless in the halted wagon, Walter and the boy already reaching for their guns, Boon came galloping back, flogging his mule with his hat, his face wild and amazed as he shouted down at them. Then the other riders came around the bend, also spurring.

"Get the dogs!" Boon cried. "Get the dogs! If he had a nub on his head, he had fourteen points! Laying right there by the road in that pawpaw thicket! If I'd a knowed he was there, I could have cut his throat with my pocket knife!"

"Maybe that's why he run," Walter said. "He saw you never had your gun." He was already out of the wagon with his rifle. Then the boy was out too with his gun, and the other riders came up and Boon got off his mule somehow and was scrabbling and clawing among the duffel in the wagon, still shouting, "Get the dogs! Get the dogs!" And it seemed to the boy too that it would take them forever to decide what to do—the old men in whom the blood ran cold and slow, in whom during the intervening years between them and himself the blood had become a different and colder substance from that which ran in him and even in Boon and Walter.

"What about it, Sam?" Major de Spain said. "Could the dogs bring him back?"

"We wont need the dogs," Sam said. "If he dont hear the dogs behind him, he will circle back in here about sundown to bed."

"All right," Major de Spain said. "You boys take the horses. We'll go on out to the road in the wagon and wait there." He and General Compson and McCaslin got into the wagon and Boon and Walter and Sam and the boy mounted the horses and turned back and out of the trail. Sam led them for an hour through the gray and unmarked afternoon whose light was little different from what it had been at dawn and which would become darkness without any graduation between. Then Sam stopped them.

"This is far enough," he said. "He'll be coming upwind, and he dont want to smell the mules." They tied the mounts in a thicket. Sam led them on foot now, unpathed through the markless afternoon, the boy pressing close behind him, the two others, or so it seemed to the boy, on his heels. But they were not. Twice Sam turned his head slightly and spoke back to him across his shoulder, still walking: "You got time. We'll get there fore he does."

So he tried to go slower. He tried deliberately to decelerate the dizzy rushing of time in which the buck which he had not even seen was moving, which it seemed to him must be carrying the buck farther and farther and more and more irretrievably away from them even though there were no dogs behind him now to make him run, even though, according to Sam, he must have completed his circle now and was heading back toward them. They went on; it could have been another hour or twice that or less than half, the boy could not have said. Then they were on a ridge. He had never been in here before and he could not see that it was a ridge. He just knew that the earth had risen slightly because the underbrush had thinned a little, the ground sloping invisibly away toward a dense wall of cane. Sam stopped. "This is it," he said. He spoke to Walter and Boon: "Follow this ridge and you will come to two crossings. You will see the tracks. If he crosses, it will be at one of these three."

Walter looked about for a moment. "I know it," he said. "I've even seen your deer. I was in here last Monday. He ain't nothing but a yearling."

"A yearling?" Boon said. He was panting from the walking. His face still looked a little wild. "If the one I saw was any yearling, I'm still in kindergarden."

"Then I must have seen a rabbit," Walter said. "I always heard you quit school altogether two years before the first grade."

Boon glared at Walter. "If you dont want to shoot him, get out of the way," he said. "Set down somewhere. By God, I—"

"Aint nobody going to shoot him standing here," Sam said quietly.

"Sam's right," Walter said. He moved, slanting the worn, silver-colored barrel of his rifle downward to walk with it again. "A little more moving and a little more quiet too. Five miles is still Hoggan-beck range, even if he wasn't downwind." They went on. The boy could still hear Boon talking, though presently that ceased too. Then once more he and Sam stood motionless together against a tremendous pin oak in a little thicket, and again there was nothing. There was only the soaring and sombre solitude in the dim light, there was the thin murmur of the faint cold rain which had not ceased all day. Then, as if it had waited for them to find their positions and become still, the wilderness breathed again. It seemed to lean inward above them, above himself and Sam and Walter and Boon in their separate lurking-places, tremendous, attentive, impartial and omniscient, the buck moving in it somewhere, not running yet since he had not been pursued, not frightened yet and never fearsome but just alert also as they were alert, perhaps already circling back, perhaps quite near, perhaps conscious also of the eye of the ancient immortal Umpire. Because he was just twelve then, and that morning something had happened to him: in less than a second he had ceased forever to be the child he was yesterday. Or perhaps that made no difference, perhaps even a city-bred man, let alone a child, could not have understood it; perhaps only a country-bred one could comprehend loving the life he spills. He began to shake again.

"I'm glad it's started now," he whispered. He did not move to speak; only his lips shaped the expiring words: "Then it will be gone when I raise the gun—"

Nor did Sam. "Hush," he said.

"Is he that near?" the boy whispered. "Do you think—"

"Hush," Sam said. So he hushed. But he could not stop the shaking. He did not try, because he knew it would go away when he needed the steadiness—had not Sam Fathers already consecrated and absolved him from weakness and regret too?—not from love and pity for all which lived and ran and then ceased to live in a second in the very midst of splendor and speed, but from weakness and regret. So they stood motionless, breathing deep and quiet and steady. If there had been any sun, it would be near to setting now; there was a condensing, a densifying, of what he had thought was the gray and unchanging light until he realised suddenly that it was his own breathing, his heart, his blood—something, all things, and that Sam Fathers had marked him indeed, not as a mere hunter, but with something Sam had had in his turn of his vanished and forgotten people. He stopped breathing then; there was only his heart, his blood, and in the following silence the wilderness ceased to breathe also, leaning, stooping overhead with its breath held, tremendous and impartial and waiting. Then the shaking stopped too, as he had known it would, and he drew back the two heavy hammers of the gun.

Then it had passed. It was over. The solitude did not breathe again yet; it had merely stopped watching him and was looking somewhere else, even turning its back on him, looking on away up the ridge at another point, and the boy knew as well as if he had seen him that the buck had come to the edge of the cane and had either seen or scented them and faded back into it. But the solitude did not breathe again. It should have suspired again then but it did not. It was still facing, watching, what it had been watching and it was not here, not where he and Sam stood; rigid, not breathing himself, he thought, cried *No! No!*, knowing already that it was too late, thinking with the old despair of two and three years ago: *I'll never get a shot.* Then he heard it—the flat single clap of Walter Ewell's rifle which never missed. Then the mellow sound of the horn came down the ridge and something went out of him and he knew then he had never expected to get the shot at all.

"I reckon that's it," he said. "Walter got him." He had raised the gun slightly without knowing it. He lowered it again and had lowered one of the hammers and was already moving out of the thicket when Sam spoke.

"Wait."

"Wait?" the boy cried. And he would remember that—how he turned upon Sam in the truculence of a boy's grief over the missed opportunity, the missed luck. "What for? Dont you hear that horn?"

And he would remember how Sam was standing. Sam had not moved. He was not tall, squat rather and broad, and the boy had been growing fast for the past year or so and there was not much difference between them in height, yet Sam was looking over the boy's head and up the ridge toward the sound of the horn and the boy knew that Sam did not even see him; that Sam knew he was still there beside him but he did not see the boy. Then the boy saw the buck. It was coming down the ridge, as if it were walking out of the very sound of the horn which related its death. It was not running, it was walking, tremendous, unhurried, slanting and tilting its head to pass the antlers through the undergrowth, and the boy standing with Sam beside him now instead of behind him as Sam always stood, and the gun still partly aimed and one of the hammers still cocked.

Then it saw them. And still it did not begin to run. It just stopped for an instant, taller than any man, looking at them; then its muscles suppled, gathered. It did not even alter its course, not fleeing, not even running, just moving with that winged and effortless ease with which deer move, passing within twenty feet of them, its head high and the eye not proud and not haughty but just full and wild and unafraid, and Sam standing beside the boy now, his right arm raised at full length, palm-outward, speaking in that tongue which the boy had learned from listening to him and Jobaker in the blacksmithshop, while up the ridge Walter Ewell's horn was still blowing them in to a dead buck.

"Oleh, Chief," Sam said. "Grandfather."

When they reached Walter, he was standing with his back toward them, quite still, bemused almost, looking down at his feet. He didn't look up at all.

"Come here, Sam," he said quietly. When they reached him he still did not look up, standing above a little spike buck which had still been a fawn last spring. "He was so little I pretty near let him go," Walter said. "But just look at the track he was making. It's pretty near big as a cow's. If there were any more tracks here beside the ones he is laying in, I would swear there was another buck here that I never even saw."

III

It was dark when they reached the road where the surrey waited. It was turning cold, the rain had stopped, and the sky was beginning to blow clear. His cousin and Major de Spain and General Compson had a fire going. "Did you get him?" Major de Spain said.

"Got a good-sized swamp-rabbit with spike horns," Walter said.

He slid the little buck down from his mule. The boy's cousin McCaslin looked at it.

"Nobody saw the big one?" he said.

"I dont even believe Boon saw it," Walter said. "He probably jumped somebody's stray cow in that thicket." Boon started cursing, swearing at Walter and at Sam for not getting the dogs in the first place and at the buck and all.

"Never mind," Major de Spain said. "He'll be here for us next fall. Let's get started home."

It was after midnight when they let Walter out at his gate two miles from Jefferson and later still when they took General Compson to his house and then returned to Major de Spain's, where he and McCaslin would spent the rest of the night, since it was still seventeen miles home. It was cold, the sky was clear now; there would be a heavy frost by sunup and the ground was already frozen beneath the horses' feet and the wheels and beneath their own feet as they crossed Major de Spain's yard and entered the house, the warm dark house, feeling their way up the dark stairs until Major de Spain found a candle and lit it, and into the strange room and the big deep bed, the still cold sheets until they began to warm to their bodies and at last the shaking stopped and suddenly he was telling McCaslin about it while McCaslin listened, quietly until he had finished. "You dont believe it," the boy said. "I know you dont—"

"Why not?" McCaslin said. "Think of all that has happened here, on this earth. All the blood hot and strong for living, pleasuring, that has soaked back into it. For grieving and suffering too, of course, but still getting something out of it for all that, getting a lot out of it, because after all you dont have to continue to bear what you believe is suffering; you can always choose to stop that, put an end to that. And even suffering and grieving is better than nothing; there is only one thing worse than not being alive, and that's shame. But you cant be alive forever, and you always wear out life long before you have exhausted the possibilities of living. And all that must be somewhere; all that could not have been invented and created just to be thrown away. And the earth is shallow; there is not a great deal of it before you come to the rock. And the earth dont want to just keep things, hoard them; it wants to use them again. Look at the seed, the acorns, at what happens even to carrion when you try to bury it: it refuses too, seethes and struggles too until it reaches light and air again, hunting the sun still. And they—" the boy saw his hand in silhouette for a moment against the window beyond which, accustomed to the darkness now, he could see sky where the scoured and icy stars glittered "—they dont want it, need it. Besides, what would it want, itself, knocking around out there, when it never had enough time about the earth as it was, when there is plenty of room about the earth, plenty of places still unchanged from what they were when the blood used and pleasured in them while it was still blood?"

"But we want them," the boy said. "We want them too. There is plenty of room for us and them too."

"That's right," McCaslin said. "Suppose they dont have substance, cant cast a shadow—"

"But I saw it!" the boy cried. "I saw him!"

"Steady," McCaslin said. For an instant his hand touched the boy's flank beneath the covers. "Steady. I know you did. So did I. Sam took me in there once after I killed my first deer."

James Joyce

1882–1941

ARABY · COUNTERPARTS · THE DEAD

James Joyce was the eldest of fourteen children in the family of a Dublin government clerk and minor politician. When James was a small boy, his father was prosperous enough to send him to the best Jesuit boarding school in Ireland. Later, because of the number of children and the father's convivial habits, the family fortunes declined rapidly. James managed to finish his education at University College, Dublin, but in the year following his graduation, trying to make his way as a writer in Paris, he was so near starvation most of the time that his health was permanently affected.

His mother's approaching death brought him back to Ireland, where he spent the two years of intellectual excitement and personal disorder so fully described in his great novel *Ulysses*. In 1904, newly married and twenty-two years old, Joyce left Ireland for good.

During the next sixteen years, always in financial difficulties, he supported himself, his wife, and two children by giving language lessons in Trieste, Rome, and Zurich. He worked stubbornly at his writing, though its breaks with convention made publication difficult, and his persisting illness of the eyes, requiring a long series of painful operations, kept him near blindness much of the time. In 1920, when his genius was beginning at last to receive recognition, Joyce moved to Paris, where he remained until the Second World War forced him to return to Zurich, his earlier wartime refuge, where he died in 1941.

Joyce had an Irish love of music and language. In a national competition in 1904 he proved himself to be one of the best young singers in Ireland. The rather conventional lyrics of *Chamber Music* (1907) are distinctive chiefly for their subtle effects of sound. Joyce learned Latin in school, studied French and Italian at the university, and taught himself Norwegian and German in order to read the plays of Henrik Ibsen and Gerhart Hauptmann in the original. At eighteen he published an article on Ibsen in a leading British journal. In the cafés of Trieste and Zurich, Joyce conversed fluently with his friends in half a dozen languages. These languages all merge into one language in the half-waking consciousness of the hero of Joyce's last and very difficult work, *Finnegans Wake*. In reaction to what he considered the parochialism of the Irish nationalist movement, Joyce refused to learn Gaelic.

Joyce's ambitions as a writer were by no means limited to experiments with language and form. Although he left the Catholic Church, his modes of thought remained Catholic, both in his respect for exact intellectual definition and in his rich use of symbols. His characters debate aesthetic and theological questions brilliantly. Similarly, although Joyce spent his life in voluntary exile he remained preoccupied with Ireland and made it the setting of all his works. At the end of the autobiographical novel *A Portrait of the Artist as a Young Man,* Stephen declares that his purpose as a writer is "to forge in the smithy of my soul the uncreated conscience of my race." Joyce was determined to outdo the great French novelists Flaubert, Balzac, and Zola in the documented particularity with which he recreated the inner and outer lives of his characters.

Joyce's first published volume of fiction was a collection of short stories, *Dubliners* (1914). These not only resemble Chekhov's stories, but were written under similar political circumstances. Joyce grew up in the period of discouraged reaction that followed the humiliation and death of the Irish independence leader Charles Stuart Parnell in 1891. In a letter to a publisher, Joyce said that his intention in *Dubliners* was to write a chapter of the moral history of his country. "I chose Dublin for the scene because that city seemed to me the center of paralysis." Very little appears to happen in some of these stories, and they often end in frustration. Through symbolic suggestion, however, and moments of unconscious self-revelation which he called "epiphanies," Joyce is able to universalize and make deeply affecting quite trivial incidents in the lives of very ordinary people.

Dubliners was followed by *A Portrait of the Artist as a Young Man* (1916), a partly lyrical, partly ironic account of the struggles of a highly sensitive young writer to become independent of family, church, and state. *Ulysses* (1921) is also autobiographical, but brings into conjunction with its hero the contrasted personality of a Dublin advertising agent named Leopold Bloom. During the course of a single day in Dublin in 1904, the experiences of its two principal characters parallel or parody the events of Homer's *Odyssey*. The work is marvelously intricate in design, and later writers were particularly influenced by its stream-of-consciousness technique.

Finnegans Wake (1939) exploits to the utmost the modern interest in psychoanalysis and myth. In his dreaming or hypnagogic state a Dublin citizen mixes up his personal history with the history first of Ireland and then of the human race. Since the connecting links are Freudian or cabalistic, and the language full of polyglot puns, the book is extremely difficult to read. This very difficulty, however, along with its wit, erudition, and comprehensiveness, makes it a persistent and exciting challenge to interpreters.

The three stories from *Dubliners* printed here are all stories of frustration, but the circumstances and meanings are very different. The young romantic in "Araby," defeated by commonplace realities and his own inexperience, judges himself far too severely. The hopelessly trapped Farrington in "Counterparts" directs his brutal aggressiveness toward others because he can no longer bear to judge himself. In "The Dead," one of the most moving of all modern short stories, Gabriel Conroy does come to see his life truly, despite his complacency, selfishness, and vanity. The way in which the shock of revelation occurs makes him able to feel not only the character of his own life, but the pathos of life generally. Because of the subtlety and complexity with which closely observed details are made to serve symbolic and thematic purposes, this story deserves very careful analysis.

ARABY

North Richmond Street, being blind, was a quiet street except at the hour when the Christian Brothers' School set the boys free. An uninhabited house of two storeys stood at the blind end, detached from its neighbours in a square ground. The other houses of the street, conscious of decent lives within them, gazed at one another with brown imperturbable faces.

The former tenant of our house, a priest, had died in the back drawing-room. Air, musty from having been long enclosed, hung in all the rooms, and the waste room behind the kitchen was littered with old useless papers. Among these I found a few paper-covered books, the pages of which were curled and damp: *The Abbot,* by Walter Scott, *The Devout Communicant* and *The Memoirs of Vidocq.* I liked the last best because its leaves were yellow. The wild garden behind the house contained a central apple-tree and a few straggling bushes under one of which I found the late tenant's rusty bicycle-pump. He had been a very charitable priest; in his will he had left all his money to institutions and the furniture of his house to his sister.

When the short days of winter came dusk fell before we had well eaten our dinners. When we met in the street the houses had grown sombre. The space of sky above us was the colour of ever-changing violet and towards it the lamps of the street lifted their feeble lanterns. The cold air stung us and we played till our bodies glowed. Our shouts echoed in the silent street. The career of our play brought us through the dark muddy lanes behind the houses where we ran the gauntlet of the rough tribes from the cottages, to the back doors of the dark dripping gardens where odours arose from the ashpits, to the dark odorous stables where a coachman smoothed and combed the horse or shook music from the buckled harness. When we re-

ARABY from *Dubliners* by James Joyce. First published 1916 by B. W. Huebsch. Reprinted by permission of The Viking Press, Inc., New York.

turned to the street light from the kitchen windows had filled the areas. If my uncle was seen turning the corner we hid in the shadow until we had seen him safely housed. Or if Mangan's sister came out on the doorstep to call her brother in to his tea we watched her from our shadow peer up and down the street. We waited to see whether she would remain or go in and, if she remained, we left our shadow and walked up to Mangan's steps resignedly. She was waiting for us, her figure defined by the light from the half-opened door. Her brother always teased her before he obeyed and I stood by the railings looking at her. Her dress swung as she moved her body and the soft rope of her hair tossed from side to side.

Every morning I lay on the floor in the front parlour watching her door. The blind was pulled down to within an inch of the sash so that I could not be seen. When she came out on the doorstep my heart leaped. I ran to the hall, seized my books and followed her. I kept her brown figure always in my eye and, when we came near the point at which our ways diverged, I quickened my pace and passed her. This happened morning after morning. I had never spoken to her, except for a few casual words, and yet her name was like a summons to all my foolish blood.

Her image accompanied me even in places the most hostile to romance. On Saturday evenings when my aunt went marketing I had to go to carry some of the parcels. We walked through the flaring streets, jostled by drunken men and bargaining women, amid the curses of labourers, the shrill litanies of shop-boys who stood on guard by the barrels of pigs' cheeks, the nasal chanting of street-singers, who sang a *come-all-you* about O'Donovan Rossa, or a ballad about the troubles in our native land. These noises converged in a single sensation of life for me: I imagined that I bore my chalice safely through a throng of foes. Her name sprang to my lips at moments in strange prayers and praises which I myself did not understand. My eyes were often full of tears (I could not tell why) and at times a flood from my heart seemed to pour itself out into my bosom. I thought little of the future. I did not know whether I would ever speak to her or not or, if I spoke to her, how I could tell her of my confused adoration. But my body was like a harp and her words and gestures were like fingers running upon the wires.

One evening I went into the back drawing-room in which the priest had died. It was a dark rainy evening and there was no sound in the house. Through one of the broken panes I heard the rain impinge upon the earth, the fine incessant needles of water playing in the sodden beds. Some distant lamp or lighted window gleamed below me. I was thankful that I could see so little. All my senses seemed to desire to veil themselves and, feeling that I was about to slip from them, I pressed the palms of my hands together until they trembled, murmuring: *"O love! O love!"* many times.

At last she spoke to me. When she addressed the first words to me I was so confused that I did not know what to answer. She asked me was I going to *Araby*. I forgot whether I answered yes or no. It would be a splendid bazaar, she said she would love to go.

"And why can't you?" I asked.

While she spoke she turned a silver bracelet round and round her wrist. She could not go, she said, because there would be a retreat that week in her convent. Her brother and two other boys were fighting for their caps and I was alone at the railings. She held one of the spikes, bowing her head towards me. The light from the lamp opposite our door caught the white curve of her neck, lit up her hair that rested there and, falling, lit up the hand upon the railing. It fell over one side of her dress and caught the white border of a petticoat, just visible as she stood at ease.

"It's well for you," she said.

"If I go," I said, "I will bring you something."

What innumerable follies laid waste my waking and sleeping thoughts after that evening! I wished to annihilate the tedious intervening days. I chafed against the work of school. At night in my bedroom and by day in the classroom her image came between me and the page I strove to read. The syllables of the word *Araby* were called to me through the silence in which my soul luxuriated and cast an Eastern enchantment over me. I asked for leave to go to the bazaar on Saturday night. My aunt was surprised and hoped it was not some Freemason affair. I answered few questions in class. I watched my master's face pass from amiability to sternness; he hoped I was not beginning to idle. I could not call my wandering thoughts together. I had hardly any patience with the serious work of life which, now that it stood between me and my desire, seemed to me child's play, ugly monotonous child's play.

On Saturday morning I reminded my uncle that I wished to go

to the bazaar in the evening. He was fussing at the hallstand, looking for the hat-brush, and answered me curtly:

"Yes, boy, I know."

As he was in the hall I could not go into the front parlour and lie at the window. I left the house in bad humour and walked slowly towards the school. The air was pitilessly raw and already my heart misgave me.

When I came home to dinner my uncle had not yet been home. Still it was early. I sat staring at the clock for some time and, when its ticking began to irritate me, I left the room. I mounted the staircase and gained the upper part of the house. The high cold empty gloomy rooms liberated me and I went from room to room singing. From the front window I saw my companions playing below in the street. Their cries reached me weakened and indistinct and, leaning my forehead against the cool glass, I looked over at the dark house where she lived. I may have stood there for an hour, seeing nothing but the brown-clad figure cast by my imagination, touched discreetly by the lamplight at the curved neck, at the hand upon the railings and at the border below the dress.

When I came downstairs again I found Mrs. Mercer sitting at the fire. She was an old garrulous woman, a pawnbroker's widow, who collected used stamps for some pious purpose. I had to endure the gossip of the tea-table. The meal was prolonged beyond an hour and still my uncle did not come. Mrs. Mercer stood up to go: she was sorry she couldn't wait any longer, but it was after eight o'clock and she did not like to be out late, as the night air was bad for her. When she had gone I began to walk up and down the room, clenching my fists. My aunt said:

"I'm afraid you may put off your bazaar for this night of Our Lord."

At nine o'clock I heard my uncle's latchkey in the halldoor. I heard him talking to himself and heard the hallstand rocking when it had received the weight of his overcoat. I could interpret these signs. When he was midway through his dinner I asked him to give me the money to go to the bazaar. He had forgotten.

"The people are in bed and after their first sleep now," he said.

I did not smile. My aunt said to him energetically:

"Can't you give him the money and let him go? You've kept him late enough as it is."

My uncle said he was very sorry he had forgotten. He said he believed in the old saying: "All work and no play makes Jack a dull boy." He asked me where I was going and, when I had told him a second time he asked me did I know *The Arab's Farewell to his Steed*. When I left the kitchen he was about to recite the opening lines of the piece to my aunt.

I held a florin tightly in my hand as I strode down Buckingham Street towards the station. The sight of the streets thronged with buyers and glaring with gas recalled to me the purpose of my journey. I took my seat in a third-class carriage of a deserted train. After an intolerable delay the train moved out of the station slowly. It crept onward among ruinous houses and over the twinkling river. At Westland Row Station a crowd of people pressed to the carriage doors; but the porters moved them back, saying that it was a special train for the bazaar. I remained alone in the bare carriage. In a few minutes the train drew up beside an improvised wooden platform. I passed out on to the road and saw by the lighted dial of a clock that it was ten minutes to ten. In front of me was a large building which displayed the magical name.

I could not find any sixpenny entrance and, fearing that the bazaar would be closed, I passed in quickly through a turnstile, handing a shilling to a weary-looking man. I found myself in a big hall girdled at half its height by a gallery. Nearly all the stalls were closed and the greater part of the hall was in darkness. I recognised a silence like that which pervades a church after a service. I walked into the centre of the bazaar timidly. A few people were gathered about the stalls which were still open. Before a curtain, over which the words *Café Chantant* were written in coloured lamps, two men were counting money on a salver. I listened to the fall of the coins.

Remembering with difficulty why I had come I went over to one of the stalls and examined porcelain vases and flowered tea-sets. At the door of the stall a young lady was talking and laughing with two young gentlemen. I remarked their English accents and listened vaguely to their conversation.

"O, I never said such a thing!"

"O, but you did!"

"O, but I didn't!"

"Didn't she say that?"

"Yes. I heard her."

"O, there's a . . . fib!"

Observing me the young lady came over and asked me did I wish to buy anything. The tone of her voice was not encouraging; she seemed to have spoken to me out of a sense of duty. I looked humbly at the great jars that stood like eastern guards at either side of the dark entrance to the stall and murmured:

"No, thank you."

The young lady changed the position of one of the vases and went back to the two young men. They began to talk of the same subject. Once or twice the young lady glanced at me over her shoulder.

I lingered before her stall, though I knew my stay was useless, to make my interest in her wares seem the more real. Then I turned away slowly and walked down the middle of the bazaar. I allowed the two pennies to fall against the sixpence in my pocket. I heard a voice call from one end of the gallery that the light was out. The upper part of the hall was now completely dark.

Gazing up into the darkness I saw myself as a creature driven and derided by vanity; and my eyes burned with anguish and anger.

COUNTERPARTS

The bell rang furiously and, when Miss Parker went to the tube, a furious voice called out in a piercing North of Ireland accent:

"Send Farrington here!"

Miss Parker returned to her machine, saying to a man who was writing at a desk:

"Mr. Alleyne wants you upstairs."

The man muttered *"Blast* him!" under his breath and pushed back his chair to stand up. When he stood up he was tall and of great bulk. He had a hanging face, dark wine-coloured, with fair eyebrows and moustache: his eyes bulged forward slightly and the whites

COUNTERPARTS from *Dubliners* by James Joyce. First published 1916 by B. W. Huebsch. Reprinted by permission of The Viking Press, Inc., New York.

of them were dirty. He lifted up the counter and, passing by the clients, went out of the office with a heavy step.

He went heavily upstairs until he came to the second landing, where a door bore a brass plate with the inscription *Mr. Alleyne*. Here he halted, puffing with labour and vexation, and knocked. The shrill voice cried:

"Come in!"

The man entered Mr. Alleyne's room. Simultaneously Mr. Alleyne, a little man wearing gold-rimmed glasses on a clean-shaven face, shot his head up over a pile of documents. The head itself was so pink and hairless it seemed like a large egg reposing on the papers. Mr. Alleyne did not lose a moment:

"Farrington? What is the meaning of this? Why have I always to complain of you? May I ask you why you haven't made a copy of that contract between Bodley and Kirwan? I told you it must be ready by four o'clock."

"But Mr. Shelley said, sir—"

"*Mr. Shelley said, sir.* . . . Kindly attend to what I say and not to what *Mr. Shelley says, sir.* You have always some excuse or another for shirking work. Let me tell you that if the contract is not copied before this evening I'll lay the matter before Mr. Crosbie. . . . Do you hear me now?"

"Yes, sir."

"Do you hear me now? . . . Ay and another little matter! I might as well be talking to the wall as talking to you. Understand once for all that you get a half an hour for your lunch and not an hour and a half. How many courses do you want, I'd like to know. . . . Do you mind me now?"

"Yes, sir."

Mr. Alleyne bent his head again upon his pile of papers. The man stared fixedly at the polished skull which directed the affairs of Crosbie & Alleyne, gauging its fragility. A spasm of rage gripped his throat for a few moments and then passed, leaving after it a sharp sensation of thirst. The man recognised the sensation and felt that he must have a good night's drinking. The middle of the month was passed and, if he could get the copy done in time, Mr. Alleyne might give him an order on the cashier. He stood still, gazing fixedly at the head upon the pile of papers. Suddenly Mr. Alleyne began to upset all the papers, searching for something. Then, as if he had been unaware of the man's presence till that moment, he shot up his head again, saying:

"Eh? Are you going to stand there all day? Upon my word, Farrington, you take things easy!"

"I was waiting to see . . ."

"Very good, you needn't wait to see. Go downstairs and do your work."

The man walked heavily towards the door and, as he went out of the room, he heard Mr. Alleyne cry after him that if the contract was not copied by evening Mr. Crosbie would hear of the matter.

He returned to his desk in the lower office and counted the sheets which remained to be copied. He took up his pen and dipped it in the ink but he continued to stare stupidly at the last words he had written: *In no case shall the said Bernard Bodley be* . . . The evening was falling and in a few minutes they would be lighting the gas: then he could write. He felt that he must slake the thirst in his throat. He stood up from his desk and, lifting the counter as before, passed out of the office. As he was passing out the chief clerk looked at him inquiringly.

"It's all right, Mr. Shelley," said the man, pointing with his finger to indicate the objective of his journey.

The chief clerk glanced at the hat-rack, but, seeing the row complete, offered no remark. As soon as he was on the landing the man pulled a shepherd's plaid cap out of his pocket, put it on his head and ran quickly down the rickety stairs. From the street door he walked on furtively on the inner side of the path towards the corner and all at once dived into a doorway. He was now safe in the dark snug of O'Neill's shop, and filling up the little window that looked into the bar with his inflamed face, the colour of dark wine or dark meat, he called out:

"Here, Pat, give us a g.p., like a good fellow."

The curate brought him a glass of plain porter. The man drank it at a gulp and asked for a caraway seed. He put his penny on the counter and, leaving the curate to grope for it in the gloom, retreated out of the snug as furtively as he had entered it.

Darkness, accompanied by a thick fog, was gaining upon the dusk of February and the lamps in Eustace Street had been lit. The man went up by the houses until he reached the door of the office, wondering whether he could finish his copy in time. On the stairs a moist pungent odour of perfumes saluted his nose: evidently Miss Dela-cour had come while he was out in O'Neill's. He crammed his cap back again into his pocket and re-entered the office, assuming an air of absentmindedness.

"Mr. Alleyne has been calling for you," said the chief clerk severely. "Where were you?"

The man glanced at the two clients who were standing at the counter as if to intimate that their presence prevented him from answering. As the clients were both male the chief clerk allowed himself a laugh.

"I know that game," he said. "Five times in one day is a little bit . . . Well, you better look sharp and get a copy of our correspondence in the Delacour case for Mr. Alleyne."

This address in the presence of the public, his run upstairs and the porter he had gulped down so hastily confused the man and, as he sat down at his desk to get what was required, he realised how hope-less was the task of finishing his copy of the contract before half past five. The dark damp night was coming and he longed to spend it in the bars, drinking with his friends amid the glare of gas and the clat-ter of glasses. He got out the Delacour correspondence and passed out of the office. He hoped Mr. Alleyne would not discover that the last two letters were missing.

The moist pungent perfume lay all the way up to Mr. Alleyne's room. Miss Delacour was a middle-aged woman of Jewish appearance. Mr. Alleyne was said to be sweet on her or on her money. She came to the office often and stayed a long time when she came. She was sitting beside his desk now in an aroma of perfumes, smoothing the handle of her umbrella and nodding the great black feather in her hat. Mr. Alleyne had swivelled his chair round to face her and thrown his right foot jauntily upon his left knee. The man put the corre-spondence on the desk and bowed respectfully but neither Mr. Al-leyne nor Miss Delacour took any notice of his bow. Mr. Alleyne tapped a finger on the correspondence and then flicked it towards him as if to say: *"That's all right: you can go."*

The man returned to the lower office and sat down again at his desk. He stared intently at the incomplete phrase: *In no case shall the said Bernard Bodley be . . .* and thought how strange it was that the last three words began with the same letter. The chief clerk began to hurry Miss Parker, saying she would never have the letters typed in time for post. The man listened to the clicking of the machine for a few minutes and then set to work to finish his copy. But his head was not clear and his mind wandered away to the glare and rattle of the public-house. It was a night for hot punches. He struggled on with his copy, but when the clock struck five he had still fourteen pages to write. Blast it! He couldn't finish it in time. He longed to execrate aloud, to bring his fist down on something violently. He was so enraged that he wrote *Bernard Bernard* instead of *Bernard Bodley* and had to begin again on a clean sheet.

He felt strong enough to clear out the whole office singlehanded. His body ached to do something, to rush out and revel in violence. All the indignities of his life enraged him. . . . Could he ask the cashier privately for an advance? No, the cashier was no good, no damn good; he wouldn't give an advance. . . . He knew where he would meet the boys: Leonard and O'Halloran and Nosey Flynn. The barometer of his emotional nature was set for a spell of riot.

His imagination had so abstracted him that his name was called twice before he answered. Mr. Alleyne and Miss Delacour were standing outside the counter and all the clerks had turned round in anticipation of something. The man got up from his desk. Mr. Alleyne began a tirade of abuse, saying that two letters were missing. The man answered that he knew nothing about them, that he had made a faithful copy. The tirade continued: it was so bitter and violent that the man could hardly restrain his fist from descending upon the head of the manikin before him:

"I know nothing about any other two letters," he said stupidly.

"*You—know—nothing*. Of course you know nothing," said Mr. Alleyne. "Tell me," he added, glancing first for approval to the lady beside him, "do you take me for a fool? Do you think me an utter fool?"

The man glanced from the lady's face to the little egg-shaped head and back again; and, almost before he was aware of it, his tongue had found a felicitous moment:

"I don't think, sir," he said, "that that's a fair question to put to me."

There was a pause in the very breathing of the clerks. Everyone was astounded (the author of the witticism no less than his neighbours) and Miss Delacour, who was a stout amiable person, began to smile broadly. Mr. Alleyne flushed to the hue of a wild rose and his mouth twitched with a dwarf's passion. He shook his fist in the man's face till it seemed to vibrate like the knob of some electric machine:

"You impertinent ruffian! You impertinent ruffian! I'll make short work of you! Wait till you see! You'll apologise to me for your impertinence or you'll quit the office instanter! You'll quit this, I'm telling you, or you'll apologise to me!"

He stood in a doorway opposite the office watching to see if the cashier would come out alone. All the clerks passed out and finally the cashier came out with the chief clerk. It was no use trying to say a word to him when he was with the chief clerk. The man felt that his position was bad enough. He had been obliged to offer an abject apology to Mr. Alleyne for his impertinence but he knew what a hornet's nest the office would be for him. He could remember the way in which Mr. Alleyne had hounded little Peake out of the office in order to make room for his own nephew. He felt savage and thirsty and revengeful, annoyed with himself and with everyone else. Mr. Alleyne would never give him an hour's rest; his life would be a hell to him. He had made a proper fool of himself this time. Could he not keep his tongue in his cheek? But they had never pulled together from the first, he and Mr. Alleyne, ever since the day Mr. Alleyne had overheard him mimicking his North of Ireland accent to amuse Higgins and Miss Parker: that had been the beginning of it. He might have tried Higgins for the money, but sure Higgins never had anything for himself. A man with two establishments to keep up, of course he couldn't. . . .

He felt his great body again aching for the comfort of the public-house. The fog had begun to chill him and he wondered could he touch Pat in O'Neill's. He could not touch him for more than a bob —and a bob was no use. Yet he must get money somewhere or other: he had spent his last penny for the g.p. and soon it would be too late for getting money anywhere. Suddenly, as he was fingering his watch-chain, he thought of Terry Kelly's pawn-office in Fleet Street. That was the dart! Why didn't he think of it sooner?

He went through the narrow alley of Temple Bar quickly, muttering to himself that they could all go to hell because he was going to have a good night of it. The clerk in Terry Kelly's said *A crown!* but the consignor held out for six shillings; and in the end the six shillings was allowed him literally. He came out of the pawn-office joyfully, making a little cylinder of the coins between his thumb and fingers. In Westmoreland Street the footpaths were crowded with young men and women returning from business and ragged urchins ran here and there yelling out the names of the evening editions. The man passed through the crowd, looking on the spectacle generally with proud satisfaction and staring masterfully at the office-girls. His head was full of the noises of tram-gongs and swishing trolleys and his nose already sniffed the curling fumes of punch. As he walked on he preconsidered the terms in which he would narrate the incident to the boys:

"So, I just looked at him—coolly, you know, and looked at her. Then I looked back at him again—taking my time, you know. 'I don't think that that's a fair question to put to me,' says I."

Nosey Flynn was sitting up in his usual corner of Davy Byrne's and, when he heard the story, he stood Farrington a half-one, saying it was as smart a thing as ever he heard. Farrington stood a drink in his turn. After a while O'Halloran and Paddy Leonard came in and the story was repeated to them. O'Halloran stood tailors of malt, hot, all round and told the story of the retort he had made to the chief clerk when he was in Callan's of Fownes's Street; but, as the retort was after the manner of the liberal shepherds in the eclogues, he had to admit that it was not as clever as Farrington's retort. At this Farrington told the boys to polish off that and have another.

Just as they were naming their poisons who should come in but Higgins! Of course he had to join in with the others. The men asked him to give his version of it, and he did so with great vivacity for the sight of five small hot whiskies was very exhilarating. Everyone roared laughing when he showed the way in which Mr. Alleyne shook his fist in Farrington's face. Then he imitated Farrington, saying, "*And here was my nabs, as cool as you please,*" while Farrington looked at the company out of his heavy dirty eyes, smiling and at times drawing forth stray drops of liquor from his moustache with the aid of his lower lip.

When that round was over there was a pause. O'Halloran had money but neither of the other two seemed to have any; so the whole party left the shop somewhat regretfully. At the corner of Duke Street Higgins and Nosey Flynn bevelled off to the left while the other three turned back towards the city. Rain was drizzling down on the cold streets and, when they reached the Ballast Office, Farrington suggested the Scotch House. The bar was full of men and loud with the noise of tongues and glasses. The three men pushed past the whining matchsellers at the door and formed a little party at the corner of the counter. They began to exchange stories. Leonard introduced them to a young fellow named Weathers who was performing at the Tivoli as an acrobat and knockabout *artiste*. Farrington stood a drink all round. Weathers said he would take a small Irish and Apollinaris. Farrington, who had definite notions of what was what, asked the boys would they have an Apollinaris too; but the boys told Tim to make theirs hot. The talk became theatrical. O'Halloran stood a round and then Farrington stood another round, Weathers protesting that the hospitality was too Irish. He promised to get them in behind the scenes and introduce them to some nice girls. O'Halloran said that he and Leonard would go, but that Farrington wouldn't go because he was a married man; and Farrington's heavy dirty eyes leered at the company in token that he understood he was being chaffed. Weathers made them all have just one little tincture at his expense and promised to meet them later on at Mulligan's in Poolbeg Street.

When the Scotch House closed they went round to Mulligan's. They went into the parlour at the back and O'Halloran ordered small hot specials all round. They were all beginning to feel mellow. Farrington was just standing another round when Weathers came back. Much to Farrington's relief he drank a glass of bitter this time. Funds were getting low but they had enough to keep them going. Presently two young women with big hats and a young man in a check suit came in and sat at a table close by. Weathers saluted them and told the company that they were out of the Tivoli. Farrington's eyes wandered at every moment in the direction of one of the young women. There was something striking in her appearance. An immense scarf of peacock-blue muslin was wound round her hat and knotted in a great bow under her chin; and she wore bright yellow gloves, reaching to the elbow. Farrington gazed admiringly at the plump arm which she moved very often and with much grace; and when, after a little time, she answered his gaze he admired still more her large dark brown eyes. The oblique staring expression in them fascinated him. She glanced at him once or twice and, when the party was leaving the room, she brushed against his chair and said *"O, pardon!"* in a London accent. He watched her leave the room in the hope that she would look back at him, but he was disappointed. He cursed his want of money and cursed all the rounds he had stood, particularly to all the whiskies and Apollinaris which he had stood to Weathers. If there was one thing that he hated it was a sponge. He was so angry that he lost count of the conversation of his friends.

When Paddy Leonard called him he found that they were talking about feats of strength. Weathers was showing his biceps muscle to to the company and boasting so much that the other two had called on Farrington to uphold the national honour. Farrington pulled up his sleeve accordingly and showed his biceps muscle to the company. The two arms were examined and compared and finally it was agreed to have a trial of strength. The table was cleared and the two men rested their elbows on it, clasping hands. When Paddy Leonard said *"Go!"* each was to try to bring down the other's hand on to the table. Farrington looked very serious and determined.

The trial began. After about thirty seconds Weathers brought his opponent's hand slowly down on to the table. Farrington's dark wine-coloured face flushed darker still with anger and humiliation at having been defeated by such a stripling.

"You're not to put the weight of your body behind it. Play fair," he said.

"Who's not playing fair?" said the other.

"Come on again. The two best out of three."

The trial began again. The veins stood out on Farrington's forehead, and the pallor of Weathers' complexion changed to peony. Their hands and arms trembled under the stress. After a long struggle Weathers again brought his opponent's hand slowly on to the table. There was a murmur of applause from the spectators. The curate, who was standing beside the table, nodded his red head towards the victor and said with stupid familiarity:

"Ah! that's the knack!"

"What the hell do you know about it?" said Farrington fiercely, turning on the man. "What do you put in your gab for?"

"Sh, sh!" said O'Halloran, observing the violent expression of Farrington's face. "Pony up, boys. We'll have just one little smahan more and then we'll be off."

A very sullen-faced man stood at the corner of O'Connell Bridge waiting for the little Sandymount tram to take him home. He was full of smouldering anger and revengefulness. He felt humiliated and discontented; he did not even feel drunk; and he had only twopence in his pocket. He cursed everything. He had done for himself in the office, pawned his watch, spent all his money; and he had not even got drunk. He began to feel thirsty again and he longed to be back again in the hot reeking public-house. He had lost his reputation as a strong man, having been defeated twice by a mere boy. His heart swelled with fury and, when he thought of the woman in the big hat who had brushed against him and said *Pardon!* his fury nearly choked him.

His tram let him down at Shelbourne Road and he steered his great body along in the shadow of the wall of the barracks. He loathed returning to his home. When he went in by the side-door he found the kitchen empty and the kitchen fire nearly out. He bawled upstairs:

"Ada! Ada!"

His wife was a little sharp-faced woman who bullied her husband when he was sober and was bullied by him when he was drunk. They had five children. A little boy came running down the stairs.

"Who is that?" said the man, peering through the darkness.

"Me, pa."

"Who are you? Charlie?"

"No, pa. Tom."

"Where's your mother?"

"She's out at the chapel."

"That's right. . . . Did she think of leaving any dinner for me?"

"Yes, pa. I—"

"Light the lamp. What do you mean by having the place in darkness? Are the other children in bed?"

The man sat down heavily on one of the chairs while the little boy lit the lamp. He began to mimic his son's flat accent, saying half to himself: "*At the chapel. At the chapel, if you please!*" When the lamp was lit he banged his fist on the table and shouted:

"What's for my dinner?"

"I'm going . . . to cook it, pa," said the little boy.

The man jumped up furiously and pointed to the fire.

"On that fire! You let the fire out! By God, I'll teach you to do that again!"

He took a step to the door and seized the walking-stick which was standing behind it.

"I'll teach you to let the fire out!" he said, rolling up his sleeve in order to give his arm free play.

The little boy cried *"O pa!"* and ran whimpering round the table, but the man followed him and caught him by the coat. The little boy looked about him wildly but, seeing no way of escape, fell upon his knees.

"Now, you'll let the fire out the next time!" said the man, striking at him vigorously with the stick. "Take that, you little whelp!"

The boy uttered a squeal of pain as the stick cut his thigh. He clasped his hands together in the air and his voice shook with fright.

"O, pa!" he cried. "Don't beat me, pa! And I'll . . . I'll say a *Hail Mary* for you. . . . I'll say a *Hail Mary* for you, pa, if you don't beat me. . . . I'll say a *Hail Mary*. . . ."

THE DEAD

Lily, the caretaker's daughter, was literally run off her feet. Hardly had she brought one gentleman into the little pantry behind the office on the ground floor and helped him off with his overcoat than the wheezy hall-door bell clanged again and she had to scamper along the bare hallway to let in another guest. It was well for her she had not to attend to the ladies also. But Miss Kate and Miss Julia had thought of that and had converted the bathroom upstairs into a ladies' dressing-room. Miss Kate and Miss Julia were there, gossiping and laughing and fussing, walking after each other to the head of the stairs, peering down over the banisters and calling down to Lily to ask her who had come.

It was always a great affair, the Misses Morkan's annual dance. Everybody who knew them came to it, members of the family, old friends of the family, the members of Julia's choir, any of Kate's

THE DEAD from *Dubliners* by James Joyce. First published 1916 by B. W. Huebsch. Reprinted by permission of The Viking Press, Inc., New York.

pupils that were grown up enough, and even some of Mary Jane's pupils too. Never once had it fallen flat. For years and years it had gone off in splendid style, as long as anyone could remember; ever since Kate and Julia, after the death of their brother Pat, had left the house in Stoney Batter and taken Mary Jane, their only niece, to live with them in the dark, gaunt house on Usher's Island, the upper part of which they had rented from Mr. Fulham, the corn-factor on the ground floor. That was a good thirty years ago if it was a day. Mary Jane, who was then a little girl in short clothes, was now the main prop of the household, for she had the organ in Haddington Road. She had been through the Academy and gave a pupils' concert every year in the upper room of the Antient Concert Rooms. Many of her pupils belonged to the better-class families on the Kingstown and Dalkey line. Old as they were, her aunts also did their share. Julia, though she was quite grey, was still the leading soprano in Adam and Eve's, and Kate, being too feeble to go about much, gave music lessons to beginners on the old square piano in the back room. Lily, the caretaker's daughter, did housemaid's work for them. Though their life was modest, they believed in eating well; the best of everything: diamond-bone sirloins, three-shilling tea and the best bottled stout. But Lily seldom made a mistake in the orders, so that she got on well with her three mistresses. They were fussy, that was all. But the only thing they would not stand was back answers.

Of course, they had good reason to be fussy on such a night. And then it was long after ten o'clock and yet there was no sign of Gabriel and his wife. Besides they were dreadfully afraid that Freddy Malins might turn up screwed. They would not wish for worlds that any of Mary Jane's pupils should see him under the influence; and when he was like that it was sometimes very hard to manage him. Freddy Malins always came late, but they wondered what could be keeping Gabriel: and that was what brought them every two minutes to the banisters to ask Lily had Gabriel or Freddy come.

"O, Mr. Conroy," said Lily to Gabriel when she opened the door for him, "Miss Kate and Miss Julia thought you were never coming. Good-night, Mrs. Conroy."

"I'll engage they did," said Gabriel, "but they forget that my wife here takes three mortal hours to dress herself."

He stood on the mat, scraping the snow from his goloshes, while Lily led his wife to the foot of the stairs and called out:

"Miss Kate, here's Mrs. Conroy."

Kate and Julia came toddling down the dark stairs at once. Both of them kissed Gabriel's wife, said she must be perished alive, and asked was Gabriel with her.

"Here I am as right as the mail, Aunt Kate! Go on up. I'll follow," called out Gabriel from the dark.

He continued scraping his feet vigorously while the three women went upstairs, laughing, to the ladies' dressing-room. A light fringe of snow lay like a cape on the shoulders of his overcoat and like toe-caps on the toes of his goloshes; and, as the buttons of his overcoat slipped with a squeaking noise through the snow-stiffened frieze, a cold, fragrant air from out-of-doors escaped from crevices and folds.

"Is it snowing again, Mr. Conroy?" asked Lily.

She had preceded him into the pantry to help him off with his overcoat. Gabriel smiled at the three syllables she had given his sur-name and glanced at her. She was a slim, growing girl, pale in com-plexion and with hay-coloured hair. The gas in the pantry made her look still paler. Gabriel had known her when she was a child and used to sit on the lowest step nursing a rag doll.

"Yes, Lily," he answered, "and I think we're in for a night of it."

He looked up at the pantry ceiling, which was shaking with the stamping and shuffling of feet on the floor above, listened for a mo-ment to the piano and then glanced at the girl, who was folding his overcoat carefully at the end of a shelf.

"Tell me, Lily," he said in a friendly tone, "do you still go to school?"

"O no, sir," she answered. "I'm done schooling this year and more."

"O, then," said Gabriel gaily, "I suppose we'll be going to your wedding one of these fine days with your young man, eh?"

The girl glanced back at him over her shoulder and said with great bitterness:

"The men that is now is only all palaver and what they can get out of you."

Gabriel coloured, as if he felt he had made a mistake and, with-out looking at her, kicked off his goloshes and flicked actively with his muffler at his patent-leather shoes.

He was a stout, tallish young man. The high colour of his cheeks pushed upwards even to his forehead, where it scattered itself in a few formless patches of pale red; and on his hairless face there scintillated restlessly the polished lenses and the bright gilt rims of the glasses which screened his delicate and restless eyes. His glossy black hair was parted in the middle and brushed in a long curve behind his ears where it curled slightly beneath the groove left by his hat.

When he had flicked lustre into his shoes he stood up and pulled his waistcoat down more tightly on his plump body. Then he took a coin rapidly from his pocket.

"O Lily," he said, thrusting it into her hands, "it's Christmas-time, isn't it? Just . . . here's a little. . . ."

He walked rapidly towards the door.

"O no, sir!" cried the girl, following him. "Really, sir, I wouldn't take it."

"Christmas-time! Christmas-time!" said Gabriel, almost trotting to the stairs and waving his hand to her in deprecation.

The girl, seeing that he had gained the stairs, called out after him: "Well, thank you, sir."

He waited outside the drawing-room door until the waltz should finish, listening to the skirts that swept against it and to the shuffling of feet. He was still discomposed by the girl's bitter and sudden retort. It had cast a gloom over him which he tried to dispel by arranging his cuffs and the bows of his tie. He then took from his waistcoat pocket a little paper and glanced at the headings he had made for his speech. He was undecided about the lines from Robert Browning, for he feared they would be above the heads of his hearers. Some quotation that they would recognise from Shakespeare or from the Melodies would be better. The indelicate clacking of the men's heels and the shuffling of their soles reminded him that their grade of culture differed from his. He would only make himself ridiculous by quoting poetry to them which they could not understand. They would think that he was airing his superior education. He would fail with them just as he had failed with the girl in the pantry. He had taken up a wrong tone. His whole speech was a mistake from first to last, an utter failure.

Just then his aunts and his wife came out of the ladies' dressing-room. His aunts were two small, plainly dressed old women. Aunt Julia was an inch or so the taller. Her hair, drawn low over the tops of her ears, was grey; and grey also, with darker shadows, was her large flaccid face. Though she was stout in build and stood erect, her slow eyes and parted lips gave her the appearance of a woman who did not know where she was or where she was going. Aunt Kate was more vivacious. Her face, healthier than her sister's, was all puckers and creases, like a shrivelled red apple, and her hair, braided in the same old-fashioned way, had not lost its ripe nut colour.

They both kissed Gabriel frankly. He was their favourite nephew, the son of their dead elder sister, Ellen, who had married T. J. Conroy of the Port and Docks.

"Gretta tells me you're not going to take a cab back to Monkstown tonight, Gabriel," said Aunt Kate.

"No," said Gabriel, turning to his wife, "we had quite enough of that last year, hadn't we? Don't you remember, Aunt Kate, what a cold Gretta got out of it? Cab windows rattling all the way, and the east wind blowing in after we passed Merrion. Very jolly it was. Gretta caught a dreadful cold."

Aunt Kate frowned severely and nodded her head at every word.

"Quite right, Gabriel, quite right," she said. "You can't be too careful."

"But as for Gretta there," said Gabriel, "she'd walk home in the snow if she were let."

Mrs. Conroy laughed.

"Don't mind him, Aunt Kate," she said. "He's really an awful bother, what with green shades for Tom's eyes at night and making him do the dumb-bells, and forcing Eva to eat the stirabout. The poor child! And she simply hates the sight of it! . . . O, but you'll never guess what he makes me wear now!"

She broke out into a peal of laughter and glanced at her husband, whose admiring and happy eyes had been wandering from her dress to her face and hair. The two aunts laughed heartily, too, for Gabriel's solicitude was a standing joke with them.

"Goloshes!" said Mrs. Conroy. "That's the latest. Whenever it's wet underfoot I must put on my goloshes. Tonight even, he wanted me to put them on, but I wouldn't. The next thing he'll buy me will be a diving suit."

Gabriel laughed nervously and patted his tie reassuringly, while Aunt Kate nearly doubled herself, so heartily did she enjoy the joke. The smile soon faded from Aunt Julia's face and her mirthless eyes were directed towards her nephew's face. After a pause she asked:

"And what are goloshes, Gabriel?"

"Goloshes, Julia!" exclaimed her sister. "Goodness me, don't you know what goloshes are? You wear them over your . . . over your boots, Gretta, isn't it?"

"Yes," said Mrs. Conroy. "Guttapercha things. We both have a pair now. Gabriel says everyone wears them on the Continent."

"O, on the Continent," murmured Aunt Julia, nodding her head slowly.

Gabriel knitted his brows and said, as if he were slightly angered:

"It's nothing very wonderful, but Gretta thinks it very funny because she says the word reminds her of Christy Minstrels."

"But tell me, Gabriel," said Aunt Kate, with brisk tact. "Of course, you've seen about the room. Gretta was saying . . ."

"O, the room is all right," replied Gabriel. "I've taken one in the Gresham."

"To be sure," said Aunt Kate, "by far the best thing to do. And the children, Gretta, you're not anxious about them?"

"O, for one night," said Mrs. Conroy. "Besides, Bessie will look after them."

"To be sure," said Aunt Kate again. "What a comfort it is to have a girl like that, one you can depend on! There's that Lily, I'm sure I don't know what has come over her lately. She's not the girl she was at all."

Gabriel was about to ask his aunt some questions on this point, but she broke off suddenly to gaze after her sister, who had wandered down the stairs and was craning her neck over the banisters.

"Now, I ask you," she said almost testily, "where is Julia going? Julia! Julia! Where are you going?"

Julia, who had gone half way down one flight, came back and announced blandly:

"Here's Freddy."

At the same moment a clapping of hands and a final flourish of the pianist told that the waltz had ended. The drawing-room door was opened from within and some couples came out. Aunt Kate drew Gabriel aside hurriedly and whispered into his ear:

"Slip down, Gabriel, like a good fellow and see if he's all right, and don't let him up if he's screwed. I'm sure he's screwed. I'm sure he is."

Gabriel went to the stairs and listened over the banisters. He could hear two persons talking in the pantry. Then he recognised Freddy Malins' laugh. He went down the stairs noisily.

"It's such a relief," said Aunt Kate to Mrs. Conroy, "that Gabriel is here, I always feel easier in my mind when he's here. . . . Julia, there's Miss Daly and Miss Power will take some refreshment. Thanks for your beautiful waltz, Miss Daly. It made lovely time."

A tall wizen-faced man, with a stiff grizzled moustache and swarthy skin, who was passing out with his partner, said:

"And may we have some refreshment, too, Miss Morkan?"

"Julia," said Aunt Kate summarily, "and here's Mr. Browne and Miss Furlong. Take them in, Julia, with Miss Daly and Miss Power."

"I'm the man for the ladies," said Mr. Browne, pursing his lips until his moustache bristled and smiling in all his wrinkles. "You know, Miss Morkan, the reason they are so fond of me is—"

He did not finish his sentence, but, seeing that Aunt Kate was out of earshot, at once led the three young ladies into the back room. The middle of the room was occupied by two square tables placed end to end, and on these Aunt Julia and the caretaker were straightening and smoothing a large cloth. On the sideboard were arrayed dishes and plates, and glasses and bundles of knives and forks and spoons. The top of the closed square piano served also as a sideboard for viands and sweets. At a smaller sideboard in one corner two young men were standing, drinking hop-bitters.

Mr. Browne led his charges thither and invited them all, in jest, to some ladies' punch, hot, strong and sweet. As they said they never took anything strong, he opened three bottles of lemonade for them. Then he asked one of the young men to move aside, and, taking hold of the decanter, filled out for himself a goodly measure of whisky. The young men eyed him respectfully while he took a trial sip.

"God help me," he said, smiling, "it's the doctor's orders."

His wizened face broke into a broader smile, and the three young ladies laughed in musical echo to his pleasantry, swaying their bodies to and fro, with nervous jerks of their shoulders. The boldest said:

"O, now, Mr. Browne, I'm sure the doctor never ordered anything of the kind."

Mr. Browne took another sip of his whisky and said, with sidling mimicry:

"Well, you see, I'm like the famous Mrs. Cassidy, who is reported to have said: 'Now, Mary Grimes, if I don't take it, make me take it, for I feel I want it.'"

His hot face had leaned forward a little too confidentially and he had assumed a very low Dublin accent so that the young ladies, with one instinct, received his speech in silence. Miss Furlong, who was one of Mary Jane's pupils, asked Miss Daly what was the name of the pretty waltz she had played; and Mr. Browne, seeing that he was ignored, turned promptly to the two young men who were more appreciative.

A red-faced young woman, dressed in pansy, came into the room, excitedly clapping her hands and crying:

"Quadrilles! Quadrilles!"

Close on her heels came Aunt Kate, crying:

"Two gentlemen and three ladies, Mary Jane!"

"O, here's Mr. Bergin and Mr. Kerrigan," said Mary Jane. "Mr. Kerrigan, will you take Miss Power? Miss Furlong, may I get you a partner, Mr. Bergin. O, that'll just do now."

"Three ladies, Mary Jane," said Aunt Kate.

The two young gentlemen asked the ladies if they might have the pleasure, and Mary Jane turned to Miss Daly.

"O, Miss Daly, you're really awfully good, after playing for the last two dances, but really we're so short of ladies tonight."

"I don't mind in the least, Miss Morkan."

"But I've a nice partner for you, Mr. Bartell D'Arcy, the tenor. I'll get him to sing later on. All Dublin is raving about him."

"Lovely voice, lovely voice!" said Aunt Kate.

As the piano had twice begun the prelude to the first figure Mary Jane led her recruits quickly from the room. They had hardly gone when Aunt Julia wandered slowly into the room, looking behind her at something.

"What is the matter, Julia?" asked Aunt Kate anxiously. "Who is it?"

Julia, who was carrying in a column of table-napkins, turned to her sister and said, simply, as if the question had surprised her:

"It's only Freddy, Kate, and Gabriel with him."

In fact right behind her Gabriel could be seen piloting Freddy Malins across the landing. The latter, a young man of about forty, was of Gabriel's size and build, with very round shoulders. His face was fleshy and pallid, touched with colour only at the thick hanging lobes of his ears and at the wide wings of his nose. He had coarse features, a blunt nose, a convex and receding brow, tumid and protruded lips. His heavy-lidded eyes and the disorder of his scanty hair made him look sleepy. He was laughing heartily in a high key at a story which he had been telling Gabriel on the stairs and at the same time rubbing the knuckles of his left fist backwards and forwards into his left eye.

"Good-evening, Freddy," said Aunt Julia.

Freddy Malins bade the Misses Morkan good-evening in what seemed an offhand fashion by reason of the habitual catch in his voice and then, seeing that Mr. Browne was grinning at him from the sideboard, crossed the room on rather shaky legs and began to repeat in an undertone the story he had just told to Gabriel.

"He's not so bad, is he?" said Aunt Kate to Gabriel.

Gabriel's brows were dark but he raised them quickly and answered: "O, no, hardly noticeable."

"Now, isn't he a terrible fellow!" she said. "And his poor mother made him take the pledge on New Year's Eve. But come on, Gabriel, into the drawing-room."

Before leaving the room with Gabriel she signalled to Mr. Browne by frowning and shaking her forefinger in warning to and fro. Mr. Browne nodded in answer and, when she had gone, said to Freddy Malins:

"Now, then, Teddy, I'm going to fill you out a good glass of lemonade just to buck you up."

Freddy Malins, who was nearing the climax of his story, waved the offer aside impatiently but Mr. Browne, having first called Freddy Malins' attention to a disarray in his dress, filled out and handed him a full glass of lemonade. Freddy Malins' left hand accepted the glass mechanically, his right hand being engaged in the mechanical readjustment of his dress. Mr. Browne, whose face was once more wrinkling with mirth, poured out for himself a glass of whisky while Freddy Malins exploded, before he had well reached the climax of his story, in a kink of high-pitched bronchitic laughter and, setting down his untasted and overflowing glass, began to rub the knuckles of his left fist backwards and forwards into his left eye, repeating words of his last phrase as well as his fit of laughter would allow him.

Gabriel could not listen while Mary Jane was playing her Academy piece, full of runs and difficult passages, to the hushed drawing-room. He liked music but the piece she was playing had no melody for him and he doubted whether it had any melody for the other listeners, though they had begged Mary Jane to play something. Four young men, who had come from the refreshment-room to stand in the doorway at the sound of the piano, had gone away quietly in couples after a few minutes. The only persons who seemed to follow the music were Mary Jane herself, her hands racing along the key-board or lifted from it at the pauses like those of a priestess in momentary imprecation, and Aunt Kate standing at her elbow to turn the page.

Gabriel's eyes, irritated by the floor, which glittered with beeswax under the heavy chandelier, wandered to the wall above the piano. A picture of the balcony scene in *Romeo and Juliet* hung there and beside it was a picture of the two murdered princes in the Tower which Aunt Julia had worked in red, blue and brown wools when she was a girl. Probably in the school they had gone to as girls that kind of work had been taught for one year. His mother had worked for him as a birthday present a waistcoat of purple tabinet, with little foxes' heads upon it, lined with brown satin and having round mulberry buttons. It was strange that his mother had had no musical talent though Aunt Kate used to call her the brains carrier of the Morkan family. Both she and Julia had always seemed a little proud of their serious and matronly sister. Her photograph stood before the pierglass. She held an open book on her knees and was pointing out something in it to Constantine who, dressed in a man-o'-war suit, lay at her feet. It was she who had chosen the names of her sons for she was very sensible of the dignity of family life. Thanks to her, Constantine was now senior curate in Balbriggan and, thanks to her, Gabriel himself had taken his degree in the Royal University. A shadow passed over his face as he remembered her sullen opposition to his marriage. Some slighting phrases she had used still rankled in his memory; she had once spoken of Gretta as being country cute and that was not true of Gretta at all. It was Gretta who had nursed her during all her last long illness in their house at Monkstown.

He knew that Mary Jane must be near the end of her piece for she was playing again the opening melody with runs of scales after every bar and while he waited for the end the resentment died down in his heart. The piece ended with a trill of octaves in the treble and a final deep octave in the bass. Great applause greeted Mary Jane as, blushing and rolling up her music nervously, she escaped from the room. The most vigorous clapping came from the four young men in the doorway who had gone away to the refreshment-room at the beginning of the piece but had come back when the piano had stopped.

Lancers were arranged. Gabriel found himself partnered with Miss Ivors. She was a frank-mannered talkative young lady, with a freckled face and prominent brown eyes. She did not wear a low-cut bodice and the large brooch which was fixed in the front of her collar bore on it an Irish device and motto.

When they had taken their places she said abruptly:

"I have a crow to pluck with you."

"With me?" said Gabriel.

She nodded her head gravely.

"What is it?" asked Gabriel, smiling at her solemn manner.

"Who is G. C.?" answered Miss Ivors, turning her eyes upon him.

Gabriel coloured and was about to knit his brows, as if he did not understand, when she said bluntly:

"O, innocent Amy! I have found out that you write for *The Daily Express*. Now, aren't you ashamed of yourself?"

"Why should I be ashamed of myself?" asked Gabriel, blinking his eyes and trying to smile.

"Well, I'm ashamed of you," said Miss Ivors frankly. "To say you'd write for a paper like that. I didn't think you were a West Briton."

A look of perplexity appeared on Gabriel's face. It was true that he wrote a literary column every Wednesday in *The Daily Express,* for which he was paid fifteen shillings. But that did not make him a West Briton surely. The books he received for review were almost more welcome than the paltry cheque. He loved to feel the covers and turn over the pages of newly printed books. Nearly every day when his teaching in the college was ended he used to wander down the quays to the second-hand booksellers, to Hickey's on Bachelor's Walk, to Web's or Massey's on Aston's Quay, or to O'Clohissey's in the bystreet. He did not know how to meet her charge. He wanted to say that literature was above politics. But they were friends of many years' standing and their careers had been parallel, first at the University and then as teachers: he could not risk a grandiose phrase with her. He continued blinking his eyes and trying to smile and murmured lamely that he saw nothing political in writing reviews of books.

When their turn to cross had come he was still perplexed and inattentive. Miss Ivors promptly took his hand in a warm grasp and said in a soft friendly tone:

"Of course, I was only joking. Come, we cross now."

When they were together again she spoke of the University question and Gabriel felt more at ease. A friend of hers had shown her his review of Browning's poems. That was how she had found out the secret: but she liked the review immensely. Then she said suddenly:

"O, Mr. Conroy, will you come for an excursion to the Aran Isles this summer? We're going to stay there a whole month. It will be splendid out in the Atlantic. You ought to come. Mr. Clancy is coming, and Mr. Kilkelly and Kathleen Kearney. It would be splendid for Gretta too if she'd come. She's from Connacht, isn't she?"

"Her people are," said Gabriel shortly.

"But you will come, won't you?" said Miss Ivors, laying her warm hand eagerly on his arm.

"The fact is," said Gabriel, "I have just arranged to go—"

"Go where?" asked Miss Ivors.

"Well, you know, every year I go for a cycling tour with some fellows and so—"

"But where?" asked Miss Ivors.

"Well, we usually go to France or Belgium or perhaps Germany," said Gabriel awkwardly.

"And why do you go to France and Belgium," said Miss Ivors, "instead of visiting your own land?"

"Well," said Gabriel, "it's partly to keep in touch with the languages and partly for a change."

"And haven't you your own language to keep in touch with—Irish?" asked Miss Ivors.

"Well," said Gabriel, "if it comes to that, you know, Irish is not my language."

Their neighbours had turned to listen to the cross-examination. Gabriel glanced right and left nervously and tried to keep his good humour under the ordeal which was making a blush invade his forehead.

"And haven't you your own land to visit," continued Miss Ivors, "that you know nothing of, your own people, and your own country?"

"O, to tell you the truth," retorted Gabriel suddenly, "I'm sick of my own country, sick of it!"

"Why?" asked Miss Ivors.

Gabriel did not answer for his retort had heated him.

"Why?" repeated Miss Ivors.

They had to go visiting together and, as he had not answered her, Miss Ivors said warmly:

"Of course, you've no answer."

Gabriel tried to cover his agitation by taking part in the dance with great energy. He avoided her eyes for he had seen a sour expression on her face. But when they met in the long chain he was surprised to feel his hand firmly pressed. She looked at him from under her brows for a moment quizzically until he smiled. Then, just as the chain was about to start again, she stood on tiptoe and whispered into his ear:

"West Briton!"

When the lancers were over Gabriel went away to a remote corner of the room where Freddy Malins' mother was sitting. She was a stout feeble old woman with white hair. Her voice had a catch in it like her son's and she stuttered slightly. She had been told that Freddy had come and that he was nearly all right. Gabriel asked her whether she had had a good crossing. She lived with her married daughter in Glasgow and came to Dublin on a visit once a year. She answered placidly that she had had a beautiful crossing and that the captain had been most attentive to her. She spoke also of the beautiful house her daughter kept in Glasgow, and of all the friends they had there. While her tongue rambled on Gabriel tried to banish from his mind all memory of the unpleasant incident with Miss Ivors. Of course the girl or woman, or whatever she was, was an enthusiast but there was a time for all things. Perhaps he ought not to have answered her like that. But she had no right to call him a West Briton before people, even in joke. She had tried to make him ridiculous before people, heckling him and staring at him with her rabbit's eyes.

He saw his wife making her way towards him through the waltzing couples. When she reached him she said into his ear:

"Gabriel, Aunt Kate wants to know won't you carve the goose as usual. Miss Daly will carve the ham and I'll do the pudding."

"All right," said Gabriel.

"She's sending in the younger ones first as soon as this waltz is over so that we'll have the table to ourselves."

"Were you dancing?" asked Gabriel.

"Of course I was. Didn't you see me? What row had you with Molly Ivors?"

"No row. Why? Did she say so?"

"Something like that. I'm trying to get that Mr. D'Arcy to sing. He's full of conceit, I think."

"There was no row," said Gabriel moodily, "only she wanted me to go for a trip to the west of Ireland and I said I wouldn't."

His wife clasped her hands excitedly and gave a little jump.

"O, do go, Gabriel," she cried. "I'd love to see Galway again."

"You can go if you like," said Gabriel coldly.

She looked at him for a moment, then turned to Mrs. Malins and said:

"There's a nice husband for you, Mrs. Malins."

While she was threading her way back across the room Mrs. Malins, without adverting to the interruption, went on to tell Gabriel what beautiful places there were in Scotland and beautiful scenery. Her son-in-law brought them every year to the lakes and they used to go fishing. Her son-in-law was a splendid fisher. One day he caught a beautiful big fish and the man in the hotel cooked it for their dinner.

Gabriel hardly heard what she said. Now that supper was coming near he began to think again about his speech and about the quotation. When he saw Freddy Malins coming across the room to visit his mother Gabriel left the chair free for him and retired into the embrasure of the window. The room had already cleared and from the back room came the clatter of plates and knives. Those who still remained in the drawing-room seemed tired of dancing and were conversing quietly in little groups. Gabriel's warm trembling fingers tapped the cold pane of the window. How cool it must be outside! How pleasant it would be to walk out alone, first along by the river and then through the park! The snow would be lying on the branches of the trees and forming a bright cap on the top of the Wellington Monument. How much more pleasant it would be there than at the supper-table!

He ran over the headings of his speech: Irish hospitality, sad memories, the Three Graces, Paris, the quotation from Browning. He repeated to himself a phrase he had written in his review: "One feels that one is listening to a thought-tormented music." Miss Ivors had praised the review. Was she sincere? Had she really any life of her own behind all her propagandism? There had never been any ill-feeling between them until that night. It unnerved him to think that she would be at the supper-table, looking up at him while he spoke with her critical quizzing eyes. Perhaps she would not be sorry to see him fail in his speech. An idea came into his mind and gave him courage. He would say, alluding to Aunt Kate and Julia: "Ladies and Gentlemen, the generation which is now on the wane among us may have had its faults but for my part I think it had certain qualities of hospitality, of humour, of humanity, which the new and very serious and hypereducated generation that is growing up around us seems to me to lack." Very good: that was one for Miss Ivors. What did he care that his aunts were only two ignorant old women?

A murmur in the room attracted his attention. Mr. Browne was advancing from the door, gallantly escorting Aunt Julia, who leaned upon his arm, smiling and hanging her head. An irregular musketry of applause escorted her also as far as the piano and then, as Mary Jane seated herself on the stool, and Aunt Julia, no longer smiling, half turned so as to pitch her voice fairly into the room, gradually ceased. Gabriel recognised the prelude. It was that of an old song of Aunt Julia's—*Arrayed for the Bridal.* Her voice, strong and clear in tone, attacked with great spirit the runs which embellish the air and though she sang very rapidly she did not miss even the smallest of the grace notes. To follow the voice, without looking at the singer's face, was to feel and share the excitement of swift and secure flight. Gabriel applauded loudly with all the others at the close of the song and loud applause was borne in from the invisible supper-table. It sounded so genuine that a little colour struggled into Aunt Julia's face as she bent to replace in the music-stand the old leather-bound songbook that had her initials on the cover. Freddy Malins, who had listened with his head perched sideways to hear her better, was still applauding when everyone else had ceased and talking animatedly to his mother who nodded her head gravely and slowly in acquiescence. At last, when he could clap no more, he stood up suddenly and hurried across the room to Aunt Julia whose hand he seized and held in both his hands, shaking it when words failed him or the catch in his voice proved too much for him.

"I was just telling my mother," he said, "I never heard you sing so well, never. No, I never heard your voice so good as it is tonight. Now! Would you believe that now? That's the truth. Upon my word and honour that's the truth. I never heard your voice sound so fresh and so . . . so clear and fresh, never."

Aunt Julia smiled broadly and murmured something about compliments as she released her hand from his grasp. Mr. Browne extended his open hand towards her and said to those who were near him in the manner of a showman introducing a prodigy to an audience:

"Miss Julia Morkan, my latest discovery!"

He was laughing very heartily at this himself when Freddy Malins turned to him and said:

"Well, Browne, if you're serious you might make a worse discovery. All I can say is I never heard her sing half so well as long as I am coming here. And that's the honest truth."

"Neither did I," said Mr. Browne. "I think her voice has greatly improved."

Aunt Julia shrugged her shoulders and said with meek pride:

"Thirty years ago I hadn't a bad voice as voices go."

"I often told Julia," said Aunt Kate emphatically, "that she was simply thrown away in that choir. But she never would be said by me."

She turned as if to appeal to the good sense of the others against a refractory child while Aunt Julia gazed in front of her, a vague smile of reminiscence playing on her face.

"No," continued Aunt Kate, "she wouldn't be said or led by anyone, slaving there in that choir night and day, night and day. Six o'clock on Christmas morning! And all for what?"

"Well, isn't it for the honour of God, Aunt Kate?" asked Mary Jane, twisting round on the piano-stool and smiling.

Aunt Kate turned fiercely on her niece and said:

"I know all about the honour of God, Mary Jane, but I think it's not at all honourable for the pope to turn out the women out of the choirs that have slaved there all their lives and put little whippersnappers of boys over their heads. I suppose it is for the good of the Church if the pope does it. But it's not just, Mary Jane, and it's not right."

She had worked herself into a passion and would have continued in defence of her sister for it was a sore subject with her but Mary Jane, seeing that all the dancers had come back, intervened pacifically:

"Now, Aunt Kate, you're giving scandal to Mr. Browne who is of the other persuasion."

Aunt Kate turned to Mr. Browne, who was grinning at this allusion to his religion, and said hastily:

"O, I don't question the pope's being right. I'm only a stupid old woman and I wouldn't presume to do such a thing. But there's such a thing as common everyday politeness and gratitude. And if I were in Julia's place I'd tell that Father Healey straight up to his face . . ."

"And besides, Aunt Kate," said Mary Jane, "we really are all hungry and when we are hungry we are all very quarrelsome."

"And when we are thirsty we are also quarrelsome," added Mr. Browne.

"So that we had better go to supper," said Mary Jane, "and finish the discussion afterwards."

On the landing outside the drawing-room Gabriel found his wife and Mary Jane trying to persuade Miss Ivors to stay for supper. But Miss Ivors, who had put on her hat and was buttoning her cloak, would not stay. She did not feel in the least hungry and she had already overstayed her time.

"But only for ten minutes, Molly," said Mrs. Conroy. "That won't delay you."

"To take a pick itself," said Mary Jane, "after all your dancing."

"I really couldn't," said Miss Ivors.

"I am afraid you didn't enjoy yourself at all," said Mary Jane hopelessly.

"Ever so much, I assure you," said Miss Ivors, "but you really must let me run off now."

"But how can you get home?" asked Mrs. Conroy.

"O, it's only two steps up the quay."

Gabriel hesitated a moment and said:

"If you will allow me, Miss Ivors, I'll see you home if you are really obliged to go."

But Miss Ivors broke away from them.

"I won't hear of it," she cried. "For goodness' sake go in to your suppers and don't mind me. I'm quite well able to take care of myself."

"Well, you're the comical girl, Molly," said Mrs. Conroy frankly.

"*Beannacht libh,*" cried Miss Ivors, with a laugh, as she ran down the staircase.

Mary Jane gazed after her, a moody puzzled expression on her face, while Mrs. Conroy leaned over the banisters to listen for the hall-door. Gabriel asked himself was he the cause of her abrupt departure. But she did not seem to be in ill humour: she had gone away laughing. He stared blankly down the staircase.

At the moment Aunt Kate came toddling out of the supper-room, almost wringing her hands in despair.

"Where is Gabriel?" she cried. "Where on earth is Gabriel? There's everyone waiting in there, stage to let, and nobody to carve the goose!"

"Here I am, Aunt Kate!" cried Gabriel, with sudden animation, "ready to carve a flock of geese, if necessary."

A fat brown goose lay at one end of the table and at the other end, on a bed of creased paper strewn with sprigs of parsley, lay a great ham, stripped of its outer skin and peppered over with crust crumbs, a neat paper frill round its shin and beside this was a round of spiced beef. Between these rival ends ran parallel lines of side-dishes: two little minsters of jelly, red and yellow; a shallow dish full of blocks of blancmange and red jam, a large green leaf-shaped dish with a stalk-shaped handle, on which lay bunches of purple raisins and peeled almonds, a companion dish on which lay a solid rectangle of Smyrna figs, a dish of custard topped with grated nutmeg, a small bowl full of chocolates and sweets wrapped in gold and silver papers and a glass vase in which stood some tall celery stalks. In the centre of the table there stood, as sentries to a fruit-stand which upheld a pyramid of oranges and American apples, two squat old-fashioned decanters of cut glass, one containing port and the other dark sherry. On the closed square piano a pudding in a huge yellow dish lay in waiting and behind it were three squads of bottles of stout and ale and minerals, drawn up according to the colours of their uniforms, the first two black, with brown and red labels, the third and smallest squad white, with transverse green sashes.

Gabriel took his seat boldly at the head of the table and, having looked to the edge of the carver, plunged his fork firmly into the goose. He felt quite at ease now for he was an expert carver and liked nothing better than to find himself at the head of a well-laden table.

"Miss Furlong, what shall I send you?" he asked. "A wing or a slice of the breast?"

"Just a small slice of the breast."

"Miss Higgins, what for you?"

'O, anything at all, Mr. Conroy."

While Gabriel and Miss Daly exchanged plates of goose and plates of ham and spiced beef Lily went from guest to guest with a dish of hot floury potatoes wrapped in a white napkin. This was Mary Jane's idea and she had also suggested apple sauce for the goose but Aunt Kate had said that plain roast goose without any apple sauce had always been good enough for her and she hoped she might never eat worse. Mary Jane waited on her pupils and saw that they got the best slices and Aunt Kate and Aunt Julia opened and carried across from the piano bottles of stout and ale for the gentlemen and bottles of minerals for the ladies. There was a great deal of confusion and laughter and noise, the noise of orders and counter-orders, of knives and forks, of corks and glass-stoppers. Gabriel began to carve second helpings as soon as he had finished the first round without serving himself. Everyone protested loudly so that he compromised by taking a long draught of stout for he had found the carving hot work. Mary Jane settled down quietly to her supper but Aunt Kate and Aunt Julia were still toddling round the table, walking on each other's heels, getting in each other's way and giving each other unheeded orders. Mr. Browne begged of them to sit down and eat their suppers and so did Gabriel but they said there was time enough, so that, at last, Freddy Malins stood up and, capturing Aunt Kate, plumped her down on her chair amid general laughter.

When everyone had been well served Gabriel said, smiling:

"Now, if anyone wants a little more of what vulgar people call stuffing let him or her speak."

A chorus of voices invited him to begin his own supper and Lily came forward with three potatoes which she had reserved for him.

"Very well," said Gabriel amiably, as he took another preparatory draught, "kindly forget my existence, ladies and gentlemen, for a few minutes."

He set to his supper and took no part in the conversation with which the table covered Lily's removal of the plates. The subject of talk was the opera company which was then at the Theatre Royal. Mr. Bartell D'Arcy, the tenor, a dark-compexioned young man with a smart moustache, praised very highly the leading contralto of the company but Miss Furlong thought she had a rather vulgar style of production. Freddy Malins said there was a Negro chieftain singing in the second part of the Gaiety pantomime who had one of the finest tenor voices he had ever heard.

"Have you heard him?" he asked Mr. Bartell D'Arcy across the table.

"No," answered Mr. Bartell D'Arcy carelessly.

"Because," Freddy Malins explained, "now I'd be curious to hear your opinion of him. I think he has a grand voice."

"It takes Teddy to find out the really good things," said Mr. Browne familiarly to the table.

"And why couldn't he have a voice too?" asked Freddy Malins sharply. "Is it because he's only a black?"

Nobody answered this question and Mary Jane led the table back to the legitimate opera. One of her pupils had given her a pass for *Mignon*. Of course it was very fine, she said, but it made her think of poor Georgina Burns. Mr. Browne could go back farther still, to the old Italian companies that used to come to Dublin—Tietjens, Ilma de Murzka, Campanini, the great Trebelli, Giuglini, Ravelli, Aramburo. Those were the days, he said, when there was something like singing to be heard in Dublin. He told too of how the top gallery of the old Royal used to be packed night after night, of how one night an Italian tenor had sung five encores to *Let me like a Soldier fall,* introducing a high C every time, and of how the gallery boys would sometimes in their enthusiasm unyoke the horses from the carriage of some great *prima donna* and pull her themselves through the streets to her hotel. Why did they never play the grand old operas now, he asked, *Dinorah, Lucrezia Borgia?* Because they could not get the voices to sing them: that was why.

"Oh, well," said Mr. Bartell D'Arcy, "I presume there are as good singers today as there were then."

"Where are they?" asked Mr. Browne defiantly.

"In London, Paris, Milan," said Mr. Bartell D'Arcy warmly. "I suppose Caruso, for example, is quite as good, if not better than any of the men you have mentioned."

"Maybe so," said Mr. Browne. "But I may tell you I doubt it strongly."

"O, I'd give anything to hear Caruso sing," said Mary Jane.

"For me," said Aunt Kate, who had been picking a bone, "there was only one tenor. To please me, I mean. But I suppose none of you ever heard of him."

"Who was he, Miss Morkan?" asked Mr. Bartell D'Arcy politely.

"His name," said Aunt Kate, "was Parkinson. I heard him when he was in his prime and I think he had then the purest tenor voice that was ever put into a man's throat."

"Strange, "said Mr. Bartell D'Arcy. "I never even heard of him."

"Yes, yes, Miss Morkan is right," said Mr. Browne. "I remember hearing of old Parkinson but he's too far back for me."

"A beautiful, pure, sweet, mellow English tenor," said Aunt Kate with enthusiasm.

Gabriel having finished, the huge pudding was transferred to the table. The clatter of forks and spoons began again. Gabriel's wife served out spoonfuls of the pudding and passed the plates down the table. Midway down they were held up by Mary Jane, who replenished them with raspberry or orange jelly or with blancmange and jam. The pudding was of Aunt Julia's making and she received praises for it from all quarters. She herself said that it was not quite brown enough.

"Well, I hope, Miss Morkan," said Mr. Browne, "that I'm brown enough for you because, you know, I'm all brown."

All the gentlemen, except Gabriel, ate some of the pudding out of compliment to Aunt Julia. As Gabriel never ate sweets the celery had been left for him. Freddy Malins also took a stalk of celery and ate it with his pudding. He had been told that celery was a capital thing for the blood and he was just then under doctor's care. Mrs. Malins, who had been silent all through the supper, said that her son was going down to Mount Melleray in a week or so. The table then spoke of Mount Melleray, how bracing the air was down there, how hospitable the monks were and how they never asked for a penny-piece from their guests.

"And do you mean to say," asked Mr. Browne incredulously, "that a chap can go down there and put up there as if it were a hotel and live on the fat of the land and then come away without paying anything?"

"O, most people give some donation to the monastery when they leave," said Mary Jane.

"I wish we had an institution like that in our Church," said Mr. Browne candidly.

He was astonished to hear that the monks never spoke, got up at two in the morning and slept in their coffins. He asked what they did it for.

"That's the rule of the order," said Aunt Kate firmly.

"Yes, but why?" asked Mr. Browne.

Aunt Kate repeated that it was the rule, that was all. Mr. Browne still seemed not to understand. Freddy Malins explained to him, as best he could, that the monks were trying to make up for the sins committed by all the sinners in the outside world. The explanation was not very clear for Mr. Browne grinned and said:

"I like that idea very much but wouldn't a comfortable spring bed do them as well as a coffin?"

"The coffin," said Mary Jane, "is to remind them of their last end."

As the subject had grown lugubrious it was buried in a silence of the table during which Mrs. Malins could be heard saying to her neighbour in an indistinct undertone:

"They are very good men, the monks, very pious men."

The raisins and almonds and figs and apples and oranges and chocolates and sweets were now passed about the table and Aunt Julia invited all the guests to have either port or sherry. At first Mr. Bartell D'Arcy refused to take either but one of his neighbours nudged him and whispered something to him upon which he allowed his glass to be filled. Gradually as the last glasses were being filled the conversation ceased. A pause followed, broken only by the noise of the wine and by unsettlings of chairs. The Misses Morkan, all three, looked down at the tablecloth. Someone coughed once or twice and then a few gentlemen patted the table gently as a signal for silence. The silence came and Gabriel pushed back his chair and stood up.

The patting at once grew louder in encouragement and then ceased altogether. Gabriel leaned his ten trembling fingers on the tablecloth and smiled nervously at the company. Meeting a row of upturned faces he raised his eyes to the chandelier. The piano was playing a waltz tune and he could hear the skirts sweeping against the drawing-room door. People, perhaps, were standing in the snow on the quay outside, gazing up at the lighted windows and listening to the waltz music. The air was pure there. In the distance lay the park where the trees were weighted with snow. The Wellington Monument wore a gleaming cap of snow that flashed westward over the white field of Fifteen Acres.

He began:

"Ladies and Gentlemen,

"It has fallen to my lot this evening, as in years past, to perform a very pleasing task but a task for which I am afraid my poor powers as a speaker are all too inadequate."

"No, no!" said Mr. Browne.

"But, however that may be, I can only ask you tonight to take the will for the deed and to lend me your attention for a few moments while I endeavour to express to you in words what my feelings are on this occasion.

"Ladies and Gentlemen, it is not the first time that we have gathered together under this hospitable roof, around this hospitable board. It is not the first time that we have been the recipients—or perhaps, I had better say, the victims—of the hospitality of certain good ladies."

He made a circle in the air with his arm and paused. Everyone laughed or smiled at Aunt Kate and Aunt Julia and Mary Jane who all turned crimson with pleasure. Gabriel went on more boldly:

"I feel more strongly with every recurring year that our country has no tradition which does it so much honour and which it should guard so jealously as that of its hospitality. It is a tradition that is unique as far as my experience goes (and I have visited not a few places abroad) among the modern nations. Some would say, perhaps, that with us it is rather a failing than anything to be boasted of. But granted even that, it is, to my mind, a princely failing, and one that I trust will long be cultivated among us. Of one thing, at least, I am sure. As long as this one roof shelters the good ladies aforesaid— and I wish from my heart it may do so for many and many a long year to come—the tradition of genuine warm-hearted courteous Irish hospitality, which our forefathers have handed down to us and which we in turn must hand down to our descendants, is still alive among us."

A hearty murmur of assent ran round the table. It shot through Gabriel's mind that Miss Ivors was not there and that she had gone away discourteously: and he said with confidence in himself:

"Ladies and Gentlemen,

"A new generation is growing up in our midst, a generation actuated by new ideas and new principles. It is serious and enthusiastic for these new ideas and its enthusiasm, even when it is misdirected, is, I believe, in the main sincere. But we are living in a sceptical and, if I may use the phrase, a thought-tormented age: and sometimes I fear that this new generation, educated or hypereducated as it is, will lack those qualities of humanity, of hospitality, of kindly humour which belonged to an older day. Listening tonight to the names of all those great singers of the past it seemed to me, I must confess, that we were living in a less spacious age. Those days might, without exaggeration, be called spacious days: and if they are gone beyond recall let us hope, at least, that in gatherings such as this we shall still speak of them with pride and affection, still cherish in our hearts the memory of those dead and gone great ones whose fame the world will not willingly let die."

"Hear, hear!" said Mr. Browne loudly.

"But yet," continued Gabriel, his voice falling into a softer inflection, "there are always in gatherings such as this sadder thoughts that will recur to our minds: thoughts of the past, of youth, of changes, of absent faces that we miss here tonight. Our path through life is strewn with many such sad memories: and were we to brood upon them always we could not find the heart to go on bravely with our work among the living. We have all of us living duties and living affections which claim, and rightly claim, our strenuous endeavours.

"Therefore, I will not linger on the past. I will not let any gloomy moralising intrude upon us here tonight. Here we are gathered together for a brief moment from the bustle and rush of our everyday routine. We are met here as friends, in the spirit of good-fellowship, as colleagues, also to a certain extent, in the true spirit of *camaraderie*, and as the guests of—what shall I call them?—the Three Graces of the Dublin musical world."

The table burst into applause and laughter at this allusion. Aunt Julia vainly asked each of her neighbours in turn to tell her what Gabriel had said.

"He says we are the Three Graces, Aunt Julia," said Mary Jane.

Aunt Julia did not understand but she looked up, smiling, at Gabriel, who continued in the same vein:

"Ladies and Gentlemen,

"I will not attempt to play tonight the part that Paris played on another occasion. I will not attempt to choose between them. The task would be an invidious one and one beyond my poor powers. For when I view them in turn, whether it be our chief hostess herself, whose good heart, whose too good heart, has become a byword with all who know her, or her sister, who seems to be gifted with perennial youth and whose singing must have been a surprise and a revelation to us all tonight, or, last but not least, when I consider our youngest hostess, talented, cheerful, hard-working and the best of nieces, I confess, Ladies and Gentlemen, that I do not know to which of them I should award the prize."

Gabriel glanced down at his aunts and, seeing the large smile on Aunt Julia's face and the tears which had risen to Aunt Kate's eyes, hastened to his close. He raised his glass of port gallantly, while every member of the company fingered a glass expectantly, and said loudly:

"Let us toast them all three together. Let us drink to their health, wealth, long life, happiness and prosperity and may they long continue to hold the proud and self-won position which they hold in their profession and the position of honour and affection which they hold in our hearts."

All the guests stood up, glass in hand, and turning towards the three seated ladies, sang in unison, with Mr. Browne as leader:

> *For they are jolly gay fellows,*
> *For they are jolly gay fellows,*
> *For they are jolly gay fellows,*
> *Which nobody can deny.*

Aunt Kate was making frank use of her handkerchief and even Aunt Julia seemed moved. Freddy Malins beat time with his pudding-fork and the singers turned towards one another, as if in melodious conference, while they sang with emphasis:

> *Unless he tells a lie,*
> *Unless he tells a lie,*

Then, turning once more towards their hostesses, they sang:

> *For they are jolly gay fellows,*
> *For they are jolly gay fellows,*
> *For they are jolly gay fellows,*
> *Which nobody can deny.*

The acclamation which followed was taken up beyond the door of the supper-room by many of the other guests and renewed time after time. Freddy Malins acting as officer with his fork on high.

The piercing morning air came into the hall where they were standing so that Aunt Kate said:

"Close the door, somebody. Mrs. Malins will get her death of cold."

"Browne is out there, Aunt Kate," said Mary Jane.

"Browne is everywhere," said Aunt Kate, lowering her voice.

Mary Jane laughed at her tone.

"Really," she said archly, "he is very attentive."

"He has been laid on here like the gas," said Aunt Kate in the same tone, "all during the Christmas."

She laughed herself this time good-humouredly and then added quickly:

"But tell him to come in, Mary Jane, and close the door. I hope to goodness he didn't hear me."

At that moment the hall-door was opened and Mr. Browne came in from the doorstep, laughing as if his heart would break. He was dressed in a long green overcoat with mock astrakhan cuffs and collar and wore on his head an oval fur cap. He pointed down the snow-covered quay from where the sound of shrill prolonged whistling was borne in.

"Teddy will have all the cabs in Dublin out," he said.

Gabriel advanced from the little pantry behind the office, struggling into his overcoat and, looking round the hall, said:

"Gretta not down yet?"

"She's getting on her things, Gabriel," said Aunt Kate.

"Who's playing up there?" asked Gabriel.

"Nobody. They're all gone."

"O no, Aunt Kate," said Mary Jane. "Bartell D'Arcy and Miss O'Callaghan aren't gone yet."

"Someone is fooling at the piano anyhow," said Gabriel.

Mary Jane glanced at Gabriel and Mr. Browne and said with a shiver:

"It makes me feel cold to look at you two gentlemen muffled up like that. I wouldn't like to face your journey home at this hour."

"I'd like nothing better this minute," said Mr. Browne stoutly, "than a rattling fine walk in the country or a fast drive with a good spanking goer between the shafts."

"We used to have a very good horse and trap at home," said Aunt Julia sadly.

"The never-to-be-forgotten Johnny," said Mary Jane, laughing.

Aunt Kate and Gabriel laughed too.

"Why, what was wonderful about Johnny?" asked Mr. Browne.

"The late lamented Patrick Morkan, our grandfather, that is," explained Gabriel, "commonly known in his later years as the old gentleman, was a glue-boiler."

"O, now, Gabriel," said Aunt Kate, laughing, "he had a starch mill."

"Well, glue or starch," said Gabriel, "the old gentleman had a horse by the name of Johnny. And Johnny used to work in the old gentleman's mill, walking round and round in order to drive the mill. That was all very well; but now comes the tragic part about Johnny. One fine day the old gentleman thought he'd like to drive out with the quality to a military review in the park."

"The Lord have mercy on his soul," said Aunt Kate compassionately.

"Amen," said Gabriel. "So the old gentleman, as I said, harnessed Johnny and put on his very best tall hat and his very best stock collar and drove out in grand style from his ancestral mansion somewhere near Back Lane, I think."

Everyone laughed, even Mrs. Malins, at Gabriel's manner and Aunt Kate said:

"O, now, Gabriel, he didn't live in Back Lane, really. Only the mill was there."

"Out from the mansion of his forefathers," continued Gabriel, "he drove with Johnny. And everything went on beautifully until Johnny came in sight of King Billy's statue: and whether he fell in love with the horse King Billy sits on or whether he thought he was back again in the mill, anyhow he began to walk round the statue."

Gabriel paced in a circle round the hall in his goloshes amid the laughter of the others.

"Round and round he went," said Gabriel, "and the old gentleman, who was a very pompous old gentleman, was highly indignant. 'Go on, sir! What do you mean, sir? Johnny! Johnny! Most extraordinary conduct! Can't understand the horse!'"

The peal of laughter which followed Gabriel's imitation of the incident was interrupted by a resounding knock at the hall door. Mary Jane ran to open it and let in Freddy Malins. Freddy Malins, with his hat well back on his head and his shoulders humped with cold, was puffing and steaming after his exertions.

"I could only get one cab," he said.

"O, we'll find another along the quay," said Gabriel.

"Yes," said Aunt Kate. "Better not keep Mrs. Malins standing in the draught."

Mrs. Malins was helped down the front steps by her son and Mr. Browne and, after many manœuvres, hoisted into the cab. Freddy Malins clambered in after her and spent a long time settling her on the seat, Mr. Browne helping him with advice. At last she was settled comfortably and Freddy Malins invited Mr. Browne into the cab. There was a good deal of confused talk, and then Mr. Browne got into the cab. The cabman settled his rug over his knees, and bent down for the address. The confusion grew greater and the cabman was directed differently by Freddy Malins and Mr. Browne, each of whom had his head out through a window of the cab. The difficulty was to know where to drop Mr. Browne along the route, and Aunt Kate, Aunt Julia and Mary Jane helped the discussion from the doorstep with cross-directions and contradictions and abundance of laughter. As for Freddy Malins he was speechless with laughter. He popped his head in and out of the window every moment to the great danger of his hat, and told his mother how the discussion was progressing, till at last Mr. Browne shouted to the bewildered cabman above the din of everybody's laughter:

"Do you know Trinity College?"

"Yes, sir," said the cabman.

"Well, drive bang up against Trinity College gates," said Mr. Browne, "and then we'll tell you where to go. You understand now?"

"Yes, sir," said the cabman.

"Make like a bird for Trinity College."

"Right, sir," said the cabman.

The horse was whipped up and the cab rattled off along the quay amid a chorus of laughter and adieus.

Gabriel had not gone to the door with the others. He was in a dark part of the hall gazing up the staircase. A woman was standing near the top of the first flight, in the shadow also. He could not see her face but he could see the terra-cotta and salmon-pink panels of her skirt which the shadow made appear black and white. It was his wife. She was leaning on the banisters, listening to something. Gabriel was surprised at her stillness and strained his ear to listen also. But he could hear little save the noise of laughter and dispute on the front steps, a few chords struck on the piano and a few notes of a man's voice singing.

He stood still in the gloom of the hall, trying to catch the air that the voice was singing and gazing up at his wife. There was grace and mystery in her attitude as if she were a symbol of something. He asked himself what is a woman standing on the stairs in the shadow, listening to distant music, a symbol of. If he were a painter he would paint her in that attitude. Her blue felt hat would show off the bronze of her hair against the darkness and the dark panels of her skirt would show off the light ones. *Distant Music* he would call the picture if he were a painter.

The hall-door was closed; and Aunt Kate, Aunt Julia and Mary Jane came down the hall, still laughing.

"Well, isn't Freddy terrible?" said Mary Jane. "He's really terrible."

Gabriel said nothing but pointed up the stairs towards where his wife was standing. Now that the hall-door was closed the voice and the piano could be heard more clearly. Gabriel held up his hand for them to be silent. The song seemed to be in the old Irish tonality and the singer seemed uncertain both of his words and of his voice. The voice, made plaintive by distance and by the singer's hoarseness, faintly illuminated the cadence of the air with words expressing grief:

> *O, the rain falls on my heavy locks*
> *And the dew wets my skin,*
> *My babe lies cold . . .*

"O," exclaimed Mary Jane. "It's Bartell D'Arcy singing and he wouldn't sing all the night. O, I'll get him to sing a song before he goes."

"O, do, Mary Jane," said Aunt Kate.

Mary Jane brushed past the others and ran to the staircase, but before she reached it the singing stopped and the piano was closed abruptly.

"O, what a pity!" she cried. "Is he coming down, Gretta?"

Gabriel heard his wife answer yes and saw her come down towards them. A few steps behind her were Mr. Bartell D'Arcy and Miss O'Callaghan.

"O, Mr. D'Arcy," cried Mary Jane, "it's downright mean of you to break off like that when we were all in raptures listening to you."

"I have been at him all the evening," said Miss O'Callaghan, "and Mrs. Conroy, too, and he told us he had a dreadful cold and couldn't sing."

"O, Mr. D'Arcy," said Aunt Kate, "now that was a great fib to tell."

"Can't you see that I'm as hoarse as a crow?" said Mr. D'Arcy roughly.

He went into the pantry hastily and put on his overcoat. The others, taken aback by his rude speech, could find nothing to say. Aunt Kate wrinkled her brows and made signs to the others to drop the subject. Mr. D'Arcy stood swathing his neck carefully and frowning.

"It's the weather," said Aunt Julia, after a pause.

"Yes, everybody has colds," said Aunt Kate readily, "everybody."

"They say," said Mary Jane, "we haven't had snow like it for thirty years; and I read this morning in the newspapers that the snow is general all over Ireland."

"I love the look of snow," said Aunt Julia sadly.

"So do I," said Miss O'Callaghan. "I think Christmas is never really Christmas unless we have the snow on the ground."

"But poor Mr. D'Arcy doesn't like the snow," said Aunt Kate, smiling.

Mr. D'Arcy came from the pantry, fully swathed and buttoned, and in a repentant tone told them the history of his cold. Everyone gave him advice and said it was a great pity and urged him to be very careful of his throat in the night air. Gabriel watched his wife, who did not join in the conversation. She was standing right under the dusty fanlight and the flame of the gas lit up the rich bronze of her hair, which he had seen her drying at the fire a few days before. She was in the same attitude and seemed unaware of the talk about her. At last she turned towards them and Gabriel saw that there was colour on her cheeks and that her eyes were shining. A sudden tide of joy went leaping out of his heart.

"Mr. D'Arcy," she said, "what is the name of that song you were singing?"

"It's called *The Lass of Aughrim*," said Mr. D'Arcy, "but I couldn't remember it properly. Why? Do you know it?"

"*The Lass of Aughrim*," she repeated. "I couldn't think of the name."

"It's a very nice air," said Mary Jane. "I'm sorry you were not in voice tonight."

"Now, Mary Jane," said Aunt Kate, "don't annoy Mr. D'Arcy. I won't have him annoyed."

Seeing that all were ready to start she shepherded them to the door, where good-night was said:

"Well, good-night, Aunt Kate, and thanks for the pleasant evening."

"Good-night, Gabriel. Good-night, Gretta!"

"Good-night, Aunt Kate, and thanks ever so much. Good-night, Aunt Julia."

"O, good-night, Gretta, I didn't see you."

"Good-night, Mr. D'Arcy. Good-night, Miss O'Callaghan."

"Good-night, Miss Morkan."

"Good-night, again."

"Good-night, all. Safe home."

"Good-night. Good night."

The morning was still dark. A dull, yellow light brooded over the houses and the river; and the sky seemed to be descending. It was slushy underfoot; and only streaks and patches of snow lay on the roofs, on the parapets of the quay and on the area railings. The lamps were still burning redly in the murky air and, across the river, the palace of the Four Courts stood out menacingly against the heavy sky.

She was walking on before him with Mr. Bartell D'Arcy, her shoes in a brown parcel tucked under one arm and her hands holding her skirt up from the slush. She had no longer any grace of attitude, but Gabriel's eyes were still bright with happiness. The blood went bounding along his veins; and the thoughts went rioting through his brain, proud, joyful, tender, valorous.

She was walking on before him so lightly and so erect that he longed to run after her noiselessly, catch her by the shoulder and say something foolish and affectionate into her ear. She seemed to him so frail that he longed to defend her against something and then to be alone with her. Moments of their secret life together burst like stars upon his memory. A heliotrope envelope was lying beside his breakfast-cup and he was caressing it with his hand. Birds were twittering in the ivy and the sunny web of the curtain was shimmering along the floor: he could not eat for happiness. They were standing on the crowded platform and he was placing a ticket inside the warm palm of her glove. He was standing with her in the cold, looking in through a grated window at a man making bottles in a roaring furnace. It was very cold. Her face, fragrant in the cold air, was quite close to his; and suddenly he called out to the man at the furnace:

"Is the fire hot, sir?"

But the man could not hear with the noise of the furnace. It was just as well. He might have answered rudely.

A wave of yet more tender joy escaped from his heart and went coursing in warm flood along his arteries. Like the tender fire of stars moments of their life together, that no one knew of or would ever know of, broke upon and illumined his memory. He longed to recall to her those moments, to make her forget the years of their dull existence together and remember only their moments of ecstasy. For the years, he felt, had not quenched his soul or hers. Their children, his writing, her household cares had not quenched all their souls' tender fire. In one letter that he had written to her then he had said: "Why is it that words like these seem to me so dull and cold? Is it because there is no word tender enough to be your name?"

Like distant music these words that he had written years before were borne towards him from the past. He longed to be alone with her. When the others had gone away, when he and she were in the room in the hotel, then they would be alone together. He would call her softly:

"Gretta!"

Perhaps she would not hear at once: she would be undressing. Then something in his voice would strike her. She would turn and look at him. . . .

At the corner of Winetavern Street they met a cab. He was glad of its rattling noise as it saved him from conversation. She was looking out of the window and seemed tired. The others spoke only a few words, pointing out some building or street. The horse galloped along wearily under the murky morning sky, dragging his old rattling box after his heels, and Gabriel was again in a cab with her, galloping to catch the boat, galloping to their honeymoon.

As the cab drove across O'Connell Bridge Miss O'Callaghan said:

"They say you never cross O'Connell Bridge without seeing a white horse."

"I see a white man this time," said Gabriel.

"Where?" asked Mr. Bartell D'Arcy.

Gabriel pointed to the statue, on which lay patches of snow. Then he nodded familiarly to it and waved his hand.

"Good-night, Dan," he said gaily.

When the cab drew up before the hotel, Gabriel jumped out and, in spite of Mr. Bartell D'Arcy's protest, paid the driver. He gave the man a shilling over his fare. The man saluted and said:

"A prosperous New Year to you, sir."

"The same to you," said Gabriel cordially.

She leaned for a moment on his arm in getting out of the cab and while standing at the curbstone, bidding the others good-night. She leaned lightly on his arm, as lightly as when she had danced with him a few hours before. He had felt proud and happy then, happy that she was his, proud of her grace and wifely carriage. But now, after the kindling again of so many memories, the first touch of her body, musical and strange and perfumed, sent through him a keen pang of lust. Under cover of her silence he pressed her arm closely to his side; and, as they stood at the hotel door, he felt that they had escaped from their lives and duties, escaped from home and friends and run away together with wild and radiant hearts to a new adventure.

An old man was dozing in a great hooded chair in the hall. He lit a candle in the office and went before them to the stairs. They followed him in silence, their feet falling in soft thuds on the thickly carpeted stairs. She mounted the stairs behind the porter, her head bowed in the ascent, her frail shoulders curved as with a burden, her skirt girt tightly about her. He could have flung his arms about her hips and held her still, for his arms were trembling with desire to seize her and only the stress of his nails against the palms of his hands held the wild impulse of his body in check. The porter halted on the stairs to settle his guttering candle. They halted, too, on the steps below him. In the silence Gabriel could hear the falling of the molten wax into the tray and the thumping of his own heart against his ribs.

The porter led them along a corridor and opened a door. Then he set his unstable candle down on a toilet-table and asked at what hour they were to be called in the morning.

"Eight," said Gabriel.

The porter pointed to the tap of the electric-bulb and began a muttered apology, but Gabriel cut him short.

"We don't want any light. We have light enough from the street. And I say," he added, pointing to the candle, "you might remove that handsome article, like a good man."

The porter took up his candle again, but slowly, for he was surprised by such a novel idea. Then he mumbled good-night and went out. Gabriel shot the lock to.

A ghastly light from the street lamp lay in a long shaft from one window to the door. Gabriel threw his overcoat and hat on a couch and crossed the room towards the window. He looked down into the street in order that his emotion might calm a little. Then he turned and leaned against a chest of drawers with his back to the light. She had taken off her hat and cloak and was standing before a large swinging mirror, unhooking her waist. Gabriel paused for a few moments, watching her, and then said:

"Gretta!"

She turned away from the mirror slowly and walked along the shaft of light towards him. Her face looked so serious and weary that the words would not pass Gabriel's lips. No, it was not the moment yet.

"You looked tired," he said.

"I am a little," she answered.

"You don't feel ill or weak?"

"No, tired: that's all."

She went on to the window and stood there, looking out. Gabriel waited again and then, fearing that diffidence was about to conquer him, he said abruptly:

"By the way, Gretta!"

"What is it?"

"You know that poor fellow Malins?" he said quickly.

"Yes. What about him?"

"Well, poor fellow, he's a decent sort of chap, after all," continued Gabriel in a false voice. "He gave me back that sovereign I lent him, and I didn't expect it, really. It's a pity he wouldn't keep away from that Browne, because he's not a bad fellow, really."

He was trembling now with annoyance. Why did she seem so abstracted? He did not know how he could begin. Was she annoyed, too, about something? If she would only turn to him or come to him of her own accord! To take her as she was would be brutal. No, he must see some ardour in her eyes first. He longed to be master of her strange mood.

"When did you lend him the pound?" she asked, after a pause.

Gabriel strove to restrain himself from breaking out into brutal language about the sottish Malins and his pound. He longed to cry to her from his soul, to crush her body against his, to overmaster her. But he said:

"O, at Christmas, when he opened that little Christmas-card shop in Henry Street."

He was in such a fever of rage and desire that he did not hear her come from the window. She stood before him for an instant, looking at him strangely. Then, suddenly raising herself on tiptoe and resting her hands lightly on his shoulders, she kissed him.

"You are a very generous person, Gabriel," she said.

Gabriel, trembling with delight at her sudden kiss and at the quaintness of her phrase, put his hands on her hair and began smoothing it back, scarcely touching it with his fingers. The washing had made it fine and brilliant. His heart was brimming over with happiness. Just when he was wishing for it she had come to him of her own accord. Perhaps her thoughts had been running with his. Perhaps she had felt the impetuous desire that was in him, and then the yielding mood had come upon her. Now that she had fallen to him so easily, he wondered why he had been so diffident.

He stood, holding her head between his hands. Then, slipping one arm swiftly about her body and drawing her towards him, he said softly:

"Gretta, dear, what are you thinking about?"

She did not answer nor yield wholly to his arm. He said again, softly:

"Tell me what it is, Gretta. I think I know what is the matter. Do I know?"

She did not answer at once. Then she said in an outburst of tears:

"O, I am thinking about that song, *The Lass of Aughrim*."

She broke loose from him and ran to the bed and, throwing her arms across the bed-rail, hid her face. Gabriel stood stock-still for a moment in astonishment and then followed her. As he passed in the way of the cheval-glass he caught sight of himself in full length, his broad, well-filled shirt-front, the face whose expression always puzzled him when he saw it in a mirror, and his glimmering gilt-rimmed eyeglasses. He halted a few paces from her and said:

"What about the song? Why does that make you cry?"

She raised her head from her arms and dried her eyes with the back of her hand like a child. A kinder note than he had intended went into his voice.

"Why, Gretta?" he asked.

"I am thinking about a person long ago who used to sing that song."

"And who was the person long ago?" asked Gabriel, smiling.

"It was a person I used to know in Galway when I was living with my grandmother," she said.

The smile passed away from Gabriel's face. A dull anger began to gather again at the back of his mind and the dull fires of his lust began to glow angrily in his veins.

"Someone you were in love with?" he asked ironically.

"It was a young boy I used to know," she answered, "named Michael Furey. He used to sing that song *The Lass of Aughrim*. He was very delicate."

Gabriel was silent. He did not wish her to think that he was interested in this delicate boy.

"I can see him so plainly," she said, after a moment. "Such eyes as he had: big, dark eyes! And such an expression in them—an expression!"

"O, then, you are in love with him?" said Gabriel.

"I used to go out walking with him," she said, "when I was in Galway."

A thought flew across Gabriel's mind.

"Perhaps that was why you wanted to go to Galway with that Ivors girl?" he said coldly.

She looked at him and asked in surprise:

"What for?"

Her eyes made Gabriel feel awkward. He shrugged his shoulders and said:

"How do I know? To see him, perhaps."

She looked away from him along the shaft of light towards the window in silence.

"He is dead," she said at length. "He died when he was only seventeen. Isn't it a terrible thing to die so young as that?"

"What was he?" asked Gabriel, still ironically.

"He was in the gasworks," she said.

Gabriel felt humiliated by the failure of his irony and by the evocation of this figure from the dead, a boy in the gasworks. While he had been full of memories of their secret life together, full of tenderness and joy and desire, she had been comparing him in her mind with another. A shameful consciousness of his own person assailed him. He saw himself as a ludicrous figure, acting as a penny-boy for his aunts, a nervous, well-meaning sentimentalist, orating to vulgarians and idealising his own clownish lusts, the pitiable fatuous fellow he had caught a glimpse of in the mirror. Instinctively he turned his back more to the light lest she might see the shame that burned upon his forehead.

He tried to keep up his tone of cold interrogation, but his voice when he spoke was humble and indifferent.

"I suppose you were in love with this Michael Furey, Gretta," he said.

"I was great with him at that time," she said.

Her voice was veiled and sad. Gabriel, feeling now how vain it would be to try to lead her whither he had purposed, caressed one of her hands and said, also sadly:

"And what did he die of so young, Gretta? Consumption, was it?"

"I think he died for me," she answered.

A vague terror seized Gabriel at this answer, as if, at that hour when he had hoped to triumph, some impalpable and vindictive being was coming against him, gathering forces against him in its vague world. But he shook himself free of it with an effort of reason and continued to caress her hand. He did not question her again, for he felt that she would tell him of herself. Her hand was warm and moist: it did not respond to his touch, but he continued to caress it just as he had caressed her first letter to him that spring morning.

"It was in the winter," she said, "about the beginning of the winter when I was going to leave my grandmother's and come up here to the convent. And he was ill at the time in his lodgings in Galway and wouldn't be let out, and his people in Oughterard were written to. He was in decline, they said, or something like that. I never knew rightly."

She paused for a moment and sighed.

"Poor fellow," she said. "He was very fond of me and he was such a gentle boy. We used to go out together, walking, you know, Gabriel, like the way they do in the country. He was going to study singing only for his health. He had a very good voice, poor Michael Furey."

"Well; and then?" asked Gabriel.

"And then when it came to the time for me to leave Galway and come up to the convent he was much worse and I wouldn't be let see him so I wrote a letter saying I was going up to Dublin and would be back in the summer, and hoping he would be better then."

She paused for a moment to get her voice under control, and then went on:

"Then the night before I left, I was in my grandmother's house in Nuns' Island, packing up, and I heard gravel thrown up against the window. The window was so wet I couldn't see, so I ran downstairs as I was and slipped out the back into the garden and there was the poor fellow at the end of the garden, shivering."

"And did you not tell him to go back?" asked Gabriel.

"I implored of him to go home at once and told him he would get his death in the rain. But he said he did not want to live. I can see his eyes as well as well! He was standing at the end of the wall where there was a tree."

"And did he go home?" asked Gabriel.

"Yes, he went home. And when I was only a week in the convent he died and he was buried in Oughterard, where his people came from. O, the day I heard that, that he was dead!"

She stopped, choking with sobs, and, overcome by emotion, flung herself face downward on the bed, sobbing in the quilt. Gabriel held her hand for a moment longer, irresolutely, and then, shy of intruding on her grief, let it fall gently and walked quietly to the window.

She was fast asleep.

Gabriel, leaning on his elbow, looked for a few moments unresentfully on her tangled hair and half-open mouth, listening to her deep-drawn breath. So she had had that romance in her life: a man had died for her sake. It hardly pained him now to think how poor a part he, her husband, had played in her life. He watched her while she slept, as though he and she had never lived together as man and wife. His curious eyes rested long upon her face and on her hair; and, as he thought of what she must have been then, in that time of her first girlish beauty, a strange, friendly pity for her entered his soul. He did not like to say even to himself that her face was no longer beautiful, but he knew that it was no longer the face for which Michael Furey had braved death.

Perhaps she had not told him all the story. His eyes moved to the chair over which she had thrown some of her clothes. A petticoat string dangled to the floor. One boot stood upright, its limp upper fallen down: the fellow of it lay upon its side. He wondered at his riot of emotions of an hour before. From what had it proceeded? From his aunt's supper, from his own foolish speech, from the wine and dancing, the merry-making when saying good-night in the hall, the pleasure of the walk along the river in the snow. Poor Aunt Julia! She, too, would soon be a shade with the shade of Patrick

Morkan and his horse. He had caught that haggard look upon her face for a moment when she was singing *Arrayed for the Bridal*. Soon, perhaps, he would be sitting in that same drawing-room, dressed in black, his silk hat on his knees. The blinds would be drawn down and Aunt Kate would be sitting beside him, crying and blowing her nose and telling him how Julia had died. He would cast about in his mind for some words that might console her, and would find only lame and useless ones. Yes, yes: that would happen very soon.

The air of the room chilled his shoulders. He stretched himself cautiously along under the sheets and lay down beside his wife. One by one, they were all becoming shades. Better pass boldly into that other world, in the full glory of some passion, than fade and wither dismally with age. He thought of how she who lay beside him had locked in her heart for so many years that image of her lover's eyes when he had told her that he did not wish to live.

Generous tears filled Gabriel's eyes. He had never felt like that himself towards any woman, but he knew that such a feeling must be love. The tears gathered more thickly in his eyes and in the partial darkness he imagined he saw the form of a young man standing under a dripping tree. Other forms were near. His soul had approached that region where dwell the vast hosts of the dead. He was conscious of, but could not apprehend, their wayward and flickering existence. His own identity was fading out into a grey impalpable world: the solid world itself, which these dead had one time reared and lived in, was dissolving and dwindling.

A few light taps upon the pane made him turn to the window. It had begun to snow again. He watched sleepily the flakes, silver and dark, falling obliquely against the lamplight. The time had come for him to set out on his journey westward. Yes, the newspapers were right: snow was general all over Ireland. It was falling on every part of the dark central plain, on the treeless hills, falling softly upon the Bog of Allen and, farther westward, softly falling into the dark mutinous Shannon waves. It was falling, too, upon every part of the lonely churchyard on the hill where Michael Furey lay buried. It lay thickly drifted on the crooked crosses and headstones, on the spears of the little gate, on the barren thorns. His soul swooned slowly as he heard the snow falling faintly through the universe and faintly falling, like the descent of their last end, upon all the living and the dead.

D. H. Lawrence

1885–1930

THE PRUSSIAN OFFICER · THE HORSE DEALER'S
DAUGHTER · THE ROCKING-HORSE WINNER

Partly because he himself was the child of an unhappy marriage, D. H. Lawrence returns again and again in his fiction to the problem of marriage, the problem of making the relationship between men and women genuinely creative and satisfying. Lawrence's father was a hearty, bearded miner in Nottingham, England, who, except for his wife's complaints, would have been quite content with his working-class life. Lawrence's mother was a former schoolteacher, determined that her children should rise in the world. Lawrence began by accepting his mother's gentility and ambitions. Later his sympathies shifted to men like his father. They possessed, he thought, a natural vitality and sensitivity that modern education more often destroys than develops. This is the theme of *Lady Chatterley's Lover* (1928).

Visits to farm country outside the bleak mill town which was his home stimulated Lawrence's extraordinary sensitivity to natural beauty. On one farm he met the Miriam of his autobiographical novel, *Sons and Lovers* (1913). After going to Nottingham University, Lawrence taught school briefly, but his literary talent was quickly recognized by London publishers. In 1912, with one novel published and another accepted, he eloped with Frieda von Richthofen, wife of one of his university teachers and daughter of a German baron. During the First World War and just after it, the Lawrences had a friendship, which was often trying and complicated, with Katherine Mansfield and her husband, John Middleton Murry. This takes fictional form in *Women in Love* (1920).

Lawrence's position in the war years was difficult because of his German wife and his lack of sympathy with the war spirit. In fact, he repudiated European civilization generally. He felt that science, modern education, and the pursuit of wealth had cut most men off from the deepest sources of imagination and feeling, making them incapable of pride, tenderness, and spontaneity. Lawrence felt a passionate need for wholeness, both personal and social. His wife introduced him to the work of Freud, but though he was fascinated by what it told of the operations of the unconscious mind, he disliked its analytic and scientific approach and turned instead to earlier mystical ideas of man's place in the cosmos. His views are expressed most directly in *Fantasia of the Unconscious* (1922), *Studies in Classical American Literature* (1923), and *Apocalypse* (1931). American critics find his book on our literature one of the most penetrating ever written by a European, though very personal and dogmatic in manner.

During the twenties the Lawrences traveled restlessly all over Europe and to Ceylon, Australia, Mexico, and the United States, looking for a place in which they could feel at home, for a way of life that could satisfy their emotional needs. They came closest to finding it at Taos, New Mexico. The ritual dances of the Pueblo and Navaho Indians represented the kind of communal, religious experience Lawrence was seeking but could never fully participate in.

From Lawrence's stay in Australia came the novel *Kangaroo* (1923), and from his stay in Mexico *The Plumed Serpent* (1926). But perhaps the best results of his travels are the essays in *Sea and Sardinia* (1921), *Mornings in Mexico* (1927), and *Etruscan Places* (1932). These show Lawrence's marvelous powers of description, his command of sensuous and metaphoric language, his ability to enter imaginatively and dramatically into whatever he is observing, whether it is a man, a plant, an animal, a landscape, or a piece of ancient art. These abilities are well displayed in "The Prussian Officer." Lawrence wrote rapidly, under the stress of strong feeling. His short stories, consequently, often have more unity of mood and more perfection of artistic form than his novels.

"The Prussian Officer" is one of the most powerful treatments in modern literature of the destructive effect of unspoken, unacknowledged passion. Lawrence knew very little about Germany when he wrote it, and nothing at first hand about army life, and yet he shows here a prophetic insight into the roots of the perverse cruelty that flourished later under the Nazis.

"The Horse Dealer's Daughter" is a remarkable love story because of the unlikeliness and yet genuineness of the passion suddenly uniting the two characters, and because of the strange symbolic scene that roused the passion. Lawrence was convinced that the most vital experiences have little to do with ordinary rationality. The physical circumstances, described with such vivid naturalness, are those that Lawrence knew as a youth.

"The Rocking-Horse Winner" is a parable on the money lusts of modern society, but it draws its magic from very ancient sources. Hobby-horses are common in folklore, and there are accounts of rituals in which their riders rocked themselves into a trance in order to attain powers of prophecy.

THE PRUSSIAN OFFICER

They had marched more than thirty kilometres since dawn, along the white, hot road where occasional thickets of trees threw a moment of shade, then out into the glare again. On either hand, the valley, wide and shallow, glittered with heat; dark green patches of rye, pale young corn, fallow and meadow and black pine woods spread in a dull, hot diagram under a glistening sky. But right in front the mountains ranged across, pale blue and very still, snow gleaming gently out of the deep atmosphere. And towards the mountains, on and on, the regiment marched between the rye fields and the meadows, between the scraggy fruit trees set regularly on either side the high road. The burnished, dark green rye threw off a suffocating heat, the mountains drew gradually nearer and more distinct. While the feet of the soldiers grew hotter, sweat ran through their hair under their helmets, and their knapsacks could burn no more in contact with their shoulders, but seemed instead to give off a cold, prickly sensation.

He walked on and on in silence, staring at the mountains ahead, that rose sheer out of the land and stood fold behind fold, half earth,

THE PRUSSIAN OFFICER. From *The Prussian Officer* by D. H. Lawrence. Reprinted by permission of The Viking Press, Inc., New York, and Pearn, Pollinger & Higham, Ltd., London.

half heaven, the heaven, the barrier with slits of soft snow, in the pale, bluish peaks.

He could now walk almost without pain. At the start, he had determined not to limp. It had made him sick to take the first steps, and during the first mile or so, he had compressed his breath, and the cold drops of sweat had stood on his forehead. But he had walked it off. What were they after all but bruises! He had looked at them, as he was getting up: deep bruises on the backs of his thighs. And since he had made his first step in the morning, he had been conscious of them, till now he had a tight, hot place in his chest, with suppressing the pain, and holding himself in. There seemed no air when he breathed. But he walked almost lightly.

The Captain's hand had trembled at taking his coffee at dawn: his orderly saw it again. And he saw the fine figure of the Captain wheeling on horseback at the farmhouse ahead, a handsome figure in pale blue uniform with facings of scarlet, and the metal gleaming on the black helmet and the sword-scabbard, and dark streaks of sweat coming on the silky bay horse. The orderly felt he was connected with that figure moving so suddenly on horseback: he followed it like a shadow, mute and inevitable and damned by it. And the officer was always aware of the tramp of the company behind, the march of his orderly among the men.

The Captain was a tall man of about forty, grey at the temples. He had a handsome, finely knit figure, and was one of the best horsemen in the West. His orderly, having to rub him down, admired the amazing riding-muscles of his loins.

For the rest, the orderly scarcely noticed the officer any more than he noticed himself. It was rarely he saw his master's face: he did not look at it. The Captain had reddish-brown, stiff hair that he wore short upon his skull. His moustache was also cut short and bristly over a full, brutal mouth. His face was rather rugged, the cheeks thin. Perhaps the man was the more handsome for the deep lines in his face, the irritable tension of his brow, which gave him the look of a man who fights with life. His fair eyebrows stood bushy over light blue eyes that were always flashing with cold fire.

He was a Prussian aristocrat, haughty and overbearing. But his mother had been a Polish Countess. Having made too many gambling debts when he was young, he had ruined his prospects in the Army, and remained an infantry captain. He had never married: his position did not allow of it, and no woman had ever moved him to it. His time he spent riding—occasionally he rode one of his own horses at the races—and at the officers' club. Now and then he took himself a mistress. But after such an event, he returned to duty with his brow still more tense, his eyes still more hostile and irritable. With the men, however, he was merely impersonal, though a devil when roused; so that, on the whole, they feared him, but had no great aversion from him. They accepted him as the inevitable.

To his orderly he was at first cold and just and indifferent: he did not fuss over trifles. So that his servant knew practically nothing about him, except just what orders he would give, and how he wanted them obeyed. That was quite simple. Then the change gradually came.

The orderly was a youth of about twenty-two, of medium height, and well built. He had strong, heavy limbs, was swarthy, with a soft, black, young moustache. There was something altogether warm and young about him. He had firmly marked eye-brows over dark, expressionless eyes that seemed never to have thought, only to have received life direct through his senses, and acted straight from instinct.

Gradually the officer had become aware of his servant's young, vigorous, unconscious presence about him. He could not get away from the sense of the youth's person, while he was in attendance. It was like a warm flame upon the older man's tense, rigid body, that had become almost unliving, fixed. There was something so free and self-contained about him, and something in the young fellow's movement, that made the officer aware of him. And this irritated the Prussian. He did not choose to be touched into life by his servant. He might easily have changed his man, but he did not. He now very rarely looked direct at his orderly, but kept his face averted, as if to avoid seeing him. And yet as the young soldier moved unthinking about the apartment, the elder watched him, and would notice the movement of his strong young shoulders under the blue cloth, the bend of his neck. And it irritated him. To see the soldier's young, brown, shapely peasant's hand grasp the loaf or the wine-bottle sent a flash of hate of or anger through the elder man's blood. It was not that the youth was clumsy: it was rather the blind, instinctive sureness of movement of an unhampered young animal that irritated the officer to such a degree.

Once, when a bottle of wine had gone over, and the red gushed

out on to the tablecloth, the officer had started up with an oath, and
his eyes, bluey like fire, had held those of the confused youth for a
moment. It was a shock for the young soldier. He felt something
sink deeper, deeper into his soul, where nothing had ever gone before. It left him rather blank and wondering. Some of his natural
completeness in himself was gone, a little uneasiness took its place.
And from that time an undiscovered feeling had held between the
two men.

Henceforward the orderly was afraid of really meeting his master.
His subconsciousness remembered those steely blue eyes and the
harsh brows, and did not intend to meet them again. So he always
stared past his master and avoided him. Also, in a little anxiety, he
waited for the three months to have gone, when his time would be
up. He began to feel a constraint in the Captain's presence, and the
soldier even more than the officer wanted to be left alone, in his neutrality as servant.

He had served the Captain for more than a year, and knew his
duty. This he performed easily, as if it were natural to him. The
officer and his commands he took for granted, as he took the sun and
the rain, and he served as a matter of course. It did not implicate him
personally.

But now if he were going to be forced into a personal interchange
with his master he would be like a wild thing caught, he felt he must
get away.

But the influence of the young soldier's being had penetrated
through the officer's stiffened discipline, and perturbed the man in
him. He, however, was a gentleman, with long, fine hands and cultivated movements, and was not going to allow such a thing as the
stirring of his innate self. He was a man of passionate temper, who
had always kept himself suppressed. Occasionally there had been a
duel, an outburst before the soldiers. He knew himself to be always
on the point of breaking out. But he kept himself hard to the idea of
the Service. Whereas the young soldier seemed to live out his warm,
full nature, to give it off in his very movements, which had a certain
zest, such as wild animals have in free movement. And this irritated
the officer more and more.

In spite of himself, the Captain could not regain his neutrality of
feeling towards his orderly. Nor could he leave the man alone. In spite
of himself, he watched him, gave him sharp orders, tried to take up

as much of his time as possible. Sometimes he flew into a rage with the young soldier, and bullied him. Then the orderly shut himself off, as it were out of earshot, and waited, with sullen, flushed face, for the end of the noise. The words never pierced to his intelligence, he made himself, protectively, impervious to the feelings of his master.

He had a scar on his left thumb, a deep seam going across the knuckle. The officer had long suffered from it, and wanted to do something to it. Still it was there, ugly and brutal on the young, brown hand. At last the Captain's reserve gave away. One day, as the orderly was smoothing out the tablecloth, the officer pinned down his thumb with a pencil, asking:

"How did you come by that?"

The young man winced and drew back at attention.

"A wood axe, Herr Hauptmann," he answered.

The officer waited for further explanation. None came. The orderly went about his duties. The elder man was sullenly angry. His servant avoided him. And the next day he had to use all his will-power to avoid seeing the scarred thumb. He wanted to get hold of it and— A hot flame ran in his blood.

He knew his servant would soon be free, and would be glad. As yet, the soldier had held himself off from the elder man. The Captain grew madly irritable. He could not rest when the soldier was away, and when he was present, he glared at him with tormented eyes. He hated those fine black brows over the unmeaning dark eyes, he was infuriated by the free movement of the handsome limbs, which no military discipline could make stiff. And he became harsh and cruelly bullying, using contempt and satire. The young soldier only grew more mute and expressionless.

"What cattle were you bred by, that you can't keep straight eyes? Look me in the eyes when I speak to you."

And the soldier turned his dark eyes to the other's face, but there was no sight in them: he stared with the slightest possible cast, holding back his sight, perceiving the blue of his master's eyes, but receiving no look from them. And the elder man went pale, and his reddish eyebrows twitched. He gave his order, barrenly.

Once he flung a heavy military glove into the young soldier's face. Then he had the satisfaction of seeing the black eyes flare up into his own, like a blaze when straw is thrown on a fire. And he had laughed with a little tremor and a sneer.

But there were only two months more. The youth instinctively tried to keep himself intact: he tried to serve the officer as if the latter were an abstract authority and not a man. All his instinct was to avoid personal contact, even definite hate. But in spite of himself the hate grew, responsive to the officer's passion. However, he put it in the background. When he had left the Army he could dare acknowledge it. By nature he was active, and had many friends. He thought what amazing good fellows they were. But, without knowing it, he was alone. Now this solitariness was intensified. It would carry him through his term. But the officer seemed to be going irritably insane, and the youth was deeply frightened.

The soldier had a sweetheart, a girl from the mountains, independent and primitive. The two walked together, rather silently. He went with her, not to talk, but to have his arm round her, and for the physical contact. This eased him, made it easier for him to ignore the Captain; for he could rest with her held fast against his chest. And she, in some unspoken fashion, was there for him. They loved each other.

The Captain perceived it, and was mad with irritation. He kept the young man engaged all the evenings long, and took pleasure in the dark look that came on his face. Occasionally, the eyes of the two men met, those of the younger sullen and dark, doggedly unalterable, those of the elder sneering with restless contempt.

The officer tried hard not to admit the passion that had got hold of him. He would not know that his feeling for his orderly was anything but that of a man incensed by his stupid, perverse servant. So, keeping quite justified and conventional in his consciousness, he let the other thing run on. His nerves, however, were suffering. At last he slung the end of a belt in his servant's face. When he saw the youth start back, the pain-tears in his eyes and the blood on his mouth, he had felt at once a thrill of deep pleasure and of shame.

But this, he acknowledged to himself, was a thing he had never done before. The fellow was too exasperating. His own nerves must be going to pieces. He went away for some days with a woman.

It was a mockery of pleasure. He simply did not want the woman. But he stayed on for his time. At the end of it, he came back in an agony of irritation, torment, and misery. He rode all the evening, then came straight into supper. His orderly was out. The officer sat with his long, fine hands lying on the table, perfectly still, and all his blood seemed to be corroding.

At last his servant entered. He watched the strong, easy young figure, the fine eyebrows, the thick black hair. In a week's time the youth had got back his old well-being. The hands of the officer twitched and seemed to be full of mad flame. The young man stood at attention, unmoving, shut off.

The meal went in silence. But the orderly seemed eager. He made a clatter with the dishes.

"Are you in a hurry?" asked the officer, watching the intent, warm face of his servant. The other did not reply.

"Will you answer my question?" said the Captain.

"Yes, sir," replied the orderly, standing with his pile of deep Army plates. The Captain waited, looked at him, then asked again:

"Are you in a hurry?"

"Yes, sir," came the answer, that sent a flash through the listener.

"For what?"

"I was going out, sir."

"I want you this evening."

There was a moment's hesitation. The officer had a curious stiffness of countenance.

"Yes, sir," replied the servant, in his throat.

"I want you tomorrow evening also—in fact, you may consider your evenings occupied, unless I give you leave."

The mouth with the young moustache set close.

"Yes, sir," answered the orderly, loosening his lips for a moment. He again turned to the door.

"And why have you a piece of pencil in your ear?"

The orderly hesitated, then continued on his way without answering. He set the plates in a pile outside the door, took the stump of pencil from his ear, and put it in his pocket. He had been copying a verse for his sweetheart's birthday card. He returned to finish clearing the table. The officer's eyes were dancing, he had a little, eager smile.

"Why have you a piece of pencil in your ear?" he asked.

The orderly took his hands full of dishes. His master was standing near the great green stove, a little smile on his face, his chin thrust forward. When the young soldier saw him his heart suddenly ran hot. He felt blind. Instead of answering, he turned dazedly to the door. As he was crouching to set down the dishes, he was pitched forward by a kick from behind. The pots went in a stream down the stairs, he clung to the pillar of the banisters. And as he was rising he was kicked heavily again, and again, so that he clung sickly to the post for some moments. His master had gone swiftly into the room and closed the door. The maid-servant downstairs looked up the staircase and made a mocking face at the crockery disaster.

The officer's heart was plunging. He poured himself a glass of wine, part of which he spilled on the floor, and gulped the remainder, leaning against the cool, green stove. He heard his man collecting the dishes from the stairs. Pale, as if intoxicated, he waited. The servant entered again. The Captain's heart gave a pang, as of pleasure, seeing the young fellow bewildered and uncertain on his feet, with pain.

"Schöner!" he said.

The soldier was a little slower in coming to attention.

"Yes, sir!"

The youth stood before him, with pathetic young moustache, and fine eyebrows very distinct on his forehead of dark marble.

"I asked you a question."

"Yes, sir."

The officer's tone bit like acid.

"Why had you a pencil in your ear?"

Again the servant's heart ran hot, and he could not breathe. With dark, strained eyes, he looked at the officer, as if fascinated. And he stood there sturdily planted, unconscious. The withering smile came into the Captain's eyes, and he lifted his foot.

"I—I forgot it—sir," panted the soldier, his dark eyes fixed on the other man's dancing blue ones.

"What was it doing there?"

He saw the young man's breast heaving as he made an effort for words.

"I had been writing."

"Writing what?"

Again the soldier looked him up and down. The officer could hear him panting. The smile came into the blue eyes. The soldier worked his dry throat, but could not speak. Suddenly the smile lit like a flame on the officer's face, and a kick came heavily against the orderly's thigh. The youth moved a pace sideways. His face went dead, with two black, staring eyes.

"Well?" said the officer.

The orderly's mouth had gone dry, and his tongue rubbed in it as on dry brown-paper. He worked his throat. The officer raised his foot. The servant went stiff.

"Some poetry, sir," came the crackling, unrecognizable sound of his voice.

"Poetry, what poetry?" asked the Captain, with a sickly smile.

Again there was the working in the throat. The Captain's heart had suddenly gone down heavily, and he stood sick and tired.

"For my girl, sir," he heard the dry, inhuman sound.

"Oh!" he said, turning away. "Clear the table."

"Click!" went the soldier's throat; then again, "Click!" and then the half-articulate:

"Yes, sir."

The young soldier was gone, looking old, and walking heavily.

The officer, left alone, held himself rigid, to prevent himself from thinking. His instinct warned him that he must not think. Deep inside him was the intense gratification of his passion, still working powerfully. Then there was a counter-action, a horrible breaking down of something inside him, a whole agony of reaction. He stood there for an hour motionless, a chaos of sensations, but rigid with a will to keep blank his consciousness, to prevent his mind grasping. And he held himself so until the worst of the stress had passed, when he began to drink, drank himself to an intoxication, till he slept obliterated. When he woke in the morning he was shaken to the base of his nature. But he had fought off the realization of what he had done. He had prevented his mind from taking it in, had suppressed it along with his instincts, and the conscious man had nothing to do with it. He felt only as after a bout of intoxication, weak, but the affair itself all dim and not to be recovered. Of the drunkenness of his passion he successfully refused remembrance. And when his orderly appeared with coffee, the officer assumed the same self he had had the morning before. He refused the event of the past night—denied it had ever been—and was successful in his denial. He had not done any such thing—not he himself. Whatever there might be, lay at the door of a stupid, insubordinate servant.

The orderly had gone about in a stupor all the evening. He drank some beer because he was parched, but not much, the alcohol made his feeling come back, and he could not bear it. He was dulled, as if nine-tenths of the ordinary man in him were inert. He crawled about disfigured. Still, when he thought of the kicks, he went sick, and when he thought of the threat of more kicking, in the room afterwards, his heart went hot and faint, and he panted, remembering the one that had come. He had been forced to say, "For my girl." He was much too done even to want to cry. His mouth hung slightly open, like an idiot's. He felt vacant, and wasted. So, he wandered at his work, painfully, and very slowly and clumsily, fumbling blindly with the brushes, and finding it difficult, when he sat down, to summon the energy to move again. His limbs, his jaw, were slack and nerveless. But he was very tired. He got to bed at last, and slept inert, relaxed, in a sleep that was rather stupor than slumber, a dead night of stupefaction shot through with gleams of anguish.

In the morning were the manoeuvres. But he woke even before the bugle sounded. The painful ache in his chest, the dryness of his throat, the awful steady feeling of misery made his eyes come awake and dreary at once. He knew, without thinking, what had happened. And he knew that the day had come again, when he must go on with his round. The last bit of darkness was being pushed out of the room. He would have to move his inert body and go on. He was so young, and had known so little trouble, that he was bewildered. He only wished it would stay night, so that he could lie still, covered up by the darkness. And yet nothing would prevent the day from coming, nothing would save him from having to get up and saddle the Captain's horse, and make the Captain's coffee. It was there, inevitable. And then, he thought, it was impossible. Yet they would not leave him free. He must go and take the coffee to the Captain. He was too stunned to understand it. He only knew it was inevitable—inevitable, however long he lay inert.

At last, after heaving at himself, for he seemed to be a mass of inertia, he got up. But he had to force every one of his movements from behind, with his will. He felt lost, and dazed, and helpless. Then he clutched hold of the bed, the pain was so keen. And looking at his thighs, he saw the darker bruises on his swarthy flesh and he knew that, if he pressed one of his fingers on one of the bruises, he should faint. But he did not want to faint—he did not want anybody to know. No one should ever know. It was between him and the Captain. There were only the two people in the world now—himself and the Captain.

Slowly, economically, he got dressed and forced himself to walk. Everything was obscure, except just what he had his hands on. But he managed to get through his work. The very pain revived his dull senses. The worst remained yet. He took the tray and went up to the Captain's room. The officer, pale and heavy, sat at the table. The orderly, as he saluted, felt himself put out of existence. He stood still for a moment submitting to his own nullification—then he gathered himself, seemed to regain himself, and then the Captain began to grow vague, unreal, and the younger soldier's heart beat up. He clung to this situation—that the Captain did not exist—so that he himself might live. But when he saw his officer's hand tremble as he took the coffee, he felt everything falling shattered. And he went away, feeling as if he himself were coming to pieces, disintegrated. And when the Captain was there on horseback, giving orders, while he himself stood, with rifle and knapsack, sick with pain, he felt as if he must shut his eyes—as if he must shut his eyes on everything. It was only the long agony of marching with a parched throat that filled him with one single, sleep-heavy intention: to save himself.

I I

He was getting used even to his parched throat. That the snowy peaks were radiant among the sky, that the whity-green glacier-river twisted through its pale shoals in the valley below, seemed almost supernatural. But he was going mad with fever and thirst. He plodded on uncomplaining. He did not want to speak, not to anybody. There were two gulls, like flakes of water and snow, over the river. The scent of green rye soaked in sunshine came like a sickness. And the march continued, monotonously, almost like a bad sleep.

At the next farm-house, which stood low and broad near the high road, tubs of water had been put out. The soldiers clustered round to drink. They took off their helmets, and the steam mounted from their wet hair. The Captain sat on horseback, watching. He needed to see his orderly. His helmet threw a dark shadow over his light, fierce eyes, but his moustache and mouth and chin were distinct in the sunshine. The orderly must move under the presence of the figure of the horseman. It was not that he was afraid, or cowed. It was as if he was disembowelled, made empty, like an empty shell. He felt himself as nothing, a shadow creeping under the sunshine. And, thirsty as he was, he could scarcely drink, feeling the Captain near him. He would not take off his helmet to wipe his wet hair. He wanted to stay in shadow, not to be forced into consciousness. Starting, he saw the light heel of the officer prick the belly of the horse; the Captain cantered away, and he himself could relapse into vacancy.

Nothing, however, could give him back his living place in the hot, bright morning. He felt like a gap among it all. Whereas the Captain was prouder, overriding. A hot flash went through the young servant's body. The Captain was firmer and prouder with life, he himself was empty as a shadow. Again the flash went through him, dazing him out. But his heart ran a little firmer.

The company turned up the hill, to make a loop for the return. Below, from among the trees, the farm-bell clanged. He saw the labourers, mowing barefoot at the thick grass, leave off their work and go downhill, their scythes hanging over their shoulders, like long, bright claws curving down behind them. They seemed like dream-people, as if they had no relation to himself. He felt as in a blackish dream: as if all the other things were there and had form, but he himself was only a consciousness, a gap that could think and perceive.

The soldiers were tramping silently up the glaring hillside. Gradually his head began to revolve, slowly, rhythmically. Sometimes it was dark before his eyes, as if he saw this world through a smoked glass, frail shadows and unreal. It gave him a pain in his head to walk.

The air was too scented, it gave no breath. All the lush green-stuff seemed to be issuing its sap, till the air was deathly, sickly with the smell of greenness. There was the perfume of clover, like pure honey and bees. Then there grew a faint acrid tang—they were near the beeches; and then a queer clattering noise, and a suffocating, hideous smell; they were passing a flock of sheep, a shepherd in a black smock, holding his crook. Why should the sheep huddle together under this fierce sun? He felt that the shepherd would not see him, though he could see the shepherd.

At last there was the halt. They stacked rifles in a conical stack, put down their kit in a scattered circle around it, and dispersed a little, sitting on a small knoll high on the hillside. The chatter began. The soldiers were steaming with heat, but were lively. He sat still, seeing the blue mountains rising upon the land, twenty kilometres away.

There was a blue fold in the ranges, then out of that, at the foot, the broad, pale bed of the river, stretches of whity-green water between pinkish-grey shoals among the dark pine woods. There it was, spread out a long way off. And it seemed to come downhill, the river. There was a raft being steered, a mile away. It was a strange country. Nearer, a red-roofed, broad farm with white base and square dots of windows crouched beside the wall of beech foliage on the wood's edge. There were long strips of rye and clover and pale green corn. And just at his feet, below the knoll, was a darkish bog, where globe flowers stood breathless still on their slim stalks. And some of the pale gold bubbles were burst, and a broken fragment hung in the air. He thought he was going to sleep.

Suddenly something moved into this coloured mirage before his eyes. The Captain, a small, light-blue and scarlet figure, was trotting evenly between the strips of corn, along the level brow of the hill. And the man making flag-signals was coming on. Proud and sure moved the horseman's figure, the quick, bright thing, in which was concentrated all the light of this morning, which for the rest lay a fragile, shining shadow. Submissive, apathetic, the young soldier sat and stared. But as the horse slowed to a walk, coming up the last steep path, the great flash flared over the body and soul of the orderly. He sat waiting. The back of his head felt as if it were weighted with a heavy piece of fire. He did not want to eat. His hands trembled slightly as he moved them. Meanwhile the officer on horseback was approaching slowly and proudly. The tension grew in the orderly's soul. Then again, seeing the Captain ease himself on the saddle, the flash blazed through him.

The Captain looked at the patch of light blue and scarlet, and dark heads, scattered closely on the hill-side. It pleased him. The command pleased him. And he was feeling proud. His orderly was among them in common subjection. The officer rose a little on his stirrups to look. The young soldier sat with averted, dumb face. The Captain relaxed on his seat. His slim-legged, beautiful horse, brown as a beechnut, walked proudly uphill. The Captain passed into the zone of the company's atmosphere: a hot smell of men, of sweat, of leather. He knew it very well. After a word with the lieutenant, he went a few paces higher, and sat there, a dominant figure, his sweat-marked horse swishing its tail, while he looked down on his men, on his orderly, a nonentity among the crowd.

The young soldier's heart was like fire in his chest, and he breathed with difficulty. The officer, looking downhill, saw three of the young soldiers, two pails of water between them, staggering across a sunny green field. A table had been set up under a tree, and there the slim lieutenant stood, importantly busy. Then the Captain summoned himself to an act of courage. He called his orderly.

The flame leaped into the young soldier's throat as he heard the command, and he rose blindly, stifled. He saluted, standing below the officer. He did not look up. But there was the flicker in the Captain's voice.

"Go to the inn and fetch me . . ." the officer gave his commands. "Quick!" he added.

At the last word, the heart of the servant leapt with a flash, and he felt the strength come over his body. But he turned in mechanical obedience, and set off at a heavy run downhill, looking almost like a bear, his trousers bagging over his military boots. And the officer watched this blind, plunging run all the way.

But it was only the outside of the orderly's body that was obeying so humbly and mechanically. Inside had gradually accumulated a core into which all the energy of that young life was compact and concentrated. He executed his commission, and plodded quickly back uphill. There was a pain in his head, as he walked, that made him twist his features unknowingly. But hard there in the centre of his chest was himself, himself, firm, and not to be plucked to pieces.

The Captain had gone up into the wood. The orderly plodded through the hot, powerfully smelling zone of the company's atmosphere. He had a curious mass of energy inside him now. The Captain was less real than himself. He approached the green entrance to the wood. There, in the half-shade, he saw the horse standing, the sunshine and the flickering shadow of leaves dancing over his brown body. There was a clearing where timber had lately been felled. Here, in the gold-green shade beside the brilliant cup of sunshine, stood two figures, blue and pink, the bits of pink showing out plainly. The Captain was talking to his lieutenant.

The orderly stood on the edge of the bright clearing, where great trunks of trees, stripped and glistening, lay stretched like naked, brown-skinned bodies. Chips of wood littered the trampled floor, like splashed light, and the bases of the felled trees stood here and there, with their raw, level tops. Beyond was the brilliant, sunlit green of a beech.

"Then I will ride forward," the orderly heard his Captain say. The lieutenant saluted and strode away. He himself went forward. A hot flash passed through his belly, as he tramped towards his officer.

The Captain watched the rather heavy figure of the young soldier stumble forward, and his veins, too, ran hot. This was to be man to man between them. He yielded before the solid, stumbling figure with bent head. The orderly stopped and put the food on a level-sawn tree-base. The Captain watched the glistening, sun-inflamed, naked hands. He wanted to speak to the young soldier but could not. The servant propped a bottle against his thigh, pressed open the cork, and poured out the beer into the mug. He kept his head bent. The Captain accepted the mug.

"Hot!" he said, as if amiably.

The flame sprang out of the orderly's heart, nearly suffocating him.

"Yes, sir," he replied, between shut teeth.

And he heard the sound of the Captain's drinking, and he clenched his fists, such a strong comment came into his wrists. Then came the faint clang of the closing of the pot-lid. He looked up. The Captain was watching him. He glanced swiftly away. Then he saw the officer stoop and take a piece of bread from the tree-base. Again the flash of flame went through the young soldier, seeing the stiff body stoop beneath him, and his hands jerked. He looked away. He could feel the officer was nervous. The bread fell as it was being broken. The officer ate the other piece. The two men stood tense and still, the master laboriously chewing his bread, the servant staring with averted face, his fist clenched.

Then the young soldier started. The officer had pressed open the lid of the mug again. The orderly watched the lid of the mug, and the white hand that clenched the handle, as if he were fascinated. It was raised. The youth followed it with his eyes. And then he saw the thin, strong throat of the elder man moving up and down as he drank, the strong jaw working. And the instinct which had been jerking at the young man's wrists suddenly jerked free. He jumped, feeling as if it were rent in two by a strong flame.

The spur of the officer caught in a tree-root, he went down backwards with a crash, the middle of his back thudding sickeningly against a sharp-edged tree-base, the pot flying away. And in a second the orderly, with serious, earnest young face, and underlip between his teeth, had got his knee in the officer's chest and was pressing the chin backward over the farther edge of the tree-stump, pressing, with all his heart behind in a passion of relief, the tension of his wrists exquisite with relief. And with the base of his palms he shoved at the chin, with all his might. And it was pleasant, too, to have that chin, that hard jaw already slightly rough with beard, in his hands. He did not relax one hair's breadth, but, all the force of all his blood exulting in his thrust, he shoved back the head of the other man, till there was a little "cluck" and a crunching sensation. Then he felt as if his head went to vapour. Heavy convulsions shook the body of the officer, frightening and horrifying the young soldier. Yet it pleased him, too, to repress them. It pleased him to keep his hands pressing back the chin, to feel the chest of the other man yield in expiration to the weight of his strong, young knees, to feel the hard twitchings of the prostrate body jerking his own whole frame, which was pressed down on it.

But it went still. He could look into the nostrils of the other man, the eyes he could scarcely see. How curiously the mouth was pushed out, exaggerating the full lips, and the moustache bristling up from them. Then, with a start, he noticed the nostrils gradually filled with blood. The red brimmed, hesitated, ran over, and went in a thin trickle down the face to the eyes.

It shocked and distressed him. Slowly, he got up. The body twitched and sprawled there, inert. He stood and looked at it in silence. It was a pity *it* was broken. It represented more than the thing which had kicked and bullied him. He was afraid to look at the eyes. They were hideous now, only the whites showing, and the blood running to them. The face of the orderly was drawn with horror at the sight. Well, it was so. In his heart he was satisfied. He had hated the face of the Captain. It was extinguished now. There was a heavy relief in the orderly's soul. That was as it should be. But he could not bear to see the long, military body lying broken over the tree-base, the fine fingers crisped. He wanted to hide it away.

Quickly, busily, he gathered it up and pushed it under the felled tree-trunks, which rested their beautiful, smooth length either end on logs. The face was horrible with blood. He covered it with the helmet. Then he pushed the limbs straight and decent, and brushed the dead leaves off the fine cloth of the uniform. So, it lay quite still in the shadow under there. A little strip of sunshine ran along the breast, from a chink between the logs. The orderly sat by it for a few moments. Here his own life also ended.

Then, through his daze, he heard the lieutenant, in a loud voice, explaining to the men outside the wood, that they were to suppose the bridge on the river below was held by the enemy. Now they were to march to the attack in such and such a manner. The lieutenant had no gift of expression. The orderly, listening from habit, got muddled. And when the lieutenant began it all again he ceased to hear.

He knew he must go. He stood up. It surprised him that the leaves were glittering in the sun, and the chips of wood reflecting white from the ground. For him a change had come over the world. But for the rest it had not—all seemed the same. Only he had left it. And he could not go back. It was his duty to return with the beer-pot and the bottle. He could not. He had left all that. The lieutenant was still hoarsely explaining. He must go, or they would overtake him. And he could not bear contact with anyone now.

He drew his fingers over his eyes, trying to find out where he was. Then he turned away. He saw the horse standing in the path. He went up to it and mounted. It hurt him to sit in the saddle. The pain of keeping his seat occupied him as they cantered through the wood. He would not have minded anything, but he could not get away from the sense of being divided from the others. The path led out of the trees. On the edge of the wood he pulled up and stood watching. There in the spacious sunshine of the valley soldiers were moving in a little swarm. Every now and then, a man harrowing on a strip of fallow shouted to his oxen, at the turn. The village and the white-towered church was small in the sunshine. And he no longer belonged to it—he sat there, beyond, like a man outside in the dark. He had gone out from everyday life into the unknown, and he could not, he even did not want to go back.

Turning from the sun-blazing valley, he rode deep into the wood. Tree-trunks, like people standing grey and still, took no notice as he went. A doe, herself a moving bit of sunshine and shadow, went running through the flecked shade. There were bright green rents in the foliage. Then it was all pine wood, dark and cool. And he was sick with pain, he had an intolerable great pulse in his head, and he was sick. He had never been ill in his life. He felt lost, quite dazed with all this.

Trying to get down from the horse, he fell, astonished at the pain and his lack of balance. The horse shifted uneasily. He jerked its bridle and sent it cantering jerkily away. It was his last connection with the rest of things.

But he only wanted to lie down and not be disturbed. Stumbling through the trees, he came on a quiet place where beeches and pine trees grew on a slope. Immediately he had lain down and closed his eyes, his consciousness went racing on without him. A big pulse of sickness beat in him as if it throbbed through the whole earth. He was burning with dry heat. But he was too busy, too tearingly active in the incoherent race of delirium to observe.

III

He came to with a start. His mouth was dry and hard, his heart beat heavily, but he had not the energy to get up. His heart beat heavily. Where was he?—the barracks—at home? There was something knocking. And, making an effort, he looked round—trees, and litter of greenery, and reddish, bright, still pieces of sunshine on the floor. He did not believe he was himself, he did not believe what he saw. Something was knocking. He made a struggle towards consciousness, but relapsed. Then he struggled again. And gradually his surroundings fell into relationship with himself. He knew, and a great pang of fear went through his heart. Somebody was knocking. He could see the heavy, black rags of a fir tree overhead. Then everything went black. Yet he did not believe he had closed his eyes. He had not. Out of the blackness sight slowly emerged again. And someone was knocking. Quickly, he saw the blood-disfigured face of his Captain, which he hated. And he held himself still with horror. Yet, deep inside, he knew that it was so, the Captain should be dead. But the physical delirium got hold of him. Someone was knocking. He lay perfectly still, as if dead, with fear. And he went unconscious.

When he opened his eyes again, he started, seeing something creeping swiftly up a tree-trunk. It was a little bird. And the bird was whistling overhead. Tap-tap-tap—it was the small, quick bird rapping the tree-trunk with its beak, as if its head were a little round hammer. He watched it curiously. It shifted sharply, in its creeping fashion. Then, like a mouse, it slid down the bare trunk. Its swift creeping sent a flash of revulsion through him. He raised his head. It felt a great weight. Then, the little bird ran out of the shadow across a still patch of sunshine, its little head bobbing swiftly, its white legs twinkling brightly for a moment. How neat it was in its build, so compact, with pieces of white on its wings. There were several of them. They were so pretty—but they crept like swift, erratic mice, running here and there among the beech-mast.

He lay down again exhausted, and his consciousness lapsed. He had a horror of the little creeping birds. All his blood seemed to be darting and creeping in his head. And yet he could not move.

He came to with a further ache of exhaustion. There was the pain in his head, and the horrible sickness, and his inability to move. He had never been ill in his life. He did not know where he was or what he was. Probably he had got sunstroke. Or what else?—he had silenced the Captain for ever—some time ago—oh, a long time ago. There had been blood on his face, and his eyes had turned upwards. It was all right, somehow. It was peace. But now he had got beyond himself. He had never been here before. Was it life, or not life? He was by himself. They were in a big, bright place, those others, and he was outside. The town, all the country, a big bright place of light: and he was outside, here, in the darkened open beyond, where each thing existed alone. But they would all have to come out there sometime, those others. Little, and left behind him, they all were. There had been father and mother and sweetheart. What did they all matter? This was the open land.

He sat up. Something scuffled. It was a little brown squirrel running in lovely, undulating bounds over the floor, its red tail completing the undulation of its body—and then, as it sat up, furling and unfurling. He watched it, pleased. It ran on again, friskily, enjoying itself. It flew wildly at another squirrel, and they were chasing each other, and making little scolding, chattering noises. The soldier wanted to speak to them. But only a hoarse sound came out of his throat. The squirrels burst away—they flew up the trees. And then he saw the one peeping round at him, half-way up a tree-trunk. A start of fear went through him, though, in so far as he was conscious, he was amused. It still stayed, its little, keen face staring at him half-way up the tree-trunk, its little ears pricked up, its clawey little hands clinging to the bark, its white breast reared. He started from it in panic.

Struggling to his feet, he lurched away. He went on walking, walking, looking for something—for a drink. His brain felt hot and inflamed for want of water. He stumbled on. Then he did not know anything. He went unconscious as he walked. Yet he stumbled on, his mouth open.

When, to his dumb wonder, he opened his eyes on the world again, he no longer tried to remember what it was. There was thick, golden light behind golden-green glitterings, and tall, grey-purple shafts, and darknesses further off, surrounding him, growing deeper. He was conscious of a sense of arrival. He was amid the reality, on the real, dark bottom. But there was the thirst burning in his brain. He felt lighter, not so heavy. He supposed it was newness. The air was muttering with thunder. He thought he was walking wonderfully swiftly and was coming straight to relief—or was it to water.

Suddenly he stood still with fear. There was a tremendous flare of gold, immense—just a few dark trunks like bars between him and it. All the young level wheat was burnished gold glaring on its silky green. A woman, full-skirted, a black cloth on her head for head-dress, was passing like a block of shadow through the glistening green corn, into the full glare. There was a farm, too, pale blue in shadow, and the timber black. And there was a church spire, nearly fused away in the gold. The woman moved on, away from him. He had no language with which to speak to her. She was the bright, solid unreality. She would make a noise of words that would confuse him, and her eyes would look at him without seeing him. She was crossing there to the other side. He stood against a tree.

When at last he turned, looking down the long, bare grove whose flat bed was already filling dark, he saw the mountains in a wonder-light, not far away, and radiant. Behind the soft, grey ridge of the nearest range the further mountains stood golden and pale grey, the snow all radiant like pure, soft gold. So still, gleaming in the sky, fashioned pure out of the ore of the sky, they shone in their silence. He stood and looked at them, his face illuminated. And like the golden, lustrous gleaming of the snow he felt his own thirst bright in him. He stood and gazed, leaning against a tree. And then everything slid away into space.

During the night the lightning fluttered perpetually, making the whole sky white. He must have walked again. The world hung livid round him for moments, fields a level sheen of grey-green light, trees in dark bulk, and the range of clouds black across a white sky. Then the darkness fell like a shutter, and the night was whole. A faint flutter of a half-revealed world, that could not quite leap out of the darkness!—Then there again stood a sweep of pallor for the land, dark shapes looming, a range of clouds hanging overhead. The world was a ghostly shadow, thrown for a moment upon the pure darkness, which returned ever whole and complete.

And the mere delirium of sickness and fever went on inside him— his brain opening and shutting like the night—then sometimes convulsions of terror from something with great eyes that stared round a tree—then the long agony of the march, and the sun decomposing his blood—then the pang of hate for the Captain, followed by a pang of tenderness and ease. But everything was distorted, born of an ache and resolving into an ache.

In the morning he came definitely awake. Then his brain flamed with the sole horror of thirstiness! The sun was on his face, the dew was steaming from his wet clothes. Like one possessed, he got up. There, straight in front of him, blue and cool and tender, the mountains ranged across the pale edge of the morning sky. He wanted them —he wanted them alone—he wanted to leave himself and be identified with them. They did not move, they were still and soft, with white, gentle markings of snow. He stood still, mad with suffering, his hands crisping and clutching. Then he was twisting in a paroxysm on the grass.

He lay still, in a kind of dream of anguish. His thirst seemed to have separated itself from him, and to stand apart, a single demand. Then the pain he felt was another single self. Then there was the clog of his body, another separate thing. He was divided among all kinds of separate beings. There was some strange, agonized connection between them, but they were drawing further apart. Then they would all split. The sun, drilling down on him, was drilling through the bond. Then they would all fall, fall through the everlasting lapse of space. Then again, his consciousness reasserted itself. He roused on to his elbow and stared at the gleaming mountains. There they ranked, all still and wonderful between earth and heaven. He stared till his eyes went black, and the mountains, as they stood in their beauty, so clean and cool, seemed to have it, that which was lost in him.

IV

When the soldiers found him, three hours later, he was lying with his face over his arm, his black hair giving off heat under the sun.

But he was still alive. Seeing the open, black mouth, the young soldiers dropped him in horror.

He died in the hospital at night, without having seen again.

The doctors saw the bruises on his legs, behind, and were silent.

The bodies of the two men lay together, side by side, in the mortuary, the one white and slender, but laid rigidly at rest, the other looking as if every moment it must rouse into life again, so young and unused, from a slumber.

THE HORSE DEALER'S DAUGHTER

"Well, Mabel, and what are you going to do with yourself?" asked Joe, with foolish flippancy. He felt quite safe himself. Without listening for an answer, he turned aside, worked a grain of tobacco to the tip of his tongue, and spat it out. He did not care about anything, since he felt safe himself.

The three brothers and the sister sat round the desolate breakfast table, attempting some sort of desultory consultation. The morning's post had given the final tap to the family fortune, and all was over. The dreary dining-room itself, with its heavy mahogany furniture, looked as if it were waiting to be done away with.

But the consultation amounted to nothing. There was a strange air of ineffectuality about the three men, as they sprawled at table, smoking and reflecting vaguely on their own condition. The girl was alone, a rather short, sullen-looking young woman of twenty-seven. She did not share the same life as her brothers. She would have been good-looking, save for the impassive fixity of her face, "bulldog," as her brothers called it.

There was a confused tramping of horses' feet outside. The three men all sprawled round in their chairs to watch. Beyond the dark holly-bushes that separated the strip of lawn from the highroad, they

THE HORSE DEALER'S DAUGHTER. From *England, My England* by D. H. Lawrence. Copyright 1922 by Thomas Seltzer, Inc., 1950 by Frieda Lawrence. Reprinted by permission of The Viking Press, Inc., New York.

could see a cavalcade of shire horses swinging out of their own yard, being taken for exercise. This was the last time. These were the last horses that would go through their hands. The young men watched with critical, callous look. They were all frightened at the collapse of their lives, and the sense of disaster in which they were involved left them no inner freedom.

Yet they were three fine, well-set fellows enough. Joe, the eldest, was a man of thirty-three, broad and handsome in a hot, flushed way. His face was red, he twisted his black moustache over a thick finger, his eyes were shallow and restless. He had a sensual way of uncovering his teeth when he laughed, and his bearing was stupid. Now he watched the horses with a glazed look of helplessness in his eyes, a certain stupor of downfall.

The great draught-horses swung past. They were tied head to tail, four of them, and they heaved along to where a lane branched off from the highroad, planting their great hoofs floutingly in the fine black mud, swinging their great rounded haunches sumptuously, and trotting a few sudden steps as they were led into the lane, round the corner. Every movement showed a massive, slumbrous strength, and a stupidity which held them in subjection. The groom at the head looked back, jerking the leading rope. And the cavalcade moved out of sight up the lane, the tail of the last horse, bobbed up tight and stiff, held out taut from the swinging great haunches as they rocked behind the hedges in a motion like sleep.

Joe watched with glazed hopeless eyes. The horses were almost like his own body to him. He felt he was done for now. Luckily he was engaged to a woman as old as himself, and therefore her father, who was steward of a neighbouring estate, would provide him with a job. He would marry and go into harness. His life was over, he would be a subject animal now.

He turned uneasily aside, the retreating steps of the horses echoing in his ears. Then, with foolish recklessness, he reached for the scraps of bacon-rind from the plates, and making a faint whistling sound, flung them to the terrier that lay against the fender. He watched the dog swallow them, and waited till the creature looked into his eyes. Then a faint grin came on his face, and in a high, foolish voice he said:

"You won't get much more bacon, shall you, you little bitch?"

The dog faintly and dismally wagged its tail, then lowered its haunches, circled round, and lay down again.

There was another helpless silence at the table. Joe sprawled uneasily in his seat, not willing to go till the family conclave was dissolved. Fred Henry, the second brother, was erect, clean-limbed, alert. He had watched the passing of the horses with more sang-froid. If he was an animal, like Joe, he was an animal which controls, not one which is controlled. He was master of any horse, and he carried himself with a well-tempered air of mastery. But he was not master of the situations of life. He pushed his coarse brown moustache upwards, off his lip, and glanced irritably at his sister, who sat impassive and inscrutable.

"You'll go and stop with Lucy for a bit, shan't you?" he asked. The girl did not answer.

"I don't see what else you can do," persisted Fred Henry.

"Go as a skivvy," Joe interpolated laconically.

The girl did not move a muscle.

"If I was her, I should go in training for a nurse," said Malcolm, the youngest of them all. He was the baby of the family, a young man of twenty-two, with a fresh, jaunty *museau*.

But Mabel did not take any notice of him. They had talked at her and round her for so many years, that she hardly heard them at all.

The marble clock on the mantelpiece softly chimed the half-hour, the dog rose uneasily from the hearthrug and looked at the party at the breakfast table. But still they sat on in ineffectual conclave.

"Oh, all right," said Joe suddenly, apropos of nothing. "I'll get a move on."

He pushed back his chair, straddled his knees with a downward jerk, to get them free, in horsey fashion, and went to the fire. Still he did not go out of the room; he was curious to know what the others would do or say. He began to charge his pipe, looking down at the dog and saying, in a high, affected voice:

"Going wi' me? Going wi' me are ter? Tha'rt goin' further tha that counts on just now, dost hear?"

The dog faintly wagged its tail, the man stuck out his jaw and covered his pipe with his hands, and puffed intently, losing himself in the tobacco, looking down all the while at the dog with an absent brown eye. The dog looked up at him in mournful distrust. Joe stood with his knees stuck out, in real horsey fashion.

"Have you had a letter from Lucy?" Fred Henry asked of his sister.

"Last week," came the neutral reply.

"And what does she say?"

There was no answer.

"Does she *ask* you to go and stop there?" persisted Fred Henry.

"She says I can if I like."

"Well, then, you'd better. Tell her you'll come on Monday."

This was received in silence.

"That's what you'll do then, is it?" said Fred Henry in some exasperation.

But she made no answer. There was a silence of futility and irritation in the room. Malcolm grinned fatuously.

"You'll have to make up your mind between now and next Wednesday," said Joe loudly, "or else find yourself lodgings on the kerbstone."

The face of the young woman darkened, but she sat on immutable.

"Here's Jack Fergusson!" exclaimed Malcolm, who was looking aimlessly out of the window.

"Where?" exclaimed Joe, loudly.

"Just gone past."

"Coming in?"

Malcolm craned his neck to see the gate.

"Yes," he said.

There was a silence. Mabel sat on like one condemned, at the head of the table. Then a whistle was heard from the kitchen. The dog got up and barked sharply. Joe opened the door and shouted:

"Come on."

After a moment a young man entered. He was muffled up in overcoat and a purple woollen scarf, and his tweed cap, which he did not remove, was pulled down on his head. He was of medium height, his face was rather long and pale, his eyes looked tired.

"Hello, Jack! Well, Jack!" exclaimed Malcolm and Joe. Fred Henry merely said, "Jack."

"What's doing?" asked the newcomer, evidently addressing Fred Henry.

"Same. We've got to be out by Wednesday. Got a cold?"

"I have—got it bad, too."

"Why don't you stop in?"

"*Me* stop in? When I can't stand on my legs, perhaps I shall have a chance." The young man spoke huskily. He had a slight Scotch accent.

"It's a knock-out, isn't it," said Joe, boisterously, "if a doctor goes round croaking with a cold. Looks bad for the patients, doesn't it?"

The young doctor looked at him slowly.

"Anything the matter with *you,* then?" he asked sarcastically.

"Not as I know of. Damn your eyes, I hope not. Why?"

"I thought you were very concerned about the patients, wondered if you might be one yourself."

"Damn it, no, I've never been patient to no flaming doctor, and hope I never shall be," returned Joe.

At this point Mabel rose from the table, and they all seemed to become aware of her existence. She began putting the dishes together. The young doctor looked at her, but did not address her. He had not greeted her. She went out of the room with the tray, her face impassive and unchanged.

"When are you off then, all of you?" asked the doctor.

"I'm catching the eleven-forty," replied Malcolm. "Are you goin' down wi' th' trap, Joe?"

"Yes, I've told you I'm going down wi' th' trap, haven't I?"

"We'd better be getting her in then. So long, Jack, if I don't see you before I go," said Malcolm, shaking hands.

He went out, followed by Joe, who seemed to have his tail between his legs.

"Well, this is the devil's own," exclaimed the doctor, when he was left alone with Fred Henry. "Going before Wednesday, are you?"

"That's the orders," replied the other.

"Where, to Northampton?"

"That's it."

"The devil," exclaimed Fergusson, with quiet chagrin.

And there was silence between the two.

"All settled up, are you?" asked Fergusson.

"About."

There was another pause.

"Well, I shall miss yer, Freddy, boy," said the young doctor.

"And I shall miss thee, Jack," returned the other.

"Miss you like hell," mused the doctor.

Fred Henry turned aside. There was nothing to say. Mabel came in again, to finish clearing the table.

"What are *you* going to do, then, Miss Pervin?" asked Fergusson. "Going to your sister's, are you?"

Mabel looked at him with her steady, dangerous eyes, that always made him uncomfortable, unsettling his superficial ease.

"No," she said.

"Well, what in the name of fortune *are* you going to do? Say what you mean to do," cried Fred Henry, with futile intensity.

But she only averted her head, and continued her work. She folded the white table-cloth, and put on the chenille cloth.

"The sulkiest bitch that ever trod!" muttered her brother.

But she finished her task with perfectly impassive face, the young doctor watching her interestedly all the while. Then she went out.

Fred Henry stared after her, clenching his lips, his blue eyes fixing in sharp antagonism, as he made a grimace of sour exasperation.

"You could bray her into bits, and that's all you'd get out of her," he said in a small, narrowed tone.

The doctor smiled faintly.

"What's she *going* to do, then?" he asked.

"Strike me if *I* know!" returned the other.

There was a pause. Then the doctor stirred.

"I'll be seeing you to-night, shall I?" he said to his friend.

"Ay—where's it to be? Are we going over to Jessdale?"

"I don't know. I've got a cold on me. I'll come round to the Moon and Stars, anyway."

"Let Lizzie and May miss their night for once, eh?"

"That's it—if I feel as I do now."

"All's one—"

The two young men went through the passage and down to the back door together. The house was large, but it was servantless now and desolate. At the back was a small bricked house-yard, and beyond that a big square, gravelled fine and red, and having stables on two sides. Sloping, dank, winter-dark fields stretched away on the open sides.

But the stables were empty. Joseph Pervin, the father of the family, had been a man of no education, who had become a fairly large horse dealer. The stables had been full of horses, there was a great turmoil and come-and-go of horses and of dealers and grooms. Then the kitchen was full of servants. But of late things had declined. The old man had married a second time, to retrieve his fortune. Now he was dead and everything was gone to the dogs, there was nothing but debt and threatening.

For months, Mabel had been servantless in the big house, keeping the home together in penury for her ineffectual brothers. She had kept house for ten years. But previously it was with unstinted means. Then, however brutal and coarse everything was, the sense of money had kept her proud, confident. The men might be foul-mouthed, the women in the kitchen might have bad reputations, her brothers might have illegitimate children. But so long as there was money, the girl herself felt established, and brutally proud, reserved.

No company came to the house, save dealers and coarse men. Mabel had no associates of her own sex, after her sister went away. But she did not mind. She went regularly to church, she attended to her father. And she lived in the memory of her mother, who had died when she was fourteen, and whom she had loved. She had loved her father, too, in a different way, depending upon him, and feeling secure in him, until at the age of fifty-four he married again. And then she had set hard against him. Now he had died and left them all hopelessly in debt.

She had suffered badly during the period of poverty. Nothing, however, could shake the curious sullen, animal pride that dominated each member of the family. Now, for Mabel, the end had come. Still she would not cast about her. She would follow her own way just the same. She would always hold the keys of her own situation. Mindless and persistent, she endured from day to day. Why should she think? Why should she answer anybody? It was enough that this was the end, and there was no way out. She need not pass any more darkly along the main street of the small town, avoiding every eye. She need not demean herself any more, going into the shops and buying the cheapest food. This was at an end. She thought of nobody, not even of herself. Mindless and persistent, she seemed in a sort of ecstasy to be coming nearer to her fulfilment, her own glorification, approaching her dead mother, who was glorified.

In the afternoon she took a little bag, with shears and sponge and a small scrubbing brush, and went out. It was a grey, wintry day, with saddened, dark green fields and an atmosphere blackened by the smoke of foundries not far off. She went quickly, darkly along the causeway, heeding nobody, through the town to the churchyard.

There she always felt secure, as if no one could see her, although as a matter of fact she was exposed to the stare of everyone who passed along under the churchyard wall. Nevertheless, once under the shadow of the great looming church, among the graves, she felt immune from the world, reserved within the thick churchyard wall as in another country.

Carefully she clipped the grass from the grave, and arranged the pinky white, small chrysanthemums in the tin cross. When this was done, she took an empty jar from a neighbouring grave, brought water, and carefully, most scrupulously sponged the marble headstone and the coping-stone.

It gave her sincere satisfaction to do this. She felt in immediate contact with the world of her mother. She took minute pains, went through the park in a state bordering on pure happiness, as if in performing this task she came into a subtle, intimate connection with her mother. For the life she followed here in the world was far less real than the world of death she inherited from her mother.

The doctor's house was just by the church. Fergusson, being a mere hired assistant, was slave to the country-side. As he hurried now to attend the outpatients in the surgery, glancing across the graveyard with his quick eye, he saw the girl at her task at the grave. She seemed so intent and remote, it was like looking into another world. Some mystical element was touched in him. He slowed down as he walked, catching her as if spell-bound.

She lifted her eyes, feeling him looking. Their eyes met. And each looked away again at once, each feeling, in some way, found out by the other. He lifted his cap and passed on down the road. There remained distinct in his consciousness, like a vision, the memory of her face, lifted from the tombstone in the churchyard, and looking at him with slow, large, portentous eyes. It *was* portentous, her face. It seemed to mesmerize him. There was a heavy power in her eyes which laid hold of his whole being, as if he had drunk some powerful drug. He had been feeling weak and done before. Now the life came back into him, he felt delivered from his own fretted, daily self.

He finished his duties at the surgery as quickly as might be, hastily filling up the bottles of the waiting people with cheap drugs. Then, in perpetual haste, he set off again to visit several cases in another part of his round, before teatime. At all times he preferred to walk if he could, but particularly when he was not well. He fancied the motion restored him.

The afternoon was falling. It was grey, deadened, and wintry, with a slow, moist, heavy coldness sinking in and deadening all the faculties. But why should he think or notice? He hastily climbed the hill and turned across the dark green fields, following the black cinder-track. In the distance, across a shallow dip in the country, the small town was clustered like smouldering ash, a tower, a spire, a heap of low, raw, extinct houses. And on the nearest fringe of the town, sloping into the dip, was Oldmeadow, the Pervins' house. He could see the stables and the outbuildings distinctly, as they lay towards him on the slope. Well, he would not go there many more times! Another resource would be lost to him, another place gone; the only company he cared for in the alien, ugly little town he was losing. Nothing but work, drudgery, constant hastening from dwelling to dwelling among the colliers and the iron-workers. It wore him out, but at the same time he had a craving for it. It was a stimulant to him to be in the homes of the working people, moving as it were through the innermost body of their life. His nerves were excited and gratified. He could come so near, into the very lives of the rough, inarticulate, powerfully emotional men and women. He grumbled, he said he hated the hellish hole. But as a matter of fact it excited him, the contact with the rough, strongly-feeling people was a stimulant applied direct to his nerves.

Below Oldmeadow, in the green, shallow, soddened hollow of fields, lay a square, deep pond. Roving across the landscape, the doctor's quick eye detected a figure in black passing through the gate of the field, down towards the pond. He looked again. It would be Mabel Pervin. His mind suddenly became alive and attentive.

Why was she going down there? He pulled up on the path on the slope above, and stood staring. He could just make sure of the small black figure moving in the hollow of the failing day. He seemed to see her in the midst of such obscurity, that he was like a clairvoyant, seeing rather with the mind's eye than with ordinary sight. Yet he could see her positively enough, whilst he kept his eye attentive. He felt, if he looked away from her, in the thick, ugly falling dusk, he would lose her altogether.

He followed her minutely as she moved, direct and intent, like something transmitted rather than stirring in voluntary activity, straight down the field towards the pond. There she stood on the bank for a moment. She never raised her head. Then she waded slowly into the water.

He stood motionless as the small black figure walked slowly and deliberately towards the centre of the pond, very slowly, gradually moving deeper into the motionless water, and still moving forward as the water got up to her breast. Then he could see her no more in the dusk of the dead afternoon.

"There!" he exclaimed. "Would you believe it?"

And he hastened straight down, running over the wet, soddened fields, pushing through the hedges, down into the depression of callous wintry obscurity. It took him several minutes to come to the pond. He stood on the bank, breathing heavily. He could see nothing. His eyes seemed to penetrate the dead water. Yes, perhaps that was the dark shadow of her black clothing beneath the surface of the water.

He slowly ventured into the pond. The bottom was deep, soft clay, he sank in, and the water clasped dead cold round his legs. As he stirred he could smell the cold, rotten clay that fouled up into the water. It was objectionable in his lungs. Still, repelled and yet not heeding, he moved deeper into the pond. The cold water rose over his thighs, over his loins, upon his abdomen. The lower part of his body was all sunk in the hideous cold element. And the bottom was so deeply soft and uncertain he was afraid of pitching with his mouth underneath. He could not swim, and was afraid.

He crouched a little, spreading his hands under the water and moving them round, trying to feel for her. The dead cold pond swayed upon his chest. He moved again, a little deeper, and again, with his hands underneath, he felt all around under the water. And he touched her clothing. But it evaded his fingers. He made a desperate effort to grasp it.

And so doing he lost his balance and went under, horribly, suffocating in the foul earthy water, struggling madly for a few moments. At last, after what seemed an eternity, he got his footing, rose again into the air and looked around. He gasped, and knew he was in the world. Then he looked at the water. She had risen near him. He grasped her clothing, and drawing her nearer, turned to take his way to land again.

He went very slowly, carefully, absorbed in the slow progress. He rose higher, climbing out of the pond. The water was now only about his legs; he was thankful, full of relief to be out of the clutches of the pond. He lifted her and staggered on to the bank, out of the horror of wet, grey clay.

He laid her down on the bank. She was quite unconscious and running with water. He made the water come from her mouth, he worked to restore her. He did not have to work very long before he could feel the breathing begin again in her; she was breathing naturally. He worked a little longer. He could feel her live beneath his hands; she was coming back. He wiped her face, wrapped her in his overcoat, looked round into the dim, dark grey world, then lifted her and staggered down the bank and across the fields.

It seemed an unthinkably long way, and his burden so heavy he felt he would never get to the house. But at last he was in the stable-yard, and then in the house-yard. He opened the door and went into the house. In the kitchen he laid her down on the hearthrug, and called. The house was empty. But the fire was burning in the grate.

Then again he kneeled to attend her. She was breathing regularly, her eyes were wide open and as if conscious, but there seemed something missing in her look. She was conscious in herself, but unconscious of her surroundings.

He ran upstairs, took blankets from a bed, and put them before the fire to warm. Then he removed her saturated, earthy-smelling clothing, rubbed her dry with a towel, and wrapped her naked in the blankets. Then he went into the dining-room, to look for spirits. There was a little whisky. He drank a gulp himself, and put some into her mouth.

The effect was instantaneous. She looked full into his face, as if she had been seeing him for some time, and yet had only just become conscious of him.

"Dr. Fergusson?" she said.

"What?" he answered.

He was divesting himself of his coat, intending to find some dry clothing upstairs. He could not bear the smell of the dead, clayey water, and he was mortally afraid for his own health.

"What did I do?" she asked.

"Walked into the pond," he replied. He had begun to shudder like one sick, and could hardly attend to her. Her eyes remained full on him, he seemed to be going dark in his mind, looking back at her helplessly. The shuddering became quieter in him, his life came back in him, dark and unknowing, but strong again.

"Was I out of my mind?" she asked, while her eyes were fixed on him all the time

"Maybe, for the moment," he replied. He felt quiet, because his strength had come back. The strange fretful strain had left him.

"Am I out of my mind now?" she asked.

"Are you?" he reflected a moment. "No," he answered truthfully. "I don't see that you are." He turned his face aside. He was afraid now, because he felt dazed, and felt dimly that her power was stronger than his, in this issue. And she continued to look at him fixedly all the time. "Can you tell me where I shall find some dry things to put on?" he asked.

"Did you dive into the pond for me?" she asked.

"No," he answered. "I walked in. But I went in overhead as well."

There was silence for a moment. He hesitated. He very much wanted to go upstairs to get into dry clothing. But there was another desire in him. And she seemed to hold him. His will seemed to have gone to sleep, and left him, standing there slack before her. But he felt warm inside himself. He did not shudder at all, though his clothes were sodden on him.

"Why did you?" she asked.

"Because I didn't want you to do such a foolish thing," he said.

"It wasn't foolish," she said, still gazing at him as she lay on the floor, with a sofa cushion under her head. "It was the right thing to do. *I* knew best, then."

"I'll go and shift these wet things," he said. But still he had not the power to move out of her presence, until she sent him. It was as if she had the life of his body in her hands, and he could not extricate himself. Or perhaps he did not want to.

Suddenly she sat up. Then she became aware of her own immediate condition. She felt the blankets about her, she knew her own limbs. For a moment it seemed as if her reason were going. She looked round, with wild eye, as if seeking something. He stood still with fear. She saw her clothing lying scattered.

"Who undressed me?" she asked, her eyes resting full and inevitable on his face.

"I did," he replied, "to bring you round."

For some moments she sat and gazed at him awfully, her lips parted.

"Do you love me, then?" she asked.

He only stood and stared at her, fascinated. His soul seemed to melt.

She shuffled forward on her knees, and put her arms round him, round his legs, as he stood there, pressing her breasts against his knees and thighs, clutching him with strange, convulsive certainty, pressing his thighs against her, drawing him to her face, her throat, as she looked up at him with flaring, humble eyes of transfiguration, triumphant in first possession.

"You love me," she murmured, in strange transport, yearning and triumphant and confident. "You love me. I know you love me, I know."

And she was passionately kissing his knees, through the wet clothing, passionately and indiscriminately kissing his knees, his legs, as if unaware of everything.

He looked down at the tangled wet hair, the wild, bare, animal shoulders. He was amazed, bewildered, and afraid. He had never thought of loving her. He had never wanted to love her. When he rescued her and restored her, he was a doctor, and she was a patient. He had no single personal thought of her. Nay, this introduction of the personal element was very distasteful to him, a violation of his professional honour. It was horrible to have her there embracing his knees. It was horrible. He revolted from it, violently. And yet—and yet—he had not the power to break away.

She looked at him again, with the same supplication of powerful love, and that same transcendent, frightening light of triumph. In view of the delicate flame which seemed to come from her face like a light, he was powerless. And yet he had never intended to love her. He had never intended. And something stubborn in him could not give way.

"You love me," she repeated, in a murmur of deep, rhapsodic assurance. "You love me."

Her hands were drawing him, drawing him down to her. He was afraid, even a little horrified. For he had, really, no intention of loving her. Yet her hands were drawing him towards her. He put out his hand quickly to steady himself, and grasped her bare shoulder. A flame seemed to burn the hand that grasped her soft shoulder. He had no intention of loving her: his whole will was against his yielding. It was horrible. And yet wonderful was the touch of her shoulders, beautiful the shining of her face. Was she perhaps mad? He had a horror of yielding to her. Yet something in him ached also.

He had been staring away at the door, away from her. But his hand remained on her shoulder. She had gone suddenly very still. He looked down at her. Her eyes were now wide with fear, with doubt, the light was dying from her face, a shadow of terrible greyness was returning. He could not bear the touch of her eyes' question upon him, and the look of death behind the question.

With an inward groan he gave way, and let his heart yield towards her. A sudden gentle smile came on his face. And her eyes, which never left his face, slowly, slowly filled with tears. He watched the strange water rise in her eyes, like some slow fountain coming up. And his heart seemed to burn and melt away in his breast.

He could not bear to look at her any more. He dropped on his knees and caught her head with his arms and pressed her face against his throat. She was very still. His heart, which seemed to have broken, was burning with a kind of agony in his breast. And he felt her slow, hot tears wetting his throat. But he could not move.

He felt the hot tears wet his neck and the hollows of his neck, and he remained motionless, suspended through one of man's eternities. Only now it had become indispensable to him to have her face pressed close to him; he could never let her go again. He could never let her head go away from the close touch of his arm. He wanted to remain like that for ever, with his heart hurting him in a pain that was also life to him. Without knowing, he was looking down on her damp, soft brown hair.

Then, as it were suddenly, he smelt the horrid stagnant smell of that water. And at the same moment she drew away from him and looked at him. Her eyes were wistful and unfathomable. He was afraid of them, and he fell to kissing her, not knowing what he was doing. He wanted her eyes not to have that terrible, wistful, unfathomable look.

When she turned her face to him again, a faint delicate flush was glowing, and there was again dawning that terrible shining of joy in her eyes, which really terrified him, and yet which he now wanted to see, because he feared the look of doubt still more.

"You love me?" she said, rather faltering.

"Yes." The word cost him a painful effort. Not because it wasn't true. But because it was too newly true, the *saying* seemed to tear open again his newly-torn heart. And he hardly wanted it to be true, even now.

She lifted her face to him, and he bent forward and kissed her on the mouth, gently, with the one kiss that is an eternal pledge. And as he kissed her his heart strained again in his breast. He never intended to love her. But now it was over. He had crossed over the gulf to her, and all that he had left behind had shrivelled and become void.

After the kiss, her eyes again slowly filled with tears. She sat still, away from him, with her face drooped aside, and her hands folded in her lap. The tears fell very slowly. There was complete silence. He too sat there motionless and silent on the hearthrug. The strange pain of his heart that was broken seemed to consume him. That he should love her? That this was love! That he should be ripped open in this way! Him, a doctor! How they would all jeer if they knew! It was agony to him to think they might know.

In the curious naked pain of the thought he looked again to her. She was sitting there drooped into a muse. He saw a tear fall, and his heart flared hot. He saw for the first time that one of her shoulders was quite uncovered, one arm bare, he could see one of her small breasts; dimly, because it had become almost dark in the room.

"Why are you crying?" he asked, in an altered voice.

She looked up at him, and behind her tears the consciousness of her situation for the first time brought a dark look of shame to her eyes.

"I'm not crying, really," she said, watching him half frightened.

He reached his hand, and softly closed it on her bare arm.

"I love you! I love you!" he said in a soft, low vibrating voice, unlike himself.

She shrank, and dropped her head. The soft, penetrating grip of his hand on her arm distressed her. She looked up at him.

"I want to go," she said. "I want to go and get you some dry things."

"Why?" he said. "I'm all right."

"But I want to go," she said. "And I want you to change your things."

He released her arm, and she wrapped herself in the blanket, looking at him rather frightened. And still she did not rise.

"Kiss me," she said wistfully.

He kissed her, but briefly, half in anger.

Then, after a second, she rose nervously, all mixed up in the blanket. He watched her in her confusion, as she tried to extricate herself and wrap herself up so that she could walk. He watched her relentlessly, as she knew. And as she went, the blanket trailing, and as he saw a glimpse of her feet and her white leg, he tried to remember her as she was when he had wrapped her in the blanket. But then he didn't want to remember, because she had been nothing to him then, and his nature revolted from remembering her as she was when she was nothing to him.

A tumbling, muffled noise from within the dark house startled him. Then he heard her voice:—"There are clothes." He rose and went to the foot of the stairs, and gathered up the garments she had thrown down. Then he came back to the fire, to rub himself down and dress. He grinned at his own appearance when he had finished.

The fire was sinking, so he put on coal. The house was now quite dark, save for the light of a street-lamp that shone in faintly from beyond the holly trees. He lit the gas with matches he found on the mantelpiece. Then he emptied the pockets of his own clothes, and threw all his wet things in a heap into the scullery. After which he gathered up her sodden clothes, gently, and put them in a separate heap on the copper-top in the scullery.

It was six o'clock on the clock. His own watch had stopped. He ought to go back to the surgery. He waited, and still she did not come down. So he went to the foot of the stairs and called.

"I shall have to go."

Almost immediately he heard her coming down. She had on her best dress of black voile, and her hair was tidy, but still damp. She looked at him—and in spite of herself, smiled.

"I don't like you in those clothes," she said.

"Do I look a sight?" he answered.

They were shy of one another.

"I'll make you some tea," she said.

"No, I must go."

"Must you?" And she looked at him again with the wide, strained, doubtful eyes. And again, from the pain of his breast, he knew how he loved her. He went and bent to kiss her, gently, passionately, with his heart's painful kiss.

"And my hair smells so horrible," she murmured in distraction. "And I'm so awful, I'm so awful. Oh, no, I'm too awful." And she broke into bitter, heart-broken sobbing. "You can't want to love me, I'm horrible."

"Don't be silly, don't be silly," he said, trying to comfort her, kissing her, holding her in his arms. "I want you, I want to marry you, we're going to be married, quickly, quickly—tomorrow if I can."

But she only sobbed terribly, and cried:

"I feel awful. I feel awful. I feel I'm horrible to you."

"No, I want you, I want you," was all he answered, blindly, with that terrible intonation which frightened her almost more than her horror lest he should *not* want her.

THE ROCKING-HORSE WINNER

There was a woman who was beautiful, who started with all the advantages, yet she had no luck. She married for love, and the love turned to dust. She had bonny children, yet she felt they had been thrust upon her, and she could not love them. They looked at her coldly, as if they were finding fault with her. And hurriedly she felt she must cover up some fault in herself. Yet what it was that she must cover up she never knew. Nevertheless, when her children were present, she always felt the centre of her heart go hard. This troubled her, and in her manner she was all the more gentle and anxious for her children, as if she loved them very much. Only she herself knew that at the centre of her heart was a hard little place that could not feel love, no, not for anybody. Everybody else said of her: "She is such a good mother. She adores her children." Only she herself, and her children themselves, knew it was not so. They read it in each other's eyes.

There were a boy and two little girls. They lived in a pleasant house, with a garden, and they had discreet servants, and felt themselves superior to anyone in the neighbourhood.

Although they lived in style, they felt always an anxiety in the house. There was never enough money. The mother had a small income, and the father had a small income, but not nearly enough for

THE ROCKING-HORSE WINNER. From *The Lovely Lady* by D. H. Lawrence. Copyright 1933 by the Estate of D. H. Lawrence. Reprinted by permission of The Viking Press, Inc., New York.

the social position which they had to keep up. The father went in to town to some office. But though he had good prospects, these prospects never materialized. There was always the grinding sense of the shortage of money, though the style was always kept up.

At last the mother said: "I will see if *I* can't make something." But she did not know where to begin. She racked her brains, and tried this thing and the other, but could not find anything successful. The failure made deep lines come into her face. Her children were growing up, they would have to go to school. There must be more money, there must be more money. The father, who was always very handsome and expensive in his tastes, seemed as if he never *would* be able to do anything worth doing. And the mother, who had a great belief in herself, did not succeed any better, and her tastes were just as expensive.

And so the house came to be haunted by the unspoken phrase: *There must be more money! There must be more money!* The children could hear it all the time, though nobody said it aloud. They heard it at Christmas, when the expensive and splendid toys filled the nursery. Behind the shining modern rocking-horse, behind the smart doll's-house, a voice would start whispering: "There *must* be more money! There *must* be more money!" And the children would stop playing, to listen for a moment. They would look into each other's eyes, to see if they had all heard. And each one saw in the eyes of the other two that they too had heard. "There *must* be more money! There *must* be more money!"

It came whispering from the springs of the still-swaying rocking-horse, and even the horse, bending his wooden, champing head, heard it. The big doll, sitting so pink and smirking in her new pram, could hear it quite plainly, and seemed to be smirking all the more self-consciously because of it. The foolish puppy, too, that took the place of the teddy-bear, he was looking so extraordinarily foolish for no other reason but that he heard the secret whisper all over the house: "There *must* be more money!"

Yet nobody ever said it aloud. The whisper was everywhere, and therefore no one spoke it. Just as no one ever says: "We are breathing!" in spite of the fact that breath is coming and going all the time.

"Mother," said the boy Paul one day, "why don't we keep a car of our own? Why do we always use uncle's, or else a taxi?"

"Because we're the poor members of the family," said the mother.

"But why *are* we, mother?"

"Well—I suppose," she said slowly and bitterly, "it's because your father has no luck."

The boy was silent for some time.

"Is luck money, mother?" he asked rather timidly.

"No, Paul. Not quite. It's what causes you to have money."

"Oh!" said Paul vaguely. "I thought when Uncle Oscar said *filthy lucker,* it meant money."

"*Filthy lucre* does mean money," said the mother. "But it's lucre, not luck."

"Oh!" said the boy. "Then what *is* luck, mother?"

"It's what causes you to have money. If you're lucky you have money. That's why it's better to be born lucky than rich. If you're rich, you may lose your money. But if you're lucky, you will always get more money."

"Oh! Will you? And is father not lucky?"

"Very unlucky, I should say," she said bitterly.

The boy watched her with unsure eyes.

"Why?" he asked.

"I don't know. Nobody ever knows why one person is lucky and another unlucky."

"Don't they? Nobody at all? Does *nobody* know?"

"Perhaps God. But He never tells."

"He ought to, then. And aren't you lucky either, mother?"

"I can't be, if I married an unlucky husband."

"But by yourself, aren't you?"

"I used to think I was, before I married. Now I think I am very unlucky indeed."

"Why?"

"Well—never mind! Perhaps I'm not really," she said.

The child looked at her, to see if she meant it. But he saw, by the lines of her mouth, that she was only trying to hide something from him.

"Well, anyhow," he said stoutly, "I'm a lucky person."

"Why?" said his mother, with a sudden laugh.

He stared at her. He didn't even know why he had said it.

"God told me," he asserted, brazening it out.

"I hope He did, dear!" she said, again with a laugh, but rather bitter

"He did, mother!"

"Excellent!" said the mother, using one of her husband's exclamations.

The boy saw she did not believe him; or, rather, that she paid no attention to his assertion. This angered him somewhat, and made him want to compel her attention.

He went off by himself, vaguely, in a childish way, seeking for the clue to "luck." Absorbed, taking no heed of other people, he went about with a sort of stealth, seeking inwardly for luck. He wanted luck, he wanted it, he wanted it. When the two girls were playing dolls in the nursery, he would sit on his big rocking-horse, charging madly into space, with a frenzy that made the little girls peer at him uneasily. Wildly the horse careered, the waving dark hair of the boy tossed, his eyes had a strange glare in them. The little girls dared not speak to him.

When he had ridden to the end of his mad little journey, he climbed down and stood in front of his rocking-horse, staring fixedly into its lowered face. Its red mouth was slightly open, its big eye was wide and glassy-bright.

"Now!" he would silently command the snorting steed. "Now, take me to where there is luck! Now take me!"

And he would slash the horse on the neck with the little whip he had asked Uncle Oscar for. He *knew* the horse could take him to where there was luck, if only he forced it. So he would mount again, and start on his furious ride, hoping at last to get there. He knew he could get there.

"You'll break your horse, Paul!" said the nurse.

"He's always riding like that! I wish he'd leave off!" said his elder sister Joan.

But he only glared down on them in silence. Nurse gave him up. She could make nothing of him. Anyhow he was growing beyond her.

One day his mother and his Uncle Oscar came in when he was on one of his furious rides. He did not speak to them.

"Hallo, you young jockey! Riding a winner?" said his uncle.

"Aren't you growing too big for a rocking-horse? You're not a very little boy any longer, you know," said his mother.

But Paul only gave a blue glare from his big, rather close-set eyes. He would speak to nobody when he was in full tilt. His mother watched him with an anxious expression on her face.

At last he suddenly stopped forcing his horse into the mechanical gallop, and slid down.

"Well, I got there!" he announced fiercely, his blue eyes still flaring, and his sturdy long legs straddling apart.

"Where did you get to?" asked his mother.

"Where I wanted to go," he flared back at her.

"That's right, son!" said Uncle Oscar. "Don't you stop till you get there. What's the horse's name?"

"He doesn't have a name," said the boy.

"Gets on without all right?" asked the uncle.

"Well, he has different names. He was called Sansovino last week."

"Sansovino, eh? Won the Ascot. How did you know his name?"

"He always talks about horse-races with Bassett," said Joan.

The uncle was delighted to find that his small nephew was posted with all the racing news. Bassett, the young gardener, who had been wounded in the left foot in the war and had got his present job through Oscar Cresswell, whose batman he had been, was a perfect blade of the "turf." He lived in the racing events, and the small boy lived with him.

Oscar Cresswell got it all from Bassett.

"Master Paul comes and asks me, so I can't do more than tell him, sir," said Bassett, his face terribly serious, as if he were speaking of religious matters.

"And does he ever put anything on a horse he fancies?"

"Well—I don't want to give him away—he's a young sport, a fine sport, sir. Would you mind asking him himself? He sort of takes a pleasure in it, and perhaps he'd feel I was giving him away, sir, if you don't mind."

Bassett was serious as a church.

The uncle went back to his nephew and took him off for a ride in the car.

"Say, Paul, old man, do you ever put anything on a horse?" the uncle asked.

The boy watched the handsome man closely.

"Why, do you think I oughtn't to?" he parried.

"Not a bit of it! I thought perhaps you might give me a tip for the Lincoln."

The car sped on into the country, going down to Uncle Oscar's place in Hampshire.

"Honour bright?" said the nephew.

"Honour bright, son!" said the uncle.

"Well, then, Daffodil."

"Daffodil! I doubt it, sonny. What about Mirza?"

"I only know the winner," said the boy. "That's Daffodil."

"Daffodil, eh?"

There was a pause. Daffodil was an obscure horse comparatively.

"Uncle!"

"Yes, son?"

"You won't let it go any further, will you? I promised Bassett."

"Bassett be damned, old man! What's he got to do with it?

"We're partners. We've been partners from the first. Uncle, he lent me my first five shillings, which I lost. I promised him, honour bright, it was only between me and him; only you gave me that ten-shilling note I started winning with, so I thought you were lucky. You won't let it go any further, will you?"

The boy gazed at his uncle from those big, hot, blue eyes, set rather close together. The uncle stirred and laughed uneasily.

"Right you are, son! I'll keep your tip private. Daffodil, eh? How much are you putting on him?"

"All except twenty pounds," said the boy. "I keep that in reserve."

The uncle thought it a good joke.

"You keep twenty pounds in reserve, do you, you young romancer? What are you betting, then?"

"I'm betting three hundred," said the boy, gravely. "But it's between you and me, Uncle Oscar! Honour bright?"

The uncle burst into a roar of laughter.

"It's between you and me all right, you young Nat Gould," he said, laughing. "But where's your three hundred?"

"Bassett keeps it for me. We're partners."

"You are, are you! And what is Bassett putting on Daffodil?"

"He won't go quite as high as I do, I expect. Perhaps he'll go a hundred and fifty."

"What, pennies?" laughed the uncle.

"Pounds," said the child, with a surprised look at his uncle. "Bassett keeps a bigger reserve than I do."

Between wonder and amusement Uncle Oscar was silent. He pursued the matter no further, but he determined to take his nephew with him to the Lincoln races.

"Now, son," he said, "I'm putting twenty on Mirza, and I'll put five for you on any horse you fancy. What's your pick?"

"Daffodil, uncle."

"No, not the fiver on Daffodil!"

"I should if it was my own fiver," said the child.

"Good! Good! Right you are! A fiver for me and a fiver for you on Daffodil."

The child had never been to a race-meeting before, and his eyes were blue fire. He pursed his mouth tight, and watched. A Frenchman just in front had put his money on Lancelot. Wild with excitement, he flayed his arms up and down, yelling *"Lancelot! Lancelot!"* in his French accent.

Daffodil came in first, Lancelot second, Mirza third. The child, flushed and with eyes blazing, was curiously serene. His uncle brought him four five-pound notes, four to one.

"What am I to do with these?" he cried, waving them before the boy's eyes.

"I suppose we'll talk to Bassett," said the boy. "I expect I have fifteen hundred now; and twenty in reserve; and this twenty."

His uncle studied him for some moments.

"Look here, son!" he said. "You're not serious about Bassett and that fifteen hundred, are you?"

"Yes, I am. But it's between you and me, uncle. Honour bright!"

"Honour bright all right, son! But I must talk to Bassett."

"If you'd like to be a partner, uncle, with Bassett and me, we could all be partners. Only, you'd have to promise, honour bright, uncle, not to let it go beyond us three. Bassett and I are lucky, and you must be lucky, because it was your ten shillings I started winning with. . . ."

Uncle Oscar took both Bassett and Paul into Richmond Park for an afternoon, and there they talked.

"It's like this, you see, sir," Bassett said. "Master Paul would get me talking about racing events, spinning yarns, you know, sir. And he was always keen on knowing if I'd made or if I'd lost. It's about a year since, now, that I put five shillings on Blush of Dawn for him— and we lost. Then the luck turned, with that ten shillings he had from you, that we put on Singhalese. And since that time, it's been pretty steady, all things considering. What do you say, Master Paul?"

"We're all right when we're sure," said Paul. "It's when we're not quite sure that we go down."

"Oh, but we're careful then," said Bassett.

"But when are you *sure?*" smiled Uncle Oscar.

"It's Master Paul, sir," said Bassett, in a secret, religious voice. "It's as if he had it from heaven. Like Daffodil, now, for the Lincoln. That was as sure as eggs."

"Did you put anything on Daffodil?" asked Oscar Cresswell.

"Yes, sir. I made my bit."

"And my nephew?"

Bassett was obstinately silent, looking at Paul.

"I made twelve hundred, didn't I, Bassett? I told uncle I was putting three hundred on Daffodil."

"That's right," said Bassett, nodding.

"But where's the money?" asked the uncle.

"I keep it safe locked up, sir. Master Paul he can have it any minute he likes to ask for it."

"What, fifteen hundred pounds?"

"And twenty! And *forty*, that is, with the twenty he made on the course."

"It's amazing!" said the uncle.

"If Master Paul offers you to be partners, sir, I would, if I were you; if you'll excuse me," said Bassett.

Oscar Cresswell thought about it.

"I'll see the money," he said.

They drove home again, and sure enough, Bassett came round to the garden-house with fifteen hundred pounds in notes. The twenty pounds reserve was left with Joe Glee, in the Turf Commission deposit.

"You see, it's all right, uncle, when I'm *sure!* Then we go strong, for all we're worth. Don't we, Bassett?"

"We do that, Master Paul."

"And when are you sure?" said the uncle, laughing.

"Oh, well, sometimes I'm *absolutely* sure, like about Daffodil," said the boy; "and sometimes I have an idea; and sometimes I haven't even an idea, have I, Bassett? Then we're careful, because we mostly go down."

"You do, do you! And when you're sure, like about Daffodil, what makes you sure, sonny?"

"Oh, well, I don't know," said the boy uneasily. "I'm sure, you know, uncle; that's all."

"It's as if he had it from heaven, sir," Bassett reiterated.

"I should say so!" said the uncle.

But he became a partner. And when the Leger was coming on, Paul was "sure" about Lively Spark, which was a quite inconsiderable horse. The boy insisted on putting a thousand on the horse, Bassett went for five hundred, and Oscar Cresswell two hundred. Lively Spark came in first, and the betting had been ten to one against him. Paul had made ten thousand.

"You see," he said, "I was absolutely sure of him."

Even Oscar Cresswell had cleared two thousand.

"Look here, son," he said, "this sort of thing makes me nervous."

"It needn't, uncle! Perhaps I shan't be sure again for a long time."

"But what are you going to do with your money?" asked the uncle.

"Of course," said the boy, "I started it for mother. She said she had no luck, because father is unlucky, so I thought if *I* was lucky, it might stop whispering."

"What might stop whispering?"

"Our house. I *hate* our house for whispering."

"What does it whisper?"

"Why—why"—the boy fidgeted—"why, I don't know. But it's always short of money, you know, uncle."

"I know it, son, I know it."

"You know people send mother writs, don't you, uncle?"

"I'm afraid I do," said the uncle.

"And then the house whispers, like people laughing at you behind your back. It's awful, that is! I thought if I was lucky . . ."

"You might stop it," added the uncle.

The boy watched him with big blue eyes, that had an uncanny cold fire in them, and he said never a word.

"Well, then!" said the uncle. "What are we doing?"

"I shouldn't like mother to know I was lucky," said the boy.

"Why not, son?"

"She'd stop me."

"I don't think she would."

"Oh!"—and the boy writhed in an odd way—"I *don't* want her to know, uncle."

"All right, son! We'll manage it without her knowing."

They managed it very easily. Paul, at the other's suggestion, handed over five thousand pounds to his uncle, who deposited it with the family lawyer, who was then to inform Paul's mother that a relative had put five thousand pounds into his hands, which sum was to be paid out a thousand pounds at a time, on the mother's birthday, for the next five years.

"So she'll have a birthday present of a thousand pounds for five successive years," said Uncle Oscar. "I hope it won't make it all the harder for her later."

Paul's mother had her birthday in November. The house had been "whispering" worse than ever lately, and, even in spite of his luck, Paul could not bear up against it. He was very anxious to see the effect of the birthday letter, telling his mother about the thousand pounds.

When there were no visitors, Paul now took his meals with his parents, as he was beyond the nursery control. His mother went into town nearly every day. She had discovered that she had an odd knack of sketching furs and dress materials, so she worked secretly in the studio of a friend who was the chief "artist" for the leading drapers. She drew the figures of ladies in furs and ladies in silk and sequins for the newspaper advertisements. This young woman artist earned several thousand pounds a year, but Paul's mother only made several hundreds, and she was again dissatisfied. She so wanted to be first in something, and she did not succeed, even in making sketches for drapery advertisements.

She was down to breakfast on the morning of her birthday. Paul watched her face as she read her letters. He knew the lawyer's letter. As his mother read it, her face hardened and became more expressionless. Then a cold, determined look came on her mouth. She hid the letter under the pile of others, and said not a word about it.

"Didn't you have anything nice in the post or your birthday, mother?" said Paul.

"Quite moderately nice," she said, her voice cold and absent.

She went away to town without saying more.

But in the afternoon Uncle Oscar appeared. He said Paul's mother had had a long interview with the lawyer, asking if the whole five thousand could not be advanced at once, as she was in debt.

"What do you think, uncle?" said the boy.

"I leave it to you, son."

"Oh, let her have it, then! We can get some more with the other," said the boy.

"A bird in the hand is worth two in the bush, laddie!" said Uncle Oscar.

"But I'm sure to *know* for the Grand National; or the Lincolnshire; or else the Derby. I'm sure to know for *one* of them," said Paul.

So Uncle Oscar signed the agreement, and Paul's mother touched the whole five thousand. Then something very curious happened. The voices in the house suddenly went mad, like a chorus of frogs on a spring evening. There were certain new furnishings, and Paul had a tutor. He was *really* going to Eton, his father's school, in the following autumn. There were flowers in the winter, and a blossoming of the luxury Paul's mother had been used to. And yet the voices in the house, behind the sprays of mimosa and almond blossom, and from under the piles of iridescent cushions, simply trilled and screamed in a sort of ecstasy: "There *must* be more money! Oh-h-h; there *must* be more money. Oh, now, now-w! Now-w-w—there *must* be more money!—more than ever! More than ever!"

It frightened Paul terribly. He studied away at his Latin and Greek with his tutors. But his intense hours were spent with Bassett. The Grand National had gone by: he had not "known," and had lost a hundred pounds. Summer was at hand. He was in agony for the Lincoln. But even for the Lincoln he didn't "know," and he lost fifty pounds. He became wild-eyed and strange, as if something were going to explode in him.

"Let it alone, son! Don't you bother about it!" urged Uncle Oscar. But it was as if the boy couldn't really hear what his uncle was saying.

"I've got to know for the Derby! I've got to know for the Derby!" the child reiterated, his big blue eyes blazing with a sort of madness.

His mother noticed how overwrought he was.

"You'd better go to the seaside. Wouldn't you like to go now to the seaside, instead of waiting? I think you'd better," she said, looking down at him anxiously, her heart curiously heavy because of him.

But the child lifted his uncanny blue eyes.

"I couldn't possibly go before the Derby, mother!" he said. "I couldn't possibly!"

"Why not?" she said, her voice becoming heavy when she was opposed. "Why not? You can still go from the seaside to see the

Derby with your Uncle Oscar, if that's what you wish. No need for you to wait here. Besides, I think you care too much about these races. It's a bad sign. My family has been a gambling family, and you won't know till you grow up how much damage it has done. But it has done damage. I shall have to send Bassett away, and ask Uncle Oscar not to talk racing to you, unless you promise to be reasonable about it; go away to the seaside and forget it. You're all nerves!"

"I'll do what you like, mother, so long as you don't send me away till after the Derby," the boy said.

"Send you away from where? Just from this house?"

"Yes," he said, gazing at her.

"Why, you curious child, what makes you care about this house so much, suddenly? I never knew you loved it."

He gazed at her without speaking. He had a secret within a secret, something he had not divulged, even to Bassett or to his Uncle Oscar.

But his mother, after standing undecided and a little bit sullen for some moments, said:

"Very well, then! Don't go to the seaside till after the Derby, if you don't wish it. But promise me you won't let your nerves go to pieces. Promise you won't think so much about horse-racing and events, as you call them!"

"Oh, no," said the boy casually. "I won't think much about them, mother. You needn't worry. I wouldn't worry, mother, if I were you."

"If you were me and I were you," said his mother, "I wonder what we *should* do!"

"But you know you needn't worry, mother, don't you?" the boy repeated.

"I should be awfully glad to know it," she said wearily.

"Oh, well, you *can,* you know. I mean, you *ought* to know you needn't worry," he insisted.

"Ought I? Then I'll see about it," she said.

Paul's secret of secrets was his wooden horse, that which had no name. Since he was emancipated from a nurse and a nursery-governess, he had had his rocking-horse removed to his own bedroom at the top of the house.

"Surely, you're too big for a rocking-horse!" his mother had remonstrated.

"Well, you see, mother, till I can have a *real* horse, I like to have *some* sort of animal about," had been his quaint answer.

"Do you feel he keeps you company?" she laughed.

"Oh, yes! He's very good, he always keeps me company, when I'm there," said Paul.

So the horse, rather shabby, stood in an arrested prance in the boy's bedroom.

The Derby was drawing near, and the boy grew more and more tense. He hardly heard what was spoken to him, he was very frail, and his eyes were really uncanny. His mother had sudden strange seizures of uneasiness about him. Sometimes, for half-an-hour, she would feel a sudden anxiety about him that was almost anguish. She wanted to rush to him at once, and know he was safe.

Two nights before the Derby, she was at a big party in town, when one of her rushes of anxiety about her boy, her first-born, gripped her heart till she could hardly speak. She fought with the feeling, might and main, for she believed in common-sense. But it was too strong. She had to leave the dance and go downstairs to telephone to the country. The children's nursery-governess was terribly surprised and startled at being rung up in the night.

"Are the children all right, Miss Wilmot?"

"Oh, yes, they are quite all right."

"Master Paul? Is he all right?"

"He went to bed as right as a trivet. Shall I run up and look at him?"

"No," said Paul's mother reluctantly. "No! Don't trouble. It's all right. Don't sit up. We shall be home fairly soon." She did not want her son's privacy intruded upon.

"Very good," said the governess.

It was about one o'clock when Paul's mother and father drove up to their house. All was still. Paul's mother went to her room and slipped off her white fur cloak. She had told her maid not to wait up for her. She heard her husband downstairs, mixing a whisky-and-soda.

And then, because of the strange anxiety at her heart, she stole upstairs to her son's room. Noiselessly she went along the upper corridor. Was there a faint noise? What was it?

She stood, with arrested muscles, outside his door, listening. There was a strange, heavy, and yet not loud noise. Her heart stood still.

It was a soundless noise, yet rushing and powerful. Something huge, in violent, hushed motion. What was it? What in God's name was it? She ought to know. She felt that she knew the noise. She knew what it was.

Yet she could not place it. She couldn't say what it was. And on and on it went, like a madness.

Softly, frozen with anxiety and fear, she turned the door-handle.

The room was dark. Yet in the space near the window, she heard and saw something plunging to and fro. She gazed in fear and amazement.

Then suddenly she switched on the light, and saw her son, in his green pyjamas, madly surging on the rocking-horse. The blaze of light suddenly lit him up, as he urged the wooden horse, and lit her up, as she stood, blonde, in her dress of pale green and crystal, in the doorway.

"Paul!" she cried. "Whatever are you doing?"

"It's Malabar!" he screamed, in a powerful, strange voice. "It's Malabar!"

His eyes blazed at her for one strange and senseless second, as he ceased urging his wooden horse. Then he fell with a crash to the ground, and she, all her tormented motherhood flooding upon her, rushed to gather him up.

But he was unconscious, and unconscious he remained, with some brain-fever. He talked and tossed, and his mother sat stonily by his side.

"Malabar! It's Malabar! Bassett, Bassett, I *know*! It's Malabar!"

So the child cried, trying to get up and urge the rocking-horse that gave him his inspiration.

"What does he mean by Malabar?" asked the heart-broken mother.

"I don't know," said the father stonily.

"What does he mean by Malabar?" she asked her brother Oscar.

"It's one of the horses running for the Derby," was the answer.

And, in spite of himself, Oscar Cresswell spoke to Bassett, and himself put a thousand on Malabar: at fourteen to one.

The third day of the illness was critical: they were waiting for a change. The boy, with his rather long, curly hair, was tossing ceaselessly on the pillow. He neither slept nor regained consciousness, and his eyes were like blue stones. His mother sat, feeling her heart had gone, turned actually into a stone.

In the evening, Oscar Cresswell did not come, but Bassett sent a message, saying could he come up for one moment, just one moment? Paul's mother was very angry at the intrusion, but on second thought she agreed. The boy was the same. Perhaps Bassett might bring him to consciousness.

The gardener, a shortish fellow with a little brown moustache, and sharp little brown eyes, tip-toed into the room, touched his imaginary cap to Paul's mother, and stole to the bedside, staring with glittering, smallish eyes, at the tossing, dying child.

"Master Paul!" he whispered. "Master Paul! Malabar came in first all right, a clean win. I did as you told me. You've made over seventy thousand pounds, you have; you've got over eighty thousand. Malabar came in all right, Master Paul."

"Malabar! Malabar! Did I say Malabar, mother? Did I say Malabar? Do you think I'm lucky, mother? I knew Malabar, didn't I? Over eighty thousand pounds! I call that lucky, don't you, mother? Over eighty thousand pounds! I knew, didn't I know I knew! Malabar came in all right. If I ride my horse till I'm sure, then I tell you, Bassett, you can go as high as you like. Did you go for all you were worth, Bassett?"

"I went a thousand on it, Master Paul."

"I never told you, mother, that if I can ride my horse, and *get there*, then I'm absolutely sure—oh, absolutely! Mother, did I ever tell you? I *am* lucky!"

"No, you never did," said the mother.

But the boy died in the night.

And even as he lay dead, his mother heard her brother's voice saying to her: "My God, Hester, you're eighty-odd thousand to the good, and a poor devil of a son to the bad. But, poor devil, poor devil, he's best gone out of a life where he rides his rocking-horse to find a winner."

Bernard Malamud

1914–

THE BILL · BEHOLD THE KEY · THE MAGIC BARREL

With the publication of his first collection of short stories, *The Magic Barrel* (1958), Bernard Malamud's distinctive qualities became generally recognized. Comparing him with Saul Bellow, James Baldwin, Daniel Fuchs, and Ralph Ellison, Alfred Kazin said, "Malamud is the most compassionate, the most concerned and involved of them all."

The writers that Kazin mentions are all ethnic writers whose principal characters usually are Jews or blacks. From the beginning of the century there has been a rich literature in America dealing with the problem of scorned or disadvantaged social minorities, but since the Second World War there has been a dramatic change in the self-awareness of these minorities themselves. Today, a large proportion of our most interesting critics, poets, and novelists are Jews or blacks, writing mostly, but not always, about the fortunes of their own people. In the previous generation, Southern writers—members of another kind of dispossessed minority—had had a similar ascendancy.

Malamud is a Jewish writer in a double sense. He writes about Jews and the particular anguish of Jewish experience, but also does it in a manner—wry, humorous, colloquial, self-deprecatory—that derives from the tradition of Yiddish writers like Singer and Sholom Aleichem. At the same time, because of the deep compassion of which Kazin speaks and the fantastic, often allegorical narrative forms in which it is dramatized, Malamud's work transcends the experience of any particular group and applies universally to human hope, suffering, alienation, and love wherever they are found. "All men are Jews," Malamud once said in an interview, "although few men know it."

Bernard Malamud is a New Yorker from Brooklyn, educated at City College and Columbia. During most of his career he has been a teacher. From 1940 to 1949 he taught at Oregon State University (which provides the background for his academic novel *A New Life*) and since then, with occasional interruptions, he has been at Bennington College in Vermont.

His first novel, *The Natural* (1952), is a remarkable fusion of American baseball lore and the myth of the quest for the Holy Grail as Sir James G. Frazer, Jessie Weston and Carl Jung interpret that quest. Roy Hobbs, a composite of Babe Ruth and other actual players, is betrayed by a woman early in his career, rises to later championship, and then in his turn betrays others, including baseball itself. In the novel *The Assistant* (1957), a non-Jew who has robbed a Jewish storekeeper tries in complicated and incompatible ways to make up for his crime. He falls in love with the storekeeper's daughter, takes over the store after the owner's death, and finally has himself circumcised as a Jew. *A New Life* (1961) describes the questing misadventures of a Jewish teacher in the alien surroundings of a far-western state university. Malamud's major novel is *The Fixer* (1966), which won both the National Book Award and Pulitzer Prize. Suggested by an actual court case that caused international concern in the last days of Russian tsardom, it recounts in highly imaginative detail the arrest and long imprisonment of a Jew falsely accused of the ritual murder of a Christian child. His 1971 novel, *The Tenants,* takes a further step in social complication by putting a Jewish novelist—resisting eviction by the landlord of a decayed New York apartment building—into disastrous conflict with a black. Though Malamud's novels vary greatly in their characters and circumstances, they all involve some sort of quest that turns into an ordeal. The ordeal, in turn, shows how difficult true morality really is, and how much love and understanding and self-sacrifice are needed to achieve it.

With the double meaning of *credit* as its theme, "The Bill" tells its story of trust and betrayal among the poorest of the poor with a direct and almost cruel simplicity that recalls Borges' "The Intruder." Capitalism is built on a structure of credit which leaves many people trapped in indebtedness all their lives. On the other hand, it is very difficult for us, in our self-centeredness, to credit other people with feelings and intentions like our own. It is right that "The Bill" should be told from Willy Schlegel's point of view rather than that of the Panessas. The story's uncompromising logic not only makes Willy's apparently senseless vindictiveness understandable, but forces us to recognize in it motives uncomfortably close to some of our own.

In more complicated circumstances "Behold the Key" reveals a similar pattern. Relentless need sets the limits for a game in which a trio of strangers are intimately and desperately involved. An American academic is made to see the Eternal City of art and the historic imagination in terms of the harsh exigencies and duplicities of present-day Roman lives. As in "The Bill," frustration ends in perverse and yet comprehensible destructiveness. The mark of the key at the end recalls the irremovable apple thrown by the father in Kafka's "The Metamorphosis."

The governing purpose of the rabbinical student in "The Magic Barrel" is even more impelling than that of the graduate student in "Behold the Key." Similarly he falls into the hands of a hungry intermediary who promises to help him, but who is more desperate and driven than the one he wants to lead. Now the quest involves marriage and the ability to love both God and woman. The amazing ending, after a series of shifts and reversals, is in the Old Testament spirit of Ezekiel or Hosea, expressed in images that might have come from the paintings of Chagall.

THE BILL

Though the street was somewhere near a river, it was landlocked and narrow, a crooked row of aged brick tenement buildings. A child throwing a ball straight up saw a bit of pale sky. On the corner, opposite the blackened tenement where Willy Schlegel worked as janitor, stood another like it except that this included the only store on the street—going down five stone steps into the basement, a small, dark delicatessen owned by Mr. and Mrs. F. Panessa, really a hole in the wall.

They had just bought it with the last of their money, Mrs. Panessa told the janitor's wife, so as not to have to depend on either of their daughters, both of whom, Mrs. Schlegel understood, were married to selfish men who had badly affected their characters. To be completely independent of them, Panessa, a retired factory worker, withdrew his three thousands of savings and bought this little delicatessen store. When Mrs. Schlegel, looking around—though she knew the delicatessen quite well for the many years she and Willy had been janitors across the way—when she asked, "Why did you buy this one?" Mrs. Panessa cheerfully replied because it was a small place and they would not have to overwork; Panessa was sixty-three. They were not here to coin money but to support themselves without working too hard. After talking it over many nights and days, they had decided that the store would at least give them a living. She gazed into Etta Schlegel's gaunt eyes and Etta said she hoped so.

She told Willy about the new people across the street who had bought out the Jew, and said to buy there if there was a chance; she meant by that they would continue to shop at the self-service, but when there was some odd or end to pick up, or something they had forgotten to buy, they could go to Panessa's. Willy did as he was told. He was tall and broad-backed, with a heavy face seamed dark from the coal and ashes he shoveled around all winter, and his hair often looked gray from the dust the wind whirled up at him out of the ash cans when he was lining them up for the sanitation truck. Always in overalls—he complained he never stopped working—he would drift across the street and down the steps when something was needed, and lighting his pipe, would stand around talking to Mrs. Panessa as her husband, a small bent man with a fitful smile, stood behind the counter waiting for the janitor after a long interval of talk to ask, upon reflection, for a dime's worth of this or that, the whole business never amounting to more than half a dollar. Then one day Willy got to talking about how the tenants goaded him all the time and what the cruel and stingy landlord could think up for him to do in that smelly five-floor dungeon. He was absorbed by what he was saying and before he knew it had run up a three-dollar order, though all he had on him was fifty cents. Willy looked like a dog that had just had a licking, but Mr. Panessa, after clearing his throat, chirped up it didn't matter, he could pay the rest whenever he wanted. He said that everything was run on credit, business and everything else, because after all what was credit but the fact that people were human beings, and if you were really a human being you gave credit to somebody else and he gave credit to you. That surprised Willy because he had never heard a storekeeper say it before. After a couple of days he paid the two fifty, but when Panessa said he could trust whenever he felt like it, Willy sucked a flame into his pipe, then began to order all sorts of things.

When he brought home two large bagfuls of stuff, Etta shouted he must be crazy. Willy answered he had charged everything and paid no cash.

"But we have to pay sometime, don't we?" Etta shouted. "And we have to pay higher prices than in the self-service." She said then what she always said, "We're poor people, Willy. We can't afford too much."

Though Willy saw the justice of her remarks, despite her scolding he still went across the street and trusted. Once he had a crumpled ten-dollar bill in his pants pocket and the amount came to less than four, but he didn't offer to pay, and let Panessa write it in the book. Etta knew he had the money so she screamed when he admitted he had bought on credit.

"Why are you doing it for? Why don't you pay if you have the money?"

He didn't answer but after a time he said there were other things he had to buy once in a while. He went into the furnace room and came out with a wrapped package which he opened, and it contained a beaded black dress.

Etta cried over the dress and said she would never wear it because the only time he ever brought her anything was when he had done something wrong. Thereafter she let him do all the grocery shopping and she did not speak when he bought on trust.

Willy continued to buy at Panessa's. It seemed they were always waiting for him to come in. They lived in three tiny rooms on the floor above the store, and when Mrs. Panessa saw him out of her window, she ran down to the store. Willy came up from his basement, crossed the street and went down the steps into the delicatessen, looming large as he opened the door. Every time he bought, it was never less than two dollars' worth and sometimes it would go as high as five. Mrs. Panessa would pack everything into a deep double bag, after Panessa had called off each item and written the price with a smeary black pencil into his looseleaf notebook. Whenever Willy walked in, Panessa would open the book, wet his finger tip and flip through a number of blank pages till he found Willy's account in the center of the book. After the order was packed and tied up, Panessa added the amount, touching each figure with his pencil, hissing to himself as he added, and Mrs. Panessa's bird eyes would follow the figuring until Panessa wrote down a sum, and the new total sum (after Panessa had glanced up at Willy and saw that Willy was looking) was twice underscored and then Panessa shut the book. Willy, with his loose unlit pipe in his mouth, did not move until the book was put away under the counter; then he roused himself and embracing the bundle—with which they offered to help him across the street though he always refused—plunged out of the store.

One day when the sum total came to eighty-three dollars and some cents, Panessa, lifting his head and smiling, asked Willy when he could pay something on account. The very next day Willy stopped buying at Panessa's and after that Etta, with her cord market bag, began to shop again at the self-service, and neither of them went across the street for as much as a pound of prunes or box of salt they had meant to buy but had forgotten.

Etta, when she returned from shopping at the self-service, scraped the wall on her side of the street to get as far away as possible from Panessa's.

Later she asked Willy if he had paid them anything.

He said no.

"When will you?"

He said he didn't know.

A month went by, then Etta met Mrs. Panessa around the corner, and though Mrs. Panessa, looking unhappy, said nothing about the bill, Etta came home and reminded Willy.

"Leave me alone," he said, "I got enough trouble of my own."

"What kind of trouble have you got, Willy?"

"The goddam tenants and the goddam landlord," he shouted and slammed the door.

When he returned he said, "What have I got that I can pay? Ain't I been a poor man every day of my life?"

She was sitting at the table and lowered her arms and put her head down on them and wept.

"With what?" he shouted, his face lit up dark and webbed. "With the meat off of my bones?

"With the ashes in my eyes. With the piss I mop up on the floors. With the cold in my lungs when I sleep."

He felt for Panessa and his wife a grating hatred and vowed never to pay because he hated them so much, especially the humpback behind the counter. If he ever smiled at him again with those goddam eyes he would lift him off the floor and crack his bent bones.

That night he went out and got drunk and lay till morning in the gutter. When he returned, with filthy clothes and bloodied eyes, Etta held up to him the picture of their four-year-old son who had died from diphtheria, and Willy, weeping splashy tears, swore he would never touch another drop.

Each morning he went out to line up the ash cans, he never looked the full way across the street.

"Give credit," he mimicked, "give credit."

Hard times set in. The landlord ordered cut down on heat, cut down on hot water. He cut down on Willy's expense money and wages. The tenants were angered. All day they pestered Willy like clusters of flies and he told them what the landlord had ordered. Then they cursed Willy and Willy cursed them. They telephoned the Board of Health but when the inspectors arrived they said the temperature was within the legal minimum though the house was drafty. However the tenants still complained they were cold and goaded Willy about it all day but he said he was cold too. He said he was freezing but no one believed him.

One day he looked up from lining up four ash cans for the truck to remove and saw Mr. and Mrs. Panessa staring at him from the store. They were staring up through the glass front door and when he looked at them at first his eyes blurred and they appeared to be two scrawny, loose-feathered birds.

He went down the block to get a wrench from another janitor, and when he got back they then reminded him of two skinny leafless bushes sprouting up through the wooden floor. He could see through the bushes to the empty shelves.

In the spring, when the grass shoots were sticking up from the cracks in the sidewalk, he told Etta, "I'm only waiting till I can pay it all."

"How, Willy?"

"We can save up."

"How?"

"How much do we save a month?"

"Nothing."

"How much have you got hid away?"

"Nothing any more."

"I'll pay them bit by bit. I will, by Jesus."

The trouble was there was no place they could get the money. Sometimes when he was trying to think of the different ways there were to get money his thoughts ran ahead and he saw what it would be like when he paid. He would wrap the wad of bills with a thick rubber band and then go up the stairs and cross the street and go down the five steps into the store. He would say to Panessa, "Here it is, little old man, and I bet you didn't think I would do it, and I don't suppose nobody else did and sometimes me myself, but here it is in bucks all held together by a fat rubber band." After hefting the wad a little, he placed it, like making a move on a checkerboard, squarely in the center of the counter, and the diminutive man and his wife both unpeeled it, squeaking and squealing over each blackened buck, and marveling that so many ones had been tied together into such a small pack.

Such was the dream Willy dreamed but he could never make it come true.

He worked hard too. He got up early and scrubbed the stairs from cellar to roof with soap and a hard brush then went over that with a wet mop. He cleaned the woodwork too and oiled the bannister till it shone the whole zigzag way down and rubbed the mailboxes in the vestibule with metal polish and a soft rag until you could see your face in them. He saw his own heavy face with a surprising yellow mustache he had recently grown and the tan felt cap he wore that a tenant had left behind in a closetful of junk when he had moved. Etta helped him and they cleaned the whole cellar and the dark courtyard under the crisscrossed clotheslines, and they were quick to respond to any kind of request, even from tenants they didn't like, for sink or toilet repairs. Both worked themselves to exhaustion every day, but as they knew from the beginning, no extra money came in.

One morning when Willy was shining up the mailboxes, he found in his own a letter for him. Removing his cap, he opened the envelope and held the paper to the light as he read the trembling writing. It was from Mrs. Panessa, who wrote her husband was sick across the street, and she had no money in the house so could he pay her just ten dollars and the rest could wait for later.

He tore the letter into bits and hid all day in the cellar. That night, Etta, who had been searching for him in the streets, found him behind the furnace amid the pipes, and she asked him what he was doing there.

He explained about the letter.

"Hiding won't do you any good at all," she said hopelessly.

"What should I do then?"

"Go to sleep, I guess."

He went to sleep but the next morning burst out of his covers, pulled on his overalls and ran out of the house with an overcoat flung over his shoulders. Around the corner he found a pawnshop, where he got ten dollars for the coat and was gleeful.

But when he ran back, there was a hearse or something across the street, and two men in black were carrying this small and narrow pine box out of the house.

"Who's dead, a child?" he asked one of the tenants.

"No, a man named Mr. Panessa."

Willy couldn't speak. His throat had turned to bone.

After the pine box was squeezed through the vestibule doors, Mrs. Panessa, grieved all over, tottered out alone. Willy turned his head away although he thought she wouldn't recognize him because of his new mustache and tan cap.

"What'd he die of?" he whispered to the tenant.

"I really couldn't say."

But Mrs. Panessa, walking behind the box, had heard.

"Old age," she shrilly called back.

He tried to say some sweet thing but his tongue hung in his mouth like dead fruit on a tree, and his heart was a black-painted window.

Mrs. Panessa moved away to live first with one stone-faced daughter, then with the other. And the bill was never paid.

BEHOLD THE KEY

One beautiful late-autumn day in Rome, Carl Schneider, a graduate student in Italian studies at Columbia University, left a real estate agent's office after a depressing morning of apartment hunting and walked up Via Veneto, disappointed in finding himself so dissatisfied in this city of his dreams. Rome, a city of perpetual surprise, had surprised unhappily. He felt unpleasantly lonely for the first time since he had been married, and found himself desiring the lovely Italian women he passed in the street, especially the few who looked as if they had money. He had been a damn fool, he thought, to come here with so little of it in his pocket.

He had, last spring, been turned down for a Fulbright fellowship and had had no peace with himself until he decided to go to Rome anyway to do his Ph.D. on the Risorgimento from first-hand sources, at the same time enjoying Italy. This plan had for years aroused his happiest expectations. Norma thought he was crazy to want to take off with two kids under six and all their savings—$3,600, most of it earned by her, but Carl argued that people had to do something different with their lives occasionally or they went to pot. He was twenty-eight—his years weighed on him—and she was thirty, and when else could they go if not now? He was confident, since he knew the language, that they could get settled satisfactorily in a short time. Norma had her doubts. It all came to nothing until her mother, a widow, offered to pay their passage across; then Norma said yes, though still with misgiving.

"We've read prices are terrible in Rome. How do we know we'll get along on what we have?"

"You got to take a chance once in a while," Carl said.

"Up to a point, with two kids," Norma replied; but she took the chance and they sailed out of season—the sixteenth of October, arriving in Naples on the twenty-sixth and going on at once to Rome, in the hope they would save money if they found an apartment quickly, though Norma wanted to see Capri and Carl would have liked to spend a little time in Pompeii.

In Rome, though Carl had no trouble getting around or making himself understood, they had immediate rough going trying to locate an inexpensive furnished flat. They had figured on a two-bedroom apartment, Carl to work in theirs; or one bedroom and a large maid's room where the kids would sleep. Although they searched across the city they could locate nothing decent within their means, fifty to fifty-five thousand lire a month, a top of about ninety dollars. Carl turned up some inexpensive places but in hopeless Trastevere sections; elsewhere there was always some other fatal flaw: no heat, missing furniture, sometimes no running water or sanitation.

To make bad worse, during their second week at the dark little pensione where they were staying, the children developed nasty intestinal disorders, little Mike having to be carried to the bathroom ten times one memorable night, and Christine running a temperature of 105; so Norma, who didn't trust the milk or cleanliness of the pensione, suggested they would be better off in a hotel. When Christine's fever abated they moved into the Sora Cecilia, a second-class albergo recommended by a Fulbright fellow they had met. It was a four-story building full of high-ceilinged, boxlike rooms. The toilets were in the hall, but the rent was comparatively low. About the only other virtue of the place was that it was near the Piazza Navona, a lovely 17th-century square, walled by many magnificently picturesque, wine-colored houses. Within the piazza three fountains played, whose water and sculpture Carl and Norma enjoyed, but which they soon became insensible to during their sad little walks with the kids, as the days passed and they still found themselves homeless.

Carl had in the beginning avoided the real estate agents to save the commission—5 per cent of the full year's rent; but when he gave in and visited their offices they said it was too late to get anything at the price he wanted to pay.

"You should have come in July," one agent said.

"I'm here now."

He threw up his hands. "I believe in miracles but who can make them?" Better to pay seventy-five thousand and so live comfortable like other Americans.

"I can't afford it, not with heat extra."

"Then you will sit out the winter in the hotel."

"I appreciate your concern." Carl left, embittered.

However, they sometimes called him to witness an occasional "miracle." One man showed him a pleasant apartment overlooking some prince or other's formal garden. The rent was sixty thousand, and Carl would have taken it had he not later learned from the tenant next door—he had returned because he distrusted the agent—that the flat was heated electrically, which would cost twenty thousand a month over the sixty thousand rent. Another "miracle" was the offer by this agent's cousin of a single studio room on the Via Margutta, for forty thousand. And from time to time a lady agent called Norma to tell her about this miraculous place in the Parioli: eight stunning rooms, three bedrooms, double service, American-style kitchen with refrigerator, garage—marvelous for an American family: price, two hundred thousand.

"Please, no more," Norma said.

"I'll go mad," said Carl. He was nervous over the way time was flying, almost a month gone, he having given none of it to his work. And Norma, washing the kids' things in the hotel sink, in an unheated, cluttered room, was obviously unhappy. Furthermore, the hotel bill last week had come to twenty thousand lire, and it was costing them two thousand more a day to eat badly, even though Norma was cooking the children's food in their room on a hotplate they had bought.

"Carl, maybe I'd better go to work?"

"I'm tired of your working," he answered. "You'll have no fun."

"What fun am I having? All I've seen is the Colosseum." She then suggested they could rent an unfurnished flat and build their own furniture.

"Where would I get the tools?" he said. "And what about the cost of wood in a country where it's cheaper to lay down marble floors? And who'll do my reading for me while I'm building and finishing the stuff?"

"All right," Norma said. "Forget I said anything."

"What about taking a seventy-five thousand place but staying only for five or six months?" Carl said.

"Can you get your research done in five or six months?"

"No."

"I thought your research was the main reason we came here."
Norma then wished she had never heard of Italy.

"That's enough of that," said Carl.

He felt helpless, blamed himself for coming—bringing all this on
Norma and the kids. He could not understand why things were
going so badly. When he was not blaming himself he was blaming
the Italians. They were aloof, evasive, indifferent to his plight. He
couldn't communicate with them in their own language, whatever
it was. He couldn't get them to say what was what, to awaken their
hearts to his needs. He felt his plans, his hopes caving in, and feared
disenchantment with Italy unless they soon found an apartment.

At the Porta Pinciana, near the tram, Carl felt himself tapped on
the shoulder. A bushy-haired Italian, clutching a worn briefcase,
was standing in the sun on the sidewalk. His hair rose in all directions. His eyes were gentle; not sad, but they had been. He wore a
clean white shirt, rag of a tie, and a black jacket that had crawled
a little up his back. His trousers were of denim, and his porous,
sharp-pointed shoes, neatly shined, were summer shoes.

"Excuse me," he said with an uneasy smile. "I am Vasco Bevilacqua. Weesh you an apotament?"

"How did you guess?" Carl said.

"I follow you," the Italian answered, making a gesture in the air,
"when you leave the agencia. I am myself agencia. I like to help
Americans. They are wonderful people."

"You're a real estate agent?"

"Eet is just."

"Parliamo italiano?"

"You spik?" He seemed disappointed. "Ma non è italiano?"

Carl told him he was an American student of Italian history and
culture, had studied the language for years.

Bevilacqua then explained that, although he had no regular office,
nor, for that matter, a car, he had managed to collect several ex-
clusive listings. He had got these, he said, from friends who knew
he was starting a business, and they made it a habit to inform him
of apartments recently vacated in their buildings or those of friends,

for which service, he of course tipped them out of his commissions. The regular agents, he went on, demanded a heartless five per cent. He requested only three. He charged less because his expenses, frankly, were low, and also because of his great affection for Americans. He asked Carl how many rooms he was looking for and what he was willing to pay.

Carl hesitated. The man, though pleasant, was no bona fide agent, probably had no license. He had heard about these two-bit operators and was about to say he wasn't interested but Bevilacqua's eyes pleaded with him not to say it.

Carl figured he had nothing to lose. Maybe he does have a place I might be interested in. He told the Italian what he was looking for and how much he expected to pay.

Bevilacqua's face lit up. "In weech zone do you seek?" he asked with emotion.

"Any place fairly decent," Carl said in Italian. "It doesn't have to be perfect."

"Not the Parioli?"

"Not the Parioli only. It would depend on the rent."

Bevilacqua held his briefcase between his knees and fished in his shirt pocket. He drew out a sheet of very thin paper, unfolded it, and read the penciled writing, with wrinkled brows. After a while he thrust the paper back into his pocket and retrieved his briefcase.

"Let me have your telephone number," he said in Italian. "I will examine my other listings and give you a ring."

"Listen," Carl said, "if you've got a good place to show me, all right. If not, please don't waste my time."

Bevilacqua looked hurt. "I give you my word," he said, placing his big hand on his chest, "tomorrow you will have your apartment. May my mother give birth to a goat if I fail you."

He put down in a little book where Carl was staying. "I'll be over at thirteen sharp to show you some miraculous places," he said.

"Can't you make it in the morning?"

Bevilacqua was apologetic. "My hours are now from thirteen to sixteen." He said he hoped to expand his time later, and Carl guessed he was working his real estate venture during his lunch and siesta time, probably from some underpaid clerk's job.

He said he would expect him at thirteen sharp.

Bevilacqua, his expression now so serious he seemed to be listening to it, bowed, and walked away in his funny shoes.

He showed up at the hotel at ten to two, wearing a small black fedora, his hair beaten down with pomade whose odor sprang into the lobby. Carl was waiting restlessly near the desk, doubting he would show up, when Bevilacqua came running through the door, clutching his briefcase.

"Ready?" he said breathlessly.

"Since one o'clock," Carl answered.

"Ah, that's what comes of not owning your own car," Bevilacqua explained. "My bus had a flat tire."

Carl looked at him but his face was deadpan. "Well, let's get on," the student said.

"I have three places to show you." Bevilacqua told him the first address, a two-bedroom apartment at just fifty thousand.

On the bus they clung to straps in a tight crowd, the Italian raising himself on his toes and looking around at every stop to see where they were. Twice he asked Carl the time, and when Carl told him, his lips moved soundlessly. After a time Bevilacqua roused himself, smiled, and remarked, "What do you think of Marilyn Monroe?"

"I haven't much thought of her," Carl said.

Bevilacqua looked puzzled. "Don't you go to the movies?"

"Once in a while."

The Italian made a short speech on the wonder of American films. "In Italy they always make us look at what we have just lived through." He fell into silence again. Carl noticed that he was holding in his hand a wooden figurine of a hunchback with a high hat, whose poor gobbo he was rubbing with his thumb, for luck.

"For us both," Carl hoped. He was still restless, still worried.

But their luck was nil at the first place, an ochre-colored house behind an iron gate.

"Third floor?" Carl asked, after the unhappy realization that he had been here before.

"Exactly. How did you guess?"

"I've seen the apartment," he answered gloomily. He remembered having seen an ad. If that was how Bevilacqua got his listings, they might as well quit now.

"But what's wrong with it?" the Italian asked, visibly disappointed.

"Bad heating."

"How is that possible?"

"They have a single gas heater in the living room but nothing in the bedrooms. They were supposed to have steam heat installed in the building in September, but the contract fell through when the price of steam pipe went up. With two kids, I wouldn't want to spend the winter in a cold flat."

"Cretins," muttered Bevilacqua. "The portiere said the heat was perfect."

He consulted his paper. "I have a place in the Prati district, two fine bedrooms and combined living and dining room. Also an American-type refrigerator in the kitchen."

"Has the apartment been advertised in the papers?"

"Absolutely no. My cousin called me about this one last night—but the rent is fifty-five thousand."

"Let's see it anyway," Carl said.

It was an old house, formerly a villa, which had been cut up into apartments. Across the street stood a little park with tall, tufted pine trees, just the thing for the kids. Bevilacqua located the portiere, who led them up the stairs, all the while saying how good the flat was. Although Carl discovered at once that there was no hot water in the kitchen sink and it would have to be carried in from the bathroom, the flat made a good impression on him. But then in the master bedroom he noticed that one wall was wet and there was a disagreeable odor in the room.

The portiere quickly explained that a water pipe had burst in the wall, but they would have it fixed in a week.

"It smells like a sewer pipe," said Carl.

"But they will have it fixed this week," Bevilacqua said.

"I couldn't live a week with that smell in the room."

"You mean you are not interested in the apartment?" the Italian said fretfully.

Carl nodded. Bevilacqua's face fell. He blew his nose and they left the house. Outside he regained his calm. "You can't trust your own mother nowadays. I called the portiere this morning and he guaranteed me the house was without a fault."

"He must have been kidding you."

"It makes no difference. I have an exceptional place in mind for you now, but we've got to hurry."

Carl half-heartedly asked where it was.

The Italian looked embarrassed. "In the Parioli, a wonderful section, as you know. Your wife won't have to look far for friends—there are Americans all over. Also Japanese and Indians, if you have international tastes."

"The Parioli," Carl muttered. "How much?"

"Only sixty-five thousand," Bevilacqua said, staring at the ground.

"Only? Still, it must be a dump at that price."

"It's really very nice—new, and with a good-size nuptial bedroom and one small, besides the usual things, including a fine kitchen. You will personally love the magnificent terrace."

"Have you seen the place?"

"I spoke to the maid and she says the owner is very anxious to rent. They are moving, for business reasons, to Turin next week. The maid is an old friend of mine. She swears the place is perfect."

Carl considered it. Sixty-five thousand meant close to a hundred and five dollars. "Well," he said after a while, "let's have a look at it."

They caught a tram and found seats together, Bevilacqua impatiently glancing out of the window whenever they stopped. On the way he told Carl about his hard life. He was the eighth of twelve children, only five now alive. Nobody was really ever not hungry, though they ate spaghetti by the bucketful. He had to leave school at ten and go to work. In the war he was wounded twice, once by the Americans advancing, and once by the Germans retreating. His father was killed in an Allied bombardment of Rome, the same that had cracked open his mother's grave in the Cimitero Verano.

"The British pinpointed their targets," he said, "but the Americans dropped bombs everywhere. This was the advantage of your great wealth."

Carl said he was sorry about the bombardments.

"Nevertheless, I like the Americans better," Bevilacqua went on. "They are more like Italians—open. That's why I like to help them when they come here. The British are more closed. They talk with tight lips." He made sounds with tight lips.

As they were walking towards Piazza Euclide, he asked Carl if he had an American cigarette on him.

"I don't smoke," Carl said apologetically.

Bevilacqua shrugged and walked faster.

The house he took Carl to was a new one on Via Archimede, an attractive street that wound up and around a hill. It was crowded with long-balconied apartment buildings in bright colors. Carl thought he would be happy to live in one of them. It was a short thought, he wouldn't let it get too long.

They rode up to the fifth floor, and the maid, a dark girl with fuzzy cheeks, showed them through the neat apartment.

"Is sixty-five thousand correct?" Carl asked her.

She said yes.

The flat was so good that Carl, moved by elation and fear, began to pray.

"I told you you'd like it," Bevilacqua said, rubbing his palms. "I'll draw up the contract tonight."

"Let's see the bedroom now," Carl said.

But first the maid led them onto a broad terrace to show them the view of the city. The sight excited Carl—the variety of architecture from ancient to modern times, where history had been and still, in its own aftermath, sensuously flowed, a sea of roofs, towers, domes; and in the background, golden-domed St. Peter's. This marvelous city, Carl thought.

"Now the bedroom," he said.

"Yes, the bedroom." The maid led them through double doors into the "camera matrimoniale," spacious, and tastefully furnished, containing handsome mahogany twin beds.

"They'll do," Carl said, to hide his joy, "though I personally prefer a double bed."

"I also," said the maid, "but you can move one in."

"These will do."

"But they won't be here," she said.

"What do you mean they won't be here?" Bevilacqua demanded.

"Nothing will be left. Everything goes to Turin."

Carl's beautiful hopes took another long dive into a dirty cellar.

Bevilacqua flung his hat on the floor, landed on it with both feet and punched himself on the head with his fists.

The maid swore she had told him on the phone that the apartment was for rent unfurnished.

He began to yell at her and she shouted at him. Carl left, broken-backed. Bevilacqua caught up with him in the street. It was a quarter to four and he had to rush off to work. He held his hat and ran down the hill.

"I weel show you a terreefic place tomorrow," he called over his shoulder.

"Over my dead body," said Carl.

On the way to the hotel he was drenched in a heavy rainfall, the first of many in the late autumn.

The next morning the hotel phone rang at seven-thirty. The children awoke, Mike crying. Carl, dreading the day, groped for the ringing phone. Outside it was still raining.

"Pronto."

It was a cheery Bevilacqua. "I call you from my job. I 'ave found for you an apotament een weech you can move tomorrow if you like."

"Go to hell."

"Cosa?"

"Why do you call so early? You woke the children."

"Excuse me," Bevilacqua said in Italian. "I wanted to give you the good news."

"What goddamn good news?"

"I have found a first-class apartment for you near the Monte Sacro. It has only one bedroom but also a combined living and dining room with a double day bed, and a glass-enclosed terrace studio for your studies, and a small maid's room. There is no garage but you have no car. Price forty-five thousand—less than you expected. The apartment is on the ground floor and there is also a garden for your children to play in. Your wife will go crazy when she sees it."

"So will I," Carl said. "Is it furnished?"

Bevilacqua coughed. "Of course."

"Of course. Have you been there?"

He cleared his throat. "Not yet. I just discovered it this minute. The secretary of my office, Mrs. Gaspari, told me about it. The apartment is directly under hers. She will make a wonderful neighbor for you. I will come to your hotel precisely at thirteen and a quarter."

"Give yourself time. Make it fourteen."

"You will be ready?"

"Yes."

But when he had hung up, his feeling of dread had grown. He felt afraid to leave the hotel and confessed this to Norma.

"Would you like me to go this time?" she asked.

He considered it but said no.

"Poor Carl."

" 'The great adventure.' "

"Don't be bitter. It makes me miserable."

They had breakfast in the room—tea, bread and jam, fruit. They were cold, but there was to be no heat, it said on a card tacked on the door, until December. Norma put sweaters on the kids. Both had colds. Carl opened a book but could not concentrate and settled for *Il Messaggero*. Norma telephoned the lady agent; she said she would ring back when there was something new to show.

Bevilacqua called up from the lobby at one-forty.

"Coming," Carl said, his heart heavy.

The Italian was standing in wet shoes near the door. He held his briefcase and a dripping large umbrella but had left his hat home. Even in the damp his bushy hair stood upright. He looked slightly miserable.

They left the hotel. Bevilacqua walking quickly by Carl's side, maneuvering to keep the umbrella over both of them. On the Piazza Navona a woman was feeding a dozen stray cats in the rain. She had spread a newspaper on the ground and the cats were grabbing hard strings of last night's macaroni. Carl felt the recurrence of his loneliness.

A packet of garbage thrown out of a window hit their umbrella and bounced off. The garbage spilled on the ground. A white-faced man, staring out of a third-floor window, pointed to the cats. Carl shook his fist at him.

Bevilacqua was moodily talking about himself. "In eight years of hard work I advanced myself only from thirty-thousand lire to fifty-five thousand a month. The cretin who sits on my left in the office has his desk at the door and makes forty thousand extra in tips just to give callers an appointment with the big boss. If I had that desk I would double what he takes in."

"Have you thought of changing jobs?"

"Certainly, but I could never start at the salary I am now earning.

And there are twenty people who will jump into my job at half the pay."

"Tough," Carl said.

"For every piece of bread, we have twenty open mouths. You Americans are the lucky ones."

"Yes, in that way."

"In what way no?"

"We have no piazzas."

Bevilacqua shrugged one shoulder. "Can you blame me for wanting to advance myself?"

"Of course not. I wish you the best."

"I wish the best to all Americans," Bevilacqua declared. "I like to help them."

"And I to all Italians and pray them to let me live among them for a while."

"Today it will be arranged. Tomorrow you will move in. I feel luck in my bones. My wife kissed St. Peter's toe yesterday."

Traffic was heavy, a stream of gnats—Vespas, Fiats, Renaults—roared at them from both directions, nobody slowing down to let them pass. They plowed across dangerously. At the bus stop the crowd rushed for the doors when the bus swerved to the curb. It moved away with its rear door open, four people hanging on the step.

I can do as well in Times Square, Carl thought.

In a half hour, after a short walk from the bus stop, they arrived at a broad, tree-lined street. Bevilacqua pointed to a yellow apartment house on the corner they were approaching. All over it were terraces, the ledges loaded with flower pots and stone boxes dropping ivy over the walls. Carl would not allow himself to think the place had impressed him.

Bevilacqua nervously rang the portiere's bell. He was again rubbing the hunchback's gobbo. A thick-set man in a blue smock came up from the basement. His face was heavy and he wore a full black mustache. Bevilacqua gave him the number of the apartment they wanted to see.

"Ah, there I can't help you," said the portiere. "I haven't got the key."

"Here we go again," Carl muttered.

"Patience," Bevilacqua counseled. He spoke to the portiere in a dialect Carl couldn't follow. The portiere made a long speech in the same dialect.

"Come upstairs," said Bevilacqua.

"Upstairs where?"

"To the lady I told you about, the secretary of my office. She lives on the first floor. We will wait there comfortably until we can get the key to the apartment."

"Where is it?"

"The portiere isn't sure. He says a certain Contessa owns the apartment but she let her lover live in it. Now the Contessa decided to get married so she asked the lover to move, but he took the key with him."

"It's that simple," said Carl.

"The portiere will telephone the Contessa's lawyer who takes care of her affairs. He must have another key. While he makes the call we will wait in Mrs. Gaspari's apartment. She will make you an American coffee. You'll like her husband too, he works for an American company."

"Never mind the coffee," Carl said. "Isn't there some way we can get a look into the flat? For all I know it may not be worth waiting for. Since it's on the ground floor maybe we can have a look through the windows?"

"The windows are covered by shutters which can be raised from the inside only."

They walked up to the secretary's apartment. She was a dark woman of thirty, with extraordinary legs, and bad teeth when she smiled.

"Is the apartment worth seeing?" Carl asked her.

"It's just like mine, with the exception of having a garden. Would you care to see mine?"

"If I may."

"Please."

She led him through her rooms. Bevilacqua remained on the sofa in the living room, his damp briefcase on his knees. He opened the straps, took out a chunk of bread, and chewed thoughtfully.

Carl admitted to himself that he liked the flat. The building was comparatively new, had gone up after the war. The one bedroom was a disadvantage, but the kids could have it and he and Norma would sleep on the day bed in the living room. The terrace studio was perfect for a workroom. He had looked out of the bedroom window and seen the garden, a wonderful place for children to play.

"Is the rent really forty-five thousand?" he asked.

"Exactly."

"And it is furnished?"

"In quite good taste."

"Why doesn't the Contessa ask more for it?"

"She has other things on her mind," Mrs. Gaspari laughed. "Oh, see," she said, "the rain has stopped and the sun is coming out. It is a good sign." She was standing close to him.

"What's in it for her?" Carl thought and then remembered she would share Bevilacqua's poor three per cent.

He felt his lips moving. He tried to stop the prayer but it went on. When he had finished, it began again. The apartment was fine, the garden just the thing for the kids. The price was better than he had hoped.

In the living room Bevilacqua was talking to the portiere. "He couldn't reach the lawyer," he said glumly.

"Let me try," Mrs. Gaspari said. The portiere gave her the number and left. She dialed the lawyer but found he had gone for the day. She got his house number and telephoned there. The busy signal came. She waited a minute, then dialed again.

Bevilacqua took two small hard apples from his briefcase and offered one to Carl. Carl shook his head. The Italian peeled the apples with his penknife and ate both. He dropped the skins and cores into his briefcase, then locked the straps.

"Maybe we could take the door down," Carl suggested. "It shouldn't be hard to pull the hinges."

"The hinges are on the inside," Bevilacqua said.

"I doubt if the Contessa would rent to you," said Mrs. Gaspari from the telephone, "if you got in by force."

"If I had the lover here," Bevilacqua said, "I would break his neck for stealing the key."

"Still busy," said Mrs. Gaspari.

"Where does the Contessa live?" Carl asked. "Maybe I could take a taxi over."

"I believe she moved recently," Mrs. Gaspari said. "I once had her address but I have no longer."

"Would the portiere know it?"

"Possibly." She called the portiere on the house phone but all he would give her was the Contessa's telephone number. The Contessa wasn't home, her maid said, so they telephoned the lawyer and again got a busy signal. Carl was by now irritated.

Mrs. Gaspari called the telephone operator, giving the Contessa's number and requesting her home address. The telephone operator found the old one but could not locate the new.

"Stupid," said Mrs. Gaspari. Once more she dialed the lawyer.

"I have him," she announced over the mouthpiece. "Buon giorno, Avvocato." Her voice was candy.

Carl heard her ask the lawyer if he had a duplicate key and the lawyer replied for three minutes.

She banged down the phone. "He has no key. Apparently there is only one."

"To hell with all this." Carl got up. "I'm going back to the United States."

It was raining again. A sharp crack of thunder split the sky, and Bevilacqua, abandoning his briefcase, rose in fright.

"I'm licked," Carl said to Norma, the next morning. "Call the agents and tell them we're ready to pay seventy-five. We've got to get out of this joint."

"Not before we speak to the Contessa. I'll tell her my troubles and break her heart."

"You'll get involved and you'll get nowhere," Carl warned her.

"Please call her anyway."

"I haven't got her number. I didn't think of asking for it."

"Find it. You're good at research."

He considered phoning Mrs. Gaspari for the number but remembered she was at work, and he didn't have that number. Recalling the address of the apartment house, he looked it up in the phone book. Then he telephoned the portiere and asked for the Contessa's address and her phone number.

"I'll call you back," said the portiere, eating as he spoke. "Give me your telephone."

"Why bother? Give me her number and save yourself the trouble."

"I have strict orders from the Contessa never to give her number to strangers. They call up on the phone and annoy her."

"I'm not a stranger. I want to rent her flat."

The portiere cleared his throat. "Where are you staying?"

"Albergo Sora Cecilia."

"I'll call you back in a quarter of an hour."

"Have it your way." He gave the portiere his name.

In forty minutes the phone rang and Carl reached for it. "Pronto."

"Signore Schneider?" It was a man's voice—a trifle high.

"Speaking."

"Permit me," the man said, in fluent though accented English. "I am Aldo De Vecchis. It would please me to speak to you in person."

"Are you a real estate agent?"

"Not precisely, but it refers to the apartment of the Contessa. I am the former occupant."

"The man with the key?" Carl asked quickly.

"It is I."

"Where are you now?"

"In the foyer downstairs."

"Come up, please."

"Excuse me, but if you will permit, I would prefer to speak to you here."

"I'll be right down."

"The lover," he said to Norma.

"Oh, God."

He rushed down in the elevator. A thin man in a green suit with cuffless trousers was waiting in the lobby. He was about forty, his face small, his hair wet black, and he wore at a tilt the brownest hat Carl had ever seen. Though his shirt collar was frayed, he looked impeccable. Into the air around him leaked the odor of cologne.

"De Vecchis," he bowed. His eyes, in a slightly pockmarked face, were restless.

"I'm Carl Schneider. How'd you get my number?"

De Vecchis seemed not to have heard. "I hope you are enjoying your visit here."

"I'd enjoy it more if I had a house to live in."

"Precisely. But what is your impression of Italy?"

"I like the people."

"There are too many of them." De Vecchis looked restlessly around. "Where may we speak? My time is short."

"Ah," said Carl. He pointed to a little room where people wrote letters. "In there."

They entered and sat at a table, alone in the room.

De Vecchis felt in his pocket for something, perhaps a cigarette, but came up with nothing. "I won't waste your time," he said. "You wish the apartment you saw yesterday? I wish you to have it, it is most desirable. There is also with it a garden of roses. You will love it on a summer night when Rome is hot. However, the practical matter is this. Are you willing to invest a few lire to obtain the privilege of entry?"

"The key?" Carl knew but asked.

"Precisely. To be frank I am not in good straits. To that is added the psychological disadvantage of the aftermath of a love affair with a most difficult woman. I leave you to imagine my present condition. Notwithstanding, the apartment I offer is attractive and the rent, as I understand, is for Americans not too high. Surely this has its value for you?" He attempted a smile but it died in birth.

"I am a graduate student of Italian studies," Carl said, giving him the facts. "I've invested all of my savings in this trip abroad to get my Ph.D. dissertation done. I have a wife to support and two children."

"I hear that your government is most generous to the Fulbright Fellows?"

"You don't understand. I am not a Fulbright Fellow."

"Whatever it is," De Vecchis said, drumming his fingertips on the table, "the price of the key is eighty-thousand lire."

Carl laughed mirthlessly.

"I beg your pardon?"

Carl rose.

"Is the price too high?"

"It's impossible."

De Vecchis rubbed his brow nervously. "Very well, since not all Americans are rich Americans—you see, I am objective—I will reduce the sum by one half. For less than a month's rent the key is yours."

"Thanks. No dice."

"Please? I don't understand your expression."

"I can't afford it. I'd still have a commission to pay the agent."

"Oh? Then why don't you forget him? I will issue orders to the portiere to allow you to move in immediately. This evening, if you prefer. The Contessa's lawyer will draw up the lease free of charge. And although she is difficult to her lovers, she is an angel to her tenants."

"I'd like to forget the agent," Carl said, "but I can't."

De Vecchis gnawed his lip. "I will make it twenty-five thousand," he said, "but this is my last and absolute word."

"No, thanks. I won't be a party to a bribe."

De Vecchis rose, his small face tight, pale. "It is people like you who drive us to the hands of the Communists. You try to buy us—our votes, our culture, and then you dare speak of bribes."

He strode out of the room and through the lobby.

Five minutes later the phone rang. "Fifteen thousand is my final offer." His voice was thick.

"Not a cent," said Carl.

Norma stared at him.

De Vecchis slammed the phone.

The portiere telephoned. He had looked everywhere, he said, but had lost the Contessa's address.

"What about her phone number?" Carl asked.

"It was changed when she moved. The numbers are confused in my mind, the old with the new."

"Look here," Carl said, "I'll tell the Contessa you sent De Vecchis to see me about her apartment."

"How can you tell her if you don't know her number?" the portiere asked with curiosity. "It isn't listed in the book."

"I'll ask Mrs. Gaspari for it when she gets home from work, then I'll call the Contessa and tell her what you did."

"What did I do? Tell me exactly."

"You sent her former lover, a man she wants to get rid of, to try to squeeze money out of me for something that is none of his business—namely her apartment."

"Is there no other way than this?" asked the portiere.

"If you tell me her address I will give you one thousand lire." Carl felt his tongue thicken.

"How shameful," Norma said from the sink, where she was washing clothes.

"Not more than one thousand?" asked the portiere.

"Not till I move in."

The portiere then told him the Contessa's last name and her new address. "Don't repeat where you got it."

Carl swore he wouldn't.

He left the hotel on the run, got into a cab, and drove across the Tiber to the Via Cassia, in the country.

The Contessa's maid admitted him into a fabulous place with mosaic floors, gilded furniture, and a marble bust of the Contessa's great-grandfather in the foyer where Carl waited. In twenty minutes the Contessa appeared, a plain-looking woman, past fifty, with dyed blonde hair, black eyebrows, and a short, tight dress. The skin on her arms was wrinkled, but her bosom was enormous and she smelled like a rose garden.

"Please, you must be quick," she said impatiently. "There is so much to do. I am preparing for my wedding."

"Contessa," said Carl, "excuse me for rushing in like this, but my wife and I have a desperate need for an apartment and we know that yours on the Via Tirreno is vacant. I'm an American student of Italian life and manners. We've been in Italy almost a month and are still living in a third-rate hotel. My wife is unhappy. The children have miserable colds. I'll be glad to pay you fifty-thousand lire, instead of the forty-five you ask, if you will kindly let us move in today."

"Listen," said the Contessa, "I come from an honorable family. Don't try to bribe me."

Carl blushed. "I mean nothing more than to give you proof of my good will."

"In any case, my lawyer attends to my real estate matters."

"He hasn't the key."

"Why hasn't he?"

"The former occupant took it with him."

"The fool," she said.

"Do you happen to have a duplicate?"

"I never keep duplicate keys. They all get mixed up and I never know which is which."

"Could we have one made?"

"Ask my lawyer."

"I called this morning but he's out of town. May I make a suggestion, Contessa? Could we have a window or a door forced? I will pay the cost of repair."

The Contessa's eyes glinted. "Of course not," she said huffily. "I will have no destruction of my property. We've had enough of that sort of thing here. You Americans have no idea what we've lived through."

"But doesn't it mean something to you to have a reliable tenant in your apartment? What good is it standing empty? Say the word and I'll bring you the rent in an hour."

"Come back in two weeks, young man, after I finish my honeymoon."

"In two weeks I may be dead," Carl said.

The Contessa laughed.

Outside, he met Bevilacqua. He had a black eye and a stricken expression.

"So you've betrayed me?" the Italian said hoarsely.

"What do you mean 'betrayed'? Who are you, Jesus Christ?"

"I hear you went to De Vecchis and begged for the key, with plans to move in without telling me."

"How could I keep that a secret with your pal Mrs. Gaspari living right over my head? The minute I moved in she'd tell you, then you'd be over on horseback to collect."

"That's right," said Bevilacqua. "I didn't think of it."

"Who gave you the black eye?" Carl asked.

"De Vecchis. He's as strong as a wild pig. I met him at the apartment and asked for the key. He called me dirty names. We had a fight and he hit me in the eye with his elbow. How did you make out with the Contessa?"

"Not well. Did you come to see her?"

"Vaguely."

"Go in and beg her to let me move in, for God's sake. Maybe she'll listen to a countryman."

"Don't ask me to eat a horse," said Bevilacqua.

That night Carl dreamed they had moved out of the hotel into the Contessa's apartment. The children were in the garden, playing among the roses. In the morning he decided to go to the portiere and offer him ten thousand lire if he would have a new key made, however they did it—door up or door down.

When he arrived at the apartment house the portiere and Bevilacqua were there with a toothless man, on his knees, poking a hooked wire into the door lock. In two minutes it clicked open.

With a gasp they all entered. From room to room they wandered like dead men. The place was a ruin. The furniture had been smashed with a dull axe. The slashed sofa revealed its inner springs. Rugs were cut up, crockery broken, books wildly torn and scattered. The white walls had been splashed with red wine, except one in the living room which was decorated with dirty words in six languages, printed in orange lipstick.

"Mamma mia," muttered the toothless locksmith, crossing himself. The portiere slowly turned yellow. Bevilacqua wept.

De Vecchis, in his pea green suit, appeared in the doorway. "Ecco la chiave!" He held it triumphantly aloft.

"Assassin!" shouted Bevilacqua. "Turd! May your bones grow hair and rot."

"He lives for my death," he cried to Carl, "I for his. This is our condition."

"You lie," said Carl. "I love this country."

De Vecchis flung the key at them and ran. Bevilacqua, the light of hatred in his eyes, ducked, and the key hit Carl on the forehead, leaving a mark he could not rub out.

THE MAGIC BARREL

Not long ago there lived in uptown New York, in a small, almost meager room, though crowded with books, Leo Finkle, a rabbinical student in the Yeshivah University. Finkle, after six years of study, was to be ordained in June and had been advised by an acquaintance that he might find it easier to win himself a congregation if he were

THE MAGIC BARREL. Reprinted with the permission of Farrar, Straus & Giroux, Inc. from *The Magic Barrel* by Bernard Malamud, copyright © 1951, 1954, 1958 by Bernard Malamud.

married. Since he had no present prospects of marriage, after two tormented days of turning it over in his mind, he called in Pinye Salzman, a marriage broker whose two-line advertisement he had read in the *Forward*.

The matchmaker appeared one night out of the dark fourth-floor hallway of the graystone rooming house where Finkle lived, grasping a black, strapped portfolio that had been worn thin with use. Salzman, who had been long in the business, was of slight but dignified build, wearing an old hat, and an overcoat too short and tight for him. He smelled frankly of fish, which he loved to eat, and although he was missing a few teeth, his presence was not displeasing, because of an amiable manner curiously contrasted with mournful eyes. His voice, his lips, his wisp of beard, his bony fingers were animated, but give him a moment of repose and his mild blue eyes revealed a depth of sadness, a characteristic that put Leo a little at ease although the situation, for him, was inherently tense.

He at once informed Salzman why he had asked him to come, explaining that his home was in Cleveland, and that but for his parents, who had married comparatively late in life, he was alone in the world. He had for six years devoted himself almost entirely to his studies, as a result of which, understandably, he had found himself without time for a social life and the company of young women. Therefore he thought it the better part of trial and error—of embarrassing fumbling—to call in an experienced person to advise him on these matters. He remarked in passing that the function of the marriage broker was ancient and honorable, highly approved in the Jewish community, because it made practical the necessary without hindering joy. Moreover, his own parents had been brought together by a matchmaker. They had made, if not a financially profitable marriage—since neither had possessed any worldly goods to speak of—at least a successful one in the sense of their everlasting devotion to each other. Salzman listened in embarrassed surprise, sensing a sort of apology. Later, however, he experienced a glow of pride in his work, an emotion that had left him years ago, and he heartily approved of Finkle.

The two went to their business. Leo had led Salzman to the only clear place in the room, a table near a window that overlooked the lamp-lit city. He seated himself at the matchmaker's side but facing him, attempting by an act of will to suppress the unpleasant tickle in his throat. Salzman eagerly unstrapped his portfolio and removed a loose rubber band from a thin packet of much-handled cards. As he flipped through them, a gesture and sound that physically hurt Leo, the student pretended not to see and gazed steadfastly out the window. Although it was still February, winter was on its last legs, signs of which he had for the first time in years begun to notice. He now observed the round white moon, moving high in the sky through a cloud menagerie, and watched with half-open mouth as it penetrated a huge hen, and dropped out of her like an egg laying itself. Salzman, though pretending through eyeglasses he had just slipped on, to be engaged in scanning the writing on the cards, stole occasional glances at the young man's distinguished face, noting with pleasure the long, severe scholar's nose, brown eyes heavy with learning, sensitive yet ascetic lips, and a certain, almost hollow quality of the dark cheeks. He gazed around at shelves upon shelves of books and let out a soft, contented sigh.

When Leo's eyes fell upon the cards, he counted six spread out in Salzman's hand.

"So few?" he asked in disappointment.

"You wouldn't believe me how much cards I got in my office," Salzman replied. "The drawers are already filled to the top, so I keep them now in a barrel, but is every girl good for a new rabbi?"

Leo blushed at this, regretting all he had revealed of himself in a curriculum vitae he had sent to Salzman. He had thought it best to acquaint him with his strict standards and specifications, but in having done so, felt he had told the marriage broker more than was absolutely necessary.

He hesitantly inquired, "Do you keep photographs of your clients on file?"

"First comes family, amount of dowry, also what kind promises," Salzman replied, unbuttoning his tight coat and settling himself in the chair. "After comes pictures, rabbi."

"Call me Mr. Finkle. I'm not yet a rabbi."

Salzman said he would, but instead called him doctor, which he changed to rabbi when Leo was not listening too attentively.

Salzman adjusted his horn-rimmed spectacles, gently cleared his throat and read in an eager voice the contents of the top card:

"Sophie P. Twenty four years. Widow one year. No children. Educated high school and two years college. Father promises eight thousand dollars. Has wonderful wholesale business. Also real estate. On the mother's side comes teachers, also one actor. Well known on Second Avenue."

Leo gazed up in surprise. "Did you say a widow?"

"A widow don't mean spoiled, rabbi. She lived with her husband maybe four months. He was a sick boy she made a mistake to marry him."

"Marrying a widow has never entered my mind."

"This is because you have no experience. A widow, especially if she is young and healthy like this girl, is a wonderful person to marry. She will be thankful to you the rest of her life. Believe me, if I was looking now for a bride, I would marry a widow."

Leo reflected, then shook his head.

Salzman hunched his shoulders in an almost imperceptible gesture of disappointment. He placed the card down on the wooden table and began to read another:

"Lily H. High school teacher. Regular. Not a substitute. Has savings and new Dodge car. Lived in Paris one year. Father is successful dentist thirty-five years. Interested in professional man. Well Americanized family. Wonderful opportunity."

"I knew her personally," said Salzman. "I wish you could see this girl. She is a doll. Also very intelligent. All day you could talk to her about books and theyater and what not. She also knows current events."

"I don't believe you mentioned her age?"

"Her age?" Salzman said, raising his brows. "Her age is thirty-two years."

Leo said after a while, "I'm afraid that seems a little too old."

Salzman let out a laugh. "So how old are you, rabbi?"

"Twenty-seven."

"So what is the difference, tell me, between twenty-seven and thirty-two? My own wife is seven years older than me. So what did I suffer?—Nothing. If Rothschild's a daughter wants to marry you, would you say on account her age, no?"

"Yes," Leo said dryly.

Salzman shook off the no in the yes. "Five years don't mean a thing. I give you my word that when you will live with her for one week you will forget her age. What does it mean five years—that she lived more and knows more than somebody who is younger?

On this girl, God bless her, years are not wasted. Each one that it comes makes better the bargain."

"What subject does she teach in high school?"

"Languages. If you heard the way she speaks French, you will think it is music. I am in the business twenty-five years, and I recommend her with my whole heart. Believe me, I know what I'm talking, rabbi."

"What's on the next card?" Leo said abruptly.

Salzman reluctantly turned up the third card:

"Ruth K. Nineteen years. Honor student. Father offers thirteen thousand cash to the right bridegroom. He is a medical doctor. Stomach specialist with marvelous practice. Brother in law owns own garment business. Particular people."

Salzman looked as if he had read his trump card.

"Did you say nineteen?" Leo asked with interest.

"On the dot."

"Is she attractive?" He blushed. "Pretty?"

Salzman kissed his finger tips. "A little doll. On this I give you my word. Let me call the father tonight and you will see what means pretty."

But Leo was troubled. "You're sure she's that young?"

"This I am positive. The father will show you the birth certificate."

"Are you positive there isn't something wrong with her?" Leo insisted.

"Who says there is wrong?"

"I don't understand why an American girl her age should go to a marriage broker."

A smile spread over Salzman's face.

"So for the same reason you went, she comes."

Leo flushed. "I am pressed for time."

Salzman, realizing he had been tactless, quickly explained. "The father came, not her. He wants she should have the best, so he looks around himself. When we will locate the right boy he will introduce him and encourage. This makes a better marriage than if a young girl without experience takes for herself. I don't have to tell you this."

"But don't you think this young girl believes in love?" Leo spoke uneasily.

Salzman was about to guffaw but caught himself and said soberly, "Love comes with the right person, not before."

Leo parted dry lips but did not speak. Noticing that Salzman had snatched a glance at the next card, he cleverly asked, "How is her health?"

"Perfect," Salzman said, breathing with difficulty. "Of course, she is a little lame on her right foot from an auto accident that it happened to her when she was twelve years, but nobody notices on account she is so brilliant and also beautiful."

Leo got up heavily and went to the window. He felt curiously bitter and upbraided himself for having called in the marriage broker. Finally, he shook his head.

"Why not?" Salzman persisted, the pitch of his voice rising.

"Because I detest stomach specialists."

"So what do you care what is his business? After you marry her do you need him? Who says he must come every Friday night in your house?"

Ashamed of the way the talk was going, Leo dismissed Salzman, who went home with heavy, melancholy eyes.

Though he had felt only relief at the marriage broker's departure, Leo was in low spirits the next day. He explained it as arising from Salzman's failure to produce a suitable bride for him. He did not care for his type of clientele. But when Leo found himself hesitating whether to seek out another matchmaker, one more polished than Pinye, he wondered if it could be—his protestations to the contrary, and although he honored his father and mother—that he did not, in essence, care for the matchmaking institution? This thought he quickly put out of mind yet found himself still upset. All day he ran around in the woods—missed an important appointment, forgot to give out his laundry, walked out of a Broadway cafeteria without paying and had to run back with the ticket in his hand; had even not recognized his landlady in the street when she passed with a friend and courteously called out, "A good evening to you, Doctor Finkle." By nightfall, however, he had regained sufficient calm to sink his nose into a book and there found peace from his thoughts.

Almost at once there came a knock on the door. Before Leo could say enter, Salzman, commercial cupid, was standing in the room. His face was gray and meager, his expression hungry, and he looked as if he would expire on his feet. Yet the marriage broker managed, by some trick of the muscles, to display a broad smile.

"So good evening. I am invited?"

Leo nodded, disturbed to see him again, yet unwilling to ask the man to leave.

Beaming still, Salzman laid his portfolio on the table. "Rabbi, I got for you tonight good news."

"I've asked you not to call me rabbi. I'm still a student."

"Your worries are finished. I have for you a first-class bride."

"Leave me in peace concerning this subject." Leo pretended lack of interest.

"The world will dance at your wedding."

"Please, Mr. Salzman, no more."

"But first must come back my strength," Salzman said weakly. He fumbled with the portfolio straps and took out of the leather case an oily paper bag, from which he extracted a hard, seeded roll and a small, smoked white fish. With a quick motion of his hand he stripped the fish out of its skin and began ravenously to chew. "All day in a rush," he muttered.

Leo watched him eat.

"A sliced tomato you have maybe?" Salzman hesitantly inquired.

"No."

The marriage broker shut his eyes and ate. When he had finished he carefully cleaned up the crumbs and rolled up the remains of the fish, in the paper bag. His spectacled eyes roamed the room until he discovered, amid some piles of books, a one-burner gas stove. Lifting his hat he humbly asked, "A glass tea you got, rabbi?"

Conscience-stricken, Leo rose and brewed the tea. He served it with a chunk of lemon and two cubes of lump sugar, delighting Salzman.

After he had drunk his tea, Salzman's strength and good spirits were restored.

"So tell me, rabbi," he said amiably, "you considered some more the three clients I mentioned yesterday?"

"There was no need to consider."

"Why not?"

"None of them suits me."

"What then suits you?"

Leo let it pass because he could give only a confused answer.

Without waiting for a reply, Salzman asked, "You remember this girl I talked to you—the high school teacher?"

"Age thirty-two?"

But, surprisingly, Salzman's face lit in a smile. "Age twenty-nine."

Leo shot him a look. "Reduced from thirty-two?"

"A mistake," Salzman avowed. "I talked today with the dentist. He took me to his safety deposit box and showed me the birth certificate. She was twenty-nine years last August. They made her a party in the mountains where she went for her vacation. When her father spoke to me the first time I forgot to write the age and I told you thirty-two, but now I remember this was a different client, a widow."

"The same one you told me about? I thought she was twenty-four?"

"A different. Am I responsible that the world is filled with widows?"

"No, but I'm not interested in them, nor for that matter, in school teachers."

Salzman pulled his clasped hands to his breast. Looking at the ceiling he devoutly exclaimed, "Yiddishe kinder, what can I say to somebody that he is not interested in high school teachers? So what then you are interested?"

Leo flushed but controlled himself.

"In what else will you be interested," Salzman went on, "if you not interested in this fine girl that she speaks four languages and has personally in the bank ten thousand dollars? Also her father guarantees further twelve thousand. Also she has a new car, wonderful clothes, talks on all subjects, and she will give you a first-class home and children. How near do we come in our life to paradise?"

"If she's so wonderful, why wasn't she married ten years ago?"

"Why?" said Salzman with a heavy laugh. "—Why? Because she is *partikiler*. This is why. She wants the *best*."

Leo was silent, amused at how he had entangled himself. But Salzman had aroused his interest in Lily H., and he began seriously to consider calling on her. When the marriage broker observed how intently Leo's mind was at work on the facts he had supplied, he felt certain they would soon come to an agreement.

Late Saturday afternoon, conscious of Salzman, Leo Finkle walked with Lily Hirschorn along Riverside Drive. He walked briskly and

erectly, wearing with distinction the black fedora he had that morning taken with trepidation out of the dusty hat box on his closet
shelf, and the heavy black Saturday coat he had thoroughly whisked
clean. Leo also owned a walking stick, a present from a distant relative, but quickly put temptation aside and did not use it. Lily,
petite and not unpretty, had on something signifying the approach
of spring. She was au courant, animatedly, with all sorts of subjects,
and he weighed her words and found her surprisingly sound—score
another for Salzman, whom he uneasily sensed to be somewhere
around, hiding perhaps high in a tree along the street, flashing the
lady signals with a pocket mirror; or perhaps a cloven-hoofed Pan,
piping nuptial ditties as he danced his invisible way before them,
strewing wild buds on the walk and purple grapes in their path,
symbolizing fruit of a union, though there was of course still none.

Lily startled Leo by remarking, "I was thinking of Mr. Salzman,
a curious figure, wouldn't you say?"

Not certain what to answer, he nodded.

She bravely went on, blushing, "I for one am grateful for his introducing us. Aren't you?"

He courteously replied, "I am."

"I mean," she said with a little laugh—and it was all in good
taste, or at least gave the effect of being not in bad—"do you mind
that we came together so?"

He was not displeased with her honesty, recognizing that she
meant to set the relationship aright, and understanding that it took
a certain amount of experience in life, and courage, to want to do it
quite that way. One had to have some sort of past to make that kind
of beginning.

He said that he did not mind. Salzman's function was traditional
and honorable—valuable for what it might achieve, which, he pointed
out, was frequently nothing.

Lily agreed with a sigh. They walked on for a while and she said
after a long silence, again with a nervous laugh, "Would you mind
if I asked you something a little bit personal? Frankly, I find the
subject fascinating." Although Leo shrugged, she went on half em-
barrassedly, "How was it that you came to your calling? I mean
was it a sudden passionate inspiration?"

Leo, after a time, slowly replied, "I was always interested in the
Law."

"You saw revealed in it the presence of the Highest?"

He nodded and changed the subject. "I understand that you spent a little time in Paris, Miss Hirschorn?"

"Oh, did Mr. Salzman tell you, Rabbi Finkle?" Leo winced but she went on, "It was ages ago and almost forgotten. I remember I had to return for my sister's wedding."

And Lily would not be put off. "When," she asked in a trembly voice, "did you become enamored of God?"

He stared at her. Then it came to him that she was talking not about Leo Finkle, but of a total stranger, some mystical figure, perhaps even passionate prophet that Salzman had dreamed up for her—no relation to the living or dead. Leo trembled with rage and weakness. The trickster had obviously sold her a bill of goods, just as he had him, who'd expected to become acquainted with a young lady of twenty-nine, only to behold, the moment he laid eyes upon her strained and anxious face, a woman past thirty-five and aging rapidly. Only his self control had kept him this long in her presence.

"I am not," he said gravely, "a talented religious person," and in seeking words to go on, found himself possessed by shame and fear. "I think," he said in a strained manner, "that I came to God not because I loved Him, but because I did not."

This confession he spoke harshly because its unexpectedness shook him.

Lily wilted. Leo saw a profusion of loaves of bread go flying like ducks high over his head, not unlike the winged loaves by which he had counted himself to sleep last night. Mercifully, then, it snowed, which he would not put past Salzman's machinations.

He was infuriated with the marriage broker and swore he would throw him out of the room the minute he reappeared. But Salzman did not come that night, and when Leo's anger had subsided, an unaccountable despair grew in its place. At first he thought this was caused by his disappointment in Lily, but before long it became evident that he had involved himself with Salzman without a true knowledge of his own intent. He gradually realized—with an emptiness that seized him with six hands—that he had called in the broker to find him a bride because he was incapable of doing it himself. This terrifying insight he had derived as a result of his meeting and conversation with Lily Hirschorn. Her probing questions had somehow irritated him into revealing—to himself more than her—the true nature of his relationship to God, and from that it had come upon him, with shocking force, that apart from his parents, he had never loved anyone. Or perhaps it went the other way, that he did not love God so well as he might, because he had not loved man. It seemed to Leo that his whole life stood starkly revealed and he saw himself for the first time as he truly was—unloved and loveless. This bitter but somehow not fully unexpected revelation brought him to a point of panic, controlled only by extraordinary effort. He covered his face with his hands and cried.

The week that followed was the worst of his life. He did not eat and lost weight. His beard darkened and grew ragged. He stopped attending seminars and almost never opened a book. He seriously considered leaving the Yeshivah, although he was deeply troubled at the thought of the loss of all his years of study—saw them like pages torn from a book, strewn over the city—and at the devastating effect of this decision upon his parents. But he had lived without knowledge of himself, and never in the Five Books and all the Commentaries—mea culpa—had the truth been revealed to him. He did not know where to turn, and in all this desolating loneliness there was no *to whom,* although he often thought of Lily but not once could bring himself to go downstairs and make the call. He became touchy and irritable, especially with his landlady, who asked him all manner of personal questions; on the other hand, sensing his own disagreeableness, he waylaid her on the stairs and apologized abjectly, until mortified, she ran from him. Out of this, however, he drew the consolation that he was a Jew and that a Jew suffered. But gradually, as the long and terrible week drew to a close, he regained his composure and some idea of purpose in life: to go on as planned. Although he was imperfect, the ideal was not. As for his quest of a bride, the thought of continuing afflicted him with anxiety and heartburn, yet perhaps with this new knowledge of himself he would be more successful than in the past. Perhaps love would now come to him and a bride to that love. And for this sanctified seeking who needed a Salzman?

The marriage broker, a skeleton with haunted eyes, returned that very night. He looked, withal, the picture of frustrated expectancy— as if he had steadfastly waited the week at Miss Lily Hirschorn's side for a telephone call that never came.

Casually coughing, Salzman came immediately to the point: "So how did you like her?"

Leo's anger rose and he could not refrain from chiding the matchmaker: "Why did you lie to me, Salzman?"

Salzman's pale face went dead white, the world had snowed on him.

"Did you not state that she was twenty-nine?" Leo insisted.

"I give you my word—"

"She was thirty-five, if a day. *At least* thirty-five."

"Of this don't be too sure. Her father told me—"

"Never mind. The worst of it was that you lied to her."

"How did I lie to her, tell me?"

"You told her things about me that weren't true. You made me out to be more, consequently less than I am. She had in mind a totally different person, a sort of semi-mystical Wonder Rabbi."

"All I said, you was a religious man."

"I can imagine."

Salzman sighed. "This is my weakness that I have," he confessed. "My wife says to me I shouldn't be a salesman, but when I have two fine people that they would be wonderful to be married, I am so happy that I talk too much." He smiled wanly. "This is why Salzman is a poor man."

Leo's anger left him. "Well, Salzman, I'm afraid that's all."

The marriage broker fastened hungry eyes on him.

"You don't want any more a bride?"

"I do," said Leo, "but I have decided to seek her in a different way. I am no longer interested in an arranged marriage. To be frank, I now admit the necessity of premarital love. That is, I want to be in love with the one I marry."

"Love?" said Salzman, astounded. After a moment he remarked, "For us, our love is our life, not for the ladies. In the ghetto they—"

"I know, I know," said Leo. "I've thought of it often. Love, I have said to myself, should be a by-product of living and worship rather than its own end. Yet for myself I find it necessary to establish the level of my need and fulfill it."

Salzman shrugged but answered, "Listen, rabbi, if you want love, this I can find you also. I have such beautiful clients that you will love them the minute your eyes will see them."

Leo smiled unhappily. "I'm afraid you don't understand."

But Salzman hastily unstrapped his portfolio and withdrew a manila packet from it.

"Pictures," he said, quickly laying the envelope on the table.

Leo called after him to take the pictures away, but as if on the wings of the wind, Salzman had disappeared.

March came. Leo had returned to his regular routine. Although he felt not quite himself yet—lacked energy—he was making plans for a more active social life. Of course it would cost something, but he was an expert in cutting corners; and when there were no corners left he would make circles rounder. All the while Salzman's pictures had lain on the table, gathering dust. Occasionally as Leo sat studying, or enjoying a cup of tea, his eyes fell on the manila envelope, but he never opened it.

The days went by and no social life to speak of developed with a member of the opposite sex—it was difficult, given the circumstances of his situation. One morning Leo toiled up the stairs to his room and stared out the window at the city. Although the day was bright his view of it was dark. For some time he watched the people in the street below hurrying along and then turned with a heavy heart to his little room. On the table was the packet. With a sudden relentless gesture he tore it open. For a half-hour he stood by the table in a state of excitement, examining the photographs of the ladies Salzman had included. Finally, with a deep sigh he put them down. There were six, of varying degrees of attractiveness, but look at them long enough and they all became Lily Hirschorn: all past their prime, all starved behind bright smiles, not a true personality in the lot. Life, despite their frantic yoohooings, had passed them by; they were pictures in a briefcase that stank of fish. After a while, however, as Leo attempted to return the photographs into the envelope, he found in it another, a snapshot of the type taken by a machine for a quarter. He gazed at it a moment and let out a cry.

Her face deeply moved him. Why, he could at first not say. It gave him the impression of youth—spring flowers, yet age—a sense of having been used to the bone, wasted; this came from the eyes, which were hauntingly familiar, yet absolutely strange. He had a vivid impression that he had met her before, but try as he might he could not place her although he could almost recall her name, as if he had read it in her own handwriting. No, this couldn't be; he would have remembered her. It was not, he affirmed, that she had an extraordinary beauty—no, though her face was attractive enough; it was that *some-thing* about her moved him. Feature for feature, even some of the ladies of the photographs could do better; but she leaped forth to his heart—had *lived,* or wanted to—more than just wanted, perhaps regretted how she had lived—had somehow deeply suffered: it could be seen in the depths of those reluctant eyes, and from the way the light enclosed and shone from her, and within her, opening realms of possibility: this was her own. Her he desired. His head ached and eyes narrowed with the intensity of his gazing, then as if an obscure fog had blown up in the mind, he experienced fear of her and was aware that he had received an impression, somehow, of evil. He shuddered, saying softly, it is thus with us all. Leo brewed some tea in a small pot and sat sipping it without sugar, to calm himself. But before he had finished drinking, again with excitement he examined the face and found it good: good for Leo Finkle. Only such a one could understand him and help him seek whatever he was seeking. She might, perhaps, love him. How she had happened to be among the discards in Salzman's barrel he could never guess, but he knew he must urgently go find her.

Leo rushed downstairs, grabbed up the Bronx telephone book, and searched for Salzman's home address. He was not listed, nor was his office. Neither was he in the Manhattan book. But Leo remembered having written down the address on a slip of paper after he had read Salzman's advertisement in the "personals" column of the *Forward.* He ran up to his room and tore through his papers, without luck. It was exasperating. Just when he needed the matchmaker he was nowhere to be found. Fortunately Leo remembered to look in his wallet. There on a card he found his name written and a Bronx address. No phone number was listed, the reason—Leo now recalled —he had originally communicated with Salzman by letter. He got on his coat, put a hat on over his skull cap and hurried to the subway station. All the way to the far end of the Bronx he sat on the edge of his seat. He was more than once tempted to take out the picture and see if the girl's face was as he remembered it, but he refrained, allowing the snapshot to remain in his inside coat pocket, content to have her so close. When the train pulled into the station he was waiting at the door and bolted out. He quickly located the street Salzman had advertised.

The building he sought was less than a block from the subway, but it was not an office building, nor even a loft, nor a store in which one could rent office space. It was a very old tenement house. Leo found Salzman's name in pencil on a soiled tag under the bell and climbed three dark flights to his apartment. When he knocked, the door was opened by a thin, asthmatic, gray-haired woman, in felt slippers.

"Yes?" she said, expecting nothing. She listened without listening. He could have sworn he had seen her, too, before but knew it was an illusion.

"Salzman—does he live here? Pinye Salzman," he said, "the matchmaker?"

She stared at him a long minute. "Of course."

He felt embarrassed. "Is he in?"

"No." Her mouth, though left open, offered nothing more.

"The matter is urgent. Can you tell me where his office is?"

"In the air." She pointed upward.

"You mean he has no office?" Leo asked.

"In his socks."

He peered into the apartment. It was sunless and dingy, one large room divided by a half-open curtain, beyond which he could see a sagging metal bed. The near side of the room was crowded with rickety chairs, old bureaus, a three-legged table, racks of cooking utensils, and all the apparatus of a kitchen. But there was no sign of Salzman or his magic barrel, probably also a figment of the imagination. An odor of frying fish made Leo weak to the knees.

"Where is he?" he insisted. "I've got to see your husband."

At length she answered, "So who knows where he is? Every time he thinks a new thought he runs to a different place. Go home, he will find you."

"Tell him Leo Finkle."

She gave no sign she had heard.

He walked downstairs, depressed.

But Salzman, breathless, stood waiting at his door.

Leo was astounded and overjoyed. "How did you get here before me?"

"I rushed."

"Come inside."

They entered. Leo fixed tea, and a sardine sandwich for Salzman.

As they were drinking he reached behind him for the packet of pictures and handed them to the marriage broker.

Salzman put down his glass and said expectantly, "You found somebody you like?"

"Not among these."

The marriage broker turned away.

"Here is the one I want." Leo held forth the snapshot.

Salzman slipped on his glasses and took the picture into his trembling hand. He turned ghastly and let out a groan.

"What's the matter?" cried Leo.

"Excuse me. Was an accident this picture. She isn't for you."

Salzman frantically shoved the manila packet into his portfolio. He thrust the snapshot into his pocket and fled down the stairs.

Leo, after momentary paralysis, gave chase and cornered the marriage broker in the vestibule. The landlady made hysterical outcries but neither of them listened.

"Give me back the picture, Salzman."

"No." The pain in his eyes was terrible.

"Tell me who she is then."

"This I can't tell you. Excuse me."

He made to depart, but Leo, forgetting himself, seized the matchmaker by his tight coat and shook him frenziedly.

"Please," sighed Salzman. *"Please."*

Leo ashamedly let him go. "Tell me who she is," he begged. "It's very important for me to know."

"She is not for you. She is a wild one—wild, without shame. This is not a bride for a rabbi."

"What do you mean wild?"

"Like an animal. Like a dog. For her to be poor was a sin. This is why to me she is dead now."

"In God's name, what do you mean?"

"Her I can't introduce to you," Salzman cried.

"Why are you so excited?"

"Why, he asks," Salzman said, bursting into tears. "This is my baby, my Stella, she should burn in hell."

Leo hurried up to bed and hid under the covers. Under the covers he thought his life through. Although he soon fell asleep he could not sleep her out of his mind. He woke, beating his breast. Though he prayed to be rid of her, his prayers went unanswered. Through days of torment he endlessly struggled not to love her; fearing success, he escaped it. He then concluded to convert her to goodness, himself to God. The idea alternately nauseated and exalted him.

He perhaps did not know that he had come to a final decision until he encountered Salzman in a Broadway cafeteria. He was sitting alone at a rear table, sucking the bony remains of a fish. The marriage broker appeared haggard, and transparent to the point of vanishing.

Salzman looked up at first without recognizing him. Leo had grown a pointed beard and his eyes were weighted with wisdom.

"Salzman," he said, "love has at last come to my heart."

"Who can love from a picture?" mocked the marriage broker.

"It is not impossible."

"If you can love her, then you can love anybody. Let me show you some new clients that they just sent me their photographs. One is a little doll."

"Just her I want," Leo murmured.

"Don't be a fool, doctor. Don't bother with her."

"Put me in touch with her, Salzman," Leo said humbly. "Perhaps I can be of service."

Salzman had stopped eating and Leo understood with emotion that it was now arranged.

Leaving the cafeteria, he was, however, afflicted by a tormenting suspicion that Salzman had planned it all to happen this way.

Leo was informed by letter that she would meet him on a certain corner, and she was there one spring night, waiting under a street lamp. He appeared, carrying a small bouquet of violets and rosebuds. Stella stood by the lamp post, smoking. She wore white with red shoes, which fitted his expectations, although in a troubled moment he had imagined the dress red, and only the shoes white. She waited uneasily and shyly. From afar he saw that her eyes—clearly her father's—were filled with desperate innocence. He pictured, in her, his own redemption. Violins and lit candles revolved in the sky. Leo ran forward with flowers outthrust.

Around the corner, Salzman, leaning against a wall, chanted prayers for the dead.

Thomas Mann

1875–1955

LITTLE HERR FRIEDEMANN · THE INFANT
PRODIGY · DISORDER AND EARLY SORROW

Thomas Mann's merchant ancestors prospered for over a century in Lübeck, Germany, ancient trading city of the Hanseatic League. His father, who died when Thomas was fifteen, was twice mayor of the city. His mother, musical and temperamental, was the daughter of a German planter in Rio de Janeiro and his Portuguese-Creole wife. As he grew up, Thomas Mann felt that the dominant qualities of his parents and their disparate traditions were at war within his nature. This is dramatized in his writing as the opposition of businessman and artist, of North and South, of life and spirit, of realism and romanticism.

At the Lübeck High School, whose Prussian military discipline he hated, Mann devoted most of his energies to a student literary magazine. When he graduated he joined his mother in Munich and soon went on to Rome, where he spent over a year in seclusion, working hard at his writing in company with his brother Heinrich, who also became an influential novelist.

Thomas Mann's magazine stories were collected in the volume *Little Herr Friedemann* when he was only twenty-three. At twenty-five he published *Buddenbrooks* (1901), a three-generation family novel which sold over a million copies in Germany alone. Like Galsworthy's later *Forsyte Saga,* it describes the gradual decay and dissolution of a patrician merchant family. As the family grows more cultivated, producing artists and men of sensibility, character and purpose tend to disappear. Mann's preoccupation with decadence is even more marked in the beautiful long short story, "Death in Venice" (1911), and in *The Magic Mountain* (1924), which is set in a tuberculosis sanitarium in Switzerland. Rich both in characterization and in explicitly discussed ideas, *The Magic Mountain* is a study of what is wrong with

European culture. The problem had fascinated Mann ever since, as a young man, he saturated himself in the philosophies of Schopenhauer and Nietzsche. In *The Magic Mountain,* as elsewhere in Mann's work, physical illness stands for spiritual illness.

Influenced by depth psychology and anthropology, Mann saw more and more clearly how myth unites present and past, the conscious and unconscious. The four-volume series *Joseph and His Brothers,* completed in 1943, retells the Biblical story of Joseph with subtle reference to Franklin D. Roosevelt and the rise of the modern welfare state. At the same time, he shows in it the power of racial memory, or of what Carl Jung calls "the collective unconscious." *Dr. Faustus* (1948) relates music, beauty, sickness, sensitivity, and decadence in the life of an imaginary composer whose biography is like that of Nietzsche. Mann's interest in music shows in the formal elements of his own stories. Certain words and images recur in association with certain characters and ideas as do *leitmotifs* in the operas of Wagner. Mann refers to this characteristic of his work in a suggestive passage, included in Appendix B, from one of his lectures. There are obvious examples in "Little Herr Friedemann."

From the time of the success of *Buddenbrooks,* with Goethe as his model, Thomas Mann took very seriously his role as one of the chief representatives of European culture. During the First World War he was still a political conservative, but during the writing of *The Magic Mountain,* where there are long debates between an authoritarian and a liberal, his views became more moderate and democratic, though still complex. In 1931, at a stormy meeting broken up by Nazi hecklers, he spoke under the auspices of the Social-Democratic Party. Mann left Germany after Hitler came to power, and broke finally with the Third Reich three years later, in a famous exchange of letters with the Dean of Philosophy at Bonn University. In 1938 he moved to the United States, where he became an American citizen.

In 1952, troubled by the tensions of the "cold war" and what he thought was increasing political reaction in the United States, Mann returned to Europe to end his days in Switzerland. His last work, published when he was eighty, is the picaresque comic novel, *The Confessions of Felix Krull, Confidence Man* (1955).

Though its melodramatic conclusion and the obviousness of some details show "Little Herr Friedemann" to be an early story, it brings together in striking form the themes and symbols that were to dominate much of Mann's work. Its picture of social manners under the Empire also points up by contrast the sense of social instability and formlessness which the professor in "Disorder and Early Sorrow" feels so acutely.

Mann liked to write about children, the abnormal, and artists. The hero of "The Infant Prodigy" is all three. He is something of a monster, though a delightful one, whose relations with his audience undoubtedly express some of the author's feelings about the role he himself—or any artist—must play.

Of Mann's four major long short stories or *novellen,* "Tonio Kröger," "Death in Venice," "Mario and the Magician," and "Disorder and Early Sorrow," the last is most universal in its theme. It is a penetrating subjective study of the unsettling effects of the inflation, which had so much to do with the disastrous events of the thirties in Germany. But as a subtle and tender expression of parental love, it transcends the merely historical.

LITTLE HERR FRIEDEMANN

It was the nurse's fault. When they first suspected, Frau Consul Friedemann had spoken to her very gravely about the need of controlling her weakness. But what good did that do? Or the glass of red wine which she got daily besides the beer which was needed for the milk? For they suddenly discovered that she even sank so low as to drink the methylated spirit which was kept for the spirit lamp. Before they could send her away and get someone to take her place, the mischief was done. One day the mother and sisters came home to find that little Johannes, then about a month old, had fallen from the couch and lay on the floor, uttering an appallingly faint little cry, while the nurse stood beside him quite stupefied.

LITTLE HERR FRIEDEMANN. Reprinted from *Stories of Three Decades* by Thomas Mann, by permission of Alfred A. Knopf, Inc. Copyright 1936 by Alfred A. Knopf, Inc.

The doctor came and with firm, gentle hands tested the little creature's contracted and twitching limbs. He made a very serious face. The three girls stood sobbing in a corner and the Frau Consul in the anguish of her heart prayed aloud.

The poor mother, just before the child's birth, had already suffered a crushing blow: her husband, the Dutch Consul, had been snatched away from her by sudden and violent illness, and now she was too broken to cherish any hope that little Johannes would be spared to her. But by the second day the doctor had given her hand an encouraging squeeze and told her that all immediate danger was over. There was no longer any sign that the brain was affected. The facial expression was altered, it had lost the fixed and staring look. . . . Of course, they must see how things went on—and hope for the best, hope for the best.

The grey gabled house in which Johannes Friedemann grew up stood by the north gate of the little old commercial city. The front door led into a large flag-paved entry, out of which a stair with a white wooden balustrade led up into the second storey. The faded wall-paper in the living-room had a landscape pattern, and straight-backed chairs and sofas in dark-red plush stood round the heavy mahogany table.

Often in his childhood Johannes sat here at the window, which always had a fine showing of flowers, on a small footstool at his mother's feet, listening to some fairy-tale she told him, gazing at her smooth grey head, her mild and gentle face, and breathing in the faint scent she exhaled. She showed him the picture of his father, a kindly man with grey side-whiskers—he was now in heaven, she said, and awaiting them there.

Behind the house was a small garden where in summer they spent much of their time, despite the smell of burnt sugar which came over from the refinery close by. There was a gnarled old walnut tree in whose shade little Johannes would sit, on a low wooden stool, cracking walnuts, while Frau Friedemann and her three daughters, now grown women, took refuge from the sun under a grey canvas tent. The mother's gaze often strayed from her embroidery to look with sad and loving eyes at her child.

He was not beautiful, little Johannes, as he crouched on his stool industriously cracking his nuts. In fact, he was a strange sight, with his pigeon breast, humped back, and disproportionately long arms. But his hands and feet were delicately formed, he had soft red-brown eyes like a doe's, a sensitive mouth, and fine, light-brown hair. His head, had it not sat so deep between his shoulders, might almost have been called pretty.

When he was seven he went to school, where time passed swiftly and uniformly. He walked every day, with the strut deformed people often have, past the quaint gabled houses and shops to the old school-house with the vaulted arcades. When he had done his preparation he would read in his books with the lovely title-page illustrations in colour, or else work in the garden, while his sisters kept house for their invalid mother. They went out too, for they belonged to the best society of the town; but unfortunately they had not married, for they had not much money nor any looks to recommend them.

Johannes too was now and then invited out by his schoolmates, but it is not likely that he enjoyed it. He could not take part in their games, and they were always embarrassed in his company, so there was no feeling of good fellowship.

There came a time when he began to hear certain matters talked about, in the courtyard at school. He listened wide-eyed and large-eared, quite silent, to his companions' raving over this or that little girl. Such things, though they entirely engrossed the attention of these others, were not, he felt, for him; they belonged in the same category as the ball games and gymnastics. At times he felt a little sad. But at length he had become quite used to standing on one side and not taking part.

But after all it came about—when he was sixteen—that he felt suddenly drawn to a girl of his own age. She was the sister of a classmate of his, a blonde, hilarious hoyden, and he met her when calling at her brother's house. He felt strangely embarrassed in her neighbourhood; she too was embarrassed and treated him with such artificial cordiality that it made him sad.

One summer afternoon as he was walking by himself on the wall outside the town, he heard a whispering behind a jasmine bush and peeped cautiously through the branches. There she sat on a bench beside a long-legged, red-haired youth of his acquaintance. They had their arms about each other and he was imprinting on her lips a kiss, which she returned amid giggles. Johannes looked, turned round, and went softly away.

His head was sunk deeper than ever between his shoulders, his hands trembled, and a sharp pain shot upwards from his chest to his throat. But he choked it down, straightening himself as well as he could. "Good," said he to himself. "That is over. Never again will I let myself in for any of it. To the others it brings joy and happiness, for me it can only mean sadness and pain. I am done with it. For me that is all over. Never again."

The resolution did him good. He had renounced, renounced forever. He went home, took up a book, or else played on his violin, which despite his deformed chest he had learned to do.

At seventeen Johannes left school to go into business, like everybody else he knew. He was apprenticed to the big lumber firm of Herr Schlievogt down on the river-bank. They were kind and considerate, he on his side was responsive and friendly, time passed with peaceful regularity. But in his twenty-first year his mother died, after a lingering illness.

This was a sore blow for Johannes Friedemann, and the pain of it endured. He cherished this grief, he gave himself up to it as one gives oneself to a great joy, he fed it with a thousand childhood memories; it was the first important event in his life and he made the most of it.

Is not life in and for itself a good, regardless of whether we may call its content "happiness"? Johannes Friedemann felt that it was so, and he loved life. He, who had renounced the greatest joy it can bring us, taught himself with infinite, incredible care to take pleasure in what it had still to offer. A walk in the springtime in the parks surrounding the town; the fragrance of a flower; the song of a bird— might not one feel grateful for such things as these?

And that we need to be taught how to enjoy, yes, that our education is always and only equal to our capacity for enjoyment—he knew that too, and he trained himself. Music he loved, and attended all the concerts that were given in the town. He came to play the violin not so badly himself, no matter what a figure of fun he made when he did it; and took delight in every beautiful soft tone he succeeded in producing. Also, by much reading he came in time to possess a literary taste the like of which did not exist in the place. He kept up with the new books, even the foreign ones; he knew how to savour the seductive rhythm of a lyric or the ultimate flavour of a subtly told tale—yes, one might almost call him a connoisseur.

He learned to understand that to everything belongs its own enjoyment and that it is absurd to distinguish between an experience which is "happy" and one which is not. With a right good will he accepted each emotion as it came, each mood, whether sad or gay. Even he cherished the unfulfilled desires, the longings. He loved them for their own sakes and told himself that with fulfilment the best of them would be past. The vague, sweet, painful yearning and hope of quiet spring evenings—are they not richer in joy than all the fruition the summer can bring? Yes, he was a connoisseur, our little Herr Friedemann.

But of course they did not know that, the people whom he met on the street, who bowed to him with the kindly, compassionate air he knew so well. They could not know that this unhappy cripple, strutting comically along in his light overcoat and shiny top hat—strange to say, he was a little vain—they could not know how tenderly he loved the mild flow of his life, charged with no great emotions, it is true, but full of a quiet and tranquil happiness which was his own creation.

But Herr Friedemann's great preference, his real passion, was for the theatre. He possessed a dramatic sense which was unusually strong; at a telling theatrical effect or the catastrophe of a tragedy his whole small frame would shake with emotion. He had his regular seat in the first row of boxes at the opera-house; was an assiduous frequenter and often took his sisters with him. Since their mother's death they kept house for their brother in the old home which they all owned together.

It was a pity they were unmarried still; but with the decline of hope had come resignation—Friederike, the eldest, was seventeen years further on than Herr Friedemann. She and her sister Henriette were over-tall and thin, whereas Pfiffi, the youngest, was too short and stout. She had a funny way, too, of shaking herself as she talked, and water came in the corners of her mouth.

Little Herr Friedemann did not trouble himself overmuch about his three sisters. But they stuck together loyally and were always of one mind. Whenever an engagement was announced in their circle they with one voice said how very gratifying that was.

Their brother continued to live with them even after he became independent, as he did by leaving Herr Schlievogt's firm and going into business for himself, in an agency of sorts, which was no great tax on his time. His offices were in a couple of rooms on the ground floor of the house so that at mealtimes he had but the pair of stairs to mount—for he suffered now and then from asthma.

His thirtieth birthday fell on a fine warm June day, and after dinner he sat out in the grey canvas tent, with a new head-rest embroidered by Henriette. He had a good cigar in his mouth and a good book in his hand. But sometimes he would put the latter down to listen to the sparrows chirping blithely in the old nut tree and look at the clean gravel path leading up to the house between lawns bright with summer flowers.

Little Herr Friedemann wore no beard, and his face had scarcely changed at all, save that the features were slightly sharper. He wore his fine light-brown hair parted on one side.

Once, as he let the book fall on his knee and looked up into the sunny blue sky, he said to himself: "Well, so that is thirty years. Perhaps there may be ten or even twenty more, God knows. They will mount up without a sound or a stir and pass by like those that are gone; and I look forward to them with peace in my heart."

Now, it happened in July of the same year that a new appointment to the office of District Commandant had set the whole town talking. The stout and jolly gentleman who had for many years occupied the post had been very popular in social circles and they saw him go with great regret. It was in compliance with goodness knows what regulations that Herr von Rinnlingen and no other was sent hither from the capital.

In any case the exchange was not such a bad one. The new Commandant was married but childless. He rented a spacious villa in the southern suburbs of the city and seemed to intend to set up an establishment. There was a report that he was very rich—which received confirmation in the fact that he brought with him four servants, five riding and carriage horses, a landau and a light hunting-cart.

Soon after their arrival the husband and wife left cards on all the best society, and their names were on every tongue. But it was not Herr von Rinnlingen, it was his wife who was the centre of interest. All the men were dazed, for the moment too dazed to pass judgment; but their wives were quite prompt and definite in the view that Gerda von Rinnlingen was not their sort.

"Of course, she comes from the metropolis, her ways would naturally be different," Frau Hagenström, the lawyer's wife, said, in conversation with Henriette Friedemann. "She smokes, and she rides. That is of course. But it is her manners—they are not only free, they are positively brusque, or even worse. You see, no one could call her ugly, one might even say she is pretty; but she has not a trace of feminine charm in her looks or gestures or her laugh—they completely lack everything that makes a man fall in love with a woman. She is not a flirt—and goodness knows I would be the last to disparage her for that. But it is strange to see so young a woman—she is only twenty-four—so entirely wanting in natural charm. I am not expressing myself very well, my dear, but I know what I mean. All the men are simply bewildered. In a few weeks, you will see, they will be disgusted."

"Well," Fräulein Friedemann said, "she certainly has everything she wants."

"Yes," cried Frau Hagenström, "look at her husband! And how does she treat him? You ought to see it—you will see it! I would be the first to approve of a married woman behaving with a certain reserve towards the other sex. But how does she behave to her own husband? She has a way of fixing him with an ice-cold stare and saying 'My dear friend!' with a pitying expression that drives me mad. For when you look at him—upright, correct, gallant, a brilliant officer and a splendidly preserved man of forty! They have been married four years, my dear."

Herr Friedemann was first vouchsafed a glimpse of Frau von Rinnlingen in the main street of the town, among all the rows of shops, at midday, when he was coming from the Bourse, where he had done a little bidding.

He was strolling along beside Herr Stephens, looking tiny and important, as usual. Herr Stephens was in the wholesale trade, a huge stocky man with round side-whiskers and bushy eyebrows. Both of them wore top hats; their overcoats were unbuttoned on account of the heat. They tapped their canes along the pavement and talked of the political situation; but half-way down the street Stephens suddenly said:

"Deuce take it if there isn't the Rinnlingen driving along."

"Good," answered Herr Friedemann in his high, rather sharp voice, looking expectantly ahead. "Because I have never set eyes on her. And here we have the yellow cart we hear so much about."

It was in fact the hunting-cart which Frau von Rinnlingen was herself driving today with a pair of thoroughbreds; a groom sat behind her, with folded arms. She wore a loose beige coat and skirt and a small round straw hat with a brown leather band, beneath which her well-waved red-blond hair, a good, thick crop, was drawn into a knot at the nape of her neck. Her face was oval, with a dead-white skin and faint bluish shadows lurking under the close-set eyes. Her nose was short but well-shaped, with a becoming little saddle of freckles; whether her mouth was as good or no could not be told, for she kept it in continual motion, sucking the lower and biting the upper lip.

Herr Stephens, as the cart came abreast of them, greeted her with a great show of deference; little Herr Friedemann lifted his hat too and looked at her with wide-eyed attention. She lowered her whip, nodded slightly, and drove slowly past, looking at the houses and shop-windows.

After a few paces Herr Stephens said:

"She has been taking a drive and was on her way home."

Little Herr Friedemann made no answer, but stared before him at the pavement. Presently he started, looked at his companion, and asked: "What did you say?"

And Herr Stephens repeated his acute remark.

Three days after that Johannes Friedemann came home at midday from his usual walk. Dinner was at half past twelve, and he would spend the interval in his office at the right of the entrance door. But the maid came across the entry and told him that there were visitors.

"In my office?" he asked.

"No, upstairs with the mistress."

"Who are they?"

"Herr and Frau Colonel von Rinnlingen."

"Ah," said Johannes Friedemann. "Then I will—"

And he mounted the stairs. He crossed the lobby and laid his hand on the knob of the high white door leading into the "landscape room." And then he drew back, turned round, and slowly returned as he had come. And spoke to himself, for there was no one else there, and said: "No, better not."

He went into his office, sat down at his desk, and took up the paper. But after a little he dropped it again and sat looking to one side out of the window. Thus he sat until the maid came to say that luncheon was ready; then he went up into the dining-room where his sisters were already waiting, and sat down in his chair, in which there were three music-books.

As she ladled the soup Henriette said:

"Johannes, do you know who were here?"

"Well?" he asked.

"The new Commandant and his wife."

"Indeed? That was friendly of them."

"Yes," said Pfiffi, a little water coming in the corners of her mouth. "I found them both very agreeable."

"And we must lose no time in returning the call," said Friederike. "I suggest that we go next Sunday, the day after tomorrow."

"Sunday," Henriette and Pfiffi said.

"You will go with us, Johannes?" asked Friederike.

"Of course he will," said Pfiffi, and gave herself a little shake. Herr Friedemann had not heard her at all; he was eating his soup, with a hushed and troubled air. It was as though he were listening to some strange noise he heard.

Next evening *Lohengrin* was being given at the opera, and everybody in society was present. The small auditorium was crowded, humming with voices and smelling of gas and perfumery. And every eyeglass in the stalls was directed towards box thirteen, next to the stage; for this was the first appearance of Herr and Frau von Rinnlingen and one could give them a good looking-over.

When little Herr Friedemann, in flawless dress clothes and glistening white pigeon-breasted shirt-front, entered his box, which was number thirteen, he started back at the door, making a gesture with his hand towards his brow. His nostrils dilated feverishly. Then he took his seat, which was next to Frau von Rinnlingen's.

She contemplated him for a little while, with her under lip stuck out; then she turned to exchange a few words with her husband, a tall, broad-shouldered gentleman with a brown, good-natured face and turned-up moustaches.

When the overture began and Frau von Rinnlingen leaned over the balustrade Herr Friedemann gave her a quick, searching side glance. She wore a light-coloured evening frock, the only one in the theatre which was slightly low in the neck. Her sleeves were full and her white gloves came up to her elbows. Her figure was statelier than it had looked under the loose coat; her full bosom slowly rose and fell and the knot of red-blond hair hung low and heavy at the nape of her neck.

Herr Friedemann was pale, much paler than usual, and little beads of perspiration stood on his brow beneath the smoothly parted brown hair. He could see Frau von Rinnlingen's left arm, which lay upon the balustrade. She had taken off her glove and the rounded, dead-white arm and ringless hand, both of them shot with pale blue veins, were directly under his eye—he could not help seeing them.

The fiddles sang, the trombones crashed, Telramund was slain, general jubilation reigned in the orchestra, and little Herr Friedemann sat there motionless and pallid, his head drawn in between his shoulders, his forefinger to his lips and one hand thrust into the opening of his waistcoat.

As the curtain fell, Frau von Rinnlingen got up to leave the box with her husband. Johannes Friedemann saw her without looking, wiped his handkerchief across his brow, then rose suddenly and went as far as the door into the foyer, where he turned, came back to his chair, and sat down in the same posture as before.

When the bell rang and his neighbours re-entered the box he felt Frau von Rinnlingen's eyes upon him, so that finally against his will he raised his head. As their eyes met, hers did not swerve aside; she continued to gaze without embarrassment until he himself, deeply humiliated, was forced to look away. He turned a shade paler and felt a strange, sweet pang of anger and scorn. The music began again.

Towards the end of the act Frau von Rinnlingen chanced to drop her fan; it fell at Herr Friedemann's feet. They both stooped at the same time, but she reached it first and gave a little mocking smile as she said: "Thank you."

Their heads were quite close together and just for a second he got the warm scent of her breast. His face was drawn, his whole body twitched, and his heart thumped so horribly that he lost his breath. He sat without moving for half a minute, then he pushed back his chair, got up quietly, and went out.

He crossed the lobby, pursued by the music; got his top hat from the cloak-room, his light overcoat and his stick, went down the stairs and out of doors.

It was a warm, still evening. In the gas-lit street the gabled houses towered towards a sky where stars were softly beaming. The pavement echoed the steps of a few passers-by. Someone spoke to him, but he heard and saw nothing; his head was bowed and his deformed chest shook with the violence of his breathing. Now and then he murmured to himself:

"My God, my God!"

He was gazing horror-struck within himself, beholding the havoc which had been wrought with his tenderly cherished, scrupulously managed feelings. Suddenly he was quite overpowered by the strength of his tortured longing. Giddy and drunken he leaned against a lamp-post and his quivering lips uttered the one word: "Gerda!"

The stillness was complete. Far and wide not a soul was to be seen. Little Herr Friedemann pulled himself together and went on, up the street in which the opera-house stood and which ran steeply down to the river, then along the main street northwards to his home.

How she had looked at him! She had forced him, actually, to cast down his eyes! She had humiliated him with her glance. But was she not a woman and he a man? And those strange brown eyes of hers— had they not positively glittered with unholy joy?

Again he felt the same surge of sensual, impotent hatred mount up in him; then he relived the moment when her head had touched his, when he had breathed in the fragrance of her body—and for the second time he halted, bent his deformed torso backwards, drew in the air through clenched teeth, and murmured helplessly, desperately, uncontrollably:

"My God, my God!"

Then went on again, slowly, mechanically, through the heavy evening air, through the empty echoing streets until he stood before his own house. He paused a minute in the entry, breathing the cool, dank inside air; then he went into his office.

He sat down at his desk by the open window and stared straight ahead of him at a large yellow rose which somebody had set there in a glass of water. He took it up and smelt it with his eyes closed, then put it down with a gesture of weary sadness. No, no. That was all over. What was even that fragance to him now? What any of all those things that up to now had been the well-springs of his joy? He turned away and gazed into the quiet street. At intervals steps passed and the sound died away. The stars stood still and glittered. He felt so weak, so utterly tired to death. His head was quite vacant, and suddenly his despair began to melt into a gentle, pervading melancholy. A few lines of a poem flickered through his head, he heard the *Lohengrin* music in his ears, he saw Frau von Rinnlingen's face and her round white arm on the red velvet—then he fell into a heavy fever-burdened sleep.

Often he was near waking, but feared to do so and managed to sink back into forgetfulness again. But when it had grown quite light, he opened his eyes and looked round him with a wide and painful gaze. He remembered everything, it was as though the anguish had never been intermitted by sleep.

His head was heavy and his eyes burned. But when he had washed up and bathed his head with cologne he felt better and sat down in his place by the still open window. It was early, perhaps only five o'clock. Now and then a baker's boy passed; otherwise there was no one to be seen. In the opposite house the blinds were down. But birds were twittering and the sky was luminously blue. A wonderfully beautiful Sunday morning.

A feeling of comfort and confidence came over little Herr Friedemann. Why had he been distressing himself? Was not everything just as it had been? The attack of yesterday had been a bad one. Granted. But it should be the last. It was not too late, he could still escape destruction. He must avoid every occasion of a fresh seizure; he felt sure he could do this. He felt the strength to conquer and suppress his weakness.

It struck half past seven and Friederike came in with the coffee, setting it on the round table in front of the leather sofa against the rear wall.

"Good morning, Johannes," said she; "here is your breakfast."

"Thanks," said little Herr Friedemann. And then: "Dear Friederike, I am sorry, but you will have to pay your call without me, I do not feel well enough to go. I have slept badly and have a headache—in short, I must ask you—"

"What a pity!" answered Friederike. "You must go another time. But you do look ill. Shall I lend you my menthol pencil?"

"Thanks," said Herr Friedemann. "It will pass." And Friederike went out.

Standing at the table he slowly drank his coffee and ate a croissant. He felt satisfied with himself and proud of his firmness. When he had finished he sat down again by the open window, with a cigar. The food had done him good and he felt happy and hopeful. He took a book and sat reading and smoking and blinking into the sunlight.

Morning had fully come, wagons rattled past, there were many voices and the sound of the bells on passing trams. With and among it all was woven the twittering and chirping; there was a radiant blue sky, a soft mild air.

At ten o'clock he heard his sisters cross the entry; the front door creaked, and he idly noticed that they passed his window. An hour went by. He felt more and more happy.

A sort of hubris mounted in him. What a heavenly air—and how the birds were singing! He felt like taking a little walk. Then suddenly, without any transition, yet accompanied by a terror namelessly sweet, came the thought: "Suppose I were to go to her!" And suppressing, as though by actual muscular effort, every warning voice within him, he added with blissful resolution: "I will go to her!"

He changed into his Sunday clothes, took his top hat and his stick, and hurried with quickened breath through the town and into the southern suburbs. Without looking at a soul he kept raising and dropping his head with each eager step, completely rapt in his exalted state until he arrived at the avenue of chestnut trees and the red brick villa with the name of Commandant von Rinnlingen on the gatepost.

But here he was seized by a tremor, his heart throbbed and pounded in his breast. He went across the vestibule and rang at the inside door. The die was cast, there was no retreating now. "Come what come may," thought he, and felt the stillness of death within him.

The door suddenly opened and the maid came towards him across the vestibule; she took his card and hurried away up the red-carpeted stair. Herr Friedemann gazed fixedly at the bright colour until she came back and said that her mistress would like him to come up.

He put down his stick beside the door leading into the salon and stole a look at himself in the glass. His face was pale, the eyes red, his hair was sticking to his brow, the hand that held his top hat kept on shaking.

The maid opened the door and he went in. He found himself in a rather large, half-darkened room, with drawn curtains. At his right was a piano, and about the round table in the centre stood several arm-chairs covered in brown silk. The sofa stood along the left-hand wall, with a landscape painting in a heavy gilt frame hanging above it. The wall-paper too was dark in tone. There was an alcove filled with potted palms.

A minute passed, then Frau von Rinnlingen opened the portières on the right and approached him noiselessly over the thick brown carpet. She wore a simply cut frock of red and black plaid. A ray of light, with motes dancing in it, streamed from the alcove and fell upon her heavy red hair so that it shone like gold. She kept her strange eyes fixed upon him with a searching gaze and as usual stuck out her under lip.

"Good morning, Frau Commandant," began little Herr Friedemann, and looked up at her, for he came only as high as her chest. "I wished to pay you my respects too. When my sisters did so I was unfortunately out . . . I regretted sincerely . . ."

He had no idea at all what else he should say; and there she stood and gazed ruthlessly at him as though she would force him to go on. The blood rushed to his head. "She sees through me," he thought, "she will torture and despise me. Her eyes keep flickering. . . ."

But at last she said, in a very high, clear voice:

"It is kind of you to have come. I have also been sorry not to see you before. Will you please sit down?"

She took her seat close beside him, leaned back, and put her arm along the arm of the chair. He sat bent over, holding his hat between his knees. She went on:

"Did you know that your sisters were here a quarter of an hour ago? They told me you were ill."

"Yes," he answered, "I did not feel well enough to go out, I thought I should not be able to. That is why I am late."

"You do not look very well even now," said she tranquilly, not shifting her gaze. "You are pale and your eyes are inflamed. You are not very strong, perhaps?"

"Oh," said Herr Friedemann, stammering, "I've not much to complain of, as a rule."

"I am ailing a good deal too," she went on, still not turning her eyes from him, "but nobody notices it. I am nervous, and sometimes I have the strangest feelings."

She paused, lowered her chin to her breast, and looked up expectantly at him. He made no reply, simply sat with his dreamy gaze directed upon her. How strangely she spoke, and how her clear and thrilling voice affected him! His heart beat more quietly and he felt as though he were in a dream. She began again:

"I am not wrong in thinking that you left the opera last night before it was over?"

"Yes, madam."

"I was sorry to see that. You listened like a music-lover—though the performance was only tolerable. You are fond of music, I am sure. Do you play the piano?"

"I play the violin, a little," said Herr Friedemann. "That is, really not very much—"

"You play the violin?" she asked, and looked past him consideringly. "But we might play together," she suddenly said. "I can accompany a little. It would be a pleasure to find somebody here—would you come?"

"I am quite at your service—with pleasure," said he, stiffly. He was still as though in a dream. A pause ensued. Then suddenly her expression changed. He saw it alter for one of cruel, though hardly perceptible mockery, and again she fixed him with that same searching, uncannily flickering gaze. His face burned, he knew not where to turn; drawing his head down between his shoulders he stared confusedly at the carpet, while there shot through him once more that strangely sweet and torturing sense of impotent rage.

He made a desperate effort and raised his eyes. She was looking over his head at the door. With the utmost difficulty he fetched out a few words:

"And you are so far not too dissatisfied with your stay in our city?"

"Oh, no," said Frau Rinnlingen indifferently. "No, certainly not; why should I not be satisfied? To be sure, I feel a little hampered, as though everybody's eyes were upon me, but—oh before I forget it," she went on quickly, "we are entertaining a few people next week, a small, informal company. A little music perhaps, and conversation. . . . There is a charming garden at the back, it runs down to the river. You and your sisters will be receiving an invitation in due course, but perhaps I may ask you now to give us the pleasure of your company?"

Herr Friedemann was just expressing his gratitude for the invitation when the door-knob was seized energetically from without and the Commandant entered. They both rose and Frau von Rinnlingen introduced the two men to each other. Her husband bowed to them both with equal courtesy. His bronze face glistened with the heat.

He drew off his gloves, addressing Herr Friedemann in a powerful, rather sharp-edged voice. The latter looked up at him with large vacant eyes and had the feeling that he would presently be clapped benevolently on the shoulder. Heels together, inclining from the waist, the Commandant turned to his wife and asked, in a much gentler tone:

"Have you asked Herr Friedemann if he will give us the pleasure of his company at our little party, my love? If you are willing I should like to fix the date for next week and I hope that the weather will remain fine so that we can enjoy ourselves in the garden."

"Just as you say," answered Frau von Rinnlingen, and gazed past him.

Two minutes later Herr Friedemann got up to go. At the door he turned and bowed to her once more, meeting her expressionless gaze still fixed upon him.

He went away, but he did not go back to the town; unconsciously he struck into a path that led away from the avenue towards the old ruined fort by the river, among well-kept lawns and shady avenues with benches.

He walked quickly and absently, with bent head. He felt intolerably hot, as though aware of flames leaping and sinking within him and his head throbbed with fatigue.

It was as though her gaze still rested on him—not vacantly as it had at the end, but with that flickering cruelty which went with the strange still way she spoke. Did it give her pleasure to put him beside himself, to see him helpless? Looking through and through him like that, could she not feel a little pity?

He had gone along the river-bank under the moss-grown wall; he sat down on a bench within a half-circle of blossoming jasmine. The sweet, heavy scent was all about him, the sun brooded upon the dimpling water.

He was weary, he was worn out; and yet within him all was tumult and anguish. Were it not better to take one last look and then to go down into that quiet water; after a brief struggle to be free and safe and at peace? Ah, peace, peace—that was what he wanted! Not peace in an empty and soundless void, but a gentle, sunlit peace, full of good, of tranquil thoughts.

All his tender love of life thrilled through him in that moment, all his profound yearning for his vanished "happiness." But then he looked about him into the silent, endlessly indifferent peace of nature, saw how the river went its own way in the sun, how the grasses quivered and the flowers stood up where they blossomed, only to fade and be blown away; saw how all that was bent submissively to the will of life; and there came over him all at once that sense of acquaintance and understanding with the inevitable which can make those who know it superior to the blows of fate.

He remembered the afternoon of his thirtieth birthday and the peaceful happiness with which he, untroubled by fears or hopes, had looked forward to what was left of his life. He had seen no light and no shadow there, only a mild twilight radiance gently declining into the dark. With what a calm and superior smile had he contemplated the years still to come—how long ago was that?

Then this woman had come, she had to come, it was his fate that she should, for she herself was his fate and she alone. He had known it from the first moment. She had come—and though he had tried his best to defend his peace, her coming had roused in him all those forces which from his youth up he had sought to suppress, feeling, as he did, that they spelled torture and destruction. They had seized upon him with frightful, irresistible power and flung him to the earth.

They were his destruction, well he knew it. But why struggle, then, and why torture himself? Let everything take its course. He would go his appointed way, closing his eyes before the yawning void, bowing to his fate, bowing to the overwhelming, anguishingly sweet, irresistible power.

The water glittered, the jasmine gave out its strong, pungent scent, the birds chattered in the tree-tops that gave glimpses among them of a heavy, velvety-blue sky. Little hump-backed Herr Friedemann sat long upon his bench; he sat bent over, holding his head in his hands.

Everybody agreed that the Rinnlingens entertained very well. Some thirty guests sat in the spacious dining-room, at the long, prettily decorated table, and the butler and two hired waiters were already handing round the ices. Dishes clattered, glasses rang, there was a warm aroma of food and perfumes. Here were comfortable merchants with their wives and daughters; most of the officers of the garrison; a few professional men, lawyers and the popular old family doctor— in short, all the best society.

A nephew of the Commandant, on a visit, a student of mathematics, sat deep in conversation with Fräulein Hagenström, whose place was directly opposite Herr Friedemann's, at the lower end of the table. Johannes Friedemann sat there on a rich velvet cushion, beside the unbeautiful wife of the Colonial Director and not far off Frau von Rinnlingen, who had been escorted to table by Consul Stephens. It was astonishing, the change which had taken place in little Herr Friedemann in these few days. Perhaps the incandescent lighting in the room was partly to blame; but his cheeks looked sunken, he made a more crippled impression even than usual, and his inflamed eyes, with their dark rings, glowed with an inexpressibly tragic light. He drank a great deal of wine and now and then addressed a remark to his neighbour.

Frau von Rinnlingen had not so far spoken to him at all; but now she leaned over and called out:

"I have been expecting you in vain these days, you and your fiddle."

He looked vacantly at her for a while before he replied. She wore a light-coloured frock with a low neck that left the white throat bare; a Maréchal Niel rose in full bloom was fastened in her shining hair. Her cheeks were a little flushed, but the same bluish shadows lurked in the corners of her eyes.

Herr Friedemann looked at his plate and forced himself to make some sort of reply; after which the school superintendent's wife asked him if he did not love Beethoven and he had to answer that too. But at this point the Commandant, sitting at the head of the table, caught his wife's eyes, tapped on his glass and said:

"Ladies and gentlemen, I suggest that we drink our coffee in the

next room. It must be fairly decent out in the garden too, and whoever wants a little fresh air, I am for him."

Lieutenant von Deidesheim made a tactful little joke to cover the
ensuing pause, and the table rose in the midst of laughter. Herr
Friedemann and his partner were among the last to quit the room;
he escorted her through the "old German" smoking-room to the dim
and pleasant living-room, where he took his leave.

He was dressed with great care: his evening clothes were irreproach-
able, his shirt was dazzlingly white, his slender, well-shaped feet were
encased in patent-leather pumps, which now and then betrayed the
fact that he wore red silk stockings.

He looked out into the corridor and saw a good many people descending the steps into the garden. But he took up a position at the
door of the smoking-room, with his cigar and coffee, where he could
see into the living-room.

Some of the men stood talking in this room, and at the right of the
door a little knot had formed round a small table, the centre of which
was the mathematics student, who was eagerly talking. He had made
the assertion that one could draw through a given point more than
one parallel to a straight line; Frau Hagenström had cried that this
was impossible, and he had gone on to prove it so conclusively that
his hearers were constrained to behave as though they understood.

At the rear of the room, on the sofa beside the red-shaded lamp,
Gerda von Rinnlingen sat in conversation with young Fräulein
Stephens. She leaned back among the yellow silk cushions with one
knee slung over the other, slowly smoking a cigarette, breathing out
the smoke through her nose and sticking out her lower lip. Fräulein
Stephens sat stiff as a graven image beside her, answering her questions with an assiduous smile.

Nobody was looking at little Herr Friedemann, so nobody saw that
his large eyes were constantly directed upon Frau von Rinnlingen.
He sat rather droopingly and looked at her. There was no passion in
his gaze nor scarcely any pain. But there was something dull and
heavy there, a dead weight of impotent, involuntary adoration.

Some ten minutes went by. Then as though she had been secretly
watching him the whole time, Frau von Rinnlingen approached and
paused in front of him. He got up as he heard her say:

"Would you care to go into the garden with me, Herr Friedemann?"

He answered:
"With pleasure, madam."

"You have never seen our garden?" she asked him as they went down the steps. "It is fairly large. I hope that there are not too many people in it; I should like to get a breath of fresh air. I got a headache during supper; perhaps the red wine was too strong for me. Let us go this way." They passed through a glass door, the vestibule, and a cool little courtyard, whence they gained the open air by descending a couple more steps.

The scent of all the flower-beds rose into the wonderful, warm, starry night. The garden lay in full moonlight and the guests were strolling up and down the white gravel paths, smoking and talking as they went. A group had gathered round the old fountain, where the much-loved old doctor was making them laugh by sailing paper boats.

With a little nod Frau von Rinnlingen passed them by, and pointed ahead of her, where the fragrant and well-cared-for garden blended into the darker park.

"Shall we go down this middle path?" asked she. At the beginning of it stood two low, squat obelisks.

In the vista at the end of the chestnut alley they could see the river shining green and bright in the moonlight. All about them was darkness and coolness. Here and there side paths branched off, all of them probably curving down to the river. For a long time there was not a sound.

"Down by the water," she said, "there is a pretty spot where I often sit. We could stop and talk a little. See the stars glittering here and there through the trees."

He did not answer, gazing, as they approached it, at the river's shimmering green surface. You could see the other bank and the park along the city wall. They left the alley and came out on the grassy slope down to the river, and she said:

"Here is our place, a little to the right, and there is no one there."

The bench stood facing the water, some six paces away, with its back to the trees. It was warmer here in the open. Crickets chirped among the grass, which at the river's edge gave way to sparse reeds. The moonlit water gave off a soft light.

For a while they both looked in silence. Then he heard her voice;

it thrilled him to recognize the same low, gentle, pensive tone of a week ago, which now as then moved him strongly: ·

"How long have you had your infirmity, Herr Friedemann? Were you born so?"

He swallowed before he replied, for his throat felt as though he were choking. Then he said, politely and gently:

"No, *gnädige Frau*. It comes from their having let me fall, when I was an infant."

"And how old are you now?" she asked again.

"Thirty years old."

"Thirty years old," she repeated. "And these thirty years were not happy ones?"

Little Herr Friedemann shook his head, his lips quivered.

"No," he said, "that was all lies and my imagination."

"Then you have thought that you were happy?" she asked.

"I have tried to be," he replied, and she responded:

"That was brave of you."

A minute passed. The crickets chirped and behind them the boughs rustled lightly.

"I understand a good deal about unhappiness," she told him. "These summer nights by the water are the best thing for it."

He made no direct answer, but gestured feebly across the water, at the opposite bank, lying peaceful in the darkness.

"I was sitting over there not long ago," he said.

"When you came from me?" she asked. He only nodded.

Then suddenly he started up from his seat, trembling all over; he sobbed and gave vent to a sound, a wail which yet seemed like a release from strain, and sank slowly to the ground before her. He had touched her hand with his as it lay beside him on the bench, and clung to it now, seizing the other as he knelt before her, this little cripple, trembling and shuddering; he buried his face in her lap and stammered between his gasps in a voice which was scarcely human:

"You know, you understand . . . let me . . . I can no longer . . . my God, oh, my God!"

She did not repulse him, neither did she bend her face towards him. She sat erect, leaning a little away, and her close-set eyes, wherein the liquid shimmer of the water seemed to be mirrored, stared beyond him into space.

Then she gave him an abrupt push and uttered a short, scornful laugh. She tore her hands from his burning fingers, clutched his arm, and flung him sidewise upon the ground. Then she sprang up and vanished down the wooded avenue.

He lay there with his face in the grass, stunned, unmanned, shudders coursing swiftly through his frame. He pulled himself together, got up somehow, took two steps, and fell again, close to the water. What were his sensations at this moment? Perhaps he was feeling that same luxury of hate which he had felt before when she had humiliated him with her glance, degenerated now, when he lay before her on the ground and she had treated him like a dog, into an insane rage which must at all costs find expression even against himself—a disgust, perhaps of himself, which filled him with a thirst to destroy himself, to tear himself to pieces, to blot himself utterly out.

On his belly he dragged his body a little further, lifted its upper part, and let it fall into the water. He did not raise his head nor move his legs, which still lay on the bank.

The crickets stopped chirping a moment at the noise of the little splash. Then they went on as before, the boughs lightly rustled, and down the long alley came the faint sound of laughter.

THE INFANT PRODIGY

The infant prodigy entered. The hall became quiet.

It became quiet and then the audience began to clap, because somewhere at the side a leader of mobs, a born organizer, clapped first. The audience had heard nothing yet, but they applauded; for a mighty publicity organization had heralded the prodigy and people were already hypnotized, whether they knew it or not.

The prodigy came from behind a splendid screen embroidered with Empire garlands and great conventionalized flowers, and climbed nimbly up to the steps of the platform, diving into the applause as

THE INFANT PRODIGY. Reprinted from *Stories of Three Decades* by Thomas Mann, by permission of Alfred A. Knopf, Inc. Copyright 1936 by Alfred A. Knopf, Inc.

into a bath; a little chilly and shivering, but yet as though into a friendly element. He advanced to the edge of the platform and smiled as though he were about to be photographed; he made a shy, charming gesture of greeting, like a little girl.

He was dressed entirely in white silk, which the audience found enchanting. The little white jacket was fancifully cut, with a sash underneath it, and even his shoes were made of white silk. But against the white socks his bare little legs stood out quite brown; for he was a Greek boy.

He was called Bibi Saccellaphylaccas. And such indeed was his name. No one knew what Bibi was the pet name for, nobody but the impresario, and he regarded it as a trade secret. Bibi had smooth black hair reaching to his shoulders; it was parted on the side and fastened back from the narrow domed forehead by a little silk bow. His was the most harmless childish countenance in the world, with an unfinished nose and guileless mouth. The area beneath his pitch-black mouselike eyes was already a little tired and visibly lined. He looked as though he were nine years old but was really eight and given out for seven. It was hard to tell whether to believe this or not. Probably everybody knew better and still believed it, as happens about so many things. The average man thinks that a little falseness goes with beauty. Where should we get any excitement out of our daily life if we were not willing to pretend a bit? And the average man is quite right, in his average brains!

The prodigy kept on bowing until the applause died down, then he went up to the grand piano, and the audience cast a last look at its programmes. First came a *Marche solonnelle,* then a *Rêverie,* and then *Le Hibou et les moineaux*—all by Bibi Saccellaphylaccas. The whole programme was by him, they were all his compositions. He could not score them, of course, but he had them all in his extraordinary little head and they possessed real artistic significance, or so it said, seriously and objectively, in the programme. The programme sounded as though the impresario had wrested these concessions from his critical nature after a hard struggle.

The prodigy sat down upon the revolving stool and felt with his feet for the pedals, which were raised by means of a clever device so that Bibi could reach them. It was Bibi's own piano, he took it everywhere with him. It rested upon wooden trestles and its polish was somewhat marred by the constant transportation—but all that only made things more interesting.

Bibi put his silk-shod feet on the pedals; then he made an artful little face, looked straight ahead of him, and lifted his right hand. It was a brown, childish little hand; but the wrist was strong and unlike a child's, with well-developed bones.

Bibi made his face for the audience because he was aware that he had to entertain them a little. But he had his own private enjoyment in the thing too, an enjoyment which he could never convey to anybody. It was that prickling delight, that secret shudder of bliss, which ran through him every time he sat at an open piano—it would always be with him. And here was the keyboard again, these seven black and white octaves, among which he had so often lost himself in abysmal and thrilling adventures—and yet it always looked as clean and untouched as a newly washed blackboard. This was the realm of music that lay before him. It lay spread out like an inviting ocean, where he might plunge in and blissfully swim, where he might let himself be borne and carried away, where he might go under in night and storm, yet keep the mastery: control, ordain—he held his right hand poised in the air.

A breathless stillness reigned in the room—the tense moment before the first note came. . . . How would it begin? It began so. And Bibi, with his index finger, fetched the first note out of the piano, a quite unexpectedly powerful first note in the middle register, like a trumpet blast. Others followed, an introduction developed—the audience relaxed.

The concert was held in the palatial hall of a fashionable first-class hotel. The walls were covered with mirrors framed in gilded arabesques, between frescoes of the rosy and fleshly school. Ornamental columns supported a ceiling that displayed a whole universe of electric bulbs, in clusters darting a brilliance far brighter than day and filling the whole space with thin, vibrating golden light. Not a seat was unoccupied, people were standing in the side aisles and at the back. The front seats cost twelve marks; for the impresario believed that anything worth having was worth paying for. And they were occupied by the best society, for it was in the upper classes, of course, that the greatest enthusiasm was felt. There were even some children, with their legs hanging down demurely from their chairs and their shining eyes staring at their gifted little white-clad contemporary.

Down in front on the left side sat the prodigy's mother, an extremely obese woman with a powdered double chin and a feather on her head. Beside her was the impresario, a man of oriental appearance with large gold buttons on his conspicuous cuffs. The princess was in the middle of the front row—a wrinkled, shrivelled little old princess but still a patron of the arts, especially everything full of sensibility. She sat in a deep, velvet-upholstered arm-chair, and a Persian carpet was spread before her feet. She held her hands folded over her grey striped-silk breast, put her head on one side, and presented a picture of elegant composure as she sat looking up at the performing prodigy. Next her sat her lady-in-waiting, in a green striped-silk gown. Being only a lady-in-waiting she had to sit up very straight in her chair.

Bibi ended in a grand climax. With what power this wee manikin belaboured the keyboard! The audience could scarcely trust its ears. The march theme, an infectious, swinging tune, broke out once more, fully harmonized, bold and showy; with every note Bibi flung himself back from the waist as though he were marching in a triumphal procession. He ended *fortissimo*, bent over, slipped sideways off the stool, and stood with a smile awaiting the applause.

And the applause burst forth, unanimously, enthusiastically; the child made his demure little maidenly curtsy and people in the front seat thought: "Look what slim little hips he has! Clap! clap! Hurrah, bravo, little chap, Saccophylax or whatever your name is! Wait, let me take off my gloves—what a little devil of a chap he is!"

Bibi had to come out three times from behind the screen before they would stop. Some late-comers entered the hall and moved about looking for seats. Then the concert continued. Bibi's *Rêverie* murmured its numbers, consisting almost entirely of arpeggios, above which a bar of melody rose now and then, weak-winged. Then came *Le Hibou et les moineaux*. This piece was brilliantly successful, it made a strong impression; it was an effective childhood fantasy, remarkably well envisaged. The bass represented the owl, sitting morosely rolling his filmy eyes; while in the treble the impudent, half-frightened sparrows chirped. Bibi received an ovation when he finished, he was called out four times. A hotel page with shiny buttons carried up three great laurel wreaths onto the stage and proffered them from one side while Bibi nodded and expressed his thanks. Even the princess shared in the applause, daintily and noiselessly pressing her palms together.

Ah, the knowing little creature understood how to make people clap! He stopped behind the screen, they had to wait for him; lingered a little on the steps of the platform, admired the long streamers on the wreaths—although actually such things bored him stiff by now. He bowed with the utmost charm, he gave the audience plenty of time to have itself out, because applause is valuable and must not be cut short. "*Le Hibou* is my drawing card," he thought—this expression he had learned from the impresario. "Now I will play the fantasy, it is a lot better than *Le Hibou*, of course, especially the C-sharp passage. But you idiots dote on the *Hibou*, though it is the first and silliest thing I wrote." He continued to bow and smile.

Next came a *Méditation* and then an *Étude*—the programme was quite comprehensive. The *Méditation* was very like the *Rêverie*—which was nothing against it—and the *Étude* displayed all of Bibi's virtuosity, which naturally fell a little short of his inventiveness. And then the *Fantaisie*. This was his favourite; he varied it a little each time, giving himself free rein and sometimes surprising even himself, on good evenings, by his own inventiveness.

He sat and played, so little, so white and shining, against the great black grand piano, elect and alone, above that confused sea of faces, above the heavy, insensitive mass soul, upon which he was labouring to work with his individual, differentiated soul. His lock of soft black hair with the white silk bow had fallen over his forehead, his trained and bony little wrists pounded away, the muscles stood out visibly on his brown childish cheeks.

Sitting there he sometimes had moments of oblivion and solitude, when the gaze of his strange little mouselike eyes with the big rings beneath them would lose itself and stare through the painted stage into space that was peopled with strange vague life. Then out of the corner of his eye he would give a quick look back into the hall and be once more with his audience.

"Joy and pain, the heights and the depths—that is my *Fantaisie*," he thought lovingly. "Listen, here is the C-sharp passage." He lingered over the approach, wondering if they would notice anything. But no, of course not, how should they? And he cast his eyes up prettily at the ceiling so that at least they might have something to look at.

All these people sat there in their regular rows, looking at the prodigy and thinking all sorts of things in their regular brains. An old gentleman with a white beard, a seal ring on his finger and a bulbous swelling on his bald spot, a growth if you like, was thinking to himself: "Really, one ought to be ashamed." He had never got any further than "Ah, thou dearest Augustin" on the piano, and here he sat now, a grey old man, looking on while this little hop-o'-my-thumb performed miracles. Yes, yes, it is a gift of God, we must remember that. God grants His gifts, or He withholds them, and there is no shame in being an ordinary man. Like with the Christ Child.—Before a child one may kneel without feeling ashamed. Strange that thoughts like these should be so satisfying—he would even say so sweet, if it was not too silly for a tough old man like him to use the word. That was how he felt, anyhow.

Art . . . the business man with the parrot-nose was thinking. "Yes, it adds something cheerful to life, a little good white silk and a little tumty-ti-ti-tum. Really he does not play so badly. Fully fifty seats, twelve marks apiece, that makes six hundred marks—and everything else besides. Take off the rent of the hall, the lighting and the programmes, you must have fully a thousand marks profit. That is worth while."

That was Chopin he was just playing, thought the piano-teacher, a lady with a pointed nose; she was of an age when the understanding sharpens as the hopes decay. "But not very original—I will say that afterwards, it sounds well. And his hand position is entirely amateur. One must be able to lay a coin on the back of the hand—I would use a ruler on him."

Then there was a young girl, at that self-conscious and chlorotic time of life when the most ineffable ideas come into the mind. She was thinking to herself: "What is it he is playing? It is expressive of passion, yet he is a child. If he kissed me it would be as though my little brother kissed me—no kiss at all. Is there such a thing as passion all by itself, without any earthly object, a sort of child's-play of passion? What nonsense! If I were to say such things aloud they would just be at me with some more codliver oil. Such is life."

An officer was leaning against a column. He looked on at Bibi's success and thought: "Yes, you are something and I am something, each in his own way." So he clapped his heels together and paid to the prodigy the respect which he felt to be due to all the powers that be.

Then there was a critic, an elderly man in a shiny black coat and turned-up trousers splashed with mud. He sat in his free seat and thought: "Look at him, this young beggar of a Bibi. As an individual he has still to develop, but as a type he is already quite complete, the artist *par excellence*. He has in himself all the artist's exaltation and his utter worthlessness, his charlatanry and his sacred fire, his burning contempt and his secret raptures. Of course I can't write all that, it is too good. Of course, I should have been an artist myself if I had not seen through the whole business so clearly."

Then the prodigy stopped playing and a perfect storm arose in the hall. He had to come out again and again from behind his screen. The man with the shiny buttons carried up more wreaths: four laurel wreaths, a lyre made of violets, a bouquet of roses. He had not arms enough to convey all these tributes, the impresario himself mounted the stage to help him. He hung a laurel wreath round Bibi's neck, he tenderly stroked the black hair—and suddenly as though overcome he bent down and gave the prodigy a kiss, a resounding kiss, square on the mouth. And then the storm became a hurricane. That kiss ran through the room like an electric shock, it went direct to peoples' marrow and made them shiver down their backs. They were carried away by a helpless compulsion of sheer noise. Loud shouts mingled with the hysterical clapping of hands. Some of Bibi's commonplace little friends down there waved their handkerchiefs. But the critic thought: "Of course that kiss had to come—it's a good old gag. Yes, good Lord, if only one did not see through everything quite so clearly—"

And so the concert drew to a close. It began at half past seven and finished at half past eight. The platform was laden with wreaths and two little pots of flowers stood on the lamp-stands of the piano. Bibi played as his last number his *Rhapsodie grecque,* which turned into the Greek national hymn at the end. His fellow-countrymen in the audience would gladly have sung it with him if the company had not been so august. They made up for it with a powerful noise and hullabaloo, a hot-blooded national demonstration. And the aging critic was thinking: "Yes, the hymn had to come too. They have to exploit every vein—publicity cannot afford to neglect any means to its end.

I think I'll criticize that as inartistic. But perhaps I am wrong, perhaps that is the most artistic thing of all. What is the artist? A jack-in-the-box. Criticism is on a higher plane. But I can't say that." And away he went in his muddy trousers.

After being called out nine or ten times the prodigy did not come any more from behind the screen but went to his mother and the impresario down in the hall. The audience stood about among the chairs and applauded and pressed forward to see Bibi close at hand. Some of them wanted to see the princess too. Two dense circles formed, one round the prodigy, the other round the princess, and you could actually not tell which of them was receiving more homage. But the court lady was commanded to go over to Bibi; she smoothed down his silk jacket a bit to make it look suitable for a court function, led him by the arm to the princess, and solemnly indicated to him that he was to kiss the royal hand. "How do you do it, child?" asked the princess. "Does it come into your head of itself when you sit down?" "*Oui, madame,*" answered Bibi. To himself he thought: "Oh, what a stupid old princess!" Then he turned round shyly and un-courtierlike and went back to his family.

Outside in the cloak-room there was a crowd. People held up their numbers and received with open arms, furs, shawls, and galoshes. Somewhere among her acquaintances the piano-teacher stood making her critique. "He is not very original," she said audibly and looked about her.

In front of one of the great mirrors an elegant young lady was being arrayed in her evening cloak and fur shoes by her brothers, two lieutenants. She was exquisitely beautiful, with her steel-blue eyes and her clean-cut, well-bred face. A really noble dame. When she was ready she stood waiting for her brothers. "Don't stand so long in front of the glass, Adolf," she said softly to one of them, who could not tear himself away from the sight of his simple, good-looking young features. But Lieutenant Adolf thinks: What cheek! He would button his overcoat in front of the glass, just the same. Then they went out on the street where the arc-lights gleamed cloudily through the white mist. Lieutenant Adolf struck up a little nigger-dance on the frozen snow to keep warm, with his hands in his slanting over-coat pockets and his collar turned up.

A girl with untidy hair and swinging arms, accompanied by a gloomy-faced youth, came out just behind them. A child! she thought.

A charming child. But in there he was an awe-inspiring . . . and aloud in a toneless voice she said: "We are all infant prodigies, we artists."

"Well, bless my soul!" thought the old gentleman who had never got further than Augustin on the piano, and whose wen was now concealed by a top hat. "What does all that mean? She sounds very oracular." But the gloomy youth understood. He nodded his head slowly.

Then they were silent and the untidy-haired girl gazed after the brothers and sister. She rather despised them, but she looked after them until they had turned the corner.

DISORDER AND EARLY SORROW

The principal dish at dinner had been croquettes made of turnip greens. So there follows a trifle, concocted out of one of those dessert powders we use nowadays, that taste like almond soap. Xaver, the youthful manservant, in his outgrown striped jacket, white woollen gloves, and yellow sandals, hands it round, and the "big folk" take this opportunity to remind their father, tactfully, that company is coming today.

The "big folk" are two, Ingrid and Bert. Ingrid is brown-eyed, eighteen, and perfectly delightful. She is on the eve of her exams, and will probably pass them, if only because she knows how to wind masters, and even headmasters, round her finger. She does not, however, mean to use her certificate once she gets it; having leanings towards the stage, on the ground of her ingratiating smile, her equally ingratiating voice, and a marked and irresistible talent for burlesque. Bert is blond and seventeen. He intends to get done with school somehow, anyhow, and fling himself into the arms of life. He will be a dancer, or a cabaret actor, possibly even a waiter—but not a waiter

DISORDER AND EARLY SORROW. Reprinted from *Stories of Three Decades* by Thomas Mann, by permission of Alfred A. Knopf, Inc. Copyright 1936 by Alfred A. Knopf, Inc.

anywhere else save at the Cairo, the night-club, whither he has once already taken flight, at five in the morning, and been brought back crestfallen. Bert bears a strong resemblance to the youthful manservant Xaver Kleinsgutl, of about the same age as himself; not because he looks common—in features he is strikingly like his father, Professor Cornelius—but by reason of an approximation of types, due in its turn to far-reaching compromises in matters of dress and bearing generally. Both lads wear their heavy hair very long on top, with a cursory parting in the middle, and give their heads the same characteristic toss to throw it off the forehead. When one of them leaves the house, by the garden gate, bareheaded in all weathers, in a blouse rakishly girt with a leather strap, and sheers off bent well over with his head on one side; or else mounts his push-bike—Xaver makes free with his employers', of both sexes, or even, in acutely irresponsible mood, with the Professor's own—Dr. Cornelius from his bedroom window cannot, for the life of him, tell whether he is looking at his son or his servant: Both, he thinks, look like young moujiks. And both are impassioned cigarette-smokers, though Bert has not the means to compete with Xaver, who smokes as many as thirty a day, of a brand named after a popular cinema star. The big folk call their father and mother the "old folk"—not behind their backs, but as a form of address and in all affection: "Hullo, old folks," they will say; though Cornelius is only forty-seven years old and his wife eight years younger. And the Professor's parents, who lead in his household the humble and hesitant life of the really old, are on the big folk's lips the "ancients." As for the "little folk," Ellie and Snapper, who take their meals upstairs with blue-faced Ann—so-called because of her prevailing facial hue—Ellie and Snapper follow their mother's example and address their father by his first name, Abel. Unutterably comic it sounds, in its pert, confiding familiarity; particularly on the lips, in the sweet accents, of five-year-old Eleanor, who is the image of Frau Cornelius's baby pictures and whom the Professor loves above everything else in the world.

"Darling old thing," says Ingrid affably, laying her large but shapely hand on his, as he presides in proper middle-class style over the family table, with her on his left and the mother opposite: "Parent mine, may I ever so gently jog your memory, for you have probably forgotten: this is the afternoon we were to have our little jollification, our turkey-trot with eats to match. You haven't a thing to do but just bear up and not funk it; everything will be over by nine o'clock."

"Oh—ah!" says Cornelius, his face falling. "Good!" he goes on, and nods his head to show himself in harmony with the inevitable. "I only meant—is this really the day? Thursday, yes. How time flies! Well, what time are they coming?"

"Half past four they'll be dropping in, I should say," answers Ingrid, to whom her brother leaves the major rôle in all dealings with the father. Upstairs, while he is resting, he will hear scarcely anything, and from seven to eight he takes his walk. He can slip out by the terrace if he likes.

"Tut!" says Cornelius deprecatingly, as who should say: "You exaggerate." But Bert puts in: "It's the one evening in the week Wanja doesn't have to play. Any other night he'd have to leave by half past six, which would be painful for all concerned."

Wanja is Ivan Herzl, the celebrated young leading man at the Stadttheater. Bert and Ingrid are on intimate terms with him, they often visit him in his dressing-room and have tea. He is an artist of the modern school, who stands on the stage in strange and, to the Professor's mind, utterly affected dancing attitudes, and shrieks lamentably. To a professor of history, all highly repugnant; but Bert has entirely succumbed to Herzl's influence, blackens the lower rim of his eyelids—despite painful but fruitless scenes with the father— and with youthful carelessness of the ancestral anguish declares that not only will he take Herzl for his model if he becomes a dancer, but in case he turns out to be a waiter at the Cairo he means to walk precisely thus.

Cornelius slightly raises his brows and makes his son a little bow —indicative of the unassumingness and self-abnegation that befits his age. You could not call it a mocking bow or suggestive in any special sense. Bert may refer it to himself or equally to his so talented friend.

"Who else is coming?" next inquires the master of the house. They mention various people, names all more or less familiar, from the city, from the suburban colony, from Ingrid's school. They still have some telephoning to do, they say. They have to phone Max. This is Max Hergesell, an engineering student; Ingrid utters his name in the nasal drawl which according to her is the traditional intonation of all the Hergesells. She goes on to parody it in the most abandonedly funny and lifelike way, and the parents laugh until they nearly choke over the wretched trifle. For even in these times when something funny happens people have to laugh.

From time to time the telephone bell rings in the Professor's study, and the big folk run across, knowing it is their affair. Many people had to give up their telephones the last time the price rose, but so far the Corneliuses have been able to keep theirs, just as they have kept their villa, which was built before the war, by dint of the salary Cornelius draws as professor of history—a million marks, and more or less adequate to the chances and changes of post-war life. The house is comfortable, even elegant, though sadly in need of repairs that cannot be made for lack of materials, and at present disfigured by iron stoves with long pipes. Even so, it is still the proper setting of the upper middle class, though they themselves look odd enough in it, with their worn and turned clothing and altered way of life. The children, of course, know nothing else; to them it is normal and regular, they belong by birth to the "villa proletariat." The problem of clothing troubles them not at all. They and their like have evolved a costume to fit the time, by poverty out of taste for innovation: in summer it consists of scarcely more than a belted linen smock and sandals. The middle-class parents find things rather more difficult.

The big folk's table-napkins hang over their chair-backs, they talk with their friends over the telephone. These friends are the invited guests who have rung up to accept or decline or arrange; and the conversation is carried on in the jargon of the clan, full of slang and high spirits, of which the old folk understand hardly a word. These consult together meantime about the hospitality to be offered to the impending guests. The Professor displays a middle-class ambitiousness: he wants to serve a sweet—or something that looks like a sweet —after the Italian salad and brown-bread sandwiches. But Frau Cornelius says that would be going too far. The guests would not expect it, she is sure—and the big folk, returning once more to their trifle, agree with her.

The mother of the family is of the same general type as Ingrid, though not so tall. She is languid; the fantastic difficulties of the housekeeping have broken and worn her. She really ought to go and take a cure, but feels incapable; the floor is always swaying under her feet, and everything seems upside down. She speaks of what is uppermost in her mind: the eggs, they simply must be bought today. Six thousand marks apiece they are, and just so many are to be had on this one day of the week at one single shop fifteen minutes' journey away. Whatever else they do, the big folk must go and fetch them immediately after luncheon, with Danny, their neighbour's son, who will soon be calling for them; and Xaver Kleinsgutl will don civilian garb and attend his young master and mistress. For no single household is allowed more than five eggs a week; therefore the young people will enter the shop singly, one after another, under assumed names, and thus wring twenty eggs from the shopkeeper for the Cornelius family. This enterprise is the sporting event of the week for all participants, not excepting the moujik Kleinsgutl, and most of all for Ingrid and Bert, who delight in misleading and mystifying their fellowmen and would revel in the performance even if it did not achieve one single egg. They adore impersonating fictitious characters; they love to sit in a bus and carry on long lifelike conversations in a dialect which they otherwise never speak, the most commonplace dialogue about politics and people and the price of food, while the whole bus listens open-mouthed to this incredibly ordinary prattle, though with a dark suspicion all the while that something is wrong somewhere. The conversation waxes ever more shameless, it enters into revolting detail about these people who do not exist. Ingrid can make her voice sound ever so common and twittering and shrill as she impersonates a shop-girl with an illegitimate child, said child being a son with sadistic tendencies, who lately out in the country treated a cow with such unnatural cruelty that no Christian could have borne to see it. Bert nearly explodes at her twittering, but restrains himself and displays a grisly sympathy; he and the unhappy shop-girl entering into a long, stupid, depraved, and shuddery conversation over the particular morbid cruelty involved; until an old gentleman opposite, sitting with his ticket folded between his index finger and his seal ring, can bear it no more and makes public protest against the nature of the themes these young folk are discussing with such particularity. He uses the Greek plural: "themata." Whereat Ingrid pretends to be dissolving in tears, and Bert behaves as though his wrath against the old gentleman was with difficulty being held in check and would probably burst out before long. He clenches his fists, he gnashes his teeth, he shakes from head to foot; and the unhappy old gentleman, whose intentions had been of the best, hastily leaves the bus at the next stop.

Such are the diversions of the big folk. The telephone plays a prominent part in them: they ring up any and everybody—members of government, opera singers, dignitaries of the Church—in the character of shop assistants, or perhaps as Lord or Lady Doolittle. They are only with difficulty persuaded that they have the wrong number. Once they emptied their parents' card-tray and distributed its contents among the neighbours' letter-boxes, wantonly, yet not without enough impish sense of the fitness of things to make it highly upsetting, God only knowing why certain people should have called where they did.

Xaver comes in to clear away, tossing the hair out of his eyes. Now that he has taken off his gloves you can see the yellow chain-ring on his left hand. And as the Professor finishes his watery eight-thousand-mark beer and lights a cigarette, the little folk can be heard scrambling down the stair, coming, by established custom, for their after-dinner call on Father and Mother. They storm the dining-room, after a struggle with the latch, clutched by both pairs of little hands at once; their clumsy small feet twinkle over the carpet, in red felt slippers with the socks falling down on them. With prattle and shoutings each makes for his own place: Snapper to Mother, to climb on her lap, boast of all he has eaten, and thump his fat little tum; Ellie to her Abel, so much hers because she is so very much his; because she consciously luxuriates in the deep tenderness—like all deep feeling, concealing a melancholy strain—with which he holds her small form embraced; in the love in his eyes as he kisses her little fairy hand or the sweet brow with its delicate tracery of tiny blue veins.

The little folk look like each other, with the strong undefined likeness of brother and sister. In clothing and hair-cut they are twins. Yet they are sharply distinguished after all, and quite on sex lines. It is a little Adam and a little Eve. Not only is Snapper the sturdier and more compact, he appears consciously to emphasize his four-year-old masculinity in speech, manner, and carriage, lifting his shoulders and letting the little arms hang down quite like a young American athlete, drawing down his mouth when he talks and seeking to give his voice a gruff and forthright ring. But all this masculinity is the result of effort rather than natively his. Born and brought up in these desolate, distracted times, he has been endowed by them with an unstable and hypersensitive nervous system and suffers greatly under life's disharmonies. He is prone to sudden anger and outbursts of bitter tears, stamping his feet at every trifle; for this reason he is his mother's special nursling and care. His round, round eyes are chest-nut brown and already inclined to squint, so that he will need glasses in the near future. His little nose is long, the mouth small—the father's nose and mouth they are, more plainly than ever since the Professor shaved his pointed beard and goes smooth-faced. The pointed beard had become impossible—even professors must make some concession to the changing times.

But the little daughter sits on her father's knee, his Eleonorchen, his little Eve, so much more gracious a little being, so much sweeter-faced than her brother—and he holds his cigarette away from her while she fingers his glasses with her dainty wee hands. The lenses are divided for reading and distance, and each day they tease her curiosity afresh.

At bottom he suspects that his wife's partiality may have a firmer basis than his own: that Snapper's refractory masculinity perhaps is solider stuff than his own little girl's more explicit charm and grace. But the heart will not be commanded, that he knows; and once and for all his heart belongs to the little one, as it has since the day she came, since the first time he saw her. Almost always when he holds her in his arms he remembers that first time: remembers the sunny room in the Women's Hospital, where Ellie first saw the light, twelve years after Bert was born. He remembers how he drew near, the mother smiling the while, and cautiously put aside the canopy of the diminutive bed that stood beside the large one. There lay the little miracle among the pillows: so well formed, so encompassed, as it were, with the harmony of sweet proportions, with little hands that even then, though so much tinier, were beautiful as now; with wide-open eyes blue as the sky and brighter than the sunshine—and almost in that very second he felt himself captured and held fast. This was love at first sight, love everlasting: a feeling unknown, unhoped for, unexpected—in so far as it could be a matter of conscious awareness; it took entire possession of him, and he understood, with joyous amazement, that this was for life.

But he understood more. He knows, does Dr. Cornelius, that there is something not quite right about this feeling, so unaware, so un-dreamed of, so involuntary. He has a shrewd suspicion that it is not by accident it has so utterly mastered him and bound itself up with his existence; that he had—even subconsciously—been preparing for it, or, more precisely, been prepared for it. There is, in short, something in him which at a given moment was ready to issue in such a feeling; and this something, highly extraordinary to relate, is his essence and quality as a professor of history. Dr. Cornelius, however, does not actually say this, even to himself; he merely realizes it, at odd times, and smiles a private smile. He knows that history professors do not love history because it is something that comes to pass, but only because it is something that *has* come to pass; that they hate a revolution like the present one because they feel it is lawless, incoherent, irrelevant—in a word, unhistoric; that their hearts belong to the coherent, disciplined, historic past. For the temper of timelessness, the temper of eternity—thus the scholar communes with himself when he takes his walk by the river before supper—that temper broods over the past; and it is a temper much better suited to the nervous system of a history professor than are the excesses of the present. The past is immortalized; that is to say, it is dead; and death is the root of all godliness and all abiding significance. Dr. Cornelius, walking alone in the dark, has a profound insight into this truth. It is this conservative instinct of his, his sense of the eternal, that has found in his love for his little daughter a way to save itself from the wounding inflicted by the times. For father love, and a little child on its mother's breast—are not these timeless, and thus very, very holy and beautiful? Yet Cornelius, pondering there in the dark, descries something not perfectly right and good in his love. Theoretically, in the interests of science, he admits it to himself. There is something ulterior about it, in the nature of it; that something is hostility, hostility against the history of today, which is still in the making and thus not history at all, in behalf of the genuine history that has already happened—that is to say, death. Yes, passing strange though all this is, yet it is true; true in a sense, that is. His devotion to this priceless little morsel of life and new growth has something to do with death, it clings to death as against life; and that is neither right nor beautiful—in a sense. Though only the most fanatical asceticism could be capable, on no other ground than such casual scientific perception, of tearing this purest and most precious of feelings out of his heart.

He holds his darling on his lap and her slim rosy legs hang down. He raises his brows as he talks to her, tenderly, with a half-teasing note of respect, and listens enchanted to her high, sweet little voice calling him Abel. He exchanges a look with the mother, who is caressing her Snapper and reading him a gentle lecture. He must be more reasonable, he must learn self-control; today again, under the manifold exasperations of life, he has given way to rage and behaved like a howling dervish. Cornelius casts a mistrustful glance at the big folk now and then, too; he thinks it not unlikely they are not unaware of those scientific preoccupations of his evening walks. If such be the case they do not show it. They stand there leaning their arms on their chair-backs and with a benevolence not untinctured with irony look on at the parental happiness.

The children's frocks are of a heavy, brick-red stuff, embroidered in modern "arty" style. They once belonged to Ingrid and Bert and are precisely alike, save that little knickers come out beneath Snapper's smock. And both have their hair bobbed. Snapper's is a streaky blond, inclined to turn dark. It is bristly and sticky and looks for all the world like a droll, badly fitting wig. But Ellie's is chestnut brown, glossy and fine as silk, as pleasing as her whole little personality. It covers her ears—and these ears are not a pair, one of them being the right size, the other distinctly too large. Her father will sometimes uncover this little abnormality and exclaim over it as though he had never noticed it before, which both makes Ellie giggle and covers her with shame. Her eyes are now golden brown, set far apart and with sweet gleams in them—such a clear and lovely look! The brows above are blond; the nose still unformed, with thick nostrils and almost circular holes; the mouth large and expressive, with a beautifully arching and mobile upper lip. When she laughs, dimples come in her cheeks and she shows her teeth like loosely strung pearls. So far she has lost but one tooth, which her father gently twisted out with his handkerchief after it had grown very wobbling. During this small operation she had paled and trembled very much. Her cheeks have the softness proper to her years, but they are not chubby; indeed, they are rather concave, due to her facial structure, with its somewhat prominent jaw. On one, close to the soft fall of her hair, is a downy freckle.

Ellie is not too well pleased with her looks—a sign that already she troubles about such things. Sadly she thinks it is best to admit it once for all, her face is "homely"; though the rest of her, "on the other hand," is not bad at all. She loves expressions like "on the other hand"; they sound choice and grown-up to her, and she likes to string them together, one after the other: "very likely," "probably," "after all." Snapper is self-critical too, though more in the moral sphere: he suffers from remorse for his attacks of rage and considers himself a tremendous sinner. He is quite certain that heaven is not for such as he; he is sure to go to "the bad place" when he dies, and no persuasions will convince him to the contrary—as that God sees the heart and gladly makes allowances. Obstinately he shakes his head, with the comic, crooked little peruke, and vows there is no place for him in heaven. When he has a cold he is immediately quite choked with mucus; rattles and rumbles from top to toe if you even look at him; his temperature flies up at once and he simply puffs. Nursy is pessimistic on the score of his constitution: such fat-blooded children as he might get a stroke any minute. Once she even thought she saw the moment at hand: Snapper had been in one of his berserker rages, and in the ensuing fit of penitence stood himself in the corner with his back to the room. Suddenly Nursy noticed that his face had gone all blue, far bluer, even, than her own. She raised the alarm, crying out that the child's all too rich blood had at length brought him to his final hour; and Snapper, to his vast astonishment, found himself, so far from being rebuked for evil-doing, encompassed in tenderness and anxiety—until it turned out that his colour was not caused by apoplexy but by the distempering on the nursery wall, which had come off on his tear-wet face.

Nursy has come downstairs too, and stands by the door, sleek-haired, owl-eyed, with her hands folded over her white apron, and a severely dignified manner born of her limited intelligence. She is very proud of the care and training she gives her nurslings and declares that they are "enveloping wonderfully." She has had seventeen suppurated teeth lately removed from her jaws and been measured for a set of symmetrical yellow ones in dark rubber gums; these now embellish her peasant face. She is obsessed with the strange conviction that these teeth of hers are the subject of general conversation, that, as it were, the sparrows on the house-tops chatter of them. "Everybody knows I've had a false set put in," she will say; "there has been a great deal of foolish talk about them." She is much given to dark hints and veiled innuendo: speaks, for instance, of a certain Dr. Bliefuss, whom every child knows, and "there are even some in the house who pretend to be him." All one can do with talk like this is charitably to pass it over in silence. But she teaches the children nursery rhymes: gems like:

> "Puff, puff, here comes the train!
> Puff, puff, toot, toot,
> Away it goes again."

Or that gastronomical jingle, so suited, in its sparseness, to the times, and yet seemingly with a blitheness of its own:

> "Monday we begin the week,
> Tuesday there's a bone to pick.
> Wednesday we're half way through,
> Thursday what a great to-do!
> Friday we eat what fish we're able,
> Saturday we dance round the table.
> Sunday brings us pork and greens—
> Here's a feast for kings and queens!"

Also a certain four-line stanza with a romantic appeal, unutterable and unuttered:

> "Open the gate, open the gate
> And let the carriage drive in.
> Who is it in the carriage sits?
> A lordly sir with golden hair."

Or, finally that ballad about golden-haired Marianne who sat on a, sat on a, sat on a stone, and combed out her, combed out her, combed out her hair; and about bloodthirsty Rudolph, who pulled out a, pulled out a, pulled out a knife—and his ensuing direful end. Ellie enunciates all these ballads charmingly, with her mobile little lips, and sings them in her sweet little voice—much better than Snapper. She does everything better than he does, and he pays her honest admiration and homage and obeys her in all things except when visited by one of his attacks. Sometimes she teaches him, instructs him upon the birds in the picture-book and tells him their proper names: "This is a chaffinch, Buddy, this is a bullfinch, this is a cowfinch." He has to repeat them after her. She gives him medical instruction too, teaches him the names of diseases, such as infammation of the lungs, infammation of the blood, infammation of the air. If he does not pay attention and cannot say the words after her, she stands him in the corner. Once she even boxed his ears, but was so ashamed that she stood herself in the corner for a long time. Yes, they are fast friends, two souls with but a single thought, and have all their adventures in common. They come home from a walk and relate as with one voice that they have seen two moollies and a teeny-weeny baby calf. They are on familiar terms with the kitchen, which consists of Xaver and the ladies Hinterhofer, two sisters once of the lower middle class who, in these evil days, are reduced to living *"au pair"* as the phrase goes and officiating as cook and housemaid for their board and keep. The little ones have a feeling that Xaver and the Hinterhofers are on much the same footing with their father and mother as they are themselves. At least sometimes, when they have been scolded, they go downstairs and announce that the master and mistress are cross. But playing with the servants lacks charm compared with the joys of playing upstairs. The kitchen could never rise to the height of the games their father can invent. For instance, there is "four gentlemen taking a walk." When they play it Abel will crook his knees until he is the same height with themselves and go walking with them, hand in hand. They never get enough of this sport; they could walk round and round the dining-room a whole day on end, five gentlemen in all, counting the diminished Abel.

Then there is the thrilling cushion game. One of the children, usually Ellie, seats herself, unbeknownst to Abel, in his seat at table. Still as a mouse she awaits his coming. He draws near with his head in the air, descanting in loud, clear tones upon the surpassing comfort of his chair; and sits down on top of Ellie. "What's this, what's this?" says he. And bounces about, deaf to the smothered giggles exploding behind him. "Why have they put a cushion in my chair? And what a queer, hard, awkward-shaped cushion it is!" he goes on. "Frightfully uncomfortable to sit on!" And keeps pushing and bouncing about more and more on the astonishing cushion and clutching behind him into the rapturous giggling and squeaking, until at last he turns round, and the game ends with a magnificent climax of discovery and recognition. They might go through all this a hundred times without diminishing by an iota its power to thrill.

Today is no time for such joys. The imminent festivity disturbs the atmosphere, and besides there is work to be done, and, above all, the eggs to be got. Ellie has just time to recite "Puff, puff," and Cornelius to discover that her ears are not mates, when they are interrupted by the arrival of Danny, come to fetch Bert and Ingrid. Xaver, meantime, has exchanged his striped livery for an ordinary coat, in which he looks rather rough-and-ready, though as brisk and attractive as ever. So then Nursy and the children ascend to the upper regions, the Professor withdraws to his study to read, as always after dinner, and his wife bends her energies upon the sandwiches and salad that must be prepared. And she has another errand as well. Before the young people arrive she has to take her shopping-basket and dash into town on her bicycle, to turn into provisions a sum of money she has in hand, which she dares not keep lest it lose all value.

Cornelius reads, leaning back in his chair, with his cigar between his middle and index fingers. First he reads Macaulay on the origin of the English public debt at the end of the seventeenth century; then an article in a French periodical on the rapid increase in the Spanish debt towards the end of the sixteenth. Both these for his lecture on the morrow. He intends to compare the astonishing prosperity which accompanied the phenomenon in England with its fatal effects a hundred years earlier in Spain, and to analyse the ethical and psychological grounds of the difference in results. For that will give him a chance to refer back from the England of William III, which is the actual subject in hand, to the time of Philip II and the Counter-Reformation, which is his own special field. He has already written a valuable work on this period; it is much cited and got him his professorship. While his cigar burns down and gets strong, he excogitates a few pensive sentences in a key of gentle melancholy, to be delivered before his class next day: about the practically hopeless struggle carried on by the belated Philip against the whole trend of history: against the new, the kingdom-disrupting power of the Germanic ideal of freedom and individual liberty. And about the persistent, futile struggle of the aristocracy, condemned by God and rejected of man, against the forces of progress and change. He savours his sentences; keeps on polishing them while he puts back the books he has been using; then goes upstairs for the usual pause in his day's work, the hour with drawn blinds and closed eyes, which he so imperatively needs. But today, he recalls, he will rest under disturbed conditions, amid the bustle of preparations for the feast. He smiles to find his heart giving a mild flutter at the thought. Disjointed phrases on the theme of black-clad Philip and his times mingle with a confused consciousness that they will soon be dancing down below. For five minutes or so he falls asleep.

As he lies and rests he can hear the sound of the garden gate and the repeated ringing at the bell. Each time a little pang goes through him, of excitement and suspense, at the thought that the young people have begun to fill the floor below. And each time he smiles at himself again—though even his smile is slightly nervous, is tinged with the pleasurable anticipations people always feel before a party. At half past four—it is already dark—he gets up and washes at the washstand. The basin has been out of repair for two years. It is supposed to tip, but has broken away from its socket on one side and cannot be mended because there is nobody to mend it; neither replaced because no shop can supply another. So it has to be hung up above the vent and emptied by lifting in both hands and pouring out the water. Cornelius shakes his head over this basin, as he does several times a day—whenever, in fact, he has occasion to use it. He finishes his toilet with care, standing under the ceiling light to polish his glasses till they shine. Then he goes downstairs.

On his way to the dining-room he hears the gramophone already going, and the sound of voices. He puts on a polite, society air; at his tongue's end is the phrase he means to utter: "Pray don't let me disturb you," as he passes directly into the dining-room for his tea. "Pray don't let me disturb you"—it seems to him precisely the *mot juste;* towards the guests cordial and considerate, for himself a very bulwark.

The lower floor is lighted up, all the bulbs in the chandelier are burning save one that has burned out. Cornelius pauses on a lower step and surveys the entrance hall. It looks pleasant and cosy in the bright light, with its copy of Marées over the brick chimney-piece, its wainscoted walls—wainscoted in soft wood—and red-carpeted floor, where the guests stand in groups, chatting, each with his tea-cup and slice of bread-and-butter spread with anchovy paste. There is a festal haze, faint scents of hair and clothing and human breath come to him across the room, it is all characteristic and familiar and highly evocative. The door into the dressing-room is open, guests are still arriving.

A large group of people is rather bewildering at first sight. The Professor takes in only the general scene. He does not see Ingrid, who is standing just at the foot of the steps, in a dark silk frock with a pleated collar falling softly over the shoulders, and bare arms. She smiles up at him, nodding and showing her lovely teeth.

"Rested?" she asks, for his private ear. With a quite unwarranted start he recognizes her, and she presents some of her friends.

"May I introduce Herr Zuber?" she says. "And this is Fräulein Plaichinger."

Herr Zuber is insignificant. But Fräulein Plaichinger is a perfect Germania, blond and voluptuous, arrayed in floating draperies. She has a snub nose, and answers the Professor's salutation in the high, shrill pipe so many stout women have.

"Delighted to meet you," he says. "How nice of you to come! A classmate of Ingrid's, I suppose?"

And Herr Zuber is a golfing partner of Ingrid's. He is in business; he works in his uncle's brewery. Cornelius makes a few jokes about the thinness of the beer and professes to believe that Herr Zuber could easily do something about the quality if he would. "But pray don't let me disturb you," he goes on, and turns towards the dining-room.

"There comes Max," says Ingrid. "Max, you sweep, what do you mean by rolling up at this time of day?" For such is the way they talk to each other, offensively to an older ear; of social forms, of hospitable warmth, there is no faintest trace. They all call each other by their first names.

A young man comes up to them out of the dressing-room and makes his bow; he has an expanse of white shirt-front and a little black string tie. He is as pretty as a picture, dark, with rosy cheeks, clean-shaven of course, but with just a sketch of side-whisker. Not a ridiculous or flashy beauty, not like a gypsy fiddler, but just charming to look at, in a winning, well-bred way, with kind dark eyes. He even wears his dinner-jacket a little awkwardly.

"Please don't scold me, Cornelia," he says; "it's the idiotic lectures." And Ingrid presents him to her father as Herr Hergesell.

Well, and so this is Herr Hergesell. He knows his manners, does Herr Hergesell, and thanks the master of the house quite ingratiatingly for his invitation as they shake hands. "I certainly seem to have missed the bus," says he jocosely. "Of course I have lectures to-day up to four o'clock; I would have; and after that I had to go home to change." Then he talks about his pumps, with which he has just been struggling in the dressing-room.

"I brought them with me in a bag," he goes on. "Mustn't tramp all over the carpet in our brogues—it's not done. Well, I was ass enough not to fetch along a shoe-horn, and I find I simply can't get in! What a sell! They are the tightest I've ever had, the numbers don't tell you a thing, and all the leather today is just cast iron. It's not leather at all. My poor finger"—he confidingly displays a reddened digit and once more characterizes the whole thing as a "sell," and a putrid sell into the bargain. He really does talk just as Ingrid said he did, with a peculiar nasal drawl, not affectedly in the least, but merely because that is the way of all the Hergesells.

Dr. Cornelius says it is very careless of them not to keep a shoe-horn in the cloak-room and displays proper sympathy with the mangled finger. "But now you *really* must not let me disturb you any longer," he goes on. "*Auf wiedersehen!*" And he crosses the hall into the dining-room.

There are guests there too, drinking tea; the family table is pulled out. But the Professor goes at once to his own little upholstered corner with the electric light bulb above it—the nook where he usually drinks his tea. His wife is sitting there talking with Bert and two other young men, one of them Herzl, whom Cornelius knows and greets; the other a typical "Wandervogel" named Möller, a youth who obviously neither owns nor cares to own the correct evening dress of the middle classes (in fact, there is no such thing any more), nor to ape the manners of a gentleman (and, in fact, there is no such thing any more either). He has a wilderness of hair, horn spectacles, and a long neck, and wears golf stockings and a belted blouse. His regular occupation, the Professor learns, is banking, but he is by way of being an amateur folk-lorist and collects folk-songs from all localities and in all languages. He sings them, too, and at Ingrid's command has brought his guitar; it is hanging in the dressing-room in an oilcloth case. Herzl, the actor, is small and slight, but he has a strong growth of black beard, as you can tell by the thick coat of powder on his cheeks. His eyes are larger than life, with a deep and melancholy glow. He has put on rouge besides the powder—those dull carmine high-lights on the cheeks can be nothing but a cosmetic. "Queer," thinks the Professor. "You would think a man would be one thing or the other—not melancholic and use face paint at the same time. It's a psychological contradiction. How can a melancholy man rouge? But here we have a perfect illustration of the abnormality of the artist soul-form. It can make possible a contradiction like this— perhaps it even consists in the contradiction. All very interesting—and no reason whatever for not being polite to him. Politeness is a primitive convention—and legitimate. . . . Do take some lemon, Herr Hofschauspieler!"

Court actors and court theatres—there are no such things any more, really. But Herzl relishes the sound of the title, notwithstanding he is a revolutionary artist. This must be another contradiction inherent in his soul-form; so, at least, the Professor assumes, and he is probably right. The flattery he is guilty of is a sort of atonement for his previous hard thoughts about the rouge.

"Thank you so much—it's really too good of you, sir," says Herzl, quite embarrassed. He is so overcome that he almost stammers; only his perfect enunciation saves him. His whole bearing towards his hostess and the master of the house is exaggeratedly polite. It is almost as though he had a bad conscience in respect of his rouge; as though an inward compulsion had driven him to put it on, but now, seeing it through the Professor's eyes, he disapproves of it himself, and thinks, by an air of humility toward the whole of unrouged society, to mitigate its effect.

They drink their tea and chat: about Möller's folk-songs, about Basque folk-songs and Spanish folk-songs; from which they pass to the new production of *Don Carlos* at the Stadttheater, in which Herzl plays the title-rôle. He talks about his own rendering of the part and says he hopes his conception of the character has unity. They go on to criticize the rest of the cast, the setting, and the production as a whole; and Cornelius is struck, rather painfully, to find the conversation trending towards his own special province, back to Spain and the Counter-Reformation. He has done nothing at all to give it this turn, he is perfectly innocent, and hopes it does not look as though he had sought an occasion to play the professor. He wonders, and falls silent, feeling relieved when the little folk come up to the table. Ellie and Snapper have on their blue velvet Sunday frocks; they are permitted to partake in the festivities up to bed-time. They look shy and large-eyed as they say how-do-you-do to the strangers and, under pressure, repeat their names and ages. Herr Möller does nothing but gaze at them solemnly, but Herzl is simply ravished. He rolls his eyes up to heaven and puts his hands over his mouth; he positively blesses them. It all, no doubt, comes from his heart, but he is so addicted to theatrical methods of making an impression and getting an effect that both words and behaviour ring frightfully false. And even his enthusiasm for the little folk looks too much like part of his general craving to make up for the rouge on his cheeks.

The tea-table has meanwhile emptied of guests, and dancing is going on in the hall. The children run off, the Professor prepares to retire. "Go and enjoy yourselves," he says to Möller and Herzl, who have sprung from their chairs as he rises from his. They shake hands and he withdraws into his study, his peaceful kingdom, where he lets down the blinds, turns on the desk lamp, and sits down to his work.

It is work which can be done, if necessary, under disturbed conditions: nothing but a few letters and a few notes. Of course, Cornelius's mind wanders. Vague impressions float through it: Herr Hergesell's refractory pumps, the high pipe in that plump body of the Plaichinger female. As he writes, or leans back in his chair and stares into space, his thoughts go back to Herr Möller's collection of Basque folk-songs, to Herzl's posings and humility, to "his" Carlos and the court of Philip II. There is something strange, he thinks, about conversations. They are so ductile, they will flow of their own accord in the direction of one's dominating interest. Often and often he has seen this happen. And while he is thinking, he is listening to the sounds next door—rather subdued, he finds them. He hears only voices, no sound of footsteps. The dancers do not glide or circle round the room; they merely walk about over the carpet, which does not hamper their movements in the least. Their way of holding each other is quite different and strange, and they move to the strains of the gramophone, to the weird music of the new world. He concentrates on the music and makes out that it is a jazz-band record, with various percussion instruments and the clack and clatter of castanets, which, however, are not even faintly suggestive of Spain, but merely jazz like the rest. No, not Spain. . . . His thoughts are back at their old round.

Half an hour goes by. It occurs to him it would be no more than friendly to go and contribute a box of cigarettes to the festivities next door. Too bad to ask the young people to smoke their own—though they have probably never thought of it. He goes into the empty dining-room and takes a box from his supply in the cupboard: not the best ones, nor yet the brand he himself prefers, but a certain long, thin kind he is not averse to getting rid of—after all, they are nothing but youngsters. He takes the box into the hall, holds it up with a smile, and deposits it on the mantel-shelf. After which he gives a look round and returns to his own room.

There comes a lull in dance and music. The guests stand about the room in groups or round the table at the window or are seated in a circle by the fireplace. Even the built-in stairs, with their worn velvet carpet, are crowded with young folk as in an amphitheatre: Max

Hergesell is there, leaning back with one elbow on the step above and gesticulating with his free hand as he talks to the shrill, voluptuous Plaichinger. The floor of the hall is nearly empty, save just in the centre: there, directly beneath the chandelier, the two little ones in their blue velvet frocks clutch each other in an awkward embrace and twirl silently round and round, oblivious of all else. Cornelius, as he passes, strokes their hair, with a friendly word; it does not distract them from their small solemn preoccupation. But at his own door he turns to glance round and sees young Hergesell push himself off the stair by his elbow—probably because he noticed the Professor. He comes down into the arena, takes Ellie out of her brother's arms, and dances with her himself. It looks very comic, without the music, and he crouches down just as Cornelius does when he goes walking with the four gentlemen, holding the fluttered Ellie as though she were grown up and taking little "shimmying" steps. Everybody watches with huge enjoyment, the gramophone is put on again, dancing becomes general. The Professor stands and looks, with his hand on the door-knob. He nods and laughs; when he finally shuts himself into his study the mechanical smile still lingers on his lips.

Again he turns over pages by his desk lamp, takes notes, attends to a few simple matters. After a while he notices that the guests have forsaken the entrance hall for his wife's drawing-room, into which there is a door from his own study as well. He hears their voices and the sounds of a guitar being tuned. Herr Möller, it seems, is to sing— and does so. He twangs the strings of his instrument and sings in a powerful bass a ballad in a strange tongue, possibly Swedish. The Professor does not succeed in identifying it, though he listens attentively to the end, after which there is great applause. The sound is deadened by the portière that hangs over the dividing door. The young bank-clerk begins another song. Cornelius goes softly in.

It is half-dark in the drawing-room; the only light is from the shaded standard lamp, beneath which Möller sits, on the divan, with his legs crossed, picking his strings. His audience is grouped easily about; as there are not enough seats, some stand, and more, among them many young ladies, are simply sitting on the floor with their hands clasped round their knees or even with their legs stretched out before them. Hergesell sits thus, in his dinner jacket, next the piano, with Fräulein Plaichinger beside him. Frau Cornelius is holding both children on her lap as she sits in her easy-chair opposite the singer.

Snapper, the Boeotian, begins to talk loud and clear in the middle of the song and has to be intimidated with hushings and finger-shakings. Never, never would Ellie allow herself to be guilty of such conduct. She sits there daintily erect and still on her mother's knee. The Professor tries to catch her eye and exchange a private signal with his little girl; but she does not see him. Neither does she seem to be looking at the singer. Her gaze is directed lower down. Möller sings the "joli tambour":

> "*Sire, mon roi, donnez-moi votre*
> *fille—*"

They are all enchanted. "How good!" Hergesell is heard to say, in the odd, nasally condescending Hergesell tone. The next one is a beggar ballad, to a tune composed by young Möller himself; it elicits a storm of applause:

> "Gypsy lassie a-goin' ' to the fair,
> Huzza!
> Gypsy laddie a-goin' to be
> there—
> Huzza, diddlety umpty dido!"

Laughter and high spirits, sheer reckless hilarity, reigns after this jovial ballad. "Frightfully good!" Hergesell comments again, as before. Follows another popular song, this time a Hungarian one; Möller sings it in its own outlandish tongue, and most effectively. The Professor applauds with ostentation. It warms his heart and does him good, this outcropping of artistic, historic, and cultural elements all amongst the shimmying. He goes up to young Möller and congratulates him, talks about the songs and their sources, and Möller promises to lend him a certain annotated book of folk songs. Cornelius is the more cordial because all the time, as fathers do, he has been comparing the parts and achievements of this young stranger with those of his own son, and being gnawed by envy and chagrin. This young Möller, he is thinking, is a capable bank-clerk (though about Möller's capacity he knows nothing whatever) and has this special gift besides, which must have taken talent and energy to cultivate. "And here is my poor Bert, who knows nothing and can do nothing and thinks of nothing except playing the clown, without even talent for that!" He tries to be just; he tells himself that, after all, Bert has innate refinement; that probably there is a good deal more to him than there is to the successful Möller; that perhaps he has even something of the poet in him, and his dancing and table-waiting are due to mere boyish folly and the distraught times. But paternal envy and pessimism win the upper hand; when Möller begins another song, Dr. Cornelius goes back to his room.

He works as before, with divided attention, at this and that, while it gets on for seven o'clock. Then he remembers a letter he may just as well write, a short letter and not very important, but letter-writing is wonderful for the way it takes up the time, and it is almost half past when he has finished. At half past eight the Italian salad will be served; so now is the prescribed moment for the Professor to go out into the wintry darkness to post his letters and take his daily quantum of fresh air and exercise. They are dancing again, and he will have to pass through the hall to get his hat and coat; but they are used to him now, he need not stop and beg them not to be disturbed. He lays away his papers, takes up the letters he has written, and goes out. But he sees his wife sitting near the door of his room and pauses a little by her easy-chair.

She is watching the dancing. Now and then the big folk or some of their guests stop to speak to her; the party is at its height, and there are more onlookers than these two: blue-faced Ann is standing at the bottom of the stairs, in all the dignity of her limitations. She is waiting for the children, who simply cannot get their fill of these unwonted festivities, and watching over Snapper, lest his all too rich blood be churned to the danger-point by too much twirling round. And not only the nursery but the kitchen takes an interest: Xaver and the two ladies Hinterhofer are standing by the pantry door looking on with relish. Fräulein Walburga, the elder of the two sunken sisters (the culinary section—she objects to being called a cook), is a whimsical, good-natured sort, brown-eyed, wearing glasses with thick circular lenses; the nose-piece is wound with a bit of rag to keep it from pressing on her nose. Fräulein Cecilia is younger, though not so precisely young either. Her bearing is as self-assertive as usual, this being her way of sustaining her dignity as a former member of the middle class. For Fräulein Cecilia feels acutely her descent into the ranks of domestic service. She positively declines to wear a cap or other badge of servitude, and her hardest trial is on the Wednesday evening when she has to serve the dinner while Xaver has his afternoon out. She hands the dishes with averted face and elevated nose—

a fallen queen; and so distressing is it to behold her degradation that one evening when the little folk happened to be at table and saw her they both with one accord burst into tears. Such anguish is unknown to young Xaver. He enjoys serving and does it with an ease born of practice as well as talent, for he was once a "piccolo." But otherwise he is a thorough-paced good-for-nothing and windbag—with quite distinct traits of character of his own, as his long-suffering employers are always ready to concede, but perfectly impossible and a bag of wind for all that. One must just take him as he is, they think, and not expect figs from thistles. He is the child and product of the disrupted times, a perfect specimen of his generation, follower of the revolution, Bolshevist sympathizer. The Professor's name for him is the "minute-man," because he is always to be counted on in any sudden crisis, if only it address his sense of humour or love of novelty, and will display therein amazing readiness and resource. But he utterly lacks a sense of duty and can as little be trained to the performance of the daily round and common task as some kinds of dog can be taught to jump over a stick. It goes so plainly against the grain that criticism is disarmed. One becomes resigned. On grounds that appealed to him as unusual and amusing he would be ready to turn out of his bed at any hour of the night. But he simply cannot get up before eight in the morning, he cannot do it, he will not jump over the stick. Yet all day long the evidence of this free and untrammelled existence, the sound of his mouth-organ, his joyous whistle, or his raucous but expressive voice lifted in song, rises to the hearing of the world above-stairs; and the smoke of his cigarettes fills the pantry. While the Hinterhofer ladies work he stands and looks on. Of a morning while the Professor is breakfasting, he tears the leaf off the study calendar—but does not lift a finger to dust the room. Dr. Cornelius has often told him to leave the calendar alone, for he tends to tear off two leaves at a time and thus to add to the general confusion. But young Xaver appears to find joy in this activity, and will not be deprived of it.

Again, he is fond of children, a winning trait. He will throw himself into games with the little folk in the garden, make and mend their toys with great ingenuity, even read aloud from their books—and very droll it sounds in his thick-lipped pronunciation. With his whole soul he loves the cinema; after an evening spent there he inclines to melancholy and yearning and talking to himself. Vague hopes stir in him that some day he may make his fortune in that gay world and belong to it by rights—hopes based on his shock of hair and his physical agility and daring. He likes to climb the ash tree in the front garden, mounting branch by branch to the very top and frightening everybody to death who sees him. Once there he lights a cigarette and smokes it as he sways to and fro, keeping a look-out for a cinema director who might chance to come along and engage him.

If he changed his striped jacket for mufti, he might easily dance with the others and no one would notice the difference. For the big folk's friends are rather anomalous in their clothing: evening dress is worn by a few, but it is by no means the rule. There is quite a sprinkling of guests, both male and female, in the same general style as Möller the ballad-singer. The Professor is familiar with the circumstances of most of this young generation he is watching as he stands beside his wife's chair; he has heard them spoken of by name. They are students at the high school or at the School of Applied Art; they lead, at least the masculine portion, that precarious and scrambling existence which is purely the product of the time. There is a tall, pale, spindling youth, the son of a dentist, who lives by speculation. From all the Professor hears, he is a perfect Aladdin. He keeps a car, treats his friends to champagne suppers, and showers presents upon them on every occasion, costly little trifles in mother-of-pearl and gold. So today he has brought gifts to the young givers of the feast: for Bert a gold lead-pencil, and for Ingrid a pair of ear-rings of barbaric size, great gold circlets that fortunately do not have to go through the little ear-lobe, but are fastened over it by means of a clip. The big folk come laughing to their parents to display these trophies; and the parents shake their heads even while they admire—Aladdin bowing over and over from afar.

The young people appear to be absorbed in their dancing—if the performance they are carrying out with so much still concentration can be called dancing. They stride across the carpet, slowly, according to some unfathomable prescript, strangely embraced; in the newest attitude, tummy advanced and shoulders high, waggling the hips. They do not get tired, because nobody could. There is no such thing as heightened colour or heaving bosoms. Two girls may dance together or two young men—it is all the same. They move to the exotic strains of the gramophone, played with the loudest needles to procure the maximum of sound: shimmies, foxtrots, one-steps, double foxes,

African shimmies, Java dances, and Creole polkas, the wild musky melodies follow one another, now furious, now languishing, a monotonous Negro programme in unfamiliar rhythm, to a clacking, clashing, and strumming orchestral accompaniment.

"What is that record?" Cornelius inquires of Ingrid, as she passes him by in the arms of the pale young speculator, with reference to the piece then playing, whose alternate languors and furies he finds comparatively pleasing and showing a certain resourcefulness in detail.

"*Prince of Pappenheim:* 'Console thee, dearest child,' " she answers, and smiles pleasantly back at him with her white teeth.

The cigarette smoke wreathes beneath the chandelier. The air is blue with a festal haze compact of sweet and thrilling ingredients that stir the blood with memories of green-sick pains and are particularly poignant to those whose youth—like the Professor's own—has been over-sensitive. . . . The little folk are still on the floor. They are allowed to stop up until eight, so great is their delight in the party. The guests have got used to their presence; in their own way, they have their place in the doings of the evening. They have separated, anyhow: Snapper revolves all alone in the middle of the carpet, in his little blue velvet smock, while Ellie is running after one of the dancing couples, trying to hold the man fast by his coat. It is Max Hergesell and Fräulein Plaichinger. They dance well, it is a pleasure to watch them. One has to admit that these mad modern dances, when the right people dance them, are not so bad after all—they have something quite taking. Young Hergesell is a capital leader, dances according to rule, yet with individuality. So it looks. With what aplomb can he walk backwards—when space permits! And he knows how to be graceful standing still in a crowd. And his partner supports him well, being unsuspectedly lithe and buoyant, as fat people often are. They look at each other, they are talking, paying no heed to Ellie, though others are smiling to see the child's persistence. Dr. Cornelius tries to catch up his little sweetheart as she passes and draw her to him. But Ellie eludes him, almost peevishly; her dear Abel is nothing to her now. She braces her little arms against his chest and turns her face away with a persecuted look. Then escapes to follow her fancy once more.

The Professor feels an involuntary twinge. Uppermost in his heart is hatred for this party, with its power to intoxicate and estrange his darling child. His love for her—that not quite disinterested, not quite unexceptionable love of his—is easily wounded. He wears a mechanical smile, but his eyes have clouded, and he stares fixedly at a point in the carpet, between the dancers' feet.

"The children ought to go to bed," he tells his wife. But she pleads for another quarter of an hour; she has promised already, and they do love it so! He smiles again and shakes his head, stands so a moment and then goes across to the cloak-room, which is full of coats and hats and scarves and overshoes. He has trouble in rummaging out his own coat, and Max Hergesell comes out of the hall, wiping his brow.

"Going out, sir?" he asks, in Hergesellian accents, dutifully helping the older man on with his coat. "Silly business this, with my pumps," he says. "They pinch like hell. The brutes are simply too tight for me, quite apart from the bad leather. They press just here on the ball of my great toe"—he stands on one foot and holds the other in his hand—"it's simply unbearable. There's nothing for it but to take them off; my brogues will have to do the business. . . . Oh, let me help you, sir."

"Thanks," says Cornelius. "Don't trouble. Get rid of your own tormentors. . . . Oh, thanks very much!" For Hergesell has gone on one knee to snap the fasteners of his snow-boots.

Once more the Professor expresses his gratitude; he is pleased and touched by so much sincere respect and youthful readiness to serve. "Go and enjoy yourself," he counsels. "Change your shoes and make up for what you have been suffering. Nobody can dance in shoes that pinch. Good-bye, I must be off to get a breath of fresh air."

"I'm going to dance with Ellie now," calls Hergesell after him. "She'll be a first-rate dancer when she grows up, and that I'll swear to."

"Think so?" Cornelius answers, already half out. "Well, you are a connoisseur, I'm sure. Don't get curvature of the spine with stooping."

He nods again and goes. "Fine lad," he thinks as he shuts the door. "Student of engineering. Knows what he's bound for, got a good clear head, and so well set up and pleasant too." And again paternal envy rises as he compares his poor Bert's status with this young man's, which he puts in the rosiest light that his son's may look the darker. Thus he sets out on his evening walk.

He goes up the avenue, crosses the bridge, and walks along the bank on the other side as far as the next bridge but one. The air is wet and cold, with a little snow now and then. He turns up his coat-collar and slips the crook of his cane over the arm behind his back. Now and then he ventilates his lungs with a long deep breath of the night air. As usual when he walks, his mind reverts to his professional preoccupations, he thinks about his lectures and the things he means to say tomorrow about Philip's struggle against the Germanic revolution, things steeped in melancholy and penetratingly just. Above all just, he thinks. For in one's dealings with the young it behoves one to display the scientific spirit, to exhibit the principles of enlightenment—not only for purposes of mental discipline, but on the human and individual side, in order not to wound them or indirectly offend their political sensibilities; particularly in these days, when there is so much tinder in the air, opinions are so frightfully split up and chaotic, and you may so easily incur attacks from one party or the other, or even give rise to scandal, by taking sides on a point of history. "And taking sides is unhistoric anyhow," so he muses. "Only justice, only impartiality is historic." And could not, properly considered, be otherwise. . . . For justice can have nothing of youthful fire and blithe, fresh, loyal conviction. It is by nature melancholy. And, being so, has secret affinity with the lost cause and the forlorn hope rather than with the fresh and blithe and loyal—perhaps this affinity is its very essence and without it it would not exist at all! . . . "And is there then no such thing as justice?" the Professor asks himself, and ponders the question so deeply that he absently posts his letters in the next box and turns round to go home. This thought of his is unsettling and disturbing to the scientific mind—but is it not after all itself scientific, psychological, conscientious, and therefore to be accepted without prejudice, no matter how upsetting? In the midst of which musings Dr. Cornelius finds himself back at his own door.

On the outer threshold stands Xaver, and seems to be looking for him.

"Herr Professor," says Xaver, tossing back his hair, "go upstairs to Ellie straight off. She's in a bad way."

"What's the matter?" asks Cornelius in alarm. "Is she ill?"

"No-o, not to say ill," answers Xaver. "She's just in a bad way and crying fit to bust her little heart. It's along o' that chap with the shirt-front that danced with her—Herr Hergesell. She couldn't be got to go upstairs peaceably, not at no price at all, and she's b'en crying bucketfuls."

"Nonsense," says the Professor, who has entered and is tossing off his things in the cloak-room. He says no more; opens the glass door and without a glance at the guests turns swiftly to the stairs. Takes them two at a time, crosses the upper hall and the small room leading into the nursery. Xaver follows at his heels, but stops at the nursery door.

A bright light still burns within, showing the gay frieze that runs all round the room, the large row of shelves heaped with a confusion of toys, the rocking-horse on his swaying platform, with red-varnished nostrils and raised hoofs. On the linoleum lie other toys—building blocks, railway trains, a little trumpet. The two white cribs stand not far apart, Ellie's in the window corner, Snapper's out in the room.

Snapper is asleep. He has said his prayers in loud, ringing tones, prompted by Nurse, and gone off at once into vehement, profound, and rosy slumber—from which a cannon-ball fired at close range could not rouse him. He lies with both fists flung back on the pillows on either side of the tousled head with its funny crooked little slumber-tossed wig.

A circle of females surrounds Ellie's bed: not only blue-faced Ann is there, but the Hinterhofer ladies too, talking to each other and to her. They make way as the Professor comes up and reveal the child sitting all pale among her pillows, sobbing and weeping more bitterly than he has ever seen her sob and weep in her life. Her lovely little hands lie on the coverlet in front of her, the nightgown with its narrow lace border has slipped down from her shoulder—such a thin, birdlike little shoulder—and the sweet head Cornelius loves so well, set on the neck like a flower on its stalk, her head is on one side, with the eyes rolled up to the corner between wall and ceiling above her head. For there she seems to envisage the anguish of her heart and even to nod to it—either on purpose or because her head wobbles as her body is shaken with the violence of her sobs. Her eyes rain down tears. The bow-shaped lips are parted, like a little *mater dolorosa's,* and from them issue long, low wails that in nothing resemble the unnecessary and exasperating shrieks of a naughty child, but rise from the deep extremity of her heart and wake in the Professor's own a sympathy that is well-nigh intolerable. He has never seen his darling so before. His feelings find immediate vent in an attack on the ladies Hinterhofer.

"What about the supper?" he asks sharply. "There must be a great deal to do. Is my wife being left to do it alone?"

For the acute sensibilities of the former middle class this is quite enough. The ladies withdraw in righteous indignation, and Xaver Kleingutl jeers at them as they pass out. Having been born to low life instead of achieving it, he never loses a chance to mock at their fallen state.

"Childie, childie," murmurs Cornelius, and sitting down by the crib enfolds the anguished Ellie in his arms. "What is the trouble with my darling?"

She bedews his face with her tears.

"Abel . . . Abel . . ." she stammers between sobs. "Why—isn't Max—my brother? Max ought to be—my brother!"

Alas, alas! What mischance is this? Is this what the party has wrought, with its fatal atmosphere? Cornelius glances helplessly up at blue-faced Ann standing there in all the dignity of her limitations with her hands before her on her apron. She purses up her mouth and makes a long face. "It's pretty young," she says, "for the female instincts to be showing up."

"Hold your tongue," snaps Cornelius, in his agony. He has this much to be thankful for, that Ellie does not turn from him now; she does not push him away as she did downstairs, but clings to him in her need, while she reiterates her absurd, bewildered prayer that Max might be her brother, or with a fresh burst of desire demands to be taken downstairs so that he can dance with her again. But Max, of course, is dancing with Fräulein Plaichinger, that behemoth who is his rightful partner and has every claim upon him; whereas Ellie—never, thinks the Professor, his heart torn with the violence of his pity, never has she looked so tiny and birdlike as now, when she nestles to him shaken with sobs and all unaware of what is happening in her little soul. No, she does not know. She does not comprehend that her suffering is on account of Fräulein Plaichinger, fat, overgrown, and utterly within her rights in dancing with Max Hergesell, whereas Ellie may only do it once, by way of a joke, although she is incomparably the more charming of the two. Yet it would be quite mad to reproach young Hergesell with the state of affairs or to make fantastic demands upon him. No, Ellie's suffering is without help or healing and must be covered up. Yet just as it is without understanding, so it is also without restraint—and that is what makes it so horribly painful. Xaver and blue-faced Ann do not feel this pain, it does not affect them—either because of native callousness or because they accept it as the way of nature. But the Professor's fatherly heart is quite torn by it, and by a distressful horror of this passion, so hopeless and so absurd.

Of no avail to hold forth to poor Ellie on the subject of the perfectly good little brother she already has. She only casts a distraught and scornful glance over at the other crib, where Snapper lies vehemently slumbering, and with fresh tears calls again for Max. Of no avail either the promise of a long, long walk tomorrow, all five gentlemen, round and round the dining-room table; or a dramatic description of the thrilling cushion games they will play. No, she will listen to none of all this, nor to lying down and going to sleep. She will not sleep, she will sit bolt upright and suffer. . . . But on a sudden they stop and listen, Abel and Ellie; listen to something miraculous that is coming to pass, that is approaching by strides, two strides, to the nursery door, that now overwhelmingly appears. . . .

It is Xaver's work, not a doubt of that. He has not remained by the door where he stood to gloat over the ejection of the Hinterhofers. No, he has bestirred himself, taken a notion; likewise steps to carry it out. Downstairs he has gone, twitched Herr Hergesell's sleeve, and made a thick-lipped request. So here they both are. Xaver, having done his part, remains by the door; but Max Hergesell comes up to Ellie's crib; in his dinner-jacket, with his sketchy side-whisker and charming black eyes; obviously quite pleased with his rôle of swan knight and fairy prince, as one who should say: "See, here am I, now all losses are restored and sorrows end."

Cornelius is almost as much overcome as Ellie herself.

"Just look," he says feebly, "look who's here. This is uncommonly good of you, Herr Hergesell."

"Not a bit of it," says Hergesell. "Why shouldn't I come to say good-night to my fair partner?"

And he approaches the bars of the crib, behind which Ellie sits struck mute. She smiles blissfully through her tears. A funny, high little note that is half a sigh of relief comes from her lips, then she looks dumbly up at her swan knight with her golden-brown eyes—tear-swollen though they are, so much more beautiful than the fat Plaichinger's. She does not put up her arms. Her joy, like her grief, is without understanding; but she does not do that. The lovely little hands lie quiet on the coverlet, and Max Hergesell stands with his arms leaning over the rail as on a balcony.

"And now," he says smartly, "she need not 'sit the livelong night and weep upon her bed'!" He looks at the Professor to make sure he is receiving due credit for the quotation. "Ha ha!" he laughs, "she's beginning young. 'Console thee, dearest child!' Never mind, you're all right! Just as you are you'll be wonderful! You've only got to grow up. . . . And you'll lie down and go to sleep like a good girl, now I've come to say good-night? And not cry any more, little Lorelei?"

Ellie looks up at him, transfigured. One birdlike shoulder is bare; the Professor draws the lace-trimmed nighty over it. There comes into his mind a sentimental story he once read about a dying child who longs to see a clown he had once, with unforgettable ecstasy, beheld in a circus. And they bring the clown to the bedside marvellously arrayed, embroidered before and behind with silver butterflies; and the child dies happy. Max Hergesell is not embroidered, and Ellie, thank God, is not going to die, she has only "been in a bad way." But, after all, the effect is the same. Young Hergesell leans over the bars of the crib and rattles on, more for the father's ear than the child's, but Ellie does not know that—and the father's feelings towards him are a most singular mixture of thankfulness, embarrassment, and hatred.

"Good night, little Lorelei," says Hergesell, and gives her his hand through the bars. Her pretty, soft, white little hand is swallowed up in the grasp of his big, strong, red one. "Sleep well," he says, "and sweet dreams! But don't dream about me—God forbid! Not at your age—ha ha!" And then the fairy clown's visit is at an end. Cornelius accompanies him to the door. "No, no, positively, no thanks called for, don't mention it," he large-heartedly protests; and Xaver goes downstairs with him, to help serve the Italian salad.

But Dr. Cornelius returns to Ellie, who is now lying down, with her cheek pressed into her flat little pillow.

"Well, wasn't that lovely?" he says as he smooths the covers. She nods, with one last little sob. For a quarter of an hour he sits beside her and watches while she falls asleep in her turn, beside the little brother who found the right way so much earlier than she. Her silky brown hair takes the enchanting fall it always does when she sleeps; deep, deep lie the lashes over the eyes that late so abundantly poured forth their sorrow; the angelic mouth with its bowed upper lip is peacefully relaxed and a little open. Only now and then comes a belated catch in her slow breathing.

And her small hands, like pink and white flowers, lie so quietly, one on the coverlet, the other on the pillow by her face—Dr. Cornelius, gazing, feels his heart melt with tenderness as with strong wine.

"How good," he thinks, "that she breathes in oblivion with every breath she draws! That in childhood each night is a deep, wide gulf between one day and the next. Tomorrow, beyond all doubt, young Hergesell will be a pale shadow, powerless to darken her little heart. Tomorrow, forgetful of all but present joy, she will walk with Abel and Snapper, all five gentlemen, round and round the table, will play the ever-thrilling cushion game."

Heaven be praised for that!

Frank O'Connor

1903–1966

JUDAS · GUESTS OF THE NATION · UPROOTED

Frank O'Connor has become so well known by his pen name that his real name, Michael O'Donovan, is rarely used. He was born and grew up in one of the poorer sections of the port city of Cork, Ireland, the only child of a family of very limited means and of peasant background. Leaving school early, he educated himself intensively, but rather haphazardly, in the public library. One youthful project, which he actually carried out, was to read the entire works of Goethe.

Like most Irish literary men, O'Connor got caught up in the excitements of Irish politics. During the savage civil war of the twenties, O'Connor opposed the Free State government of Southern Ireland, which had agreed to become part of the British Commonwealth of Nations. He fought on the side of the Republicans, who wanted immediate independence for a united Ireland. Arrested by the government, he spent a year in prison camp. But later his frank and lively biography, *Death in Dublin* (1937), presents a sympathetic picture of James Michael Collins, the Free State military leader.

O'Connor first became widely known for *Guests of the Nation* (1931), a collection of short stories about the period when British troops were trying to suppress the revolutionary movement in Ireland. After 1931 he published more than a book a year, and saw several of his plays produced. Besides many short stories and some novels, he wrote both original poems and translations of Gaelic poetry into English, made brilliant descriptive studies of Ireland and Irish social conditions, and showed his powers as a critic in *Towards an Appreciation of Literature* (1945), *The Art of the Theatre* (1947), *The Mirror in the Roadway* (1956), a lively and unorthodox study of the modern novel, and *The Lonely Voice: A Study of the Short Story* (1963). He wrote two volumes of autobiography, *My Father's Son* (1968) and *An Only Child* (1961).

O'Connor married an American and lived for many years in the United States, though he returned frequently to Ireland to refresh his imagination at its sources. He taught writing courses at Northwestern and at Harvard and was a frequent contributor to *The New Yorker*. His collections, *The Stories of Frank O'Connor* (1952) and *More Stories by Frank O'Connor* (1954) were enthusiastically received by American critics.

From 1935 to 1939, with the support of William Butler Yeats, O'Connor was the courageous and creative director of the Abbey Theatre, the principal theater in Ireland, and always a center of cultural and political controversy. Though O'Connor had the approval of both Yeats and "A. E.," George Russell, his attitude toward Ireland and Irish culture was very different from that of the leaders of the Celtic Renaissance, which flourished at the beginning of the century. That movement, mystical and more or less opposed to middle-class democracy, was preoccupied with ancient Irish myths and legends, with the folklore of the more primitive peasants, and with the revival of Gaelic. While O'Connor shows his sympathy with peasant character and the satisfactions of the earlier Irish way of life in "Uprooted," he is primarily interested in describing the universal human condition as it reveals itself in Irish circumstances. He feels that modern Ireland's development must parallel that of the other Western democracies, and that though strength can be drawn from the cultural past, it is a mistake to try to return to that past.

O'Connor is a master of the Gaelic story-telling manner. Moreover, his experiences in writing and producing plays gave him, he said, "a lasting passion for technique." But he uses technique to reveal and express meanings that at first he has sensed intuitively in his material. He disliked stories that seem logically calculated in advance. Having great respect and affection for the persons he wrote about, he revised a story from five to fifty times until he felt he had done them and their situations full justice. He liked to tell stories in the first person, but each "I" has his own distinct personality and background.

Many of O'Connor's stories reveal the pains and passionate incoherences of youthful love. "Judas" is one of the most profound and yet amusing of these. It is a wry, sad, boisterous study of the conflict D. H. Lawrence describes in *Sons and Lovers*. Here the conflict is treated from a more detached view of the relations of love, maturity, and a sense of reality. Although the ironic title "Guests of the Nation" suggests a political attitude, the compassion O'Connor expresses is purely human. Without melodrama or sentimentality, he presents a classic example of the contradiction—particularly terrible in our own period—between personal feelings and political imperatives. This story may be compared with Thomas Hardy's poem "The Man I Killed." "Uprooted," probably O'Connor's best story, contrasts the two Irelands, urban and peasant. The brothers' journey into the past of their parents and grandparents shows the irreversibility of psychological and cultural time. And yet O'Connor throws a magic, nostalgic light over what the brothers are forced to reject— a light reflected in the delicate beauty of Cait's face.

JUDAS

I'll forget a lot of things before I forget that night. As I was going out the mother said: "Sure, you won't be late, Jerry?" and I only laughed at her and said: "Am I ever late?" As I went down the road I was thinking it was months since I had taken her to the pictures. You might think that funny, Michael John, but after the father's death we were thrown together a lot. And I knew she hated being alone in the house after dark.

At the same time I had troubles of my own. You see, Michael John, being an only child, I never knocked round with girls the way others did. All the chaps in the office went with girls, or at any rate they let on they did. They said: "Who was the old doll I saw you with last night, Jerry? Aha, Jerry, you'd better mind yourself, boy, or you'll be getting into trouble!" Paddy Kinnane, for instance, talked like that, and he never saw how it upset me. I think he thought it was a great compliment. It wasn't until years after that I began to suspect that Paddy's acquaintance with dolls was about of one kind with my own.

Then I met Kitty Doherty. Kitty was a hospital nurse, and all the

JUDAS. Reprinted from *More Stories by Frank O'Connor,* by permission of Alfred A. Knopf, Inc. Copyright 1948, 1954 by Frank O'Connor.

chaps in the office said a fellow should never go with hospital nurses —they knew too much. I knew when I met Kitty that that was a lie. She was a well-educated, superior girl; she lived up the river in a posh locality, and her mother was on all sorts of councils and committees. She was small and wiry; a good-looking girl, always in good humor, and when she talked, she hopped from one thing to another like a robin on a frosty morning.

Anyway, she had me dazzled. I used to meet her in the evenings up the river road, as if I was walking there by accident and very surprised to see her. "Fancy meeting you!" I'd say, or "Well, well, isn't this a great surprise?" Then we'd stand talking for half an hour and I'd see her home. Several times she asked me in, but I was too nervous. I knew I'd lose my head, break the china, use some dirty word, and then go home and cut my throat. Of course, I never asked her to come to the pictures or anything like that. I knew she was above that. My only hope was that if I waited long enough I might be able to save her from drowning, the White Slave Traffic, or something of the sort. That would show in a modest, dignified way how I felt about her. Of course, I knew at the same time I ought to stay at home more with the mother, but the very thought that I might be missing an opportunity like that would be enough to spoil a whole evening on me.

This night in particular I was nearly distracted. It was three weeks since I'd seen Kitty. You know what three weeks are at that age. I was sure that at the very least the girl was dying and asking for me and that no one knew my address. A week before, I'd felt I simply couldn't bear it any longer, so I made an excuse and went down to the post-office. I rang up the hospital and asked for her. I fully expected them to say that she was dead, and I got a shock when the girl at the other end asked my name. "I'm afraid," I said, "I'm a stranger to Miss Doherty, but I have an important message for her." Then I got completely panic-stricken. What could a girl like Kitty make of a damned deliberate lie like that? What else was it but a trap laid by an old and cunning hand. I held the receiver out and looked at it. "Moynihan," I said to it, "you're mad. An asylum, Moynihan, is the only place for a fellow like you." Then I heard her voice, not in my ear at all, but in the telephone booth as if she were standing before me, and I nearly dropped the receiver with terror. I put it to my ear and asked in a disguised voice: "Who is that speaking, please?" "This is Kitty Doherty," she said rather impatiently. "Who are you?" "I am Monsieur Bertrand," said I, speaking in what I hoped was a French accent. "I am afraid I have de wrong number." Then I put down the receiver carefully and thought how nice it would be if only I had a penknife handy to cut my throat with. It's funny, but from the moment I met Kitty I was always coveting sharp things like razors and penknives.

After that an awful idea dawned on my mind. Of course, I should have thought of it before, but, as you've probably guessed, I wasn't exactly knowledgeable. I began to see that I wasn't meeting Kitty for the very good reason that Kitty didn't want to meet me. That filled me with terror. I examined my conscience to find out what I might have said to her. You know what conscience is at that age. I remembered every remark I'd made and they were all brutal, indecent or disgusting. I had talked of Paddy Kinnane as a fellow who "went with dolls." What could a pure-minded girl think of a chap who naturally used such a phrase except—what, unfortunately, was true—that he had a mind like a cesspit.

It was a lovely summer evening, with views of hillsides and fields between the gaps in the houses, and that raised my spirits a bit. Maybe I was wrong, maybe she hadn't found out the sort I was and wasn't avoiding me, maybe we might meet and walk home together. I walked the full length of the river road and back, and then started off to walk it again. The crowds were thinning out as fellows and girls slipped off up the lanes or down to the river. As the streets went out like lamps about me I grew desperate. I saw clearly that she was avoiding me; that she knew I wasn't the quiet, good-natured chap I let on to be but a volcano of brutality and lust. "Lust, lust, lust!" I hissed to myself, clenching my fists.

Then I glanced up and saw her on a tram. I forgot instantly about the lust and smiled and waved my cap at her, but she was looking ahead and didn't see me. I ran after the car, intending to jump on it, to sit on one of the back seats on top and then say as she was getting off: "Fancy meeting you here!" (Trams were always a bit of a problem. If you sat beside a girl and paid for her, it might be considered forward; if you didn't, it looked mean. I never quite knew.) But as if the driver knew what was in my mind, he put on speed and away went the tram, tossing and screeching down the straight, and I stood panting in the middle of the road, smiling as if missing a tram was the best joke in the world and wishing all the time I had the penknife and the courage to use it. My position was hopeless. Then I must have gone a bit mad, for I started to race the tram. There were still lots of people out walking, and they stared after me, so I lifted my fists to my chest in the attitude of a professional runner and dropped into a comfortable stride which I hoped vaguely would delude them into the belief that I was in training for a big race.

Between the running and the halts I just managed to keep the tram in view all the way through town and out at the other side. When I saw Kitty get off and go up a hilly street I collapsed and was just able to drag myself after her. When she went into a house on a terrace I sat on the curb with my head between my knees till the panting stopped. At any rate I felt safe. I could now walk up and down before the house till she came out, and accost her with an innocent smile and say: "Fancy meeting you!"

But my luck was dead out that night. As I was walking up and down out of range of the house I saw a tall chap come strolling up at the opposite side and my heart sank. It was Paddy Kinnane.

"Hullo, Jerry," he chuckled with that knowing grin he put on whenever he wanted to compliment you on being discovered in a compromising situation, "what are you doing here?"

"Ah, just waiting for a chap I had a date with, Paddy," I said, trying to sound casual.

"Begor," said Paddy, "you look to me more like a man that was waiting for an old doll. Still waters run deep. . . . What time are you supposed to be meeting him?"

"Half eight," I said at random.

"Half eight?" said Paddy in surprise. " 'Tis nearly nine now."

"I know," said I, "but as I waited so long I may as well give him another few minutes."

"Ah, I'll wait along with you," said Paddy, leaning against the wall and taking out a packet of fags. "You might find yourself stuck by the end of the evening. There's people in this town and they have no consideration for anyone."

That was Paddy all out; no trouble too much for him if he could do you a good turn.

"As he kept me so long," I said hastily, "I don't think I'll bother with him. It only struck me this very minute that there's a chap up the Asragh road that I have to see on urgent business. You'll excuse me, Paddy. I'll tell you about it another time."

And away I went hell for leather to the tram. When I reached the tram-stop below Kitty's house I sat on the river wall in the dusk. The moon was rising, and every quarter of an hour the trams came grunting and squeaking over the old bridge and then went black out while the conductors switched the trolleys. I stood on the curb in the moonlight searching for Kitty. Then a bobby came along, and as he seemed to be watching me, I slunk slowly off up the hill and stood against a wall in the shadow. There was a high wall at the other side too, and behind it the roofs of a house shining in the moon. Every now and then a tram would come in and people would pass in the moonlight, and the snatches of conversation I caught were like the warmth from an open door to the heart of a homeless man. It was quite clear now that my position was hopeless. The last tram came and went, and still there was no Kitty and still I hung on.

Then I heard a woman's step. I couldn't even pretend to myself that it might be Kitty till she shuffled past me with that hasty little walk of hers. I started and called out her name; she glanced over her shoulder and, seeing a man emerging from the shadow, took fright and ran. I ran too, but she put on speed and began to outdistance me. At that I despaired. I stood on the pavement and shouted after her at the top of my voice.

"Kitty!" I cried. "Kitty, for God's sake, wait for me!"

She ran a few steps further and then halted, turned, and came back slowly down the path.

"Jerry Moynihan!" she whispered, lifting her two arms to her breasts as if I had found her with nothing on. "What in God's name are you doing here?"

I was summoning up strength to tell her that I just happened to be taking a stroll in that direction and was astonished to see her when I realized the improbability of it and began to cry instead. Then I laughed. I suppose it was nerves. But Kitty had had a bad fright and now that she was getting over it she was as cross as two sticks.

"What's wrong with you, I say," she snapped. "Are you out of your senses or what?"

"Well, you see," I stammered awkwardly, half in dread I was going to cry again, "I didn't see you in town."

"No," she replied with a shrug, "I know you didn't. I wasn't out. What about it?"

"I thought it might be something I said to you," I said desperately.

"No," said Kitty candidly, "it wasn't anything to do with you. It's Mother."

"Why?" I asked almost joyously. "Is there something wrong with her?"

"I don't mean that," said Kitty impatiently. "It's just that she made such a fuss, I felt it wasn't worth it."

"But what did she make a fuss about?" I asked.

"About you, of course," said Kitty in exasperation. "What did you think?"

"But what did I do?" I asked, clutching my head. This was worse than anything I'd ever imagined. This was terrible.

"You didn't do anything," said Kitty, "but people were talking about us. And you wouldn't come in and be introduced to her like anyone else. I know she's a bit of a fool, and her head is stuffed with old nonsense about her family. I could never see that they were different to anyone else, and anyway, she married a commercial herself, so she has nothing much to boast about. Still, you needn't be so superior. There's no obligation to buy, you know."

I didn't. There were cold shivers running through me. I had thought of Kitty as a secret between God, herself, and me and that she only knew the half of it. Now it seemed I didn't even know the half. People were talking about us! I was superior! What next?

"But what has she against me?" I asked despairingly.

"She thinks we're doing a tangle, of course," snapped Kitty as if she was astonished at my stupidity, "and I suppose she imagines you're not grand enough for a great-great-grandniece of Daniel O'Connell. I told her you were a different sort of fellow entirely and above all that sort of thing, but she wouldn't believe me. She said I was a deep, callous, crafty little intriguer and that I hadn't a drop of Daniel O'Connell's blood in my veins." Kitty began to giggle at the thought of herself as an intriguer.

"That's all she knows," I said bitterly.

"I know," said Kitty with a shrug. "The woman has no sense. And anyway she has no reason to think I'm telling lies. Cissy and I always had fellows, and we spooned with them all over the shop under her very nose, so why should she think I'm lying to her now?"

At that I began to laugh like an idiot. This was worse than appalling. This was a nightmare. Kitty, whom I had thought so angelic, talking in cold blood about "spooning" with fellows all over the house. Even the bad women in the books I'd read didn't talk about love in that cold-blooded way. Madame Bovary herself had at least the decency to pretend that she didn't like it. It was like another door opening on the outside world, but Kitty thought I was laughing at her and started to apologize.

"Of course I had no sense," she said. "You're the first fellow I ever met that treated me properly. The others only wanted to fool around with me, and now because I don't like it, Mother thinks I'm getting stuck-up. I told her I liked you better than any fellow I knew, but that I'd grown out of all that sort of thing."

"And what did she say to that?" I asked fiercely. It was—how can I describe it?—like a man who'd lived all his life in a dungeon getting into the sunlight for the first time and afraid of every shadow.

"Ah, I told you the woman was silly," said Kitty, getting embarrassed.

"Go on!" I shouted. "I want to know everything. I insist on knowing everything."

"Well," said Kitty with a demure little grin, "she said you were a deep, designing guttersnipe who knew exactly how to get round feather-pated little idiots like me. . . . You see," she added with another shrug, "it's quite hopeless. The woman is common. She doesn't understand."

"But I tell you she does understand," I shouted frantically. "She understands better than you do. I only wish to God I was deep and designing so that I'd have some chance with you."

"Do you really?" asked Kitty, opening her eyes wide. "To tell you the truth," she added after a moment, "I thought you were a bit keen the first time, but then I didn't know. When you didn't kiss me or anything, I mean."

"God," I said bitterly, "when I think of what I've been through in the past couple of weeks!"

"I know," said Kitty, biting her lip. "I was the same." And then we said nothing for a few moments.

"You're sure you're serious?" she asked suspiciously.

"I tell you, girl," I shouted, "I was on the point of committing suicide."

"What good would that be?" she asked with another shrug, and then she looked at me and laughed outright—the little jade!

It is all as clear in my mind as if it had happened last night. I told Kitty about my prospects. She didn't care, but I insisted on telling her. It was as if a stone had been lifted off my heart, and I went home in the moonlight singing. Then I heard the clock strike, and the singing stopped. I remembered the mother at home, waiting, and began to run again. This was desperation too, but a different sort.

The door was ajar and the kitchen in darkness. I saw her sitting before the fire by herself, and just as I was going to throw my arms about her, I smelt Kitty's perfume round me and was afraid to go near her. God help us, as if it would have told her anything!

"Hallo, Mum," I said with a laugh, rubbing my hands, "you're all in darkness."

"You'll have a cup of tea?" she said.

"I might as well," said I.

"What time is it?" she said, lighting the gas. "You're very late."

"Ah, I met a fellow from the office," I said, but at the same time I was stung by the complaint in her tone.

"You frightened me," she said with a little whimper. "I didn't know what happened you. What kept you at all?"

"Oh, what do you think?" I said, goaded into retorting. "Drinking and blackguarding as usual."

I could have bitten my tongue off when I'd said it; it sounded so cruel, as if some stranger had said it instead of me. She turned to me for a moment with a frightened stare as if she was seeing the stranger too, and somehow I couldn't bear it.

"God Almighty," I said, "a fellow can have no life in his own house," and away with me upstairs.

I lit the candle, undressed and got into bed. I was wild. A chap could be a drunkard and blackguard and not be made to suffer more reproach than I was for being late one single night. That, I felt, was what you got for being a good son.

"Jerry," she called from the foot of the stairs, "will I bring you up your cup?"

"I don't want it now, thanks," I said.

I heard her give a heavy sigh and turn away. Then she locked the two doors front and back. She didn't wash up, and I knew my cup of tea was standing there on the table with a saucer on top in case

I changed my mind. She came slowly up the stairs, and she walked like an old woman. I blew out the candle before she reached the landing in case she came in to ask me if I wanted anything else, and the moonlight came in the attic window and brought me memories of Kitty. But every time I tried to imagine her face while she grinned up at me, waiting for me to kiss her, it was the mother's face that came up with that look like a child's when you strike him the first time—as if he suddenly saw the stranger in you. I remembered all our life together from the night the father—God rest him! —died; our early Mass on Sunday; our visits to the pictures; our plans for the future, and Christ, Michael John, it was as if I was inside her mind and she sitting by the fire, waiting for the blow to fall! And now it had fallen, and I was a stranger to her, and nothing I ever did could make us the same to each other again. There was something like a cannon-ball stuck in my chest, and I lay awake till the cocks started crowing. Then I couldn't bear it any longer. I went out on to the landing and listened.

"Are you awake, Mother?" I asked in a whisper.

"What is it, Jerry?" she said in alarm, and I knew she hadn't slept any more than I had.

"I only came to say I was sorry," I said, opening the room door, and then as I saw her sitting up in bed under the Sacred Heart lamp, the cannon-ball burst inside me and I began to bawl like a kid.

"Oh, child, child," she cried out, "what are you crying for at all, my little boy?" and she spread out her arms to me. I went to her and she hugged me and rocked me just as she did when I was only a nipper. "Oh, oh, oh," she was saying to herself in a whisper, "my storeen bawn, my little man!"—all the names she hadn't called me since I was a kid. That was all we said. I couldn't bring myself to tell her what I'd done, and she wouldn't confess to me that she was jealous; all she could do was to try and comfort me for the way I'd hurt her, to make up to me for the nature she'd given me. "My storeen bawn," she said. "My little man!"

GUESTS OF THE NATION

At dusk the big Englishman, Belcher, would shift his long legs out of the ashes and say "Well, chums, what about it?" and Noble or me would say "All right, chum" (for we had picked up some of their curious expressions), and the little Englishman, Hawkins, would light the lamp and bring out the cards. Sometimes Jeremiah Donovan would come up and supervise the game and get excited over Hawkins's cards, which he always played badly, and shout at him as if he was one of our own "Ah, you divil, you, why didn't you play the tray?"

But ordinarily Jeremiah was a sober and contented poor devil like the big Englishman, Belcher, and was looked up to only because he was a fair hand at documents, though he was slow enough even with them. He wore a small cloth hat and big gaiters over his long pants, and you seldom saw him with his hands out of his pockets. He reddened when you talked to him, tilting from toe to heel and back, and looking down all the time at his big farmer's feet. Noble and me used to make fun of his broad accent, because we were from the town.

I couldn't at the time see the point of me and Noble guarding Belcher and Hawkins at all, for it was my belief that you could have planted that pair down anywhere from this to Claregalway and they'd have taken root there like a native weed. I never in my short experience seen two men to take to the country as they did.

They were handed on to us by the Second Battalion when the search for them became too hot, and Noble and myself, being young, took over with a natural feeling of responsibility, but Hawkins made us look like fools when he showed that he knew the country better than we did.

"You're the bloke they calls Bonaparte," he says to me. "Mary Brigid O'Connell told me to ask you what you done with the pair of her brother's socks you borrowed."

GUESTS OF THE NATION. From *Guests of the Nation* by Frank O'Connor. Reprinted by permission of St. Martin's Press, Inc., New York, and A. D. Peters, London.

For it seemed, as they explained it, that the Second used to have little evenings, and some of the girls of the neighbourhood turned in, and, seeing they were such decent chaps, our fellows couldn't leave the two Englishmen out of them. Hawkins learned to dance "The Walls of Limerick," "The Siege of Ennis," and "The Waves of Tory" as well as any of them, though, naturally, he couldn't return the compliment, because our lads at that time did not dance foreign dances on principle.

So whatever privileges Belcher and Hawkins had with the Second they just naturally took with us, and after the first day or two we gave up all pretence of keeping a close eye on them. Not that they could have got far, for they had accents you could cut with a knife and wore khaki tunics and overcoats with civilian pants and boots. But it's my belief that they never had any idea of escaping and were quite content to be where they were.

It was a treat to see how Belcher got off with the old woman of the house where we were staying. She was a great warrant to scold, and cranky even with us, but before ever she had a chance of giving our guests, as I may call them, a lick of her tongue, Belcher had made her his friend for life. She was breaking sticks, and Belcher, who hadn't been more than ten minutes in the house, jumped up from his seat and went over to her.

"Allow me, madam," he says, smiling his queer little smile, "please allow me"; and he takes the bloody hatchet. She was struck too paralytic to speak, and after that, Belcher would be at her heels, carrying a bucket, a basket, or a load of turf, as the case might be. As Noble said, he got into looking before she leapt, and hot water, or any little thing she wanted, Belcher would have it ready for her. For such a huge man (and though I am five foot ten myself I had to look up at him) he had an uncommon shortness—or should I say lack?—of speech. It took us some time to get used to him, walking in and out, like a ghost, without a word. Especially because Hawkins talked enough for a platoon, it was strange to hear big Belcher with his toes in the ashes come out with a solitary "Excuse me, chum," or "That's right, chum." His one and only passion was cards, and I will say for him that he was a good card-player. He could have fleeced myself and Noble, but whatever we lost to him Hawkins lost to us, and Hawkins played with the money Belcher gave him.

Hawkins lost to us because he had too much old gab, and we probably lost to Belcher for the same reason. Hawkins and Noble would spit at one another about religion into the early hours of the morning, and Hawkins worried the soul out of Noble, whose brother was a priest, with a string of questions that would puzzle a cardinal. To make it worse, even in treating of holy subjects, Hawkins had a deplorable tongue. I never in all my career met a man who could mix such a variety of cursing and bad language into an argument. He was a terrible man, and a fright to argue. He never did a stroke of work, and when he had no one else to talk to, he got stuck in the old woman.

He met his match in her, for one day when he tried to get her to complain profanely of the drought, she gave him a great come-down by blaming it entirely on Jupiter Pluvius (a deity neither Hawkins nor I had ever heard of, though Noble said that among the pagans it was believed that he had something to do with the rain). Another day he was swearing at the capitalists for starting the German war when the old lady laid down her iron, puckered up her little crab's mouth, and said: "Mr. Hawkins, you can say what you like about the war, and think you'll deceive me because I'm only a simple poor countrywoman, but I know what started the war. It was the Italian Count that stole the heathen divinity out of the temple in Japan. Believe me, Mr Hawkins, nothing but sorrow and want can follow the people that disturb the hidden powers."

A queer old girl, all right.

<h3 style="text-align:center">II</h3>

We had our tea one evening, and Hawkins lit the lamp and we all sat into cards. Jeremiah Donovan came in too, and sat down and watched us for a while, and it suddenly struck me that he had no great love for the two Englishmen. It came as a great surprise to me, because I hadn't noticed anything about him before.

Late in the evening a really terrible argument blew up between Hawkins and Noble, about capitalists and priests and love of your country.

"The capitalists," says Hawkins with an angry gulp, "pays the priests to tell you about the next world so as you won't notice what the bastards are up to in this."

"Nonsense, man!" says Noble, losing his temper. "Before ever a capitalist was thought of, people believed in the next world."

Hawkins stood up as though he was preaching a sermon.

"Oh, they did, did they?" he says with a sneer. "They believed all the things you believe, isn't that what you mean? And you believe that God created Adam, and Adam created Shem, and Shem created Jehoshophat. You believe all that silly old fairytale about Eve and Eden and the apple. Well, listen to me, chum. If you're entitled to hold a silly belief like that, I'm entitled to hold my silly belief—which is that the first thing your God created was a bleeding capitalist, with morality and Rolls-Royce complete. Am I right, chum?" he says to Belcher.

"You're right, chum," says Belcher with his amused smile, and got up from the table to stretch his long legs into the fire and stroke his moustache. So, seeing that Jeremiah Donovan was going, and that there was no knowing when the argument about religion would be over, I went out with him. We strolled down to the village together, and then he stopped and started blushing and mumbling and saying I ought to be behind, keeping guard on the prisoners. I didn't like the tone he took with me, and anyway I was bored with life in the cottage, so I replied by asking him what the hell we wanted guarding them at all for. I told him I'd talked it over with Noble, and that we'd both rather be out with a fighting column.

"What use are those fellows to us?" says I.

He looked at me in surprise and said: "I thought you knew we were keeping them as hostages."

"Hostages?" I said.

"The enemy have prisoners belonging to us," he says, "and now they're talking of shooting them. If they shoot our prisoners, we'll shoot theirs."

"Shoot them?" I said.

"What else did you think we were keeping them for?" he says.

"Wasn't it very unforeseen of you not to warn Noble and myself of that in the beginning?" I said.

"How was it?" says he. "You might have known it."

"We couldn't know it, Jeremiah Donovan," says I. "How could we when they were on our hands so long?"

"The enemy have our prisoners as long and longer," says he.

"That's not the same thing at all," says I.

"What difference is there?" says he.

I couldn't tell him, because I knew he wouldn't understand. If it was only an old dog that was going to the vet's, you'd try and not get too fond of him, but Jeremiah Donovan wasn't a man that would ever be in danger of that.

"And when is this thing going to be decided?" says I.

"We might hear tonight," he says. "Or tomorrow or the next day at latest. So if it's only hanging round here that's a trouble to you, you'll be free soon enough."

It wasn't the hanging round that was a trouble to me at all by this time. I had worse things to worry about. When I got back to the cottage the argument was still on. Hawkins was holding forth in his best style, maintaining that there was no next world, and Noble was maintaining that there was; but I could see that Hawkins had had the best of it.

"Do you know what, chum?" he was saying with a saucy smile. "I think you're just as big a bleeding unbeliever as I am. You say you believe in the next world, and you know just as much about the next world as I do, which is sweet damn-all. What's heaven? You don't know. Where's heaven? You don't know. You know sweet damn-all! I ask you again, do they wear wings?"

"Very well, then," says Noble, "they do. Is that enough for you? They do wear wings."

"Where do they get them, then? Who makes them? Have they a factory for wings? Have they a sort of store where you hands in your chit and takes your bleeding wings?"

"You're an impossible man to argue with," says Noble. "Now, listen to me—" And they were off again.

It was long after midnight when we locked up and went to bed. As I blew out the candle I told Noble what Jeremiah Donovan was after telling me. Noble took it very quietly. When we'd been in bed about an hour he asked me did I think we ought to tell the Englishmen. I didn't think we should, because it was more than likely that the English wouldn't shoot our men, and even if they did, the brigade officers, who were always up and down with the Second Battalion and knew the Englishmen well, wouldn't be likely to want them plugged. "I think so too," says Noble. "It would be great cruelty to put the wind up them now."

"It was very unforeseen of Jeremiah Donovan anyhow," says I.

It was next morning that we found it so hard to face Belcher and Hawkins. We went about the house all day scarcely saying a word. Belcher didn't seem to notice; he was stretched into the ashes as usual, with his usual look of waiting in quietness for something unforeseen to happen, but Hawkins noticed and put it down to Noble's being beaten in the argument of the night before.

"Why can't you take a discussion in the proper spirit?" he says severely. "You and your Adam and Eve! I'm a Communist, that's what I am. Communist or anarchist, it all comes to much the same thing." And for hours he went round the house, muttering when the fit took him. "Adam and Eve! Adam and Eve! Nothing better to do with their time than picking bleeding apples!"

III

I don't know how we got through that day, but I was very glad when it was over, the tea things were cleared away, and Belcher said in his peaceable way: "Well, chums, what about it?" We sat round the table and Hawkins took out the cards, and just then I heard Jeremiah Donovan's footstep on the path and a dark presentiment crossed my mind. I rose from the table and caught him before he reached the door.

"What do you want?" I asked.

"I want those two soldier friends of yours," he says, getting red.

"Is that the way, Jeremiah Donovan?" I asked.

"That's the way. There were four of our lads shot this morning, one of them a boy of sixteen."

"That's bad," I said.

At that moment Noble followed me out, and the three of us walked down the path together, talking in whispers. Feeney, the local intelligence officer, was standing by the gate.

"What are you going to do about it?" I asked Jeremiah Donovan.

"I want you and Noble to get them out; tell them they're being shifted again; that'll be the quietest way."

"Leave me out of that," says Noble under his breath.

Jeremiah Donovan looks at him hard.

"All right," he says. "You and Feeney get a few tools from the shed and dig a hole by the far end of the bog. Bonaparte and myself will be after you. Don't let anyone see you with the tools. I wouldn't like it to go beyond ourselves."

We saw Feeney and Noble go round to the shed and went in ourselves. I left Jeremiah Donovan to do the explanations. He told them that he had orders to send them back to the Second Battalion.

Hawkins let out a mouthful of curses, and you could see that though Belcher didn't say anything, he was a bit upset too. The old woman was for having them stay in spite of us, and she didn't stop advising them until Jeremiah Donovan lost his temper and turned on her. He had a nasty temper, I noticed. It was pitch-dark in the cottage by this time, but no one thought of lighting the lamp, and in the darkness the two Englishmen fetched their topcoats and said good-bye to the old woman.

"Just as a man makes a home of a bleeding place, some bastard at headquarters thinks you're too cushy and shunts you off," says Hawkins, shaking her hand.

"A thousand thanks, madam," says Belcher. "A thousand thanks for everything"—as though he'd made it up.

We went round to the back of the house and down towards the bog. It was only then that Jeremiah Donovan told them. He was shaking with excitement.

"There were four of our fellows shot in Cork this morning and now you're to be shot as a reprisal."

"What are you talking about?" snaps Hawkins. "It's bad enough being mucked about as we are without having to put up with your funny jokes."

"It isn't a joke," says Donovan. "I'm sorry, Hawkins, but it's true," and begins on the usual rigmarole about duty and how unpleasant it is.

I never noticed that people who talk a lot about duty find it much of a trouble to them.

"Oh, cut it out!" says Hawkins.

"Ask Bonaparte," says Donovan, seeing that Hawkins isn't taking him seriously. "Isn't it true, Bonaparte?"

"It is," I say, and Hawkins stops.

"Ah, for Christ's sake, chum!"

"I mean it, chum," I say.

"You don't sound as if you meant it."

"If he doesn't mean it, I do," says Donovan, working himself up.

"What have you against me, Jeremiah Donovan?"

"I never said I had anything against you. But why did your people take out four of our prisoners and shoot them in cold blood?"

He took Hawkins by the arm and dragged him on, but it was impossible to make him understand that we were in earnest. I had the Smith and Wesson in my pocket and I kept fingering it and wondering what I'd do if they put up a fight for it or ran, and wishing to God they'd do one or the other. I knew if they did run for it, that I'd never fire on them. Hawkins wanted to know was Noble in it, and when we said yes, he asked us why Noble wanted to plug him. Why did any of us want to plug him? What had he done to us? Weren't we all chums? Didn't we understand him and didn't he understand us? Did we imagine for an instant that he'd shoot us for all the so-and-so officers in the so-and-so British Army?

By this time we'd reached the bog, and I was so sick I couldn't even answer him. We walked along the edge of it in the darkness, and every now and then Hawkins would call a halt and begin all over again, as if he was wound up, about our being chums, and I knew that nothing but the sight of the grave would convince him that we had to do it. And all the time I was hoping that something would happen; that they'd run for it or that Noble would take over the responsibility from me. I had the feeling that it was worse on Noble than on me.

I V

At last we saw the lantern in the distance and made towards it. Noble was carrying it, and Feeney was standing somewhere in the darkness behind him, and the picture of them so still and silent in the bogland brought it home to me that we were in earnest, and banished the last bit of hope I had.

Belcher, on recognizing Noble, said: "Hallo, chum," in his quiet way, but Hawkins flew at him at once, and the argument began all over again, only this time Noble had nothing to say for himself and stood with his head down, holding the lantern between his legs.

It was Jeremiah Donovan who did the answering. For the twentieth time, as though it was haunting his mind, Hawkins asked if anybody thought he'd shoot Noble.

"Yes, you would," says Jeremiah Donovan.

"No, I wouldn't, damn you!"

"You would, because you'd know you'd be shot for not doing it."

"I wouldn't, not if I was to be shot twenty times over. I wouldn't shoot a pal. And Belcher wouldn't—isn't that right, Belcher?"

"That's right, chum," Belcher said, but more by way of answering the question than of joining in the argument. Belcher sounded as though whatever unforeseen thing he'd always been waiting for had come at last.

"Anyway, who says Noble would be shot if I wasn't? What do you think I'd do if I was in his place, out in the middle of a blasted bog?"

"What would you do?" asks Donovan.

"I'd go with him wherever he was going, of course. Share my last bob with him and stick by him through thick and thin. No one can ever say of me that I let down a pal."

"We had enough of this," says Jeremiah Donovan, cocking his revolver. "Is there any message you want to send?"

"No, there isn't."

"Do you want to say your prayers?"

Hawkins came out with a cold-blooded remark that even shocked me and turned on Noble again.

"Listen to me, Noble," he says. "You and me are chums. You can't come over to my side, so I'll come over to your side. That show you I mean what I say? Give me a rifle and I'll go along with you and the other lads."

Nobody answered him. We knew that was no way out.

"Hear what I'm saying?" he says. "I'm through with it. I'm a deserter or anything else you like. I don't believe in your stuff, but it's no worse than mine. That satisfy you?"

Noble raised his head, but Donovan began to speak and he lowered it again without replying.

"For the last time, have you any messages to send?" says Donovan in a cold, excited sort of voice.

"Shut up, Donovan! You don't understand me, but these lads do. They're not the sort to make a pal and kill a pal. They're not the tools of any capitalist."

I alone of the crowd saw Donovan raise his Webley to the back of Hawkins's neck, and as he did so I shut my eyes and tried to pray. Hawkins had begun to say something else when Donovan fired, and as I opened my eyes at the bang, I saw Hawkins stagger at the knees and lie out flat at Noble's feet, slowly and as quiet as a kid falling asleep, with the lantern-light on his lean legs and bright farmer's boots. We all stood very still, watching him settle out in the last agony.

Then Belcher took out a handkerchief and began to tie it about his own eyes (in our excitement we'd forgotten to do the same for Hawkins), and, seeing it wasn't big enough, turned and asked for the loan of mine. I gave it to him and he knotted the two together and pointed with his foot at Hawkins.

"He's not quite dead," he says. "Better give him another."

Sure enough, Hawkins's left knee is beginning to rise. I bend down and put my gun to his head; then, recollecting myself, I get up again. Belcher understands what's in my mind.

"Give him his first," he says. "I don't mind. Poor bastard, we don't know what's happening to him now."

I knelt and fired. By this time I didn't seem to know what I was doing. Belcher, who was fumbling a bit awkwardly with the handkerchiefs, came out with a laugh as he heard the shot. It was the first time I heard him laugh and it sent a shudder down my back; it sounded so unnatural.

"Poor bugger!" he said quietly. "And last night he was so curious about it all. It's very queer, chums, I always think. Now he knows as much about it as they'll ever let him know, and last night he was all in the dark."

Donovan helped him to tie the handkerchiefs about his eyes. "Thanks, chum," he said. Donovan asked if there were any messages he wanted sent.

"No, chum," he says. "Not for me. If any of you would like to write to Hawkins's mother, you'll find a letter from her in his pocket. He and his mother were great chums. But my missus left me eight years ago. Went away with another fellow and took the kid with her. I like the feeling of a home, as you may have noticed, but I couldn't start again after that."

It was an extraordinary thing, but in those few minutes Belcher said more than in all the weeks before. It was just as if the sound of the shot had started a flood of talk in him and he could go on the whole night like that, quite happily, talking about himself. We stood round like fools now that he couldn't see us any longer. Donovan looked at Noble, and Noble shook his head. Then Donovan raised his Webley, and at that moment Belcher gives his queer laugh again. He may have thought we were talking about him, or perhaps he noticed the same thing I'd noticed and couldn't understand it.

"Excuse me, chums," he says. "I feel I'm talking the hell of a lot, and so silly, about my being so handy about a house and things like that. But this thing came on me suddenly. You'll forgive me, I'm sure."

"You don't want to say a prayer?" asks Donovan.

"No, chum," he says. "I don't think it would help. I'm ready, and you boys want to get it over."

"You understand that we're only doing our duty?" says Donovan.

Belcher's head was raised like a blind man's, so that you could only see his chin and the tip of his nose in the lantern-light.

"I never could make out what duty was myself," he said. "I think you're all good lads, if that's what you mean. I'm not complaining."

Noble, just as if he couldn't bear any more of it, raised his fist at Donovan, and in a flash Donovan raised his gun and fired. The big man went over like a sack of meal, and this time there was no need of a second shot.

I don't remember much about the burying, but that it was worse than all the rest because we had to carry them to the grave. It was all mad lonely with nothing but a patch of lantern-light between ourselves and the dark, and birds hooting and screeching all round, disturbed by the guns. Noble went through Hawkins's belongings to find the letter from his mother, and then joined his hands together. He did the same with Belcher. Then, when we'd filled in the grave, we separated from Jeremiah Donovan and Feeney and took our tools back to the shed. All the way we didn't speak a word. The kitchen was dark and cold as we'd left it, and the old woman was sitting over the hearth, saying her beads. We walked past her into the room, and Noble struck a match to light the lamp. She rose quietly and came to the doorway with all her cantankerousness gone.

"What did ye do with them?" she asked in a whisper, and Noble started so that the match went out in his hand.

"What's that?" he asked without turning round.

"I heard ye," she said.

"What did you hear?" asked Noble.

"I heard ye. Do ye think I didn't hear ye, putting the spade back in the houseen?"

Noble struck another match and this time the lamp lit for him.

"Was that what ye did to them?" she asked.

Then, by God, in the very doorway, she fell on her knees and began praying, and after looking at her for a minute or two Noble did the same by the fireplace. I pushed my way out past her and left them at it. I stood at the door, watching the stars and listening to the shrieking of the birds dying out over the bogs. It is so strange what you feel at times like that that you can't describe it. Noble says he saw everything ten times the size, as though there were nothing in the whole world but that little patch of bog with the two Englishmen stiffening into it, but with me it was as if the patch of bog where the Englishmen were was a million miles away, and even Noble and the old woman, mumbling behind me, and the birds and the bloody stars were all far away, and I was somehow very small and very lost and lonely like a child astray in the snow. And anything that happened me afterwards, I never felt the same about again.

UPROOTED

Spring had only come and already he was tired to death; tired of the city, tired of his job. He had come up from the country intending to do wonders, but he was as far as ever from that. He would be lucky if he could carry on, be at school each morning at half past nine and satisfy his half-witted principal.

He lodged in a small red-brick house in Rathmines that was kept by a middle-aged brother and sister who had been left a bit of money and thought they would end their days enjoyably in a city. They did not enjoy themselves, regretted their little farm in Kerry, and were glad of Ned Keating because he could talk to them about all the things they remembered and loved.

Keating was a slow, cumbrous young man with dark eyes and a dark cow's-lick that kept tumbling into them. He had a slight stammer and ran his hand through his long limp hair from pure nervousness. He had always been dreamy and serious. Sometimes on market days you saw him standing for an hour in Nolan's shop, turning the pages of a schoolbook. When he could not afford it he put it back with a sigh and went off to find his father in a pub, just raising his

UPROOTED. Reprinted from *The Stories of Frank O'Connor,* by permission of Alfred A. Knopf, Inc. Copyright 1944, 1952 by Frank O'Connor.

eyes to smile at Jack Nolan. After his elder brother Tom had gone for the church he and his father had constant rows. Nothing would do Ned now but to be a teacher. Hadn't he all he wanted now? his father asked. Hadn't he the place to himself? What did he want going teaching? But Ned was stubborn. With an obstinate, almost despairing determination he had fought his way through the training college into a city job. The city was what he had always wanted. And now the city had failed him. In the evenings you could still see him poking round the second-hand bookshops on the quays, but his eyes were already beginning to lose their eagerness.

It had all seemed so clear. But then he had not counted on his own temper. He was popular because of his gentleness, but how many concessions that involved! He was hesitating, good-natured, slow to see guile, slow to contradict. He felt he was constantly underestimating his own powers. He even felt he lacked spontaneity. He did not drink, smoked little, and saw dangers and losses everywhere. He blamed himself for avarice and cowardice. The story he liked best was about the country boy and the letter box. "Indeed, what a fool you think I am! Put me letther in a pump!"

He was in no danger of putting his letter in a pump or anywhere else for the matter of that. He had only one friend, a nurse in Vincent's Hospital, a wild, light-hearted, light-headed girl. He was very fond of her and supposed that some day when he had money enough he would ask her to marry him; but not yet: and at the same time something that was both shyness and caution kept him from committing himself too far. Sometimes he planned excursions beside the usual weekly walk or visit to the pictures but somehow they seldom came to anything.

He no longer knew why he had come to the city, but it was not for the sake of the bed-sitting-room in Rathmines, the oblong of dusty garden outside the window, the trams clanging up and down, the shelf full of second-hand books, or the occasional visit to the pictures. Half humorously, half despairingly, he would sometimes clutch his head in his hands and admit to himself that he had no notion of what he wanted. He would have liked to leave it all and go to Glasgow or New York as a labourer, not because he was romantic, but because he felt that only when he had to work with his hands for a living and was no longer sure of his bed would he find out what all his ideals and emotions meant and where he could fit them into the scheme of his life.

But no sooner did he set out for school next morning, striding slowly along the edge of the canal, watching the trees become green again and the tall claret-coloured houses painted on the quiet surface of the water, than all his fancies took flight. Put his letter in a pump indeed! He would continue to be submissive and draw his salary and wonder how much he could save and when he would be able to buy a little house to bring his girl into; a nice thing to think of on a spring morning: a house of his own and a wife in the bed beside him. And his nature would continue to contract about him, every ideal, every generous impulse another mesh to draw his head down tighter to his knees till in ten years' time it would tie him hand and foot.

I I

Tom who was a curate in Wicklow wrote and suggested that they might go home together for the long weekend, and on Saturday morning they set out in Tom's old Ford. It was Easter weather, pearly and cold. They stopped at several pubs on the way and Tom ordered whiskies. Ned was feeling expansive and joined him. He had never quite grown used to his brother, partly because of old days when he felt that Tom was getting the education he should have got, partly because his ordination seemed to have shut him off from the rest of the family, and now it was as though he were trying to surmount it by his boisterous manner and affected bonhomie. He was like a man shouting to his comrades across a great distance. He was different from Ned; lighter in colour of hair and skin; fat-headed, fresh-complexioned, deep-voiced, and autocratic; an irascible, humorous, friendly man who was well-liked by those he worked for. Ned, who was shy and all tied up within himself, envied him his way with men in garages and barmaids in hotels.

It was nightfall when they reached home. Their father was in his shirtsleeves at the gate waiting to greet them, and immediately their mother rushed out as well. The lamp was standing in the window and threw its light as far as the whitewashed gateposts. Little Brigid, the girl from up the hill who helped their mother now she was growing old, stood in the doorway in half-silhouette. When her eyes caught theirs she bent her head in confusion.

Nothing was changed in the tall, bare, whitewashed kitchen. The harness hung in the same place on the wall, the rosary on the same nail in the fireplace, by the stool where their mother usually sat; table under the window, churn against the back door, stair without banisters mounting straight to the attic door that yawned in the wall—all seemed as unchanging as the sea outside. Their mother sat on the stool, her hands on her knees, a coloured shawl tied tightly about her head, like a gypsy woman with her battered yellow face and loud voice. Their father, fresh-complexioned like Tom, stocky and broken-bottomed, gazed out the front door, leaning with one hand on the dresser in the pose of an orator while Brigid wet the tea.

"I said ye'd be late," their father proclaimed triumphantly, twisting his moustache. "Didn't I, woman? Didn't I say they'd be late?"

"He did, he did," their mother assured them. " 'Tis true for him."

"Ah, I knew ye'd be making halts. But damn it, if I wasn't put astray by Thade Lahy's car going east!"

"And was that Thade Lahy's car?" their mother asked in a shocked tone.

"I told ye 'twas Thade Lahy's," piped Brigid, plopping about in her long frieze gown and bare feet.

"Sure I should know it, woman," old Tomas said with chagrin. "He must have gone into town without us noticing him."

"Oye, and how did he do that?" asked their mother.

"Leave me alone now," Tomas said despairingly. "I couldn't tell you, I could not tell you."

"My goodness, I was sure that was the Master's car," their mother said wonderingly, pulling distractedly at the tassels of her shawl.

"I'd know the rattle of Thade Lahy's car anywhere," little Brigid said very proudly and quite unregarded.

It seemed to Ned that he was interrupting a conversation that had been going on since his last visit, and that the road outside and the sea beyond it, and every living thing that passed before them, formed a pantomime that was watched endlessly and passionately from the darkness of the little cottage.

"Wisha, I never asked if ye'd like a drop of something," their father said with sudden vexation.

"Is it whisky?" boomed Tom.

"Why? Would you sooner whisky?"

"Can't you pour it out first and ask us after?" growled Tom.

"The whisky, is it?"

" 'Tis not. I didn't come all the ways to this place for what I can get better at home. You'd better have a bottle ready for me to take back."

"Coleen will have it. Damn it, wasn't it only last night I said to Coleen that you'd likely want a bottle? Some way it struck me you would. Oh, he'll have it, he'll have it."

"Didn't they catch that string of misery yet?" asked Tom with the cup to his lips.

"Ah, man alive, you'd want to be a greyhound to catch him. God Almighty, hadn't they fifty police after him last November, scouring the mountains from one end to the other and all they caught was a glimpse of the white of his ass. Ah, but the priest preached a terrible sermon against him—by name, Tom, by name!"

"Is old Murphy blowing about it still?" growled Tom.

"Oh, let me alone now!" Tomas threw his hands to heaven and strode to and fro in his excitement, his bucket-bottom wagging. Ned knew to his sorrow that his father could be prudent, silent, and calculating; he knew only too well the cock of the head, the narrowing of the eyes, but, like a child, the old man loved innocent excitement and revelled in scenes of the wildest passion, all about nothing. Like an old actor he turned everything to drama. "The like of it for abuse was never heard, never heard, never heard! How Coleen could ever raise his head again after it! And where the man got the words from! Tom, my treasure, my son, you'll never have the like."

"I'd spare my breath to cool my porridge," Tom replied scornfully. "I dare say you gave up your own still so?"

"I didn't, Tom, I didn't. The drop I make, 'twould harm no one. Only a drop for Christmas and Easter."

The lamp was in its own place on the rear wall, and made a circle of brightness on the fresh lime wash. Their mother was leaning over the fire with joined hands, lost in thought. The front door was open and night thickening outside, the coloured night of the west; and as they ate their father walked to and fro in long ungainly strides, pausing each time at the door to give a glance up and down the road and at the fire to hoist his broken bottom to warm. Ned heard steps come up the road from the west. His father heard them too. He returned to the door and glued his hand to the jamb. Ned covered his eyes with his hands and felt that everything was as it had always been. He could hear the noise of the strand as a background to the voices.

"God be with you, Tomas," the voice said.

"God and Mary be with you, Teig." (In Irish they were speaking.) "What way are you?"

"Well, honour and praise be to God. 'Tis a fine night."

" 'Tis, 'tis, 'tis so indeed. A grand night, praise be to God."

"Musha, who is it?" their mother asked, looking round.

" 'Tis young Teig," their father replied, looking after him.

"Shemus's young Teig?"

" 'Tis, 'tis, 'tis."

"But where would Shemus's young Teig be going at this hour of night? 'Tisn't to the shop?"

"No, woman, no, no, no. Up to the uncle's I suppose."

"Is it Ned Willie's?"

"He's sleeping at Ned Willie's," Brigid chimed in in her high-pitched voice, timid but triumphant. " 'Tis since the young teacher came to them."

There was no more to be said. Everything was explained and Ned smiled. The only unfamiliar voice, little Brigid's, seemed the most familiar of all.

III

Tom said first Mass next morning and the household, all but Brigid, went. They drove, and Tomas in high glee sat in front with Tom, waving his hand and shouting greetings at all they met. He was like a boy, so intense was his pleasure. The chapel was perched high above the road. Outside the morning was grey and beyond the windy edge of the cliff was the sea. The wind blew straight in, setting cloaks and petticoats flying.

After dinner as the two boys were returning from a series of visits to the neighbours' houses their father rushed down the road to meet them, shaking them passionately by the hand and asking were they well. When they were seated in the kitchen he opened up the subject of his excitement.

"Well," he said, "I arranged a grand little outing for ye tomorrow, thanks be to God," and to identify further the source of his inspiration he searched at the back of his neck for the peak of his cap and raised it solemnly.

"Musha, what outing are you talking about?" their mother asked angrily.

"I arranged for us to go over the bay to your brother's."

"And can't you leave the poor boys alone?" she bawled. "Haven't they only the one day? Isn't it for the rest they came?"

"Even so, even so, even so," Tomas said with mounting passion. "Aren't their own cousins to lay eyes on them?"

"I was in Carriganassa for a week last summer," said Tom.

"Yes, but I wasn't, and Ned wasn't. 'Tis only decent."

" 'Tisn't decency is worrying you at all but drink," growled Tom.

"Oh!" gasped his father, fishing for the peak of his cap to swear with, "that I might be struck dead!"

"Be quiet, you old heathen!" crowed his wife. "That's the truth, Tom my pulse. Plenty of drink is what he wants where he won't be under my eye. Leave ye stop at home."

"I can't stop at home, woman," shouted Tomas. "Why do you be always picking at me? I must go whether they come or not. I must go, I must go, and that's all there is about it."

"Why must you?" asked his wife.

"Because I warned Red Pat and Dempsey," he stormed. "And the woman from the island is coming as well to see a daughter of hers that's married there. And what's more, I borrowed Cassidy's boat and he lent it at great inconvenience, and 'twould be very bad manners for me to throw his kindness back in his face. I must go."

"Oh, we may as well all go," said Tom.

It blew hard all night and Tomas, all anxiety, was out at break of day to watch the whitecaps on the water. While the boys were at breakfast he came in and, leaning his arms on the table with hands joined as though in prayer, he announced in a caressing voice that it was a beautiful day, thank God, a pet day with a moist gentle little bit of a breezheen that would only blow them over. His voice would have put a child to sleep, but his wife continued to nag and scold, and he stumped out again in a fury and sat on the wall with his back to the house and his legs crossed, chewing his pipe. He was dressed in his best clothes, a respectable blue tailcoat and pale frieze trousers with only one patch on the seat. He had turned his cap almost right way round so that the peak covered his right ear.

He was all over the boat like a boy. Dempsey, a haggard, pock-marked, melancholy man with a soprano voice of astounding penetration, took the tiller and Red Patrick the sail. Tomas clambered into the bows and stood there with one knee up, leaning forward like a figurehead. He knew the bay like a book. The island woman was perched on the ballast with her rosary in her hands and her shawl over her eyes to shut out the sight of the waves. The cumbrous old boat took the sail lightly enough and Ned leaned back on his elbows against the side, rejoicing in it all.

"She's laughing," his father said delightedly when her bows ran white.

"Whose boat is that, Dempsey?" he asked, screwing up his eyes as another brown sail tilted ahead of them.

"'Tis the island boat," shrieked Dempsey.

"'Tis not, Dempsey. 'Tis not indeed, my love. That's not the island boat."

"Whose boat is it then?"

"It must be some boat from Carriganassa, Dempsey."

"'Tis the island boat I tell you."

"Ah, why will you be contradicting me, Dempsey, my treasure? 'Tis not the island boat. The island boat has a dark brown sail; 'tis only a month since 'twas tarred, and that's an old tarred sail, and what proves it out and out, Dempsey, the island-boat sail has a patch in the corner."

He was leaning well over the bows, watching the rocks that fled beneath them, a dark purple. He rested his elbow on his raised knee and looked back at them, his brown face sprinkled with spray and lit from below by the accumulated flickerings of the water. His flesh seemed to dissolve, to become transparent, while his blue eyes shone with extraordinary brilliance. Ned half-closed his eyes and watched sea and sky slowly mount and sink behind the red-brown, sun-filled sail and the poised and eager figure.

"Tom!" shouted his father, and the battered old face peered at them from under the arch of the sail, with which it was almost one in tone, the silvery light filling it with warmth.

"Well?" Tom's voice was an inexpressive boom.

"You were right last night, Tom, my boy. My treasure, my son, you were right. 'Twas for the drink I came."

"Ah, do you tell me so?" Tom asked ironically.

"'Twas, 'twas, 'twas," the old man said regretfully. "'Twas for the drink. 'Twas so, my darling. They were always decent people, your mother's people, and 'tis her knowing how decent they are makes her so suspicious. She's a good woman, a fine woman, your poor mother, may the Almighty God bless her and keep her and watch over her."

"Aaaa-men," Tom chanted irreverently as his father shook his old cap piously towards the sky.

"But Tom! Are you listening, Tom?"

"Well, what is it now?"

"I had another reason."

"Had you indeed?" Tom's tone was not encouraging.

"I had, I had, God's truth, I had. God blast the lie I'm telling you, Tom, I had."

"'Twas boasting out of the pair of ye," shrieked Dempsey from the stern, the wind whipping the shrill notes from his lips and scattering them wildly like scraps of paper.

"'Twas so, Dempsey, 'twas so. You're right, Dempsey. You're always right. The blessing of God on you, Dempsey, for you always had the true word." Tomas's laughing leprechaun countenance gleamed under the bellying, tilting, chocolate-coloured sail and his powerful voice beat Dempsey's down. "And would you blame me?"

"The O'Donnells hadn't the beating of them in their own hand," screamed Dempsey.

"Thanks be to God for all His goodness and mercy," shouted Tomas, again waving his cap in a gesture of recognition towards the spot where he felt the Almighty might be listening, "they have not. They have not so, Dempsey. And they have a good hand. The O'Donnells are a good family and an old family and a kind family, but they never had the like of my two sons."

"And they were stiff enough with you when you came for the daughter," shrieked Dempsey.

"They were, Dempsey, they were. They were stiff. They were so. You wouldn't blame them, Dempsey. They were an old family and I was nothing only a landless man." With a fierce gesture the old man pulled his cap still further over his ear, spat, gave his moustache a tug and leaned at a still more precarious angle over the bow, his blue eyes dancing with triumph. "But I had the gumption, Dempsey. I had the gumption, my love."

The islands slipped past; the gulf of water narrowed and grew calmer, and white cottages could be seen scattered under the tall ungainly church. It was a wild and rugged coast, the tide was full, and they had to pull in as best they could among the rocks. Red Patrick leaped lightly ashore to draw in the boat. The others stepped after him into several inches of water and Red Patrick, himself precariously poised, held them from slipping. Rather shamefastly, Ned and Tom took off their shoes.

"Don't do that!" shrieked their father. "We'll carry ye up. Mother of God, yeer poor feet!"

"Will you shut your old gob?" Tom said angrily.

They halted for a moment at the stile outside Caheragh's. Old Caheragh had a red beard and a broad, smiling face. Then they went on to O'Donnell's who had two houses, modern and old, separated by a yard. In one lived Uncle Maurice and his family and in the other Maurice's married son, Sean. Ned and Tom remained with Sean and his wife. Tom and he were old friends. When he spoke he rarely looked at Tom, merely giving him a sidelong glance that just reached to his chin and then dropped his eyes with a peculiar timid smile. " 'Twas," Ned heard him say, and then: "He did," and after that: "Hardly." Shuvaun was tall, nervous and matronly. She clung to their hands with an excess of eagerness as though she couldn't bear to let them go, uttering ejaculations of tenderness, delight, astonishment, pity, and admiration. Her speech was full of diminutives: "childeen," "handeen," "boateen." Three young children scrambled about the floor with a preoccupation scarcely broken by the strangers. Shuvaun picked her way through them, filling the kettle and cutting the bread, and then, as though afraid of neglecting Tom, she clutched his hand again. Her feverish concentration gave an impression that its very intensity bewildered her and made it impossible for her to understand one word they said. In three days' time it would all begin to drop into place in her mind and then she would begin quoting them.

Young Niall O'Donnell came in with his girl; one of the Deignans from up the hill. She was plump and pert; she had been in service in town. Niall was a well-built boy with a soft, wild-eyed, sensuous face and a deep mellow voice of great power. While they were having a cup of tea in the parlour where the three or four family photos were skyed, Ned saw the two of them again through the back window. They were standing on the high ground behind the house with the spring sky behind them and the light in their faces. Niall was asking her something but she, more interested in the sitting-room window, only shook her head.

"Ye only just missed yeer father," said their Uncle Maurice when they went across to the other house for dinner. Maurice was a tight-lipped little man with a high bald forehead and a snappy voice. "He went off to Owney Pat's only this minute."

"The devil!" said Tom. "I knew he was out to dodge me. Did you give him whisky?"

"What the hell else could I give him?" snapped Maurice. "Do you think 'twas tea the old coot was looking for?"

Tom took the place of honour at the table. He was the favourite. Through the doorway into the bedroom could be seen a big canopy bed and on the whiteness of a raised pillow a skeleton face in a halo of smoke-blue hair surmounted with what looked suspiciously like a mauve tea-cosy. Sometimes the white head would begin to stir and everyone fell silent while Niall, the old man's pet, translated the scarcely audible whisper. Sometimes Niall would go in with his stiff ungainly swagger and repeat one of Tom's jokes in his drawling, powerful bass. The hens stepped daintily about their feet, poking officious heads between them, and rushing out the door with a wild flutter and shriek when one of the girls hooshed them. Something timeless, patriarchal and restful about it made Ned notice everything. It was as though he had never seen his mother's house before.

"Tell me," Tom boomed with mock concern, leaning over confidentially to his uncle and looking under his brows at young Niall, "speaking as a clergyman and for the good of the family and so on, is that son of yours coorting Delia Deignan?"

"Why? Was the young blackguard along with her again?" snapped Maurice in amusement.

"Of course I might be mistaken," Tom said doubtfully.

"You wouldn't know a Deignan, to be sure," Sean said dryly.

"Isn't any of them married yet?" asked Tom.

"No, by damn, no," said Maurice. "Isn't it a wonder?"

"Because," Tom went on in the same solemn voice, "I want someone to look after this young brother of mine. Dublin is a wild sort of place and full of temptations. Ye wouldn't know a decent little girl I could ask?"

"Cait! Cait!" they all shouted, Niall's deep voice loudest of all.

"Now all the same, Delia looks a smart little piece," said Tom.

"No, Cait! Cait! Delia isn't the same since she went to town. She has notions of herself. Leave him marry Cait!"

Niall rose gleefully and shambled in to the old man. With a gamesome eye on the company Tom whispered:

"Is she a quiet sort of girl? I wouldn't like Ned to get anyone rough."

"She is, she is," they said, "a grand girl!"

Sean rose quietly and went to the door with his head bowed.

"God knows, if anyone knows he should know and all the times he manhandled her."

Tom sat bolt upright with mock indignation while the table rocked. Niall shouted the joke into his grandfather's ear. The mauve tea-cosy shook; it was the only indication of the old man's amusement.

I V

The Deignans' house was on top of a hill high over the road and commanded a view of the countryside for miles. The two brothers with Sean and the O'Donnell girls reached it by a long winding boreen that threaded its way uncertainly through little grey rocky fields and walls of unmortared stone which rose against the sky along the edges of the hill like lacework. On their way they met another procession coming down the hill. It was headed by their father and the island woman, arm in arm, and behind came two locals with Dempsey and Red Patrick. All the party except the island woman were well advanced in liquor. That was plain when their father rushed forward to shake them all by the hand and ask them how they were. He said that divil such honourable and kindly people as the people of Carriganassa were to be found in the whole world, and of these there was no one a patch on the O'Donnells; kings and sons of kings as you could see from one look at them. He had only one more call to pay and promised to be at Caheragh's within a quarter of an hour.

They looked over the Deignans' half-door. The kitchen was empty. The girls began to titter. They knew the Deignans must have watched them coming from Maurice's door. The kitchen was a beautiful room; woodwork and furniture, homemade and shapely, were painted a bright red-brown and the painted dresser shone with pretty ware. They entered and looked about them. Nothing was to be heard but the tick of the cheap alarm-clock on the dresser. One of the girls began to giggle hysterically. Sean raised his voice.

"Are ye in or are ye out, bad cess to ye!"

For a moment there was no reply. Then a quick step sounded in the attic and a girl descended the stairs at a run, drawing a black knitted shawl tighter about her shoulders. She was perhaps twenty-eight or thirty, with a narrow face, sharp like a ferret's, and blue nervous eyes. She entered the kitchen awkwardly sideways, giving the customary greetings but without looking at anyone.

"A hundred welcomes. . . . How are ye? . . . 'Tis a fine day."

The O'Donnell girls giggled again. Nora Deignan looked at them in astonishment, biting nervously at the tassel of her shawl. She had tiny sharp white teeth.

"What is it, aru?" she asked.

"Musha, will you stop your old cimeens," boomed Tom, "and tell us where's Cait from you? You don't think 'twas to see your ugly puss that we came up here?"

"Cait!" Nora called in a low voice.

"What is it?" another voice replied from upstairs.

"Damn well you know what it is," bellowed Tom, "and you cross-eyed expecting us since morning. Will you come down out of that or will I go up and fetch you?"

There was the same hasty step and a second girl descended the stairs. It was only later that Ned was able to realize how beautiful she was. She had the same narrow pointed face as her sister, the same slight features sharpened by a sort of animal instinct, the same blue eyes with their startled brightness; but all seemed to have been differently composed, and her complexion had a transparency as though her whole nature were shining through it. "Child of Light, thy limbs are burning through the veil which seems to hide them," Ned found himself murmuring. She came on them in the same hostile way, blushing furiously. Tom's eyes rested on her; soft, bleary, emotional eyes incredibly unlike her own.

"Have you nothing to say to me, Cait?" he boomed, and Ned thought his very voice was soft and clouded.

"Oh, a hundred welcomes." Her blue eyes rested for a moment on him with what seemed a fierce candour and penetration and went past him to the open door. Outside a soft rain was beginning to fall; heavy clouds crushed down the grey landscape, which grew clearer as it merged into one common plane; the little grey bumpy fields with the walls of grey unmortared stone that drifted hither and over across them like blown sand, the whitewashed farmhouses lost to the sun sinking back into the brown-grey hillsides.

"Nothing else, my child?" he growled, pursing his lips.

"How are you?"

"The politeness is suffocating you. Where's Delia?"

"Here I am," said Delia from the doorway immediately behind him. In her furtive way she had slunk round the house. Her bland impertinence raised a laugh.

"The reason we called," said Tom, clearing his throat, "is this young brother of mine that's looking for a wife."

Everyone laughed again. Ned knew the oftener a joke was repeated the better they liked it, but for him this particular joke was beginning to wear thin.

"Leave him take me," said Delia with an arch look at Ned who smiled and gazed at the floor.

"Be quiet, you slut!" said Tom. "There are your two sisters before you."

"Even so, I want to go to Dublin. . . . Would you treat me to lemonade, mister?" she asked Ned with her impudent smile. "This is a rotten hole. I'd go to America if they left me."

"America won't be complete without you," said Tom. "Now, don't let me hurry ye, ladies, but my old fellow will be waiting for us in Johnny Kit's."

"We'll go along with you," said Nora, and the three girls took down three black shawls from inside the door. Some tension seemed to have gone out of the air. They laughed and joked between themselves.

"Ye'll get wet," said Sean to the two brothers.

"Cait will make room for me under her shawl," said Tom.

"Indeed I will not," she cried, starting back with a laugh.

"Very shy you're getting," said Sean with a good-natured grin.

" 'Tisn't that at all but she'd sooner the young man," said Delia.

"What's strange is wonderful," said Nora.

Biting her lip with her tiny front teeth, Cait looked angrily at her sisters and Sean, and then began to laugh. She glanced at Ned and smilingly held out her shawl in invitation, though at the same moment angry blushes chased one another across her forehead like squalls across the surface of a lake. The rain was a mild, persistent drizzle and a strong wind was blowing. Everything had darkened and grown lonely and, with his head in the blinding folds of the shawl, which reeked of turf-smoke, Ned felt as if he had dropped out of Time's pocket.

They waited in Caheragh's kitchen. The bearded old man sat in one chimney corner and a little barelegged boy in the other. The dim blue light poured down the wide chimney on their heads in a shower with the delicacy of light on old china, picking out surfaces one rarely saw; and between them the fire burned a bright orange in the great whitewashed hearth with the black, swinging bars and pothook. Outside the rain fell softly, almost soundlessly, beyond the half door. Delia, her black shawl trailing from her shoulders, leaned over it, acting the part of watcher as in a Greek play. Their father's fifteen minutes had strung themselves out to an hour and two little bare-footed boys had already been sent to hunt him down.

"Where are they now, Delia?" one of the O'Donnells would ask.

"Crossing the fields from Patsy Kit's."

"He wasn't there so."

"He wouldn't be," the old man said. "They'll likely go on to Ned Kit's now."

"That's where they're making for," said Delia. "Up the hill at the far side of the fort."

"They'll find him there," the old man said confidently.

Ned felt as though he were still blanketed by the folds of the turf-reeking shawl. Something seemed to have descended on him that filled him with passion and loneliness. He could scarcely take his eyes off Cait. She and Nora sat on the form against the back wall, a composition in black and white, the black shawl drawn tight under the chin, the cowl of it breaking the curve of her dark hair, her shadow on the gleaming wall behind. She did not speak except to answer some question of Tom's about her brother, but sometimes Ned caught her looking at him with naked eyes. Then she smiled swiftly and secretly and turned her eyes again to the door, sinking back into pensiveness. Pensiveness or vacancy? he wondered. While he gazed at her face with the animal instinctiveness of its overdelicate features it seemed like a mirror in which he saw again the falling rain, the rocks and hills and angry sea.

The first announced by Delia was Red Patrick. After him came the island woman. Each had last seen his father in a different place. Ned chuckled at a sudden vision of his father, eager and impassioned and aflame with drink, stumping with his broken bottom across endless fields through pouring rain with a growing procession behind him. Dempsey was the last to come. He doubted if Tomas would be in a condition to take the boat at all.

"What matter, aru?" said Delia across her shoulder. "We can find room for the young man."

"And where would we put him?" gaped Nora.

"He can have Cait's bed," Delia said innocently.

"Oye, and where would Cait sleep?" Nora asked and then skitted and covered her face with her shawl. Delia scoffed. The men laughed and Cait, biting her lip furiously, looked at the floor. Again Ned caught her eyes on him and again she laughed and turned away.

Tomas burst in unexpected on them all like a sea-wind that scattered them before him. He wrung Tom's hand and asked him how he was. He did the same to Ned. Ned replied gravely that he was very well.

"In God's holy name," cried his father, waving his arms like a windmill, "what are ye all waiting for?"

The tide had fallen. Tomas grabbed an oar and pushed the boat on to a rock. Then he raised the sail and collapsed under it and had to be extricated from its drenching folds, glauming and swearing at Cassidy's old boat. A little group stood on a naked rock against a grey background of drifting rain. For a long time Ned continued to wave back to the black shawl that was lifted to him. An extraordinary feeling of exultation and loss enveloped him. Huddled up in his overcoat he sat with Dempsey in the stern, not speaking.

"It was a grand day," his father declared, swinging himself to and fro, tugging at his Viking moustache, dragging the peak of his cap farther over his ear. His gestures betrayed a certain lack of rhythmical cohesion; they began and ended abruptly. "Dempsey, my darling, wasn't it a grand day?"

"'Twas a grand day for you," shrieked Dempsey as if his throat would burst.

"'Twas, my treasure, 'twas a beautiful day. I got an honourable reception and my sons got an honourable reception."

By this time he was flat on his belly, one leg completely over the edge of the boat. He reached back a clammy hand to his sons.

"'Twas the best day I ever had," he said. "I got porter and I got whisky and I got poteen. I did so, Tom, my calf. Ned, my brightness, I went to seven houses and in every house I got seven drinks and with every drink I got seven welcomes. And your mother's people are a hand of trumps. It was no slight they put on me at all even if I was nothing but a landless man. No slight, Tom. Nó slight at all."

Darkness had fallen, the rain had cleared, the stars came out of a pitch-black sky under which the little tossing, nosing boat seemed lost beyond measure. In all the waste of water nothing could be heard but the splash of the boat's sides and their father's voice raised in tipsy song.

> "The evening was fair and the sunlight was yellow,
> I halted, beholding a maiden bright
> Coming to me by the edge of the mountain,
> Her cheeks had a berry-bright rosy light."

v

Ned was the first to wake. He struck a match and lit the candle. It was time for them to be stirring. It was just after dawn, and at half past nine he must be in his old place in the schoolroom before the rows of pinched little city-faces. He lit a cigarette and closed his eyes. The lurch of the boat was still in his blood, the face of Cait Deignan in his mind, and as if from far away he heard a line of the wild love-song his father had been singing: "And we'll drive the geese at the fall of night."

He heard his brother mumble something and nudged him. Tom looked big and fat and vulnerable with his fair head rolled sideways and his heavy mouth dribbling on to the sleeve of his pyjamas. Ned slipped quietly out of bed, put on his trousers, and went to the window. He drew the curtains and let in the thin cold daylight. The bay was just visible and perfectly still. Tom began to mumble again in a frightened voice and Ned shook him. He started out of his sleep with a cry of fear, grabbing at the bedclothes. He looked first at Ned, then at the candle and drowsily rubbed his eyes.

"Did you hear it too?" he asked.

"Did I hear what?" asked Ned with a smile.

"In the room," said Tom.

"There was nothing in the room," replied Ned. "You were ramaishing so I woke you up."

"Was I? What was I saying?"

"You were telling no secrets," said Ned with a quiet laugh.

"Hell!" Tom said in disgust and stretched out his arm for a cigarette. He lit it at the candle flame, his drowsy red face puckered and distraught. "I slept rotten."

"Oye!" Ned said quietly, raising his eyebrows. It wasn't often Tom spoke in that tone. He sat on the edge of the bed, joined his hands and leaned forward, looking at Tom with wide gentle eyes.

"Is there anything wrong?" he asked.

"Plenty."

"You're not in trouble?" Ned asked without raising his voice.

"Not that sort of trouble. The trouble is in myself."

Ned gave him a look of intense sympathy and understanding. The soft emotional brown eyes were searching him for a judgment. Ned had never felt less like judging him.

"Ay," he said gently and vaguely, his eyes wandering to the other side of the room while his voice took on its accustomed stammer, "the trouble is always in ourselves. If we were contented in ourselves the other things wouldn't matter. I suppose we must only leave it to time. Time settles everything."

"Time will settle nothing for me," Tom said despairingly. "You have something to look forward to. I have nothing. It's the loneliness of my job that kills you. Even to talk about it would be a relief but there's no one you can talk to. People come to you with their troubles but there's no one you can go to with your own."

Again the challenging glare in the brown eyes and Ned realized with infinite compassion that for years Tom had been living in the same state of suspicion and fear, a man being hunted down by his own nature; and that for years to come he would continue to live in this way, and perhaps never be caught again as he was now.

"A pity you came down here," stammered Ned flatly. "A pity we went to Carriganassa. 'Twould be better for both of us if we went somewhere else."

"Why don't you marry her, Ned?" Tom asked earnestly.

"Who?" asked Ned.

"Cait."

"Yesterday," said Ned with the shy smile he wore when he confessed something, "I nearly wished I could."

"But you can, man," Tom said eagerly, sitting upon his elbow. Like all men with frustration in their hearts he was full of schemes for others. "You could marry her and get a school down here. That's what I'd do if I was in your place."

"No," Ned said gravely. "We made our choice a long time ago. We can't go back on it now."

Then with his hands in his trouser pockets and his head bowed he went out to the kitchen. His mother, the coloured shawl about her head, was blowing the fire. The bedroom door was open and he could see his father in shirtsleeves kneeling beside the bed, his face raised reverently toward a holy picture, his braces hanging down behind. He unbolted the half-door, went through the garden and out on to the road. There was a magical light on everything. A boy on a horse rose suddenly against the sky, a startling picture. Through the apple-green light over Carriganassa ran long streaks of crimson, so still they might have been enamelled. Magic, magic, magic! He saw it as in a children's picture-book with all its colours intolerably bright; something he had outgrown and could never return to, while the world he aspired to was as remote and intangible as it had seemed even in the despair of youth.

It seemed as if only now for the first time was he leaving home; for the first time and forever saying good-bye to it all.

Eudora Welty

1909–

PETRIFIED MAN · A WORN PATH · THE
DEMONSTRATORS

Like William Faulkner, Eudora Welty was born in Mississippi, and has lived there most of her life. Her stories have a Southern locale and a distinctive Southern quality. After two years at college in Mississippi and two years at the University of Wisconsin, Miss Welty studied advertising at Columbia University until she rebelled at using imaginative language simply to make people buy things. Back in Mississippi, she worked for a while as a newspaper reporter and radio writer, but found the writing of fiction more satisfying. She is also a photographer and painter. Before she became known as a writer, she had an exhibit in New York City of her photographs of Mississippi scenes.

In the excellent library of her father, a wealthy Jackson, Mississippi, insurance man, Miss Welty began reading the classic European writers while she was still a child. She started her own writing fresh from her discovery of William Butler Yeats and Virginia Woolf. As one might guess from the qualities of her fiction, her favorite writers include Chekhov, Katherine Mansfield, Thomas Mann, and D. H. Lawrence. Miss Welty creates the kind of effect that Wordsworth and Coleridge set out to achieve in their *Lyrical Ballads*. She makes the fantastic seem real, seem part of us, and exposes the strangeness, even unreality, of everyday life. Though some of her stories are dreamlike, they are never merely dreams. They imply a dreamer with a particular history and personality, and so rearrange and reimagine the actualities of his life that they enable us to penetrate to new depths of psychological reality. This is true, for instance, in one of her stories, "A Traveling Salesman," which anticipated, more succinctly and lyrically, the far more famous play by Arthur Miller.

The vivid originality and beauty of her first magazine stories made Miss Welty a subject of much discussion even before her collection *A Curtain of Green* appeared in 1941. But when critics saw the seventeen stories in that volume all together, they were amazed at the tremendous range in material, mood, style, and point of view, and at the technical skill with which these elements were managed so that each story had its own appropriate kind of unity.

The Robber Bridegroom (1942) is a short novel in the manner of a folk ballad, describing the romance of a bandit chief and a Mississippi planter's daughter. It introduces legendary heroes like Mike Fink, the flat-boat bully, and plays fancifully with the customs and hazards of American frontier life. The eight stories in *The Wide Net* (1943) are nearly as varied as those in *A Curtain of Green,* but they all have some connection with the Natchez Trace, an old trading road which still cuts deep through some of the Mississippi forests. In one story, "A Still Moment," three historic figures, Audubon, the naturalist, Murrell, the outlaw, and Lorenzo Dow, the preacher, come into dramatic confrontation on the Trace, though the drama is more spiritual than physical. In the novel *Delta Wedding* (1946), three generations of family life are reconstituted in the mind of a young cousin of the bride as she watches the family gather for a plantation wedding. *The Golden Apples* (1949) is a group of seven interrelated stories about the main families of Morgana, Mississippi.

With successive volumes Miss Welty's ability to suggest precise visual appearances and to capture peculiar speech idioms and inflections has grown steadily more brilliant. Occasionally a story has been told in such an indirect or fragmentary way, and with such free use of unexplained symbols, that some critics have felt the mystification was deliberate, and that the technical means got in the way of the total imaginative effect. In her latest novel, *Losing Battles* (1970), a long and apparently leisurely account of a Southern family gathering, Miss Welty shows again that when an author really sees and cares what people do and say, the result is not only irresistibly comic, but reveals how unique— and often very strangely so—each human being is.

"Petrified Man" is a ruthlessly objective, circumstantial study of vulgarity of spirit. In its setting and manner it closely resembles Ring Lardner's famous "Haircut." But though apparently more preoccupied than Lardner with picturesquely unpleasant detail, Miss Welty is actually treating human meanness and callousness in a more complicated way that does not allow the reader such an easy sense of moral superiority. Miss Welty does not like obvious moralizing in fiction, but all her work is based on unshakable moral realities which she feels exist so unquestionably that any true picture must represent them; they do not need to be argued. "A Worn Path" is a beautifully sympathetic insight into the mind of a very old black woman. In her illiterate shrewdness, simplicity, suffering, and imagination, she has to deal as best she can with the white representatives of a largely alien culture.

"The Demonstrators" is a deeply honest and thoughtful story, with a quiet manner deliberately contrasted to the violence of some of its contents. Its portrayal of the blacks is very like that of the peasants in Chekhov's "The New Villa," and with the same implication that reformers cannot be effective unless they appreciate the realities—and especially the psychological realities—of the situations that they are trying to change. They must appreciate the extent to which, as Maupassant says, each man carries his own reality inside him, and realize that this holds for reformers, too.

"The Demonstrators" may seem unsympathetic unless we notice that the story is written entirely from the doctor's perspective and unless we know Miss Welty's own point of view from such stories as "Where Is the Voice Coming From?" which is based on the shooting of Medgar Evers. In "The Demonstrators," she has been able to imagine how the town, its people, and the issues raised on all sides, must look to a man who knows all there is to know about the region but whose own life has lost its meaning with the loss of his wife and daughter—a man whose lights have gone out like those of the streets through which he drives.

PETRIFIED MAN

"Reach in my purse and git me a cigarette without no powder in it if you kin, Mrs. Fletcher, honey," said Leota to her ten o'clock shampoo-and-set customer. "I don't like no perfumed cigarettes."

Mrs. Fletcher gladly reached over to the lavender shelf under the lavender-framed mirror, shook a hair net loose from the clasp of the patent-leather bag, and slapped her hand down quickly on a powder puff which burst out when the purse was opened.

"Why, look at the peanuts, Leota!" said Mrs. Fletcher in her marvelling voice.

"Honey, them goobers has been in my purse a week if they's been in it a day. Mrs. Pike bought them peanuts."

"Who's Mrs. Pike?" asked Mrs. Fletcher, settling back. Hidden in this den of curling fluid and henna packs, separated by a lavender swing-door from the other customers, who were being gratified in other booths, she could give her curiosity its freedom. She looked expectantly at the black part in Leota's yellow curls as she bent to light the cigarette.

"Mrs. Pike is this lady from New Orleans," said Leota, puffing, and pressing into Mrs. Fletcher's scalp with strong red-nailed fingers. "A friend, not a customer. You see, like maybe I told you last time, me and Fred and Sal and Joe all had us a fuss, so Sal and Joe up and moved out, so we didn't do a thing but rent out their room. So we rented it to Mrs. Pike. And Mr. Pike." She flicked an ash into the basket of dirty towels. "Mrs. Pike is a very decided blonde. *She* bought me the peanuts."

"She must be cute," said Mrs. Fletcher.

"Honey, 'cute' ain't the word for what she is. I'm tellin' you, Mrs. Pike is attractive. She has her a good time. She's got a sharp eye out, Mrs. Pike has."

She dashed the comb through the air, and paused dramatically as a cloud of Mrs. Fletcher's hennaed hair floated out of the lavender teeth like a small storm-cloud.

"Hair fallin'."

"Aw, Leota."

"Uh-huh, commencin' to fall out," said Leota, combing again, and letting fall another cloud.

"Is it any dandruff in it?" Mrs. Fletcher was frowning, her hairline eyebrows diving down toward her nose, and her wrinkled, beady-lashed eyelids batting with concentration.

"Nope." She combed again. "Just fallin' out."

"Bet it was that last perm'nent you gave me that did it," Mrs. Fletcher said cruelly. "Remember you cooked me fourteen minutes."

"You had fourteen minutes comin' to you," said Leota with finality.

"Bound to be somethin'," persisted Mrs. Fletcher. "Dandruff, dandruff. I couldn't of caught a thing like that from Mr. Fletcher, could I?"

"Well," Leota answered at last, "you know what I heard in here yestiddy, one of Thelma's ladies was settin' over yonder in Thelma's booth gittin' a machineless, and I don't mean to insist or insinuate or anything, Mrs. Fletcher, but Thelma's lady just happ'med to throw out—I forgotten what she was talkin' about at the time—that you was p-r-e-g., and lots of times that'll make your hair do awful funny, fall out and God knows what all. It just ain't our fault, is the way I look at it."

There was a pause. The women stared at each other in the mirror.

"Who was it?" demanded Mrs. Fletcher.

"Honey, I really couldn't say," said Leota. "Not that you look it."

"Where's Thelma? I'll get it out of her," said Mrs. Fletcher.

"Now, honey, I wouldn't go and git mad over a little thing like that," Leota said, combing hastily, as though to hold Mrs. Fletcher down by the hair. "I'm sure it was somebody didn't mean no harm in the world. How far gone are you?"

"Just wait," said Mrs. Fletcher, and shrieked for Thelma, who came in and took a drag from Leota's cigarette.

"Thelma, honey, throw your mind back to yestiddy if you kin," said Leota, drenching Mrs. Fletcher's hair with a thick fluid and catching the overflow in a cold wet towel at her neck.

"Well, I got my lady half wound for a spiral," said Thelma doubtfully.

"This won't take but a minute," said Leota. "Who is it you got in there, old Horse Face? Just cast your mind back and try to remember who your lady was yestiddy who happ'm to mention that my customer was pregnant, that's all. She's dead to know."

Thelma drooped her blood-red lips and looked over Mrs. Fletcher's head into the mirror. "Why, honey, I ain't got the faintest," she breathed. "I really don't recollect the faintest. But I'm sure she meant no harm. I declare, I forgot my hair finally got combed and thought it was a stranger behind me."

"Was it that Mrs. Hutchinson?" Mrs. Fletcher was tensely polite.

"Mrs. Hutchinson? Oh, Mrs. Hutchinson." Thelma batted her eyes. "Naw, precious, she come on Thursday and didn't ev'm mention your name. I doubt if she ev'm knows you're on the way."

"Thelma!" cried Leota staunchly.

"All I know is, whoever it is 'll be sorry some day. Why, I just barely knew it myself!" cried Mrs. Fletcher. "Just let her wait!"

"Why? What're you gonna do to her?"

It was a child's voice, and the women looked down. A little boy was making tents with aluminum wave pinchers on the floor under the sink.

"Billy Boy, hon, mustn't bother nice ladies," Leota smiled. She slapped him brightly and behind her back waved Thelma out of the booth. "Ain't Billy Boy a sight? Only three years old and already just nuts about the beauty-parlor business."

"I never saw him here before," said Mrs. Fletcher, still unmollified.

"He ain't been here before, that's how come," said Leota. "He belongs to Mrs. Pike. She got her a job but it was Fay's Millinery. He oughtn't to try on those ladies' hats, they come down over his eyes like I don't know what. They just git to look ridiculous, that's what, an' of course he's gonna put 'em on: hats. They tole Mrs. Pike they didn't appreciate him hangin' around there. Here, he couldn't hurt a thing."

"Well! I don't like children that much," said Mrs. Fletcher.

"Well!" said Leota moodily.

"Well! I'm almost tempted not to have this one," said Mrs. Fletcher. "That Mrs. Hutchinson! Just looks straight through you when she sees you on the street and then spits at you behind your back."

"Mr. Fletcher would beat you on the head if you didn't have it now," said Leota reasonably. "After going this far."

Mrs. Fletcher sat up straight. "Mr. Fletcher can't do a thing with me."

"He can't!" Leota winked at herself in the mirror.

"No, siree, he can't. If he so much as raises his voice against me, he knows good and well I'll have one of my sick headaches, and then I'm just not fit to live with. And if I really look that pregnant already—"

"Well, now, honey, I just want you to know—I habm't told any of my ladies and I ain't goin' to tell 'em—even that you're losin' your hair. You just get you one of those Stork-a-Lure dresses and stop worryin'. What people don't know don't hurt nobody, as Mrs. Pike says."

"Did you tell Mrs. Pike?" asked Mrs. Fletcher sulkily.

"Well, Mrs. Fletcher, look, you ain't ever goin' to lay eyes on Mrs. Pike or her lay eyes on you, so what diffunce does it make in the long run?"

"I knew it!" Mrs. Fletcher deliberately nodded her head so as to destroy a ringlet Leota was working on behind her ear. "Mrs. Pike!"

Leota sighed. "I reckon I might as well tell you. It wasn't any more Thelma's lady tole me you was pregnant than a bat."

"Not Mrs. Hutchinson?"

"Naw, Lord! It was Mrs. Pike."

"Mrs. Pike!" Mrs. Fletcher could only sputter and let curling fluid roll into her ear. "How could Mrs. Pike possibly know I was pregnant or otherwise, when she doesn't even know me? The nerve of some people!"

"Well, here's how it was. Remember Sunday?"

"Yes," said Mrs. Fletcher.

"Sunday, Mrs. Pike an' me was all by ourself. Mr. Pike and Fred had gone over to Eagle Lake, sayin' they was goin' to catch 'em some fish, but they didn't a course. So we was settin' in Mrs. Pike's car, it's a 1939 Dodge—"

"1939, eh," said Mrs. Fletcher.

"—An' we was gettin' us a Jax beer apiece—that's the beer that Mrs. Pike says is made right in N.O., so she won't drink no other kind. So I seen you drive up to the drugstore an' run in for just a secont, leavin' I reckon Mr. Fletcher in the car, an' come runnin' out with looked like a perscription. So I says to Mrs. Pike, just to be makin' talk, 'Right yonder's Mrs. Fletcher, and I reckon that's Mr. Fletcher—she's one of my regular customers,' I says."

"I had on a figured print," said Mrs. Fletcher tentatively.

"You sure did," agreed Leota. "So Mrs. Pike, she give you a good look—she's very observant, a good judge of character, cute as a minute, you know—and she says, 'I bet you another Jax that lady's three months on the way.'"

"What gall!" said Mrs. Fletcher. "Mrs. Pike!"

"Mrs. Pike ain't goin' to bite you," said Leota. "Mrs. Pike is a lovely girl, you'd be crazy about her, Mrs. Fletcher. But she can't sit still a minute. We went to the travellin' freak show yestiddy after work. I got through early—nine o'clock. In the vacant store next door. What, you ain't been?"

"No, I despise freaks," declared Mrs. Fletcher.

"Aw. Well, honey, talkin' about bein' pregnant an' all, you ought to see those twins in a bottle, you really owe it to yourself."

"What twins?" asked Mrs. Fletcher out of the side of her mouth.

"Well, honey, they got these two twins in a bottle, see? Born joined plumb together—dead a course." Leota dropped her voice into a soft lyrical hum. "They was about this long—pardon—must of been full time, all right, wouldn't you say?—an' they had these two heads an' two faces an' four arms an' four legs, all kind of joined *here.* See, this face looked this-a-way, and the other face looked that-a-way, over their shoulder, see. Kinda pathetic."

"Glah!" said Mrs. Fletcher disapprovingly.

"Well, ugly? Honey, I mean to tell you—their parents was first cousins and all like that. Billy Boy, git me a fresh towel from off Teeny's stack—this 'n's wringin' wet—an' quit ticklin' my ankles with that curler. I declare! He don't miss nothin'."

"Me and Mr. Fletcher aren't one speck of kin, or he could never of had me," said Mrs. Fletcher placidly.

"Of course not!" protested Leota. "Neither is me an' Fred, not that we know of. Well, honey, what Mrs. Pike liked was the pygmies. They've got these pygmies down there, too, an' Mrs. Pike was just wild about 'em. You know, the teeniniest men in the universe? Well, honey, they can just rest back on their little bohunkus an' roll around an' you can't hardly tell if they're sittin' or standin'. That'll give you some idea. They're about forty-two years old. Just suppose it was your husband!"

"Well, Mr. Fletcher is five foot nine and one half," said Mrs. Fletcher quickly.

"Fred's five foot ten," said Leota, "but I tell him he's still a shrimp, account of I'm so tall." She made a deep wave over Mrs. Fletcher's other temple with the comb. "Well, these pygmies are a kind of a dark brown, Mrs. Fletcher. Not bad-lookin' for what they are, you know."

"I wouldn't care for them," said Mrs. Fletcher. "What does that Mrs. Pike see in them?"

"Aw, I don't know," said Leota. "She's just cute, that's all. But they got this man, this petrified man, that ever'thing ever since he was nine years old, when it goes through his digestion, see, somehow Mrs. Pike says it goes to his joints and has been turning to stone."

"How awful!" said Mrs. Fletcher.

"He's forty-two too. That looks like a bad age."

"Who said so, that Mrs. Pike? I bet she's forty-two," said Mrs. Fletcher.

"Naw," said Leota, "Mrs. Pike's thirty-three, born in January, an Aquarian. He could move his head—like this. A course his head and mind ain't a joint, so to speak, and I guess his stomach ain't, either —not yet, anyways. But see—his food, he eats it, and it goes down, see, and then he digests it"—Leota rose on her toes for an instant— "and it goes out to his joints and before you can say 'Jack Robinson,' it's stone—pure stone. He's turning to stone. How'd you like to be married to a guy like that? All he can do, he can move his head just a quarter of an inch. A course he *looks* just *terrible*."

"I should think he would," said Mrs. Fletcher frostily. "Mr. Fletcher takes bending exercises every night of the world. I make him."

"All Fred does is lay around the house like a rug. I wouldn't be surprised if he woke up some day and couldn't move. The petrified man just sat there moving his quarter of an inch though," said Leota reminiscently.

"Did Mrs. Pike like the petrified man?" asked Mrs. Fletcher.

"Not as much as she did the others," said Leota deprecatingly. "And then she likes a man to be a good dresser, and all that."

"Is Mr. Pike a good dresser?" asked Mrs. Fletcher sceptically.

"Oh, well, yeah," said Leota, "but he's twelve or fourteen years older'n her. She ast Lady Evangeline about him."

"Who's Lady Evangeline?" asked Mrs. Fletcher.

"Well, it's this mind reader they got in the freak show," said Leota. "Was real good. Lady Evangeline is her name, and if I had another dollar I wouldn't do a thing but have my other palm read. She had what Mrs. Pike said was the 'sixth mind' but she had the worst manicure I ever saw on a living person."

"What did she tell Mrs. Pike?" asked Mrs. Fletcher.

"She told her Mr. Pike was as true to her as he could be and be-sides, would come into some money."

"Humph!" said Mrs. Fletcher. "What does he do?"

"I can't tell," said Leota, "because he don't work. Lady Evangeline didn't tell me enough about my nature or anything. And I would like to go back and find out some more about this boy. Used to go with this boy until he got married to this girl. Oh, shoot, that was about three and a half years ago, when you was still goin' to the Robert E. Lee Beauty Shop in Jackson. He married her for her money. Another fortune-teller tole me that at the time. So I'm not in love with him any more, anyway, besides being married to Fred, but Mrs. Pike thought, just for the hell of it, see, to ask Lady Evangeline was he happy."

"Does Mrs. Pike know everything about you already?" asked Mrs. Fletcher unbelievingly. "Mercy!"

"Oh, yeah, I tole her ever'thing about ever'thing, from now on back to I don't know when—to when I first started goin' out," said Leota. "So I ast Lady Evangeline for one of my questions, was he happily married, and she says, just like she was glad I ask her, 'Honey,' she says, 'naw, he idn't. You write down this day, March 8, 1941,' she says, 'and mock it down: three years from today him and her won't be occupyin' the same bed.' There it is, up on the wall with them other dates—see, Mrs. Fletcher? And she says, 'Child, you ought to be glad you didn't git him, because he's so mercenary.' So I'm glad I married Fred. He sure ain't mercenary, money don't mean a thing to him. But I sure would like to go back and have my other palm read."

"Did Mrs. Pike believe in what the fortune-teller said?" asked Mrs. Fletcher in a superior tone of voice.

"Lord, yes, she's from New Orleans. Ever'body in New Orleans believes ever'thing spooky. One of 'em in New Orleans before it was raided says to Mrs. Pike one summer she was goin' to go from State to State and meet some grey-headed men, and, sure enough, she says she went on a beautician convention up to Chicago. . . ."

"Oh!" said Mrs. Fletcher. "Oh, is Mrs. Pike a beautician too?"

"Sure she is," protested Leota. "She's a beautician. I'm goin' to git her in here if I can. Before she married. But it don't leave you. She says sure enough, there was three men who was a very large part of making her trip what it was, and they all three had grey in their hair and they went in six States. Got Christmas cards from 'em. Billy Boy, go see if Thelma's got any dry cotton. Look how Mrs. Fletcher's a-drippin'."

"Where did Mrs. Pike meet Mr. Pike?" asked Mrs. Fletcher primly.

"On another train," said Leota.

"I met Mr. Fletcher, or rather he met me, in a rental library," said Mrs. Fletcher with dignity, as she watched the net come down over her head.

"Honey, me an' Fred, we met in a rumble seat eight months ago and we was practically on what you might call the way to the altar inside of half an hour," said Leota in a guttural voice, and bit a bobby pin open. "Course it don't last. Mrs. Pike says nothin' like that ever lasts."

"Mr. Fletcher and myself are as much in love as the day we married," said Mrs. Fletcher belligerently as Leota stuffed cotton into her ears.

"Mrs. Pike says it don't last," repeated Leota in a louder voice. "Now go git under the dryer. You can turn yourself on, can't you? I'll be back to comb you out. Durin' lunch I promised to give Mrs. Pike a facial. You know—free. Her bein' in the business, so to speak."

"I bet she needs one," said Mrs. Fletcher, letting the swing-door fly back against Leota. "Oh, pardon me."

A week later, on time for her appointment, Mrs. Fletcher sank heavily into Leota's chair after first removing a drug-store rental book, called *Life Is Like That,* from the seat. She stared in a discouraged way into the mirror.

"You can tell it when I'm sitting down, all right," she said.

Leota seemed preoccupied and stood shaking out a lavender cloth. She began to pin it around Mrs. Fletcher's neck in silence.

"I said you sure can tell it when I'm sitting straight on and coming at you this way," Mrs. Fletcher said.

"Why, honey, naw you can't," said Leota gloomily. "Why, I'd never know. If somebody was to come up to me on the street and say, 'Mrs. Fletcher is pregnant!' I'd say, 'Heck, she don't look it to me.'"

"If a certain party hadn't found it out and spread it around, it wouldn't be too late even now," said Mrs. Fletcher frostily, but Leota was almost choking her with the cloth, pinning it so tight, and she couldn't speak clearly. She paddled her hands in the air until Leota wearily loosened her.

"Listen, honey, you're just a virgin compared to Mrs. Montjoy," Leota was going on, still absent-minded. She bent Mrs. Fletcher back in the chair and, sighing, tossed liquid from a teacup on to her head and dug both hands into her scalp. "You know Mrs. Montjoy—her husband's that premature-grey-headed fella?"

"She's in the Trojan Garden Club, is all I know," said Mrs. Fletcher.

"Well, honey," said Leota, but in a weary voice, "she come in here not the week before and not the day before she had her baby—she come in here the very selfsame day, I mean to tell you. Child, we was all plumb scared to death. There she was! Come for her shampoo an' set. Why, Mrs. Fletcher, in an hour an' twenty minutes she was layin' up there in the Babtist Hospital with a seb'm-pound son. It was that close a shave. I declare, if I hadn't been so tired I would of drank up a bottle of gin that night."

"What gall," said Mrs. Fletcher. "I never knew her at all well."

"See, her husband was waitin' outside in the car, and her bags was all packed an' in the back seat, an' she was all ready, 'cept she wanted her shampoo an' set. An' havin' one pain right after another. Her husband kep' comin' in here, scared-like, but couldn't do nothin' with her a course. She yelled bloody murder, too, but she always yelled her head off when I give her a perm'nent."

"She must of been crazy," said Mrs. Fletcher. "How did she look?"

"Shoot!" said Leota.

"Well, I can guess," said Mrs. Fletcher. "Awful."

"Just wanted to look pretty while she was havin' her baby, is all," said Leota airily. "Course, we was glad to give the lady what she was after—that's our motto—but I bet a hour later she wasn't payin' no mind to them little end curls. I bet she wasn't thinkin' about she ought to have on a net. It wouldn't of done her no good if she had."

"No, I don't suppose it would," said Mrs. Fletcher.

"Yeah man! She was a-yellin'. Just like when I give her perm'nent."

"Her husband ought to make her behave. Don't it seem that way to you?" asked Mrs. Fletcher. "He ought to put his foot down."

"Ha," said Leota. "A lot he could do. Maybe some women is soft."

"Oh, you mistake me, I don't mean for her to get soft—far from it! Women have to stand up for themselves, or there's just no telling. But now you take me—I ask Mr. Fletcher's advice now and then, and he appreciates it, especially on something important, like is it time for a permanent—not that I've told him about the baby. He says, 'Why, dear, go ahead!' Just ask their *advice*."

"Huh! If I ever ast Fred's advice we'd be floatin' down the Yazoo

River on a houseboat or somethin' by this time," said Leota. "I'm sick of Fred. I told him to go over to Vicksburg."

"Is he going?" demanded Mrs. Fletcher.

"Sure. See, the fortune-teller—I went back and had my other palm read, since we've got to rent the room agin—said my lover was goin' to work in Vicksburg, so I don't know who she could mean, unless she meant Fred. And Fred ain't workin' here—that much is so."

"Is he going to work in Vicksburg?" asked Mrs. Fletcher. "And—"

"Sure. Lady Evangeline said so. Said the future is going to be brighter than the present. He don't want to go, but I ain't gonna put up with nothin' like that. Lays around the house an' bulls—did bull—with that good-for-nuthin' Mr. Pike. He says if he goes who'll cook, but I says I never get to eat anyway—not meals. Billy Boy, take Mrs. Grover that *Screen Secrets* and leg it."

Mrs. Fletcher heard stamping feet go out the door.

"Is that that Mrs. Pike's little boy here again?" she asked, sitting up gingerly.

"Yeah, that's still him." Leota stuck out her tongue.

Mrs. Fletcher could hardly believe her eyes. "Well! How's Mrs. Pike, your attractive new friend with the sharp eyes who spreads it around town that perfect strangers are pregnant?" she asked in a sweetened tone.

"Oh, Mizziz Pike." Leota combed Mrs. Fletcher's hair with heavy strokes.

"You act like you're tired," said Mrs. Fletcher.

"Tired? Feel like it's four o'clock in the afternoon already," said Leota. "I ain't told you the awful luck we had, me and Fred? It's the worst thing you ever heard of. Maybe *you* think Mrs. Pike's got sharp eyes. Shoot, there's a limit! Well, you know, we rented out our room to this Mr. and Mrs. Pike from New Orleans when Sal an' Joe Fentress got mad at us 'cause they drank up some home-brew we had in the closet—Sal an' Joe did. So, a week ago Sat'day Mr. and Mrs. Pike moved in. Well, I kinda fixed up the room, you know —put a sofa pillow on the couch and picked some ragged robbins and put in a vase, but they never did say they appreciated it. Anyway, then I put some old magazines on the table."

"I think that was lovely," said Mrs. Fletcher.

"Wait. So, come night 'fore last, Fred and this Mr. Pike, who Fred just took up with, was back from they said they was fishin', bein' as neither one of 'em has got a job to his name, and we was all settin' around in their room. So Mrs. Pike was settin' there, readin' a old *Startling G-Man Tales* that was mine, mind you, I'd bought it myself, and all of a sudden she jumps!—into the air—you'd 'a' thought she'd set on a spider—an' says, 'Canfield'—ain't that silly, that's Mr. Pike—'Canfield, my God A'mighty,' she says, 'honey,' she says, 'we're rich, and you won't have to work.' Not that he turned one hand anyway. Well, me and Fred rushes over to her, and Mr. Pike, too, and there she sets, pointin' her finger at a photo in my copy of *Startling G-Man.* 'See that man?' yells Mrs. Pike. 'Remember him, Canfield?' 'Never forget a face,' says Mr. Pike. 'It's Mr. Petrie, that we stayed with him in the apartment next to ours in Toulouse Street in N.O. for six weeks. Mr. Petrie.' 'Well,' says Mrs. Pike, like she can't hold out one secont longer, 'Mr. Petrie is wanted for five hundred dollars cash, for rapin' four women in California, and I know where he is.' "

"Mercy!" said Mrs. Fletcher. "Where was he?"

At some time Leota had washed her hair and now she yanked her up by the back locks and sat her up.

"Know where he was?"

"I certainly don't," Mrs. Fletcher said. Her scalp hurt all over.

Leota flung a towel around the top of her customer's head. "Nowhere else but in that freak show! I saw him just as plain as Mrs. Pike. *He* was the petrified man!"

"Who would ever have thought that!" cried Mrs. Fletcher sympathetically.

"So Mr. Pike says, 'Well whatta you know about that,' an' he looks real hard at the photo and whistles. And she starts dancin' and singin' about their good luck. She meant our bad luck! I made a point of tellin' that fortune-teller the next time I saw her. I said, 'Listen, that magazine was layin' around the house for a month, and there was the freak show runnin' night an' day, not two steps away from my own beauty parlor, with Mr. Petrie just sittin' there waitin'. An' it had to be Mr. and Mrs. Pike, almost perfect strangers.' "

"What gall," said Mrs. Fletcher. She was only sitting there, wrapped in a turban, but she did not mind.

"Fortune-tellers don't care. And Mrs. Pike, she goes around actin' like she thinks she was Mrs. God," said Leota. "So they're goin' to leave tomorrow, Mr. and Mrs. Pike. And in the meantime I got to keep that mean, bad little ole kid here, gettin' under my feet ever' minute of the day an' talkin' back too."

"Have they gotten the five hundred dollars' reward already?" asked Mrs. Fletcher.

"Well," said Leota, "at first Mr. Pike didn't want to do anything about it. Can you feature that? Said he kinda liked that ole bird and said he was real nice to 'em, lent 'em money or somethin'. But Mrs. Pike simply tole him he could just go to hell, and I can see her point. She says, 'You ain't worked a lick in six months, and here I make five hundred dollars in two seconts, and what thanks do I get for it? You go to hell, Canfield,' she says. So," Leota went on in a despondent voice, "they called up the cops and they caught the ole bird, all right, right there in the freak show where I saw him with my own eyes, thinkin' he was petrified. He's the one. Did it under his real name —Mr. Petrie. Four women in California, all in the month of August. So Mrs. Pike gits five hundred dollars. And my magazine, and right next door to my beauty parlor. I cried all night, but Fred said it wasn't a bit of use and to go to sleep, because the whole thing was just a sort of coincidence—you know: can't do nothin' about it. He says it put him clean out of the notion of goin' to Vicksburg for a few days till we rent out the room agin—no tellin' who we'll git this time."

"But can you imagine anybody knowing this old man, that's raped four women?" persisted Mrs. Fletcher, and she shuddered audibly. "Did Mrs. Pike *speak* to him when she met him in the freak show?"

Leota had begun to comb Mrs. Fletcher's hair. "I says to her, I says, 'I didn't notice you fallin' on his neck when he was the petrified man—don't tell me you didn't recognize your fine friend?' And she says, 'I didn't recognize him with that white powder all over his face. He just looked familiar,' Mrs. Pike says, 'and lots of people look familiar.' But she says that ole petrified man did put her in mind of somebody. She wondered who it was! Kep' her awake, which man she'd ever knew it reminded her of. So when she seen the photo, it all come to her. Like a flash. Mr. Petrie. The way he'd turn his head and look at her when she took him in his breakfast."

"Took him in his breakfast!" shrieked Mrs. Fletcher. "Listen— don't tell me. I'd 'a' felt something."

"Four women. I guess those women didn't have the faintest notion at the time they'd be worth a hunderd an' twenty-five bucks a piece

some day to Mrs. Pike. We ast her how old the fella was then, an'
she says he musta had one foot in the grave, at least. Can you beat
it?"

"Not really petrified at all, of course," said Mrs. Fletcher medita-
tively. She drew herself up. "I'd 'a' felt something," she said proudly.

"Shoot! I did feel somethin'," said Leota. "I tole Fred when I got
home I felt so funny. I said, 'Fred, that ole petrified man sure did
leave me with a funny feelin'.' He says, 'Funny-haha or funny-
peculiar?' and I says, 'Funny-peculiar.' " She pointed her comb into
the air emphatically.

"I'll bet you did," said Mrs. Fletcher.

They both heard a crackling noise.

Leota screamed, "Billy Boy! What you doin' in my purse?"

"Aw, I'm just eatin' these ole stale peanuts up," said Billy Boy.

"You come here to me!" screamed Leota, recklessly flinging down
the comb, which scattered a whole ashtray full of bobby pins and
knocked down a row of Coca-Cola bottles. "This is the last straw!"

"I caught him! I caught him!" giggled Mrs. Fletcher. "I'll hold
him on my lap. You bad, bad boy, you! I guess I better learn how to
spank little old bad boys," she said.

Leota's eleven o'clock customer pushed open the swing-door upon
Leota paddling him heartily with the brush, while he gave angry but
belittling screams which penetrated beyond the booth and filled the
whole curious beauty parlor. From everywhere ladies began to gather
round to watch the paddling. Billy Boy kicked both Leota and Mrs.
Fletcher as hard as he could, Mrs. Fletcher with her new fixed smile.

Billy Boy stomped through the group of wild-haired ladies and
went out the door, but flung back the words. "If you're so smart,
why ain't you rich?"

A WORN PATH

It was December—a bright frozen day in the early morning. Far out in the country there was an old Negro woman with her head tied in a red rag, coming along a path through the pinewoods. Her name was Phoenix Jackson. She was very old and small and she walked slowly in the dark pine shadows, moving a little from side to side in her steps, with the balanced heaviness and lightness of a pendulum in a grandfather clock. She carried a thin, small cane made from an umbrella, and with this she kept tapping the frozen earth in front of her. This made a grave and persistent noise in the still air, that seemed meditative like the chirping of a solitary little bird.

She wore a dark striped dress reaching down to her shoe tops, and an equally long apron of bleached sugar sacks, with a full pocket: all neat and tidy, but every time she took a step she might have fallen over her shoelaces, which dragged from her unlaced shoes. She looked straight ahead. Her eyes were blue with age. Her skin had a pattern all its own of numberless branching wrinkles and as though a whole little tree stood in the middle of her forehead, but a golden color ran underneath, and the two knobs of her cheeks were illumined by a yellow burning under the dark. Under the red rag her hair came down on her neck in the frailest of ringlets, still black, and with an odor like copper.

Now and then there was a quivering in the thicket. Old Phoenix said, "Out of my way, all you foxes, owls, beetles, jack rabbits, coons and wild animals! . . . Keep out from under these feet, little bob-whites. . . . Keep the big wild hogs out of my path. Don't let none of those come running my direction. I got a long way." Under her small black-freckled hand her cane, limber as a buggy whip, would switch at the brush as if to rouse up any hiding things.

On she went. The woods were deep and still. The sun made the pine needles almost too bright to look at, up where the wind rocked.

The cones dropped as light as feathers. Down in the hollow was the mourning dove—it was not too late for him.

The path ran up a hill. "Seem like there is chains about my feet, time I get this far," she said, in the voice of argument old people keep to use with themselves. "Something always take a hold of me on this hill—pleads I should stay."

After she got to the top she turned and gave a full, severe look behind her where she had come. "Up through pines," she said at length. "Now down through oaks."

Her eyes opened their widest, and she started down gently. But before she got to the bottom of the hill a bush caught her dress.

Her fingers were busy and intent, but her skirts were full and long, so that before she could pull them free in one place they were caught in another. It was not possible to allow the dress to tear. "I in the thorny bush," she said. "Thorns, you doing your appointed work. Never want to let folks pass, no sir. Old eyes thought you was a pretty little *green* bush."

Finally, trembling all over, she stood free, and after a moment dared to stoop for her cane.

"Sun so high!" she cried, leaning back and looking, while the thick tears went over her eyes. "The time getting all gone here."

At the foot of this hill was a place where a log was laid across the creek.

"Now comes the trial," said Phoenix.

Putting her right foot out, she mounted the log and shut her eyes. Lifting her skirt, leveling her cane fiercely before her, like a festival figure in some parade, she began to march across. Then she opened her eyes and she was safe on the other side.

"I wasn't as old as I thought," she said.

But she sat down to rest. She spread her skirts on the bank around her and folded her hands over her knees. Up above her was a tree in a pearly cloud of mistletoe. She did not dare to close her eyes, and when a little boy brought her a plate with a slice of marble-cake on it she spoke to him. "That would be acceptable," she said. But when she went to take it there was just her own hand in the air.

So she left that tree, and had to go through a barbed-wire fence. There she had to creep and crawl, spreading her knees and stretching her fingers like a baby trying to climb the steps. But she talked loudly to herself: she could not let her dress be torn now, so late in the day, and she could not pay for having her arm or her leg sawed off if she got caught fast where she was.

At last she was safe through the fence and risen up out in the clearing. Big dead trees, like black men with one arm, were standing in the purple stalks of the withered cotton field. There sat a buzzard.

"Who you watching?"

In the furrow she made her way along.

"Glad this not the season for bulls," she said, looking sideways, "and the good Lord made his snakes to curl up and sleep in the winter. A pleasure I don't see no two-headed snake coming around that tree, where it come once. It took a while to get by him, back in the summer."

She passed through the old cotton and went into a field of dead corn. It whispered and shook and was taller than her head. "Through the maze now," she said, for there was no path.

Then there was something tall, black, and skinny there, moving before her.

At first she took it for a man. It could have been a man dancing in the field. But she stood still and listened, and it did not make a sound. It was as silent as a ghost.

"Ghost," she said sharply, "who be you the ghost of? For I have heard of nary death close by."

But there was no answer—only the ragged dancing in the wind.

She shut her eyes, reached out her hand, and touched a sleeve. She found a coat and inside that an emptiness, cold as ice.

"You scarecrow," she said. Her face lighted. "I ought to be shut up for good," she said with laughter. "My senses is gone. I too old. I the oldest people I ever know. Dance, old scarecrow," she said, "while I dancing with you."

She kicked her foot over the furrow, and with mouth drawn down, shook her head once or twice in a little strutting way. Some husks blew down and whirled in streamers about her skirts.

Then she went on, parting her way from side to side with the cane, through the whispering field. At last she came to the end, to a wagon track where the silver grass blew between the red ruts. The quail were walking around like pullets, seeming all dainty and unseen.

"Walk pretty," she said. "This the easy place. This the easy going."

She followed the track, swaying through the quiet bare fields, through the little strings of trees silver in their dead leaves, past cabins silver from weather, with the doors and windows boarded shut, all like old women under a spell sitting there. "I walking in their sleep," she said, nodding her head vigorously.

In a ravine she went where a spring was silently flowing through a hollow log. Old Phoenix bent and drank. "Sweet-gum makes the water sweet," she said, and drank more. "Nobody know who made this well, for it was here when I was born."

The track crossed a swampy part where the moss hung as white as lace from every limb. "Sleep on, alligators, and blow your bubbles." Then the track went into the road.

Deep, deep the road went down between the high green-colored banks. Overhead the live-oaks met, and it was as dark as a cave.

A black dog with a lolling tongue came up out of the weeds by the ditch. She was meditating, and not ready, and when he came at her she only hit him a little with her cane. Over she went in the ditch, like a little puff of milkweed.

Down there, her senses drifted away. A dream visited her, and she reached her hand up, but nothing reached down and gave her a pull. So she lay there and presently went to talking. "Old woman," she said to herself, "that black dog come up out of the weeds to stall you off, and now there he sitting on his fine tail, smiling at you."

A white man finally came along and found her—a hunter, a young man, with his dog on a chain.

"Well, Granny!" he laughed. "What are you doing there?"

"Lying on my back like a June-bug waiting to be turned over, mister," she said, reaching up her hand.

He lifted her up, gave her a swing in the air, and set her down. "Anything broken, Granny?"

"No sir, them old dead weeds is springy enough," said Phoenix, when she had got her breath. "I thank you for your trouble."

"Where do you live, Granny?" he asked, while the two dogs were growling at each other.

"Away back yonder, sir, behind the ridge. You can't even see it from here."

"On your way home?"

"No sir, I going to town."

"Why, that's too far! That's as far as I walk when I come out myself, and I get something for my trouble." He patted the stuffed bag he carried, and there hung down a little closed claw. It was one of the bob-whites, with its beak hooked bitterly to show it was dead. "Now you go on home, Granny!"

"I bound to go to town, mister," said Phoenix. "The time come around."

He gave another laugh, filling the whole landscape. "I know you old colored people! Wouldn't miss going to town to see Santa Claus!"

But something held old Phoenix very still. The deep lines in her face went into a fierce and different radiation. Without warning, she had seen with her own eyes a flashing nickel fall out of the man's pocket onto the ground.

"How old are you, Granny?" he was saying.

"There is no telling, mister," she said, "no telling."

Then she gave a little cry and clapped her hands and said, "Git on away from here, dog! Look! Look at that dog!" She laughed as if in admiration. "He ain't scared of nobody. He a big black dog." She whispered, "Sic him!"

"Watch me get rid of that cur," said the man. "Sic him, Pete! Sic him!"

Phoenix heard the dogs fighting, and heard the man running and throwing sticks. She even heard a gunshot. But she was slowly bending forward by that time, further and further forward, the lids stretched down over her eyes, as if she were doing this in her sleep. Her chin was lowered almost to her knees. The yellow palm of her hand came out from the fold of her apron. Her fingers slid down and along the ground under the piece of money with the grace and care they would have in lifting an egg from under a setting hen. Then she slowly straightened up, she stood erect, and the nickel was in her apron pocket. A bird flew by. Her lips moved. "God watching me the whole time. I come to stealing."

The man came back, and his own dog panted about them. "Well, I scared him off that time," he said, and then he laughed and lifted his gun and pointed it at Phoenix.

She stood straight and faced him.

"Doesn't the gun scare you?" he said, still pointing it.

"No, sir, I seen plenty go off closer by, in my day, and for less than what I done," she said, holding utterly still.

He smiled, and shouldered the gun. "Well, Granny," he said, "you must be a hundred years old, and scared of nothing. I'd give you a dime if I had any money with me. But you take my advice and stay home, and nothing will happen to you."

"I bound to go on my way, mister," said Phoenix. She inclined her head in the red rag. Then they went in different directions, but she could hear the gun shooting again and again over the hill.

She walked on. The shadows hung from the oak trees to the road like curtains. Then she smelled wood-smoke, and smelled the river, and she saw a steeple and the cabins on their steep steps. Dozens of little black children whirled around her. There ahead was Natchez shining. Bells were ringing. She walked on.

In the paved city it was Christmas time. There were red and green electric lights strung and crisscrossed everywhere, and all turned on in the daytime. Old Phoenix would have been lost if she had not distrusted her eyesight and depended on her feet to know where to take her.

She paused quietly on the sidewalk where people were passing by. A lady came along in the crowd, carrying an armful of red-, green- and silver-wrapped presents; she gave off perfume like the red roses in hot summer, and Phoenix stopped her.

"Please, missy, will you lace up my shoe?" She held up her foot.

"What do you want, Grandma?"

"See my shoe," said Phoenix. "Do all right for out in the country, but wouldn't look right to go in a big building."

"Stand still then, Grandma," said the lady. She put her packages down on the sidewalk beside her and laced and tied both shoes tightly.

"Can't lace 'em with a cane," said Phoenix. "Thank you, missy. I doesn't mind asking a nice lady to tie up my shoe, when I gets out on the street."

Moving slowly and from side to side, she went into the big building, and into a tower of steps, where she walked up and around and around until her feet knew to stop.

She entered a door, and there she saw nailed up on the wall the document that had been stamped with the gold seal and framed in the gold frame, which matched the dream that was hung up in her head.

"Here I be," she said. There was a fixed and ceremonial stiffness over her body.

"A charity case, I suppose," said an attendant who sat at the desk before her.

But Phoenix only looked above her head. There was sweat on her face, the wrinkles in her skin shone like a bright net.

"Speak up, Grandma," the woman said. "What's your name? We must have your history, you know. Have you been here before? What seems to be the trouble with you?"

Old Phoenix only gave a twitch to her face as if a fly were bothering her.

"Are you deaf?" cried the attendant.

But then the nurse came in.

"Oh, that's just old Aunt Phoenix," she said. "She doesn't come for herself—she has a little grandson. She makes these trips just as regular as clockwork. She lives away back off the Old Natchez Trace." She bent down. "Well, Aunt Phoenix, why don't you just take a seat? We won't keep you standing after your long trip." She pointed.

The old woman sat down, bolt upright in the chair.

"Now, how is the boy?" asked the nurse.

Old Phoenix did not speak.

"I said, how is the boy?"

But Phoenix only waited and stared straight ahead, her face very solemn and withdrawn into rigidity.

"Is his throat any better?" asked the nurse. "Aunt Phoenix, don't you hear me? Is your grandson's throat any better since the last time you came for the medicine?"

With her hands on her knees, the old woman waited, silent, erect and motionless, just as if she were in armor.

"You mustn't take up our time this way, Aunt Phoenix," the nurse said. "Tell us quickly about your grandson, and get it over. He isn't dead, is he?"

At last there came a flicker and then a flame of comprehension across her face, and she spoke.

"My grandson. It was my memory had left me. There I sat and forgot why I made my long trip."

"Forgot?" The nurse frowned. "After you came so far?"

Then Phoenix was like an old woman begging a dignified forgiveness for waking up frightened in the night. "I never did go to school, I was too old at the Surrender," she said in a soft voice. "I'm an old woman without an education. It was my memory fail me. My little grandson, he is just the same, and I forgot it in the coming."

"Throat never heals, does it?" said the nurse, speaking in a loud, sure voice to old Phoenix. By now she had a card with something written on it, a little list. "Yes. Swallowed lye. When was it?— January—two-three years ago—"

Phoenix spoke unasked now. "No, missy, he not dead, he just the same. Every little while his throat begin to close up again, and he not able to swallow. He not get his breath. He not able to help himself. So the time come around, and I go on another trip for the soothing medicine."

"All right. The doctor said as long as you came to get it, you could have it," said the nurse. "But it's an obstinate case."

"My little grandson, he sit up there in the house all wrapped up, waiting by himself," Phoenix went on. "We is the only two left in the world. He suffer and it don't seem to put him back at all. He got a sweet look. He going to last. He wear a little patch quilt and peep out holding his mouth open like a little bird. I remembers so plain now. I not going to forget him again, no, the whole enduring time. I could tell him from all the others in creation."

"All right." The nurse was trying to hush her now. She brought her a bottle of medicine. "Charity," she said, making a check mark in a book.

Old Phoenix held the bottle close to her eyes, and then carefully put it into her pocket.

"I thank you," she said.

"It's Christmas time, Grandma," said the attendant. "Could I give you a few pennies out of my purse?"

"Five pennies is a nickel," said Phoenix stiffly.

"Here's a nickel," said the attendant.

Phoenix rose carefully and held out her hand. She received the nickel and then fished the other nickel out of her pocket and laid it beside the new one. She stared at her palm closely, with her head on one side.

Then she gave a tap with her cane on the floor.

"This is what come to me to do," she said. "I going to the store and buy my child a little windmill they sells, made out of paper. He going to find it hard to believe there such a thing in the world. I'll march myself back where he waiting, holding it straight up in this hand."

She lifted her free hand, gave a little nod, turned around, and walked out of the doctor's office. Then her slow step began on the stairs, going down.

THE DEMONSTRATORS

Near eleven o'clock that Saturday night the doctor stopped again by his office. He had recently got into playing a weekly bridge game at the club, but tonight it had been interrupted for the third time, and he'd just come from attending to Miss Marcia Pope. Now bedridden, scorning all medication and in particular tranquillizers, she had a seizure every morning before breakfast and often on Saturday night for some reason, but had retained her memory; she could amuse herself by giving out great wads of Shakespeare and "*Arma virumque cano,*" or the like. The more forcefully Miss Marcia Pope declaimed, the more innocent grew her old face—the lines went right out.

"She'll sleep naturally now, I think," he'd told the companion, still in her rocker.

Mrs. Warrum did well, perhaps hadn't hit yet on an excuse to quit that suited her. She failed to be alarmed by Miss Marcia Pope, either in convulsions or in recitation. From where she lived, she'd never gone to school to this lady, who had taught three generations of Holden, Mississippi, its Latin, civics, and English, and who had carried, for forty years, a leather satchel bigger than the doctor's bag.

As he'd snapped his bag shut tonight, Miss Marcia had opened her eyes and spoken distinctly: "Richard Strickland? I have it on my report that Irene Roberts is not where she belongs. Now which of you wants the whipping?"

"It's all right, Miss Marcia. She's still my wife," he'd said, but could not be sure the answer got by her.

In the office, he picked up the city newspaper he subscribed to— seeing as he did so the picture on the front of a young man burning his draft card before a camera—and locked up, ready to face home.

As he came down the stairway onto the street, his sleeve was plucked.

It was a Negro child. "We got to hurry," she said.

His bag was still in the car. She climbed into the back and stood there behind his ear as he drove down the hill. He met the marshal's car as both bounced over the railroad track—no passenger rode with the marshal that he could see—and the doctor asked the child, "Who got hurt? Whose house?" But she could only tell him how to get there, an alley at a time, till they got around the cottonseed mill.

Down here, the street lights were out tonight. The last electric light of any kind appeared to be the one burning in the vast shrouded cavern of the gin. His car lights threw into relief the dead goldenrod that stood along the road and made it look heavier than the bridge across the creek.

As soon as the child leaned on his shoulder and he had stopped the car, he heard men's voices; but at first his eyes could make out little but an assembly of white forms spaced in the air near a low roof—chickens roosting in a tree. Then he saw the reds of cigarettes. A dooryard was as packed with a standing crowd as if it were funeral time. They were all men. Still more people seemed to be moving from the nearby churchyard and joining onto the crowd in front of the house.

The men parted before them as he went following the child up broken steps and across a porch. A kerosene lamp was being held for him in the doorway. He stepped into a roomful of women. The child kept going, went to the foot of an iron bed and stopped. The lamp came up closer behind him and he followed a path of newspapers laid down on the floor from the doorway to the bed.

A dark quilt was pulled up to the throat of a girl alive on the bed. A pillow raised her at the shoulders. The dome of her forehead looked thick as a battering ram, because of the rolling of her eyes.

Dr. Strickland turned back the quilt. The young, very black-skinned woman lay in a white dress with her shoes on. A maid? Then he saw that of course the white was not the starched material of a uniform but shiny, clinging stuff, and there was a banner of some kind crossing it in a crumpled red line from the shoulder. He unfastened the knot at the waist and got the banner out of the way. The skintight satin had been undone at the neck already; as he parted it farther, the girl kicked at the foot of the bed. He exposed the breast and then, before her hand had pounced on his, the wound below the breast. There was a small puncture with little evidence of external bleeding. He had seen splashes of blood on the dress, now almost dry.

"Go boil me some water. Too much excitement to send for the doctor a little earlier?"

The girl clawed at his hand with her sticky nails.

"Have you touched her?" he asked.

"See there? And she don't want you trying it, either," said a voice in the room.

A necklace like sharp and pearly teeth was fastened around her throat. It was when he took that off that the little girl who had been sent for him cried out. "I bid that!" she said, but without coming nearer. He found no other wounds.

"Does it hurt you to breathe?" He spoke almost absently as he addressed the girl.

The nipples of her breasts cast shadows that looked like figs; she would not take a deep breath when he used the stethoscope. Sweat in the airless room, in the bed, rose and seemed to weaken and unstick the newspapered walls like steam from a kettle already boiling; it glazed his own white hand, his tapping fingers. It was the stench of sensation. The women's faces coming nearer were streaked in the hot lamplight. Somewhere close to the side of his head something glittered; hung over the knob of the bedpost, where a boy would have tossed his cap, was a tambourine. He let the stethoscope fall, and heard women's sighs travel around the room, domestic sounds like a broom being flirted about, women getting ready for company.

"Stand back," he said. "You got a fire on in here?" Warm as it was, crowded as it was in here, he looked behind him and saw the gas heater burning, half the radiants burning blue. The girl, with lips turned down, lay pulling away while he took her pulse.

The child who had been sent for him and then had been sent to heat the water brought the kettle in from the kitchen too soon and had to be sent back to make it boil. When it was ready and in the pan, the lamp was held closer; it was beside his elbow as if to singe his arm.

"Stand back," he said. Again and again the girl's hand had to be forced away from her breast. The wound quickened spasmodically as if it responded to light.

"Icepick?"

"You right this time," said voices in the room.

"Who did this to her?"

The room went quiet; he only heard the men in the yard laughing together. "How long ago?" He looked at the path of newspapers spread on the floor. "Where? Where did it happen? How did she get here?"

He had an odd feeling that somewhere in the room somebody was sending out beckoning smiles in his direction. He lifted, half turned his head. The elevated coal that glowed at regular intervals was the pipe of an old woman in a boiled white apron standing near the door. He persisted. "Has she coughed up anything yet?"

"Don't you know her?" they cried, as if he never was going to hit on the right question.

He let go the girl's arm, and her hand started its way back again to her wound. Sending one glowing look at him, she covered it again. As if she had spoken, he recognized her.

"Why, it's Ruby," he said.

Ruby Gaddy *was* the maid. Five days a week she cleaned up on the second floor of the bank building where he kept his office and consulting rooms.

He said to her, "Ruby, this is Dr. Strickland. What have you been up to?"

"*Nothin'!*" everybody cried for her.

The girl's eyes stopped rolling and rested themselves on the expressionless face of the little girl, who again stood at the foot of the bed watching from this restful distance. Look equalled look: sisters.

"Am I supposed to just know?" The doctor looked all around him. An infant was sitting up on the splintery floor near his feet, he now saw, on a clean newspaper, a spoon stuck pipelike in its mouth. From out in the yard at that moment came a regular guffaw, not much different from the one that followed the telling of a dirty story or a race story by one of the clowns in the Elks' Club. He frowned at the baby; and the baby, a boy, looked back over his upside down spoon and gave it a long audible suck.

"She married? Where's her husband? That where the trouble was?"

Now, while the women in the room, too, broke out in sounds of amusement, the doctor stumbled where he stood. "What the devil's running in here? Rats?"

"You wrong there."

Guinea pigs were running underfoot, not only in this room but on the other side of the wall, in the kitchen where the water had finally got boiled. Somebody's head turned toward the leaf end of a stalk of celery wilting on top of the Bible on the table.

"Catch those things!" he exclaimed.

The baby laughed; the rest copied the baby.

"They lightning. Get away from you so fast!" said a voice.

"Them guinea pigs ain't been caught since they was born. Let you try."

"Know why? 'Cause they's Dove's. Dove left 'em here when he move out, just to be in the way."

The doctor felt the weight recede from Ruby's fingers, and saw it flatten her arm where it lay on the bed. Her eyes had closed. A little boy with a sanctimonious face had taken the bit of celery and knelt down on the floor; there was scrambling about and increasing laughter until Dr. Strickland made himself heard in the room.

"All right. I heard you. Is Dove who did it? Go on. Say."

He heard somebody spit on the stove. Then:

"It's Dove."

"Dove."

"Dove."

"Dove."

"You got it right that time."

While the name went around, passed from one mouth to the other, the doctor drew a deep breath. But the sigh that filled the room was the girl's own, luxuriously uncontained.

"Dove Collins? I believe you. I've had to sew him up enough times on Sunday morning, you all know that," said the doctor. "I know Ruby, I know Dove, and if the lights would come back on I can tell you the names of the rest of you and you know it." While he was speaking, his eyes fell on Oree, a figure of the Holden square for twenty years, whom he had inherited—sitting here in the room in her express wagon, the flowered skirt spread down from her lap and tucked in over the stumps of her knees.

While he was preparing the hypodermic, he was aware that more watchers, a row of them dressed in white with red banners like

Ruby's, were coming in to fill up the corners. The lamp was lifted—higher than the dipping shadows of their heads, a valentine tacked on the wall radiated color—and then, as he leaned over the bed, the lamp was brought down closer and closer to the girl, like something that would devour her.

"Now I can't see what I'm doing," the doctor said sharply, and as the light jumped and swung behind him he thought he recognized the anger as a mother's.

"Look to me like the fight's starting to go out of Ruby mighty early," said a voice.

Still her eyes stayed closed. He gave the shot.

"Where'd he get to—Dove? Is the marshal out looking for him?" he asked.

The sister moved along the bed and put the baby down on it close to Ruby's face.

"Remove him," said the doctor.

"She don't even study him," said the sister. "Poke her," she told the baby.

"Take him out of here," ordered Dr. Strickland.

The baby opened one of his mother's eyes with his fingers. When she shut it on him he cried, as if he knew it to be deliberate of her.

"Get that baby out of here and all the kids, I tell you," Dr. Strickland said into the room. "This ain't going to be pretty."

"Carry him next door, Twosie," said a voice.

"I ain't. You all promised me if I leave long enough to get the doctor I could stand right here until." The child's voice was loud.

"O.K. Then you got to hold Roger."

The baby made a final reach for his mother's face, putting out a hand with its untrimmed nails, gray as the claw of a squirrel. The woman who had held the lamp set that down and grabbed the baby out of the bed herself. His legs began churning even before she struck him a blow on the side of the head.

"You trying to raise him an idiot?" the doctor flung out.

"*I* ain't going to raise him," the mother said toward the girl on the bed.

The deliberation had gone out of her face. She was drifting into unconsciousness. Setting her hand to one side, the doctor inspected the puncture once more. It was clean as the eye of a needle. While he stood there watching her, he lifted her hand and washed it—the wrist, horny palm, blood-caked fingers one by one.

But as he again found her pulse, he saw her eyes opening. As long as he counted he was aware of those eyes as if they loomed larger than the watch face. They were filled with the unresponding gaze of ownership. She knew what she had. Memory did not make the further effort to close the lids when he replaced her hand, or when he took her shoes off and set them on the floor, or when he stepped away from the bed and again the full lamplight struck her face.

The twelve-year-old stared on, over the buttress of the baby she held to her chest.

"Can you ever hush that baby?"

A satisfied voice said, "He going to keep-a-noise till he learn better."

"Well, I'd like a little peace and consideration to be shown!" the doctor said. "Try to remember there's somebody in here with you that's going to be pumping mighty hard to breathe." He raised a finger and pointed it at the old woman in the boiled apron whose pipe had continued to glow with regularity by the door. "You stay. You sit here and watch Ruby," he called. "The rest of you clear out of here."

He closed his bag and straightened up. The woman stuck the lamp hot into his own face.

"Remember Lucille? I'm Lucille. I was washing for your mother when you was born. Let me see you do something," she said with fury. "You ain't even tied her up! You sure ain't your daddy!"

"Why, she's bleeding inside," he retorted. "What do you think *she's* doing?"

They hushed. For a minute all he heard was the guinea pigs racing. He looked back at the girl; her eyes were fixed with possession. "I gave her a shot. She'll just go to sleep. If she doesn't, call me and I'll come back and give her another one. One of you kindly bring me a drink of water," the doctor continued in the same tone.

With a crash, hushed off like cymbals struck by mistake, something was moved on the kitchen side of the wall. The little boy who had held the celery to catch the guinea pigs came in carrying a tea-cup. He passed through the room and out onto the porch, where he could be heard splashing fresh water from a pump. He came back inside and at arm's length held the cup out to the doctor.

Dr. Strickland drank with a thirst they all could and did follow. The cup, though it held the whole smell of this house in it, was of thin china, was an old one.

Then he stepped across the gaze of the girl on the bed as he would have had to step over a crack yawning in the floor.

"Fixing to leave?" asked the old woman in the boiled white apron, who still stood up by the door, the pipe gone from her lips. He then remembered her. In the days when he travelled East to medical school, she used to be the sole factotum at the Holden depot when the passenger train came through sometime between two and three in the morning. It was always late. Circling the pewlike benches of the waiting rooms, she carried around coffee which she poured boiling hot into paper cups out of a white-enamelled pot that looked as long as her arm. She wore then, in addition to the apron, a white and flaring head covering—something between a chef's cap and a sunbonnet. As the train at last steamed in, she called the stations. She didn't use a loud-speaker but just the power of her lungs. In all the natural volume of her baritone voice she thundered them out to the scattered and few who had waited under lights too poor to read by—first in the colored waiting room, then in the white waiting room, to echo both times from the vault of the roof: ". . . Meridian. Birmingham. Chattanooga. Bristol. Lynchburg. Washington. Baltimore. Philadelphia. And New York." Seizing all the bags, two by two, in her own hands, walking slowly in front of the passengers, she saw to it that they left.

He said to her, "I'm going, but you're not. You're keeping a watch on Ruby. Don't let her slide down in the bed. Call me if you need me." As a boy, had he never even wondered what her name was— this tyrant? He didn't know it now. He put the cup into her reaching hand. "Aren't you ready to leave?" he asked Oree, the legless woman. She still lived by the tracks where the train had cut off her legs.

"I ain't in no hurry," she replied and as he passed her she called her usual "Take it easy, Doc."

When he stepped outside onto the porch, he saw that there was moonlight everywhere. Uninterrupted by any lights from Holden, it filled the whole country lying out there in the haze of the long rainless fall. He himself stood on the edge of Holden. Just one house and one church farther, the Delta began, and the cotton fields ran into the scattered paleness of a dimmed-out Milky Way.

Nobody called him back, yet he turned his head and got a sideways glimpse all at once of a row of dresses hung up across the front of the house, starched until they could have stood alone (as his mother complained), and in an instant had recognized his mother's gardening dress, his sister Annie's golf dress, his wife's favorite duster that she liked to wear to the breakfast table, and more dresses, less substantial. Elevated across the front of the porch, they were hung again between him and the road. With sleeves spread wide, trying to scratch his forehead with the tails of their skirts, they were flying around this house in the moonlight.

The moment of vertigo passed, as a small black man came up the steps and across the porch wearing heeltaps on his shoes.

"Sister Gaddy entered yet into the gates of joy?"

"No, Preacher, you're in time," said the doctor.

As soon as he left the house, he heard it become as noisy as the yard had been, and the men in the yard went quiet to let him through. From the road, he saw the moon itself. It was above the tree with the chickens in it; it might have been one of the chickens flown loose. He scraped children off the hood of his car, pulled another from position at the wheel, and climbed inside. He turned the car around in the churchyard. There was a flickering light inside the church. Flat-roofed as a warehouse, it had its shades pulled down like a bedroom. This was the church where the sounds of music and dancing came from habitually on many another night besides Sunday, clearly to be heard on top of the hill.

He drove back along the road, across the creek, its banks glittering now with the narrow bottles, the size of harmonicas, in which paregoric was persistently sold under the name of Mother's Helper. The telephone wires along the road were hung with shreds of cotton, the sides of the road were strewn with them too, as if the doctor were out on a paper chase.

He passed the throbbing mill, working on its own generator. No lights ever shone through the windowless and now moonlit sheet iron, but the smell came out freely and spread over the town at large—a cooking smell, like a dish ordered by a man with an endless appetite. Pipes hung with streamers of lint fed into the moonlit gin, and wagons and trucks heaped up round as the gypsy caravans or circus wagons of his father's, or even his grandfather's, stories, stood this way and that, waiting in the yard outside.

Far down the railroad track, beyond the unlighted town, rose the pillowshaped glow of a grass fire. It was gaseous, unveined, unblotted by smoke, a cloud with the November flush of the sedge grass by day, sparkless and nerveless, not to be confused with a burning church, but like anesthetic made visible.

Then a long beam of electric light came solid as a board from behind him to move forward along the long loading platform, to some bales of cotton standing on it, some of them tumbled one against the others as if pushed by the light; then it ran up the wall of the dark station so you could read the name, "Holden." The hooter sounded. This was a grade crossing with a bad record, and it seemed to the doctor that he had never started over it in his life that something was not bearing down. He stopped the car, and as the train in its heat began to pass in front of him he saw it to be a doubleheader, a loaded freight this time. It was going right on through Holden.

He cut off his motor. One of the sleepers rocked and complained with every set of wheels that rolled over it. Presently the regular, slow creaking reminded the doctor of an old-fashioned porch swing holding lovers in the dark.

He had been carried a cup tonight that might have been his own mother's china or his wife's mother's—the rim not a perfect round, a thin, porcelain cup his lips and his fingers had recognized. In that house of murder, comfort had been brought to him at his request. After drinking from it he had all but reeled into a flock of dresses stretched wide-sleeved across the porch of that house like a child's drawing of angels.

Faintly rocked by the passing train, he sat bent at the wheel of the car, and the feeling of well-being persisted. It increased, until he had come to the point of tears.

The doctor was the son of a doctor, practicing in his father's office; all the older patients, like Miss Marcia Pope—and like Lucille and Oree—spoke of his father, and some confused the young doctor with the old; but not they. The watch he carried was the gold one that had belonged to his father. Richard had grown up in Holden, married "the prettiest girl in the Delta." Except for his years at the university and then at medical school and during his internship, he had lived here at home and had carried on the practice—the only practice in town. Now his father and his mother both were dead, his sister had married and moved away, a year ago his child had died. Then, back in the summer, he and his wife had separated, by her wish.

Sylvia had been their only child. Until her death from pneumonia last Christmas, at the age of thirteen, she had never sat up or spoken. He had loved her and mourned her all her life; she had been injured at birth. But Irene had done more; she had dedicated her life to Sylvia, sparing herself nothing, tending her, lifting her, feeding her, everything. What do you do after giving all your devotion to something that cannot be helped, and that has been taken away? You give all your devotion to something else that cannot be helped. But you shun all the terrible reminders, and turn not to a human being but to an idea.

Last June, there had come along a student, one of the civil-rights workers, calling at his office with a letter of introduction. For the sake of an old friend, the doctor had taken him home to dinner. (He had been reminded of him once tonight, already, by a photograph in the city paper.) He remembered that the young man had already finished talking about his work. They had just laughed around the table after Irene had quoted the classic question the governor-before-this-one had asked, after a prison break: "If you can't trust a trusty, who can you trust?" Then the doctor had remarked, "Speaking of who can you trust, what's this I read in your own paper, Philip? It said some of your outfit over in the next county were forced at gunpoint to go into the fields at hundred-degree temperature and pick cotton. Well, that didn't happen—there isn't any cotton in June."

"I asked myself the same question you do. But I told myself, 'Well, they won't know the difference where the paper is read,'" said the young man.

"It's lying, though."

"We are dramatizing your hostility," the young bearded man had corrected him. "It's a way of reaching people. Don't forget—what they *might* have done to us is even worse."

"Still—you're not justified in putting a false front on things, in my opinion," Dr. Strickland had said. "Even for a good cause."

"*You* won't tell Herman Fairbrothers what's the matter with him," said his wife, and she jumped up from the table.

Later, as a result of this entertainment, he supposed, broken glass had been spread the length and breadth of his driveway. He hadn't seen in time what it wouldn't have occurred to him to look for, and Irene, standing in the door, had suddenly broken into laughter. . . .

He had eventually agreed that she have her wish and withdraw herself for as long as she liked. She was back now where she came from, where, he'd heard, they were all giving parties for her. He had offered to be the one to leave. "Leave Holden without its Dr. Strickland? You wouldn't to save your soul, would you?" she had replied. But as yet it was not divorce.

He thought he had been patient, but patience had made him tired. He was so increasingly tired, so sick and even bored with the bitterness, intractability that divided everybody and everything.

And suddenly, tonight, things had seemed just the way they used to seem. He had felt as though someone had stopped him on the street and offered to carry his load for a while—had insisted on it—some old, trusted, half-forgotten family friend that he had lost sight of since youth. Was it the sensation, now returning, that there was still allowed to everybody on earth a *self*—savage, death-defying, private? The pounding of his heart was like the assault of hope, throwing itself against him without a stop, merciless.

It seemed a long time that he had sat there, but the cars were still going by. Here came the caboose. He had counted them without knowing it—seventy-two cars. The grass fire at the edge of town came back in sight.

The doctor's feeling gradually ebbed away, like nausea put down. He started up the car and drove across the track and on up the hill.

Candles, some of them in dining-room candelabra, burned clear across the upstairs windows in the Fairbrothers' house. His own house, next door, was of course dark, and while he was wondering where Irene kept candles for emergencies he had driven on past his driveway for the second time that night. But the last place he wanted to go now was back to the club. He'd only tried it anyway to please his sister Annie. Now that he'd got by Miss Marcia Pope's dark window, he smelled her sweet-olive tree, solid as the bank building.

Here stood the bank, with its doorway onto the stairs to Drs. Strickland & Strickland, their names in black and gilt on three windows. He passed it. The haze and the moonlight were one over the squares, over the row of storefronts opposite with the line of poles thin as matchsticks rising to prop the one long strip of tin over the sidewalk, the drygoods store with its ornamental top that looked like opened paper fans held up by acrobats. He slowly started around the square. Behind its iron railings, the courthouse-and-jail stood barely emerging from its black cave of trees and only the slicked iron steps of the stile caught the moon. He drove on, past the shut-down movie house with all the light bulbs unscrewed from the sign that spelled out in empty sockets "BROADWAY." In front of the new post office the flagpole looked feathery, like the track of a jet that is already gone from the sky. From in front of the fire station, the fire chief's old Buick had gone home.

What was there, who was there, to keep him from going home? The doctor drove on slowly around. From the center of the deserted pavement, where cars and wagons stood parked helter-skelter by day, rose the water tank, pale as a balloon that might be only tethered here. A clanking came out of it, for the water supply too had been a source of trouble this summer—a hollow, irregular knocking now and then from inside, but the doctor no longer heard it. In turning his car, he saw a man lying prone and colorless in the arena of moonlight.

The lights of the car fastened on him and his clothes turned golden yellow. The man looked as if he had been sleeping all day in a bed of flowers and rolled in their pollen and were sleeping there still, with his face buried. He was covered his length in cottonseed meal.

Dr. Strickland stopped the car short and got out. His footsteps made the only sound in town. The man raised up on his hands and looked at him like a seal. Blood laced his head like a net through which he had broken. His wide tongue hung down out of his mouth. But the doctor knew the face.

"So you're alive, Dove, you're still alive?"

Slowly, hardly moving his tongue, Dove said: "Hide me." Then he hemorrhaged through the mouth.

Through the other half of the night, the doctor's calls came to him over the telephone—all chronic cases. Eva Duckett Fairbrothers telephoned at daylight.

"Feels low in his mind? Of course he feels low in his mind," he had finally shouted at her. "If I had what Herman has, I'd go down in the back yard and shoot myself!"

The *Sentinel,* owned and edited by Horatio Duckett, came o t on Tuesdays. The next week's back-page headline read, "TWO DEAD,

ONE ICEPICK. FREAK EPISODE AT NEGRO CHURCH." The subhead read, "No Racial Content Espied."

The doctor sat at the table in his dining room, finishing breakfast as he looked it over.

An employee of the Fairbrothers Cotton Seed Oil Mill and a Holden maid, both Negroes, were stabbed with a sharp instrument judged to be an icepick in a crowded churchyard here Saturday night. Both later expired. The incident was not believed by Mayor Herman Fairbrothers to carry racial significance.

"It warrants no stir," the Mayor declared.

The mishap boosted Holden's weekend death toll to 3. Billy Lee Warrum Jr. died Sunday before reaching a hospital in Jackson where he was rushed after being thrown from his new motorcycle while on his way there. He was the oldest son of Mrs. Billy Lee Warrum, Rt. 1. Reputedly en route to see his fiance he was pronounced dead on arrival. Multiple injuries was listed as the cause, the motorcycle having speeded into an interstate truck loaded to capacity with holiday turkeys. (See eye-witness account, page 1.)

As Holden marshal Curtis "Cowboy" Stubblefield reconstructed the earlier mishap, Ruby Gaddy, 21, was stabbed in full view of the departing congregation of the Holy Gospel Tabernacle as she attempted to leave the church when services were concluded at approximately 9:30 P.M. Saturday.

Witnesses said Dave Collins, 25, appeared outside the church as early as 9:15 P.M. having come directly from his shift at the mill where he had been employed since 1959. On being invited to come in and be seated he joked and said he preferred to wait outdoors as he was only wearing work clothes until the Gaddy woman, said to be his common-law wife, came outside the frame structure.

In the ensuing struggle at the conclusion of the services, the woman, who was a member of the choir, is believed to have received fatal icepick injuries to a vital organ, then to have wrested the weapon from her assailant and paid him back in kind. The Gaddy woman then walked to her mother's house but later collapsed.

Members of the congregation said they chased Collins 13 or 14 yds. in the direction of Snake Creek on the South side of the church then he fell to the ground and rolled approximately ten feet down the bank, rolling over six or seven times. Those present believed him to have succumbed since it was said the pick while in the woman's hand had been seen to drive in and pierce either his ear or his eye, either of which, is in close approximation to the brain. However, Collins later managed to crawl unseen from the creek and to make his way undetected up Railroad Avenue and to the Main St. door of an office occupied by Richard Strickland, M.D., above the Citizens Bank & Trust.

Witnesses were divided on which of the Negroes struck the first blow, Percy McAtee, pastor of the church, would not take sides but declared on being questioned by Marshal Stubblefield he was satisfied no outside agitators were involved and no arrests were made.

Collins was discovered on his own doorstep by Dr. Strickland who had been spending the evening at the Country Club. Collins is reported by Dr. Strickland to have expired shortly following his discovery, alleging his death to chest wounds.

"He offered no statement," Dr. Strickland said in response to a query.

Interviewed at home where he is recuperating from an ailment, Mayor Fairbrothers stated that he had not heard of there being trouble of any description at the Mill. "We are not trying to ruin our good reputation by inviting any, either," he said. "If the weatherman stays on our side we expect to attain capacity production in the latter part of next month," he stated. Saturday had been pay day as usual.

When Collins' body was searched by officers the pockets were empty however.

An icepick, reportedly the property of the Holy Gospel Tabernacle, was later found by Deacon Gaddy, 8, brother of Ruby Gaddy, covered with blood and carried it to Marshal Stubblefield. Stubblefield said it had been found in the grounds of the new $100,000.00 Negro school. It is believed to have served as the instrument in the twin slayings, the victims thus virtually succeeding in killing each other.

"Well, I'm surprised didn't more of them get hurt," said Rev. Alonzo Duckett, pastor of the Holden First Baptist Church. "And yet they expect to be seated in our churches." County Sheriff Vince Lasseter, reached fishing at Lake Bourne, said: "That's one they can't pin the blame on us for. That's how they treat their own kind. Please take note our conscience is clear."

Members of the Negro congregation said they could not account for Collins having left Snake Creek at the unspecified time. "We stood there a while and flipped some bottle caps down at him and threw his cap down after him right over his face and didn't get a stir out of him," stated an official of the congregation. "The way he acted, we figured he was dead. We would not have gone off and left him if we had known he was able to subsequently crawl up the hill." They stated Collins was not in the habit of worshipping at Holy Gospel Tabernacle.

The Gaddy woman died later this morning, also from chest wounds. No cause was cited for the fracas.

The cook had refilled his cup without his noticing. The doctor dropped the paper and carried his coffee out onto the little porch; it was still his morning habit.

The porch was at the back of the house, screened on three sides.

Sylvia's daybed used to stand here; it put her in the garden. No other houses were in sight; the gin could not be heard or even the traffic whining on the highway up off the bypass.

The roses were done for, the perennials too. But the surrounding crapemyrtle tree, the redbud, the dogwood, the Chinese tallow tree, and the pomegranate bush were bright as toys. The ailing pear tree had shed its leaves ahead of the rest. Past a falling wall of Michaelmas daisies that had not been tied up, a pair of flickers were rifling the grass, the cock in one part of the garden, the hen in another, picking at the devastation right through the bright leaves that appeared to have been left lying there just for them, probing and feeding. They stayed year round, he supposed, but it was only in the fall of the year that he ever noticed them. He was pretty sure that Sylvia had known the birds were there. Her eyes would follow birds when they flew across the garden. As he watched, the cock spread one wing, showy as a zebra's hide, and with a turn of his head showed his red seal.

Dr. Strickland swallowed the coffee and picked up his bag. It was all going to be just about as hard as seeing Herman and Eva Fairbrothers through. He thought that in all Holden, as of now, only Miss Marcia Pope was still quite able to take care of herself—or such was her own opinion.

Appendix A
Stories for Comparison

Invisible Man, by Ralph Ellison (b. 1914), is the best novel of black experience written so far in this country. Paradoxically, his story "Flying Home" is in many ways more detached in its treatment of the interracial situation than such stories by white authors as Faulkner's "Dry September" and "The Demonstrators" by Eudora Welty. The central encounter is between two blacks, Todd and Jefferson, and not between blacks and whites. The complex symbolism of constraint and of flight (by angels, aviators, and buzzards) gives an impression of metaphoric displacement. Written in 1943, in the middle of the Second World War, and going back through Todd's memories to a period well before this, the story provides a long perspective on racial antagonism in the United States, on what has changed in the past forty or fifty years, and what remains the same.

In the period between the world wars, the reputation of Ernest Hemingway (1898–1961) was even greater than Faulkner's, and in Europe his short stories were prized more highly than any of his other work. (Only the restrictions of his publisher prevent his being represented in this volume by the full quota of three stories, as in the first edition.) His use of a repetitive, vernacular style suggests a debt to Gertrude Stein and Sherwood Anderson, while his reserve and indirectness in expressing emotion reflect his pleasure in upper-class British understatement. Hemingway's characters, like their creator, are often sportsmen, soldiers, or both. His favorite theme is the need to maintain courage, pride in craft, and certain limited codes of conduct in a disordered and often apparently meaningless world. A very pure example of his mode of expressing these concerns, "In Another Country" is much more subtly patterned structurally than might at first appear.

Franz Kafka (1883–1924) was a German-speaking Jew who grew up in Prague in the days of the Austro-Hungarian empire. His anguished private obsessions, dramatized in his novels *The Trial* and *The Castle* and the short story "The Metamorphosis," came to symbolize the experience of Western man after the rise of communist and fascist totalitarianism. A devoted reader of the Danish theologian Kierkegaard, and acquainted also with Freudianism, Kafka expressed the psychic helplessness of the individual before the inexorable judgments passed upon him by society, by divine law, and by his own superego. Kafka's attitude toward experience is fundamentally religious, but for him religion remains the realm of the hidden, the incommensurable. His sense of an in-between state, neither of this world nor the next, is projected in "The Hunter Gracchus." As in so many of Kafka's stories—"The Country Doctor," for instance—its events have the vivid clarity and arbitrariness of a dream.

When he was in his early twenties, Rudyard Kipling (1865–1936) won an international reputation with his poems and short stories about the British in India. He had immense narrative skill, a journalistic flair for phrase, a painter's eye for local color, and a serious appreciation of the opposing cultures in India. His tales for children, *The Jungle Book* and *Just So Stories,* make delightful use of the classic Eastern modes of oral narration. As he grew older, and especially after the outbreak of the First World War, Kipling often chose—as did Tolstoy in his later years—to treat fundamental human experience with simple directness, in the manner of a fable. Such a story is "The Gardener," which evokes a type of Christianity almost totally incompatible with the frightening literalism of "The Tree" by Dylan Thomas.

Vladimir Nabokov was born in Russia, where his father was a wealthy, courageous liberal. The elder Nabokov fled abroad from the Bolsheviki only to be assassinated by rightists in Berlin. The son has lived in many countries, longest in America where, while lecturing at Cornell, he produced his best novels, *Pnin* (1957) and *Lolita* (1958) . He is not only a lepidopterist of scientific distinction (*Lolita* has been shown to parallel exactly his quest for a certain butterfly in its immature or nymphet stage), a poet (*Pale Fire*) and a vivid autobiographer (*Speak, Memory*), but also a phenomenal scholar and linguist. He translated Pushkin's *Eugene Onegin,* adding two fat volumes of commentary. His mastery of English as a second language equals Conrad's. Nearly all his fiction and poetry conceals an elaborate puzzle; he plays constantly with problems of time, reality, and moral responsibility. Though "That in Aleppo Once . . ." is on its surface a poignant tale of refugee lovers during the Second World War, it reaches the same metaphysical depths as Borges' "The Garden of Forking Paths."

Although Grace Paley's intense political activity—recently in support of draft resisters—has kept her literary output relatively small (*The Little Disturbances of Man, 1960*, was an unchanged reissue of an earlier book), she is one of the wittiest and most compassionate members of what may be called the New York or Bronx school of fiction. "The Loudest Voice" is held skillfully to the child's point of view, and while apparently lighthearted and humorous is actually a deeply sympathetic interethnic rendering of the Christian story, refracted through the speeches of deftly individualized characters. Principal among them, of course, is the child's eloquent father.

Regally beautiful, a wise critic, Katherine Anne Porter (b. 1890) was a greatly admired literary figure of the thirties and forties, the time of her best stories. She has been a model for younger Southern writers, among them Eudora Welty, Carson McCullers, and Truman Capote. Born in Texas of Southern forebears, Miss Porter lived for a long time in Mexico, where she knew and mirrored in her fiction such international figures as the painter Diego Rivera and the film-maker Sergei Eisenstein. Among her best stories are "Noon Wine," "Flowering Judas," and "María Concepción." Though so much less explicitly dramatic, "The Grave" resembles Ellison's "Flying Home" in its complex mingling of elements that are at once literal and figurative—the buried memories that came out of an actual grave, and the beautiful tiny rabbits killed wantonly by a male hunter before they could be born.

Dylan Thomas (1914–53) was the first poet since Hopkins to write with such manifest joy in the richness of the English language. His stories are as lyrical as his verse, but with a clarity of form and theme that is sometimes missing in his poems, which tend to be difficult. "The Tree" is a terrifying tribute to the power of imagination when it has been taken over by mythic forces in a complete break—as in Kafka—with the everyday reality that still supplies the materials through which these forces work.

Leo Tolstoy (1828–1910) had always been concerned with religious and moral questions, but these had become a dominant preoccupation by the time he wrote "After the Ball" in 1903. They led him in *What Is Art* (1898) at the age of seventy-five to reject as decadent aestheticism many of the best elements of the plays of Shakespeare and of his own great novels *War and Peace* (1869) and *Anna Karenina* (1877). In "After the Ball" he uses an actual experience of his student days in the Tartar city of Kazan. Despite the doctrine quoted from him in Appendix B: The Writers on Their Art, he does not hesitate to tell straightforwardly a tale of evil, of the inconsistency of human values, and let the implications speak for themselves. This is a profound story that goes to the source of the anguished soul-searching into which Americans have been forced by the tragic events of our period.

Flying Home

RALPH ELLISON

When Todd came to, he saw two faces suspended above him in a sun so hot and blinding that he could not tell if they were black or white. He stirred, feeling a pain that burned as though his whole body had been laid open to the sun which glared into his eyes. For a moment an old fear of being touched by white hands seized him. Then the very sharpness of the pain began slowly to clear his head. Sounds came to him dimly. He done come to. Who are they? he thought. Naw he ain't, I coulda sworn he was white. Then he heard clearly:

"You hurt bad?"

Something within him uncoiled. It was a Negro sound.

"He's still out," he heard.

"Give 'im time. . . . Say, son, you hurt bad?"

Was he? There was that awful pain. He lay rigid, hearing their breathing and trying to weave a meaning between them and his being stretched painfully upon the ground. He watched them warily, his mind traveling back over a painful distance. Jagged scenes, swiftly unfolding as in a movie trailer, reeled through his mind, and he saw himself piloting a tailspinning plane and landing and falling from the cockpit and trying to stand. Then, as in a great silence, he remembered the sound of crunching bone, and now, looking up into the anxious faces of an old Negro man and a boy from where he lay in the same field, the memory sickened him and he wanted to remember no more.

"How you feel, son?"

Todd hesitated, as though to answer would be to admit an inacceptable weakness. Then, "It's my ankle," he said.

"Which one?"

"The left."

With a sense of remoteness he watched the old man bend and remove his boot, feeling the pressure ease.

"That any better?"

"A lot. Thank you."

He had the sensation of discussing someone else, that his concern was with some far more important thing, which for some reason escaped him.

"You done broke it bad," the old man said. "We have to get you to a doctor."

He felt that he had been thrown into a tailspin. He looked at his watch; how long had he been here? He knew there was but one important thing in the world, to get the plane back to the field before his officers were displeased.

"Help me up," he said. "Into the ship."

"But it's broke too bad. . . ."

"Give me your arm!"

"But, son . . ."

Clutching the old man's arm he pulled himself up, keeping his left leg clear, thinking, "I'd never make him understand," as the leather-smooth face came parallel with his own.

"Now, let's see."

He pushed the old man back, hearing a bird's insistent shrill. He swayed giddily. Blackness washed over him, like infinity.

"You best sit down."

"No, I'm O.K."

"But, son. You jus' gonna make it worse. . . ."

It was a fact that everything in him cried out to deny, even against the flaming pain in his ankle. He would have to try again.

"You mess with that ankle they have to cut your foot off," he heard.

Holding his breath, he started up again. It pained so badly that he had to bite his lips to keep from crying out and he allowed them to help him down with a pang of despair.

"It's best you take it easy. We gon' git you a doctor."

Of all the luck, he thought. Of all the rotten luck, now I have done it. The fumes of high-octane gasoline clung in the heat, taunting him.

"We kin ride him into town on old Ned," the boy said.

Ned? He turned, seeing the boy point toward an ox team browsing where the buried blade of a plow marked the end of a furrow. Thoughts of himself riding an ox through the town, past streets full of white faces, down the concrete runways of the airfield made swift images of humiliation in his mind. With a pang he remembered his girl's last letter. "Todd," she had written, "I don't need the papers to tell me you had the intelligence to fly. And I have always known you to be as brave as anyone else. The papers annoy me. Don't you be contented to prove over and over again that you're brave or skillful just because you're black, Todd. I think they keep beating that dead horse because they don't want to say why you boys are not yet fighting. I'm really disappointed, Todd. Anyone with brains can learn to fly, but then what? What about using it, and who will you use it for? I wish, dear, you'd write about this. I sometimes think they're playing a trick on us. It's very humiliating. . . ." He wiped cold sweat from his face, thinking, What does she know of humiliation? She's never been down South. Now the humiliation would come. When you must have them judge you, knowing that they never accept your mistakes as your own, but hold it against your whole race—that was humiliation. Yes, and humiliation was when you could never be simply yourself, when you were always a part of this old black ignorant man. Sure, he's all right. Nice and kind and helpful. But he's not you. Well, there's one humiliation I can spare myself.

"No," he said, "I have orders not to leave the ship. . . ."

"Aw," the old man said. Then turning to the boy, "Teddy, then you better hustle down to Mister Graves and get him to come. . . ."

"No, wait!" he protested before he was fully aware. Graves might be white. "Just have him get word to the field, please. They'll take care of the rest."

He saw the boy leave, running.

"How far does he have to go?"

"Might' nigh a mile."

He rested back, looking at the dusty face of his watch. But now they know something has happened, he thought. In the ship there was a perfectly good radio, but it was useless. The old fellow would never operate it. That buzzard knocked me back a hundred years, he thought. Irony danced within him like the gnats circling the old man's head. With all I've learned I'm dependent upon this "peasant's" sense of time and space. His leg throbbed. In the plane, instead of time being measured by the rhythms of pain and a kid's legs, the instruments would have told him at a glance. Twisting upon his elbows he saw where dust had powdered the plane's fuselage, feeling the lump form in his throat that was always there when he thought of flight. It's crouched there, he thought, like the abandoned shell of a locust. I'm naked without it. Not a machine, a suit of clothes you wear. And with a sudden embarrassment and wonder he whispered, "It's the only dignity I have. . . ."

He saw the old man watching, his torn overalls clinging limply to him in the heat. He felt a sharp need to tell the old man what he felt. But that would be meaningless. If I tried to explain why I need to fly back, he'd think I was simply afraid of white officers. But it's more than fear . . . a sense of anguish clung to him like the veil of sweat that hugged his face. He watched the old man, hearing him humming snatches of a tune as he admired the plane. He felt a furtive sense of resentment. Such old men often came to the field to watch the pilots with childish eyes. At first it had made him proud; they had been a meaningful part of a new experience. But soon he realized they did not understand his accomplishments and they came to shame and embarrass him, like the distasteful praise of an idiot. A part of the meaning of flying had gone then, and he had not been able to regain it. If I were a prizefighter I would be more human, he thought. Not a monkey doing tricks, but a man. They were pleased simply that he was a Negro who could fly, and that was not enough. He felt cut off from them by age, by understanding, by sensibility, by technology and by his need to measure himself against the mirror of other men's appreciation. Somehow he felt betrayed, as he had when as a child he grew to discover that his father was dead. Now for him any real appreciation lay with his white officers; and with them he could never be sure. Between ignorant black men and condescending whites, his course of flight seemed mapped by the nature of things

away from all needed and natural landmarks. Under some sealed
orders, couched in ever more technical and mysterious terms, his
path curved swiftly away from both the shame the old man symbol-
ized and the cloudy terrain of white men's regard. Flying blind, he
knew but one point of landing and there he would receive his wings.
After that the enemy would appreciate his skill and he would assume
his deepest meaning, he thought sadly, neither from those who con-
descended nor from those who praised without understanding, but
from the enemy who would recognize his manhood and skill in terms
of hate. . . .

He sighed, seeing the oxen making queer, prehistoric shadows
against the dry brown earth.

"You just take it easy, son," the old man soothed. "That boy
won't take long. Crazy as he is about airplanes."

"I can wait," he said.

"What kinda airplane you call this here'n?"

"An Advanced Trainer," he said, seeing the old man smile. His
fingers were like gnarled dark wood against the metal as he touched
the low-slung wing.

"'Bout how fast can she fly?"

"Over two hundred an hour."

"Lawd! That's so fast I bet it don't seem like you moving!"

Holding himself rigid, Todd opened his flying suit. The shade had
gone and he lay in a ball of fire.

"You mind if I take a look inside? I was always curious to see. . . ."

"Help yourself. Just don't touch anything."

He heard him climb upon the metal wing, grunting. Now the
questions would start. Well, so you don't have to think to answer. . . .

He saw the old man looking over into the cockpit, his eyes bright
as a child's.

"You must have to know a lot to work all these here things."

He was silent, seeing him step down and kneel beside him.

"Son, how come you want to fly way up there in the air?"

Because it's the most meaningful act in the world . . . because
it makes me less like you, he thought.

But he said: "Because I like it, I guess. It's as good a way to fight
and die as I know."

"Yeah? I guess you right," the old man said. "But how long you think before they gonna let you all fight?"

He tensed. This was the question all Negroes asked, put with the same timid hopefulness and longing that always opened a greater void within him than that he had felt beneath the plane the first time he had flown. He felt light-headed. It came to him suddenly that there was something sinister about the conversation, that he was flying unwillingly into unsafe and uncharted regions. If he could only be insulting and tell this old man who was trying to help him to shut up!

"I bet you one thing . . ."

"Yes?"

"That you was plenty scared coming down."

He did not answer. Like a dog on a trail the old man seemed to smell out his fears and he felt anger bubble within him.

"You sho' scared me. When I seen you coming down in that thing with it a-rollin' and a-jumpin' like a pitchin' hoss, I thought sho' you was a goner. I almost had me a stroke!"

He saw the old man grinning, "Ever'thin's been happening round here this morning, come to think of it."

"Like what?" he asked.

"Well, first thing I know, here come two white fellers looking for Mister Rudolph, that's Mister Graves's cousin. That got me worked up right away. . . ."

"Why?"

"Why? 'Cause he done broke outta the crazy house, that's why. He liable to kill somebody," he said. "They oughta have him by now though. Then here you come. First I think it's one of them white boys. Then doggone if you don't fall outta there. Lawd, I'd done heard about you boys but I haven't never seen one o' you-all. Cain't tell you how it felt to see somebody what look like me in a airplane!"

The old man talked on, the sound streaming around Todd's thoughts like air flowing over the fuselage of a flying plane. You were a fool, he thought, remembering how before the spin the sun had blazed bright against the billboard signs beyond the town, and how a boy's blue kite had bloomed beneath him, tugging gently in the wind like a strange, odd-shaped flower. He had once flown such kites himself and tried to find the boy at the end of the invisible cord. But he had been flying too high and too fast. He had climbed steeply away in exultation. Too steeply, he thought. And one of the first rules you learn is that if the angle of thrust is too steep the plane goes into a spin. And then, instead of pulling out of it and going into a dive you let a buzzard panic you. A lousy buzzard!

"Son, what made all that blood on the glass?"

"A buzzard," he said, remembering how the blood and feathers had sprayed back against the hatch. It had been as though he had flown into a storm of blood and blackness.

"Well, I declare! They's lots of 'em around here. They after dead things. Don't eat nothing what's alive."

"A little bit more and he would have made a meal out of me," Todd said grimly.

"They bad luck all right. Teddy's got a name for 'em, calls 'em jimcrows," the old man laughed.

"It's a damned good name."

"They the damnedest birds. Once I seen a hoss all stretched out like he was sick, you know. So I hollers, 'Gid up from there, suh!' Just to make sho! An' doggone, son, if I don't see two ole jimcrows come flying right up outa that hoss's insides! Yessuh! The sun was shinin' on 'em and they couldn't a been no greasier if they'd been eating barbecue."

Todd thought he would vomit, his stomach quivered.

"You made that up," he said.

"Nawsuh! Saw him just like I see you."

"Well, I'm glad it was you."

"You see lots a funny things down here, son."

"No, I'll let you see them," he said.

"By the way, the white folks round here don't like to see you boys up there in the sky. They ever bother you?"

"No."

"Well, they'd like to."

"Someone always wants to bother someone else," Todd said. "How do you know?"

"I just know."

"Well," he said defensively, "no one has bothered us."

Blood pounded in his ears as he looked away into space. He tensed, seeing a black spot in the sky, and strained to confirm what he could not clearly see.

"What does that look like to you?" he asked excitedly.

"Just another bad luck, son."

Then he saw the movement of wings with disappointment. It was gliding smoothly down, wings outspread, tail feathers gripping the air, down swiftly—gone behind the green screen of trees. It was like a bird he had imagined there, only the sloping branches of the pines remained, sharp against the pale stretch of sky. He lay barely breathing and stared at the point where it had disappeared, caught in a spell of loathing and admiration. Why did they make them so disgusting and yet teach them to fly so well? It's like when I was up in heaven, he heard, starting.

The old man was chuckling, rubbing his stubbled chin.

"What did you say?"

"Sho', I died and went to heaven . . . maybe by time I tell you about it they be done come after you."

"I hope so," he said wearily.

"You boys ever sit around and swap lies?"

"Not often. Is this going to be one?"

"Well, I ain't so sho', on account of it took place when I was dead."

The old man paused, "That wasn't no lie 'bout the buzzards, though."

"All right," he said.

"Sho' you want to hear 'bout heaven?"

"Please," he answered, resting his head upon his arm.

"Well, I went to heaven and right away started to sproutin' me some wings. Six good ones, they was. Just like them the white angels had. I couldn't hardly believe it. I was so glad that I went off on some clouds by myself and tried 'em out. You know, 'cause I didn't want to make a fool outta myself the first thing. . . ."

It's an old tale, Todd thought. Told me years ago. Had forgotten. But at least it will keep him from talking about buzzards.

He closed his eyes, listening.

". . . First thing I done was to git up on a low cloud and jump off. And doggone, boy, if them wings didn't work! First I tried the right; then I tried the left; then I tried 'em both together. Then Lawd, I started to move on out among the folks. I let 'em see me. . . ."

He saw the old man gesturing flight with his arms, his face full of mock pride as he indicated an imaginary crowd, thinking, It'll be in the newspapers, as he heard, ". . . so I went and found me some colored angels—somehow I didn't believe I was an angel till I seen a real black one, ha, yes! Then I was sho'—but they tole me I better come down 'cause us colored folks had to wear a special kin' a harness when we flew. That was how come they wasn't flyin'. Oh yes, an' you had to be extra strong for a black man even, to fly with one of them harnesses. . . ."

This is a new turn, Todd thought, what's he driving at?

"So I said to myself, I ain't gonna be bothered with no harness! Oh naw! 'Cause if God let you sprout wings you oughta have sense enough not to let nobody make you wear something what gits in the way of flyin'. So I starts to flyin'. Heck, son," he chuckled, his eyes twinkling, "you know I had to let eve'ybody know that old Jefferson could fly good as anybody else. And I could too, fly smooth as a bird! I could even loop-the-loop—only I had to make sho' to keep my long white robe down roun' my ankles. . . ."

Todd felt uneasy. He wanted to laugh at the joke, but his body refused, as of an independent will. He felt as he had as a child when after he had chewed a sugar-coated pill which his mother had given him, she had laughed at his efforts to remove the terrible taste.

". . . Well," he heard, "I was doing all right 'til I got to speeding. Found out I could fan up a right strong breeze, I could fly so fast. I could do all kin'sa stunts too. I started flying up to the stars and divin' down and zooming roun' the moon. Man, I like to scare the devil outa some ole white angels. I was raisin' hell. Not that I meant any harm, son. But I was just feeling good. It was so good to know I was free at last. I accidentally knocked the tips offa some stars and they tell me I caused a storm and a coupla lynchings down here in Macon County—though I swear I believe them boys what said that was making up lies on me. . . ."

He's mocking me, Todd thought angrily. He thinks it's a joke. Grinning down at me . . . His throat was dry. He looked at his watch; why the hell didn't they come? Since they had to, why? One day I was flying down one of them heavenly streets. You got yourself into it, Todd thought. Like Jonah in the whale.

"Justa throwin' feathers in everybody's face. An' ole Saint Peter called me in. Said, 'Jefferson, tell me two things, what you doin' flyin' without a harness; an' how come you flyin' so fast?' So I tole him I was flyin' without a harness 'cause it got in my way, but I couldn'ta been flyin' so fast, 'cause I wasn't usin' but one wing. Saint Peter said, 'You wasn't flyin' with but one wing?' 'Yessuh,' I says, scared-like. So he says, 'Well, since you got sucha extra fine pair of wings you can leave off yo' harness awhile. But from now on none of that there one-wing flyin', 'cause you gittin' up too damn much speed!' "

And with one mouth full of bad teeth you're making too damned much talk, thought Todd. Why don't I send him after the boy? His body ached from the hard ground and seeking to shift his position he twisted his ankle and hated himself for crying out.

"It gittin' worse?"

"I . . . I twisted it," he groaned.

"Try not to think about it, son. That's what I do."

He bit his lip, fighting pain with counter-pain as the voice resumed its rhythmical droning. Jefferson seemed caught in his own creation.

". . . After all that trouble I just floated roun' heaven in slow motion. But I forgot, like colored folks will do, and got to flyin' with one wing again. This time I was restin' my old broken arm and got to flyin' fast enough to shame the devil. I was comin' so fast, Lawd, I got myself called befo' ole Saint Peter again. He said, 'Jeff, didn't I warn you 'bout that speedin'?' 'Yessuh,' I says, 'but it was an accident.' He looked at me sad-like and shook his head and I knowed I was gone. He said, 'Jeff, you and that speedin' is a danger to the heavenly community. If I was to let you keep on flyin', heaven wouldn't be nothin' but uproar. Jeff, you got to go!' Son, I argued and pleaded with that old white man, but it didn't do a bit of good. They rushed me straight to them pearly gates and gimme a parachute and a map of the state of Alabama . . .' "

Todd heard him laughing so that he could hardly speak, making a screen between them upon which his humiliation glowed like fire.

"Maybe you'd better stop awhile," he said, his voice unreal.

"Ain't much more," Jefferson laughed. "When they gimme the parachute ole Saint Peter ask me if I wanted to say a few words before I went. I felt so bad I couldn't hardly look at him, specially with all them white angels standin' around. Then somebody laughed and made me mad. So I tole him, 'Well, you done took my wings. And you puttin' me out. You got charge of things so's I can't do nothin' about it. But you got to admit just this: While I was up here I was the flyinest sonofabitch what ever hit heaven!' "

At the burst of laughter Todd felt such an intense humiliation that only great violence would wash it away. The laughter which shook the old man like a boiling purge set up vibrations of guilt within him which not even the intricate machinery of the plane would have been adequate to transform and he heard himself screaming, "Why do you laugh at me this way?"

He hated himself at that moment, but he had lost control. He saw Jefferson's mouth fall open, "What—?"

"Answer me!"

His blood pounded as though it would surely burst his temples and he tried to reach the old man and fell, screaming, "Can I help it because they won't let us actually fly? Maybe we are a bunch of buzzards feeding on a dead horse, but we can hope to be eagles, can't we? Can't we?"

He fell back, exhausted, his ankle pounding. The saliva was like straw in his mouth. If he had the strength he would strangle this old man. This grinning, gray-headed clown who made him feel as he felt when watched by the white officers at the field. And yet this old man had neither power, prestige, rank nor technique. Nothing that could rid him of this terrible feeling. He watched him, seeing his face struggle to express a turmoil of feeling.

"What you mean, son? What you talking 'bout . . . ?"

"Go away. Go tell your tales to the white folks."

"But I didn't mean nothing like that. . . . I . . . I wasn't tryin' to hurt your feelings. . . ."

"Please. Get the hell away from me!"

"But I didn't, son. I didn't mean all them things a-tall."

Todd shook as with a chill, searching Jefferson's face for a trace of the mockery he had seen there. But now the face was somber and tired and old. He was confused. He could not be sure that there had ever been laughter there, that Jefferson had ever really laughed in his whole life. He saw Jefferson reach out to touch him and shrank away, wondering if anything except the pain, now causing his vision to waver, was real. Perhaps he had imagined it all.

"Don't let it get you down, son," the voice said pensively.

He heard Jefferson sigh wearily, as though he felt more than he could say. His anger ebbed, leaving only the pain.

"I'm sorry," he mumbled.

"You just wore out with pain, was all. . . ."

He saw him through a blur, smiling. And for a second he felt the embarrassed silence of understanding flutter between them.

"What you was doin' flyin' over this section, son? Wasn't you scared they might shoot you for a cow?"

Todd tensed. Was he being laughed at again? But before he could decide, the pain shook him and a part of him was lying calmly behind the screen of pain that had fallen between them, recalling the first time he had ever seen a plane. It was as though an endless series of hangars had been shaken ajar in the air base of his memory and from each, like a young wasp emerging from its cell, arose the memory of a plane.

The first time I ever saw a plane I was very small and planes were new in the world. I was four-and-a-half and the only plane that I had ever seen was a model suspended from the ceiling of the automobile exhibit at the State Fair. But I did not know that it was only a model. I did not know how large a real plane was, nor how expensive. To me it was a fascinating toy, complete in itself, which my mother said could only be owned by rich little white boys. I stood rigid with admiration, my head straining backwards as I watched the gray little plane describing arcs above the gleaming tops of the automobiles. And I vowed that, rich or poor, someday I would own such a toy. My mother had to drag me out of the exhibit and not even the merry-go-round, the Ferris wheel, or the racing horses could hold my attention for the rest of the Fair. I was too busy imitating the tiny drone of the plane with my lips, and imitating with my hands the motion, swift and circling, that it made in flight.

After that I no longer used the pieces of lumber that lay about our back yard to construct wagons and autos . . . now it was used for airplanes. I built biplanes, using pieces of board for wings, a small box for the fuselage, another piece of wood for the rudder. The trip to the Fair had brought something new into my small world. I asked my mother repeatedly when the Fair would come back again. I'd lie in the grass and watch the sky, and each fighting bird became a soaring plane. I would have been good a year just to have seen a plane again. I became a nuisance to everyone with my questions about airplanes. But planes were new to the old folks, too, and there was little that they could tell me. Only my uncle knew some of the answers. And better still, he could carve propellers from pieces of wood that would whirl rapidly in the wind, wobbling noisily upon oiled nails.

I wanted a plane more than I'd wanted anything; more than I wanted the red wagon with rubber tires, more than the train that ran on a track with its train of cars. I asked my mother over and over again:

"Mamma?"

"What do you want, boy?" she'd say.

"Mamma, will you get mad if I ask you?" I'd say.

"What do you want now? I ain't got time to be answering a lot of fool questions. What you want?"

"Mamma, when you gonna get me one . . . ?" I'd ask.

"Get you one what?" she'd say.

"You know, Mamma; what I been asking you. . . ."

"Boy," she'd say, "if you don't want a spanking you better come on an' tell me what you talking about so I can get on with my work."

"Aw, Mamma, you know. . . ."

"What I just tell you?" she'd say.

"I mean when you gonna buy me a airplane."

"Airplane! Boy, is you crazy? How many times I have to tell you to stop that foolishness. I done told you them things cost too much. I bet I'm gon' wham the living daylight out of you if you don't quit worrying me 'bout them things!"

But this did not stop me, and a few days later I'd try all over again.

Then one day a strange thing happened. It was spring and for some reason I had been hot and irritable all morning. It was a beautiful spring. I could feel it as I played barefoot in the backyard. Blossoms hung from the thorny black locust trees like clusters of fragrant white grapes. Butterflies flickered in the sunlight above the short new dew-wet grass. I had gone in the house for bread and butter and coming out I heard a steady unfamiliar drone. It was unlike anything I had ever heard before. I tried to place the sound. It was no use. It was a sensation like that I had when searching for my father's watch, heard ticking unseen in a room. It made me feel as though I had forgotten to perform some task that my mother had ordered . . . then I located it, overhead. In the sky, flying quite low and about a hundred yards off was a plane! It came so slowly that it seemed barely to move. My mouth hung wide; my bread and butter fell into the dirt. I wanted to jump up and down and cheer. And when the idea struck I trembled with excitement: "Some little white boy's plane's done flew away and all I got to do is stretch out my hands and it'll be mine!" It was a little plane like that at the Fair, flying no higher than the eaves of our roof. Seeing it come steadily forward I felt the world grow warm with promise. I opened the screen and climbed over it and clung there, waiting. I would catch the plane as it came over and swing down fast and run into the house before anyone could see me. Then no one could come to claim the plane. It droned nearer. Then when it hung like a silver cross in the blue directly above me I stretched out my hand and grabbed. It was like sticking my finger through a soap bubble. The plane flew on, as though I had simply blown my breath after it. I grabbed again, frantically, trying to catch the tail. My fingers clutched the air and disappointment surged tight and hard in my throat. Giving one last desperate grasp, I strained forward. My fingers ripped from the screen. I was falling. The ground burst hard against me. I drummed the earth with my heels and when my breath returned, I lay there bawling.

My mother rushed through the door.

"What's the matter, chile! What on earth is wrong with you?"

"It's gone! It's gone!"

"What gone?"

"The airplane . . ."

"Airplane?"

"Yessum, jus' like the one at the Fair. . . . I . . . I tried to stop it an' it kep' right on going. . . ."

"When, boy?"

"Just now," I cried, through my tears.

"Where it go, boy, what way?"

"Yonder, there . . ."

She scanned the sky, her arms akimbo and her checkered apron flapping in the wind as I pointed to the fading plane. Finally she looked down at me, slowly shaking her head.

"It's gone! It's gone!" I cried.

"Boy, is you a fool?" she said. "Don't you see that there's a real airplane 'stead of one of them toy ones?"

"Real . . . ?" I forgot to cry. "Real?"

"Yass, real. Don't you know that thing you reaching for is bigger'n a auto? You here trying to reach for it and I bet it's flying 'bout two hundred miles higher'n this roof." She was disgusted with me. "You come on in this house before somebody else sees what a fool you done turned out to be. You must think these here lil ole arms of you'n is mighty long. . . ."

I was carried into the house and undressed for bed and the doctor was called. I cried bitterly, as much from the disappointment of finding the plane so far beyond my reach as from the pain.

When the doctor came I heard my mother telling him about the plane and asking if anything was wrong with my mind. He explained that I had had a fever for several hours. But I was kept in bed for a week and I constantly saw the plane in my sleep, flying just beyond my fingertips, sailing so slowly that it seemed barely to move. And each time I'd reach out to grab it I'd miss and through each dream I'd hear my grandma warning:

> *Young man, young man,*
> *Yo' arms too short*
> *To box with God. . . .*

"Hey, son!"

At first he did not know where he was and looked at the old man pointing, with blurred eyes.

"Ain't that one of you-all's airplanes coming after you?"

As his vision cleared he saw a small black shape above a distant field, soaring through waves of heat. But he could not be sure and with the pain he feared that somehow a horrible recurring fantasy of being split in twain by the whirling blades of a propeller had come true.

"You think he sees us?" he heard.

"See? I hope so."

"He's coming like a bat outa hell!"

Straining, he heard the faint sound of a motor and hoped it would soon be over.

"How you feeling?"

"Like a nightmare," he said.

"Hey, he's done curved back the other way!"

"Maybe he saw us," he said. "Maybe he's gone to send out the ambulance and ground crew." And, he thought with despair, maybe he didn't even see us.

"Where did you send the boy?"

"Down to Mister Graves," Jefferson said. "Man what owns this land."

"Do you think he phoned?"

Jefferson looked at him quickly.

"Aw sho'. Dabney Graves is got a bad name on accounta them killings but he'll call though. . . ."

"What killings?"

"Them five fellers . . . ain't you heard?" he asked with surprise.

"No."

"Everybody knows 'bout Dabney Graves, especially the colored. He done killed enough of us."

Todd had the sensation of being caught in a white neighborhood after dark.

"What did they do?" he asked.

"Thought they was men," Jefferson said. "An' some he owed money, like he do me. . . ."

"But why do you stay here?"

"You black, son."

"I know, but . . ."

"You have to come by the white folks, too."

He turned away from Jefferson's eyes, at once consoled and accused. And I'll have to come by them soon, he thought with despair. Closing his eyes, he heard Jefferson's voice as the sun burned blood-red upon his lips.

"I got nowhere to go," Jefferson said, "an' they'd come after me if I did. But Dabney Graves is a funny fellow. He's all the time making jokes. He can be mean as hell, then he's liable to turn right around and back the colored against the white folks. I seen him do it. But me, I hates him for that more'n anything else. 'Cause just as soon as he gits tired helping a man he don't care what happens to him. He just leaves him stone cold. And then the other white folks is double hard on anybody he done helped. For him it's just a joke. He don't give a hilla beans for nobody—but hisself. . . ."

Todd listened to the thread of detachment in the old man's voice. It was as though he held his words arm's length before him to avoid their destructive meaning.

"He'd just as soon do you a favor and then turn right around and have you strung up. Me, I stays outa his way 'cause down here that's what you gotta do."

If my ankle would only ease for a while, he thought. The closer I spin toward the earth the blacker I become, flashed through his mind. Sweat ran into his eyes and he was sure that he would never see the plane if his head continued whirling. He tried to see Jefferson, what it was that Jefferson held in his hand? It was a little black man, another Jefferson! A little black Jefferson that shook with fits of belly-laughter while the other Jefferson looked on with detachment. Then Jefferson looked up from the thing in his hand and turned to speak, but Todd was far away, searching the sky for a plane in a hot dry land on a day and age he had long forgotten. He was going mysteriously with his mother through empty streets where black faces peered from behind drawn shades and someone was rapping at a window and he was looking back to see a hand and a frightened face frantically beckoning from a cracked door and his mother was looking down the empty perspective of the street and shaking her head and hurrying him along and at first it was only a flash he saw and a motor was droning as through the sun-glare he saw it gleaming silver as it circled and he was seeing a burst like a puff of white smoke·and hearing his mother yell, Come along, boy, I got no time for them fool airplanes, I got no time, and he saw it a second time, the plane flying high, and the burst appeared suddenly and fell slowly, billowing out and sparkling like fireworks and he was watching and being hurried along as the air filled with a flurry of white pinwheeling cards that caught in the wind and scattered over the rooftops and into the gutters and a woman was running and snatching a card and reading it and screaming and he darted into the shower, grabbing as in winter he grabbed for snow-flakes and bounding away at his mother's, Come on here, boy! Come on, I say! and he was watching as she took the card away, seeing her face grow puzzled and turning taut as her voice quavered, "Niggers Stay From The Polls," and died to a moan of terror as he saw the eyeless sockets of a white hood staring at him from the card and above he saw the plane spiraling gracefully, agleam in the sun like a fiery sword. And seeing it soar he was caught, transfixed between a terrible horror and a horrible fascination.

The sun was not so high now, and Jefferson was calling and gradually he saw three figures moving across the curving roll of the field.

"Look like some doctors, all dressed in white," said Jefferson.

They're coming at last, Todd thought. And he felt such a release of tension within him that he thought he would faint. But no sooner did he close his eyes than he was seized and he was struggling with three white men who were forcing his arms into some kind of coat. It was too much for him, his arms were pinned to his sides and as the pain blazed in his eyes, he realized that it was a straitjacket. What filthy joke was this?

"That oughta hold him, Mister Graves," he heard.

His total energies seemed focused in his eyes as he searched their faces. That was Graves; the other two wore hospital uniforms. He was poised between two poles of fear and hate as he heard the one called Graves saying, "He looks kinda purty in that there suit, boys. I'm glad you dropped by."

"This boy ain't crazy, Mister Graves," one of the others said. "He needs a doctor, not us. Don't see how you led us way out here anyway. It might be a joke to you, but your cousin Rudolph liable to kill somebody. White folks or niggers, don't make no difference. . . ."

Todd saw the man turn red with anger. Graves looked down upon him, chuckling.

"This niggah belongs in a straitjacket, too, boys. I knowed that the minit Jeff's kid said something 'bout a nigguh flyer. You all know you cain't let the nigguh git up that high without his going crazy. The nigguh brain ain't built right for high altitudes. . . ."

Todd watched the drawling red face, feeling that all the unnamed horror and obscenities that he had ever imagined stood materialized before him.

"Let's git outta here," one of the attendants said.

Todd saw the other reach toward him, realizing for the first time that he lay upon a stretcher as he yelled.

"Don't put your hands on me!"

They drew back, surprised.

"What's that you say, nigguh?" asked Graves.

He did not answer and thought that Graves's foot was aimed at his head. It landed on his chest and he could hardly breathe. He coughed helplessly, seeing Graves's lips stretch taut over his yellow teeth, and tried to shift his head. It was as though a half-dead fly was dragging slowly across his face and a bomb seemed to burst within him. Blasts of hot, hysterical laughter tore from his chest, causing his eyes to pop and he felt that the veins in his neck would surely burst. And then a part of him stood behind it all, watching the surprise in Graves's red face and his own hysteria. He thought he would never stop, he would laugh himself to death. It rang in his ears like Jefferson's laughter and he looked for him, centering his eyes desperately upon his face, as though somehow he had become his sole salvation in an insane world of outrage and humiliation. It brought a certain relief. He was suddenly aware that although his body was still contorted it was an echo that no longer rang in his ears. He heard Jefferson's voice with gratitude.

"Mister Graves, the Army done tole him not to leave his airplane."

"Nigguh, Army or no, you gittin' off my land! That airplane can stay 'cause it was paid for by taxpayers' money. But you gittin' off. An' dead or alive, it don't make no difference to me."

Todd was beyond it now, lost in a world of anguish.

"Jeff," Graves said, "you and Teddy come and grab holt. I want you to take this here black eagle over to that nigguh airfield and leave him."

Jefferson and the boy approached him silently. He looked away, realizing and doubting at once that only they could release him from his overpowering sense of isolation.

They bent for the stretcher. One of the attendants moved toward Teddy.

"Think you can manage it, boy?"

"I think I can, suh," Teddy said.

"Well, you better go behind then, and let yo' pa go ahead so's to keep that leg elevated."

He saw the white men walking ahead as Jefferson and the boy carried him along in silence. Then they were pausing and he felt a hand wiping his face; then he was moving again. And it was as though he had been lifted out of his isolation, back into the world of men. A new current of communication flowed between the man and boy and himself. They moved him gently. Far away he heard a mockingbird liquidly calling. He raised his eyes, seeing a buzzard poised unmoving in space. For a moment the whole afternoon seemed suspended and he waited for the horror to seize him again. Then like a song within his head he heard the boy's soft humming and saw the dark bird glide into the sun and glow like a bird of flaming gold.

In Another Country

ERNEST HEMINGWAY

In the fall the war was always there, but we did not go to it any more. It was cold in the fall in Milan and the dark came very early. Then the electric lights came on, and it was pleasant along the streets looking in the windows. There was much game hanging outside the shops, and the snow powdered in the fur of the foxes and the wind blew their tails. The deer hung stiff and heavy and empty, and small birds blew in the wind and the wind turned their feathers. It was a cold fall and the wind came down from the mountains.

We were all at the hospital every afternoon, and there were different ways of walking across the town through the dusk to the hospital. Two of the ways were alongside canals, but they were long. Always, though, you crossed a bridge across a canal to enter the hospital. There was a choice of three bridges. On one of them a woman sold roasted chestnuts. It was warm, standing in front of her charcoal fire, and the chestnuts were warm afterward in your pocket. The hospital was very old and very beautiful, and you entered through a gate and walked across a courtyard and out a gate on the other side. There were usually funerals starting from the courtyard. Beyond the old hospital were the new brick pavilions, and there we met every afternoon and were all very polite and interested in what was the matter, and sat in the machines that were to make so much difference.

The doctor came up to the machine where I was sitting and said: "What did you like best to do before the war? Did you practise a sport?"

I said: "Yes, football."

The Editor regrets that the permissions policy of Ernest Hemingway's publisher is such that only one story by Mr. Hemingway may appear in this third edition of *Ten Modern Masters.*

"Good," he said. "You will be able to play football again better than ever."

My knee did not bend and the leg dropped straight from the knee to the ankle without a calf, and the machine was to bend the knee and make it move as in riding a tricycle. But it did not bend yet, and instead the machine lurched when it came to the bending part. The doctor said: "That will all pass. You are a fortunate young man. You will play football again like a champion."

In the next machine was a major who had a little hand like a baby's. He winked at me when the doctor examined his hand, which was between two leather straps that bounced up and down and flapped the stiff fingers, and said: "And will I too play football, captain-doctor?" He had been a very great fencer, and before the war the greatest fencer in Italy.

The doctor went to his office in a back room and brought a photograph which showed a hand that had been withered almost as small as the major's, before it had taken a machine course, and after was a little larger. The major held the photograph with his good hand and looked at it very carefully. "A wound?" he asked.

"An industrial accident," the doctor said.

"Very interesting, very interesting," the major said, and handed it back to the doctor.

"You have confidence?"

"No," said the major.

There were three boys who came each day who were about the same age I was. They were all three from Milan, and one of them was to be a lawyer, and one was to be a painter, and one had intended to be a soldier, and after we were finished with the machines, sometimes we walked back together to the Café Cova, which was next door to the Scala. We walked the short way through the communist quarter because we were four together. The people hated us because we were officers, and from a wine-shop some one called out, "A basso gli ufficiali!" as we passed. Another boy who walked with us sometimes and made us five wore a black silk handkerchief across his face because he had no nose then and his face was to be rebuilt. He had gone out to the front from the military academy and been wounded within an hour after he had gone into the front line for the first time. They rebuilt his face, but he came from a very old family and they could never get the nose exactly right. He went to South America and worked in a bank. But this was a long time ago, and then we did not any of us know how it was going to be afterward. We only knew then that there was always the war, but that we were not going to it any more.

We all had the same medals, except the boy with the black silk bandage across his face, and he had not been at the front long enough to get any medals. The tall boy with a very pale face who was to be a lawyer had been a lieutenant of Arditi and had three medals of the sort we each had only one of. He had lived a very long time with death and was a little detached. We were all a little detached, and there was nothing that held us together except that we met every afternoon at the hospital. Although, as we walked to the Cova through the tough part of town, walking in the dark, with light and singing coming out of the wine-shops, and sometimes having to walk into the street when the men and women would crowd together on the sidewalk so that we would have had to jostle them to get by, we felt held together by there being something that had happened that they, the people who disliked us, did not understand.

We ourselves all understood the Cova, where it was rich and warm and not too brightly lighted, and noisy and smoky at certain hours, and there were always girls at the tables and the illustrated papers on a rack on the wall. The girls at the Cova were very patriotic, and I found that the most patriotic people in Italy were the café girls—and I believe they are still patriotic.

The boys at first were very polite about my medals and asked me what I had done to get them. I showed them the papers, which were written in very beautiful language and full of *fratellanza* and *abnegazione,* but which really said, with the adjectives removed, that I had been given the medals because I was an American. After that their manner changed a little toward me, although I was their friend against outsiders. I was a friend, but I was never really one of them after they had read the citations, because it had been different with them and they had done very different things to get their medals. I had been wounded, it was true; but we all knew that being wounded, after all, was really an accident. I was never ashamed of the ribbons, though, and sometimes, after the cocktail hour, I would imagine myself having done all the things they had done to get their medals; but walking home at night through the empty streets with the cold wind and all the shops closed, trying to keep near the street lights, I knew that I would never have done such things, and I was very much afraid to die, and often lay in bed at night by myself, afraid to die and wondering how I would be when I went back to the front again.

The three with the medals were like hunting-hawks; and I was not a hawk, although I might seem a hawk to those who had never hunted; they, the three, knew better and so we drifted apart. But I stayed good friends with the boy who had been wounded his first day at the front, because he would never know now how he would have turned out; so he could never be accepted either, and I liked him because I thought perhaps he would not have turned out to be a hawk either.

The major, who had been the great fencer, did not believe in bravery, and spent much time while we sat in the machines correcting my grammar. He had complimented me on how I spoke Italian, and we talked together very easily. One day I had said that Italian seemed such an easy language to me that I could not take a great interest in it; everything was so easy to say. "Ah, yes," the major said. "Why, then, do you not take up the use of grammar?" So we took up the use of grammar, and soon Italian was such a difficult language that I was afraid to talk to him until I had the grammar straight in my mind.

The major came very regularly to the hospital. I do not think he ever missed a day, although I am sure he did not believe in the machines. There was a time when none of us believed in the machines, and one day the major said it was all nonsense. The machines were new then and it was we who were to prove them. It was an idiotic idea, he said, "a theory, like another." I had not learned my grammar, and he said I was a stupid impossible disgrace, and he was a fool to have bothered with me. He was a small man and he sat straight up in his chair with his right hand thrust into the machine and looked straight ahead at the wall while the straps thumped up and down with his fingers in them.

"What will you do when the war is over if it is over?" he asked me. "Speak grammatically!"

"I will go to the States."

"Are you married?"

"No, but I hope to be."

"The more of a fool you are," he said. He seemed very angry. "A man must not marry."

"Why, Signor Maggiore?"

"Don't call me 'Signor Maggiore.' "

"Why must not a man marry?"

"He cannot marry. He cannot marry," he said angrily. "If he is to lose everything, he should not place himself in a position to lose that. He should not place himself in a position to lose. He should find things he cannot lose."

He spoke very angrily and bitterly, and looked straight ahead while he talked.

"But why should he necessarily lose it?"

"He'll lose it," the major said. He was looking at the wall. Then he looked down at the machine and jerked his little hand out from between the straps and slapped it hard against his thigh. "He'll lose it," he almost shouted. "Don't argue with me!" Then he called to the attendant who ran the machines. "Come and turn this damned thing off."

He went back into the other room for the light treatment and the massage. Then I heard him ask the doctor if he might use his telephone and he shut the door. When he came back into the room, I was sitting in another machine. He was wearing his cape and had his cap on, and he came directly toward my machine and put his arm on my shoulder.

"I am so sorry," he said, and patted me on the shoulder with his good hand. "I would not be rude. My wife has just died. You must forgive me."

"Oh—" I said, feeling sick for him. "I am *so* sorry."

He stood there biting his lower lip. "It is very difficult," he said. "I cannot resign myself."

He looked straight past me and out through the window. Then he began to cry. "I am utterly unable to resign myself," he said and choked. And then crying, his head up looking at nothing, carrying himself straight and soldierly, with tears on both his cheeks and biting his lips, he walked past the machines and out the door.

The doctor told me that the major's wife, who was very young and whom he had not married until he was definitely invalided out of the war, had died of pneumonia. She had been sick only a few days. No one expected her to die. The major did not come to the hospital for three days. Then he came at the usual hour, wearing a black band on the sleeve of his uniform. When he came back, there were large framed photographs around the wall, of all sorts of wounds before and after they had been cured by the machines. In front of the machine the major used were three photographs of hands like his that were completely restored. I do not know where the doctor got them. I always understood we were the first to use the machines. The photographs did not make much difference to the major because he only looked out of the window.

The Hunter Gracchus

FRANZ KAFKA

Two boys were sitting on the harbour wall playing with dice. A man was reading a newspaper on the steps of the monument, resting in the shadow of a hero who was flourishing his sword on high. A girl was filling her bucket at the fountain. A fruit-seller was lying beside his scales, staring out to sea. Through the vacant window and door openings of a café one could see two men quite at the back drinking their wine. The proprietor was sitting at a table in front and dozing. A bark was silently making for the little harbour, as if borne by invisible means over the water. A man in a blue blouse climbed ashore and drew the rope through a ring. Behind the boatman two other men in dark coats with silver buttons carried a bier, on which, beneath a great flower-patterned tasselled silk cloth, a man was apparently lying.

Nobody on the quay troubled about the newcomers; even when they lowered the bier to wait for the boatman, who was still occupied with his rope, nobody went nearer, nobody asked them a question, nobody accorded them an inquisitive glance.

The pilot was still further detained by a woman who, a child at her breast, now appeared with loosened hair on the deck of the boat. Then

THE HUNTER GRACCHUS. From *The Great Wall of China* by Franz Kafka; translated by Willa and Edwin Muir. Copyright 1946 by Schocken Books, Inc. Reprinted by permission of Schocken Books, Inc., New York.

he advanced and indicated a yellowish two-storeyed house that rose abruptly on the left beside the sea; the bearers took up their burden and bore it to the low but gracefully pillared door. A little boy opened a window just in time to see the party vanishing into the house, then hastily shut the window again. The door too was now shut; it was of black oak, and very strongly made. A flock of doves which had been flying round the belfry alighted in the street before the house. As if their food were stored within, they assembled in front of the door. One of them flew up to the first storey and pecked at the window-pane. They were bright-hued, well-tended, beautiful birds. The woman on the boat flung grain to them in a wide sweep; they ate it up and flew across to the woman.

A man in a top hat tied with a band of crêpe now descended one of the narrow and very steep lanes that led to the harbour. He glanced round vigilantly, everything seemed to displease him, his mouth twisted at the sight of some offal in a corner. Fruit skins were lying on the steps of the monument; he swept them off in passing with his stick. He rapped at the house door, at the same time taking his top hat from his head with his black-gloved hand. The door was opened at once, and some fifty little boys appeared in two rows in the long entry-hall, and bowed to him.

The boatman descended the stairs, greeted the gentleman in black, conducted him up to the first storey, led him round the bright and elegant loggia which encircled the courtyard, and both of them entered, while the boys pressed after them at a respectful distance, a cool spacious room looking towards the back, from whose window no habitation, but only a bare, blackish grey rocky wall was to be seen. The bearers were busied in setting up and lighting several long candles at the head of the bier, yet these did not give light, but only scared away the shadows which had been immobile till then, and made them flicker over the walls. The cloth covering the bier had been thrown back. Lying on it was a man with wildly matted hair, who looked somewhat like a hunter. He lay without motion and, it seemed, without breathing, his eyes closed; yet only his trappings indicated that this man was probably dead.

The gentleman stepped up to the bier, laid his hand on the brow of the man lying upon it, then kneeled down and prayed. The boatman made a sign to the bearers to leave the room; they went out, drove away the boys who had gathered outside, and shut the door.

But even that did not seem to satisfy the gentleman, he glanced at the boatman; the boatman understood, and vanished through a side door into the next room. At once the man on the bier opened his eyes, turned his face painfully towards the gentleman, and said: "Who are you?" Without any mark of surprise the gentleman rose from his kneeling posture and answered: "The Burgomaster of Riva."

The man on the bier nodded, indicated a chair with a feeble movement of his arm, and said, after the Burgomaster had accepted his invitation: "I knew that, of course, Burgomaster, but in the first moments of returning consciousness I always forget, everything goes round before my eyes, and it is best to ask about anything even if I know. You too probably know that I am the hunter Gracchus."

"Certainly," said the Burgomaster. "Your arrival was announced to me during the night. We had been asleep for a good while. Then towards midnight my wife cried: 'Salvatore'—that's my name—'look at that dove at the window.' It was really a dove, but as big as a cock. It flew over me and said in my ear: 'To-morrow the dead hunter Gracchus is coming; receive him in the name of the city.' "

The hunter nodded and licked his lips with the tip of his tongue: "Yes, the doves flew here before me. But do you believe, Burgomaster, that I shall remain in Riva?"

"I cannot say that yet," replied the Burgomaster. "Are you dead?"

"Yes," said the hunter, "as you see. Many years ago, yes, it must be a great many years ago, I fell from a precipice in the Black Forest —that is in Germany—when I was hunting a chamois. Since then I have been dead."

"But you are alive too," said the Burgomaster.

"In a certain sense," said the hunter, "in a certain sense I am alive too. My death ship lost its way; a wrong turn of the wheel, a moment's absence of mind on the pilot's part, a longing to turn aside towards my lovely native country, I cannot tell what it was; I only know this, that I remained on earth and that ever since my ship has sailed earthly waters. So I, who asked for nothing better than to live among my mountains, travel after my death through all the lands of the earth."

"And you have no part in the other world?" asked the Burgomaster, knitting his brow.

"I am for ever," replied the hunter, "on the great stair that leads up to it. On that infinitely wide and spacious stair I clamber about, sometimes up, sometimes down, sometimes on the right, sometimes on the left, always in motion. The hunter has been turned into a butterfly. Do not laugh."

"I am not laughing," said the Burgomaster in self-defence.

"That is very good of you," said the hunter. "I am always in motion. But when I make a supreme flight and see the gate actually shining before me I awaken presently on my old ship, still stranded forlornly in some earthly sea or other. The fundamental error of my one-time death grins at me as I lie in my cabin. Julia, the wife of the pilot, knocks at the door and brings me on my bier the morning drink of the land whose coasts we chance to be passing. I lie on a wooden pallet, I wear—it cannot be a pleasure to look at me—a filthy winding sheet, my hair and beard, black tinged with grey, have grown together inextricably, my limbs are covered with a great flower-patterned woman's shawl with long fringes. A sacramental candle stands at my head and lights me. On the wall opposite me is a little picture, evidently of a Bushman who is aiming his spear at me and taking cover as best he can behind a beautifully painted shield. On shipboard one is often a prey to stupid imaginations, but that is the stupidest of them all. Otherwise my wooden case is quite empty. Through a hole in the side wall come in the warm airs of the southern night, and I hear the water slapping against the old boat.

"I have lain here ever since the time when, as the hunter Gracchus living in the Black Forest, I followed a chamois and fell from a precipice. Everything happened in good order. I pursued, I fell, bled to death in a ravine, died, and this ship should have conveyed me to the next world. I can still remember how gladly I stretched myself out on this pallet for the first time. Never did the mountains listen to such songs from me as these shadowy walls did then.

"I had been glad to live and I was glad to die. Before I stepped aboard, I joyfully flung away my wretched load of ammunition, my knapsack, my hunting rifle that I had always been proud to carry, and I slipped into my winding sheet like a girl into her marriage dress. I lay and waited. Then came the mishap."

"A terrible fate," said the Burgomaster, raising his hand defensively. "And you bear no blame for it?"

"None," said the hunter. "I was a hunter; was there any sin in that? I followed my calling as a hunter in the Black Forest, where there were still wolves in those days. I lay in ambush, shot, hit my mark, flayed the skins from my victims: was there any sin in that? My labours were blessed. 'The great hunter of the Black Forest' was the name I was given. Was there any sin in that?"

"I am not called upon to decide that," said the Burgomaster, "but to me also there seems to be no sin in such things. But, then whose is the guilt?"

"The boatman's," said the hunter. "Nobody will read what I say here, no one will come to help me; even if all the people were commanded to help me, every door and window would remain shut, everybody would take to bed and draw the bedclothes over his head, the whole earth would become an inn for the night. And there is sense in that, for nobody knows of me, and if anyone knew he would not know where I could be found, and if he knew where I could be found, he would not know how to deal with me, he would not know how to help me. The thought of helping me is an illness that has to be cured by taking to one's bed.

"I know that, and so I do not shout to summon help, even though at moments—when I lose control over myself, as I have done just now, for instance—I think seriously of it. But to drive out such thoughts I need only look round me and verify where I am, and—I can safely assert—have been for hundreds of years."

"Extraordinary," said the Burgomaster, "extraordinary.—And now do you think of staying here in Riva with us?"

"I think not," said the hunter with a smile, and, to excuse himself, he laid his hand on the Burgomaster's knee. "I am here, more than that I do not know, further than that I cannot go. My ship has no rudder, and it is driven by the wind that blows in the undermost regions of death."

The Gardener

RUDYARD KIPLING

Every one in the village knew that Helen Turrell did her duty by all her world, and by none more honourably than by her only brother's unfortunate child. The village knew, too, that George Turrell had tried his family severely since early youth, and were not surprised to be told that, after many fresh starts given and thrown away, he, an Inspector of Indian Police, had entangled himself with the daughter of a retired non-commissioned officer, and had died of a fall from a horse a few weeks before his child was born. Mercifully, George's father and mother were both dead, and though Helen, thirty-five and independent, might well have washed her hands of the whole disgraceful affair, she most nobly took charge, though she was, at the time, under threat of lung trouble which had driven her to the South of France. She arranged for the passage of the child and a nurse from Bombay, met them at Marseilles, nursed the baby through an attack of infantile dysentery due to the carelessness of the nurse, whom she had had to dismiss, and at last, thin and worn but triumphant, brought the boy late in the autumn, wholly restored, to her Hampshire home.

All these details were public property, for Helen was as open as the day, and held that scandals are only increased by hushing them up. She admitted that George had always been rather a black sheep, but things might have been much worse if the mother had insisted on her right to keep the boy. Luckily, it seemed that people of that class would do almost anything for money, and, as George had always turned to her in his scrapes, she felt herself justified—her friends agreed with her—in cutting the whole non-commissioned officer connection, and giving the child every advantage. A christening, by the

Rector, under the name of Michael, was the first step. So far as she knew herself, she was not, she said, a child-lover, but, for all his faults, she had been very fond of George, and she pointed out that little Michael had his father's mouth to a line; which made something to build upon.

As a matter of fact, it was the Turrell forehead, broad, low, and well-shaped, with the widely-spaced eyes beneath it, that Michael had most faithfully reproduced. His mouth was somewhat better cut than the family type. But Helen, who would concede nothing good to his mother's side, vowed he was a Turrell all over, and, there being no one to contradict, the likeness was established.

In a few years Michael took his place, as accepted as Helen had always been—fearless, philosophical, and fairly good-looking. At six, he wished to know why he could not call her "Mummy," as other boys called their mothers. She explained that she was only his auntie, and that aunties were not quite the same as mummies, but that, if it gave him pleasure, he might call her "Mummy" at bedtime, for a pet-name between themselves.

Michael kept his secret most loyally, but Helen, as usual, explained the fact to her friends; which when Michael heard, he raged.

"Why did you tell? *Why* did you tell?" came at the end of the storm.

"Because it's always best to tell the truth," Helen answered, her arm round him as he shook in his cot.

"All right, but when the troof's ugly I don't think it's nice."

"Don't you, dear?"

"No, I don't, and"—she felt the small body stiffen—"now you've told, I won't call you 'Mummy' any more—not even at bedtimes."

"But isn't that rather unkind?" said Helen, softly.

"I don't care! I don't care! You've hurted me in my insides and I'll hurt you back. I'll hurt you as long as I live!"

"Don't, oh, don't talk like that, dear! You don't know what—"

"I will! And when I'm dead I'll hurt you worse!"

"Thank goodness, I shall be dead long before you, darling."

"Huh! Emma says, ' 'Never know your luck.' " (Michael had been talking to Helen's elderly, flat-faced maid.) "Lots of little boys die quite soon. So'll I. *Then* you'll see!"

Helen caught her breath and moved towards the door, but the wail of "Mummy! Mummy!" drew her back again, and the two wept together.

At ten years old, after two terms at a prep school, something or somebody gave him the idea that his civil status was not quite regular. He attacked Helen on the subject, breaking down her stammered defences with the family directness.

"Don't believe a word of it," he said, cheerily, at the end. "People wouldn't have talked like they did if my people had been married. But don't you bother, Auntie. I've found out all about my sort in English Hist'ry and the Shakespeare bits. There was William the Conqueror to begin with, and—oh, heaps more, and they all got on first-rate. 'Twon't make any difference to you, my being *that*—will it?"

"As if anything could—" she began.

"All right. We won't talk about it any more if it makes you cry." He never mentioned the thing again of his own will, but when, two years later, he skilfully managed to have measles in the holidays, as his temperature went up to the appointed one hundred and four he muttered of nothing else, till Helen's voice, piercing at last his delirium, reached him with assurance that nothing on earth or beyond could make any difference between them.

The terms at his public school and the wonderful Christmas, Easter, and summer holidays followed each other, variegated and glorious as jewels on a string; and as jewels Helen treasured them. In due time Michael developed his own interests, which ran their courses and gave way to others; but his interest in Helen was constant and increasing throughout. She repaid it with all that she had of affection or could command of counsel and money; and since Michael was no fool, the war took him just before what was like to have been a most promising career.

He was to have gone up to Oxford, with a scholarship, in October. At the end of August he was on the edge of joining the first holocaust of public-school boys who threw themselves into the Line; but the captain of his O.T.C., where he had been sergeant for nearly a year, headed him off and steered him directly to a commission in a battalion so new that half of it still wore the old Army red, and the other half was breeding meningitis through living overcrowdedly in damp tents. Helen had been shocked at the idea of direct enlistment.

"But it's in the family," Michael laughed.

"You don't mean to tell me that you believed that old story all this time?" said Helen. (Emma, her maid, had been dead now several years.) "I gave you my word of honour—and I give it again—that—that it's all right. It is indeed."

"Oh, *that* doesn't worry me. It never did," he replied valiantly. "What I meant was, I should have got into the show earlier if I'd enlisted—like my grandfather."

"Don't talk like that! Are you afraid of its ending so soon, then?"

"No such luck. You know what K. says."

"Yes. But my banker told me last Monday it couldn't *possibly* last beyond Christmas—for financial reasons."

" 'Hope he's right, but our Colonel—and he's a Regular—says it's going to be a long job."

Michael's battalion was fortunate in that, by some chance which meant several "leaves," it was used for coast-defence among shallow trenches on the Norfolk coast; thence sent north to watch the mouth of a Scotch estuary, and, lastly, held for weeks on a baseless rumour of distant service. But, the very day that Michael was to have met Helen for four whole hours at a railway-junction up the line, it was hurled out, to help make good the wastage of Loos, and he had only just time to send her a wire of farewell.

In France luck again helped the battalion. It was put down near the Salient, where it led a meritorious and unexacting life, while the Somme was being manufactured; and enjoyed the peace of the Armentières and Laventie sectors when that battle began. Finding that it had sound views on protecting its own flanks and could dig, a prudent Commander stole it out of its own Division, under pretence of helping to lay telegraphs, and used it round Ypres at large.

A month later, and just after Michael had written Helen that there was nothing special doing and therefore no need to worry, a shell-splinter dropping out of a wet dawn killed him at once. The next shell uprooted and laid down over the body what had been the foundation of a barn wall, so neatly that none but an expert would have guessed that anything unpleasant had happened.

By this time the village was old in experience of war, and, English fashion, had evolved a ritual to meet it. When the postmistress handed her seven-year-old daughter the official telegram to take to Miss Turrell, she observed to the Rector's gardener: "It's Miss Helen's turn now." He replied, thinking of his own son: "Well, he's lasted longer than some." The child herself came to the front-door weeping aloud, because Master Michael had often given her sweets. Helen, presently, found herself pulling down the house-blinds one after one with great care, and saying earnestly to each: "Missing *always* means dead." Then she took her place in the dreary procession that was impelled to go through an inevitable series of unprofitable emotions. The Rector, of course, preached hope and prophesied word, very soon, from a prison camp. Several friends, too, told her perfectly truthful tales, but always about other women, to whom, after months and months of silence, their missing had been miraculously restored. Other people urged her to communicate with infallible Secretaries of organisations who could communicate with benevolent neutrals, who could extract accurate information from the most secretive of Hun prison commandants. Helen did and wrote and signed everything that was suggested or put before her.

Once, on one of Michael's leaves, he had taken her over a munition factory, where she saw the progress of a shell from blank-iron to the all but finished article. It struck her at the time that the wretched thing was never left alone for a single second; and "I'm being manufactured into a bereaved next-of-kin," she told herself, as she prepared her documents.

In due course, when all the organisations had deeply or sincerely regretted their inability to trace, etc., something gave way within her and all sensation—save of thankfulness for the release—came to an end in blessed passivity. Michael had died and her world had stood still and she had been one with the full shock of that arrest. Now she was standing still and the world was going forward, but it did not concern her—in no way or relation did it touch her. She knew this by the ease with which she could slip Michael's name into talk and incline her head to the proper angle, at the proper murmur of sympathy.

In the blessed realisation of that relief, the Armistice with all its bells broke over her and passed unheeded. At the end of another year she had overcome her physical loathing of the living and returned young, so that she could take them by the hand and almost sincerely wish them well. She had no interest in any aftermath, national or personal, of the War, but, moving at an immense distance, she sat on various relief committees and held strong views—she heard herself delivering them—about the site of the proposed village War Memorial.

Then there came to her, as next of kin, an official intimation, backed by a page of a letter to her in indelible pencil, a silver identity-disc, and a watch, to the effect that the body of Lieutenant Michael Turrell had been found, identified, and re-interred in Hagenzeele Third Military Cemetery—the letter of the row and the grave's number in that row duly given.

So Helen found herself moved on to another process of the manufacture—to a world full of exultant or broken relatives, now strong in the certainty that there was an altar upon earth where they might lay their love. These soon told her, and by means of time-tables made clear, how easy it was and how little it interfered with life's affairs to go and see one's grave.

"*So* different," as the Rector's wife said, "if he'd been killed in Mesopotamia, or even Gallipoli."

The agony of being waked up to some sort of second life drove Helen across the Channel, where, in a new world of abbreviated titles, she learnt that Hagenzeele Third could be comfortably reached by an afternoon train which fitted in with the morning boat, and that there was a comfortable little hotel not three kilometres from Hagenzeele itself, where one could spend quite a comfortable night and see one's grave next morning. All this she had from a Central Authority who lived in a board and tarpaper shed on the skirts of a razed city full of whirling lime-dust and blown papers.

"By the way," said he, "you know your grave, of course?"

"Yes, thank you," said Helen, and showed its row and number typed on Michael's own little typewriter. The officer would have checked it, out of one of his many books; but a large Lancashire woman thrust between them and bade him tell her where she might find her son, who had been corporal in the A.S.C. His proper name, she sobbed, was Anderson, but, coming of respectable folk, he had of course enlisted under the name of Smith; and had been killed at Dickiebush, in early 'Fifteen. She had not his number nor did she know which of his two Christian names he might have used with his alias; but her Cook's tourist ticket expired at the end of Easter week, and if by then she could not find her child she should go mad.

Whereupon she fell forward on Helen's breast; but the officer's wife came out quickly from a little bedroom behind the office, and the three of them lifted the woman on to the cot.

"They are often like this," said the officer's wife, loosening the tight bonnet-strings. "Yesterday she said he'd been killed at Hooge. Are you sure you know your grave? It makes such a difference."

"Yes, thank you," said Helen, and hurried out before the woman on the bed should begin to lament again.

Tea in a crowded mauve and blue striped wooden structure, with a false front, carried her still further into the nightmare. She paid her bill beside a stolid, plain-featured Englishwoman, who, hearing her inquire about the train to Hagenzeele, volunteered to come with her.

"I'm going to Hagenzeele myself," she explained. "Not to Hagenzeele Third; mine is Sugar Factory, but they call it La Rosière now. It's just south of Hagenzeele Three. Have you got your room at the hotel there?"

"Oh yes, thank you. I've wired."

"That's better. Sometimes the place is quite full, and at others there's hardly a soul. But they've put bathrooms into the old Lion d'Or—that's the hotel on the west side of Sugar Factory—and it draws off a lot of people, luckily."

"It's all new to me. This is the first time I've been over."

"Indeed! This is my ninth time since the Armistice. Not on my own account. *I* haven't lost any one, thank God—but, like every one else, I've a lot of friends at home who have. Coming over as often as I do, I find it helps them to have some one just look at the—the place and tell them about it afterwards. And one can take photos for them, too. I get quite a list of commissions to execute." She laughed nervously and tapped her slung Kodak. "There are two or three to see at Sugar Factory this time, and plenty of others in the cemeteries all about. My system is to save them up, and arrange them, you know. And when I've got enough commissions for one area to make it worth while, I pop over and execute them. It *does* comfort people."

"I suppose so," Helen answered, shivering as they entered the little train.

"Of course it does. (Isn't it lucky we've got window-seats?) It must do or they wouldn't ask one to do it, would they? I've a list of quite twelve or fifteen commissions here"—she tapped the Kodak again—"I must sort them out to-night. Oh, I forgot to ask you. What's yours?"

"My nephew," said Helen. "But I was very fond of him."

"Ah yes! I sometimes wonder whether *they* know after death? What do you think?"

"Oh, I don't—I haven't dared to think much about that sort of thing," said Helen, almost lifting her hands to keep her off.

"Perhaps that's better," the woman answered. "The sense of loss must be enough, I expect. Well, I won't worry you any more."

Helen was grateful, but when they reached the hotel Mrs. Scarsworth (they had exchanged names) insisted on dining at the same table with her, and after the meal, in the little, hideous salon full of low-voiced relatives, took Helen through her "commissions" with biographies of the dead, where she happened to know them, and sketches of their next of kin. Helen endured till nearly half-past nine, ere she fled to her room.

Almost at once there was a knock at her door and Mrs. Scarsworth entered; her hands, holding the dreadful list, clasped before her.

"Yes—yes—*I* know," she began. "You're sick of me, but I want to tell you something. You—you aren't married are you? Then perhaps you won't. . . . But it doesn't matter. I've *got* to tell some one. I can't go on any longer like this."

"But please—" Mrs. Scarsworth had backed against the shut door, and her mouth worked dryly.

"In a minute," she said. "You—you know about these graves of mine I was telling you about downstairs, just now? They really *are* commissions. At least several of them are." Her eye wandered round the room. "What extraordinary wall-papers they have in Belgium, don't you think? . . . Yes. I swear they are commissions. But there's *one,* d'you see, and—and he was more to me than anything else in the world. Do you understand?"

Helen nodded.

"More than any one else. And, of course, he oughtn't to have been. He ought to have been nothing to me. But he *was.* He *is.* That's why I do the commissions, you see. That's all."

"But why do you tell me?" Helen asked desperately.

"Because I'm *so* tired of lying. Tired of lying—always lying—year in and year out. When I don't tell lies I've got to act 'em and I've got to think 'em always. *You* don't know what that means. He was everything to me that he oughtn't to have been—the one real thing —the only thing that ever happened to me in all my life; and I've had to pretend he wasn't. I've had to watch every word I said, and think out what lie I'd tell next, for years and years!"

"How many years?" Helen asked.

"Six years and four months before, and two and three-quarters after. I've gone to him eight times, since. To-morrow'll make the ninth, and—and I can't—I *can't* go to him again with nobody in the world knowing. I want to be honest with some one before I go. Do you understand? It doesn't matter about *me*. I was never truthful, even as a girl. But it isn't worthy of *him*. So—so I—I had to tell you. I can't keep it up any longer. Oh, I can't!"

She lifted her joined hands almost to the level of her mouth, and brought them down sharply, still joined, to full arms' length below her waist. Helen reached forward, caught them, bowed her head over them, and murmured: "Oh, my dear! My dear!" Mrs. Scarsworth stepped back, her face all mottled.

"My God!" said she. "Is *that* how you take it?"

Helen could not speak, the woman went out; but it was a long while before Helen was able to sleep.

Next morning Mrs. Scarsworth left early on her round of commissions, and Helen walked alone to Hagenzeele Third. The place was still in the making, and stood some five or six feet above the metalled road, which it flanked for hundreds of yards. Culverts across a deep ditch served for entrances through the unfinished boundary wall. She climbed a few wooden-faced earthen steps and then met the entire crowded level of the thing in one held breath. She did not know that Hagenzeele Third counted twenty-one thousand dead already. All she saw was a merciless sea of black crosses, bearing little strips of stamped tin at all angles across their faces. She could distinguish no order or arrangement in their mass; nothing but a waist-high wilderness as of weeds stricken dead, rushing at her. She went forward, moved to the left and the right hopelessly, wondering by what guidance she should ever come to her own. A great distance away there was a line of whiteness. It proved to be a block of some two or three hundred graves whose headstones had already been set, whose flowers were planted out, and whose new-sown grass showed green. Here she could see clear-cut letters at the ends of the rows, and, referring to her slip, realised that it was not here she must look.

A man knelt behind a line of headstones—evidently a gardener, for he was firming a young plant in the soft earth. She went towards him, her paper in her hand. He rose at her approach and without prelude or salutation asked: "Who are you looking for?"

"Lieutenant Michael Turrell—my nephew," said Helen slowly and word for word, as she had many thousands of times in her life.

The man lifted his eyes and looked at her with infinite compassion before he turned from the fresh-sown grass towards the naked black crosses.

"Come with me," he said, "and I will show you where your son lies."

When Helen left the Cemetery she turned for a last look. In the distance she saw the man bending over his young plants; and she went away, supposing him to be the gardener.

"That in Aleppo Once . . ."

VLADIMIR NABOKOV

Dear V.—Among other things, this is to tell you that at last I am here, in the country whither so many sunsets have led. One of the first persons I saw was our good old Gleb Alexandrovich Gekko gloomily crossing Columbus Avenue in quest of the *petit café du coin* which none of us three will ever visit again. He seemed to think that somehow or other you were betraying our national literature, and he gave me your address with a deprecatory shake of his gray head, as if you did not deserve the treat of hearing from me.

I have a story for you. Which reminds me—I mean putting it like

"THAT IN ALEPPO ONCE . . ." From *Nabokov's Dozen* by Vladimir Nabokov, copyright 1943 by The Atlantic Monthly Company. Reprinted by permission of Doubleday & Company, Inc.

this reminds me—of the days when we wrote our first udder-warm bubbling verse, and all things, a rose, a puddle, a lighted window, cried out to us: "I'm a rhyme!" Yes, this is a most useful universe. We play, we die: *ig-rhyme, umi-rhyme*. And the sonorous souls of Russian verbs lend a meaning to the wild gesticulation of trees or to some discarded newspaper sliding and pausing, and shuffling again, with abortive flaps and apterous jerks along an endless wind-swept embankment. But just now I am not a poet. I come to you like that gushing lady in Chekhov who was dying to be described.

I married, let me see, about a month after you left France and a few weeks before the gentle Germans roared into Paris. Although I can produce documentary proofs of matrimony, I am positive now that my wife never existed. You may know her name from some other source, but that does not matter: it is the name of an illusion. Therefore, I am able to speak of her with as much detachment as I would of a character in a story (one of your stories, to be precise).

It was love at first touch rather than at first sight, for I had met her several times before without experiencing any special emotion; but one night, as I was seeing her home, something quaint she had said made me stoop with a laugh and lightly kiss her on the hair— and of course we all know of that blinding blast which is caused by merely picking up a small doll from the floor of a carefully abandoned house: the soldier involved hears nothing; for him it is but an ecstatic soundless and boundless expansion of what had been during his life a pin point of light in the dark center of his being. And really, the reason we think of death in celestial terms is that the visible firmament, especially at night (above our blacked-out Paris with the gaunt arches of its Boulevard Exelmans and the ceaseless Alpine gurgle of desolate latrines), is the most adequate and ever-present symbol of that vast silent explosion.

But I cannot discern her. She remains as nebulous as my best poem—the one you made such gruesome fun of in the *Literaturnïe Zapiski*. When I want to imagine her, I have to cling mentally to a tiny brown birthmark on her downy forearm, as one concentrates upon a punctuation mark in an illegible sentence. Perhaps, had she used a greater amount of make-up or used it more constantly, I might have visualized her face today, or at least the delicate transverse furrows of dry, hot rouged lips; but I fail, I fail—although I still feel their elusive touch now and then in the blindman's bluff of my senses, in that sobbing sort of dream when she and I clumsily clutch at each other through a heartbreaking mist and I cannot see the color of her eyes for the blank luster of brimming tears drowning their irises.

She was much younger than I—not as much younger as was Nathalie of the lovely bare shoulders and long earrings in relation to swarthy Pushkin; but still there was a sufficient margin for that kind of retrospective romanticism which finds pleasure in imitating the destiny of a unique genius (down to the jealousy, down to the filth, down to the stab of seeing her almond-shaped eyes turn to her blond Cassio behind her peacock-feathered fan) even if one cannot imitate his verse. She liked mine though, and would scarcely have yawned as the other was wont to do every time her husband's poem happened to exceed the length of a sonnet. If she has remained a phantom to me, I may have been one to her: I suppose she had been solely attracted by the obscurity of my poetry; then tore a hole through its veil and saw a stranger's unlovable face.

As you know, I had been for some time planning to follow the example of your fortunate flight. She described to me an uncle of hers who lived, she said, in New York: he had taught riding at a Southern college and had wound up by marrying a wealthy American woman; they had a little daughter born deaf. She said she had lost their address long ago, but a few days later it miraculously turned up, and we wrote a dramatic letter to which we never received any reply. This did not much matter, as I had already obtained a sound affidavit from Professor Lomchenko of Chicago; but little else had been done in the way of getting the necessary papers, when the invasion began, whereas I foresaw that if we stayed on in Paris some helpful compatriot of mine would sooner or later point out to the interested party sundry passages in one of my books where I argued that, with all her many black sins, Germany was still bound to remain forever and ever the laughing stock of the world.

So we started upon our disastrous honeymoon. Crushed and jolted amid the apocalyptic exodus, waiting for unscheduled trains that were bound for unknown destinations, walking through the stale stage setting of abstract towns, living in a permanent twilight of physical exhaustion, we fled; and the farther we fled, the clearer it became that what was driving us on was something more than a booted and buckled fool with his assortment of variously propelled junk—something of which he was a mere symbol, something monstrous and impalpable, a timeless and faceless mass of immemorial horror that still keeps coming at me from behind even here, in the green vacuum of Central Park.

Oh, she bore it gamely enough—with a kind of dazed cheerfulness. Once, however, quite suddenly she started to sob in a sympathetic railway carriage. "The dog," she said, "the dog we left. I cannot forget the poor dog." The honesty of her grief shocked me, as we have never had any dog. "I know," she said, "but I tried to imagine we had actually bought that setter. And just think, he would be now whining behind a locked door." There had never been any talk of buying a setter.

I should also not like to forget a certain stretch of high-road and the sight of a family of refugees (two women, a child) whose old father, or grandfather, had died on the way. The sky was a chaos of black and flesh-colored clouds with an ugly sunburst beyond a hooded hill, and the dead man was lying on his back under a dusty plane tree. With a stick and their hands the women had tried to dig a roadside grave, but the soil was too hard; they had given it up and were sitting side by side, among the anemic poppies, a little apart from the corpse and its upturned beard. But the little boy was still scratching and scraping and tugging until he tumbled a flat stone and forgot the object of his solemn exertions as he crouched on his haunches, his thin, eloquent neck showing all its vertebrae to the headsman, and watched with surprise and delight thousands of minute brown ants seething, zigzagging, dispersing, heading for places of safety in the Gard, and the Aude, and the Drome, and the Var, and the Basses-Pyrénées—we two paused only in Pau.

Spain proved too difficult and we decided to move on to Nice. At a place called Faugères (a ten-minute stop) I squeezed out of the train to buy some food. When a couple of minutes later I came back, the train was gone, and the muddled old man responsible for the atrocious void that faced me (coal dust glittering in the heat between naked indifferent rails, and a lone piece of orange peel) brutally told me that, anyway, I had had no right to get out.

In a better world I could have had my wife located and told what to do (I had both tickets and most of the money); as it was, my nightmare struggle with the telephone proved futile, so I dismissed the whole series of diminutive voices barking at me from afar, sent two or three telegrams which are probably on their way only now, and late in the evening took the next local to Montpellier, farther than which her train would not stumble. Not finding her there, I had to choose between two alternatives: going on because she might have boarded the Marseilles train which I had just missed, or going back because she might have returned to Faugères. I forget now what tangle of reasoning led me to Marseilles and Nice.

Beyond such routine action as forwarding false data to a few unlikely places, the police did nothing to help: one man bellowed at me for being a nuisance; another sidetracked the question by doubting the authenticity of my marriage certificate because it was stamped on what he contended to be the wrong side; a third, a fat *commissaire* with liquid brown eyes confessed that he wrote poetry in his spare time. I looked up various acquaintances among the numerous Russians domiciled or stranded in Nice. I heard those among them who chanced to have Jewish blood talk of their doomed kinsmen crammed into hell-bound trains; and my own plight, by contrast, acquired a commonplace air of irreality while I sat in some crowded café with the milky blue sea in front of me and a shell-hollow murmur behind telling and retelling the tale of massacre and misery, and the gray paradise beyond the ocean, and the ways and whims of harsh consuls.

A week after my arrival an indolent plain-clothes man called upon me and took me down a crooked and smelly street to a black-stained house with the word "hotel" almost erased by dirt and time; there, he said, my wife had been found. The girl he produced was an absolute stranger, of course; but my friend Holmes kept on trying for some time to make her and me confess we were married, while her taciturn and muscular bed-fellow stood by and listened, his bare arms crossed on his striped chest.

When at length I got rid of those people and had wandered back to my neighborhood, I happened to pass by a compact queue waiting at the entrance of a food store; and there, at the very end, was my wife, straining on tiptoe to catch a glimpse of what exactly was being sold. I think the first thing she said to me was that she hoped it was oranges.

Her tale seemed a trifle hazy, but perfectly banal. She had returned to Faugères and gone straight to the Commissariat instead of making inquiries at the station, where I had left a message for her. A party of refugees suggested that she join them; she spent the night in a bicycle shop with no bicycles, on the floor, together with three elderly women who lay, she said, like three logs in a row. Next day she realized that she had not enough money to reach Nice. Eventually she borrowed some from one of the log-women. She got into the wrong train, however, and traveled to a town the name of which she could not remember. She had arrived at Nice two days ago and had found some friends at the Russian church. They had told her I was somewhere around, looking for her, and would surely turn up soon.

Some time later, as I sat on the edge of the only chair in my garret and held her by her slender young hips (she was combing her soft hair and tossing her head back with every stroke), her dim smile changed all at once into an odd quiver and she placed one hand on my shoulder, staring down at me as if I were a reflection in a pool, which she had noticed for the first time.

"I've been lying to you, dear," she said. "*Ya lgunia.* I stayed for several nights in Montpellier with a brute of a man I met on the train. I did not want it at all. He sold hair lotions."

The time, the place, the torture. Her fan, her gloves, her mask. I spent that night and many others getting it out of her bit by bit, but not getting it all. I was under the strange delusion that first I must find out every detail, reconstruct every minute, and only then decide whether I could bear it. But the limit of desired knowledge was unattainable, nor could I ever foretell the approximate point after which I might imagine myself satiated, because of course the denominator of every fraction of knowledge was potentially as infinite as the number of intervals between the fractions themselves.

Oh, the first time she had been too tired to mind, and the next had not minded because she was sure I had deserted her; and she apparently considered that such explanations ought to be a kind of consolation prize for me instead of the nonsense and agony they really were. It went on like that for eons, she breaking down every now and then, but soon rallying again, answering my unprintable questions in a breathless whisper or trying with a pitiful smile to wriggle into the semisecurity of irrelevant commentaries, and I crushing and crushing the mad molar till my jaw almost burst with pain, a flaming pain which seemed somehow preferable to the dull, humming ache of humble endurance.

And mark, in between the periods of this inquest, we were trying to get from reluctant authorities certain papers which in their turn would make it lawful to apply for a third kind which would serve as a steppingstone toward a permit enabling the holder to apply for yet other papers which might or might not give him the means of discovering how and why it had happened. For even if I could imagine the accursed recurrent scene, I failed to link up its sharp-angled grotesque shadows with the dim limbs of my wife as she shook and rattled and dissolved in my violent grasp.

So nothing remained but to torture each other, to wait for hours on end in the Prefecture, filling forms, conferring with friends who had already probed the innermost viscera of all visas, pleading with secretaries, and filling forms again, with the result that her lusty and versatile traveling salesman became blended in a ghastly mix-up with rat-whiskered snarling officials, rotting bundles of obsolete records, the reek of violet ink, bribes slipped under gangrenous blotting paper, fat flies tickling moist necks with their rapid cold padded feet, new-laid clumsy concave photographs of your six subhuman doubles, the tragic eyes and patient politeness of petitioners born in Slutzk, Starodub, or Bobruisk, the funnels and pulleys of the Holy Inquisition, the awful smile of the bald man with the glasses, who had been told that his passport could not be found.

I confess that one evening, after a particularly abominable day, I sank down on a stone bench weeping and cursing a mock world where millions of lives were being juggled by the clammy hands of consuls and *commissaires*. I noticed she was crying too, and then I told her that nothing would really have mattered the way it mattered now, had she not gone and done what she did.

"You will think me crazy," she said with a vehemence that, for a second, almost made a real person of her, "but I didn't—I swear that I didn't. Perhaps I live several lives at once. Perhaps I wanted to test you. Perhaps this bench is a dream and we are in Saratov or on some star."

It would be tedious to niggle the different stages through which I passed before accepting finally the first version of her delay. I did not talk to her and was a good deal alone. She would glimmer and fade, and reappear with some trifle she thought I would appreciate— a handful of cherries, three precious cigarettes or the like—treating me with the unruffled mute sweetness of a nurse that trips from and to a gruff convalescent. I ceased visiting most of our mutual friends because they had lost all interest in my passport affairs and seemed to have turned vaguely inimical. I composed several poems. I drank all the wine I could get. I clasped her one day to my groaning breast, and we went for a week to Caboule and lay on the round pink pebbles of the narrow beach. Strange to say, the happier our new relations seemed, the stronger I felt an undercurrent of poignant sadness, but I kept telling myself that this was an intrinsic feature of all true bliss.

In the meantime, something had shifted in the moving pattern of our fates and at last I emerged from a dark and hot office with a couple of plump *visas de sortie* cupped in my trembling hands. Into these the U.S.A. serum was duly injected, and I dashed to Marseilles and managed to get tickets for the very next boat. I returned and tramped up the stairs. I saw a rose in a glass on the table—the sugar pink of its obvious beauty, the parasitic air bubbles clinging to its stem. Her two spare dresses were gone, her comb was gone, her checkered coat was gone, and so was the mauve hairband with a mauve bow that had been her hat. There was no note pinned to the pillow, nothing at all in the room to enlighten me, for of course the rose was merely what French rhymsters call *une cheville*.

I went to the Veretennikovs, who could tell me nothing; to the Hellmans, who refused to say anything; and to the Elagins, who were not sure whether to tell me or not. Finally the old lady—and you know what Anna Vladimirovna is like at crucial moments—asked for her rubber-tipped cane, heavily but energetically dislodged her bulk from her favorite armchair, and took me into the garden. There she informed me that, being twice my age, she had the right to say I was a bully and a cad.

You must imagine the scene: the tiny graveled garden with its blue Arabian Nights jar and solitary cypress; the cracked terrace where the old lady's father had dozed with a rug on his knees when he retired from his Novgorod governorship to spend a few last evenings in Nice; the pale-green sky; a whiff of vanilla in the deepening dusk; the crickets emitting their metallic trill pitched at two octaves above middle C; and Anna Vladimirovna, the folds of her cheeks jerkily dangling as she flung at me a motherly but quite undeserved insult.

During several preceding weeks, my dear V., every time she had visited by herself the three or four families we both knew, my ghostly wife had filled the eager ears of all those kind people with an extraordinary story. To wit: that she had madly fallen in love with a young Frenchman who could give her a turreted home and a crested name; that she had implored me for a divorce and I had refused; that in fact I had said I would rather shoot her and myself than sail to New York alone; that she had said her father in a similar case had acted like a gentleman; that I had answered I did not give a hoot for her *cocu de père.*

There were loads of other preposterous details of the kind—but they all hung together in such a remarkable fashion that no wonder the old lady made me swear I would not seek to pursue the lovers with a cocked pistol. They had gone, she said, to a château in Lozère. I inquired whether she had ever set eyes upon the man. No, but she had been shown his picture. As I was about to leave, Anna Vladimirovna, who had slightly relaxed and had even given me her five fingers to kiss, suddenly flared up again, struck the gravel with her cane, and said in her deep strong voice: "But one thing I shall never forgive you—her dog, that poor beast which you hanged with your own hands before leaving Paris."

Whether the gentleman of leisure had changed into a traveling salesman, or whether the metamorphosis had been reversed, or whether again he was neither the one nor the other, but the nondescript Russian who had courted her before our marriage—all this was absolutely inessential. She had gone. That was the end. I should have been a fool had I begun the nightmare business of searching and waiting for her all over again.

On the fourth morning of a long and dismal sea voyage, I met on the deck a solemn but pleasant old doctor with whom I had played chess in Paris. He asked me whether my wife was very much incommoded by the rough seas. I answered that I had sailed alone; whereupon he looked taken aback and then said he had seen her a couple of days before going on board, namely in Marseilles, walking, rather aimlessly he thought, along the embankment. She said that I would presently join her with bag and tickets.

This is, I gather, the point of the whole story—although if you write it, you had better not make him a doctor, as that kind of thing has been overdone. It was at that moment that I suddenly knew for certain that she had never existed at all. I shall tell you another thing. When I arrived I hastened to satisfy a certain morbid curiosity: I went to the address she had given me once; it proved to be an anonymous gap between two office buildings; I looked for her uncle's name in the directory; it was not there; I made some inquiries, and Gekko, who knows everything, informed me that the man and his horsey wife existed all right, but had moved to San Francisco after their deaf little girl had died.

Viewing the past graphically, I see our mangled romance engulfed in a deep valley of mist between the crags of two matter-of-fact mountains: life had been real before, life will be real from now on, I hope. Not tomorrow, though. Perhaps after tomorrow. You, happy mortal, with your lovely family (how is Ines? how are the twins?) and your diversified work (how are the lichens?), can hardly be expected to puzzle out my misfortune in terms of human communion, but you may clarify things for me through the prism of your art.

Yet the pity of it. Curse your art, I am hideously unhappy. She keeps on walking to and fro where the brown nets are spread to dry on the hot stone slabs and the dappled light of the water plays on the side of a moored fishing boat. Somewhere, somehow, I have made some fatal mistake. There are tiny pale bits of broken fish scales glistening here and there in the brown meshes. It may all end in *Aleppo* if I am not careful. Spare me, V.: you would load your dice with an unbearable implication if you took that for a title.

Boston, 1943

The Loudest Voice

GRACE PALEY

There is a certain place where dumb-waiters boom, doors slam, dishes crash; every window is a mother's mouth bidding the street shut up, go skate somewhere else, come home. My voice is the loudest.

There, my own mother is still as full of breathing as me and the grocer stands up to speak to her. "Mrs. Abramowitz," he says, "people should not be afraid of their children."

"Ah, Mr. Bialik," my mother replies, "if you say to her or her father 'Ssh,' they say, 'In the grave it will be quiet.' "

"From Coney Island to the cemetery," says my papa. "It's the same subway; it's the same fare."

I am right next to the pickle barrel. My pinky is making tiny whirlpools in the brine. I stop a moment to announce: "Campbell's Tomato Soup. Campbell's Vegetable Beef Soup. Campbell's S-c-otch Broth . . ."

"Be quiet," the grocer says, "the labels are coming off."

"Please, Shirley, be a little quiet," my mother begs me.

In that place the whole street groans: Be quiet! Be quiet! but steals from the happy chorus of my inside self not a tittle or a jot.

There, too, but just around the corner, is a red brick building that has been old for many years. Every morning the children stand before it in double lines which must be straight. They are not insulted. They are waiting anyway.

I am usually among them. I am, in fact, the first, since I begin with "A."

One cold morning the monitor tapped me on the shoulder. "Go to Room 409, Shirley Abramowitz," he said. I did as I was told. I went in a hurry up a down staircase to Room 409, which contained sixth-graders. I had to wait at the desk without wiggling until Mr. Hilton, their teacher, had time to speak.

After five minutes he said, "Shirley?"

"What?" I whispered.

He said, "My! My! Shirley Abramowitz! They told me you had a particularly loud, clear voice and read with lots of expression. Could that be true?"

"Oh yes," I whispered.

"In that case, don't be silly; I might very well be your teacher someday. Speak up, speak up."

"Yes," I shouted.

"More like it," he said. "Now, Shirley, can you put a ribbon in your hair or a bobby pin? It's too messy."

"Yes!" I bawled.

"Now, now, calm down." He turned to the class. "Children, not a sound. Open at page 39. Read till 52. When you finish, start again." He looked me over once more. "Now, Shirley, you know, I suppose, that Christmas is coming. We are preparing a beautiful play. Most of the parts have been given out. But I still need a child with a strong voice, lots of stamina. Do you know what stamina is? You do? Smart kid. You know, I heard you read 'The Lord is my shepherd' in Assembly yesterday. I was very impressed. Wonderful delivery. Mrs. Jordan, your teacher, speaks highly of you. Now listen to me, Shirley Abramowitz, if you want to take the part and be in the play, repeat after me, 'I swear to work harder than I ever did before.' "

I looked to heaven and said at once, "Oh, I swear." I kissed my pinky and looked at God.

"That is an actor's life, my dear," he explained. "Like a soldier's, never tardy or disobedient to his general, the director. Everything," he said "absolutely everything will depend on you."

That afternoon, all over the building, children scraped and scrubbed the turkeys and the sheaves of corn off the schoolroom windows. Goodbye Thanksgiving. The next morning a monitor brought red paper and green paper from the office. We made new shapes and hung them on the walls and glued them to the doors.

The teachers became happier and happier. Their heads were ringing like the bells of childhood. My best friend Evie was prone to evil, but she did not get a single demerit for whispering. We learned "Holy Night" without an error. "How wonderful!" said Miss Glacé, the student teacher. "To think that some of you don't even speak the language!" We learned "Deck the Halls" and "Hark! The Herald Angels." . . . They weren't ashamed and we weren't embarrassed.

Oh, but when my mother heard about it all, she said to my father: "Misha, you don't know what's going on there. Cramer is the head of the Tickets Committee."

"Who?" asked my father. "Cramer? Oh yes, an active woman."

"Active? Active has to have a reason. Listen," she said sadly, "I'm surprised to see my neighbors making tra-la-la for Christmas."

My father couldn't think of what to say to that. Then he decided: "You're in America! Clara, you wanted to come here. In Palestine the Arabs would be eating you alive. Europe you had pogroms. Argentina is full of Indians. Here you got Christmas. . . . Some joke, ha?"

"Very funny, Misha. What is becoming of you? If we came to a new country a long time ago to run away from tyrants, and instead we fall into a creeping pogrom, that our children learn a lot of lies, so what's the joke? Ach, Misha, your idealism is going away."

"So is your sense of humor."

"That I never had, but idealism you had a lot of."

"I'm the same Misha Abramovitch, I didn't change an iota. Ask anyone."

"Only ask me," says my mama, may she rest in peace. "I got the answer."

Meanwhile the neighbors had to think of what to say too.

Marty's father said: "You know, he has a very important part, my boy."

"Mine also," said Mr. Sauerfeld.

"Not my boy!" said Mrs. Klieg. "I said to him no. The answer is no. When I say no! I mean no!"

The rabbi's wife said, "It's disgusting!" But no one listened to her. Under the narrow sky of God's great wisdom she wore a strawberry-blond wig.

Every day was noisy and full of experience. I was Right-hand Man. Mr. Hilton said: "How could I get along without you, Shirley?"

He said: "Your mother and father ought to get down on their knees every night and thank God for giving them a child like you."

He also said: "You're absolutely a pleasure to work with, my dear, dear child."

Sometimes he said: "For God's sakes, what did I do with the script? Shirley! Shirley! Find it."

Then I answered quietly: "Here it is, Mr. Hilton."

Once in a while, when he was very tired, he would cry out: "Shirley, I'm just tired of screaming at those kids. Will you tell Ira Pushkov not to come in till Lester points to that star the second time?"

Then I roared: "Ira Pushkov, what's the matter with you? Dope! Mr. Hilton told you five times already, don't come in till Lester points to that star the second time."

"Ach, Clara," my father asked, "what does she do there till six o'clock she can't even put the plates on the table?"

"Christmas," said my mother coldly.

"Ho! Ho!" my father said. "Christmas. What's the harm? After all, history teaches everyone. We learn from reading this is a holiday from pagan times also, candles, lights, even Chanukah. So we learn it's not altogether Christian. So if they think it's a private holiday, they're only ignorant, not patriotic. What belongs to history, belongs to all men. You want to go back to the Middle Ages? Is it better to shave your head with a secondhand razor? Does it hurt Shirley to learn to speak up? It does not. So maybe someday she won't live between the kitchen and the shop. She's not a fool."

I thank you, Papa, for your kindness. It is true about me to this day. I am foolish but I am not a fool.

That night my father kissed me and said with great interest in my career, "Shirley, tomorrow's your big day. Congrats."

"Save it," my mother said. Then she shut all the windows in order to prevent tonsillitis.

In the morning it snowed. On the street corner a tree had been decorated for us by a kind city administration. In order to miss its chilly shadow our neighbors walked three blocks east to buy a loaf of bread. The butcher pulled down black window shades to keep the colored lights from shining on his chickens. Oh, not me. On the way to school, with both my hands I tossed it a kiss of tolerance. Poor thing, it was a stranger in Egypt.

I walked straight into the auditorium past the staring children. "Go ahead, Shirley!" said the monitors. Four boys, big for their age, had already started work as propmen and stagehands.

Mr. Hilton was very nervous. He was not even happy. Whatever he started to say ended in a sideward look of sadness. He sat slumped in the middle of the first row and asked me to help Miss Glacé. I did this, although she thought my voice too resonant and said, "Show-off!"

Parents began to arrive long before we were ready. They wanted to make a good impression. From among the yards of drapes I peeked out at the audience. I saw my embarrassed mother.

Ira, Lester, and Meyer were pasted to their beards by Miss Glacé. She almost forgot to thread the star on its wire, but I reminded her. I coughed a few times to clear my throat. Miss Glacé looked around and saw that everyone was in costume and on line waiting to play his part. She whispered, "All right . . . " Then:

Jackie Sauerfeld, the prettiest boy in first grade, parted the curtains with his skinny elbow and in a high voice sang out:

> Parents dear
> We are here
> To make a Christmas play in time.
> It we give
> In narrative
> And illustrate with pantomime.

He disappeared.

My voice burst immediately from the wings to the great shock of Ira, Lester, and Meyer, who were waiting for it but were surprised all the same.

"I remember, I remember, the house where I was born . . ."

Miss Glacé yanked the curtain open and there it was, the house— an old hayloft, where Celia Kornbluh lay in the straw with Cindy Lou, her favorite doll. Ira, Lester, and Meyer moved slowly from the wings toward her, sometimes pointing to a moving star and sometimes ahead to Cindy Lou.

It was a long story and it was a sad story. I carefully pronounced all the words about my lonesome childhood, while little Eddie Braunstein wandered upstage and down with his shepherd's stick, looking for sheep. I brought up lonesomeness again, and not being understood at all except by some women everybody hated. Eddie was too small for that and Marty Groff took his place, wearing his father's prayer shawl. I announced twelve friends, and half the boys in the fourth grade gathered round Marty, who stood on an orange crate while my voice harangued. Sorrowful and loud, I declaimed about love and God and Man, but because of the terrible deceit of Abie Stock we came suddenly to a famous moment. Marty, whose remembering tongue I was, waited at the foot of the cross. He stared desperately at the audience. I groaned, "My God, my God, why hast thou forsaken me?" The soldiers who were sheiks grabbed poor Marty to pin him up to die, but he wrenched free, turned again to the audience, and spread his arms aloft to show despair and the end. I murmured at the top of my voice, "The rest is silence, but as everyone in this room, in this city—in this world—now knows, I shall have life eternal."

That night Mrs. Kornbluh visited our kitchen for a glass of tea.

"How's the virgin?" asked my father with a look of concern.

"For a man with a daughter, you got a fresh mouth, Abramovitch."

"Here," said my father kindly, "have some lemon, it'll sweeten your disposition."

They debated a little in Yiddish, then fell in a puddle of Russian and Polish. What I understood next was my father, who said, "Still and all, it was certainly a beautiful affair, you have to admit, introducing us to the beliefs of a different culture."

"Well, yes," said Mrs. Kornbluh. "The only thing . . . you know Charlie Turner—that cute boy in Celia's class—a couple others? They got very small parts or no part at all. In very bad taste, it seemed to me. After all, it's their religion."

"Ach," explained my mother, "what could Mr. Hilton do? They got very small voices; after all, why should they holler? The English language they know from the beginning by heart. They're blond like angels. You think it's so important they should get in the play? Christmas . . . the whole piece of goods . . . they own it."

I listened and listened until I couldn't listen any more. Too sleepy, I climbed out of bed and kneeled. I made a little church of my hands and said, "Hear, O Israel . . ." Then I called out in Yiddish, "Please, good night, good night. Ssh." My father said, "Ssh yourself," and slammed the kitchen door.

I was happy. I fell asleep at once. I had prayed for everybody: my talking family, cousins far away, passers-by, and all the lonesome Christians. I expected to be heard. My voice was certainly the loudest.

The Grave

KATHERINE ANNE PORTER

The grandfather, dead for more than thirty years, had been twice disturbed in his long repose by the constancy and possessiveness of his widow. She removed his bones first to Louisiana and then to Texas as if she had set out to find her own burial place, knowing well she would never return to the places she had left. In Texas she set up a small cemetery in a corner of her first farm, and as the family connection grew, and oddments of relations came over from Kentucky to settle, it contained at last about twenty graves. After the grandmother's death, part of her land was to be sold for the benefit of certain of her children, and the cemetery happened to lie in the part set aside for sale. It was necessary to take up the bodies and bury them again in the family plot in the big new public cemetery, where the grandmother had been buried. At last her husband was to lie beside her for eternity, as she had planned.

The family cemetery had been a pleasant small neglected garden of tangled rose bushes and ragged cedar trees and cypress, the simple flat stones rising out of uncropped sweet-smelling wild grass. The graves were lying open and empty one burning day when Miranda and her brother Paul, who often went together to hunt rabbits and doves, propped their twenty-two Winchester rifles carefully against the rail fence, climbed over and explored among the graves. She was nine years old and he was twelve.

They peered into the pits all shaped alike with such purposeful accuracy, and looking at each other with pleased adventurous eyes, they said in solemn tones: "These were graves!" trying by words to shape a special, suitable emotion in their minds, but they felt nothing except an agreeable thrill of wonder: they were seeing a new sight, doing something they had not done before. In them both there was also a small disappointment at the entire commonplaceness of the actual spectacle. Even if it had once contained a coffin for years upon years, when the coffin was gone a grave was just a hole in the ground. Miranda leaped into the pit that had held her grandfather's bones. Scratching around aimlessly and pleasurably as any young animal, she scooped up a lump of earth and weighed it in her palm. It had a pleasantly sweet, corrupt smell, being mixed with cedar needles and small leaves, and as the crumbs fell apart, she saw a silver dove no larger than a hazel nut, with spread wings and a neat fan-shaped tail. The breast had a deep round hollow in it. Turning it up to the fierce sunlight, she saw that the inside of the hollow was cut in little whorls. She scrambled out, over the pile of loose earth that had fallen back into one end of the grave, calling to Paul that she had found something, he must guess what . . . His head appeared smiling over the rim of another grave. He waved a closed hand at her. "I've got something too!" They ran to compare treasures, making a game of it, so many guesses each, all wrong, and a final show-down with opened palms. Paul had found a thin wide gold ring carved with intricate flowers and leaves. Miranda was smitten at sight of the ring and wished to have it. Paul seemed more impressed by the dove. They made a trade, with some little bickering. After he had got the dove in his hand, Paul said, "Don't you know what this is? This is a screw head for a *coffin!* . . . I'll bet nobody else in the world has one like this!"

Miranda glanced at it without covetousness. She had the gold ring on her thumb; it fitted perfectly. "Maybe we ought to go now," she said, "maybe one of the niggers'll see us and tell somebody." They knew the land had been sold, the cemetery was no longer theirs, and they felt like trespassers. They climbed back over the fence, slung their rifles loosely under their arms—they had been shooting at targets with various kinds of firearms since they were seven years old—and set out to look for the rabbits and doves or whatever small game might happen along. On these expeditions Miranda always followed at Paul's heels along the path, obeying instructions about handling her gun when going through fences; learning how to stand it up properly so it would not slip and fire unexpectedly; how to wait her turn for a shot and not just bang away in the air without looking, spoiling shots for Paul, who really could hit things if given a chance. Now and then, in her excitement at seeing birds whizz up suddenly before her face, or a rabbit leap across her very toes, she lost her head, and almost without sighting she flung her rifle up and pulled the trigger. She hardly ever hit any sort of mark. She had no proper sense of hunting at all. Her brother would be often completely disgusted with her. "You don't care whether you get your bird or not," he said. "That's no way to hunt." Miranda could not understand his indignation. She had seen him smash his hat and yell with fury when he had missed his aim. "What I like about shooting," said Miranda, with exasperating inconsequence, "is pulling the trigger and hearing the noise."

"Then, by golly," said Paul, "whyn't you go back to the range and shoot at bulls-eyes?"

"I'd just as soon," said Miranda, "only like this, we walk around more."

"Well, you just stay behind and stop spoiling my shots," said Paul, who, when he made a kill, wanted to be certain he had made it.

Miranda, who alone brought down a bird once in twenty rounds, always claimed as her own any game they got when they fired at the same moment. It was tiresome and unfair and her brother was sick of it.

"Now, the first dove we see, or the first rabbit, is mine," he told her. "And the next will be yours. Remember that and don't get smarty."

"What about snakes?" asked Miranda idly. "Can I have the first snake?"

Waving her thumb gently and watching her gold ring glitter, Miranda lost interest in shooting. She was wearing her summer roughing outfit: dark blue overalls, a light blue shirt, a hired-man's straw hat, and thick brown sandals. Her brother had the same outfit except his was a sober hickory-nut color. Ordinarily Miranda preferred her overalls to any other dress, though it was making rather a scandal in the countryside, for the year was 1903, and in the back country the law of female decorum had teeth in it. Her father had been criticized for letting his girls dress like boys and go careering around astride barebacked horses. Big sister Maria, the really independent and fearless one, in spite of her rather affected ways, rode at a dead run with only a rope knotted around her horse's nose. It was said the motherless family was running down, with the Grandmother no longer there to hold it together. It was known that she had discriminated against her son Harry in her will, and that he was in straits about money. Some of his old neighbors reflected with vicious satisfaction that now he would probably not be so stiffnecked, nor have any more high-stepping horses either. Miranda knew this, though she could not say how. She had met along the road old women of the kind who smoked corn-cob pipes, who had treated her grandmother with most sincere respect. They slanted their gummy old eyes side-ways at the grand-daughter and said, "Ain't you ashamed of yoself, Missy? It's against the Scriptures to dress like that. What yo Pappy thinkin about?" Miranda, with her powerful social sense, which was like a fine set of antennae radiating from every pore of her skin, would feel ashamed because she knew well it was rude and ill-bred to shock anybody, even bad-tempered old crones, though she had faith in her father's judgment and was perfectly comfortable in the clothes. Her father had said, "They're just what you need, and they'll save your dresses for school . . ." This sounded quite simple and natural to her. She had been brought up in rigorous economy. Wastefulness was vulgar. It was also a sin.

These were truths; she had heard them repeated many times and never once disputed.

Now the ring, shining with the serene purity of fine gold on her rather grubby thumb, turned her feelings against her overalls and sockless feet, toes sticking through the thick brown leather straps. She wanted to go back to the farmhouse, take a good cold bath, dust herself with plenty of Maria's violet talcum powder—provided Maria was not present to object, of course—put on the thinnest, most becoming dress she owned, with a big sash, and sit in a wicker chair under the trees . . . These things were not all she wanted, of course; she had vague stirrings of desire for luxury and a grand way of living which could not take precise form in her imagination but were founded on family legend of past wealth and leisure. These immediate comforts were what she could have, and she wanted them at once. She lagged rather far behind Paul, and once she thought of just turning back without a word and going home. She stopped, thinking that Paul would never do that to her, and so she would have to tell him. When a rabbit leaped, she let Paul have it without dispute. He killed it with one shot.

When she came up with him, he was already kneeling, examining the wound, the rabbit trailing from his hands. "Right through the head," he said complacently, as if he had aimed for it. He took out his sharp, competent bowie knife and started to skin the body. He did it very cleanly and quickly. Uncle Jimbilly knew how to prepare the skins so that Miranda always had fur coats for her dolls, for though she never cared much for her dolls she liked seeing them in fur coats. The children knelt facing each other over the dead animal. Miranda watched admiringly while her brother stripped the skin away as if he were taking off a glove. The flayed flesh emerged dark scarlet, sleek, firm; Miranda with thumb and finger felt the long fine muscles with the silvery flat strips binding them to the joints. Brother lifted the oddly bloated belly. "Look," he said, in a low amazed vioce. "It was going to have young ones."

Very carefully he slit the thin flesh from the center ribs to the flanks, and a scarlet bag appeared. He slit again and pulled the bag open, and there lay a bundle of tiny rabbits, each wrapped in a thin scarlet veil. The brother pulled these off and there they were, dark gray, their sleek wet down lying in minute even ripples, like a baby's head just washed, their unbelievably small delicate ears folded close, their little blind faces almost featureless.

Miranda said, "Oh, I want to *see*," under her breath. She looked and looked—excited but not frightened, for she was accustomed to the sight of animals killed in hunting—filled with pity and astonishment and a kind of shocked delight in the wonderful little creatures for their own sakes, they were so pretty. She touched one of them ever so carefully, "Ah, there's blood running over them," she said and began to tremble without knowing why. Yet she wanted most deeply to see and to know. Having seen, she felt at once as if she had known all along. The very memory of her former ignorance faded, she had always known just this. No one had ever told her anything outright, she had been rather unobservant of the animal life around her because she was so accustomed to animals. They seemed simply disorderly and unaccountably rude in their habits, but altogether natural and not very interesting. Her brother had spoken as if he had known about everything all along. He may have seen all this before. He had never said a word to her, but she knew now a part at least of what he knew. She understood a little of the secret, formless intuitions in her own mind and body, which had been clearing up, taking form, so gradually and so steadily she had not realized that she was learning what she had to know. Paul said cautiously, as if he were talking about something forbidden: "They were just about ready to be born." His voice dropped on the last word. "I know," said Miranda, "like kittens. I know, like babies." She was quietly and terribly agitated, standing again with her rifle under her arm, looking down at the bloody heap. "I don't want the skin," she said, "I won't have it." Paul buried the young rabbits again in their mother's body, wrapped the skin around her, carried her to a clump of sage bushes, and hid her away. He came out again at once and said to Miranda, with an eager friendliness, a confidential tone quite unusual in him, as if he were taking her into an important secret on equal terms: "Listen now. Now you listen to me, and don't ever forget. Don't you ever tell a living soul that you saw this. Don't tell a soul. Don't tell Dad because I'll get into trouble. He'll say I'm leading you into things you ought not to do. He's always saying that. So now don't you go and forget and blab out sometime the way you're always doing . . . Now, that's a secret. Don't you tell."

Miranda never told, she did not even wish to tell anybody. She thought about the whole worrisome affair with confused unhappiness for a few days. Then it sank quietly into her mind and was heaped over by accumulated thousands of impressions, for nearly twenty years. One day she was picking her path among the puddles and crushed refuse of a market street in a strange city of a strange country, when without warning, plain and clear in its true colors as if she looked through a frame upon a scene that had not stirred nor changed since the moment it happened, the episode of that far-off day leaped from its burial place before her mind's eye. She was so reasonlessly horrified she halted suddenly staring, the scene before her eyes dimmed by the vision back of them. An Indian vendor had held up before her a tray of dyed sugar sweets, in the shapes of all kinds of small creatures: birds, baby chicks, baby rabbits, lambs, baby pigs. They were in gay colors and smelled of vanilla, maybe. . . . It was a very hot day and the smell in the market, with its piles of raw flesh and wilting flowers, was like the mingled sweetness and corruption she had smelled that other day in the empty cemetery at home: the day she had remembered always until now vaguely as the time she and her brother had found treasure in the opened graves. Instantly upon this thought the dreadful vision faded, and she saw clearly her brother, whose childhood face she had forgotten, standing again in the blazing sunshine, again twelve years old, a pleased sober smile in his eyes, turning the silver dove over and over in his hands.

The Tree

DYLAN THOMAS

Rising from the house that faced the Jarvis hills in the long distance, there was a tower for the day-birds to build in and for the owls to fly around at night. From the village the light of the tower window shone like a glowworm through the panes; but the room under the

THE TREE. Dylan Thomas, *Adventures in the Skin Trade.* Copyright 1955 by New Directions Publishing Corporation. Reprinted by permission of New Directions Publishing Corporation.

sparrows' nests was rarely lit; webs were spun over its unwashed ceilings; it stared over twenty miles of the up-and-down country, and the corners kept their secrets where there were claw marks in the dust.

The child knew the house from roof to cellar; he knew the irregular lawns and the gardener's shed where flowers burst out of their jars; but he could not find the key that opened the door of the tower.

The house changed to his moods, and a lawn was the sea or the shore or the sky or whatever he wished it. When a lawn was a sad mile of water, and he was sailing on a broken flower down the waves, the gardener would come out of his shed near the island of bushes. He, too, would take a stalk, and sail. Straddling a garden broom, he would fly wherever the child wished. He knew every story from the beginning of the world.

In the beginning, he would say, there was a tree.

What kind of tree?

The tree where that blackbird's whistling.

A hawk, a hawk, cried the child.

The gardener would look up at the tree, seeing a monstrous hawk perched on a bough or an eagle swinging in the wind.

The gardener loved the Bible. When the sun sank and the garden was full of people, he would sit with a candle in his shed, reading of the first love and the legend of apples and serpents. But the death of Christ on a tree he loved most. Trees made a fence around him, and he knew of the changing of the seasons by the hues on the bark and the rushing of sap through the covered roots. His world moved and changed as spring moved along the branches, changing their nakedness; his God grew up like a tree from the apple-shaped earth, giving bud to His children and letting His children be blown from their places by the breezes of winter; winter and death moved in one wind. He would sit in his shed and read of the crucifixion, looking over the jars on his window-shelf into the winter nights. He would think that love fails on such nights, and that many of its children are cut down.

The child transfigured the blowsy lawns with his playing. The gardener called him by his mother's name, and seated him on his knee, and talked to him of the wonders of Jerusalem and the birth in the manger.

In the beginning was the village of Bethlehem, he whispered to the child before the bell rang for tea out of the growing darkness.

Where is Bethlehem?

Far away, said the gardener, in the East.

To the east stood the Jarvis hills, hiding the sun, their trees drawing up the moon out of the grass.

The child lay in bed. He watched the rocking horse and wished that it would grow wings so that he could mount it and ride into the Arabian sky. But the winds of Wales blew at the curtains, and crickets made a noise in the untidy plot under the window. His toys were dead. He started to cry and then stopped, knowing no reason for tears. The night was windy and cold, he was warm under the sheets; the night was as big as a hill, he was a boy in bed.

Closing his eyes, he stared into a spinning cavern deeper than the darkness of the garden where the first tree on which the unreal birds had fastened stood alone and bright as fire. The tears ran back under his lids as he thought of the first tree that was planted so near him, like a friend in the garden. He crept out of bed and tiptoed to the door. The rocking horse bounded forward on its springs, startling the child into a noiseless scamper back to bed. The child looked at the horse and the horse was quiet; he tiptoed again along the carpet, and reached the door, and turned the knob around, and ran on to the landing. Feeling blindly in front of him, he made his way to the top of the stairs; he looked down the dark stairs into the hall, seeing a host of shadows curve in and out of the corners, hearing their sinuous voices, imagining the pits of their eyes and their lean arms. But they would be little and secret and bloodless, not cased in invisible armour but wound around with cloths as thin as a web; they would whisper as he walked, touch him on the shoulder, and say S in his ear. He went down the stairs; not a shadow moved in the hall, the corners were empty. He put out his hand and patted the darkness, thinking to feel some dry and velvet head creep under the fingers and edge, like a mist, into the nails. But there was nothing. He opened the front door, and the shadows swept into the garden.

Once on the path, his fears left him. The moon had lain down on the unweeded beds, and her frosts were spread on the grass. At last he came to the illuminated tree at the long gravel end, older even than the marvel of light, with the woodlice asleep under the bark, with the boughs standing out from the body like the frozen arms of a woman. The child touched the tree; it bent as to his touch. He saw a star, brighter than any in the sky, burn steadily above the first birds' tower, and shine on nowhere but on the leafless boughs and the trunk and the travelling roots.

The child had not doubted the tree. He said his prayers to it, with knees bent on the blackened twigs the night wind fetched to the ground. Then, trembling with love and cold, he ran back over the lawns towards the house.

There was an idiot to the east of the county who walked the land like a beggar. Now at a farmhouse and now at a widow's cottage he begged for his bread. A parson gave him a suit, and it lopped round his hungry ribs and shoulders and waved in the wind as he shambled over the fields. But his eyes were so wide and his neck so clear of the country dirt that no one refused him what he asked. And asking for water, he was given milk.

Where do you come from?

From the east, he said.

So they knew he was an idiot, and gave him a meal to clean the yards.

As he bent with a rake over the dung and the trodden grain, he heard a voice rise in his heart. He put his hand into the cattle's hay, caught a mouse, rubbed his hand over its muzzle, and let it go away.

All day the thought of the tree was with the child; all night it stood up in his dreams as the star stood above its plot. One morning towards the middle of December, when the wind from the farthest hills was rushing around the house, and the snow of the dark hours had not dissolved from lawns and roofs, he ran to the gardener's shed. The gardener was repairing a rake he had found broken. Without a word, the child sat on a seedbox at his feet, and watched him tie the teeth, and knew that the wire would not keep them together. He looked at the gardener's boots, wet with snow, at the patched knees of his trousers, at the undone buttons of his coat, and the folds of his belly under the patched flannel shirt. He looked at his hands as they busied themselves over the golden knots of wire; they were hard, brown hands, with the stains of the soil under the broken nails and the stains of tobacco on the tips of the fingers. Now the lines of the gardener's face were set in determination as time upon time he knotted the iron teeth only to feel them shake insecurely from the handle. The child was frightened of the strength and uncleanliness of the old man; but, looking at the long, thick beard, unstained and white as fleece, he soon became reassured. The beard was the beard of an apostle.

I prayed to the tree, said the child.

Always pray to a tree, said the gardener, thinking of Calvary and Eden.

I pray to the tree every night.

Pray to a tree.

The wire slid over the teeth.

I pray to that tree.

The wire snapped.

The child was pointing over the glasshouse flowers to the tree that, alone of all the trees in the garden, had no sign of snow.

An elder, said the gardener, but the child stood up from his box and shouted so loud that the unmended rake fell with a clatter on the floor.

The first tree. The first tree you told me of. In the beginning was the tree, you said. I heard you, the child shouted.

The elder is as good as another, said the gardener, lowering his voice to humour the child.

The first tree of all, said the child in a whisper.

Reassured again by the gardener's voice, he smiled through the window at the tree, and again the wire crept over the broken rake.

God grows in strange trees, said the old man. His trees come to rest in strange places.

As he unfolded the story of the twelve stages of the cross, the tree waved its boughs to the child. An apostle's voice rose out of the tarred lungs.

So they hoisted him up on a tree, and drove nails through his belly and his feet.

There was the blood of the noon sun on the trunk of the elder, staining the bark.

The idiot stood on the Jarvis hills, looking down into the immaculate valley from whose waters and grasses the mists of morning rose and were lost. He saw the dew dissolving, the cattle staring into the stream, and the dark clouds flying away at the rumour of the sun. The sun turned at the edges of the thin and watery sky like a sweet in a glass of water. He was hungry for light as the first and almost invisible rain fell on his lips; he plucked at the grass, and, tasting it, felt it lie green on his tongue. So there was light in his mouth, and light was a sound at his ears, and the whole dominion of light in the valley that had such a curious name. He had known of the Jarvis hills; their shapes rose over the slopes of the county to be seen for miles around, but no one had told him of the valley lying under the hills. Bethlehem, said the idiot to the valley, turning over the sounds of the word and giving it all the glory of the Welsh morning. He brothered the world around him, sipped at the air, as a child newly born sips and brothers the light. The life of the Jarvis valley, steaming up from the body of the grass and the trees and the long hand of the stream, lent him a new blood. Night had emptied the idiot's veins, and dawn in the valley filled them again.

Bethlehem, said the idiot to the valley.

The gardener had no present to give the child, so he took out a key from his pocket and said, This is the key to the tower. On Christmas Eve I will unlock the door for you.

Before it was dark, he and the child climbed the stairs to the tower, the key turned in the lock, and the door, like the lid of a secret box, opened and let them in. The room was empty. Where are the secrets? asked the child, staring up at the matted rafters and into the spiders' corners and along the leaden panes of the window.

It is enough that I have given you the key, said the gardener, who believed the key of the universe to be hidden in his pocket along with the feathers of birds and the seeds of flowers.

The child began to cry because there were no secrets. Over and over again he explored the empty room, kicking up the dust to look for a colourless trap-door, tapping the unpanelled walls for the hollow voice of a room beyond the tower. He brushed the webs from the window, and looked out through the dust into the snowing Christmas Eve. A world of hills stretched far away into the measured sky, and the tops of the hills he had never seen climbed up to meet the falling flakes. Woods and rocks, wide seas of barren land, and a new tide of mountain sky sweeping through the black beeches, lay before him. To the east were the outlines of nameless hill creatures and a den of trees.

Who are they? Who are they?

They are the Jarvis hills, said the gardener, which have been from the beginning.

He took the child by the hand and led him away from the window. The key turned in the lock.

That night the child slept well; there was power in snow and darkness; there was unalterable music in the silence of the stars; there was a silence in the hurrying wind. And Bethlehem had been nearer than he expected.

On Christmas morning the idiot walked into the garden. His hair was wet and his flaked and ragged shoes were thick with the dirt of the fields. Tired from the long journey from the Jarvis hills, and weak for the want of food, he sat down under the elder-tree where the gardener had rolled a log. Clasping his hands in front of him, he saw the desolation of the flower-beds and the weeds that grew in profusion on the edges of the paths. The tower stood up like a tree of stone and glass over the red eaves. He pulled his coat-collar round his neck as a fresh wind sprang up and struck the tree; he looked down at his hands and saw that they were praying. Then a fear of the garden came over him, the shrubs were his enemies, and the trees that made an avenue down to the gate lifted their arms in horror. The place was too high, peering down on to the tall hills; the place was too low, shivering up at the plumed shoulders of a new mountain. Here the wind was too wild, fuming about the silence, raising a Jewish voice out of the elder boughs; here the silence beat like a human heart. And as he sat under the cruel hills, he heard a voice that was in him cry out: Why did you bring me here?

He could not tell why he had come; they had told him to come and had guided him, but he did not know who they were. The voice of a people rose out of the garden beds, and rain swooped down from heaven.

Let me be, said the idiot, and made a little gesture against the sky. There is rain on my face, there is wind on my cheeks. He brothered the rain.

So the child found him under the shelter of the tree, bearing the torture of the weather with a divine patience, letting his long hair blow where it would, with his mouth set in a sad smile.

Who was the stranger? He had fires in his eyes, the flesh of his neck under the gathered coat was bare. Yet he smiled as he sat in his rags under a tree on Christmas Day.

Where do you come from? asked the child.

From the east, answered the idiot.

The gardener had not lied, and the secret of the tower was true; this dark and shabby tree, that glistened only in the night, was the first tree of all.

But he asked again:

Where do you come from?

From the Jarvis hills.

Stand up against the tree.

The idiot, still smiling, stood up with his back to the elder.

Put out your arms like this.

The idiot put out his arms.

The child ran as fast as he could to the gardener's shed, and, returning over the sodden lawns, saw that the idiot had not moved but stood, straight and smiling, with his back to the tree and his arms stretched out.

Let me tie your hands.

The idiot felt the wire that had not mended the rake close round his wrists. It cut into the flesh, and the blood from the cuts fell shining on to the tree.

Brother, he said. He saw that the child held silver nails in the palm of his hand.

After the Ball

LEO TOLSTOY

"—And you say that a man cannot, of himself, understand what is good and evil; that it is all environment, that the environment swamps the man. But I believe it is all chance. Take my own case . . ."

Thus spoke our excellent friend, Ivan Vasilievich, after a conversation between us on the impossibility of improving individual character without a change of the conditions under which men live. Nobody had actually said that one could not of oneself understand good and evil; but it was a habit of Ivan Vasilievich to answer in this way the thoughts aroused in his own mind by conversation, and to illustrate those thoughts by relating incidents in his own life. He often quite forgot the reason for his story in telling it; but he always told it with great sincerity and feeling.

He did so now.

"Take my own case. My whole life was moulded, not by environment, but by something quite different."

"By what, then?" we asked.

"Oh, that is a long story. I should have to tell you about a great many things to make you understand."

"Well, tell us then."

Ivan Vasilievich thought a little, and shook his head.

"My whole life," he said, "was changed in one night, or, rather, morning."

"Why, what happened?" one of us asked.

"What happened was that I was very much in love. I have been in love many times, but this was the most serious of all. It is a thing of the past; she has married daughters now. It was Varinka B—." Ivan Vasilievich mentioned her surname. "Even at fifty she is remarkably handsome; but in her youth, at eighteen, she was exquisite —tall, slender, graceful, and stately. Yes, stately is the word; she held herself very erect, by instinct as it were; and carried her head high, and that together with her beauty and height gave her a queenly air in spite of being thin, even bony one might say. It might indeed have been deterring had it not been for her smile, which was always gay and cordial, and for the charming light in her eyes and for her youthful sweetness."

"What an entrancing description you give, Ivan Vasilievich!"

"Description, indeed! I could not possibly describe her so that you could appreciate her. But that does not matter; what I am going to tell you happened in the forties. I was at that time a student in a provincial university. I don't know whether it was a good thing or no, but we had no political clubs, no theories in our universities then. We were simply young and spent our time as young men do, studying and amusing ourselves. I was a very gay, lively, careless fellow, and had plenty of money too. I had a fine horse, and used to go tobogganing with the young ladies. Skating had not yet come into fashion. I went to drinking parties with my comrades—in those days we drank nothing but champagne—if we had no champagne we drank nothing at all. We never drank vodka, as they do now. Evening parties and balls were my favourite amusements. I danced well, and was not an ugly fellow."

"Come, there is no need to be modest," interrupted a lady near him. "We have seen your photograph. Not ugly, indeed! You were a handsome fellow."

"Handsome, if you like. That does not matter. When my love for her was at its strongest, on the last day of the carnival, I was at a ball at the provincial marshal's, a good-natured old man, rich and hospitable, and a court chamberlain. The guests were welcomed by his wife, who was as good-natured as himself. She was dressed in puce-coloured velvet, and had a diamond diadem on her forehead, and her plump, old white shoulders and bosom were bare like the portraits of Empress Elizabeth, the daughter of Peter the Great.

"It was a delightful ball. It was a splendid room, with a gallery for the orchestra, which was famous at the time, and consisted of serfs belonging to a musical landowner. The refreshments were magnificent, and the champagne flowed in rivers. Though I was fond of champagne I did not drink that night, because without it I was drunk with love. But I made up for it by dancing waltzes and polkas till I was ready to drop—of course, whenever possible, with Varinka. She wore a white dress with a pink sash, white shoes, and white kid gloves, which did not quite reach to her thin pointed elbows. A disgusting engineer named Anisimov robbed me of the mazurka with her—to this day I cannot forgive him. He asked her for the dance the minute she arrived, while I had driven to the hairdresser's to get a pair of gloves, and was late. So I did not dance the mazurka with her, but with a German girl to whom I had previously paid a little attention; but I am afraid I did not behave very politely to her that evening. I hardly spoke or looked at her, and saw nothing but the tall, slender figure in a white dress, with a pink sash, a flushed, beaming, dimpled face, and sweet, kind eyes. I was not alone; they were all looking at her with admiration, the men and women alike, although she outshone all of them. They could not help admiring her.

"Although I was not nominally her partner for the mazurka, I did as a matter of fact dance nearly the whole time with her. She always came forward boldly the whole length of the room to pick me out. I flew to meet her without waiting to be chosen, and she thanked me with a smile for my intuition. When I was brought up to her with somebody else, and she guessed wrongly, she took the other man's hand with a shrug of her slim shoulders, and smiled at me regretfully.

"Whenever there was a waltz figure in the mazurka, I waltzed with her for a long time, and breathing fast and smiling, she would say, '*Encore*'; and I went on waltzing and waltzing, as though unconscious of any bodily existence."

"Come now, how could you be unconscious of it with your arm round her waist? You must have been conscious, not only of your own existence, but of hers," said one of the party.

Ivan Vasilievich cried out, almost shouting in anger: "There you are, moderns all over! Nowadays you think of nothing but the body. It was different in our day. The more I was in love the less corporeal was she in my eyes. Nowadays you see legs, ankles, and I don't know what. You undress the women you are in love with. In my eyes, as Alphonse Karr said—and he was a good writer—'the one I loved was always draped in robes of bronze.' We never thought of doing so; we tried to veil her nakedness, like Noah's good-natured son. Oh, well, you can't understand."

"Don't pay any attention to him. Go on," said one of them.

"Well, I danced for the most part with her, and did not notice how time was passing. The musicians kept playing the same mazurka tunes over and over again in desperate exhaustion—you know what it is towards the end of a ball. Papas and mammas were already getting up from the card-tables in the drawing-room in expectation of supper, the men-servants were running to and fro bringing in things. It was nearly three o'clock. I had to make the most of the last minutes. I chose her again for the mazurka, and for the hundredth time we danced across the room.

" 'The quadrille after supper is mine,' I said, taking her to her place.

" 'Of course, if I am not carried off home,' she said, with a smile.

" 'I won't give you up,' I said.

" 'Give me my fan, anyhow,' she answered.

" 'I am so sorry to part with it,' I said, handing her a cheap white fan.

" 'Well, here's something to console you,' she said, plucking a feather out of the fan, and giving it to me.

"I took the feather, and could only express my rapture and gratitude with my eyes. I was not only pleased and gay, I was happy, delighted; I was good, I was not myself but some being not of this earth, knowing nothing of evil. I hid the feather in my glove, and stood there unable to tear myself away from her.

" 'Look, they are urging father to dance,' she said to me, pointing to the tall, stately figure of her father, a colonel with silver epaulettes, who was standing in the doorway with some ladies.

" 'Varinka, come here!' exclaimed our hostess, the lady with the diamond *ferronnière* and with shoulders like Elizabeth, in a loud voice.

"Varinka went to the door, and I followed her.

" 'Persuade your father to dance the mazurka with you, *ma chère*. —Do, please, Peter Valdislavovich,' she said, turning to the colonel.

"Varinka's father was a very handsome, well-preserved old man. He had a good colour, moustaches curled in the style of Nicolas I, and white whiskers which met the moustaches. His hair was combed on to his forehead, and a bright smile, like his daughter's, was on his lips and in his eyes. He was splendidly set up, with a broad military chest, on which he wore some decorations, and he had powerful shoulders and long slim legs. He was that ultra-military type produced by the discipline of Emperor Nicolas I.

"When we approached the door the colonel was just refusing to dance, saying that he had quite forgotten how; but at that instant he smiled, swung his arm gracefully around to the left, drew his sword from its sheath, handed it to an obliging young man who stood near, and smoothed his suède glove on his right hand.

" 'Everything must be done according to rule,' he said with a smile. He took the hand of his daughter, and stood one-quarter turned, waiting for the music.

"At the first sound of the mazurka, he stamped one foot smartly, threw the other forward, and, at first slowly and smoothly, then buoyantly and impetuously, with stamping of feet and clicking of boots, his tall, imposing figure moved the length of the room. Varinka swayed gracefully beside him, rhythmically and easily, making her steps short or long, with her little feet in their white satin slippers.

"All the people in the room followed every movement of the couple. As for me I not only admired, I regarded them with enraptured sympathy. I was particularly impressed with the old gentleman's boots. They were not the modern pointed affairs, but were made of cheap leather, squared-toed, and evidently built by the regimental cobbler. In order that his daughter might dress and go out in society, he did not buy fashionable boots, but wore home-made ones, I thought, and his square toes seemed to me most touching. It was obvious that in his time he had been a good dancer; but now he was too heavy, and his legs had not spring enough for all the beautiful steps he tried to take. Still, he contrived to go twice round the room. When at the end, standing with legs apart, he suddenly clicked his feet together and fell on one knee, a bit heavily, and she danced gracefully around him, smiling and adjusting her skirt, the whole room applauded.

"Rising with an effort, he tenderly took his daughter's face between his hands. He kissed her on the forehead, and brought her to me, under the impression that I was her partner for the mazurka. I said I was not. 'Well, never mind. Just go around the room once with her,' he said, smiling kindly, as he replaced his sword in the sheath.

"As the contents of a bottle flow readily when the first drop has been poured, so my love for Varinka seemed to set free the whole force of loving within me. In surrounding her it embraced the world. I loved the hostess with her diadem and her shoulders like Elizabeth, and her husband and her guests and her footmen, and even the engineer Anisimov who felt peevish towards me. As for Varinka's father, with his home-made boots and his kind smile, so like her own, I felt a sort of tenderness for him that was almost rapture.

"After supper I danced the promised quadrille with her, and though I had been infinitely happy before, I grew still happier every moment.

"We did not speak of love. I neither asked myself nor her whether she loved me. It was quite enough to know that I loved her. And I had only one fear—that something might come to interfere with my great joy.

"When I went home, and began to undress for the night, I found it quite out of the question. I held the little feather out of her fan in my hand, and one of her gloves which she gave me when

I helped her into the carriage after her mother. Looking at these things, and without closing my eyes I could see her before me as she was for an instant when she had to choose between two partners. She tried to guess what kind of person was represented in me, and I could hear her sweet voice as she said, 'Pride—am I right?' and merrily gave me her hand. At supper she took the first sip from my glass of champagne, looking at me over the rim with her caressing glance. But, plainest of all, I could see her as she danced with her father, gliding along beside him, and looking at the admiring observers with pride and happiness.

"He and she were united in my mind in one rush of pathetic tenderness.

"I was living then with my brother, who has since died. He disliked going out, and never went to dances; and besides, he was busy preparing for his last university examinations, and was leading a very regular life. He was asleep. I looked at him, his head buried in the pillow and half covered with the quilt; and I affectionately pitied him—pitied him for his ignorance of the bliss I was experiencing. Our serf Petrusha had met me with a candle, ready to undress me, but I sent him away. His sleepy face and tousled hair seemed to me so touching. Trying not to make a noise, I went to my room on tiptoe and sat down on my bed. No, I was too happy; I could not sleep. Besides, it was too hot in the rooms. Without taking off my uniform, I went quietly into the hall, put on my overcoat, opened the front door and stepped out into the street.

"It was after four when I had left the ball; going home and stopping there a while had occupied two hours, so by the time I went out it was dawn. It was regular carnival weather—foggy, and the road full of water-soaked snow just melting, and water dripping from the eaves. Varinka's family lived on the edge of town near a large field, one end of which was a parade ground: at the other end was a boarding-school for young ladies. I passed through our empty little street and came to the main thoroughfare, where I met pedestrians and sledges laden with wood, the runners grating the road. The horses swung with regular paces beneath their shining yokes, their backs covered with straw mats and their heads wet with rain; while the drivers, in enormous boots, splashed through the mud beside the sledges. All this, the very horses themselves, seemed to me stimulating and fascinating, full of suggestion.

"When I approached the field near their house, I saw at one end of it, in the direction of the parade ground, something very huge and black, and I heard sounds of fife and drum proceeding from it. My heart had been full of song, and I had heard in imagination the tune of the mazurka, but this was very harsh music. It was not pleasant.

" 'What can that be?' I thought, and went towards the sound by a slippery path through the centre of the field. Walking about a hundred paces, I began to distinguish many black objects through the mist. They were evidently soldiers. 'It is probably a drill,' I thought.

"So I went along in that direction in company with a blacksmith, who wore a dirty coat and an apron, and was carrying something. He walked ahead of me as we approached the place. The soldiers in black uniforms stood in two rows, facing each other motionless, their guns at rest. Behind them stood the fifes and drums, incessantly repeating the same unpleasant tune.

" 'What are they doing?' I asked the blacksmith, who halted at my side.

" 'A Tartar is being beaten through the ranks for his attempt to desert,' said the blacksmith in an angry tone, as he looked intently at the far end of the line.

"I looked in the same direction, and saw between the files something horrid approaching me. The thing that approached was a man, stripped to the waist, fastened with cords to the guns of two soldiers who were leading him. At his side an officer in overcoat and cap was walking, whose figure had a familiar look. The victim advanced under the blows that rained upon him from both sides, his whole body plunging, his feet dragging through the snow. Now he threw himself backward, and the subalterns who led him thrust him forward. Now he fell forward, and they pulled him up short; while ever at his side marched the tall officer, with firm and nervous pace. It was Varinka's father, with his rosy face and white moustache.

"At each stroke the man, as if amazed, turned his face, grimacing with pain, towards the side whence the blow came, and showing his white teeth repeated the same words over and over. But I could only hear what the words were when he came quite near. He did not speak them, he sobbed them out,—

" 'Brothers, have mercy on me! Brothers, have mercy on me!' But the brothers had no mercy, and when the procession came close to me, I saw how a soldier who stood opposite me took a firm step forward and lifting his stick with a whirr, brought it down upon the man's back. The man plunged forward, but the subalterns pulled him back, and another blow came down from the other side, then from this side and then from the other. The colonel marched beside him, and looking now at his feet and now at the man, inhaled the air, puffed out his cheeks, and breathed it out between his protruded lips. When they passed the place where I stood, I caught a glimpse between the two files of the back of the man that was being punished. It was something so many-coloured, wet, red, unnatural, that I could hardly believe it was a human body.

" 'My God!' muttered the blacksmith.

"The procession moved farther away. The blows continued to rain upon the writhing, falling creature; the fifes shrilled and the drums beat, and the tall imposing figure of the colonel moved alongside the man, just as before. Then, suddenly, the colonel stopped, and rapidly approached a man in the ranks.

" 'I'll teach you to hit him gently,' I heard his furious voice say. 'Will you pat him like that? Will you?' and I saw how his strong hand in the suède glove struck the weak, bloodless, terrified soldier for not bringing down his stick with sufficient strength on the red neck of the Tartar.

" 'Bring new sticks!' he cried, and looking round, he saw me. Assuming an air of not knowing me, and with a ferocious, angry frown, he hastily turned away. I felt so utterly ashamed that I didn't know where to look. It was as if I had been detected in a disgraceful act. I dropped my eyes, and quickly hurried home. All the way I had the drums beating and the fifes whistling in my ears. And I heard the words, 'Brothers, have mercy on me!' or 'Will you pat him? Will you?' My heart was full of physical disgust that was almost sickness. So much so that I halted several times on my way, for I had the feeling that I was going to be really sick from all the horrors that possessed me at that sight. I do not remember how I got home and got to bed. But the moment I was about to fall asleep I heard and saw again all that had happened, and I sprang up.

" 'Evidently he knows something I do not know,' I thought about the colonel. 'If I knew what he knows I should certainly grasp—

understand—what I have just seen, and it would not cause me such suffering.'

"But however much I thought about it, I could not understand the thing that the colonel knew. It was evening before I could get to sleep, and then only after calling on a friend and drinking till I was quite drunk.

"Do you think I had come to the conclusion that the deed I had witnessed was wicked? Oh, no. Since it was done with such assurance, and was recognised by every one as indispensable, they doubtless knew something which I did not know. So I thought, and tried to understand. But no matter, I could never understand it, then or afterwards. And not being able to grasp it, I could not enter the service as I had intended. I don't mean only the military service: I did not enter the Civil Service either. And so I have been of no use whatever, as you can see."

"Yes, we know how useless you've been," said one of us. "Tell us, rather, how many people would be of any use at all if it hadn't been for you."

"Oh, that's utter nonsense," said Ivan Vasilievich, with genuine annoyance.

"Well; and what about the love affair?"

"My love? It decreased from that day. When, as often happened, she looked dreamy and meditative, I instantly recollected the colonel on the parade ground, and I felt so awkward and uncomfortable that I began to see her less frequently. So my love came to naught. Yes; such chances arise, and they alter and direct a man's whole life," he said in summing up. "And you say . . ."

Appendix B

*The Writers
on Their Art*

JORGE LUIS BORGES

How "The Intruder" Was Written

In the fall of 1965, the Buenos Aires bibliophile Gustavo Fillol Day asked me for a short story to be published by him in one of those fine and secret editions meant for the happy few. Around that time I had been rereading Kipling's *Plain Tales from the Hills,* and I told Fillol that I had a story in mind. The brevity and straightforwardness of the young Kipling tempted me, since I had always written very involved and many-faceted narratives. A few months later I was ready to get down to work, and at the beginning of 1966 I dictated "The Intruder" to my mother.

Without my suspecting it, the hint for this story—perhaps the best I have ever written—came out of a chance conversation with my friend Don Nicolás Paredes sometime back in the late twenties. Commenting on the decadence of tango lyrics, which even then went in for "loud self-pity" among sentimental *compadritos* betrayed by their wenches, Paredes remarked dryly, "Any man who thinks five minutes straight about a woman is no man—he's a queer." Love among such people was obviously ruled out; I knew that their real passion would be friendship. Out of this rather abstract set of ideas I evolved my story. I placed it in an almost nameless town to the south of Buenos Aires more than seventy years ago so that nobody could dispute the details. Really there are only two characters—the two brothers. Of them, we are allowed to hear only what the elder brother says; it is he who takes all the decisions, even the last one. I made them brothers for the sake of likelihood and, of course, to avoid unsavory implications.

I was stuck at the end of the story, unsure of the words Cristián would say. My mother, who from the outset thoroughly disliked the tale, at that point gave me the words I needed without a moment's hesitation.

"The Intruder" was, by the way, the first of my new ventures into straightforward storytelling. From this beginning I went on to write many others, ultimately collecting them under the title *El informe de Brodie* (Doctor Brodie's Report).[1]

ANTON CHEKHOV

Moonlight on a Broken Bottle

In my opinion descriptions of Nature should be very brief and have an incidental character. Commonplaces like: "The setting sun, bathing in the waves of the darkening sea, flooded with purple and gold," etc. . . . "The swallows, flying over the surface of the water, chirped merrily"—such commonplaces should be finished with. In descriptions of Nature one has to snatch at small details, grouping them in such a manner that after reading them one can obtain the picture on closing one's eyes.

For instance, you will get a moonlight night if you write that on the dam of the mill a fragment of broken bottle flashed like a small bright star, and there rolled by, like a ball, the black shadow of a dog, or a wolf—and so on. Nature appears animated if you do not disdain to use comparisons of its phenomena with those of human actions, etc.

The same, too, in the sphere of psychology. God defend you from generalizations. Best of all, avoid describing the psychological state of the characters; one should contrive that this is clear from their actions. One should not hunt after an abundance of characters. The centre of gravity should be two: he and she.[2]

[1] From the book *The Aleph And Other Stories: 1939–1969* by Jorge Luis Borges. Eng. trans. copyright © 1968, 1969, 1970 by Emecé Editores, S.A. and Norman Thomas di Giovanni; copyright © 1970 by Jorge Luis Borges, Adolfo, Bioy-Caseres, and Norman Thomas di Giovanni. Published by E. P. Dutton & Co., Inc. and used with their permission.

[2] From *The Life and Letters of Anton Tchekhov*, trans. and ed. by Koteliansky and Tomlinson. Reprinted by permission of Routledge & Kegan Paul, Ltd., London.

Moralizing in Short Stories

You abuse me for objectivity, calling it indifference to good and evil, lack of ideals and ideas, and so on. You would have me, when I describe horse-thieves, say: "Stealing horses is an evil." But that has been known for ages without my saying so. Let the jury judge them; it's my job simply to show what sort of people they are. I write: You are dealing with horse-thieves, so let me tell you that they are not beggars but well-fed people, that they are people of a special cult, and that horse-stealing is not simply theft but a passion. Of course it would be pleasant to combine art with a sermon, but for me personally it is extremely difficult and almost impossible, owing to the conditions of technique. You see, to depict horse-thieves in seven hundred lines I must all the time speak and think in their tone and feel in their spirit, otherwise, if I introduce subjectivity, the image becomes blurred and the story will not be as compact as all short stories ought to be. When I write, I reckon entirely upon the reader to add for himself the subjective elements that are lacking in the story.[3]

JOSEPH CONRAD

The Difficulty of Creation

29th March, 1898

My Dear Garnett,

I am ashamed of myself. I ought to have written to you before, but the fact is I have not written anything at all. When I received your letter together with part IInd of The Rescuer I was in bed—this beastly nervous trouble. Since then I've been better but have been unable to write. I sit down religiously every morning, I sit down for eight hours every day—and the sitting down is all. In the course of that working day of 8 hours, I write 3 sentences which I erase before leaving the table in despair. There's not a single word to send you. Not one! And time passes—and McClure waits—not to speak of

[3] From *Letters on the Short Story, the Drama and Other Literary Topics,* ed. by Louis S. Friedland. Copyright, 1924, by G. P. Putnam's Sons. Reprinted by permission of the publishers.

Eternity, for which I don't care a damn. Of McClure however I am afraid.

I ask myself sometimes whether I am bewitched, whether I am the victim of an evil eye? But there is no "jettatura" in England—is there? I assure you—speaking soberly and on my word of honour—that sometimes it takes all my resolution and power of self-control to refrain from butting my head against the wall. I want to howl and foam at the mouth, but I daren't do it for fear of waking the baby and alarming my wife. It's no joking matter. After such crises of despair I doze for hours still half conscious that there is that story I am unable to write. Then I wake up, try again—and at last go to bed completely done-up. So the days pass and nothing is done. At night I sleep. In the morning I get up with the horror of that powerlessness I must face through a day of vain efforts.

In these circumstances you imagine I feel not much inclination to write letters. As a matter of fact I have a great difficulty in writing the most commonplace note. I seem to have lost all *sense* of style and yet I am haunted, mercilessly haunted, by the *necessity* of style. And that story I can't write weaves itself into all I see, into all I speak, into all I think, into the lines of every book I try to read. I haven't read for days. You know how bad it is when one *feels* one's liver, or lungs. Well, I feel my brain. I am distinctly conscious of the contents of my head. My story is there in a fluid—in an evading shape. I can't get hold of it. It is all there—to bursting, yet I can't get hold of it, any more than you grasp a handful of water.

There! I've told you all and feel better. While I write this I am amazed to see that I can write. It looks as though the spell were broken, but I must hasten, hasten lest it should in five minutes or in half an hour be laid again.[4]

Fiction at Its Highest

All art, therefore, appeals primarily to the senses, and the artistic aim when expressing itself in written words must also make its appeal through the senses, if its high desire is to reach the secret spring of responsive emotions. It must strenuously aspire to the plasticity of sculpture, to the colour of painting, and to the magic suggestiveness

[4] From *Notes on Life and Letters* by Joseph Conrad. Reprinted by permission of J. M. Dent & Sons, Ltd., London.

of music—which is the art of arts. And it is only through complete, unswerving devotion to the perfect blending of form and substance; it is only through an unremitting never-discouraged care for the shape and ring of sentences that an approach can be made to plasticity, to colour, and that the light of magic suggestiveness may be brought to play for an evanescent instant over the commonplace surface of words: of the old, old words, worn thin, defaced by ages of careless usage.

The sincere endeavour to accomplish that creative task, to go as far on that road as his strength will carry him, to go undeterred by faltering, weariness or reproach, is the only valid justification for the worker in prose. And if his conscience is clear, his answer to those who in the fulness of a wisdom which looks for immediate profit, demand specifically to be edified, consoled, amused; who demand to be promptly improved, or encouraged, or frightened, or shocked, or charmed, must run thus:—My task which I am trying to achieve is, by the power of the written word to make you hear, to make you feel—it is, before all, to make you *see*. That—and no more, and it is everything. If I succeed, you shall find there according to your deserts: encouragement, consolation, fear, charm—all you demand—and, perhaps, also that glimpse of truth for which you have forgotten to ask.

To snatch in a moment of courage, from the remorseless rush of time, a passing phase of life, is only the beginning of the task. The task approached in tenderness and faith is to hold up unquestioningly, without choice and without fear, the rescued fragment before all eyes in the light of a sincere mood. It is to show its vibration, its colour, its form; and through its movement, its form, and its colour, reveal the substance of its truth—disclose its inspiring secret: the stress and passion within the core of each convincing moment. In a single-minded attempt of that kind, if one be deserving and fortunate, one may perchance attain to such clearness of sincerity that at last the presented vision of regret or pity, of terror or mirth, shall awaken in the hearts of the beholders that feeling of unavoidable solidarity; of the solidarity in mysterious origin, in toil, in joy, in hope, in uncertain fate, which binds men to each other and all mankind to the visible world.[5]

[5] Preface to *The Nigger of the Narcissus* by Joseph Conrad. Reprinted by permission of J. M. Dent & Sons, Ltd., London.

WILLIAM FAULKNER

The Things Worth Writing About

I feel that this award [6] was not made to me as a man but to my work—a life's work in the agony and sweat of the human spirit, not for glory and least of all for profit, but to create out of the materials of the human spirit something which did not exist there before. So this award is only mine in trust. It will not be difficult to find a dedication for the money part of it commensurate with the purpose and significance of its origin. But I would like to do the same with the acclaim, too, by using this moment as a pinnacle from which I might be listened to by the young men and women already dedicated to the same anguish and travail, among whom is already that one who will some day stand here where I am standing.

Our tragedy today is a general and a universal physical fear so long sustained by now that we can even bear it. There are no longer problems of the spirit. There is only the question: When will I be blown up? Because of this, the young man or woman writing today has forgotten the problems of the human heart in conflict with itself which alone can make good writing because only that is worth writing about, worth the agony and the sweat.

He must learn them again. He must teach himself that the basest of all things is to be afraid; and, teaching himself that, forget it forever, leaving no room in his workshop for anything but the old verities and truths of the heart, the old universal truths lacking which any story is ephemeral and doomed—love and honor and pity and pride and compassion and sacrifice. Until he does so he labors under a curse. He writes not of love, but of lust, of defeats in which nobody loses anything of value, of victories without hope and worst of all without pity or compassion. His griefs grieve on no universal bones, leaving no scars. He writes not of the heart but of the glands.

Until he relearns these things he will write as though he stood among and watched the end of man. I decline to accept the end of man. It is easy enough to say that man is immortal simply because he will endure; that when the last ding-dong of doom has clanged

[6] This is Faulkner's speech accepting the Nobel Prize for Literature in Stockholm, December 10, 1950.

and faded from the last worthless rock hanging tideless in the last red and dying evening, that even then there will still be one more sound: that of his puny inexhaustible voice still talking. I refuse to accept this. I believe that man will not merely endure: he will prevail. He is immortal, not because he alone among creatures has an inexhaustible voice, but because he has a soul, a spirit capable of compassion and sacrifice and endurance. The poet's, the writer's, duty is to write about these things. It is his privilege to help man endure by lifting his heart, by reminding him of the courage and honor and hope and pride and compassion and pity and sacrifice which have been the glory of his past. The poet's voice need not merely be the record of man, it can be one of the props, the pillars to help him endure and prevail.

JAMES JOYCE

Young Dedalus on Tragedy

After a pause Stephen began:
—Aristotle has not defined pity and terror. I have. I say . . .
Lynch halted and said bluntly:
—Stop! I won't listen! I am sick. I was out last night on a yellow drunk with Horan and Goggins.—
Stephen went on:
—Pity is the feeling which arrests the mind in the presence of whatsoever is grave and constant in human sufferings and unites it with the human sufferer. Terror is the feeling which arrests the mind in the presence of whatsoever is grave and constant in human sufferings and unites it with the secret cause.—
—Repeat—said Lynch.
Stephen repeated the definitions slowly.
—A girl got into a hansom a few days ago—he went on—in London. She was on her way to meet her mother whom she had not seen for many years. At the corner of a street the shaft of a lorry shivered the window of the hansom in the shape of a star. A long fine needle of the shivered glass pierced her heart. She died on the instant. The reporter called it a tragic death. It is not. It is remote from terror and pity according to the terms of my definitions.
—The tragic emotion, in fact, is a face looking two ways, towards

terror and towards pity, both of which are phases of it. You see I use the word *arrest*. I mean that the tragic emotion is static. Or rather the dramatic emotion is. The feelings excited by improper art are kinetic, desire or loathing. Desire urges us to possess, to go to something; loathing urges us to abandon, to go from something. The arts which excite them, pornographical or didactic, are therefore improper arts. The esthetic emotion (I used the general term) is therefore static. The mind is arrested and raised above desire and loathing.—

—You say that art must not excite desire—said Lynch—I told you that one day I wrote my name in pencil on the backside of the Venus of Praxiteles in the Museum. Was that not desire?—

—I speak of normal natures—said Stephen.

The Triumph of the Impersonal

. . . Even in literature, the highest and most spiritual art, the forms are often confused. The lyrical form is in fact the simplest verbal vesture of an instant of emotion, a rhythmical cry such as ages ago cheered on the man who pulled at the oar or dragged stones up a slope. He who utters it is more conscious of the instant of emotion than of himself as feeling emotion. The simplest epical form is seen emerging out of lyrical literature when the artist prolongs and broods upon himself as the centre of an epical event and this form progresses till the centre of emotional gravity is equidistant from the artist himself and from others. The narrative is no longer purely personal. The personality of the artist passes into the narration itself, flowing round and round the persons and the action like a vital sea. This progress you will see easily in that old English ballad *Turpin Hero,* which begins in the first person and ends in the third person. The dramatic form is reached when the vitality which has flowed and eddied round each person fills every person with such vital force that he or she assumes a proper and intangible esthetic life. The personality of the artist, at first a cry or a cadence or a mood and then a fluid and lambent narrative, finally refines itself out of existence, impersonalizes itself, so to speak. The esthetic image in the dramatic form is life purified in and reprojected from the human imagination. The mystery of esthetic like that of material creation is accomplished. The artist, like the God of the creation, remains within or behind or beyond or above his handiwork, invisible, refined out of existence, indifferent, paring his fingernails.—[7]

D. H. LAWRENCE

The Cosmic Sense

For man, the vast marvel is to be alive. For man, as for flower and beast and bird, the supreme triumph is to be most vividly, most perfectly alive. Whatever the unborn and the dead may know, they cannot know the beauty, the marvel of being alive in the flesh. . . . We ought to dance with rapture that we should be alive and in the flesh, and part of the living, incarnate cosmos. I am part of the sun as my eye is part of me. That I am part of the earth my feet know perfectly, and my blood is part of the sea. My soul knows that I am part of the human race, my soul is an organic part of the great human soul, as my spirit is part of my nation. In my own very self, I am part of my family. There is nothing of me that is alone and absolute except in my mind, and we shall find that the mind has no existence by itself, it is only the glitter of the sun on the surface of the waters.

So that my individualism is really an illusion. I am part of the great whole, and I can never escape. But I *can* deny my connections, break them, and become a fragment. Then I am wretched.

What we want is to destroy our false, inorganic connections, especially those related to money, and re-establish the living organic connections with the cosmos, the sun and earth, with mankind and nation and family. Start with the sun, and the rest will slowly happen.[8]

[7] From *A Portrait of the Artist as a Young Man* by James Joyce. Copyright 1916 by B. W. Huebsch, Inc., 1944 by Nora Joyce. Reprinted by permission of The Viking Press, Inc.

[8] From Apocalypse by D. H. Lawrence. Copyright 1931 by The Estate of David Herbert Lawrence, © renewed 1960 by The Viking Press, Inc. All rights reserved. Reprinted by permission of The Viking Press, Inc.

BERNARD MALAMUD

The Source and Purpose of Art

What moves me moves me to art. What moves me to art I may deal with in whatever forms, whatever means of achieving a fiction, I am able to use. To say that this is the world and it is present is hardly satisfying or sufficient. What a fool I'd be not to say what I think of the world! . . . What one gives to fiction is what he has to give, not what is prescribed. One gives all he can; he limits as art demands, not definition.

I welcome, as I said before, the seeking for new forms in fiction. However, no form dies; they are all eternally available to the artist to use in a manner original to him. He reinvents then as he uses them. A 19th-century form used by a 20th-century writer becomes a 20th-century form. Nothing is outdated if it creates art. The best form for an artist is that which compels him to use his greatest strength.

That the world is present is only a small portion of the truth available to art. In the novel the world appears in language, itself a form of interpretation. Therefore, why should it not be further valued, explained—experienced? One cannot sit on language; it moves beyond the presence of things into the absence of things, the illusion of things. Art must interpret, or it is mindless. Mindlessness is not mystery, it is the absence of mystery. Content cannot be disinvented. Presentation of the world, or history, or society is not enough when it may be necessary to proscribe them.

If the world, as some say, is ultimately an esthetic phenomenon, so, too, in its way, is humanity. One might even argue that there is such a thing as an esthetic of behavior. Wasn't it Santayana who said that the purpose of love is to increase beauty? Morality may have more than one source of beauty. Art is, moreover, the invention of the human artist, not an act of God or nature. To preserve it must, in a variety of subtle ways, conserve the artist through sanctifying human life and freedom.[9]

[9] Adapted from Bernard Malamud's speech accepting the National Book Award for *The Fixer* in March 1967. Copyright © 1967 by Bernard Malamud. Reprinted by permission of the author.

THOMAS MANN

The Leitmotif or Thematic Phrase

Every morning, one step ahead, every morning, one more passage written—that has become my way of work, and it has its inner necessity. In a kind and unusually sensitive review which a critic has recently given my literary efforts . . . , he drew attention to my methods of composition, and described how I had perfected and deepened the much-used artistic device of the "Leitmotif," how with me it no longer remains a mere identifying tag, a cue to remind the reader of external circumstances or to suggest a mood. On the contrary, it is used in a directly musical way, and determines the whole mode of presentation and the coloring of the style. . . .

Now this method alone is sufficient to explain my slowness. It is the result neither of anxiety nor of indolence, but of an extraordinarily keen conscientiousness in the choice of every word, the coining of every phrase, a conscientiousness which requires perfect freshness, and which, after two hours' work, prefers not to undertake an important sentence. For which sentence is important, and which not? Can one know beforehand whether a sentence, or part of a sentence, may not be called upon to serve as Motif, link, symbol, citation or association? And a sentence which must be heard twice must be fashioned accordingly. It must—I do not speak of beauty—possess a certain symbolic suggestion and level of meaning which will make it worthy to sound again in any epic future. So every bit of ground gained is also a taking-off point, every adjective, a decision. It is clear that such work is not to be produced off-hand.[10]

FRANK O'CONNOR

Story vs. Novel

About story v. novel. With me it's a difficulty of temperament. Mine is lyrical, explosive. I write a story with a feeling of slight regret

[10] From *Rede und Antwort* by Thomas Mann. Reprinted by permission of Alfred A. Knopf, Inc.

for poor Shakespeare's lack of talent and wake up with a hangover that makes poteen look like cold water. Then, having cursed life and forsworn literature, I start rewriting. If I can work up the Shakespeare mood often enough I may get it right in six revisions. If I don't I may have to rewrite it fifty times. This isn't exaggeration, and it's not a question of polishing. By the time the story is finished I've usually forgotten the number I started with. In "Traveller's Samples" there's a story which I published twice, once in Ireland, once in America, and neither version bears much resemblance to the other or to the version in the book. As I have now not seen it for six months, I have a wild hope that I really may have got it out of my system. Now, I ask you, how could I write a novel? . . .

Story vs. Author

I think I like the instinctual as against the intellectual. I don't think I like my short stories "unified"—your word [11]—any more than I'd like my Keats or Shelley unified. George Crabbe is unified. Isn't "unified" by definition minor? (Don't mind me, I'm only arguing.) As a writer I like the feeling I get when some story which I've been trying to bring up in the right way gets on its own feet and tells me to go to hell. You don't imagine any story in "Dubliners" told Joyce to get to hell, do you? It wouldn't have the nerve. I'm for the democratic way of life in literature as well as politics. Writers are leaders, not dictators.[12]

EUDORA WELTY

Form and D. H. Lawrence

A story with a "pattern," an exact kind of design, may lack a more compelling over-all quality that is what we mean by form. Edgar A. Poe and other writers whose ultimate aim depended on pattern, on

[11] O'Connor is replying to a letter from Harvey Breit, writer for *The New York Times.*
[12] From "Story vs. Novel," by Frank O'Connor, *The New York Times Book Review,* June 24, 1951. Reprinted by permission of *The New York Times* and A. D. Peters, London.

a perfect and dove-tailing structure (note the relation to puzzles and to detection and mystery here) might have felt real horror at a story by D. H. Lawrence first of all because of the unmitigated shapeless-ness of Lawrence's narrative. . . . And what about his characters? Are they real, recognizable, neat men and women? Would you know them if you saw them? Not even, I think, if they began to speak on the street as they speak in the stories, in the very words—they would only appear as deranged people. For the truth seems to be that Lawrence's characters don't really speak their words—not conversa-tionally, not to one another—they are *not* speaking on the street, but are playing like fountains or radiating like the moon or storming like the sea, or their silence is the silence of wicked rocks. It is borne home to us that Lawrence is writing of our human relationships on earth in terms of eternity, and these terms set Lawrence's form. The author himself appears in authorship in phases like the moon, and sometimes smites us while we stand there under him. But we see his plots and his characters are alike sacrificed to something; there is something which Lawrence considers as transcending them both. Others besides him have thought that something does. But Lawrence alone, that I have knowledge of now, thinks the transcending thing is found direct through the senses. It is the world of the senses that Lawrence writes in, works in, thinks in, takes as his medium—and if that is strange to us, isn't the loss ours? Through this world he will send his story— it is the plot too—it is his story's reason for being, with sex the chan-nel the senses most deeply, mysteriously, run through, cutting down through layers and centuries and country after country of hypocrisy.

What Makes Beauty

Could it be that one who carps at difficulties in a writer ("Why didn't he write it like this? Why didn't he write another story?"), at infringements on the rules and lack of performance of duty, fails to take note of beauty? And fails to see straight off that beauty springs from deviation, from desire not to comply but to act inevi-tably, as long as truth is in sight, whatever that inevitability may mean?

Where does beauty come from, in the short story? Beauty is of form, development of idea, of after-effect . . . It often comes from carefulness, lack of confusion, elimination of waste—and yes, those are the rules. But that can be on occasion a cold kind of beauty, when there are warm kinds. And beware of tidiness. Sometimes spontaneity is the most sparkling kind of beauty—Katherine Mansfield had it—and no more than the flush of health or the bloom of youth can spontaneity be imitated. It is a fortuitous circumstance attending the birth of some stories, like a fairy godmother that has—this time—accepted the standing invitation and come smiling in.

Beauty may be missed or forgotten sometimes by the analysers because it is not a means, not a way of getting the story along, or furthering a thing in the world. For beauty is a result—as form is a result. It *comes*. We are lucky when beauty comes, for often we try and it should come, it could, we think, but then when the virtues of our story are counted, beauty is standing behind the door. I think it may be wrong to try for beauty; that we should try for other things, and then hope.[13]

RALPH ELLISON

Art and Protest

INTERVIEWERS: Then you consider your novel a purely literary work as opposed to one in the tradition of social protest.

ELLISON: Now mind! I recognize no dichotomy between art and protest. Dostoievsky's *Notes from Underground* is, among other things, a protest against the limitations of nineteenth-century rationalism; *Don Quixote, Man's Fate, Oedipus Rex, The Trial*—all these embody protest, even against the limitation of human life itself. If social protest is antithetical to art, what then shall we make of Goya, Dickens and Twain? One hears a lot of complaints about the so-called protest novel, especially when written by Negroes; but it seems to me that the critics could more accurately complain about their lack of craftsmanship and their provincialism.

INTERVIEWERS: But isn't it going to be difficult for the Negro writer

[13] From "On Short Stories" by Eudora Welty. Reprinted by permission of Random House, Inc.

to escape provincialism when his literature is concerned with a minority?

ELLISON: All novels are about certain minorities: the individual is a minority. The universal in the novel—and isn't that what we're all clamoring for these days?—is reached only through the depiction of the specific circumstance.

INTERVIEWERS: But still, how is the Negro writer, in terms of what is expected of him by critics and readers, going to escape his particular need for social protest and reach the "universal" you speak of?

ELLISON: If the Negro, or any other writer, is going to do what is expected of him, he's lost the battle before he takes the field. I suspect that all the agony that goes into writing is borne precisely because the writer longs for acceptance—but it must be acceptance on his own terms. Perhaps, though, this thing cuts both ways: the Negro novelist draws his blackness too tightly around him when he sits down to write —that's what the anti-protest critics believe—but perhaps the white reader draws his whiteness around himself when he sits down to read. He doesn't want to identify himself with Negro characters in terms of our immediate racial and social situation, though on the deeper human level, identification can become compelling when the situation is revealed artistically. The white reader doesn't want to get too close, not even in an imaginary re-creation of society. Negro writers have felt this and it has led to much of our failure.

Too many books by Negro writers are addressed to a white audience. By doing this the authors run the risk of limiting themselves to the audience's presumptions of what a Negro is or should be; the tendency is to become involved in polemics, to plead the Negro's humanity. You know, many white people question that humanity but I don't think that Negroes can afford to indulge in such a false issue. For us the question should be, What are the specific forms of that humanity, and what in our background is worth preserving or abandoning.[14]

[14] From Writers At Work: The Paris Review Interviews, Second Series. Copyright © 1963 by The Paris Review, Inc. All rights reserved. Reprinted by permission of the Viking Press, Inc.

RUDYARD KIPLING

The Virtues of Excision

I forget who started the notion of my writing a series of Anglo-Indian tales, but I remember our council over the naming of the series. They were originally much longer than when they appeared, but the shortening of them, first to my own fancy after rapturous re-readings, and next to the space available, taught me that a tale from which pieces have been raked out is like a fire that has been poked. One does not know that the operation has been performed, but everyone feels the effect. Note, though, that the excised stuff must have been honestly written for inclusion. I found that when, to save trouble, I "wrote short" *ab initio* much salt went out of the work. This supports the theory of the chimaera which, having bombinated and been removed, is capable of producing secondary causes *in vacuo*.

This leads me to the Higher Editing. Take of well-ground Indian Ink as much as suffices and a camel-hair brush proportionate to the interspaces of your lines. In an auspicious hour, read your final draft and consider faithfully every paragraph, sentence and word, blacking out where requisite. Let it lie by to drain as long as possible. At the end of that time, re-read and you should find that it will bear a second shortening. Finally, read it aloud alone and at leisure. Maybe a shade more brushwork will then indicate or impose itself. If not, praise Allah and let it go, and "when thou hast done, repent not." The shorter the tale, the longer the brushwork and, normally, the shorter the lie-by, and *vice versa*. The longer the tale, the less brush but the longer lie-by. I have had tales by me for three or five years which shortened themselves almost yearly. The magic lies in the Brush and the Ink. For the Pen, when it is writing, can only scratch; and bottled ink is not to compare with the ground Chinese stick. *Experto crede*.[15]

[15] From *Something of Myself* by Rudyard Kipling. Copyright 1937 by Caroline Kipling. Reprinted by permission of Mrs. George Bambridge, Doubleday & Co., Inc., and the Macmillan Company of Canada Ltd.

FRANZ KAFKA

Uncapturable Exaltations

November 15. Yesterday evening, already with a sense of foreboding, pulled the cover off the bed, lay down and again became aware of all my abilities as though I were holding them in my hand; they tightened my chest, they set my head on fire, for a short while, to console myself for not getting up to work, I repeated: "That's not healthy, that's not healthy," and with almost visible purpose tried to draw sleep over my head. . . .

It is certain that everything I have conceived in advance, even when I was in a good mood, whether word for word or just casually, but in specific words, appears dry, wrong, inflexible, embarrassing to everybody around me, timid, but above all incomplete when I try to write it down at my desk, although I have forgotten nothing of the original conception. This is naturally related in large part to the fact that I conceive something good away from paper only in a time of exaltation, a time more feared than longed for, much as I do long for it; but then the fulness is so great that I have to give up. Blindly and arbitrarily I snatch handfuls out of the stream so that when I write it down calmly, my acquisition is nothing in comparison with the fulness in which it lived, is incapable of restoring this fulness, and thus is bad and disturbing because it tempts to no purpose.[16]

ERNEST HEMINGWAY

How to Look at Violence

I was trying to write then and I found the greatest difficulty, aside from knowing truly what you really felt, rather than what you were supposed to feel, and had been taught to feel, was to put down what really happened in action; what the actual things were which produced the emotion that you experienced. In writing for a newspaper you told what happened and, with one trick and another, you com-

[16] From *The Diaries of Franz Kafka, 1910–1913*, ed. by Max Brod and published by Schocken Books, Inc., New York.

municated the emotion aided by the element of timeliness which gives a certain emotion to any account of something that has happened on that day; but the real thing, the sequence of motion and fact which made the emotion and which would be as valid in a year or in ten years or, with luck and if you stated it purely enough, always, was beyond me and I was working very hard to try to get it. The only place where you could see life and death, i.e., violent death now that the wars were over, was in the bull ring and I wanted very much to go to Spain where I could study it. I was trying to learn to write, commencing with the simplest things, and one of the simplest things of all and the most fundamental is violent death. It has none of the complications of death by disease, or so-called natural death, or the death of a friend or some one you have loved or have hated, but it is death nevertheless, one of the subjects that a man may write of. I had read many books in which, when the author tried to convey it, he only produced a blur, and I decided that this was because either the author had never seen it clearly or at the moment of it, he had physically or mentally shut his eyes, as one might do if he saw a child that he could not possibly reach or aid, about to be struck by a train. In such a case I suppose he would probably be justified in shutting his eyes as the mere fact of the child being about to be struck by the train was all that he could convey, the actual striking would be an anti-climax, so that the moment before striking might be as far as he could represent. But in the case of an execution by a firing squad, or a hanging, this is not true, and if these very simple things were to be made permanent, as, say, Goya tried to make them in *Los Desastros de la Guerra*, it could not be done with any shutting of the eyes.[17]

GRACE PALEY

Notes for Students of Writing

1. Literature has something to do with language. There's probably a natural grammar at the tip of your tongue. You may not believe it but if you say what's on your mind in the language that comes to

[17] Reprinted from *Death in the Afternoon* by Ernest Hemingway (copyright 1932 Charles Scribner's Sons) by permission of the publishers.

you from your parents and your street and friends you'll probably say something beautiful. Still, if you weren't a tough recalcitrant kid, that language may have been destroyed by the tongues of school-teachers who were ashamed of interesting homes, inflection, and language and left them all for correct usage.

2. A first assignment: To be repeated whenever necessary, by me or the class. Write a story, a first person narrative in the tongue of someone with whom you're in conflict. Someone who disturbs you, worries you, someone you don't understand. Use a situation you don't understand.

3. No personal journals, please, for about a year. Why? Boring to me. When you find yourself interesting, you're boring. When I find myself interesting, I'm a conceited bore. When I'm interested in you, I'm interesting.

4. This year, I want to *tell* stories. I ask my father, now that he's old and not so busy, to tell me stories, so I can learn how. I try to remember my grandmother's stories, the faces of her dead children. A first assignment for *this* year: Tell a story in class, something that your grandmother told you about a life that preceded yours. That will remind us of our home language. Also—because of time shortage and advanced age, neither your father or your grandmother will bother to tell unimportant stories.

5. It's possible to write about anything in the world, but the slight-est story ought to contain the facts of money and blood in order to be interesting to adults. That is—everybody continues on this earth by courtesy of certain economic arrangements, people are rich or poor, make a living or don't have to, are useful to systems, or superfluous— And blood—the way people live as families or outside families or in the creations of family, sisters, sons, fathers, the bloody ties. Trivial work ignores these two FACTS and is never comic or tragic.

May you do trivial work? [18]

[18] From "Some Notes on Teaching: Probably Spoken" by Grace Paley from *Writers As Teachers/Teachers As Writers* edited by Jonathan Baumback and published by Holt, Rinehart and Winston, Inc.

VLADIMIR NABOKOV

The Card-Carrying Snail

QUESTION: Could you tell us something about your work habits as a writer, and the way you compose your novels. Do you use an outline? Do you have a full sense of where a fiction is heading even while you are in the early stages of composition?

ANSWER: In my twenties and early thirties, I used to write, dipping pen in ink and using a new nib every other day, in exercise books, crossing out, inserting, striking out again, crumpling the page, rewriting every page three or four times, then copying out the novel in a different ink and a neater hand, then revising the whole thing once more, re-copying it with new corrections, and finally dictating it to my wife who has typed out all my stuff. Generally speaking, I am a slow writer, a snail carrying its house at the rate of two hundred pages of final copy per year (one spectacular exception was the Russian original of *Invitation to a Beheading,* the first draft of which I wrote in one fortnight of wonderful excitement and sustained inspiration). In those days and nights I generally followed the order of chapters when writing a novel but even so, from the very first, I relied heavily on mental composition, constructing whole paragraphs in my mind as I walked in the streets or sat in my bath, or lay in bed, although often deleting or rewriting them later. In the late 'thirties, beginning with *The Gift,* and perhaps under the influence of the many notes needed, I switched to another, physically more practical, method— that of writing with an eraser-capped pencil on index cards. Since I always have at the very start a curiously clear preview of the entire novel before me or above me, I find cards especially convenient when not following the logical sequence of chapters but preparing instead this or that passage at any point of the novel and filling in the gaps in no special order. I am afraid to get mixed up with Plato whom I do not care for, but I do think that in my case it is true that the entire book, before it is written, seems to be ready ideally in some other, now transparent, now dimming, dimension, and my job is to take down as much of it as I can make out and as precisely as I am humanly able to. The greatest happiness I experience in composing is when I feel I cannot understand, or rather catch myself not understanding (without the presupposition of an already existing creation) how or why that image or structural move has just come to me. It is sometimes rather amusing to find my readers trying to elucidate in a matter-of-fact way these wild workings of my not very efficient mind.[19]

KATHERINE ANNE PORTER

Women and Criticism

All art comes out of human nature, not just one part, but every cell of it; and so does criticism. You seem to speak as if criticism was some sort of purely scientific apparatus, like a surgeon's kit or a chemistry laboratory, where art, the human organism or tissue is subjected to a purely impersonal or abstract analysis. There is no such thing as the purely abstract or the purely intellectual, anyway. Even criticism such as yours of Gertrude Stein's work carries such a charge of the sensory and personal it fairly pulsates through and between the lines. Judging merely by what I read of criticism, whether by men or women, men are quite as motivated by these forces as women; if you are not a good critic, it is for precisely the same reason that I am not—our minds and feelings work better in other ways, and why this is so, nobody knows at all. It occurs to me sometimes that the real difference between the sexes, emotionally and intellectually considered, is that women feel less need for asserting themselves by analyzing and judging everything—they do not, in a word, feel a need to be God. This could have some relation perhaps to their biological function, it has been advanced as theory, but no one really knows.[20]

[19] From "An Interview with Vladimir Nabokov," conducted by Alfred Appel, Jr., in Nabokov: The Man and His Work, L. J. Dembo, editor (Madison: The University of Wisconsin Press; © 1967 by the Regents of the University of Wisconsin), pp. 24–25.
[20] From "Ole Woman River: A Correspondence," copyright © 1959 by Katherine Anne Porter, from *The Collected Essays And Occasional Writings of Katherine Anne Porter*. A Seymour Lawrence Book/Delacorte Press. Reprinted by permission of the publisher.

DYLAN THOMAS

Beginning with the Word

I am tortured to-day by every doubt and misgiving that an hereditarily twisted imagination, an hereditary thirst and a commercial quenching, a craving for a body not my own, a chequered education and too much egocentric poetry, and a wild, wet day in a tided town, are capable of conjuring up out of their helly deeps. Helly deeps. There is torture in words, torture in their linking and spelling, in the snail of their course on stolen papers, in their sound that the four winds double, and in my knowledge of their inadequacy. With a priggish weight on the end, the sentence falls. All sentences fall when the weight of the mind is distributed unevenly among the holy consonants and vowels. In the beginning was a word I can't spell, not a reversed Dog, or a physical light, but a word as long as Glastonbury and as short as pith. Nor does it lisp like the last word, break wind like Balzac through a calligraphied window, but speaks out sharp and everlastingly with the intonations of death and doom on the magnificent syllables. I wonder whether I love your word, the word of your hair—by loving hair I reject all Oscardom, for homosexuality is as bald as a coot—the word of your voice. The word of your flesh, and the word of your presence. However good, I can never love you as earth. The good earth of your blood is always there, under the skin I love, but it is two worlds. There must be only half a world tangible, audible, and visible to the illiterate. And is that the better half? Or is it the wholly ghostly past? And does the one-eyed ferryman, who cannot read a printed word, row over a river of words, where the syllables of the fish dart out and are caught on his rhyming hook, or feel himself a total ghost in a world that's as matter-of-fact as a stone? If these were the only questions, I could be happy, for they are answered quickly with a twisting sense into the old metaphysics. But there are other and more dreadful questions I am frightened to answer. I am whimsy enough today to imagine that the oyster-catchers flying over the pearliest mudbanks are questioning all the time. I know the question and the answer, but I'm going to tell you neither, for it would make you sad to know how easily the answer drops off the tip of the brain.

Fill up the pan of the skull with millet seed. Each seed shall be a grain of truth, and the mating grains pop forth an answer.[21]

LEO TOLSTOY

Truth as God's Will

Verbal compositions are good and necessary, not when they describe what has happened, but when they show what ought to be; not when they tell what people have done, but when they set a value on what is good and evil—when they show men the narrow path of God's will, which leads to life.

And in order to show that path one must not describe merely what happens in the world. The world abides in evil and is full of offence. If one is to describe the world as it is, one will describe much evil and the truth will be lacking. In order that there may be truth in what one describes, it is necessary to write not about the truth of what is, but of the kingdom of God which is drawing nigh unto us but is not as yet. That is why there are mountains of books in which we are told what really has happened or might have happened, yet they are all false if those who write them do not themselves know what is good and what is evil, and do not know and do not show the one path which leads to the kingdom of God. And there are fairy-tales, parables, fables, legends, in which marvelous things are described which never happened or ever could happen, and these legends, fairy-tales, and fables, are true, because, they show wherein the will of God has always been, and is, and will be: they show the truth of the kingdom of God.[22]

[21] From Selected Letters of Dylan Thomas, edited by Constantine Fitzgibbon. Copyright © 1965 by The Trustees for the Copyrights of Dylan Thomas. Reprinted by permission of New Directions Publishing Corporation.
[22] From What Is Art? 1898 and Essays on Art 1861–1905 by Leo Tolstoy, translated by Louise and Aylmer Maude and published by Oxford University Press.